Praise for *Scholar*

"Modesitt's latest addition to his fantasy saga focuses on the complex character of its hero, an unlikely combination of serious scholar and, when need be, ruthless opponent. The author excels in creating worlds that are believable down to the last detail and characters whose vitality expresses itself in actions that have resounding consequences." —*Library Journal*

Praise for the Imager Portfolio

"Meticulous world-building . . . The world is fascinating, and the imagers themselves are extraordinary." —*RT Book Reviews* on *Imager*

"Modesitt capably integrates believable fantasy elements into a story centered on characters who work at real jobs and have private lives. . . . Consistently, well, *intriguing* in every sense." —*Kirkus Reviews* on *Imager's Intrigue*

"The Imager Portfolio features some of the best characters Modesitt has ever created, real enough to make you consider what you'd do in their places." —*Booklist* on *Imager's Challenge*

"Modesitt writes some of the most interesting characters in fantasy. He is a master. . . . Fans of the author's Recluce and Corus series will enjoy this series as well." —*SFRevu* on *Imager's Challenge*

TOR BOOKS BY L. E. MODESITT, JR.

Scholar

The Fourth Book of the Imager Portfolio

L. E. MODESITT, JR.

A TOM DOHERTY ASSOCIATES BOOK
NEW YORK

This is a work of fiction. All of the characters, organizations, and events portrayed in this novel are either products of the author's imagination or are used fictitiously.

SCHOLAR: THE FOURTH BOOK OF THE IMAGER PORTFOLIO

Copyright © 2011 by L. E. Modesitt, Jr.

All rights reserved.

Edited by David G. Hartwell

A Tor Book
Published by Tom Doherty Associates, LLC
175 Fifth Avenue
New York, NY 10010

www.tor-forge.com

Tor® is a registered trademark of Tom Doherty Associates, LLC.

ISBN 978-1-2508-3732-5

First Edition: November 2011
First Mass Market Edition: October 2012

Characters

Bhayar	Lord of Telaryn
Aelina	Wife of Bhayar
Vaelora	Youngest sister of Bhayar
Quaeryt	Scholar and friend of Bhayar
Voltyr	Imager
Kharst	Rex of Bovaria
Aliaro	Autarch of Antiago
Rescalyn	Governor of Tilbor
Straesyr	Princeps of Tilbor
Myskyl	Regimental Commander, Tilbor
Zirkyl	Post Commander, Boralieu
Pulaskyr	Post Commander, Midcote
Skarpa	Major, Sixth Battalion
Meinyt	Captain, Sixth Battalion
Gauswn	Undercaptain, Sixth Battalion
Phargos	Chorister of the Nameless
Phaeryn	Master Scholar of the Ecoliae
Zarxes	Scholar Princeps of the Ecoliae

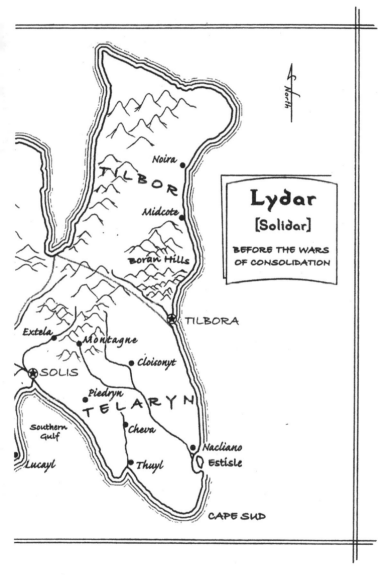

North

Noira

TILBOR

Midcote

Boran Hills

Lydar
[Solidar]

BEFORE THE WARS
OF CONSOLIDATION

Extela

Montagne

TILBORA

Cloisonyt

SOLIS

Piedryn

TELARYN

Southern
Gulf

Cheva

Nacliano

Estisle

Lucayl

Thuyl

CAPE SUD

Scholar

1

"You'd think the Tilborans would have more sense," snapped Bhayar. "Some of them, anyway." His dark blue eyes appeared almost black in the dim light of the small study that adjoined his receiving chamber. In the midafternoon of summer, the air barely moved, even with the high arched ceilings, and when it did, it only brought the smells of the city up the hill to the palace overlooking the harbor of Solis. He walked to the map displayed on the wooden stand, scowled, and then looked to the man in scholar's brown.

"Why would you think that?" Quaeryt replied in the formal Bovarian in which he'd been addressed, as always. He smiled politely, his thin lips quirking up slightly at the corners. Despite the itching of his slightly-too-long nose, he did not scratch it.

"Don't bait me, scholar." The Lord of Telaryn added only a slight emphasis to the last word. "Tell me what you have in mind."

"Only your best interests, my lord." Quaeryt shifted his weight off his slightly shorter left leg. The higher heel of his left boot helped, but the leg ached when he stood for long periods.

"When you talk like that, you remind me of the sycophants who surrounded my sire in his last days."

"Why might they have talked like that?"

"Answer my question!"

"Have you considered why I—or they—would

avoid answering a demand delivered so forcefully?"
Quaeryt grinned.

Abruptly, Bhayar laughed. "There are times . . .
friend or no friend . . ."

"Every time anything went wrong in Tilbor immediately after your sire conquered it, his first solution was
to issue an edict. If that didn't work, he killed people."

"It worked, didn't it?"

"It did indeed. It still does. But . . . exactly how
many of your soldiers are stationed in Tilbor and not
on the borders with Bovaria? How many weeks would
it take to get the companies from Tilbora or Noira to
Solis—if you had enough ships to carry them?"

"I could commandeer merchantmen."

"How long before they became as unhappy with
you as the Tilborans are?"

"They won't turn to Kharst." Bhayar laughed.

"Not until they forget what he did to the Pharsi
merchants in Eshtora. How long will that be? As long
as you've had garrisons in Tilbor?"

"Quaeryt! Enough of your questions. You're as bad
as Uhlyn was. Scholars and imagers! A ruler can't live
with them, and a strong one can't live without them.
You'll turn my hair as white as yours." A fist outsized
for the lord's wiry frame slammed onto the pale goldenwood of the desk.

That was always Bhayar's rejoinder when he tired
of dealing with the issues behind the questions, Quaeryt mused behind a pleasant smile, and never mind the
fact that Quaeryt's hair was white blond and that he
was actually a year younger than Bhayar, who had
just turned thirty.

"Namer's demons, I hate Solis in the summer. I'd
even prefer the mist stench of Extela when the winds
blow off the mountain."

Mist stench? Abruptly, Quaeryt recalled that some of the ancient volcanoes north of the old capital occasionally still belched ash and fumes.

Bhayar blotted his forehead with a linen cloth already soiled in more places than not, for all that it had been fresh and white at noon. "Instead of raising all these questions, why don't you offer an answer?"

Quaeryt grinned. "I don't recall your asking for one."

"I'm asking now. What do you suggest, my friend, the so-knowledgeable scholar? Tell me what I can do to remove the troops from Tilbor without immediately inviting another rebellion?"

"Let me think about it."

"Don't think too long."

"After breakfast—eighth glass of the morning," suggested Quaeryt, knowing that was too late for the early-rising lord.

"Seventh glass. I still don't see why you don't want to stay in the palace. I've offered far better quarters than you have on Scholarium Hill . . ."

"The quarters are indeed better, but I'd end up being of no help to you." *Or to me.* "And rulers soon tire of friends or retainers who outlive their usefulness." That was accurate, but not the real reason for his determination to avoid the palace for as long as possible. "Besides, you'd want me to get up at the Namer-fired glass that you do."

"You're not that lazy. You just like me to think you are."

You and everyone else. "But I am. I don't work the way you do. I'm just an itinerant scholar fortunate enough to have schooled some with the Lord of Telaryn."

"Bah . . . we'll let everyone else think that. . . ." Bhayar blotted his forehead again. "Why did he insist on moving the capitol here?" Before Quaeryt could have answered, not that he had any intention of doing so, the lord went on, "I know. I know. A port city on a big river and a good harbor makes more sense for trade and for moving armies. And Grandmere . . ." He shook his head. "I don't have to like it."

Quaeryt wondered about what Bhayar might have said about his grandmother, but decided not to ask. He'd pressed enough. "Tomorrow at seventh glass, then, sire?"

"Go!" Bhayar shook his head, but then grinned again.

"I hear and obey." Quaeryt's words were light, verging on the sardonic.

As he left the study and entered the private corridor separating the receiving hall from the study, Quaeryt forced himself to walk without limping, uncomfortable as it was, but he tried never to limp in the palace or when he was around Bhayar. He glanced into the large chamber, on the third level, the highest one in the palace, where, when necessary, Bhayar sat on the gilded throne that had been brought from Extela by his sire sixteen years before and received visitors or handed down formal pronouncements or sentences. Even the wide windows didn't help much in keeping the chamber cool in the height of summer.

Quaeryt made his way to the west end of the private corridor, where the palace guard unlocked the iron-grille door, allowing the scholar to make his way down the windowless and stifling staircase, past the grille door on the second level to the main-level grille door. Another guard unlocked that door as well. Quaeryt stepped carefully along the shaded and colonnaded walk that bordered the west end of the palace gardens, taking his time so that he could enjoy the cooler air created by the fountains. His enjoyment was always tempered by the knowledge that oxen— and sometimes prisoners—turned the capstan-like pumps that lifted the water to the reservoirs on the up- permost level at the rear of the palace. He was careful not to look into the gardens. After passing the guard at the top of the side steps, he walked down to the gate used by favored vendors and visitors to the palace.

"Good day, scholar," offered the taller soldier of the two at the gate in accented Bovarian.

"The same to you. I don't envy you in this heat."

"Some of the mist from the gardens drifts down here. It's better than the main gate, let me tell you."

"I can imagine." Quaeryt smiled and stepped out onto the wide stone sidewalk below the wall, a side- walk that bordered the north side of the stone-paved avenue.

Across the avenue to the south and below the pal- ace were the public gardens, open to those suitably attired, according to the judgment of the palace guards stationed at the two entrances. There weren't that many fountains there, and the cooler venues would already be taken. He turned right and started back toward the hill to the west, close to a vingt away, that held the Scholarium Solum . . . and the Scholars' House.

The one-legged beggar boy was a good two blocks west of the palace grounds. Beggars weren't allowed any closer.

Quaeryt flipped a copper to the beggar boy. "That's from Lord Bhayar." His words were in common Tellan.

The beggar frowned.

The scholar flipped a second copper. "And that's

from me, but you wouldn't have either without your lord."

The beggar looked at the coppers. "Could you a gotten 'em any dirtier, lord scholar?"

"Complaints, yet? Next time I might try." Privately, Quaeryt was pleased. It was easier to image a shiny copper than a worn and grubby one, not that anyone would have cared about coppers, but coppers added up to silvers, and silvers to golds, and few would think that a scholar who had dirty coppers was actually imaging them.

The scholar studied the avenue ahead of him, taking in the pair of youthful cutpurses, seemingly playing at bones, on the far side of the flower vendor, and the drunken lout who lurched out of the tavern. His appearance was timed too well and he was just a tad too tipsy. Quaeryt imaged a patch of fish oil onto the heels and soles of his polished boots, just before the fellow reached him.

The man's heels slipped from under him, and the slam-thief flailed before hitting the stones of the sidewalk. "Friggin' . . . sow-slut . . ."

Obviously, the would-be grabber was having a slow day. Otherwise, he wouldn't even have bothered with a scholar . . . unless he knew who Quaeryt was. That could be a problem.

"Do you need help?" Quaeryt asked, expecting the usual knife.

As the man tried to scramble to his feet and the knife appeared, Quaeryt imaged out a sliver of steel, and the useless blade separated from the hilt, and haft and blade clunked on the stones—just as the thief's boots slid out from under him again and he crashed face-first onto the sidewalk. He moaned, but didn't move for a moment, and Quaeryt skirted his prone figure, stepping into the avenue and barely avoiding a carriage before regaining the sidewalk. He'd gotten a good look. He just hoped he didn't have to deal with the thief again. That was one problem with using imaging to create accidents. Some people didn't learn. They just blamed their bad luck and went on doing stupid or dangerous things.

Although Quaeryt walked at a good pace, he didn't strain, and he was only sweating moderately when he reached the point where the avenue passed in front of the hill on which the so-called Scholarium Solum was set. The Scholars' House was halfway down the hill on the west side. Quaeryt glanced up the hill to the dark red brick building that held the Scholarium Solum as he walked past it to the winding walk up to the Scholars' House, no longer bothering to hide the slight limp he'd always had.

The brick steps of the front entry had shifted slightly over time, and Quaeryt had to take care as he climbed them onto the front porch because his bad leg had a tendency to drag. The wide-roofed porches that encircled the Scholars' House were designed to pick up the sea breezes, but since the sea breezes brought red flies in the day and mosquitoes at twilight, not to mention all the less than savory smells of the harbor, few scholars ventured out onto the porches once the sun dropped behind the warehouses and factorages to the west.

Quaeryt made his way to the east porch, the most shaded one in the afternoon.

There a younger man in a grayish purple shirt and trousers looked up from his wooden straight-backed chair. "It's a hot walk from the palace. I still don't see why Lord Bhayar doesn't offer you quarters." Voltyr spoke in Bovarian, as did all scholars, at least with each other and in dealing with the palace and other high officials. He was several years younger than Quaeryt, how many Quaeryt didn't know exactly. He'd never asked.

"Would you want to live in the palace, Voltyr?" asked Quaeryt as he settled into the chair across from the younger man.

"No. You know that. You're a scholar. Scholars' Houses are the only place for imagers, and they're not even half-safe in some cities, even here at times. Do you know what it was like when my parents discovered I could image a copper?"

"I imagine they were upset and pleased all at once." Quaeryt had heard enough that when he'd done his first imaging—after hearing about imagers from old Scholar Geis, he'd tried to image a cake, and it had tasted like mud—he'd done it alone. But then, all his imaging had been in secret and painfully discovered by trial and error when the scholars who raised him were not around.

"They were just upset. In a month, I was here, being told not to image until I was older . . . but no one could help me. They just told me to be careful."

"There aren't that many imagers. What about Uhlyn?"

"The only thing he ever said was not to image large things and not to try imaging anything out of metal until I had a beard and then to begin with small items." Voltyr laughed harshly. "He was so careful about his imaging, but look what happened to him, even with Bhayar's protection."

"He wasn't careful about other things. He flaunted being an imager." Even as Quaeryt spoke, he understood how many people feared imagers and their seemingly wondrous ability to visualize something and then have it appear. What so few wanted to understand was how painfully few imagers there were or how much skill and strength and concentration it took to image the smallest of objects, and how most imagers could do little beyond that. But . . . those who could . . . they were feared and shunned, and often the target of anyone who knew their abilities.

"Oh . . . and it's all right for merchants and High Holders to flaunt what they are, but not imagers? Even scholars can flaunt their knowledge."

"Not without risk," returned Quaeryt. "People don't like to be reminded of what they don't know. That's why Scholars' Houses are also the safest place for scholars. Good scholars ask questions. Questions upset rulers and those who fawn on them."

"Scholars in favor can gather in golds," pointed out Voltyr.

"Golds aren't much use to a headless man."

"Don't ask questions."

"What's the point of being a scholar, then?"

"How about the good life . . . or the best life possible for someone who wasn't born a High Holder?"

"High Holders are captive to their wealth."

"Quaeryt . . . I'd like to be held captive like that."

The scholar laughed, then sat there for several moments before asking, "What do you know about Tilbor?"

"Most of it is cold. The people are rude and crude, and they don't like strangers. They don't like scholars and imagers, except that they like Telaryn soldiers even less. They like to fight a lot, except when they're drinking, and they do a lot of that in the winter because it's too cold to do anything else. Even Antiagon

Fire wouldn't warm Noira in midwinter." The imager frowned. "Why are you asking?"

"I'm thinking of going there."

"Why, for the sake of the Nameless?"

"To learn about it, to try to resolve something for Lord Bhayar. Besides, I've been seen at the palace too much in the past few seasons. That's getting to be a problem."

"That's a problem half the High Holders in Telaryn would like to have."

"They only think they want that problem. They don't know Bhayar."

Voltyr frowned. "He's not that arbitrary or cruel. Certainly not like his father, is he?"

"He's generally very fair. Most High Holders aren't. But neither forgets *anything*."

"Oh . . ."

Quaeryt stood. "Do you want to go down to Amphora later? I have a few spare coppers."

"How could I refuse such an invitation?"

"You can't," laughed the scholar. "Half past fifth glass? I have work to do later."

"You're paying."

With a last smile, Quaeryt turned and walked toward the north porch, hoping the nook by the north chimney wall would be vacant. Both Bhayar's and Voltyr's comments about imagers had played into the half-formed idea in his thoughts. Why, indeed, did imagers have to move and act with such care? Could he do anything about that? Or, at least, about his own position?

2

"Good night." Quaeryt nodded to Voltyr as they stepped out of Amphora.

"Where are you headed? You said you had work to do."

"I do. I don't want to keep her waiting."

"That's not work," protested Voltyr.

"With all that's expected of me . . . it's work." With a wave, Quaeryt turned down the street, south from both Amphora and the Scholarium. Even though he and Voltyr had spent almost two glasses at the café, the sun was barely touching the tops of the shops and dwellings to the west.

Quaeryt had not been jesting about the work ahead of him. That was why, at Amphora, he had eaten a domchana, whose batter-fried crust was light but filling, although he felt that the fowl strips inside were tough and the peppers stringy. The tangy cheese helped, if not enough. The two lagers had also helped.

When he reached the harbor, he walked to the seawall that ran between the third and fourth piers. There he sat on the stone wall, in a spot almost exactly between the two piers and directly above one of the spots where silt and debris collected, enough so that it mounded close enough to the surface that the water actually broke over it in little wavelets. While the sun had not set, shadows were stealing across the entire harbor, leaving the topmasts of the tallest vessels in light while shading the lower masts and decks. Sailors were beginning to leave their ships and hurry in along the piers toward the cafés, taprooms, and taverns that filled the streets just north of the harbor.

As Quaeryt sat there, he concentrated on the image of a copper. One appeared on the stone beside his hand. He waited a time and concentrated again. A second appropriately dingy copper manifested itself. He managed seven more coppers before he felt light-headed, a sign that there was not that much left in the way of copper fragments and minute bits in the harbor basin and debris nearby.

He blotted his damp forehead with an old linen square, then eased the nine coppers into his wallet. He remained sitting on the seawall for over a glass, resting and enjoying the sunset . . . and absently recalling how long it had taken him to learn to focus and concentrate on every detail on each side of a copper . . . and how, once he'd mastered it, he'd left the Scholarium, thinking that he could get by as a sailor and not have to listen to grumpy scholars any longer.

He shook his head ruefully at the memory.

Then, in the fast-fading light, for twilight did not last long in Solis, he stood and stretched. He walked northward for several blocks before turning west, making his way among and around the sailors from the vessels tied up at the piers. Few paid any attention to him, their thoughts and doubtless their emotions elsewhere. Once Quaeryt left the harbor area, despite the warmth of the air, as the evening darkened into night, he pulled his cowl up. His white-blond hair, cut short as it was, still stood out too much in the darkness, and that could be a problem in the narrow streets.

He glanced to the western sky where the reddish

half disc of Erion hung just above a low cloud. Artiema had not yet risen, and that was fine with him. He'd passed the area that held the better factorages, cafés, and crafters' shops, and was headed into the oldest area of Solis, where sagging houses with crooked shutters or even boarded-up windows sat side by side with shells of dwellings and ruined buildings.

A block ahead were the ruins of an old smelter, little more than piles of rubble overgrown with thornweed and knifegrass. While it was slightly safer during the day, far too many people would have asked questions, and Quaeryt preferred to be the one asking, not the one having to answer.

He sensed the movement in the alley some yards away, and he stopped beside a wall that would keep anyone from coming up behind him. He just waited as the man in tattered grays and a long knife held at waist height edged toward him.

"What do you want?" Quaeryt let his voice quaver.

"Old father . . . I'm sure you'd be having some coins." The man's grin revealed more broken and blackened teeth than white or yellow ones.

"You'd not be wanting to bother me."

"That I'd not once I've your coins." The knife flashed toward Quaeryt's gut.

The scholar darted back and imaged bread into the man's windpipe and throat. Then he stepped back, glancing around. No one else emerged from the shadows of the alley as the thief flailed silently for quite some time, then grasped at his throat, before collapsing against the side of the lane. Once the man was dead, since he would have no further use for his coins, Quaeryt quickly examined his wallet. He found five coppers and a silver, which he transferred to his own wallet, before straightening and continuing down the dark lane toward the ruins of the old smelter.

He didn't need to get too near, choosing to stand close to the section of wall that had once held a wagon gate. Not even the iron hinges remained, only holes in the crumbling bricks and mortar. From where he stood, he began to concentrate. First, he tried to image a silver. The first was easy, and so was the second. After a clear strain with the third, he paused and slipped the coins into his wallet, then blotted his forehead.

He waited in the shadows almost a quarter glass, checking the lane in both directions, before he resumed imaging. Eleven coppers later, he stopped and blotted his forehead again.

He was tired, but not exhausted. Metal imaging was far harder than the other imaging he'd tried. Imaging earth and soil into place was far easier. He'd learned that as a boy forced to garden, although he'd had to grub up his hands so that the scholars who appeared to check his efforts hadn't learned how he'd kept the garden so free of weeds.

His wallet wasn't sagging as he made his way back along the dim alley, giving the dead man a wide berth, but it was definitely heavy.

All in all, it had been a good night's work. More coppers and silvers for his wallet, and one less thief to trouble people who didn't need that sort of difficulty.

3

More than a half glass before seven on Mardi morning, Quaeryt reached the side gate of the palace. As he'd calculated, Jhoal was on duty.

"Pleasant morning to you," offered Quaeryt with a smile. "For now."

"Be as hot as an Antiagon's balls by midmorning, scholar, maybe sooner." The sentry's Bovarian held the harshness of a Tellan native speaker.

"It's still early Juyn, and harvest is hotter than summer. Wait until Agostos."

"You're not cheering me up," replied the guard, glancing toward the tower on the southeast side corner of the wall and then using his sleeve to blot his forehead. "Got two more glasses before Dhuar relieves me."

"The first watch is easier."

"In summer."

"Were you ever posted in Tilbor?" Quaeryt already knew the answer.

"We all were. Old Lord Chayar wouldn't have any guards who hadn't seen battle. Lord Bhayar's the same."

"He might have to change that before long, unless the Tilborans revolt or there's another war."

"Nah ... they're still fighting there. Stiff-necked bunch. Worse than they say the Bovarians are."

"Don't you think there are people like that everywhere? You must see it here."

"More 'n you'd believe, scholar. More 'n you'd believe."

"High Holders mostly?"

Jhoal shook his head. "They're mannered folk. Might look down on you, but most don't swell out of their britches." After another furtive glance toward the tower, the guard scratched his neck, just below the bronze ceremonial helmet. "Most, anyway."

"Except High Holder Khervar? Isn't he here all the time?"

"He is." The slightest hint of a smile crossed the older guard's face. "He's young."

"I'd better be careful," replied Quaeryt. "I'm not that old, myself."

"You were never that young, I'd be thinking."

Quaeryt hoped not. "I suppose I'd better go inside. I wouldn't want to be late."

Jhoal stepped back and opened the narrow gate. "Take care, scholar."

"You, too."

Quaeryt walked up the steps leading to the roofed colonnades that flanked the garden. The guard at the top of the steps studied the scholar, then nodded. Quaeryt took his time, but did not loiter, especially when he saw Savaityl—the palace seneschal—standing beside the grille to the private staircase, quietly talking to the guard. The staircase guard looked straight ahead, not at Savaityl and not at Quaeryt.

Even so, Savaityl turned. "You're a quarter glass early, scholar. You can wait here." A good ten years older than the scholar, the seneschal had a face that would have fit an ax, hard and smooth, with flinty gray eyes under coal-black hair cut short enough that it lay flat on his scalp, barely covering it. His Bovarian was precise and flawless, like everything else he cultivated.

"Certainly. I wouldn't want to intrude. I just didn't want to be late."

"Lord Bhayar appreciates your punctuality. So do I. There is a difference between being slightly early and far too early . . . especially when one is here so very often."

Quaeryt nodded respectfully. There were times when responding verbally was worse than unnecessary. Savaityl had served Chayar, and now served his son. Both lords sent those who didn't meet their standards to handle unpleasant and marginally meaningful tasks in even less pleasant locales. Bhayar was an enlightened lord. He did not believe in torture. Those who failed were exiled to distant locales. Those who stole or did worse vanished forever.

While he stood waiting, Quaeryt considered again his plan. Would it work? Who knew? What he did know was that Bhayar had little real regard for scholars and a wariness combined with contempt for imagers. On top of that, he had little patience for advisors—or anyone—who loitered around the palace providing little but pronouncements without ever undertaking anything of risk or value. Savaityl's last words had reinforced that.

A time later, but before the chimes rang out announcing the glass, Savaityl returned and nodded. The guard unlocked the private staircase, and Quaeryt started up the steep and narrow steps and made his way up to the private corridor on the upper level. There the walls were of goldenwood bleached out until it was a faint tannish off-white. The floor was of pale blue tile, edged in dark blue. There were no hangings, no paintings, and no other decorations. In fact, mused Quaeryt, except in the receiving hall, he'd never seen any art or sculpture, and all that was displayed in the one chamber had been gifted to the Lord of Telaryn.

One of the assistant stewards stood by the half-open door to the study. He inclined his head, then turned and announced, "Scholar Quaeryt Rytersyn to see you, Lord."

There was no answer, only a gesture. As was his wont, Bhayar was not seated behind the overly ornate carved goldenwood desk, but standing. He had been perusing the map of Lydar affixed to the map stand.

"Good morning, Lord." Quaeryt bowed.

"Good morning. Do you have an answer to my question, scholar?" Bhayar's voice was jovial, meaning that he'd had a good evening with his lady. Everyone knew when he didn't.

"I do have a proposal, Lord. Who's the governor of Tilbor Province?"

"I asked for an answer, not more questions."

Quaeryt inclined his head respectfully and waited.

Bhayar sighed, but it was a deep sigh, for effect, and not the tight short sigh that meant displeasure. "Rescalyn. He's a good troop commander, doesn't put up with local nonsense."

"Who's the deputy governor or the assistant governor?"

"Straesyr. He's the princeps. He was a solid marshal, not brilliant. He's good with golds and supplies."

"Why don't you send me to Tilbora as a scholar advisor to Straesyr?"

"You *want* to go to Tilbora?"

"No. But I can't give you a recommendation without going there." Quaeryt laughed. "I can't even ask the right questions."

Bhayar fingered his clean-shaven chin. "Anyone who wants to go to that forsaken place ..." He paused. "What do you have in mind?"

"Finding out if there's a way to stop the incidents without killing people—or a way to do it with fewer troops."

"You can't calculate that from here?"

"Did your father conquer Tilbor by staying in Solis?"

"More questions . . . Your questions will be the death of me." Bhayar shook his head. "I'll write you an appointment. The pay won't be much, a half gold a week and a room in the barracks. Do you want to travel with the next dispatch riders?"

Quaeryt shook his head. "I'd like to go by sea and look around some before I present myself."

Bhayar nodded. "How long will you . . ." He broke off his words. "Be back by the end of winter, or don't bother."

"You're worried about the Bovarians?"

"Who wouldn't be after what Kharst did in Khel?"

"In time, that could be your opportunity."

"How do you see that? I don't know that the Pharsi will look to me as their savior, and the Bovarians were pleased to see the Pharsi brought down."

"You don't have to be a savior. Just don't make all the mistakes Rex Kharst has." *Or your father did in Tilbor.*

"And just what would you have done with the Pharsi?"

"I'd have to think about that," Quaeryt admitted, "but don't you think that after the war is over and you've made people part of your land, you need to find a way to make them want you as their ruler?"

"That's why you're going to Tilbora, I suppose? Rather than say that I should go?"

"Can you think of a better reason?"

"Not at the moment. What's in it for you?"

"Your appreciation, if I succeed, and your willingness to agree, again, if I succeed, that scholars are occasionally useful." Quaeryt grinned. "Also enough coin and gratitude that I don't have to become an itinerant scholar, always looking over my shoulder."

"You might get one out of two, and half of the other." Bhayar rose. "I'll have your commission and appointment ready on Jeudi, with a few golds for travel. Come by in the late afternoon, fourth glass or so."

"You have that look. Which minister are you meeting with next?"

"Thrachis. The factors are protesting that I'm spending golds on roads that make travel easy for the High Holders, but not for trade. They're never happy."

"Some people are only happy when they're complaining," observed Quaeryt. "Sometimes they're right, but when you address their complaint, they'll soon find another. You might have him ask them, if you address their problem, how long it will be before they find another."

Bhayar laughed.

Quaeryt could see the calculation in his eyes. "By your leave, Lord?"

Bhayar nodded, a movement somewhere between indifference and brusqueness. "You may go."

The scholar offered a respectful bow before turning and departing.

4

Meredi found Quaeryt in what was called the library in the Scholarium Solum. A pretentious name, not only for the repository of miscellaneous volumes, but for the location itself, suggesting that the large but decrepit old building held the one body of scholars in all Telaryn, he thought, as he brushed a moldering bit of plaster from his shoulder with one hand, while brushing the cobwebs off a tome on the shelf before him. He eased the volume out and opened it, reading the title: *Rholan, Synthesizing the Esoteric and Exoteric?*

While it was far from what he was seeking, he read through several pages. One paragraph did catch his attention.

> Although so little is known of Rholan the Unnamer that he might as well be apocryphal, the stories and sayings attributed to him are a remarkable fusion of the exoteric and esoteric, as if he were attempting to instill spirituality within the most pragmatic of human group functions and interactions. . . . Yet, for all the impact he has had upon history and belief, the man himself remains more evanescent than morning fog in summer. . . . We only know that he lived in Montagne and was presumably born there, although no records exist, and that he vanished after traveling to Cloisonyt in his fifty-third year, according to the historian Jletyr Vladomsyn . . .

"More evanescent than morning fog, yet he single-handedly made Lydar a bastion of the Nameless," murmured Quaeryt to himself.

He closed the volume and continued his search, absently wondering, far from the first time, why so many books in a library supposedly used and perused by scholars had been untouched for so long, and why many had never been opened. He quickly looked at and discarded several other volumes—*Time of the Champions: Caldor and Hengyst*; *The Five Ports of*

Lydar; Historical Inaccuracies in the Accounts of Tholym; Natural Remedies from Telaryn Flora.

He couldn't help but wince at one—*Imaging as a Manifestation of Naming.*

In time, he did discover a volume that would suffice for his purposes—*Historical Commentary on Tilbor.* It had the added benefit of the title on the cover and a seal indicating it had never been opened. It might even be informative as well. Finding it was likely to be the easy part. While he could have taken it past the gate desk to the library under a concealment shield, or removed it by even more covert means, either could raise questions later, when he would not wish them to surface. He decided to try the direct approach first.

He walked to the desk set beside the locked door gate to the library and looked to the young student scholar seated there.

"Yes, sir?"

"I'd like to borrow this volume."

"Sir . . . I cannot grant that."

Quaeryt knew that. He even knew the answer to the question he had to ask. "Who can?"

"I'll have to check with Scholar Parelceus, sir. He is the only one who can decide." The youth's voice did not quite quaver.

"Please do. I'll leave it here with you, and come back late this afternoon."

"Ah . . . he won't be back until late tonight . . . after the library is locked."

"Then I'll come by in the morning." Quaeryt handed the book to the young man. "Don't break the seal, either."

"Ah . . . no, sir."

"Thank you." Quaeryt smiled and departed.

Outside the Scholarium, the day was already hot, despite high hazy clouds.

Quaeryt turned his steps toward the harbor, knowing full well that later it would be even hotter, and the hazy clouds meant that there would be little breeze at all.

The hillside that held the Scholarium flattened into the lower city after Quaeryt had walked less than two hundred yards, just past the anomen of the Nameless that was almost as old as the Scholarium, but far less decrepit. Once he was among the welter of shops and cafés and establishments even less reputable, the last traces of the morning breeze vanished, leaving him walking steadfastly through a haze that held the pungency of onions fried in grease close to rancid; the smoke of various types of incenses, likely from one of the countries located on the southern continent of Otelyrn; the faint but acrid bitterness of elveweed; the more welcome smell of roasting fowl; and dozens of other less identifiable odors, the origins of many on which few would wish to dwell.

Quaeryt stepped past a bent old man standing beside a cart that held folded scarves, neckerchiefs, and smaller pocket squares. The vendor did not return his smile. Then he dodged around two heavyset women who balanced bundles of laundry on their heads as they strode toward the cross street that led to a public fountain two long blocks to the west.

Close to three-quarters of a glass later, and feeling far warmer, Quaeryt slowed as he approached the establishment on the unnamed street that everyone called "second street," since it was the second one back from and north of Harbor Avenue. The sign displayed a rat in a sailor's sleeveless jacket lifting a gray tankard. The illustration had been recently repainted. The Tellan words underneath—"The Wharf Rat"— had not. Quaeryt nodded and stepped inside.

The unlit and dim taproom was empty, except for an angular gray-haired woman in black trousers and a plain faded blue shirt-blouse. She smiled as she saw Quaeryt. "Scholar." Except the Tellan word meant something more like "learned rascal."

"Quaeryt. Always been Quaeryt to you, Zaenyi." He grinned. "You always make me do that."

"It's a harmless game. These days, what's harmless is good. Better than most of what passes for games."

"Business isn't that bad, is it?"

"It's been better. It's also been worse."

"You get many Tilborans in here lately?"

"A sailor's a sailor. If they behave and have coin, we serve them. If they don't, Kuisad gets them to leave." She paused. "Why do you ask?"

"I may have to go there."

"I thought you gave up the sea when you became a scholar. Now even your words reek of the Bovarian."

"Zaenyi . . . you're cruel."

Her smile was mischievous.

"Traveling to Tilbora," he finally replied, "isn't the same as going back to sea."

"You can't ever stay put, can you?"

"Too much of a target if you do."

"Kuisad said you'd been named a Scholar of the Lord. Many would become Bilbryn's apprentice for that."

Quaeryt merely nodded to that. So many thought the historic imager a disciple of the Namer that there was little point in protesting. "It brings in a few silvers a week. Lord Bhayar's a fair man. He's not a patient man. He's getting impatient. It's not a good time for a scholar to be around. He's thinking I might be of use studying things in Tilbora. I'm considering taking him up on it." Quaeryt shrugged. "What should I know that's been happening here?"

"There was an Antiagon crew in here last night. They were boasting about how they privateered a fat Bovarian merchanter. They captured something. They were free with their coins, and the silvers were Bovarian."

"Were they truly Antiagons?"

"They all spoke that low tongue."

Quaeryt nodded again. The "low tongue" was a bastard Bovarian dialect spoken in Antiago and southern Bovaria, mainly in Kherseilles and Ephra and the lands between. "No Bovarians lately?"

"Not since mid-Mayas."

In the remaining half glass or so that they talked, Zaenyi didn't add anything more to what she'd said earlier, and it was close to noon when Quaeryt left and walked the two blocks to the harbor proper. When Lord Chayar had moved the capital from Extela to Solis, he had also rebuilt the harbor. All the piers were accessed off the stone-paved and stone-walled Harbor Avenue, and all four long piers were not only of solid stone with stone footings, but were widely separated.

Quaeryt knew the kind of ship he was looking for—not the biggest, nor the fanciest, but a modest-sized, tight-rigged, and older Telaryn or Tilboran vessel in outstanding repair.

The first and southernmost pier in the harbor was the smallest, and the vessels who tied up there were either local coasters or fishermen. Quaeryt started with the second pier, even though that meant walking farther. He thought the second ship from the foot of the pier was Tilboran, what with the high sides and sturdy timbers, but planks at the waterline were green and the gunwales were neither oiled nor varnished, and she creaked too much even in the gentle swells of the harbor. While a Tilboran vessel would have been ideal, he wasn't about to trust one whose maintenance had clearly been slighted.

Next was a sleek northern vessel, most likely Jariolan, with shorter sloop-rigged masts to deal with the force of northern gales. Quaeryt had to wonder if she was a spice trader, stopping in Solis for repairs, in order to avoid the high porting tariffs imposed by the Rex of Bovaria. Beyond the Jariolan was a bulky Ferran barque whose crew looked to be re-rigging the foremast.

"Good-looking ship," he murmured, even if he had no intention of sailing under a Ferran ensign.

The ship at the end of the pier on the seaward side had to be Antiagon—much smaller and sloop-rigged. Quaeryt had to admit that she was trim and well-kept, but he needed a Telaryn vessel, and he didn't like the idea of a smaller craft in the rougher waters off the eastern coast.

He trudged back down the second pier and started studying vessels on the third pier, the most likely one for his needs, since the fourth pier held both of Bhayar's warships, used solely if the Lord wished to travel somewhere by sea, and several of the larger ocean clippers designed for faster ocean crossings and unlikely to be calling on coastal ports—even had he wanted to pay their exorbitant rates for passage.

Halfway out the third pier, he spied a ship that was close to what he sought, a three-masted barque, a few years older than he would have liked, but the care and cleanliness showed. The fantail plaque proclaimed her as *Diamond Naclia*, suggesting she was ported out of either Nacliano or Estisle. She might be outbound from there, but then again, she might be headed back, and if she weren't headed north from her home port, he'd have a chance to pick up a Tilboran ship there.

The gangway was down, and two heavy wagons were blocked in place roughly opposite where the forward-hold hatch was likely to be located. The teamster of the forward wagon was unfastening the canvas from his wagon bed.

Quaeryt stopped at the base of the gangway and looked to the sailor at the opening in the railing, a mate judging from the sleeveless jacket with the black cloth stripes angled up toward his neck. "Permission to come aboard." His words were Tellan.

"Polite now, aren't you, scholar?" replied the mate in Tellan. "That brown shirt and trousers says you're that, right?"

"That's right."

The mate gestured, and Quaeryt limped up the gangway to the area that would have been called the quarterdeck on a passenger ship.

"What can I do for you, scholar?"

"I'm trying to get to Tilbora. . . ."

"You are? And you'd be wanting to work your way, I suppose?"

The top of the mate's head was barely level with Quaeryt's nose, but the scholar wouldn't have wanted to tangle with the sailor, not with his knotted muscles and unscarred face.

Quaeryt laughed. "I'm a scholar. I can write letters, copy manifests and waybills, total shipment values, but I've got a bad leg, and I'm clumsy when I carry heavy things because of it. You look to be headed back to Estisle, perhaps farther. . . ."

"Passage to Nacliano would be a gold, plus two coppers a day for the crew's fare, four for the captain's."

"I didn't say I couldn't be helpful," replied Quaeryt. "Years ago . . ."

"What? Cabin boy?"

"Quartermaster stryker. I can do navigation calculations, and, if you've got the tables, double moon triangulation . . . or just spell your lookouts."

"With Artiema full twenty degrees above the horizon in the west and Erion at the zenith, and the Triad fifteen above the water . . ."

Quaeryt let himself grin. "You'd not be seeing the Triad in the morning light . . ."

A faint smile crossed the mate's lips. "How about Artiema twenty degrees above the horizon in the east . . . ?"

For close to half a glass, the mate asked questions about navigation. Abruptly, he stopped. "I'll have to talk to the captain. If he agrees, a half gold, and a copper a day for fare, and you can have the bunk in the fantail storage locker. We'll be casting off at dawn on Vendrei. No extra cost if you want to sleep aboard tomorrow night."

"I'll come by tomorrow to see if he agrees."

The mate nodded. "I'm Ghoryn."

"Quaeryt."

After he left the *Diamond*, the scholar found himself smiling. He'd enjoyed the navigation exam and puzzles posed by Ghoryn.

The smile faded as he considered that, while he had the beginnings of an idea to deal with his problems, he still didn't have a real solution to Bhayar's difficulties, even though he'd known he wouldn't until he'd spent time in Tilbora. Still . . .

5

A little after eighth glass on Jeudi, Quaeryt presented himself at the library gate desk.

The student scholar looked up and swallowed. "Scholar Quaeryt? Ah . . . sir. Scholar Parelceus has the book in his study, sir."

Quaeryt smiled politely. "Thank you."

As he walked from the gate desk down the dingy corridor to the study claimed by the principal assistant scholar to the princeps of the Scholarium Solum, Quaeryt reflected that even the seemingly simplest tasks often required more effort to accomplish within laws and procedures than outside them, a fact overlooked by too many rulers, governors, and chiefs of patrollers . . . or officious scholars.

He knocked on the proper door, then opened it, and entered without waiting for an acknowledgment.

"Scholar Quaeryt . . . this is most untoward." Parelceus was the rotund form of scholar with chubby red cheeks, the brown hair on the sides of his head slicked into place with a scented grease pomade. His brown eyes were as hard as the top of his balding skull as he looked up from where he sat behind a desk so ancient that the wood was more black than its likely original brown finish.

"Untoward?" Quaeryt let a puzzled expression appear on his face. "Untoward? In what fashion, Scholar Parelceus?"

For a moment, the assistant to the princeps said

nothing, his mouth opening once slightly before closing with almost a snap. Finally, he spoke. "The library assistant said that you wished to remove this valuable reference tome from the library." As he pointed to the ancient leather-bound volume, Parelceus shook his head. "Surely you know, Scholar Quaeryt, that all books, volumes, folios, and maps must remain within the confines of the library. Otherwise, before long, we would have nothing remaining."

"I understand, Scholar Parelceus." Quaeryt smiled. "In the years I have been here, first as a student, and then as a scholar, have I ever asked for that privilege?" Quaeryt refrained from pointing out the years he had been away from Solis.

"That is not the point. Rules are rules. What is the point of having rules if they can be broken?"

"Have you looked at the book?"

"What do you mean?"

"Until I picked it up yesterday, it had not been read since it was placed in the library. I left the original seal in place."

Parelceus frowned.

"Is not the purpose of a book to be useful?"

"Of course. Of course . . . but within the rules of the Scholarium."

"The book would be useful to me in a commission for Lord Bhayar. You may recall that he did name me his scholar?"

"Ah . . . I did hear something about that."

"I'd be most happy to sign a pledge that I will return the book upon the completion of this commission."

"But that would violate the rules of the Scholarium."

"I know the permanent removal is forbidden, and that makes great sense. You are right. If anyone could remove any number of books, before long there would be no library." Quaeryt paused. "But where is it written that borrowing a single book in pursuit of a commission of the Lord of Telaryn is prohibited?"

"There is the matter of tradition . . ." protested Parelceus.

"Would it be in the interests of the Scholarium Solum to refuse on the grounds of tradition . . . over a single book?"

A calculating look appeared in the hard brown eyes. "You would sign a pledge . . . and perhaps a deposit . . ."

"A pledge . . . yes. A deposit would be most unnecessary. If I fail to return the book, then you could deny me all privileges accorded me as a scholar. Before long I would not be welcome in any community of scholars. Why would I risk that over a single book when I struggled so long to become a scholar?"

"But . . . the rules . . . others . . . ?"

"I can borrow the book, or I can tell Lord Bhayar that I could not. That's your choice. Of course, you could always ask the princeps." Quaeryt looked calmly at Parelceus and waited.

After a long moment, Parelceus sighed. "I suppose it is a matter of practicality. I will need two copies of your pledge, one for the files here, and one for the princeps."

"I'll write them out here and now."

Parelceus sighed again.

Almost a glass later, Quaeryt was seated in the shielded corner of the north porch of the Scholars' House, reading through the *Historical Commentary on Tilbor*. He'd studied the seal and imaged several duplicates before he'd opened the book and broken the seal.

Sections of the opening pages suggested that, while the book contained information he'd never seen elsewhere, connecting it to real history was likely to be a laborious process.

One paragraph struck him as particularly representative.

> . . . while it can be debated whether Hengyst's methodology in the razing of Noveault was accepted as typical of the border skirmishes between Ryntar and Tilbor or whether it was typicality carried to excess as a result of the Tilboran massacre of Ryntaran peasants outside of Bluodyn the previous spring, there is little question that Hengyst wished to remove all threats, real or perceived, along the border with Tilbor before he embarked on his decade-long war of consolidation against Tela that eventually, if uneasily and in a fashion that required considerable martial prowess on the part of his descendants, both son and grandson, in maintaining stability, resulted in the foundation of the larger state of Telaryn, and laid the crumbling foundation of governance later undermined and superseded with great effect by the Yaran warlords of the Montagne province, whose ascension to power and the Lordship of Telaryn, while not necessarily acclaimed, especially given their fire and passion, reputedly bestowed on them because they inhabited a land where the mountains still spewed fire, was most obviously accepted with relief by the majority of the populace . . .

Quaeryt blotted his forehead, not necessarily from the heat. Still, he'd found no other comparatively voluminous history of Tilbor in the library, nor one so handsomely bound. *It had to be written by the third son of a wealthy High Holder ... or the fourth or fifth.*

He kept reading for another three glasses, before he returned to his small cubby on the second floor of the house. There he imaged a hole in the false wall he'd imaged into place in the nook that held his bed pallet, removed the strongbox and unlocked it, placed the tome inside, and then locked and replaced the strongbox. After imaging away the hole in the wall, he descended to the main floor, from where he made his way out into another sweltering day and down the hill to Vinara, one of the tavernas he frequented when he wanted neither to spend many coppers nor to risk severe indigestion.

He nodded politely to the civic patroller he passed. The patroller barely nodded in return.

While some cafés and tavernas closed from second glass to fourth glass, especially in summer, Vinara was not one of them, perhaps because it was located in an old thick-walled dwelling that had a small fountain in its shaded courtyard. Or it might have been that Celina and her husband simply saw an opportunity. Either way, Quaeryt was glad the taverna was one of those that fit his habits.

He had no more than stepped into the dimness of the front entry when Celina appeared, flashing a coquettish smile for all that her figure was definitely excessively matronly. "There is a small table by the fountain, scholar." Her Tellan was that of old Solis, softer and recalling a vanished time.

"I would like that." He returned the smile. "And you will serve me?"

"Who else would dare with all your words and improper behavior?" The proprietress did not quite flounce out into the courtyard, where she pointed to the circular table so close to the fountain that one edge held a sheen of dampness.

"Thank you, gracious mistress." Quaeryt grinned.

"Would that you would ever be that fortunate." Her tone was severe, but there was a glint in her eyes.

"A man can dream . . ."

"A man's dreams are often a maiden's nightmares."

"I'm far kinder than that." He paused. "Is the cucumber sauce fresh?"

"Less than a glass ago, scholar."

"Then I'll have the lamb flatbread with it and the mild rice fries."

"And the pale lager?"

"That, too."

Celina hurried off, and Quaeryt followed her steps for a moment. Sitting in the shade by the courtyard fountain was the most comfortable he'd felt in days. He wasn't looking forward to meeting with Bhayar again, and especially not to what likely awaited him in Tilbora, but unless the weather was truly unseasonal, the voyage to Nacliano would be more pleasant than sweltering through the summer in Solis—or riding along the dusty and all too winding roads that led to the eastern coast of Telaryn.

The lager and lamb-filled flatbread arrived quickly, and Quaeryt took his time, enjoying both . . . as well as bantering with Celina. The extra pair of coppers he left were worth it, and he reminded himself that they had taken only a bit of effort.

He was reluctant to depart Vinara, but well aware of the dangers of being late to the palace. Bhayar might keep him waiting, but the Lord of Telaryn got more than testy with those who were not available at his beck and call—and that was another reason why going to Tilbora was a good idea, since Bhayar had been testier than usual of late.

Quaeryt arrived at the private gate to the palace at a quarter to fourth glass. After a few pleasantries with Fherad, another of the guards he knew in passing, he made his way through the gate and up the steps to the second guard. After he passed the man, as he was walking along the colonnaded passage toward the locked interior staircase, a woman addressed him.

"Scholar?" The voice was somewhere between girlish and womanly, yet slightly husky.

Quaeryt debated not halting, but courtesy, caution, and curiosity won out. He stopped and looked past the marble column and through the lacy screen of ferns, some of which had browned edges despite their nearness to the fountains.

Beyond the ferns, the not-quite-gangly girl-woman who wore riding pants and a woman's light riding jacket to conceal her figure sat in the shade of a tall fern less than three yards from the fountain that supposedly depicted a sea sprite, with water geysering from its blowhole and from its barbed tail. A riding hat with a veil rested on a well-shaped leg. Her light brown hair held natural waves, but not excessive curls. Beside her sat a gray-haired duenna, who turned and regarded Quaeryt with a disapproving expression.

"You can enter the gardens. Take the next archway." Her words were offered in formal Bovarian, rather than Tellan or far less common Pharsi, and the language and the light honeyed shade to her clear skin suggested not only her background but who she happened to be.

"As you wish, mistress," replied Quaeryt.

"It *is* my wish, scholar."

He bowed his head, then turned and walked the ten yards or so to the first archway.

Two guards stood there.

"The young mistress requested my presence."

"Wait," said one.

The other turned and disappeared past another bank of ferns. In moments he returned and nodded. Both stepped aside, but as Quaeryt walked past, he could feel their eyes on his back.

He kept walking until he reached the young woman. "You requested my presence, mistress?" Quaeryt avoided looking directly into her eyes, as required when addressing a woman of stature.

"You're going to see my brother, aren't you?" Her voice was pleasant, with that hint of huskiness he found attractive. Her face was also well-shaped, neither too long nor too round.

"My presence has been requested by Lord Bhayar. I could not presume your position. Many women have brothers," he replied. "I only know that you are favored to be here in the fountain gardens."

"Favored? One might say that. You are a scholar. Tell me something."

"About what, mistress?"

"Aunt Nerya"—the girl-woman nodded to the duenna—"claims that for an unmarried woman to ride in public without her parents or a male relative is as bad a sin as Naming. Is it? Are there any writings that declare that? Has any high chorister of the Nameless proclaimed it?" Her light brown eyes studied him with an intensity he found unsettling, yet oddly pleasing.

"I have read none, mistress, yet I am not a scholar of the Nameless, but of history and of the physical world. You would do better to ask a high chorister."

Nerya nodded.

"Are you a coward to refuse an opinion?" The young woman's voice remained pleasant, a tone more suited to asking about the weather or the time to dine, but with the slightest undertone of amusement.

"Any man is a fool to offer advice on how a woman behaves with regard to her family, unless he is her husband. In that case, he might still be foolhardy. I would far rather be called a coward than to be a fool."

"So you're afraid of Bhayar?"

"I respect Lord Bhayar, and only a fool would not have a healthy respect for a lord as accomplished and powerful as he is. I also respect his willingness to learn and to listen." *Even if his lack of patience limits both.*

"Do you ride, scholar?"

"At times, mistress. There is little call for scholars to ride."

"I had heard differently." She offered a smile, one not quite inviting, nor yet dismissive. "In time, perhaps I can persuade my brother to have you accompany us on a ride somewhere . . . suitable." There was a slight pause before she extended a sealed missive. "Since you are a scholar of history, you might find this of some amusement. If you do, I will take your comments. You may return them to me, directly, if we happen to encounter each other, or you may pass them to Nerya."

Historical comments from her? Quaeryt took the sealed document and inclined his head. "I will do so."

After a moment, she added, "You may go."

"By your leave, mistress."

"You didn't use my name," she said.

Quaeryt smiled. "It's not my place to presume." *Although doing so would be a pleasure . . . if most dangerous.*

"Go." The single word held a tone of amusement . . . and perhaps something more.

He bowed and then turned, slipping the document inside his tunic and making his way from the fountain gardens, wondering exactly what Vaelora had really wanted . . . and even more of concern, what was in the missive or document. He hadn't seen her in years, and then only a handful of times from a distance, but Bhayar's other three surviving sisters were all much older—and married. The oldest, Chaerila, had been married to the Autarch of Antiago and had died in childbirth a year after the wedding. The autarch had promptly remarried—a niece of Rex Kharst, another matter of continuing concern to Bhayar.

Still . . . there was definitely something about Vaelora . . . far beyond mere attractiveness, although she was certainly good-looking. She might have been raised to be married off for political purposes, but whoever married her would have his hands full, and then some, Quaeryt suspected.

Enough . . . you'd best not even dream about her.

He concentrated on what he would say to Bhayar as he approached the private staircase.

Savaityl was not there, but the guard nodded politely. "Lord Bhayar is currently occupied."

Still thinking about Vaelora and what she wanted, and wondering why on Terahnar she had reached out to him, Quaeryt waited for a good half glass before the bell beside the grille gate rang and the guard unlocked it. He nodded politely and started up the staircase, seemingly as hot as an oven. When he reached the third level, he was drenched in his own sweat. He stopped and blotted his forehead before he walked slowly to where an assistant steward stood outside the open study door.

"The scholar is here, Lord."

"Send him in."

Quaeryt stepped past the man and walked toward the desk Bhayar stood behind, looking down and examining a musket laid out on the wooden surface.

"There ought to be a better way of making these," mused Bhayar. "Do you think they could be imaged?"

"I would doubt it. A good imager *might* be able to image each piece perfectly, but they'd still have to be put together, and if any piece happened to be the slightest bit out of true . . ."

"It wouldn't work. Or worse, would misfire." Bhayar shook his head. "It must have taken Kharst's smiths years to hammer out the parts for the muskets he supposedly used at Khel. They take forever to load, and they're not very accurate. I'd wager that they were mostly for effect, and that his cavalry was what routed the Pharsi."

"It could be."

"You don't sound convinced, scholar."

"The Pharsi won most of the battles where cavalry were important. Rex Kharst had to have done something different at Khel."

"Maybe he just had more cavalry by then. Or imagers."

"That's very possible."

"I understand my sister summoned you," Bhayar said evenly, "and gave you a document detailing her thoughts on history."

"She did. I thought it unwise to refuse it."

Bhayar laughed. "I have found it unwise to refuse her more reasonable requests as well. Yet you were most proper. Even Savaityl thought so, and he is not generous in his judgments. Most proper. Were it not for your reputation, scholar, one might think that your interests did not lie in women."

"I have great interests in women, and your sister is most attractive. Most attractive. It is not my place to make advances to her or to respond to such."

"You're right. You also have good judgment in that and in many other matters." Bhayar picked a leather pouch off the desk and extended it. "Your silvers and golds for travel." He then handed Quaeryt a thin leather folder. "That holds your appointment as scholar assistant to the princeps. I thought an easily concealed case would be more suitable."

"Thank you." Quaeryt bowed his head. "I appreciate your thoughtfulness."

"I also have sent a dispatch telling both Rescalyn and Straesyr to expect you. Upon your return, I want a detailed report on the state of matters in Tilbor. An honest report." A chuckle followed. "Knowing you, that is doubtless an unnecessary warning. I still felt compelled to make it."

"You've never left much to chance."

"With you around, how could I?" Bhayar shook his head again. "Go. Go and pester my governor and princeps with your questions."

Sensing both exasperation and humor in Bhayar's words, Quaeryt bowed. "At your command, Lord."

Quaeryt was almost to the study door when Bhayar added in a low voice, "And take care of yourself. If you think it necessary—and it had better be—I will come to Tilbor."

"Thank you . . . and don't be too hard on those who ask questions while I'm gone."

"Only those who ask stupid ones."

Quaeryt smiled, but kept walking. He still had to meet with Ghoryn . . . and he wanted to read whatever it was Vaelora had written—if only to be able to protect himself.

Are you certain that's the only reason? He didn't laugh softly to himself until he was walking down the private staircase.

6

Once he left the palace, Quaeryt immediately made his way back to his chamber in the Scholarium, where he could read Vaelora's missive without interruption. Before he met with the mate of the *Diamond Naclia*, and parted with silvers, he wanted to know why Bhayar's sister was sending him a missive . . . and what she had in mind. While it might be exactly what she had claimed, he had more than casual doubts—far more. Vaelora might be only nineteen, going on twenty, but not a one of that family was lacking in brains and cunning, and for a mere scholar to get drawn into whatever might be on the young woman's mind was bound to be risky.

But she definitely is attractive. He pushed that thought away.

Once he closed the door and slid the lock plate, just for practice, he imaged the seal from where it joined the edges of the paper to a point slightly lower, then opened the two sheets and began to read.

Dear Scholar Quaeryt—

Many, including Lord Bhayar himself, have noted that you possess a quiet but pervasive understanding of both history and those who would make it, whether those persons be men or women. It is said that history is written by those who have triumphed. That is often so, but it is also true that, at times, it is written by those who have not. They are the ones who have survived others' triumphs and then their decline.

What then is triumph? The momentary accession to power, followed by a constant struggle to increase or maintain that power? Or is such triumph always followed by an inevitable loss of power, whether such a decline is visible to observers at the time? Can power be merely maintained by a wise ruler? Or is that a fiction created by such rulers? Or must it always be increased, or lost? Are the wisest of rulers those who quietly surround themselves with men and women of ability, and listen to them, choosing what serves their ends most judiciously? Yet how is this possible, when so many men of ability seek to further their own ends, rather than those of another?

Quaeryt stopped and reread the clear and graceful writing of the previous paragraph once again.

"'Men and women of ability,'" he murmured, "yet 'so many men of ability seek to further their own ends.'" *An accidental choice of words? Not likely. Not at all.*

A woman of ability must subordinate herself to a man, if indirectly, in order to obtain her ends, while a man may seek to make his own destiny. Thus, a ruler must always ask of a man who ostensibly serves him whose ends that underling truly works for and in what circumstances, while the ruler can ask with which man a woman is allied and how her acts and requests might benefit the man in question.

"I don't know about that . . . a woman can flatter one man while serving another." *But that's what's she's saying.*

This is not as simple as it may appear, for a mother may have desires for her husband or her lover or her children. The honest woman is the one who is direct with the one she loves the most, but do men respect such honesty?

Another good question. Quaeryt kept reading.

In historical tomes, one often reads of how effectively a ruler must treat with allies and enemies. Seldom is there ever reference to the effectiveness in dealing with those closest to a ruler, save when a ruler cold-bloodedly removes all those whose bloodlines might supplant his own. Yet Lord Chayar was most successful in not resorting to such familial bloodletting, as was his father and as has been his son. Why do those who study history not remark upon such?

Because Chayar had only a single son and because his father Lhayar sent all his sons into battle against the descendants of Hengyst until but one son remained.

Or is it because they use circumstances in quiet ways to limit familial rivalries before they can threaten the internal harmonies necessary for a successful ruler?

These are mere thoughts, offered for your consideration.

The signature was a single letter—"V."

When he had finished, Quaeryt folded the missive carefully, then slipped it inside the document case Bhayar had given him.

What exactly did Vaelora have in mind? What she had written wasn't a flattering treatise on his intellect or insight. Nor was it seductive—except in the sense of showing that she could indeed think . . . and raise issues without revealing, at least directly, even who she was. The document was unlike anything he had ever read, and it was incredible, so incredible that he had to wonder if Vaelora had composed it herself.

Yet . . . who else could have? From the brief meeting, he had doubts that Nerya had, and none of Vaelora's sisters had been in residence in Solis in years. That meant that the document reflected either Vaelora or the presence in the palace of another woman of intellect and perception. Perhaps Aelina?

Quaeryt nodded. That was possible. Was the document suggesting that some of the better of Bhayar's decisions had come from his Lady?

Either way, the missive had raised many of the key issues of ruling, including perhaps the most important, that of assuring an orderly succession. Hengyst had been a great ruler, and yet within a few generations, his successors had been anything but great. Supposedly, the same had been true of Caldor, the founder of Bovaria. Kharst had come from a cadet lineage that had scarcely been noted a few generations earlier, when suddenly, all the direct descendants of Caldor had suffered various fatalities that had never been explained satisfactorily, perhaps because anyone who raised such issues also vanished.

Was the letter a form of indirect communication from Bhayar?

He shook his head. While he certainly couldn't discount the possibility, Vaelora's words to him and the tone of the letter mitigated that likelihood. Besides, Bhayar had never minced words with him, not ever. He had hinted, upon occasion, that his youngest sister was proving to be difficult—a greater and greater problem for which he had no easy solution. Because of her intellect? That was all too possible.

Was Vaelora interested in Quaeryt? Perhaps . . . but

why? He was essentially a scholar with a modest income, very modest, and she had no idea that he had a limited ability, through his imaging, to do somewhat better than that—but certainly not the ability to keep her in the style to which she was accustomed. Nor could Bhayar afford to waste an asset like Vaelora on a mere scholar, even one the Lord was familiar with and friendly to.

As for some sort of liaison, Vaelora's words had almost hinted at that . . . but, as Quaeryt had as much as indicated to Bhayar, giving in to such an impulse, even if Vaelora were interested, would be tantamount to Quaeryt sentencing himself to a distant exile . . . or even death. That was certainly not his plan, not when he had so much he wanted to accomplish . . . somehow. In any case, he would not even have a chance to see Vaelora before he sailed, yet she had asked for his comments.

He sat down and took out a short sheet of paper, thinking, and then finally writing.

Dear Mistress Vaelora—

Your missive raised most of the issues of historical interest in assessing the problems facing a ruler, as well as those facing women who are close to such rulers or who may have power in their own right.

Inasmuch as I am departing immediately on a task assigned to me, I cannot comment at length on your words, but the depth and perception of your insights are indeed remarkable, and when I return I would hope to discuss them, if that is agreeable to all concerned.

He signed it as she had signed hers, with his initial. Finally, he left his chamber, heading for the harbor. It was later than he would have liked, and he still needed to meet with Ghoryn and confirm with silver his passage on the *Diamond Naclia*. Then he would have to return to the palace and arrange for his reply to go to Nerya. He wasn't about to address the outside of his reply directly to Vaelora. Not at all.

7

After meeting with Ghoryn late on Jeudi afternoon to confirm his space on the *Diamond*, and then returning to the palace, and spending several silvers to reach Nerya, who accepted the missive silently, Quaeryt returned to the Scholars' House to sleep there on Jeudi night, knowing that the bunk in the fantail locker would have been as hot and steamy as the inside of a boiling cookpot. He'd also melted some wax to waterproof the leather case Bhayar had given him, which now held both his credentials and Vaelora's missive. He was up well before dawn on Vendrei, walking toward the harbor with a sailor's duffel, the canvas strap over his shoulder, the duffel almost on his hip. While he had the silvers for Shuld, the captain, in his wallet, the golds were in hidden slots in his belt, boots, and the sheath of his belt knife.

Until he reached the unmarked way that was "second street," he saw almost no one on the avenues and streets, and but one patroller. Except around the harbor, and in the palace, Solis was not a morning city. Because it was not, he had to worry less about slamthieves and cutpurses.

Even from the pier in the gray light before dawn,

Quaeryt could see that the crew of the *Diamond Naclia* was busy with the last tasks before casting off. The land breeze was light, but enough to get the barque out of the harbor.

"That duffel yours, scholar?" asked Ghoryn as Quaeryt walked up the gangplank. "From back when?"

"It is. Never found anything better for traveling."

"Looks like it's seen a few ports."

"A few," agreed Quaeryt amiably. He turned as the angular figure he had met once approached. There were three black stripes with the crescent moon above them on the front shoulder of the sleeveless dark gray linen jacket.

The scholar slipped his fingers inside his own brown traveling jacket and came up with the coins. "I believe you agreed to these, Captain. The other half of the passage and fare for ten days." Quaeryt handed across four silvers to the lanky captain.

"You're a man of your word, scholar." Shuld smiled humorously, his surprisingly white and full set of teeth contrasting with his square-cut black beard.

"Sometimes that's all we have."

"Looks like you've a bit more than that."

"A patron commissioned a history of Tilbor. Commissions like that don't come often."

"How often?" asked Ghoryn.

"This is my first and probably my last," replied Quaeryt with a laugh.

Shuld nodded and walked away, turning his attention toward the fo'c's'le. "Careful with those capstan bars!"

Ghoryn turned. "Baeryn! Show the scholar the fantail locker."

"Yes, sir." A ragged-haired youth in breeches that

barely covered his knees hurried across the deck and stopped a yard away. He was barefoot. "This way, sir!"

Baeryn quickly clambered up the ladder to the poop deck, keeping well to starboard as they passed the helm, and then dropped down the half ladder.

The youth opened the locker, which, as he did, Quaeryt could see had two doors, rather than hatches, one on the starboard side and one on the port. "There you are, sir."

Quaeryt did not enter the locker, but studied it from the open door. The bunk, such as it was, consisted of a narrow plank shelf, with a canvas pallet, and three ropes anchoring the forward side to the overhead. Under the shelf bunk were spare sails, and against the forward bulkhead were lines and cables. Everything was stowed neatly and fastened in place. There were no portholes in the locker itself, only several sets of shielded and louvered openings to provide ventilation. He noted that the door opened so that it was flat against the outside bulkhead and that there was a cleat there, as well as one on the inside of the door, doubtless one pair of two so that the doors could be tied open in fair weather to air out the locker. On each side of the locker in the aft bulkhead that ran down from the poop deck to the main deck were three brass-framed portholes, clearly going into the captain's and other quarters. All were open.

Quaeryt set the duffel on the narrow deck between the railing and the bulkhead. "How long have you been on the *Diamond*, Baeryn?"

"Near-on three years, sir. My da was a top-rigger on the *Emerald* back when the captain was first mate."

From the way the youth spoke, Quaeryt suspected his father was no longer alive, but now was not the time to ask. "Are all the ships out of Nacliano with jewel names in the same fleet?"

"Don't know as it's rightly a fleet, sir. There's six, I hear, and High Holder Ghasphar owns 'em all." He grinned. "The *Diamond*'s the best."

"She's well-kept and clean. Can you tell me the other mates besides Ghoryn?"

"He's the first. Wealhyr's the second, and Zoeryl's the bosun."

Quaeryt concentrated, committing the names to memory. "Thank you. I won't keep you longer. I'm sure you've duties to attend to in getting under way."

"Yes, sir." After a quick nod, the youth scrambled back up the ladder and headed forward across the poop deck.

Quaeryt stowed his duffel in the locker in a narrow cubby at the end of the shelf bunk on the port side. Then he closed the locker and made his way up the ladder. The helmsman was standing by the wheel, and the captain was forward of him, surveying the ship and crew. Keeping well clear of both, Quaeryt made his way to the main deck, below the poop near the port ladder, where he would be out of the crew's way. He listened as the bosun called out the orders.

"Single up!"

"Gangway aboard. . . ."

Quaeryt noted that the captain used only the topsails in clearing the port and heading down the channel out into the bay, but that made sense, given the long and comparatively narrow channel toward deeper water. The scholar looked back as the white-orange light of dawn crept over Solis, turning the palace on the hill a pinkish orange.

Not for the first time since he'd decided on his course of action, he wondered if the goals he had in mind were worth the risk—or if they were even attainable. He also couldn't help but worry about whether he should have replied to Vaelora . . . yet not replying might well have been worse.

But . . . she is attractive and bright . . . and few women are both.

8

Sometime before dawn on Solayi, nine days into the voyage, Quaeryt was awakened from an uneasy sleep by the sound of boots on the poop deck, far more boots than there should have been at that glass. He immediately pulled on his shirt, trousers, jacket, and boots, and stowed the remainder of his gear in his cubby. Then he eased open the locker, slipped out the starboard door, and closed it behind him.

He studied the sky, but could see no stars, let alone either moon, and since Artiema was still close to full—or, more properly, barely beginning to wane— that meant that the clouds were fairly thick, at least to the west. The wind was light, but steady, out of the west, and the swells were low, no more than a yard from crest to trough at the most.

After a moment, Quaeryt made his way forward, climbing the ladder to the poop deck, forward on the upper deck, and then down to the main deck, since the side of the poop deck was flush with the hull and the only way forward was over the poop.

The bosun stood aft of the main cargo hatch, and

Ghoryn stood above him, at the poop deck forward railing, watching as men scurried up the masts.

Eight crewmen wrestled a huge bronze long-gun into position on the starboard side, just forward of midships, while two others were rigging hawsers from heavy iron rings that were probably anchored into the frame of the ship itself. Quaeryt wasn't sure, but he thought he caught sight of grooves at the end of the muzzle of the cannon as they turned it.

One gun? Just one, despite its rather sizable proportions?

The shot for the cannon didn't look like anything Quaeryt had seen before, either. The ten objects in the wooden cradle were more like short cylinders with rounded points, instead of regular round cannonballs, not that he'd seen all that many cannon or cannonballs. Most merchanters didn't carry cannon.

Quaeryt risked a question. "What's the trouble?"

Zoeryl glanced toward the scholar, then back toward the foremast. "Pirates. Off to the west, just above the horizon. Like as not out of Lucayl. They hole up in the coves south of the cape. Some have caves that open to the sea and will hold a small ship."

Quaeryt studied the sea to the west, finally making out a low, sloop-rigged craft running at an angle to the wind. For a moment, he didn't understand why the captain hadn't turned downwind, but another look at the rapidly nearing craft explained that. The pirate craft was designed and rigged so that she'd be far faster, and Shuld wanted to maneuver so as to put the *Diamond* where the barque's greater sail expanse would offset the cleaner lines and rigging of the pirate.

After several moments, Quaeryt asked, "They try to grapple and board on a single pass with their speed?"

"When they get close, they'll try to use sailshot to disable us first."

Sailshot? The scholar hadn't heard of that, but it was probably a version of grapeshot or chainshot or even wadding designed to rip through the merchanter's sails.

"You right with weapons? We've got a spare cutlass or two and a shipstaff. Hope we won't need them. If the captain's as good as usual, they won't get close enough to board," said the bosun.

"I'm better with a shipstaff."

"Comes to that, you'll have one." The bosun turned from the scholar.

Ghoryn's voice rose over the others. "Mind the fore topsail!"

Behind and above Quaeryt, Shuld was giving orders, and the scholar strained to hear the captain's orders to the helmsman.

"Another point to port. . . ."

Quaeryt watched the pirate vessel—dark-hulled with gray sails and even grayed masts—slowly draw nearer.

"Gun crew to the foredeck!" Shuld hurried down the ladder from the upper deck.

Behind him, Ghoryn moved aft to direct the helmsman.

A puff of smoke issued from the oncoming vessel, less than a vingt away, then a second. Quaeryt saw only the single gout of water a good fifty yards short of the *Diamond* and more than a hundred yards forward of the bow.

Shuld was issuing directions to the gun crew. "Second wedge! One right."

Quaeryt watched, intrigued, while the crewman acting as gun captain tapped the wedge-shaped quoin in place. They weren't firing point-blank, but he judged the elevation to be low. He hadn't seen the shell rammed in place, but it must have been.

"Match at the ready!"

"Match ready."

Shuld was using a device like a sextant, which he lowered. "Two right!"

Two of the gun crew cranked a small winch attached to lines on the gun carriage to turn the gun.

"Fire!"

The cannon's recoil, was restricted by wooden wheels and the heavy hawsers attached to the frame of the vessel itself.

Quaeryt watched. From what he could tell, the first shell landed long, well aft of the pirate sloop.

Two more puffs of smoke from the pirate were followed by a cannonball tearing through the foresail.

Quaeryt winced.

"First wedge, three right."

The second shot from the *Diamond* landed in the water some fifty yards in front of the pirate.

"Hold! Match ready!"

At that moment, Baeryn scurried across the deck and thrust a shipstaff at the scholar. Quaeryt accepted it almost unthinkingly as his eyes fixed on the black-hulled ship bearing down on the *Diamond*.

The pirate was less than half a vingt from the *Diamond* before Shuld again ordered, "Fire!"

The shell ripped into the fo'c's'le of the pirate, and almost instantly, crimson-green-yellow flames surged up. There was . . . something . . . about that unnatural fire. *Antiagon Fire? In a shell?* Quaeryt repressed a shiver.

"Fire!" ordered Shuld.

A second shell exploded on the low fantail of the

pirate sloop, and it too erupted in flames that raced skyward into the rigging.

The pirate vessel seemed to shudder, then swing to the south, as if to parallel the *Diamond*'s heading. Then the sails and rigging began to catch fire, and men started to jump and dive off the burning ship. Part of the bow exploded.

Powder magazine? wondered Quaeryt.

"Steady as she goes!" called out Ghoryn.

"Stow the shells!" ordered Shuld. "On the double!"

Quaeryt turned to watch as the gun crew quickly removed the six shells remaining in the wooden cradle inboard and aft of the shining bronze gun. Once the shells disappeared below, Shuld seemed to be less tense.

The scholar risked another look at the sinking and flaming hulk that had been a pirate vessel, then eased toward the captain, still watching as the crew cleaned the gun and began to unfasten the recoil hawsers. "What was in those shells?" He thought he knew, but wanted to make sure.

"Antiagon Fire," replied the captain quietly, his eyes straying aft to the still-burning hulk that had been a pirate vessel.

"You keep it on board?"

"The magazine is steel-sheathed and lead-lined. The shells are cast iron and copper-lined."

"And the gun is very special," added Quaeryt. "A fine gun, Captain, and better gunnery."

"We were fortunate. Usually takes more than a few shots to get the range. Especially in the gray before dawn. They were too eager, kept a steady course."

Quaeryt nodded. As he stood there on the deck in the growing light of dawn, the wind in his face off the starboard quarter, he realized, if belatedly, why Shuld's gun and shells were so effective. There had been no survivors, and from the coordination of the gun crew, it was far from the first time they'd been used. Yet he knew that none of the privateers commissioned by Bhayar had shells like the ones Shuld had used. And he doubted that either of Bhayar's two warships had shells such as those, or bronze cannon.

"Puzzled, aren't you, scholar?" asked the captain.

"I have to admit I am. Why don't more ships have guns and shells like that?"

Shuld laughed. "More than a few reasons. Each shell costs a gold, maybe a bit more. I have no idea what the gun cost. I was told not to ask and not to lose it—ever. Pirates can't afford guns and shells like that. Most merchanters can't, either. Even if they could, who would they get to make the Antiagon Fire? It takes an imager who's also an armorer and an alchemist. There are but a handful in all Terahnar, and all are employed by High Holders or rulers."

"Such as High Holder Ghasphar?"

Shuld nodded.

"Still . . . they would make fearful armament for warships."

"They would, until everyone had them." Shuld smiled ironically. "Only the Antiagons have ever bothered with large numbers of warships, and they have but a triple handful."

Put that way, it made sense, all too much sense. Antiagon Fire was useless against stone and earth ramparts, and that was why no fortifications were ever wooden. But it was effective against large bodies of men on foot, and that was one reason why most rulers used cavalry or mounted infantry that could scatter quickly. Quaeryt and every other scholar for generations had known that. The threat of Antiagon

Fire had also affected the way war was waged, but Quaeryt was amazed and more than a little irritated at himself for not realizing why there had been so few naval conflicts. Yet it was obvious. Why would anyone want to build a fleet of warships that could be destroyed so quickly? If every ruler built and armed ships with cannons that shot Antiagon Fire shells, a war would ruin them all.

"You understand, I see."

"I never thought of it that way," Quaeryt admitted.

"No one cares if pirate vessels vanish, and we just hoist the Jewel ensign if privateers get too close. If they ignore it . . . well, then they're pirates."

"I imagine the jewel fleet is profitable."

"Rather our losses are far less, and we keep good crews that way."

"Do you see pirates on every voyage in or out of Solis?"

"Namer's demons, no. One passage in ten is more like it, but we could see two on a single transit, and not another for years." Shuld turned to the bosun. "You can handle it from here, Zoeryl. If you would excuse me, scholar?"

"Oh . . . I didn't mean to get in the way, Captain. Thank you." Quaeryt inclined his head and stepped back.

Then he eased his way to the railing just forward of midships and looked back to the west. Only a rapidly dispersing plume of mixed gray and black smoke remained of the pirate vessel.

9

The sun on Jeudi—the second Jeudi Quaeryt had spent on board—had been blistering hot, especially in the late afternoon, so hot that the fantail locker was still radiating heat well after sundown. That was only one of the reasons why Quaeryt stood on the poop, just short of where the two railings met on the forward port corner, looking out into a darkness little relieved by the reddish crescent of Erion. The other reason was that the captain had asked him to stand a watch as the port lookout and offer navigation calculations.

So far, over the past glass, he'd seen no other vessels and no inclement weather creeping up from any horizon, not that he would have expected that, not on a cloudless night with a mild following wind and only moderate swells.

According to the tables, at the longitude of Cape Sud, on Jeudi, the twenty-sixth of Juyn, Artiema should rise at two quints past eighth glass. By checking the deck glass, illuminated by a shielded lantern, Quaeryt could then determine how far west the *Diamond* was from the cape. That was only an approximation, of course, because even in a stabilized box, the glass sands did not run smoothly, but it was a start. Then, by sighting both moons, he could get an idea of their latitude.

"Scholar . . . I thought you might be here." Ghoryn's

voice was barely audible above the sound of the ship cutting through the increasingly larger swells that the *Diamond* was encountering as the ship neared Cape Sud.

"It should be a bit before Artiema rises, but I wanted to sight Erion first. . . ." Quaeryt glanced toward the horizon again.

"Where do you feel we are?"

"I'd say we're seventy to eighty milles west of Cape Sud, and twenty south. I'll know better when I see Artiema."

"Oh? And why do you think that?"

"The captain wants to be far enough offshore for us not to be seen, but not too far, just beyond sight from the cliffs. He'd be holding a course a half point north of southeast to keep us even with the coast. . . ."

Ghoryn chuckled. "We'll see in a bit, won't we?"

"That we will."

"Don't see many scholars at sea," offered the first mate.

"I've never run across another scholar who went to sea," admitted Quaeryt. *Or much of anywhere if they didn't have to.* "Then there are more sailors than scholars." He grinned in the darkness. "Why do you think that might be?"

Ghoryn laughed. "Most folk would say that there's need of more sailors, and perhaps a need for fewer scholars."

"Well put," agreed Quaeryt. "There's a need for scholars, but too many scholars in one place are like too many cooks in the kitchen."

"You never did say much about why you needed to get to Tilbora. Not that I heard, anyways."

"No. I didn't. I think I told you I had a patron who commissioned a more recent history of Tilbor." Quaeryt kept scanning the sea to port. He was still supposed to be a lookout.

"He'd pay for that?"

"Of course. Why do you think the frontispieces of so many books give the name of the patron who commissioned the work? That's so that everyone who reads it for generations to come will see his name."

"Sounds sort of like Naming," mused Ghoryn.

"Ah . . . but he can claim that he is merely advancing human knowledge. A patron isn't erecting a huge stone monument that everyone would immediately see as evidence of selling one's integrity to the Namer."

"A clever way of Naming, then. And you'd do it?"

"What's a name in a book compared to saving knowledge that would otherwise be lost?" asked Quaeryt. "We all have to do things that aren't ideal. Don't you think that there were probably some crewmen on that pirate vessel that had little choice if they wanted to survive? But didn't the good of saving the *Diamond* and her crew and cargo outweigh the evil of killing a handful of comparative innocents among the guilty?"

"You scholars . . . you could argue that Erion was the spirit of mercy, and not the great red hunter, and then you'd make out Artiema to be the evil moon."

"I could," replied Quaeryt with a laugh, "but I wouldn't. There's a big difference between light gray and black, and sometimes there's an even bigger difference between those who claim to follow pure white and those who prefer slightly grayed white."

"I have the feeling you're not a follower of the Nameless, then."

"Oh . . . but I am." *At least of the tenets, even if you're unsure if there even is a Nameless.* "Life is shades of gray. Those who claim to follow the absolute of pure white are disciples of the Namer, because insisting on absolutes in an imperfect world is another form of Naming." He glanced eastward again, catching a glimmer of pearly white on the horizon, just about where he expected it. He'd have to approximate, because moonrise was calculated as that time when the highest limb of the moon's orb cleared the plane of the horizon, and that was almost impossible to determine precisely from a ship's deck, even one pitching so comparatively slightly as was the *Diamond*.

"Excuse me," he said to Ghoryn before hurrying across the deck to the lantern-lit glass.

He checked the time—two and a quarter quints past.

"Where are we, scholar?" asked the mate, who had followed Quaeryt across the deck to stand behind the helm.

"If the glass is correct, we're closer to Cape Sud than I'd thought, more like sixty milles, and I'd judge we're closer to thirty south of the cape." Quaeryt shrugged. "That's an approximation, though."

Ghoryn nodded. "We both have us close to the same position."

"We don't seem to be traveling that fast."

"Captain knows the currents."

Quaeryt had to admit he hadn't thought about currents. He just laughed softly.

"Glad to see there are some things you don't know, scholar."

"There are more than a few." *Far more than a few.* Quaeryt walked back to his position as lookout.

The mate did not follow, but retreated belowdecks, as if the only reason he'd come up had been to check moonrise. But then, it probably had been.

10

Once the *Diamond Naclia* rounded Cape Sud, she faced heavy seas and headwinds, day in and day out. Quaeryt had to lash himself into his bunk every night, waking up frequently, and rising with bruises in places he hadn't had bruises since his last voyage, some ten years earlier. By the end of every day his clothes were damp, if not soaked, and nothing seemed to dry completely. The fare was salted mutton and hard biscuits, with occasional dried lemon and orange rinds. All in all, sailing the three hundred milles from Cape Sud to the calmer waters off Estisle took over a week. During that time, Quaeryt reflected more than a few times on the reasons behind his trip . . . and upon Vaelora's missive, clearly an expression of interest of some sort. But what? And why?

The skies were gray as Shuld guided the *Diamond* around the northern tip of Estisle and toward the harbor at Nacliano, but the early-afternoon air was warm and dry, for which Quaeryt was thankful.

Nacliano was the oldest port on the east coast of Lydar. Even before Shuld eased the *Diamond* into place at the end of a pier that creaked with every swell that rolled under it, Quaeryt was reminded of that antiquity by not only the odors, but by aged brown and gray stone buildings that jumbled themselves across the hills on the north side of the River Acliano. From the pier, the patchwork of roof tiles was all too obvious. There also seemed to be little rhyme or reason as

to what ship was moored where on what pier. Inshore
from the *Diamond* was a fishing craft, little more than
fifteen yards from stem to stern, and opposite was a
broad-beamed three-masted square-rigger.

Quaeryt waited until the *Diamond* was doubled up
and the gangway was down before carrying his duffel
over to the base of the forward ladder where Ghoryn
stood.

"Do you have any thoughts on ships that will get
me to Tilbora?" Quaeryt looked to the first mate as he
handed over the last silvers he owed.

Ghoryn smiled wryly. "Depends on how you want
-to get there, scholar."

"Safely, but without stopping at every little coastal
port along the way."

"You could start by talking to Caarlon. He's the
first on the *Azurite Naclia*. Saw them a pier over, and
they were just winding up loading out. Odds are that
they'll be heading north. Captain Whuylor does a lot
of iron runs."

Iron runs? "And you don't?"

"That's heavy gear. Sawmill blades, axes, crosscut
saws, even iron pigs. They're hard on a ship, and harder
on the crew. Captain Shuld prefers cargoes that have
more . . . value for their weight."

"Scented oils, perfumes . . . ?" ventured Quaeryt.

"Medicinals from Antiago, worked silver from
Eshtora . . . Anyway, if the *Azurite*'s not headed north,
you might try Fhular. He's been taking the *Regia Nord*
that way for years. More of a coaster, but he's a solid
master. Doesn't stop at more than a port or two each
way. Then . . . if you're really desperate, there's always
Chexar on the *Moon's Son*."

The way Ghoryn' mentioned Chexar, Quaeryt
hoped he wasn't ever desperate enough to have to rely

on the *Moon's Son* to get to Tilbora. Even the ship's name was worrisome, at least if one believed in folk-tales. The Pharsi believed that certain women—daughters of Artiema, the greater moon—were specially gifted, but Quaeryt had never heard of a son of the moon, except in muttered terms, and no tales about the lesser moon—Erion, the hunter—mentioned either sons or daughters.

Since Ghoryn had no other suggestions, and a well-meant but short "Good fortune," Quaeryt hoisted his duffel and headed down the gangway, turning toward the foot of the pier. He glanced at the big square-rigger, flying a Tiempran ensign from the stern staff above a nameplate that was unreadable, at least to him.

Beyond the Tiempran vessel was one flying an ensign that Quaeryt thought was Caenenan. The crew was unloading barrels and kegs, and a mixture of scents drifted across the pier, suggesting that the cargo was largely spices . . . and that at least one keg had broken or cracked.

As he neared the inshore end of the pier, he began to angle his way southward in order to make his way back onto the adjoining pier where the *Azurite* was purported to be tied up.

"You there! What do you think you're doing? Get over here." A heavyset figure in a washed-out green uniform, with a black leather harness and belt, a black-billed visored green cap, and scuffed black boots, gestured with an iron-tipped truncheon for Quaeryt to move toward him. He spoke in the harsh Tellan of the east.

Quaeryt recognized the uniform as that of the local patrol, the colors dating back to the time of Hengyst and the Ryntarian despots. The scholar moved care-fully, leaving his hands exposed, stopping a yard short of the patroller. He set the duffel on the worn wood of the pier, holding the strap loosely.

"How did you get here?" The patroller's voice was deep, but cuttingly nasal.

"I was a passenger on the *Diamond*. She just ported."

"With that duffel? Likely as not, you've jumped ship. We don't need people like you here with your fancy words and your pretty way of trying to talk like real people."

Quaeryt could see the problems ahead. If he showed coin, then the patroller would mark him for a confederate not on the Patrol to deprive him of coin and possibly life. If he didn't, he'd likely end up in gaol for some trumped-up reason. "I'm a scholar, patroller. All scholars wear brown, you might recall."

"Don't get fancy with me, fellow. Scholars can't afford ship passage unless they're up to no good."

"Why don't we walk back to the ship? You can ask the captain or the mate if what I said was true." Quaeryt turned just slightly, noting that another, even larger patroller was moving toward him, also with a truncheon.

"We don't need to do that to deal with trash like you."

The loaders and the four vendors on the northern side of the pier edged away from the three. That told Quaeryt more than he wanted to know, but what to expect.

"You're going to come with us, *scholar*." The patroller emphasized the already derogatory Tellan term for scholar.

"Might I ask why?"

"No. Your type doesn't need answers."

"Where do you want me to go?" Too many people had seen him and probably noted the scholar's browns.

That meant he was limited in what he could do in public. Yet he certainly didn't want to go with the pair of patrollers, not the way they were looking for an excuse to use their truncheons.

"That's for us to say. Pick up that duffel."

Quaeryt started to lean forward when he saw the second patroller's truncheon slashing toward him. He jumped back and imaged pepper juice into the man's eyes, and then into the first patroller's eyes as well.

"Sow-sucking bastard!"

Both patrollers lurched, and the larger man stumbled and sprawled across the duffel.

"Thief! Killer!" yelled one of them.

Quaeryt looked beyond the end of the pier, but two more patrollers had appeared there. There was no help for it. He turned and ran back down the pier, dodging around two vendors and alongside a wagon whose wheels were blocked in place opposite an ancient brig.

"Loaders! Stop him! A silver to anyone who catches him!"

For a silver they well might hazard tackling him. Quaeryt saw an opening in between two groups of men who had turned at the patrollers' calls and dashed between them, jumping off the pier in the space between the brig and the square-rigger, just hoping that the water was deep enough.

He went under, and down perhaps three yards, then struggled underwater back toward the pier—except his hands encountered a rough stone wall. He concentrated, trying to move along the wall underwater until he could find a space between the sections of the pier built on solid stone and rock supports and the patches of water between them and the wooden supports sunk into the harbor bottom.

His lungs were bursting when he finally surfaced under the pier, but he came up as quietly as he could, immediately creating a slight concealment shield that he hoped just showed water, if anyone tried to look down through the few narrow gaps in the heavy wood of the pier above.

He'd been in dirtier water before, but not in years, and he had to use one hand to clamp his nose to keep from sneezing. The fingers of the other held to an edge in the rough stone.

"He went in over there!"

"More like by the square-rigger."

"Go after him, Walthar. It's a silver."

"In that water? Patrollers can keep their silver. 'Sides, he hasn't even come up. No sight of him. No sounds. You go in if you want."

"Where did he go?" demanded a harsh voice.

"He jumped off the pier. Never came up."

"He might be right underneath you, for all you know."

"We looked. Don't see anything."

"There's a silver reward for whoever turns him in."

"We get it if we find his body?"

"Only if he's alive. He has to answer to the Patrol."

"What'd he do?"

"Never mind that!"

Quaeryt kept breathing easily and waiting, but it had to have been close to two quints before the patrollers left. He still had no idea why the patroller and his partner had decided to go after him. He'd been polite, and he hadn't done a single thing except walk down the pier with a duffel. Years before, he'd never had any trouble in Nacliano. Why now?

Once the crowd above slowly dispersed, he eased his way to the other side of the pier, still holding shields, and made his way inshore, half-swimming, half-pulling himself hand over hand along the stone foundations, sometimes having to squeeze through the narrow spaces between pier supports and hulls, until he finally found a ladder up the side of one of the stone pier supports. He took his time climbing it because, while his shield might conceal him, he'd still be leaving a trail of water behind.

He simply rested on the top of the ladder, out of the way, watching and listening, but he saw no patrollers, and the various vendors, loaders, and teamsters traveling the pier appeared to have forgotten the commotion that had occurred half a glass earlier.

Once his browns had dried enough that water droplets did not leave a trail, Quaeryt climbed from the ladder to the edge of the pier and, still holding his concealment shield, walked slowly toward the base of the pier.

Two patrollers walked back and forth on the stone causeway beyond the end of the pier, glancing along it, clearly still looking for Quaeryt.

"Haelan . . . he drowned. . . . Even if he didn't, he's not going to walk down here toward us. . . ."

"Scholars . . . Duultyn said they were trouble . . . as bad as Pharsi traders or imagers."

"Duultyn's pretty hard on 'em," offered the younger patroller.

"Don't matter. Can't have anyone attacking patrollers."

"Suppose not. . . ."

"You don't want Duultyn saying you love scholars. Next thing you know . . ."

Quaeryt eased by the pair unseen and slowly made his way toward the next pier. There were no patrollers at its base and he walked more quickly out toward the far end where the *Azurite* was berthed. He passed a brig and a barque, both with Telaryn ensigns, and then a Ferran brig. When he came to where the *Azurite* had been ... the berth was empty.

He stood there looking at the *Azurite* sailing slowly out into the harbor.

What vessel leaves port in midafternoon? The winds are better in the morning and evening.

That might well be, but the *Azurite* was gone, and there was no help for it. He'd have to try Captain Fhular and the *Regia Nord* ... if the coaster even happened to be ported at the present.

His browns were almost dry, enough so that most wouldn't notice, even if his feet felt like they were still sloshing inside his boots. Still holding concealment shields, he eased along the side of the pier until he was in the shadow of a bollard, where he released the shields, several yards from where three loaders stood, watching as two dray horses pulled a wagon slowly toward the two-masted schooner in the berth inboard from where the *Azurite* had been. He was a little light-headed, both from his exertions in escaping the two patrollers and from having to hold the shields as long as he had.

One of the loaders turned and looked at Quaeryt, a puzzled expression on his face.

"I was trying to reach the *Azurite* before she cast off," the scholar explained.

"The jewel ships don't wait for no one."

"Have you seen the *Regia Nord*?"

"Fhular's boat? Nah ... hasn't ported yet."

"Or the *Moon's Son*?"

"Haven't seen Chexar's boat lately. Fhular left for Shacchal, let's see, day before yesterday." He turned to the man beside him. "Was on Samedi, wasn't it?"

"What was?"

"Fhular leavin', coldass."

"Coldass, yourself. Yah . . . Samedi."

"Loaders!" called the teamster.

"You know if the schooner there is headed north?" asked Quaeryt.

The loader shrugged.

Quaeryt took a deep breath.

He'd have to cover all the piers to discover if any ships were ported that might be sailing north—and he'd have to keep a constant watch for the patrollers.

11

By late afternoon on Lundi, Quaeryt had learned two things. First, there were no ships currently ported in Nacliano that would be headed to Tilbora, or anywhere close, and, second, that the patrollers stayed off the piers unless they observed a malefactor or chased one. As the better part of wisdom, he parted with a silver and bought a dark green shirt of less than perfect quality from a pier vendor and immediately stripped off the scholar's brown tunic. His sleeveless brown jacket wasn't identifiable as a scholar's without the customary brown tunic shirt, which he'd let dry and then wrapped around his midsection under the green shirt.

The vendor had only said, in common Tellan, "Wise man. The patrollers don't like brown."

"So I've heard. Do you know why?"

The gray-haired vendor shook his head and offered

a sad smile. "There is much they do not like. That is why my son rows me to the pier each day. That way I can avoid them. They demand coin for no reason."

"But they don't come on the piers?"

"Only to chase someone who has done what they think wrong in the city."

Is that a rule of the local council? Quaeryt didn't ask. "Are there any inns that are honest?" He knew nothing of the inns in Nacliano. He'd been in the port only a few times more than ten years ago, and he'd slept in his hammock aboard ship.

The vendor shook his head. "There are but two kinds. There are those who charge too much, and there are those who cheat those who stay."

"What might be the cheapest of those that charge too much?"

"The Tankard is said not to be too bad. All say to avoid the Silver Bowl."

"Thank you."

As he walked away, Quaeryt counted his duffel and spare clothes as lost—and the history as well, but he still had the leather commission case. It was hardly even damp on the outside, because of the wax coating and oilcloth wrapping.

He made his way off the second pier, where he'd purchased the shirt, using an empty wagon as a partial shield from the pier patrollers, although he was ready to lift a concealment shield at any moment. He moved with the air of a man who knew where he was headed, although he remembered so little of Nacliano that he had no idea. It didn't matter; he only needed to find a chandlery where he could purchase a few items. The sun was low in the sky and in his eyes when he finally found one on a side lane. The door squeaked as he stepped inside, but the red-haired man standing by a side counter barely looked in his direction as he counted out coppers to a customer.

Quaeryt immediately located a small stained and scuffed canvas bag, but it took him far longer to find a small steel razor in a battered leather case. The blade was worn, but still sharp, but even so, it was likely not to be inexpensive. Still, he did need to replace the one lost with the duffel. Any beard he grew was itchy, and before long his skin began to develop sores.

He also found a pair of drawers, a small square of boot wax, and an equally small square of hard soap.

The chandler watched as Quaeryt carried his items over to the counter. "Three for the bag, two silvers and a half for the razor, two for the wax, one for the soap, seven for the drawers—you ought to have a strop for the razor . . . ruin it quick otherwise."

"It's been a long trip," said Quaeryt with a wry smile.

"You take this strop." With a smile, the chandler held up a strop as worn as the razor case. "I'll call it even for four silvers."

"How about if you throw in a second square of soap?"

"Done."

Quaeryt eased out a gold. He hated revealing that, but it was likely safer to do so in the chandler's shop than in the inn, and he only had two silvers left in his wallet.

"You must have had a rough passage coming south," offered the chandler, taking the gold and returning six silvers.

"It wasn't what I expected," temporized Quaeryt.

"It never is." The chandler laughed. "Never is. Best of fortune."

"I just might need that." Quaeryt paused as he

slipped his wallet inside his trousers, mostly behind the heavy and wide belt. "Where's the best honest fare?"

"The best is the Silver Bowl, but you'll go through those silvers faster 'n their wine. Good wine, but it ought to be. The Tankard and the Overdeck are solid. Cheapest is the Red Lantern, but you'll need a gut tougher than bullhide. Tankard's a block south, Overdeck one north, and the Silver Bowl two west."

Quaeryt nodded. "Thank you."

He slowed just as he opened the door to the chandlery, checking the street, but there was no one that close when he stepped outside into the lengthening shadows indicating sunset was not that far off. Keeping an eye out for cutpurses and slam-thieves, Quaeryt turned south at the corner.

The Tankard was a narrow three-story timber and brick building, some three streets back from the harbor, almost directly west from the pier on which the *Diamond* had tied up, and faced on a small square that held a timeworn statue of Hengyst the Unifier.

Quaeryt looked at the statue. *If he happened to be such a great unifier, why was Lydar still split into five lands after he became the unifier?* He shook his head. That wasn't a useful question.

Carrying his small bag, he walked into the Tankard and toward a woman who stood behind a narrow upright writing desk. Just above her head, on a narrow railed shelf to her left, were two vases, both about a hand and a half high, each a simple curving shape rising from a circular base into a trumpet-like opening slanted at an angle. One was glazed in shimmering silver, the other in a deep blue.

Quaeryt managed not to stare at the pair. *Where did she ever get those?* They had to be Cloisonyt pieces dating back centuries. He forced his eyes to the woman, who wore gray trousers and shirt. Her eyes were gray, and her hair was iron gray. "Yes?"

"I'm looking for a room for several days."

"Missed a ship, did you?" asked the gray lady.

"That I did."

"We've two rooms free. Second-floor corner with a wide bed, and a third-floor back side, not much more than a bed and a place to sleep. Five coppers for the second floor, and three for the third. No locks, but you can bar·the door at night."

"I'd like to see the third-floor one."

"Suit yourself. It's empty. Straight back from the stairs with the number three on the door." The gray lady pointed down the narrow hall. "Stairs are at the end."

"Thank you." Quaeryt nodded.

He walked up a staircase so narrow that his shoulders almost brushed the walls on each side. Every other step creaked, but the risers did not give under his boots. The chamber was more like a garret, with less than a yard between the narrow pallet bed and the wall, not even as large as the fantail locker on the *Diamond*. The plank door struck the bottom of the bed if opened all the way. There was a wall shelf between the window frame and the wall against which the bed was set, with a pitcher and bowl, both tin, and several pegs for hanging clothes on the opposite wall. The single narrow window was unglazed and had warped shutters.

Quaeryt checked the pallet, then made his way back down to the front hall, where the gray lady looked at him.

"I'll take it."

"Every night in advance," replied the gray lady.

"Two nights for now, and, after I eat, I'd like a tub of clean water to wash some things."

The old woman squinted. "You smell as you could use some washing yourself. I could have the girls bring up the tub and water for another two coppers—and a bucket for rinse water. Slice of soap be another copper."

"If that's the way it is . . . it's the way it is." He handed over a silver.

"Best of the fare tonight is the duck goulash." She returned a copper.

"Thank you." He made his way to the public room, where he found a corner table.

The duck goulash with thick noodles wasn't bad, and it wasn't too peppery. Quaeryt approved. He'd never liked food spiced so much that he couldn't taste anything except the spices. Of course, that was how some places disguised bad meat.

Once he'd eaten, and limited himself to a single lager with his meal, he made his way back to the gray lady.

"Have the water up in a bit."

He nodded and climbed the stairs. His feet were sore, as much for having walked in damp boots for too long as for the distance he had covered. When he reached the small room, he pulled off his boots and waited.

About half a glass later, two wiry girls appeared with a narrow tin tub less than a yard long and little more than half that wide, with a bucket. The tub barely fit between the bed and the wall, and it took the girls three trips with buckets to get enough water into it.

"Thank you." Quaeryt smiled and gave each girl a copper.

"Much obliged, sir," the two chorused in thick country Tellan, before leaving him.

After dipping the pitcher in the tub to set aside some of the water for shaving, and a bucket of rinse water, he washed himself, then shaved, before washing and then rinsing all the garments except the green shirt. He spread them across the wall pegs to dry, then eased the tub and buckets out into the narrow hallway, and barred the door.

He was more than ready to sleep while the clothes dried. He'd been attacked and chased by a vengeful patroller for no reason at all, lost his duffel, taken a swim in the harbor, and was spending coin faster than he wanted. The weather to the north was bad. The best ship had already left, and he still had to watch out for angry patrollers. And . . . he was little more than halfway to Tilbora.

Quaeryt stretched out on the narrow bed and tried not to think about all that.

12

Quaeryt sat alone in the public room of the Tankard on Mardi morning, finishing off what the serving girl had called a ham-fry—stale bread wrapped around a slice of cheese and a slice of ham and dipped in egg batter, and then fried until it was deep brown. For a breakfast, accompanied by a lager, it was adequate.

"You seen any scholars, swamp lily?" boomed a deep nasal voice from outside the public room.

"And if I had?"

"You'd tell me. If I find you've put up one, I'll close you down."

"You try it, and not even your Namer-damned uncle will save you. And that's if you have better fortune with the next scholar than you did with the first."

Abruptly, a crashing sound followed.

"I'm so sorry . . . swamp lily. Accidents do happen. Just remember that." A cruel laugh followed the cynical words.

Quaeryt recognized the voice, and the cruelty behind it. He forced himself to finish the ham-fry and the last of the lager—and he left a copper for the serving girl.

When he did leave the public room, he paused for only an instant to glance back toward the writing stand. The gray lady was carefully picking up pieces of blue ceramic, although the silver vase appeared untouched. He concealed a wince and quickly headed toward the stairs. The patroller had destroyed a vase that was worth perhaps a hundred golds to a collector, one of beauty that could never be replaced.

Once in the small third-floor room, he folded those now-dry garments he wasn't wearing and eased them into the canvas bag, along with the razor, strop, and soap. Then he made his way back down to the main level. The gray lady, the broken vase, and the silver one were nowhere in sight when he left the Tankard.

He walked toward the harbor and the piers with the gait, if limping, of a man who had a destination and a purpose, watching for patrollers, and then picked the third pier, because that was the one without any green uniforms in sight. Unfortunately, there were also no new ships ported there. Using his concealment shield—and transport wagons rolling onto the piers—to get past the patrollers watching the base of the other two piers, he checked the other ships in port, but the three new arrivals were headed south and east.

With no immediate transport in sight, he slipped off the pier, past a pair of patrollers, neither of whom happened to be the nasal-voiced one. In fact, Quaeryt hadn't encountered the obnoxious and overbearing one since he'd overheard him at the inn.

The incident with the vase bothered Quaeryt, in some ways far more than the attempt by the nasal-voiced patroller to assault Quaeryt. Was that because the patroller was abusing those whom he was charged to protect? Or because he would destroy an ancient object of beauty without a second thought as a means to pursue a personal agenda?

Since there weren't any ships going in the direction he needed to travel, his next priority was to find a place where he could image some coppers, somewhere that had copper wastes or scraps in an old building or the ground around it. With that preparation, he'd found that imaging coppers was not too difficult. Sometimes he could manage silvers. The one time he'd tried golds, he'd nearly died, and he wasn't about to try that again.

Once he was well clear of the harborfront and the piers, he turned south, toward where the Acliano River ran northwest from the south side of the harbor, thinking that there might be some locations suitable for his imaging somewhere along the riverfront. Usually, there were some places that handled metals, or at least a ruined building or two. He kept to the streets that were better traveled, and by late morning he was walking northwest along the riverside road. While many of the buildings had seen better days, almost all were still in use, from a factorage dealing in oils to a lumber and timber yard, both with their own small river docks for unloading barges, to a newer stone building where loaders were rolling barrels off a barge.

He walked almost a mille before finally coming to a ruined and roofless structure surrounded by a palisade fence with gaps here and there, if mostly too small for him to slip through. The large square chimneys suggested it had been some sort of metalworking facility, although they were but half the height they once had likely been, and the space between the remaining walls was filled with grasses and weeds, mostly tan and dried from the heat of a long summer. He kept walking, nodding to a teamster guiding a wagon pulled by four dray horses, until he saw a wider gap in the fence.

Just to be on the safe side, he stepped behind a twisted oak in front of the battered palisade fence and raised a concealment screen. Only then did he move toward the gap in the fence. Once through, he surveyed the ruins and the hint of a path toward the nearest chimney.

He took several steps. His trousers brushed the tinder-dry weeds, and they crackled.

"Someone's coming! Run!" The voice was low, but high-pitched, like a child's.

He didn't see whoever had raised the alarm, only the swaying of high grasses and weeds between the tumbled-down foundation walls before him.

Quaeryt stopped and waited, listening, but the children had apparently hurried between the walls and hidden downhill, possibly under the sagging wharf whose end barely protruded over the muddy water of the river. He stepped into another set of shadows beside a section of stone and yellow-brick wall that remained and released the concealment shield. He tried imaging a copper, and one appeared in his hand.

Nodding, he continued until he had fourteen in his wallet, and he was beginning to sweat profusely. Then he wiped his forehead and stood in the shade until he was cooler. Only then did he raise the concealment shield and retrace his steps through the fallen stone, weeds, and grass and back through the fence. He stood behind the oak once more, waiting until no wagons or pedestrians were nearby before releasing the concealment and stepping out onto the edge of the road to continue his walk.

At the next street heading north, he crossed the road, waiting for a coach and then hurrying across to avoid a collier's wagon. After covering less than twenty yards, he could see that the street he traveled was one catering to cloth factors of various sorts.

He still wondered about the one patroller's fixation on and hatred of scholars. Would someone at the local Scholars' House be able to shed some light on that?

After walking another block, he saw an older man adjusting the shutters on the side windows of a small shop that looked to be a lace factorage. When he neared the graying and stout factor, he stopped and waited for the other to finish.

"What can I do for you?" The man did not smile.

"Pardon me," Quaeryt began. "Could you tell me the way to the Scholars' House here in Nacliano?"

The factor frowned, and his eyes narrowed. "You're a stranger here, aren't you?"

"From Solis."

"A word of advice. Don't be asking about scholars here in Nacliano. You want to know why, just walk some three blocks north and two west, and that'll tell you." The factor nodded brusquely, turned, and left Quaeryt standing outside the shop.

The scholar managed not to gape. He'd traveled much of Telaryn over the years, and he'd never gotten that kind of answer.

Five blocks farther on, he understood better the factor's words. What had been the Scholars' House was a blackened ruin, and clearly had been for at least several years. The only thing that identified it as such was the cracked granite plaque-stone, only half of which remained, with only the chiseled letters SCHOLAR left. Scavengers had taken everything except the core of the walls and timbers so blackened that they were useless.

Quaeryt noticed something else as well—an abandoned anomen across the street, but the anomen had not been gutted and salvaged the way the Scholars' House had, perhaps because there was at least some respect for a place of worship of the Nameless, even if it had been the anomen of the scholars. For a time, he stood in the shade cast by the tinsmith's shop and watched the various passersby. To a person, not a one looked at either the anomen or the ruined Scholars' House, as if neither existed.

Lord Bhayar could be skeptical of both choristers and scholars, but Quaeryt knew that Bhayar would have been displeased with both the patroller and the apparent public hatred of scholars, if only because such public hatred too often led to unrest and dissatisfaction with the ruler.

Quaeryt turned back toward the harbor—and in the direction of the Tankard, he hoped. He needed to listen and watch—and think—while he waited for a ship.

13

Although Quaeryt walked through the harbor district until close to twilight on Mardi, he did not see the patroller he was seeking. He didn't expect to, because it was likely the man was on early duty. He did locate the Patrol building, with the barred windows that signified that it was also a gaol, some six blocks south of the Tankard and one back toward the harbor, tucked away between a stable that catered to teamsters and a café without a name. He did find it ironic that the building that served the patrollers faced away from the harbor.

On Meredi morning, Quaeryt was up and ate early, then made his way to the tall desk, above which the wall shelf remained empty. He waited until the gray lady appeared.

"What can I do for you?"

"It looks like I'll be here at least one more night." He extended three coppers. "For tonight."

She took them with a nod.

"You're Lily?" he asked.

"Was once. How'd you know? I never told you."

Quaeryt smiled. "I listened. Years back, I used to be a sailor. I discovered that if you listen people will answer some of the questions you'd otherwise ask."

"You still have that look, but you speak better than any sailor I've ever met, and you've got a slight accent that might say you're Bovarian."

"I'm not Bovarian. I am from Solis."

"Now what do you do?"

"Whatever I must. I have a patron. He dispatched me to Tilbora to locate something, but I missed the *Azurite Naclia*. Took longer coming up from Cape Sud."

Lily smiled. "Always does, except in fall. Winds turn then."

"Is there a good patisserie anywhere?"

"Patisserie? Oh . . . one of those fancy bakeries? Not around here. You want to walk a good mille, you can take the next street north and go west until you get to the Hill Square. There's two within a block or so of the square."

Quaeryt nodded. "Thank you. Until later." With that, he turned and left the Tankard, walking quickly to the north. Once he turned the corner, he stopped to look at some copperware displayed in a window, then eased to where he could watch the Tankard's front door while seemingly waiting on the corner for someone.

He waited for almost half a glass before a pair of patrollers strolled by. While he was ready to head for the nearest alleyway and vanish behind a concealment shield, neither looked more than passingly in his direction. Nor was either the round-faced and heavyset patroller who had attacked him.

Since it was unlikely that another and different pair of patrollers would be following the first any time soon, Quaeryt turned and headed toward the harbor. There, at the first pier, he observed a second pair of patrollers, but not the man for whom he was looking. Keeping well away from them, but not in an obviously apparent fashion, he walked onto the pier. He wasn't exactly hopeful about finding a ship headed north, not when almost half the berths at the pier were vacant, but he covered the entire pier, making inquiries and having no success.

When he left the first pier, the patrollers were no longer at the base, but he found they had moved to watch the second pier, although neither seemed especially attentive, and he eased past them. The long pier held but four vessels, and not a single one was headed north. He did use concealment to leave the pier, although it might not have been necessary.

There were no patrollers at the base of the third pier, and, again, he made his way out and inquired of the ships tied at the pier, but not a single one was headed north.

As he turned to head back down the pier, away from a schooner that had just arrived from Thuyl, a voice called out. "Dried fruits . . . the best dried fruit in the east! You can't do better, sir!"

Quaeryt smiled as he looked at the bent old man. He liked the man's cheerfulness, as well as his clean tan shirt and trousers, and the clean tannish cloth that covered his tray. "I doubt I could. What's the best?"

"Depends on your taste, sir. I'm a tad partial to the sour cherries, but I've got some sweet ones, too, and the dried apple keeps well if you're going on a long voyage."

"A copper's worth of the sour ones." Quaeryt tendered the coin and received a small pile of dried cherries on a clean but small cloth square—a rag, in fact. "You keep track of the ships?"

"I wouldn't say that I keep track of them. I see some more often than not."

"I've been looking for vessels heading to Tilbora. I heard that the *Moon's Son* sails there often."

"Right regular, she does, excepting she's not in yet."

"Where might she tie up?"

"Over on the second pier, way in . . . cheaper there. That's because the end berths are easier to catch the wind . . ."

When the old vendor finished, and Quaeryt had eaten all the dried cherries, he handed the cloth back. "Thank you."

"My pleasure, sir." The old man nodded.

Quaeryt grinned before heading back toward the base of the pier. He wasn't about to ask about the nasal-voiced patroller who hated scholars. People usually remembered when strangers asked about such, and he didn't want anyone remembering anything, and since he had the time, it was better not to ask.

He was vaguely surprised to find that the pair of patrollers who had attacked him had stationed themselves at the shore end of the third pier in the time that he'd been on the pier, although that might have been because there looked to be more vessels tied up there than at the other two piers, and the pier was more crowded with vendors, teamsters and wagons, and loaders, as well as at least some travelers. Quaeryt moved back and tried to blend into the nearest bollard, listening as he did.

". . . *Sparrow*'s back . . ."

"Just sails three ports—Kephria, Hassyl, and here . . . must like those Antiagonan women . . ."

"Nuanyt likes more than that."

". . . don't see anyone in brown . . ."

"Not many these days . . . suppose the word's out. Might as well swing by the Sailrigger."

"Why? Be dead as dead till . . ." The larger patroller shook his head. "Might have known . . ."

As the two turned, Quaeryt raised a concealment and waited until they were headed away, both swinging the iron-tipped truncheons from their leather straps. Then he followed, if at a distance, as the two walked along the avenue fronting the harbor, heading southward. After passing a small café that looked to be closed, the two stopped in front of a legless man sitting on a low-backed stool with stubby legs less than a hand long and strumming a mandolin.

"Pharlon! Seen any scholars lately?" asked the nasal-voiced patroller.

"No, sir."

"You will let me know if you do, won't you?"

"Yes, sir."

"That's a good fellow." The patroller bent and scooped a coin from the bowl set before the disabled musician, then continued to the next corner, where both patrollers turned away from the harbor. Two women carrying laundry baskets on their heads hurried across the narrow street and down an alleyway to avoid the patrollers.

A block later, the two patrollers slowed as they neared a larger building with a painted signboard proclaiming it as the Sailrigger. The place was definitely a taproom, but one with dancers attired more than suggestively, if the painting on the signboard happened to be an indication, although there was an open courtyard in front, enclosed by a chest-high yellow brick wall, where some sort of food could be served. All the tables were empty.

The patrollers walked through the untended open courtyard gate. Quaeryt followed so far as the gate, then stopped, holding his concealment and waiting.

"Saerysa!" called the nasal-voiced patroller.

No one appeared, although Quaeryt thought he saw one of the closed shutters on a window on the wall of the taproom adjoining the courtyard vibrate.

"You wouldn't want to make the Patrol unhappy, would you, Saerysa?"

After several moments, a woman appeared, wearing a thin cotton robe. She was dark-haired and small, but even with the loose robe, it was obvious she was well-formed, most likely one of the dancers. Quaeryt doubted that her duties were limited to dancing. She stopped a yard or so outside the door leading into the building, leaving it open behind her.

"Aren't you going to come and greet me?" The nasal-voiced patroller stepped past several tables but stopped a good three yards short of the dancer. He eased the truncheon into his belt sheath.

"You're here early. I just got up." Her voice was low and husky.

"Fancy that. You need to come over and greet me. Just like you would when you want a sailor to spend his silvers on you."

"I'm not even really awake, Duultyn."

"You really should come here."

Saerysa took two steps and halted just out of the patroller's easy reach.

"You're shy this morning."

"I told you I was tired."

Abruptly, the patroller moved and grabbed both her wrists, pulling them down and pressing her against him. The girl tried to knee him in the groin, but he turned his body and took the knee on his thigh, then shifted his grip and pinned both arms with one large hand, and ran the other hand across her body.

"You need to be more friendly, Saerysa."

The dancer slumped, as if surrendering, then tried to bite Duultyn's shoulder.

As the patroller pushed the dancer back and twisted away from her teeth, Quaeryt did his best to imitate the "caaw" of a raven, then imaged a sordid mass that he hoped resembled a large and soggy raven dropping less than a yard above the patroller. It dropped and spread across the patroller's green shirt with a splatting sound.

While a few bits of the "dropping" splattered on the dancer, Saerysa pulled back, then wrenched free of Duultyn's grasp as the patroller gaped at the mess across the front of his uniform. She turned and ran through the door into the building.

"Shit!"

"That's right." The other patroller stifled a laugh, but did shake his head. "That raven really got you."

"Ravens don't do that!" snapped Duultyn.

"I heard it, and you've seen it."

"I didn't see any raven, and you can't miss birds that big."

"He didn't miss you."

An older woman appeared with two large towels, one damp and one dry. "Sir . . . perhaps these would help."

Duultyn glared at her. "Where's Saerysa?"

"You scared her. She ran off. She is no longer here."

"She is, too."

The other patroller cleared his throat. "Duultyn . . ."

"Shit . . ." Duultyn looked at the older woman. "Tell your little dancer she has a big debt to pay. And she'd better." He took the damp towel and began to sponge off his shirt.

The older woman retreated into the Sailrigger, closing the door behind her.

"Namer-cursed sow . . ." muttered Duultyn. "Name 'em all!"

"She's pretty enough, but is she worth all the trouble?" asked the taller patroller.

"It's a matter of principle. How would Burchal feel if he knew . . ." Duultyn glanced down and shook his head. "Still going to have a stain here."

"Glad the chief's not a relation of mine."

"It comes in handy at times." Duultyn threw the damp towel on the nearest table and blotted his shirt with the dry one. "Old lady Shaalya knows I can find a reason to close her down if Saerysa isn't more co-operative. You'll see."

The dry towel followed the first, then dropped to the brick-paved courtyard floor. Duultyn did not pick it up, but turned toward the gate.

Once the two patrollers left the Sailrigger's courtyard, Quaeryt followed. He could have done far worse, but he needed Duultyn in good health, at least until he discovered more.

The only problem was that, while he followed the pair for more than three glasses, he learned little that he had not already seen. Duultyn did take coin from two other beggars along the way, speaking cheerfully to both. Just before noon, perhaps a quint before tenth glass, the two returned to the Patrol building.

Quaeryt took a table at a café a half block away, where he ordered a lager and a domchana. The batter-fried ham and fresh yellow and red pepper sandwich wasn't bad, although he'd had better. But then, he'd also eaten far worse.

He did wonder just how long he'd have to wait for the two patrollers before they left the patrol station.

After lingering over his midday meal, Quaeryt waited until Duultyn and his partner reappeared and followed them for another two glasses. He learned little more. He then returned to the harbor and visited the two ships that had ported since the morning. Neither was heading north.

He debated returning to the Sailrigger, but decided that he wouldn't learn what he needed to know even if Duultyn did return there after his duty shift. Instead, he decided to look to see if he could find a bookseller.

That took more than a glass, because, after one look of disgust from a cabinetmaker who displayed a bookcase in his window, when Quaeryt inquired about a bookstore, he decided that asking was anything but the best policy. In the end, he stumbled onto it, because he had decided that at least a few people who liked good pastries might like books as well and he had made his way to the area around Hill Square. He had just walked by one of the bakeries mentioned by Lily and had noted that it was close to being a patisserie, but he decided he could always stop later.

He had turned the corner and was walking down a narrow side street, passing a felter's shop, when he noticed that the next building had iron grates on the windows, and an iron-grated door, although the grated outer door was swung back and latched open. Above the door was a sign that read "Cooper." That was what the faded and stylized letters seemed to signify. The windows were so grimy that he could see nothing, perhaps because there were no lamps lit within the building.

Yet, when Quaeryt slowed and peered through the open doors, he saw bookshelves, despite the pair of half barrels against each side of the entry foyer.

He stopped and considered. The bookshop, if it were indeed that, was well away from the harbor, but less than two blocks from Hill Square. It was also tiny, less than four yards wide, wedged between the felter's and a cordwainer's shop.

Finally, he shrugged and decided to enter, if cautiously.

When he stepped inside, Quaeryt was almost overwhelmed by the mustiness, an odor stronger than that in the dankest corner of the library of the Scholarium in Solis. He paused for a moment, then glanced at the shelves, then at the tall silent man standing at the back of the shop, who held a knife with a shimmering blade.

"Go ahead and look," said another voice, one filled with age.

Quaeryt glanced to his right, locating a man with wispy white hair perched on a stool chair behind a high desk. "I'm sorry. Your guard took me by surprise. So did the sign for a cooper."

"That's all right. It's better that most think it's the place of a cooper who's given up coopering. You'd be an outlander, even to come in here."

"If no one comes in here . . . ?"

"Oh . . . there are plenty of folk who'd like books. Most of them just don't walk in. They send notes to a friend of mine, along with the coin, and Eltaar delivers them at night. These days, no one likes being thought much like a scholar."

"Could you tell me why?"

"I can, and, unlike others in this fear-ridden city, I'd be pleased to tell you." The white-haired bookseller gestured to a high-backed stool in front of his desk. "That is, if you would care to join me."

As he saw the gesture, Quaeryt also noted that the bookseller wore tightly fitted gray gloves that ran from his fingertips up under the sleeves of the pale gray shirt and that there were whitish welts on the front of his neck, revealed but slightly by the high-collared shirt.

"I'd like to hear the story," Quaeryt admitted as he moved toward the stool. He did turn the stool slightly, so that he could keep an eye on the guard out of the corners of his eyes.

"Stories here, you understand," began the bookseller, "always begin with a phrase such as, 'In the time of . . . whoever was famous, it came to pass that . . .' I suppose every place has a phrase to signify a story." A chuckle followed. "In the time of the first years of Lord Bhayar of Telaryn, a strong man became the head of the City Patrol of Nacliano, and that man's name was Burchal. He had the strength of two men and the cunning of both a weasel and a fox, and like a serpent, he could strike from the darkness. At first, everyone rejoiced, because the Patrol stopped the loaders from soliciting bribes from the shipmasters and teamsters. They were also glad when the taprooms and cafés that drugged the sailors burned to the ground. No one was displeased when the number of beggars was limited to one on each pier, and only to those beggars missing arms or legs or eyes, and with each beggar being given but one day a week to beg . . ."

Quaeryt listened as the bookseller went through a listing of changes created by Burchal, but he kept his attention split between the storyteller and the guard.

". . . and then, one day, a scholar from Cloisonyt arrived in Nacliano. At first, no one even knew he had come to the city, for he repaired to the House of Scholars, but, in time, he began to visit the harbor and to teach some of the women to read, and one of those women was the young wife of Burchal, who was a beautiful girl from outside of Cheva. She could not read and begged the old scholar, and he was old, with hair of silver and a kind face, to teach her to read and to do her numbers so that she could help her husband with the household accounts." The bookseller laughed ironically. "And from that day was Burchal's happiness diminished, for the young woman was bright as well as beautiful, and she began to read, and then to look at the account books of the household, and then at another account book." The bookseller shook his head. "Then she disappeared, never to be seen again, and one week to the day later, a great fire burned down the House of Scholars, and all the scholars within were said to have perished, including the old scholar who had taught the girl to read." The bookseller stopped.

"That's it? And no one has done anything?"

"What else would there be to say?" asked the bookseller. "The House of Scholars burned, and there are no scholars left in Nacliano."

"Or none who dare call themselves scholars," replied Quaeryt.

"One who does not acknowledge who and what he is cannot claim to be such, can he?"

"That is a point many have debated, including Rholan, who said that a name did not equal deeds."

"Perhaps I should have said that one who neither acknowledges who or what he is nor acts as such cannot claim to be what he believes himself to be."

Quaeryt nodded. "I prefer to believe that acts rather than words define the man . . . or woman."

The bookseller laughed, a sound soft but ironic and edged with a hint of bitterness. "You are neither innocent enough nor cynical enough, for all acts come from words."

"Perhaps," said Quaeryt, easing himself from the stool, "but the words need not come from the one who acts, nor the deeds from the one who speaks." He smiled. "It is always better when someone else tells the story."

"I take it you have no interest in purchasing a book?"

"A traveler should only purchase books when he is home and can provide for them." Quaeryt bowed. "I thank you for the story."

"And I for your patience."

Despite the apparent politeness of the bookseller, Quaeryt remained ill at ease on the entire walk back to the Tankard, not because he doubted the story, but because he believed it . . . as well as what had not been said, but suggested, and not spoken, by the bookseller himself. More than that, the hidden semi-parable about the woman who learned to read and what came of it bothered him as well, especially in light of the missive from Vaelora sealed within the document case.

14

Again on Jeudi, Quaeryt rose and ate early, and plied Lily with another three coppers to save the garret chamber for yet another night. Unlike the previous day, he immediately headed toward the harbor Patrol building. He reached there even before the patrollers going on duty left the building. Duultyn and his partner were among the last to leave, and they headed in the direction of the Sailrigger.

Using his concealment shield, Quaeryt followed more closely. After several days, he was beginning to understand the rougher Tellan of the east more clearly.

". . . never said what happened last night . . ."

"She wasn't there. Old lady Shaalya took me into every room in the place."

"Then she's gone."

Duultyn shook his head. "Just for now. She'll be back. Then she'll pay. More than she wants."

"Your uncle said not to—"

"I told him that she'd been seeing that scholar we chased."

"Oh .·. still don't understand what he has against them. Except for the one . . . don't seem any worse than anyone else."

"They're worse." Low as Duultyn's voice was, the venom was far stronger than the words. "Worse even than imagers."

"You, I understand. But him? You've never said why he—"

"You don't want to know. Leave it, Thuaylt. Just leave it."

Duultyn stopped and looked at the taproom, with its shutters and doors all closed. "Be a shame, a real shame, if the place caught fire."

"Too many people know what happened yesterday."

"I can be patient. Long enough for people to forget. . . ." Duultyn turned and resumed his strolling walk toward the piers.

Neither patroller spoke for a time.

"You're fortunate, Thuaylt," Duultyn finally said. "Pretty wife who wouldn't look past you, no matter what."

"Thank the Nameless for ·that every day," agreed the taller patroller.

"I still wonder why . . ." Duultyn shook his head. "Never will understand women."

Even from what he'd overheard, Quaeryt knew why the patroller never would.

"Been a hot week."

"So was last week," replied Duultyn. "I'll be glad when tomorrow's rounds are done."

"That makes two of us."

By the time Duultyn and Thuaylt stopped at another café for a midday meal, Quaeryt was convinced that he'd discovered all that he was going to by following the pair, and he returned to the first pier. Two more ships had ported, and he inquired about the destination of each. One was heading east, and the other was a Ferran brig headed homeward via Westisle.

Then he eased past another pair of patrollers to get onto the second pier, where a single worn brig had just tied up at the innermost bollard. Even before he reached the ship, he had the sinking feeling that the vessel was the *Moon's Son*.

He stood back and studied the ship, but he had to admit, worn as she looked, she was also trim, and nothing looked out of place or in ill repair. While the gangway was already down, he watched the crew for a time before he finally made his way up the plank and requested permission to board from the bosun.

"Come on aboard."

"I'm looking for passage to Tilbora."

The bosun replied, "We port there, but best you talk to the captain."

"That's Chexar?"

"Aye." The bosun turned. "Captain . . . the gent here is looking for passage."

The man who walked across the deck toward Quaeryt was of average height and build and not notable in any attribute, except for the copper-red brush mustache that matched neither the dull red of his hair nor the brownish red of his eyebrows. "Yes?" His voice was a raspy baritone.

"I understand you might be heading to Tilbora," offered Quaeryt.

"That we would be, but not until a glass before dawn on Samedi. Passage costs a gold, and three coppers a day for fare. That gets you a bunk cabin in the fantail and the same meals as the rest of us."

Quaeryt handed across two silvers. "That's to hold it, the rest when I come on board Vendrei night."

Chexar took the silvers. "Done. What do we call you?"

"Quaeryt."

The captain frowned. "Had a mate once, kept talking about a quartermaster type who left to be a scholar . . . name like that. Said he'd have been a good mate."

Quaeryt wasn't surprised. Even halfway decent quartermasters were rare, and captains kept their ears open about mates and others of possible value.

"Might have been me." Quaeryt smiled wryly. "Might have been someone else."

Chexar nodded. "Why might you be headed north?"

"I have a patron who sent me there. I need to do what he wants and return before the turn of winter."

"Might have been better staying a quartermaster," replied Chexar.

"True enough, Captain, but we can't live over what we might have done."

"All too right." Chexar nodded again, brusquely. "Be aboard before eighth glass tomorrow night."

"That I will, Captain."

Chexar turned and walked forward, toward where the bosun was overseeing the off-loading from the forward hatch.

Quaeryt walked down the gangway and headed back toward the harbor Patrol building. When he passed the Sailrigger, he noted that all the doors and shutters remained tightly closed.

Once he reached the street across from the Patrol building, he began to watch, moving from point to point, occasionally using a concealment shield. He continued his surveillance until almost a glass past midday, changing his position, using a concealment shield at times until a coach pulled up. The coach was green and trimmed in polished brass. Quaeryt once more raised a concealment screen and eased along the uneven brick sidewalk until he was within a few yards of the coach, if with his back to the wall of the adjoining café.

Shortly, a tall, burly, and gray-haired patroller in greens, with a gold seven-pointed star on each collar, emerged from the building, accompanied by another patroller, and walked toward the waiting coach.

"... don't care what's wrong with his wife. . . . He keeps the schedule, or he can take an early stipend. . . . Tell him that."

"Yes, Chief."

Just from his body posture, the few words, and the chief's tone of voice, Quaeryt didn't care any more for the chief than for Duultyn, who, apparently, was Burchal's nephew. *That family tree has more than its share of sour lemons.*

After the coach pulled away, Quaeryt decided to walk back to Hill Square, as much because he wanted to look around a nicer part of Nacliano as because there was little more he could learn by watching the Patrol building. Besides, he couldn't hold the concealment shield for long, long periods without getting exhausted, and remaining near the Patrol building without concealment might call too much notice to himself.

As he walked along the even yellow-brick sidewalks

. that bordered the equally uneven yellow-brick surface of the streets, he couldn't help but notice a certain almost furtive air displayed by many of those he passed, who moved with their eyes shifting quickly from point to point. Yet few eyes rested long on Quaeryt, as if those who did look at him quickly dismissed him and looked away.

When he neared Hill Square, he began looking for the narrow street that held the bookshop, then turned down it. He walked past the felter's shop, then stopped. The dilapidated building between the felter's and the cordwainer's was closed, the iron-grated door locked. It looked abandoned, and as if it had been for years. Yet he had been there the day before. Abruptly, he nodded. Clearly, the use of the "cooperage" as a bookstore was a tacit accommodation between Burchal and the bookseller, who had to have once been other than a mere vendor of tomes.

He retraced his steps back uphill in the direction of the nearer pastry shop. Less than a quint later, he - stood inside a white-walled shop filled with the scents of baking bread, almonds, and other nuts and spices.

A dark-haired girl who could not have stood to his shoulder looked over the counter at him. "Might I help you, sir?"

"What's the best pastry you have?" he asked.

"The lime tarts are good, and so are the orange ones . . . or perhaps the walnut-honey layers . . ." The woman girl smiled shyly.

Lime tarts reminded him of sour lemons, and so might an orange one, especially if it were the slightest bit bitter. "I'll try one of the walnut-honey pastries."

"A walnut-honey layer it is. Two coppers."

Two coppers? The shop definitely catered to the wealthier citizens of Nacliano. Quaeryt handed over the coppers and received in return a square of layers of thin pastry interspersed with honey and ground nuts and placed on a larger square of brown paper.

"There you are."

Quaeryt took the pastry outside and walked slowly in the direction of the Tankard, not that he was in any hurry. He took a small bite of the walnut-honey layer, chewing it slowly.

For all its sweetness, the pastry tasted bitter.

Like Nacliano.

He finished the last crumbs and licked his fingers, then continued eastward toward the Tankard, which, for all its lack of comfort, somehow felt more honest than did Hill Square.

15

On Vendrei morning, Quaeryt did not get up quite so early. He didn't see much point in tracking the patrollers exceptionally close to dawn. He had overheard that Duultyn was on duty, but, if that had changed, it wasn't something that he could control. Still, he washed up and shaved and finished breakfast before seventh glass, then went out to the high desk in the front hall. The wall shelf remained empty of any pottery or other decorations.

When the gray lady appeared, he said, "Thank you. I won't be staying tonight."

"You find a ship?" asked Lily.

"I did."

"Chexar's *Moon's Son*, I'd wager. He's one of the

few that goes north in summer. Good master, but not the most fortunate, I've heard tell."

"And he's still sailing?"

"He's one of the best at sea. He hasn't always picked the right cargoes at the right time."

Quaeryt nodded. He understood that, and he didn't care as much about the cargoes as arriving safely in Tilbora.

"Best of fortune."

"Thank you."

After making a few small purchases, including a large number of apricots, Quaeryt arrived across the street from the harbor Patrol building two quints before the ten bells of midday rang out. He took a seat at the café from where he could watch the Patrol building, set his small canvas bag between his boots, and ordered a lager and a domchana. He paid the server immediately in case he needed to depart in a hurry. Then, between bites and sips, he just watched.

The only places where the sidewalks were uncrowded were those fronting the Patrol building. Likewise, there were no street vendors there, either.

Quaeryt smiled as he watched a young bootblack persuade a couple to have their boots shined. He wasn't quite so pleased when he saw a pleasant-faced young woman cozy up to a teamster about to unload his wagon, but he needn't have worried, because the burly fellow backhanded her cutpurse companion with enough force to throw him into the wagon and leave him stunned. The two thieves scurried off, but their haste was unnecessary because there were no patrollers nearby, even in front of the Patrol building, and the teamster didn't call for any.

Quaeryt ordered a second lager, not that he intended to drink it all, and kept watching, but also looking toward the harbor time and again, as if he were waiting for someone.

As on the previous day, Burchal did not leave at noon, but at just before a single bell struck the first glass of the afternoon, and he was accompanied by two other patrollers. No coach arrived, for which Quaeryt was grateful, although he had been prepared to follow the coach on foot, since Nacliano's streets were narrow and crowded enough that coach or wagon movement near the harbor was slow.

As soon as he glimpsed the chief, Quaeryt stood and left, slipping a pair of coppers to the serving girl as he passed her. He moved into a shadowed doorway for a moment and raised a concealment shield, hoping that anyone looking in his direction would simply have thought he had entered the confectionery shop, while anyone watching from inside the shop would think that he had hurried away.

The three patrollers had covered less than twenty yards before Quaeryt had closed enough to overhear parts of their conversation.

". . . talk about it later."

"Yes, Chief."

"What do you say we go to Ufyeryl's?"

"The fare's good there."

"So are the servers," replied Burchal with a deep rolling laugh. "It's close, and I need to be back before half past second glass."

No more than a block later, the three entered a large café. Ufyeryl had to have been the owner or the proprietor, because the signboard outside the stone-faced structure declared it to be the Sea Sprite. Unlike at most eating establishments in Nacliano, the windows were glazed and the shutters painted, if a shiny gray.

Quaeryt had to squeeze in behind the last patroller because he didn't want people seeing a door open and close with no one apparently there.

"We have your favorite table available, Chief Burchal," offered a corpulent man in a white shirt and purple vest, gesturing toward the left side of the dining area.

Burchal said nothing, but one of the two patrollers following murmured to the other, "As if he dared otherwise."

The table was set off from the others by two half walls that were head-high, except for a column at the outer end of each, with pale purple drapes hanging from brackets and filling the space between the half walls and the ceiling.

Quaeryt stood back, as close as he could to the narrow column at the end of the half wall on the side toward the kitchen.

"How about some of that Montagne red, Ufyeryl?" asked Burchal, as he seated himself, in a tone that was more demand than request.

"You will have it," the proprietor said cheerfully. "Dhaela . . . the good Montagne red!"

Quaeryt's eyes flicked to the serving girl addressed by Ufyeryl. He doubted she could have been much over sixteen, for all of her clearly feminine figure, accentuated as it was by the nearly sheer formfitting purple cotton blouse and tight trousers.

In moments, Dhaela reappeared with two carafes, setting both in the center of the table, and leaning forward while doing so in a way to show her charms to their best advantage. Then she hurried off, only to return with three heavy goblets. "Here you are." Her voice was cheerful, if sultry.

Burchal's right hand slid down from her waist and

caressed her momentarily, before she straightened and eased away.

"We have the special lamb . . ."

Quaeryt watched the three patrollers as Dhaela recited the available fare, then took their orders, and then slipped away.

Burchal grasped the nearer carafe, filled his goblet, and handed the carafe to the patroller on his right.

"See what you mean by the fare and the servers," said the youngest-looking patroller.

"They're definitely fair," countered the other patroller, filling his goblet.

"They treat me well." Burchal's voice held satisfaction.

Quaeryt mentally supplied the words that the chief had not spoken. *Because they know what's good for them.* Then the scholar had to flatten himself against the side of the half wall as a server hurried by.

The patroller across from Burchal looked up and frowned, then shook his head.

"What is it?" demanded the chief.

"The hangings . . . they were moving."

The other patroller leaned back. "No one there."

"Can't be too careful," said Burchal cheerfully. "That's why you don't talk about anything important in public—or with women. There are ears everywhere. We're here to eat." He lifted the goblet, sniffed it, and took a small sip. He nodded and took a larger swallow. "Good as always."

"Heard your nephew found another scholar. Didn't know there were any left."

"That's part of his job. We need to make sure that imagers and scholars and other undesirable sorts don't bother folks here."

"Be easier if Estisle felt the same way."

"It would indeed."

Although Burchal's tone was cheerfully even, there was something behind it, almost as if the chief had plans that extended beyond Nacliano.

Quaeryt nodded to himself. While he could have imaged pitricin or blueacid into Burchal's gut, what he had in mind was far better for the situation.

Before long Dhaela returned with another server, a young man, and set platters before the three patrollers, as well as a large basket of bread.

After another caress of Dhaela, Burchal looked at the platter before him and smiled. "This is the best lamb in Nacliano."

The other two exchanged quick glances, then nodded.

Quaeryt watched as the chief took several mouthfuls, then, after Burchal took another swallow of wine, and another mouthful of wine, imaged chunks of lamb into Burchal's lower windpipe.

Burchal swallowed, then tried to swallow again. He lurched to his feet, upsetting the chair behind him and knocking over the goblet so that red wine poured over the pale purple table linens.

The patroller to his right jumped to his feet and pounded the chief on the back, but Burchal had turned red. His mouth was open, but no sound issued forth.

The older patroller stood and pulled his own chair in front of the chief, trying to bend the chief forward over the back of the chair, but Burchal pushed him away and put his hand into his mouth. The chief staggered, trying to remove the lamb that was beyond his grasp.

Quaeryt waited and watched until Burchal pitched forward.

One of the servers screamed.

Once he was certain that the chief was dead, amid the chaos and with his concealment shield Quaeryt had no trouble in slipping out of the Sea Sprite. He did not release the concealment shield until he was in an alleyway two blocks away in the direction of the harbor.

Now all he needed to do was to locate Duultyn.

He began to walk toward the harbor.

Duultyn and Thuaylt weren't at the foot of pier one, nor of pier two . . . nor even pier three. Was Vendrei the patroller's day off? That seemed unlikely to Quaeryt, given what he'd overheard on Jeudi, especially since Duultyn did enjoy some favoritism from his uncle. But what if Duultyn had gotten ill? After what Burchal had said, Quaeryt didn't see that as likely, yet . . . where was Duultyn? Quaeryt wanted to shake his head. Any possible or practical way of tracking the patroller down would require asking questions, and questions would leave tracks, and that was the last thing he wanted to do. Nor could he afford to wait for yet another ship heading north.

After retracing his steps to check the first two piers again, Quaeryt was about ready to head in the direction of the Sailrigger when he finally spotted the two patrollers as they approached the second pier. He remained in the shadows of the awning of the chandlery next to which he'd taken a position until the two passed him, moving toward the pier. Then he raised a concealment shield and followed.

". . . still think that scholar escaped?"

". . . know he must have . . ."

"Why?"

"Because he jumped into the water like he knew what he was doing . . . knew we couldn't follow him . . . will find him."

"What if he shipped out already?"

"I have a feeling he hasn't."

". . . might be better if he had . . ." murmured Thuaylt.

"What did you say?"

"Just that it might have been better for him if he had."

"I don't care about what's good for scholars. I know what's best for them, and that's to get rid of as many as possible."

From where he followed the pair, Quaeryt shook his head, then imaged a jolt of pitricin into the patroller's stomach.

Duultyn's step faltered for a moment. Then he shook his head.

"What is it?" asked Thuaylt.

"Must have been that pepper fowl I ate. Gut-ache. It'll pass."

"Are you all right?" Thuaylt's voice held concern.

"I said I'll be fine." Even as irritation filled Duultyn's voice, his free hand went to his forehead. His steps became more uneven.

"Duultyn!"

"Sow-named fowl! Spoiled meat. Bastard Xeryl fed me spoiled meat." Duultyn staggered to the seawall and leaned over it, gagging uncontrollably. His body began to convulse.

Thuaylt leaned, took several steps toward his partner, then halted, as if uncertain as what to do. "Duultyn?"

There was no response, except for several more convulsions before the patroller slumped over the seawall. Before long, even his breathing stopped.

Quaeryt slipped around the pair and made his way onto the second pier, holding the concealment shield while he reached the shadow cast by the first vessel tied there, a coastal schooner. He eased the grass bag holding the remains of the apricots over the side of the pier, but the splash was so small that no one could have heard it, then waited until no one was near or looking before releasing the shield.

He walked purposefully toward the next ship—the *Moon's Son.*

16

For all of Chexar's talk about leaving well before dawn, the *Moon's Son* had barely left the harbor behind when the leading edge of the sun peered over the eastern waters on Samedi morning, but the ship was sailing almost directly before the wind, and the swells in the gulf beyond the harbor were moderate. The "bunk cabin" was far smaller than the space in the fantail locker on the *Diamond,* but, although there were two bunks against the aft bulkhead, Quaeryt was the only passenger. For that, he was grateful.

As orangish light flooded diffusely over the ship, he stood by the starboard railing on the poop deck, looking to the southeast at the northern end of the rocky island of Estisle, which held the port of the same name. He couldn't help but reflect on the past week. Two aspects of his time in Nacliano particularly bothered him. First was the possibility that an innocent café owner might be blamed for poisoning Duultyn. Quaeryt hadn't considered the fact that Duultyn would immediately blame someone when he felt unwell. He should have. People like Duultyn blamed others for everything. Second was the concern that the Patrol chief who followed Burehal might be even worse. While that seemed unlikely, in places like Nacliano the same factors that allowed a man like Burchal to abuse power made it more likely that someone similar would succeed him. On the other hand, Quaeryt was only one man, and a scholar and hidden imager at that, and he couldn't be everywhere to try to improve things. That was another reason why he had to prove his greater usefulness to Bhayar. That was the first step in what he planned.

Besides, he told himself, *it's better to do something when no one else has done anything than hope that what's bad will improve itself.*

Still . . . he worried.

His eyes drifted back to Estisle, which had begun as a haven for pirates and smugglers centuries ago— before they all discovered that trading was more profitable and less fatal . . . and Hengyst had granted them amnesty for their support.

Quaeryt sensed someone and turned to see the captain standing a few yards away, looking forward, then to the helm, before returning his gaze to the scholar no longer attired as such—and who wouldn't be until after he disembarked from the *Moon's Son.*

"You were on board right early yesterday," observed Chexar. "You in haste to get to Tilbora?" The captain spoke Tellan with what Quaeryt suspected was the thick accent of Tilbor.

Quaeryt laughed. "Not so much that as in haste to leave Nacliano. I've seen friendlier ports in my day."

Chexar nodded. "It didn't used to be that way. Now . . ." The captain shrugged. "Most of the crew stays close to the ship these days. We try to off-load and load as quick as we can."

"What happened? You must know. You've spent more than a few days tied up in Nacliano over the years."

"That's hard to say. Things happened. Someone burned down the Scholars' House, and all the scholars left . . . maybe some of them stayed permanently, you might say. A couple of the older factorages closed. Another caught fire. Who knows? It just isn't the same. People look strange-like at anyone they don't know."

"I saw this one patroller who jumped at anyone wearing brown. . . ."

Chexar shook his head. "That had to be Duultyn. He hates scholars. Scholars wear brown. His wife, pretty thing she was, ran off with one."

"He hates scholars and men who wear brown just for that?"

"The scholar was the kind who studied all the old martial arts. It was weeks before Duultyn could walk straight." Chexar grinned. "They say that he lost more than his wife." The grin faded. "Don't think he's quite right in the head, but he's the nephew or some such of the City Patrol chief."

"He sounds like a patroller to avoid."

"If you're a seafarer, they're all to be avoided," replied Chexar wryly.

"Even in Tilbora? What's it like there?"

"It's colder there. More like harvest in summer, fall in harvest, winter in fall, and you don't really want to be there in winter." He laughed. "I don't, and most of the crew doesn't, and we grew up there."

"I was thinking about the patrollers. . . ."

"The ones in Tilbora aren't like those in Nacliano. They're like those in most ports. You don't bother them, and they don't bother you."

"What about the governor?"

"I've never seen him. They say he keeps pretty much to the Telaryn Palace—used to be the Khanar's Palace. Stay away from the Telaryn armsmen, though. . They can be nasty pieces of work."

"Why? Do they think Tilbor is going to revolt or something?"

"That's the way they act. Me . . . I never saw anything like that. We Tilborans are stiff-necked. That doesn't mean that we're troublemakers. Oh . . . there are a few, call themselves partisans or some such, but most of the real partisans went back to work once things settled down after the war. Life's tough enough in the north without making trouble for yourself. Except for the hill folk. They've always been trouble. The rest of us, we just want to get by. You want troublemakers, go to Antiago or Bovaria."

Quaeryt nodded. "I've never been to Tilbor. What's a good dish to eat . . . and what should I avoid?"

Chexar laughed. "Most is like anywhere else, but I'd avoid the white cod. Never liked it as a boy. Still don't. Looks and tastes like fish jerky seasoned in lye. That's because it is. It'll keep forever . . ." Abruptly, he turned. "Gelas! Bring her a half point more to port."

"Aye, Captain!" returned the helmsman.

Chexar continued, without looking at Quaeryt, "We need to stay well north of the Wreckers' Rocks. That's not really a problem with the weather as fair as it is."

"I heard that the seas are rougher north of here. How soon will we hit them?"

"On the trip south . . . we got to calmer weather

some four days out of Nacliano. Likely enough, that hasn't changed all that much."

"How rough?" asked Quaeryt.

"Not that bad. Swells a yard or two at most. Winter seas, you see swells five to ten yards all the time." Chexar laughed softly. "That's why we do winter runs from Nacliano to the south. There aren't many who run to Tilbora in the winter, and none who sail farther north."

Since the shortest overland routes from Tilbora to Solis ran through the mountains, Quaeryt wasn't going to have as much time as he would have liked in Tilbor, not and meet Bhayar's request for his return. Yet . . . staying longer in Solis would not have suited either his needs or Bhayar's, and from what he'd already seen in Nacliano, there were more than a few problems of which the Lord of Telaryn was woefully unaware.

"How late do you leave Tilbora for the last time in the fall?"

Chexar shrugged. "That depends on the weather and the signs." He grinned wryly. "And if anyone has a good cargo. If things look spare, we leave a few weeks before the end of Finitas, never later than the twenty-third." The captain nodded, then turned and walked back toward the helm.

Quaeryt thought. It was already the thirty-fifth of Juyn, the last day of summer. That left the two months of harvest and a little over seven weeks of fall— seventeen weeks in all—and it would likely take more than a week to reach Tilbora . . . if nothing untoward happened.

That seemed more than possible, but . . . still.

17

After four days aboard the *Moon's Son*, Quaeryt had to admit that the often-dour Chexar was a good shiphandler. The fare was adequate, and the weather slightly rough, but bearable. The ocean was getting colder. That was obvious from the fine spray that flew from the bow when the ship encountered a larger swell. Late on Meredi afternoon, he managed to catch Chaenyr, the second mate, in a talkative mood . . . or what passed for one.

"Will you have any time away from the ship when you port?"

"Depends on what we can load and how long it takes. It's early in harvest." The mate shrugged. "That means fewer cargoes. I wouldn't mind a few days home."

"You're from Tilbora?"

"You might say that, excepting as I grew up in Slaegyn. That's a hamlet some ten milles to the north of Tilbora, on the Highlands."

"Is that near Haestal?"

The mate nodded. "Just south of there."

"And it's in the Highlands?" From Quaeryt's study of the maps of Tilbor, Haestal was on the coast, but didn't have a harbor.

"Aye . . . the east cliffs drop near on three hundred yards into the sea. There's not even shingle at the base of the cliffs, and in a nor'easter, the waves might break halfway up."

"Is a nor'easter likely this time of year?"

Chaenyr laughed. "You can get a nor'easter any time of year. They happen more in fall and winter, and they're worse then."

Quaeryt glanced forward. "No clouds in sight now, but the wind's freshened and shifted. It's more out of the east now. That's usually a sign of a change in the weather."

"The weather changes all the time once you get a few days north of Estisle." Chaenyr cocked his head, his eyes squinting. "Might be a blow coming. Might not. Might just be a shift to a sou'easterly. We could use that. Calmer seas and a mostly following wind."

The scholar looked to port where, just on the western horizon, there was the thinnest line of darkness— the coastline of eastern Telaryn. "Where are we now?"

"We passed the headland at Edcloin just after sunrise . . . most likely we'll be coming in sight of the Barrens before long. They'll be hard to see. The captain'll be turning some to the east. Won't want the winds and currents to fetch us up there."

"The Barrens? Are those low sandspits or islands?"

"Hundreds of 'em. Stretch for a good three hundred milles, and that doesn't count the shallows to the north. They say there were once more towns and good harbors there, but the waters changed and filled them with sand, and the folks all left, most of them, anyway. I'd dare say more ships been lost to the shallows than to the Barrens. One good thing that the Lords of Telaryn did—they cleaned out most of the shipbreakers and their false lights and fires. Still some on the Shallows Coast, though." The mate spat over the rail. "About the only good thing the Telaryns did."

"Doesn't sound like the Telaryns are much liked in Tilbor."

"Telaryns are fine. We could do without the arms-men and the extra tariffs. Some folks wouldn't even mind the tariffs if the coin went to building better roads or replacing the breakwater in Tilbora. All they see is the parties and balls in the Telaryn Palace." Chaenyr frowned. "Where are you from?"

Quaeryt laughed. "I can't say as I know. The schol-ars in Solis took me in when I was too young to re-member. They told me later I could speak a few words, but no one knew what because I didn't speak what-ever it was properly."

"You know a bit about the sea."

"I spent a few years before the mast, then went back and studied some more with the scholars. That didn't turn out quite the way I thought it might."

"You a scholar, then?"

"I could claim that." Quaeryt laughed again. "I kept leaving the Scholars' House often enough that they never bothered to de-scholar me. Then I found a patron, and they decided it wasn't worth the trouble." All of that was true, if not precisely in the way or or-der in which he'd related it.

"Why are you headed to Tilbor?"

Quaeryt offered a rueful expression. "There are good things and bad things about having a patron. The best thing is that you know you'll be provided for. The worst thing is that they often want things done . . . or obtained . . . or looked into . . ."

Chaenyr laughed. "Some ways I prefer dealing with the captain. It's clear what he wants, when he wants it, and how."

"Everyone I talked to, asking about shipmasters heading north, said he was a fine mariner and ship-handler."

"That he is, no question about it. And if others

were as honest as he is, he'd have more than the *Moon's Son*."

Quaeryt nodded and waited, sensing that a question would close off learning more.

"But most folk aren't so much honest as self-serving and trying not to seem so. That's the way of the world, and you and I and the captain just have to do the best we can." Chaenyr turned. "I'd best be checking with the bosun. . . ." With a nod, the mate headed forward.

Quaeryt looked to the northeast. The sky above the horizon was clear.

18

For the next four days the skies remained largely clear and the winds generally out of the east, but the seas gradually became heavier, so that the swells were running a good three yards in height, and sometimes more, by midday on Solayi. By midafternoon, everything changed. Within the space of two quints, the wind abruptly shifted and increased markedly, coming hard out of the northeast, while dark clouds scudded toward the ship from the north-northeast. Chexar changed course so that the *Moon's Son* swung to the south.

Just what I needed, thought Quaeryt. Running before what looked to be a solid storm was certainly the wisest course, but in even a few glasses, they'd cover more milles to the south than they had in a day heading northward. Still, essentially reversing course was better than fighting a storm.

Less than a glass later, the entire sky was overcast, and the swells were closer to four yards in height and far less regular. The blue of the ocean had turned blue-black, the darkness emphasized by the white of the foam on the waves. Then rain began to pelt the ship, if in intermittent wave-like gusts.

Quaeryt hated the thought of being belowdecks in a blow. That was one thing that hadn't changed over the years. At the same time, there was little sense in remaining topside and getting soaked through. So he returned to the tiny bunk cabin to wait out the storm.

After spending close to a glass getting bounced around and hanging on to the bunk supports, Quaeryt made his way back to the hatchway, from where he could take a look. Things were even worse than he feared.

He could barely hear Chexar yelling out orders, but the riggers had understood, and they had furled the sails, set a storm jib, then set storm sails in place of the main courses on both the fore- and mainmasts. Even so, the ship seemed not to lose any speed, although it was clear that the storm was moving far faster than the *Moon's Son*.

You would have to disregard superstitions. . . .

"Hold tight!" yelled someone.

Quaeryt glanced around, only to see a wall of water that had to be at least twenty yards high about to break over the ship from the port side. He forced the hatch shut, tightening it as much as he quickly could, then braced himself in the narrow passageway. The entire ship rolled and then pitched forward. Water sprayed past the edges of the hatch and sloshed down the passageway.

Quaeryt had the feeling that the entire ship was underwater for a time before she sluggishly righted herself. When there was no more water coming under or around the hatch, Quaeryt opened it, only to see that the mainmast was broken and splintered no more than a few yards above the deck, jutting out over the starboard side at an angle, held in that odd position by the stays, sheets, and what else remained of the rigging. Both storm sails were shreds, but the storm jib had somehow survived, although one sheet had parted.

"Cut away!" bellowed Chexar.

Quaeryt understood that. In a calmer sea, the captain would have wanted to save what he could, but not in the storm that buffeted the damaged ship.

"Drogue's away, Captain!" called another voice, that of the bosun.

The crew managed to get another storm sail in place on the foremast—or it could have been a reefed main course—and the *Moon's Son* began to gain some headway, rather than being tossed by the waves. Chexar kept the vessel from getting swamped—and the crew from being washed overboard—for the next several quints. Somehow the upper section of the mainmast and the tangled stays and rigging were cut away.

Quaeryt never saw exactly what happened, because he dogged the hatch shut and waited. Then another wave crashed across the decks, and after the ship struggled to right herself, and he looked again, the broken section was gone. So were several riggers. The wind continued to rise until it became a howling force that blotted out all other sounds, and every swell threatened the ship slightly more than the previous one.

The brig began to ride more deeply in the water, a sure sign that the seams had been strained or hatch covers pounded open by the force of the storm—or perhaps both. Then, almost abruptly, the ship swung sideways to the swells.

Chaenyr hauled himself hand over hand along the port railing, his eyes looking to the helm. "Rudder's gone! Tie yourself to something topside, or you'll drown when she founders!"

Quaeryt found line in the inside locker, but cutting it was difficult, and he almost cut himself before he put away the knife and just imaged out a piece of the rope, rather than cutting it. Then he had to follow Chaenyr's example and struggle up to the railing on the low upper deck that barely merited the term "upper" or "poop." By then he was soaked, but soaked was more to his liking than drowned belowdecks.

He'd barely managed to lash himself to the railing when another massive wave towered over the ship. He threw both arms around the railing and waited, taking a deep breath at the last moment before the dark chill of the water crashed down, thrusting him against the railing, then trying to rip him away from it. A second wave followed the first, and Quaeryt's lungs were burning when he could finally breathe again.

When he could see again, after the foam subsided, although the main deck looked barely above water, Quaeryt squinted and tried to make out Chaenyr—or anyone—but he seemed to be the only one left on the upper deck, and the helm scarcely moved. Either the rudder had been torn away, or the steering cables had snapped, and sooner or later another wave would swamp the ship, rolling uncontrollably, first in the trough of one wave, then being submerged by another.

The skies were almost as dark as full night.

How many glasses later it was, Quaeryt had no idea, but some time later he could see spray foaming upward as well as hear what sounded like surf above the wail and whine of the wind. He looked to the starboard side of the helpless derelict, where less than a hundred yards away spray cascaded upward, then receded.

Whether they were being carried onto a reef, one of the sandbars the mate had talked about, or even the coast, Quaeryt had no idea, except there were no cliffs, and there looked to be waters beyond the foam and spume. Another massive swell lifted the ship's hull, then smashed it down. The impact jarred every bone in Quaeryt's body and strained his muscles.

Rocks, not sand.

Spray, foam, and water swirled over and around Quaeryt, then receded . . . but only for a moment, before another cascade surged over him.

For a brief time, he could breathe without having to grab mouthfuls of air between the surges of waves and surf, but he felt a warmer wetness. Belatedly, he realized that it was rain. He hadn't even noticed it with all the seawater pounding him.

Then another huge swell lifted the battered hull and dropped it again. Grinding, jarring impact followed impact, until what was left of the ship's stem and bowsprit broke away.

Quaeryt decided to stay with his section of wreckage, at least for a time. He could swim, unlike many sailors, but no swimmer would last in that tempest, especially not when being thrashed by the surf and pounded against the rocks.

The storm had to end . . . sometime.

He just hoped he could outlast it . . . and that wherever he was stranded was some place from which he could extricate himself.

Quaeryt husbanded his strength and trusted to the

rope that held him tethered to the remnants of the
stern section of the *Moon's Sun*. At some point full
darkness lifted, and the wind dropped from a gale to a
strong wind. The surging surf receded enough that
only occasional spray dampened the scholar, and what
remained of the ship no longer shifted with the movement of the water. At that point, he cut the rope,
which took almost all of his strength, and surveyed
the hulk. The rocks on which the ship had broached
were still covered with swirling water, and he could
see no other sign of land through the dim light.

So he struggled back to the quarters under the upper deck. The captain's cabin was empty, as were the
two cabins for the mates. All were damp.

Quaeryt would have shrugged, except he was far
too tired. Instead, he collapsed on the damp pallet.
Sleep might help, and he could use it for what lay
ahead.

19

When Quaeryt woke, his lips were cracked and dry,
and he could taste salt everywhere. Every muscle
ached, and his clothes and jacket were still wet, but
not soaked. He could hear the sea, if barely, as he
rolled off the still-damp pallet and up onto the sloping
deck. He had to brace himself to keep his footing as
he made his way to the hatchway, now missing the
hatch itself.

He peered out. A misty drizzle surrounded the hulk,
and patches of fog or low clouds obscured his view,

but from what he could see, it seemed to be early, possibly less than a glass after sunrise. He definitely hoped that was the case.

What remained of the ship rested on a stretch of rock that, surprisingly, appeared dark and level, and stretched in an arc toward a sandy shore. He estimated that the long curve of stone was close to a half mille in length, and was less than a yard underwater. He glanced seaward, but the natural rock causeway ended no more than fifty yards from the hulk of the *Moon's Son*.

Was it natural? Or had some ancient imager created it as a pier or a seawall for a long-vanished town? He shook his head. Whatever had created it didn't matter now. Since the causeway that had broken the back of the *Moon's Son* also provided a way to shore, he needed to take it. He had no intention of staying on board the hulk. As even a passenger, he represented the sole barrier to the local ship reavers claiming salvage rights over what remained of ship and cargo, and if they found him, his survival was less than assured, particularly since, in his present condition, it was unlikely he could do much imaging, not and be in any shape to do much of anything else.

He spent less than a quint rummaging through the captain's cabin, where he found a pouch of silvers, and the galley. The galley yielded some squares of hard cheese and even more durable hardtack, and a tin water bottle with water in it. With his canvas bag not quite bulging he made his way back on deck, then over the side, trying to ease himself down onto the rock below, where the water swirled somewhere between ankle-deep and knee-deep.

He still ended up sliding across the angled planking of the hulk, but managed to land on his boots, if with a jarring impact. His boots slid out from under him, so that his backside hit the water and stone too, hard enough that he'd be bruised and sore there as well. He staggered to his feet and began wading through the calf-deep water over the stone toward the shore, his eyes scanning the narrow sandy beach beyond and beside the end of the causeway, which, near the water's edge, straightened and continued due west. The patchy fog and mist limited his sight, but he did see detritus and debris scattered along the sand—but no reavers. Not yet.

He placed each boot carefully, well aware that the seemingly shallow water likely concealed deeper potholes. Yet for all the likelihood of holes or gaps in the stone, he found none on the long walk to where the stone ended, some forty yards shoreward from the water's edge. Except, he realized, the causeway did not end, but extended under a sand dune covered with coarse grass. How much farther it continued, he had no idea, although he wondered if more of a harbor, even with the ruins of buildings, lay under the dunes that bordered the narrow beach.

Glancing around, he looked for a trail or path that might point the way to a place of habitation, or a town or hamlet, finally catching sight of what appeared to be a track through the waist-high grass. The track had not been used since the storm had lifted. That was clear from the lack of clear prints in the damp sand. That did not mean that someone might not be coming the other way before long. Quaeryt forced himself to hurry up through the sand until he neared the top of the dune, where he slowed and listened.

He moved more deliberately until he was at the top and could look down. What he saw were more sandy dunes or hills, stretching a good mille, or so it seemed. Beyond them looked to be rolling rises of grassland, with some scattered trees. He took a deep breath and continued.

When he reached the last line of dunes, or the first line of hills with thick grass and soil as well as sand, he paused at the crest and studied the land beyond, noticing immediately downhill and to his right a small cot was tucked away on the south side of the hill, with earthen berms to the east and west, and a lower one to the south, all positioned to protect the gardens there.

He started down toward the cot, but a white-haired head popped up before Quaeryt could even consider a raising concealment, and the woman, wearing a faded gray shirt and trousers, studied the scholar as he approached.

"How did the garden fare with the storm?" he asked, stopping short of the weathered wooden gate that afforded the sole break in the earthen walls.

"A fair bit better than you, from the looks of you. A sight you are." The white-haired woman's voice was younger than her looks, but the eyes were a hard flint gray.

"It happens when your ship gets broken on the rocks and you get washed ashore." Quaeryt didn't trust the woman in the slightest, but wanted to appear pleasant.

"You'd be the first to make land alive. Vaolyn said they'd found two corpses on the sands well south of the Namer's Causeway. The menfolk'll find the ship afore long, I'd judge. You're more than welcome to stay here and rest."

"I'm far too late in getting where I'm supposed to be." Besides, while Quaeryt had no doubt that what Vaolyn, whoever that was, had said was now likely true, he had great doubts whether the two had been dead when Vaolyn had found them. Nor was he especially eager to find out . . . or encounter Vaolyn. "If the Namer's Causeway is that stretch of stone that heads into the ocean and then curves, that's where part of the ship broke and broached."

The woman frowned. "Never heard of a ship breaking there. They usually fetch up on the shallows north or south. There's little enough left of the old channel."

"Why do they call it the Namer's Causeway?" Quaeryt couldn't help but ask.

"Some say because it looks promising and leads nowhere. Others say it's because the old ones built a harbor there on the promises of the Namer. It's been called that from well before my time."

"How far south are we from Tilbora?"

"Be a ride of three-four days, if you had a mount, and you don't, by all looks."

"Is there a village or a hamlet nearby where I could catch a wagon or the like headed in that direction?"

"Nearby? Aye, but the closest place on a road that leads to Tilbora is Fairby, and that is more than ten milles north. You might be best served by waiting here till the weather clears."

"I'll have to take my chances. Point me in the right direction, good lady, if you would." Quaeryt paused. "And if you could spare some water, it would be good to drink some without the taste of salt."

"Water I can spare, young fellow."

Quaeryt wasn't about to point out that he wasn't all that young, not when he must have seemed that way to her. Besides, he wanted to get away from the possibility of ship reavers as quickly as possible.

Although he was ready to raise concealment at any time, he waited by the gate while she walked back into the cottage. Shortly, she returned with a small bucket and a dipper.

He took the dipper and drank a small sip, tasting the water, then took more. When he finished, he returned the dipper. "Thank you. That was much appreciated."

"The least one should do for a thirsty traveler. We don't see many these days."

"I imagine not. Which way to the road leading to Fairby?"

"The local road is at the end of the lane at the end of the path there." She pointed south. "You go left, and it will lead you to Khasyl. To the right is the long walk to Fairby."

"Thank you."

"You might want to sit on that bench there and rest your legs," she offered, pointing to a plank resting between two hillocks of earth just inside the gate.

While he was tired, Quaeryt replied, "I thank you for your kindness, but I must be on my way." He inclined his head politely, picked up his canvas bag, and then stepped back before walking toward the path she had indicated. He could sense her eyes on his back.

While he had his doubts about her directions, or her intentions, since north was where he needed to go, he stayed on the path, and then the lane until it joined the road. Just before he reached the road, he passed one other cot that looked to have been long abandoned.

At the crossroads, if it could be called that, he glanced southward, but the foggy mist shrouded everything more than a half mille away, and he turned in

the direction that felt generally northward, and doubtless had to be, since it was roughly parallel to the
coast. The road was little more than a dirt track, rutted and uneven, and he ended up walking on the
shoulder.

Less than a mille later, although he couldn't be certain, for there were no millestones or other distance
markers, he thought he heard the sound of footsteps
behind him. He looked back, but the misty fog was
thick enough that he could only see a few hundred
yards.

Then he heard the bay of a dog.

Frigging horse dung! They would have a hound.
Concealment shields didn't hide scent, and they didn't
erase tracks in or along a wet and muddy road.

He began to look for a tree large enough for him to
climb. Needless to say, he didn't see one immediately
close. So he forced himself to pick up his pace, tired as
he was, as he searched for a tree or some other place
with height.

He covered another fifty yards or so through the
patchy fog, with the baying of the dog coming ever
closer, without catching sight of a tree or anything
that might serve his purposes. Then he caught sight of
a tree ahead on the right, but it turned out to be a
scrawny juniper. He forced himself into a faster walk.

After another hundred yards, he saw several trees
through the mist, up a gentle slope to his left. One
might be large enough for him to climb up out of easy
reach. He turned and hurried up the slope of grass
and low bushes, on one of which his trousers caught,
enough that he had to stop and pull them free.

The baying of the hound was markedly louder, but
he did not head for the taller tree, but the shortest,

which he circled, and then the next taller, before he
began to climb the tallest one. The storm had shred-
ded some of the leaves, but there were enough remaining to offer some cover. The problem was that the tree
wasn't a sturdy oak or the like, but a softwood of
some sort, and by the time his feet were less than three
yards off the ground the branches were swaying under
his weight. Carrying the canvas bag didn't make matters any easier, either. He decided against climbing
higher and braced himself against the unsteady main
trunk. Then he waited for the pursuers to come to
him, hoping that there were not too many of them.

As they drew nearer, between the baying of the
hound, he could hear some of what was said, but
the thick accent he did not recognize made it harder.

"He's left the road . . . has to have heard the
hound . . ."

"Maergyt said he was headed north . . ."

". . . don't see what the trouble is . . . just wants to
put the wreck behind him . . ."

"Vaolyn says better to have no witnesses . . ."

". . . lot of the cargo spoiled . . ."

"Not the oils . . . worth a fair piece."

". . . still don't know why she wants him tracked
down and taken out . . ."

Vaolyn was a woman? Quaeryt shrugged. Reaver
queens weren't unknown, just rare, but they tended to
be more ruthless than their male counterparts, probably out of necessity.

"Hound's on to something! Must be getting close."

Quaeryt peered through the leaves, trying to get a
good look at his pursuers as they moved up the slope,
slowing as they neared the clump of trees. There were
three men—all young, lean, and hard. The one with

the dog on a rope lead carried a club. The other two held blades. One looked to be a cutlass, another a sabre of some sort.

"... think he's in the trees?"

"Where else?"

"Give the dog more rope. . . ."

Quaeryt concentrated on the man at the back of the group, then imaged an oblong of wood into the man's chest, right-where his heart should be. The reaver offered a strangled cry and pitched forward. When the second man turned, Quaeryt managed a second imaging. His head was pounding as the second attacker clutched at his chest.

The man with the hound stopped, looking around.

The third imaging left Quaeryt's guts turning inside out, and his vision dimmed. He just hung on to the tree.

The hound stopped baying and looked toward the fallen man, around whose wrist the lead rope was wrapped. Then the dog lurched toward the base of the tree in which Quaeryt perched and resumed baying, if with a more desperate edge to the sound. The rope did not allow the hound quite to reach the trunk of the tree, but the dog kept baying . . . and baying.

Finally Quaeryt imaged a chunk of wood into its heart as well. That bothered him . . . far more than dealing with the reavers, but he dared not have the baying call more attention to where he was.

His eyes were burning, his guts were churning, and it was all he could do not to puke and to hold his position in the tree, hoping that no one else would happen along soon, and that the fog and mist would cloak him for a while until his guts settled and he could eat some of the hardtack and cheese and regain some strength.

20

Worried as he was, Quaeryt remained in the tree and rested, grateful that the misty fog, while beginning to lift, still remained thick in places. After a time, certainly less than a glass, he sipped water from the tin bottle and then slowly chewed some of the hardtack. A good quint later, he was finally recovered enough to ease himself down from the tree and to resume walking. The one thing he was sure of was that he needed to get as far from the wreck as he could . . . and as quickly as possible.

The first mille or so from the tree was almost pleasant. By the second he was feeling warm, although the air was still cool. By the third mille, a good glass or so later, the dampness combined with his own body heat and the lack of a breeze to make him feel uncomfortably hot, and he loosened his shirt and jacket. His arms were getting tired from carrying the canvas bag, even though he was switching it from hand to hand as he kept walking.

To keep his mind away from how he felt, he went back over what had happened. He hadn't been thinking as well as he should have been. He should have imaged red pepper into his scent, so that the hound wouldn't have been able to smell anything at all for a time. That just showed how tired he was. Yet he definitely needed to put as much distance as he could between himself and the dead reavers and the poor hound, whose only fault had been its masters.

For a time, he concentrated on just putting one foot in front of the other.

After perhaps another half glass, he came to the ruins of a cot, one that had been burned, it appeared, and then razed. He looked along the road, only to realize that he stood at the southern edge of a small hamlet where every building had been fired and leveled. The destruction had not been too recent because scraggly grass grew up to the remaining foundation and wall stones and the only path was the well-worn one from the road to the ruin, but it had happened within the past few years, because the soot on the mud bricks had not faded that much.

Despite his feeling feverish, or possibly because he was, Quaeryt shivered, then shook his head. The destruction merely refueled his intention to put the Shallows Coast behind him. Even so, he forced himself to sit down on a flat portion of the cot wall and to drink some of the water and eat more of the hardtack. The very thought of eating any of the cheese gave him a queasy feeling.

After taking that brief refreshment, he rose and made his way along the road and through the ruins. He couldn't help but note that not a wall remained standing above knee height. What had been the cause of such devastation? Reavers usually just raided and departed. They weren't known for such thorough destruction, even when villagers resisted. Had the village been burned because of a recurrence of plague? That didn't make sense because no one would have stayed around afterward to level the walls.

Nothing else he saw as he passed the twenty-odd ruined buildings shed any more light on the reason for the destruction. There were no signs of animals, either, except that the rolling hills to the north of the hamlet had been recently grazed.

He kept walking, but he had to pause more frequently as the day grew somewhat warmer and the fog and mist lifted into low clouds. For all the greenness of the land, he saw no cots or holdings—none at all. While he did see signs the grass had been grazed, he saw no herds or flocks. The lack of human habitation bothered him, because there seemed to be no reason for it, yet he knew full well that such an emptiness was anything but natural and had to have a cause.

Sometime around midday, he passed through another village that had been leveled and burned, and it seemed slightly larger than the first he had encountered. Once more, he stopped and rested. This time, he had to force himself to stand and resume walking, and when he did, he had to stop for several moments because he coughed so violently he almost retched. Yet the cough was dry and hacking. Still, the coughing stopped, and he was able to keep walking.

He felt more than warm, more like feverish. Was that because he'd imaged more than his body could bear at a time? Or was it because he was sick?

More likely sick. But there was little point in stopping in the middle of nowhere with little food and less water.

His pace slowed some, but he kept trudging along.

In midafternoon, he came to a large stream, or small river, crossed by an old stone bridge with two spans anchored in the middle by a stone and brick pier. The bridge was barely wide enough for a wagon and a team, and there was no sign that any carts, wagons, or mounts had passed that way recently.

He decided against refilling the water bottle that

was close to empty. Who knew what lay upstream? He certainly didn't want to court a flux on top of whatever illness he was fighting.

Less than a mille past the bridge, after he'd followed the road up a gentle slope, he saw a small cot down a lane to the west of the road, and then several dwellings along the top of the next rise on the east side of the road. When he walked past the lane, he saw hoofprints and cart or wagon wheel tracks in the road for the first time since he'd scrambled ashore.

He could feel his steps slowing as he clambered up the next rise toward the hamlet, but when he reached the top, he paused to catch his breath after another spell of dry hacking coughs. While he recovered, he studied the buildings and realized that the place was not a hamlet at all, but a single holding. Four mud-brick outbuildings with thick thatched roofs surrounded a large and sprawling one-story dwelling, also thatched, situated on the highest point of the rise to the east of the road. On the south side of the dwelling, less than a hundred yards away, was a small orchard.

The clouds had lifted enough that, beyond the sandy hills that bordered the grasslands east of the holding, Quaeryt could see the ocean, still a dull gray under the clouds. Finally, he began to walk again, directing his steps along the road until he reached the brick-paved narrow lane that led to the main house of the holding.

He was halfway to the front entry of the main house when a tall and broad-shouldered, but gray-haired, man carried a large basket of fruit—late cherries, Quaeryt suspected—out of the small orchard and set it down in a small cart. He walked swiftly to meet Quaeryt.

"Greetings!" The single word was spoken in what

Quaeryt thought of as unaccented Tellan, and his voice was cheerful as he stopped short of the scholar. His smile turned to a worried frown. "You look a sight. . . ."

"I'm sure I do. . . ." Quaeryt's voice was hoarse and felt raw. "I was set upon. . . . Lost my mount." Quaeryt looked over his shoulder toward the south.

"You don't speak Tellan like a native. Do you speak Bovarian?" the man asked in that tongue, if with a heavy Tellan accent.

"I do."

"Then I will. I need the practice. You traveled through the Shallows Coast?" The man shook his head. "Not even the Lord's armsmen go there, except in force."

"The reavers? They're not a problem for you?"

"These days they don't come north of the Ayerne."

"That's the little river with the bridge?"

"It is indeed. Vaolyn keeps her folk south of there. We had to burn a few hamlets to get that across."

"Is there anywhere I might find a mount?" Quaeryt's throat felt rawer with every word.

"Nawlyn's the closest. Times, Zachys will part with a horse. . . ." The holder paused. "If I do say so, you'd not be looking ready to ride."

"Where is Fairby? I must have missed it."

The holder laughed. "Don't see as how you could have found it. That was one of the places we burned . . . razed the very stones."

When Quaeryt tried to look at the man closely, his eyes burned, and flashes of light that jabbed like needles pierced his eyes. He could also feel heat pouring off his forehead. "I wondered . . . why . . . who . . ."

"We didn't have much choice. Some people just won't be reasonable."

Quaeryt's legs felt weak and very unsteady. "I beg your pardon . . . I think . . . I need to sit down."

"You need more than that, friend. Best you come with me. Oh . . . I'm Rhodyn."

"This is . . . your holding?"

"Don't know as it's a holding. The lands have been in the family forever. We don't even know how long." The holder paused. "I'd not wish to be forward, but I could carry that bag for you."

For a moment, Quaeryt thought about demurring, but the way he felt, he wasn't going anywhere any time soon. "Thank you. It's been a long hike." He extended the canvas bag.

Rhodyn took it. "Heavy to be carrying across the Shallows Coast. This way. . . . We'll go around to the side door and get you something to drink. . . . I think Darlinka's still in the kitchen, but if she's not, Raisa or Shaentyla will be."

"You're most kind. . . ."

"Nonsense. We don't get many travelers here, even those that didn't mean to be traveling our roads. . . ."

Quaeryt made it to the stained and oiled side door, with the polished brass lever handle. Then the sky fell, and hot rain and darkness swirled around him.

21

When Quaeryt woke, he was in a small chamber in a narrow bed. His head was a mass of fire, and his body ached all over. While flashes of light flickered across his eyes, he could see a dark-haired woman was blotting his forehead with a damp cloth. The coolness was welcome, neither chilling nor tepid.

"Where . . ."

"Hush . . . you've been fevered. You still are. You don't need to talk. You need to rest. Just lean back and rest."

Quaeryt had to strain to make out the colloquial Tellan. "But where . . . ?"

"You're in one of Master Rhodyn's guest chambers, and before long you'll be better."

Fevered as he was, Quaeryt wondered about that. How . . . how had he gotten so ill?

". . . not a normal fever for the croup you've got . . . or not one that's all of nature . . . you're better now . . ." The woman blotted his forehead again, with the coolness that relieved the heat that poured off his forehead.

". . . thank you . . ."

"Not to be thanking me for what any good person should do . . . just close your eyes and rest . . ."

He tried to keep his eyes open, but they felt so heavy, and he was so tired. What had happened? There had to be more questions . . . if he could only remember what they were. If only . . . but he could not. All he could think of was that they were taking care of him, and for the moment, that was enough, and more than he could ask.

He let his eyes close.

Waves of heat and chill swept over him, and coughing spells that he half-remembered, as if in a daze or stupor where his body reacted. He thought he said words, but he could not remember what they were or what they meant.

The next time he remembered waking, he was alone in the small chamber, and his forehead was warm, but not burning the way it had been, and a light sheet of good cotton covered his body. He realized he'd been undressed down to his drawers, although he didn't remember that ever happening. The light was low, as if just after sunset or before sunrise.

A younger woman, if older than Quaeryt himself, peered through the open door. "Oh . . . you're awake. Let me tell the master." With that, she was gone.

Quaeryt managed to prop himself up slightly on the single pillow before the gray-haired holder stepped into the chamber. Quaeryt mentally groped for his name. Rhodyn, that was it. "I am in your debt. . . ."

"Nonsense. Where would the world be if doing what one ought to do put people in debt?" asked Rhodyn in his accented Bovarian. He smiled openly and warmly. "How are you feeling?"

"Better . . . weak as a newborn lamb."

"That's not surprising. You're an ill man, and not just from the croup you have. Darlinka thinks you were poisoned somehow, but you've sweated most of that out. For a day or two, we weren't certain."

A day or two? How long had he been out of his mind? And poisoned? The water from the old woman? He wanted to laugh, but he was afraid it would cause more coughing. And to think that he'd been worried about getting a flux from stream water.

"You're also a bit more than you seem. You're carrying a pouch with silvers and have hidden golds in your belt and a leather case sealed with wax. Looks like a dispatch case of the sort Telaryn officers carry. Your body bears scars of the kind that come from warfare, but there's a tunic shirt of the kind only scholars wear." The holder laughed. "You're safe here. I'd not wish harm on any traveler, and not on one who walked through the Shallows Coast. Nor one who might be on

Lord Bhayar's affairs." He paused. "I can't say I believe your tale about losing a mount, unless you lost it with a ship. Your clothes were coated in salt."

"You have me, sir." Quaeryt's voice came out hoarse and raspy. "The reavers were chasing me." His eyes stopped focusing, and he had trouble making out the holder. "But . . . the rest . . ." He started coughing.

Rhodyn waited until the fit subsided, then handed him a mug from the small bedside table. "Watered lager. It helps."

"Thank . . . you . . ." Quaeryt took a sip, then a small swallow before replacing the mug on the plain wooden table.

". . . Rest, and we'll hear the whole story when you're better. Just know that you're safe here."

Quaeryt wasn't sure he was safe anywhere, but he was so feverish and tired that he doubted he could have taken a handful of steps. Like it or not, he had to trust his keepers. Once again, his eyes closed without his wanting them to.

22

Although the feverishness subsided, it did not totally disappear over the next few days, and the same was true of the coughing. For all that, Rhodyn and his household were both patient and solicitous. They also fed Quaeryt well.

On Lundi afternoon, a week after he had collapsed literally on Rhodyn's doorstep, Quaeryt sat on the covered porch on the northeast corner of the main house, from where he could see the ocean. The sky was silvered with the haze of high thin clouds, and not a vessel was in sight on the dull gray-blue waters. Across the table from him was Rhodyn's wife Darlinka.

She waited for him to set down the beaker that was still half-filled with lager before she said, "You don't like to talk about yourself, do you?" Her Tellan was clear and concise, the way he'd learned it. "You gave the bare-bones account of your escape from the reavers."

The shorter explanation had been necessary, and he'd minimized his confrontation with the three reavers and the dog, just saying that he'd heard a dog in the distance and that he had run and pressed as much as he could until he'd had to deal with but one and had disabled him and then managed to make his way north and cross the Ayerne. "How many people are truly interested?" he replied in Tellan, smiled, then added, "There are some, but how many do you know who wish to know that much about another? How many of those want to know for the sake of knowing, and how many wish to learn in order to gain an advantage of some sort?"

"There are some, and they are worth knowing."

"You and Rhodyn are among the first I've encountered in some time, and I find myself very fortunate that I have. Might I ask what enables you two to be so?"

"You might indeed, and I will even try to answer. Even if it is a way for you to avoid talking about yourself." Her smile combined warmth and humor.

Quaeryt didn't bother hiding his grin, but he didn't say a word.

"Rhodyn was born here, but when he was young, his father sent him to school in Cloisonyt, just as we have sent Syndar and Lankyt to study in Tilbora. Back then, of course, going to school in Tilbora was not possible. He was as guarded as a young man as you are. Through an acquaintance of his father, he met a young woman who was so unguarded that she might have been prey to anyone. Together, they began to see the world as it was." She smiled again.

"And you never stopped seeing it together?"

"There is a time to question, and a time to answer questions, Scholar Quaeryt. We were fortunate to learn that together."

"It wasn't easy for you two, was it?"

"Not so hard as you might think. Four eyes and two hearts who can trust each other are better than one." After the slightest pause, she went on, calmly. "You're not a man who trusts many, are you? It frets at you to be depending on the goodness of others."

"And how did you notice that?" Quaeryt kept his voice light, still trying not to cough when he spoke.

"That'd be another thing." The older woman smiled. "You answer with questions. You'd think that your parents named you knowing that."

"They didn't name me. If they did, I don't know what that name might have been. They died in the Great Plague, and the scholars took me in. They gave me the name because I asked questions as soon as I could talk in their tongue."

"That would explain much. You are a scholar, yet you were not wearing that garb."

"No." He offered a rueful smile. "When I disembarked from a ship in Nacliano, a harbor patroller tried to attack me because I was a scholar. I think he would have killed me if he could have. I had to dive into the harbor and hide under the piers . . . and avoid the patrollers. That caused me to miss the ship I planned to take, and that led me to take the vessel I did, and that resulted in getting caught in the storm and getting wrecked on something called the Namer's Causeway."

"You were the only one who escaped the reavers, Rhodyn said."

"I don't know that. The old reaver woman, the one I think might have poisoned me, said that two crewmen were found dead on the sands. There was no one else on the wreck when I left, but anyone else who might have survived could have left before I recovered enough to be aware of what had happened. After the worst of the storm hit and the ship struck the causeway, I never saw anyone else. I'd just tied myself to the ship to wait it out." Quaeryt's eyes drifted to the nearer mud-brick building, the one that he'd thought was a barn or some such, and wasn't, but a long building with quarters for many of those who worked the holding. "Don't your workers find this . . . lonely?"

"Some do, and they're free to leave. Some of those return before long. Even with Rhodyn requiring training in arms for the men and boys, most like living here. We don't have winters near so cold as Tilbora, and the women like the calmer life."

"Do you have any daughters?"

"Just one. She lives some five milles north on the old stead."

"From your family?" guessed Quaeryt.

"A crotchety uncle. It's mostly orchard, and Caella always did well with trees. She has a knack with them, even taught her husband some."

"She's the oldest, then?"

"Except for Jorem. He's a produce factor in Bhorael."

Quaeryt tried to remember where Bhorael was, then nodded. "That's just south of Tilbora, on the other side of the river, isn't it?"

Darlinka nodded, then stood. "I need to see about supper and how Liexa is doing. You just stay right there. It won't be long before Rhodyn comes in, and it's a real pleasure for him to have someone not from around here to talk with."

"I don't know that I've been that entertaining . . . more like a burden . . ."

"Nonsense." With that she was gone.

Quaeryt couldn't help but smile. He did worry about the time it was taking him to recover, but his walks about the holding had convinced him that he needed a few more days to regain his strength. He also had to admit that he enjoyed talking to Rhodyn and Darlinka. It also made him wonder what he'd missed in growing up. But then, would his parents have been like the holder and his wife? He suspected few were, and even if he had sickened himself on more than one occasion trying to puzzle out imaging, would parents have helped . . . or turned him out, as some did when they found a child was an imager?

He didn't have to wait long before the holder appeared. Rhodyn carried a large goblet of a red wine out to the shaded table and settled into one of the wooden armchairs across from Quaeryt.

"You look like you've had a long hard day."

"Long and tedious, but not hard. We got in the last of the late cherries. I fear that those baskets will make better wine than anything else." Rhodyn had insisted on speaking Bovarian, saying he needed the practice.

"There's nothing wrong with cherry wine, is there?"

"Besides the fact that unless you make it perfectly,

it doesn't keep well, doesn't sell well, and few people truly enjoy it? No." Rhodyn's voice was cheerfully sarcastic, but not bitter. "Darlinka and Caella like it, and it's rare enough that when I send some to Jorem, he can sell it to a few people who like it. So it's not all a loss. We do better with the honey, though. It keeps, and people like sweets."

Quaeryt nodded and took a swallow of the lager.

"You haven't said much about why you're headed to Tilbora," said Rhodyn conversationally.

"I haven't. That's true. Your wife says I avoid answering questions with questions, but I'm still going to ask a question first. How do you think the Tilborans feel about having so many of Lord Bhayar's armsmen still in Tilbor more than ten years after the fighting stopped?"

"I'd imagine they wouldn't like it. No one likes having armsmen too close at hand. If they aren't kept busy they get into trouble, especially with the local girls, and that leads to more trouble with the local young men. If they are kept busy, and what they're doing is makework, they get angry because they're being kept from the local girls. If you allow them to marry the locals, then that causes a different kind of trouble."

"So how do you keep the locals from rebelling without armsmen?"

"Buy goods from them. Hire them to fix everything that's broken or to build things they need. I'd wager that's cheaper than paying armsmen to do nothing." Rhodyn laughed. "Besides, if things get repaired and they get new market squares or better piers or wider roads that they didn't have before . . ."

"They might be happier."

"Some people are never happy, except when they're

causing trouble. Those you have to get rid of, but in ways that others accept. There was one old fellow who used to get into fights every Samedi night. My sire stopped that. He paid him an extra two coppers to watch the flocks on Samedi night, and told his woman about it. She'd insist he work on Samedi night, and he found out that he had twice as many coins because he wasn't drinking them, either." The holder smiled. "He saved enough to lease a morgen of land in the hills, and his son has an apple orchard there."

"That doesn't always work."

"No. No one thing always works. You have to find what works for each man and each woman. You also have to learn to recognize those for whom nothing will work." Rhodyn's laugh turned bitter. "That was why we had to raze Fairby and the other hamlets to the south."

"I take it that was costly."

"It was. So much so that I would prefer we not talk about it."

Quaeryt was in no position to insist. "My apologies. I did not mean . . ."

"I was the one who brought it up. You needed to know about how evil the ship reavers are. But then, I believe your own experience has reinforced my mere words."

Quaeryt smiled wryly. "You do have a way of putting things, sir. And yes, my experience was quite convincing."

"Experience often trumps words, and that is why what schooling and scholars can do is limited. Some people, perhaps most, only learn from their own mistakes, even when they see others make the very mistakes they will later make because they cannot learn from the failures of others."

"Rhodyn, dear . . . scholar . . . if you would join us for supper!" called Darlinka.

"We'd be delighted!" returned Rhodyn.

As Quaeryt rose, he considered the holder's words. Certainly, what Rhodyn said made sense, but finding out what worked for all Tilbor . . . when he knew so little? He was finding problems in Telaryn that he never knew existed—and he doubted that Bhayar did, either, and Quaeryt hadn't even arrived in Tilbora.

23

Four days later, and with three golds fewer in his belt, Quaeryt rode toward the southern edge of Bhorael, a town set on low hills on the south side of the Albhor River, across which lay the far larger city of Tilbora. While the holdings and the cots and the croppers' houses along the road to the town were neat and well-kept, and mostly of lightly fired mud brick of a yellowish brown, Quaeryt noted that almost none were new or recently built. Likewise, the main avenue that looked to be leading to the river was brick-paved, but many of the bricks were cracked or replaced with others of a different shade. Not until he was close to the river, where he could catch glimpses of brownish gray water at the end of several streets sloping downhill, did he begin to pass any buildings above a single story.

Even though he had directions from Rhodyn, it took him close to a glass to find the "river market square," because all the buildings devoted to trade seemed to run in a swath paralleling the river. By then it was after the third glass of the afternoon. The "square" he sought turned out to be a wide and open paved space two blocks south of the river and the ferry piers to Tilbora. There was not even a raised platform for end-day vendors, nor a statue or fountain, but the square and the buildings fronting it were higher than the area surrounding it, as if a low hill had been flattened, so that Quaeryt again found himself looking down a gentle slope when he glanced toward the river.

The produce factorage had no name on the signboard across the front, just paintings of various kinds of produce—onions, potatoes, carrots, peppers, gourds. The paintings had been recently done and showed an attention to detail that Quaeryt appreciated. The two-story building itself was older, but looked to be in good repair, and the windows on both the lower and the upper level were both glazed and shuttered, but the only windows Quaeryt observed on the lower level were two large oblongs flanking the open front door, a door protected from the sun by a roofed porch. Two backless wooden benches graced the unrailed porch. Both were vacant as Quaeryt dismounted and tied the horse to the iron hitching post.

He walked stiffly up the single stone step to the porch, limping more than he usually did, the stiffness the result of too much riding with too little practice in recent years, not that he'd ever had that much experience in the saddle. The wooden planks of the porch creaked slightly as he walked over them and into the factorage itself.

Long and simple wooden tables in rows filled the front half of the building, and on each table were rows of baskets. After a moment, Quaeryt realized that each table held a different kind of produce—with differing kinds of onions and shallots on one, and a range of peppers on anther, potatoes on a third, different root vegetables on another. There were apricots, early apples, a single basket of late cherries.

He turned toward the rear of the factorage and said in Tellan, "I'm looking for Factor Jorem."

A man who had been bending over a table straightened, then walked forward. He was broad-shouldered and square-chinned, with light brown hair and a slightly tanned face. He showed a far more marked resemblance to Darlinka than to his father, and there was a thin pink scar that ran down the left side of his face from cheekbone to jaw. Quaeryt judged that he was several years younger than Quaeryt himself, and that seemed young to have built or bought such an impressive factorage in a desirable location.

"Yes? What is it?"

"I have a letter here from your family," said Quaeryt, extending the folded and sealed paper. "They were kind to me in my travels, and since I was coming this way, I offered to carry any messages they might have."

Jorem took the missive, although his face betrayed concern and curiosity. "It's not often travelers come from the Ayerne. Nor are such travelers usually scholars."

"That wasn't my plan, either. I was on a ship that was wrecked on the Shallows Coast. I barely escaped the reavers, but I fell ill on my escape. I fear that my acquaintance with your parents came because I collapsed on their doorstep while talking to your father. They were most kind and helped me in every way possible to recover."

Jorem frowned. "You're not an easterner, are you?"

"No. I'm from Solis. I was traveling to Tilbora

when the ship ran afoul of a storm and fetched up on something called the Namer's Causeway."

"I've heard of that . . . never saw it, of course." Jorem paused. "Please look around, if you would, while I read the letter. Oh . . . and thank you for bringing it."

"It was truly the least I could do for them." Quaeryt stepped back and then began to look over the remaining tables of produce. The leeks looked especially good, as did a variety of apples that were a mottled green and red. He didn't see any cherry wine . . . or anything similar, but perhaps the factor kept special goods in another part of the factorage.

He also wondered about the specific instructions that Rhodyn had given him with the three letters—that Jorem was not to be told of the letters to Syndar and Lankyt and the two sons studying in Tilbora were not to be told of Jorem's letter. Obviously, there were problems of some sort, but since Quaeryt wasn't so sure he would have survived without the care and concern of Rhodyn and Darlinka, he intended to respect the holder's wishes, particularly since he had sensed what he would have called a wistful melancholy in Rhodyn's voice when he had asked Quaeryt to carry the missives.

He looked up as Jorem hurried toward him.

"I'm sorry. I was perhaps too brief." The younger man offered an embarrassed smile. "My father thinks highly of you. He seldom offers that observation. You must have impressed him greatly."

"He impressed me," said Quaeryt. "So did your mother. They're both rather thoughtful people."

"He writes that you are traveling on behalf of Lord Bhayar."

"I do have a commission from him for a task in Tilbora."

"You must join us for supper and tell us about your visit. It has been almost two years since I saw them."

There was something sad behind Jorem's words, but Quaeryt only said, "If it would not be an imposition, I would be glad to do so. Thus far, the only truly enjoyable part of my travels was with your parents—after the first few days, when I was so ill that I do not remember much."

"They are known for their kindness." Jorem smiled. "Come, I will tell Hailae, and then we will stable your horse. There is an extra stall in the stable in back. He will be safer there while we eat, and you can groom him so that you won't have to later."

"She's actually a mare," admitted Quaeryt. "I purchased a well-behaved horse, not a cavalry charger."

Jorem laughed as he led the way toward a door at the back of the front chamber. He opened it, revealing a wide staircase to the upper level. He stopped and called, "Hailae, we have a guest for supper!"

There was no answer.

"Hailae!"

"I heard you, dear," came a feminine voice holding a trace of irritation. "It will be another glass . . ."

"We'll come up and talk while you finish fixing it . . . after we stable his horse."

"I will be here."

Jorem closed the door and turned to Quaeryt. "I'll meet you in back."

"Closing early won't hurt your business?" asked Quaeryt. "I wouldn't want to . . ."

"All those I'd expect on a Vendrei afternoon have already come. Tomorrow morning will be busy, but I see few late on Vendrei—sometimes, no one at all."

"You're certain?"

"Very certain. A factor who doesn't know when those who want his goods are likely to want them will not be a factor all that long."

"How long have you had the factorage?"

"Hailae and I have been the ones operating it for seven years. Her parents had it for twenty-five years, and her grandparents before them."

"Very established, then. You're carrying on a tradition."

"A long tradition. I'll see you in back."

Quaeryt nodded and turned. Once he was outside, he untied the mare and walked her down the narrow alleyway to the small courtyard in the rear of the factorage. The stable was on the north side, just beyond the single large loading dock and door.

Jorem stood by the stable door.

While Quaeryt unsaddled the mare, Jorem added grain and hay to the feed trough. The other stall was occupied by a broad dray horse far larger than the mare. In the shed area beyond the stalls was a high-sided wagon—its side panels painted in the same design as the signboard of the factorage.

"That's a handsome wagon, and the painting is well done."

"Hailae did that. She has quite a hand." Jorem's voice held both pride and affection.

"Do you deliver produce as well or is the wagon for collecting it from growers?"

"Both. Hailae often makes those collections, especially from Groryan. It takes two of us to keep things going here."

Again, Quaeryt had the feeling that Jorem had left much unspoken, but he did not press and went to work grooming the mare. Even so, it was almost two quints later by the time he reentered the factorage, washed up on the lower level, and headed up the stairs behind Jorem.

As Quaeryt reached the top of the steps, he caught the last few words spoken by a child.

"... eat with you?"

"If you're good. Father is bringing company. You must listen and not talk unless someone asks you something."

"I'll be good. I promise."

The steps opened onto a foyer with a wide window looking westward, from which the early-evening harvest sun flooded in.

Jorem gestured to the right. "There's the parlor, but, if you don't mind, we'll join Hailae in the kitchen so that she can hear what you have to say." After a moment he added, "Our daughter is likely there also. She's usually good." Those words were followed by a gentle laugh as he walked through a dining chamber that held but a long table and ten plain straight-backed wooden chairs—and a single tall sideboard on the wall opposite the pair of west-facing windows.

The door at the end of the chamber was ajar. Jorem pushed it open and stepped into the kitchen, where he stopped and said, "Hailae, this is Scholar Quaeryt. He is traveling to Tilbora, and he brought a letter from my parents."

Quaeryt bowed.

The young woman who stood before a table in the kitchen that occupied the southwest corner of the second floor had black hair braided and coiled above an angular face dominated by large black eyes and a skin that was a faint golden almond. Behind her stood a small girl, her face almost a child's replica of her mother's, save that her eyes were dark gray and her hair far shorter and unbraided.

Could Hailae be the reason for all the melancholy and sadness between Jorem and his parents and brothers? Quaeryt wondered.

The mother's eyes widened as she looked at Quaeryt, and she spoke.

He understood the words—though he had not heard them in more than twenty years—and he instinctively inclined his head and replied, again with a phrase he recalled, but only understood vaguely. Then he added in Tellan, "That's all I remember. I was very young when they died. "

"I am so sorry," replied Hailae in Tellan. "I did not mean to bring up unpleasant memories."

Quaeryt smiled. "The memories were not unpleasant. What happened after was not always so pleasurable."

"But . . . he's blond . . ." said Jorem.

"There are blond Pharsi, and they have the white-blond hair. . . . That is how I know. They are the lost ones. Besides . . . can you not tell? His eyes are as black as mine."

Jorem laughed, self-deprecatingly, and turned to Quaeryt. "My wife is far more perceptive. I saw an educated scholar. She saw more. She often does."

What Quaeryt saw was that Jorem adored his wife.

"My Jorem," interjected Hailae quickly, "he is trusting and trustworthy." Her smile was warm and open.

Quaeryt said nothing for a moment, envying them both. "You are well suited to each other, it would seem."

"Oh . . . and this is Daerlae," said Jorem, gesturing

to the girl, who now held to her mother's gray trousers with one hand.

"Daerlae, I'm very happy to meet you." Quaeryt inclined his head once more.

Daerlae lowered her eyes for a moment, then peered back at Quaeryt.

"He's a scholar," declared Jorem.

"Uncle Lankyt is a scholar."

"Uncle Lankyt is studying to be a scholar," corrected Jorem. "So is Uncle Syndar."

"If we are to eat before the stars appear," said Hailae gently, "I must finish." She glanced toward the small ceramic tiled stove.

"Why don't you tell us how you came to meet my parents?" suggested Jorem. "That way Hailae can hear the story while she's getting things ready—and I can help as well." He looked to Daerlae. "And you can hear more about your grandparents. If you're good."

Quaeryt couldn't help smiling.

Jorem hurried into the dining room and returned with one of the chairs. "Here . . ."

After taking a seat, Quaeryt cleared his throat. "I never thought that I would ever be close to the Ayerne, or meet your parents—and grandparents—when I took passage on a brig out of Nacliano called the *Moon's Son* . . ." Quaeryt took his time in telling the story, trying to emphasize details that might interest Daerlae, while avoiding revealing how he had escaped the reavers by telling exactly what he had told Rhodyn and Darlinka. He also tried to time the story to how the meal preparation was going so that he was close to ending when he saw Hailae nod to Jorem. ". . . and then the mare carried me up to the front of a factorage that had a wonderful signboard painted with all kinds of fruits and vegetables." He looked to

Daerlae again. "And do you know whose factorage that was?"

"Mother and Father's!"

"Exactly! And that is how I came to be here."

· "And now it's time for dinner." Jorem turned to Quaeryt. "Thank you. You speak well."

Once they were seated at the long table, with Jorem at the head and Hailae to his left with Daerlae beside her and Quaeryt across from Hailae, Jorem looked to his wife.

She lowered her head and spoke. "For the grace that we all owe each other, in times both fair and ill, for the bounty of the land of which we are about to partake, for good faith among all peoples, and especially for mercies great and small. For all these, we offer thanks and gratitude, both now and ever more, in the spirit of that which cannot be named or imaged . . ."

"In peace and harmony," Quaeryt replied almost in unison with both Jorem and Daerlae.

The blessing had to be of Pharsi origins, because the wording was somewhat different from any Quaeryt had heard before, yet not jarringly unfamiliar. Was he really Pharsi? At times, he'd wondered if there had been some Pharsi in his background, because he'd never seen anyone else with black eyes who hadn't been Pharsi, but with his white-blond hair, he'd only assumed he was part Pharsi at most.

Jorem handed a carafe to Quaeryt. "It's a decent red."

"I'm sure it's more than decent," replied Quaeryt, "and whatever it is that you prepared, dear lady," he added, looking at Hailae, "it smells wonderful, especially to a tired traveler."

"It's just a fowl ragout that we have for supper

often. If I'd known Jorem was inviting company, I could have fixed something special."

"For me, this is very special." Quaeryt's words were heartfelt.

Jorem dished out a large helping of the ragout and handed the platter to the scholar. "The olive bread is a family tradition, too."

"You're both most kind, and I can't tell you how much I appreciate your asking me to supper."

"Nonsense," replied Jorem, with an intonation that recalled his mother to Quaeryt.

Hailae smiled.

For a time after everyone was served and had taken bread, there was a silence. From the first mouthful Quaeryt enjoyed the ragout—covered with a flaky pastry crust and with a filling consisting more of vegetables and leeks than fowl. Even so, it was tasty, if more subtle in flavor than most of the dishes in Solis, and the olive bread enhanced the flavor of the ragout.

"Your father mentioned your brothers in Tilbora—do you see them often?" Quaeryt finally asked.

"Lankyt takes one of the ferries down to see us when he can, every other week or so," replied Jorem. "We usually send him back with fruit, or in the winter, dried fruit. He doesn't get much of that from the scholars."

Quaeryt glanced to Daerlae. "Do you like your uncle Lankyt?"

"He's nice. Sometimes, he brings me things. He brought me a doll for my birthday."

"Uncles should do things like that." Quaeryt smiled, then shifted his glance back to Jorem. "Does he say much about how things are in Tilbora these days?"

"He doesn't talk much about Tilbora. He tells us about his studies."

"Do you go there often? To Tilbora?"

Jorem and Hailae exchanged the briefest of glances before Jorem replied. "We haven't been north of the river in years. It takes all our time to keep things going here. We've been fortunate enough that some of the cafés in Tilbora send buyers for our specialties almost every week."

"They always want the anise leeks," added Hailae, "and the sweet red onions."

"I take it there are more cafés in Tilbora."

"We have some here," replied Jorem. "The Painted Pony is good, and so is Brambles. They also are good customers."

"Do you see many armsmen here?"

Jorem shook his head.

"Do they do much to keep the peace in Tilbora, or do they just chase the local girls?" Quaeryt injected light sarcasm into his voice.

"Most girls know enough to stay away from them," answered Hailae.

"Some years back," said Jorem, "a few of them decided that Pharsi girls couldn't protect themselves."

"They were wrong," interjected Hailae.

"But the governor razed an entire block of Pharsi houses when two soldiers were killed, and three were wounded," continued Jorem. "Almost all the Pharsi families around there moved to places in Bhorael."

"Your family was already here, though, wasn't it?" Quaeryt asked Hailae.

"They were."

The simplicity of the answer suggested that Hailae didn't really want to say more, but Quaeryt thought an indirect question might shed some light on the matter, from what he knew of Pharsi customs. "I imagine you had some cousins who decided to move."

"They've been much happier here," she replied.

"I'm glad, and you both seem to like Bhorael."

"It's much friendlier than Tilbora," said Jorem.

"Is there anything you think I should be aware of in Tilbora?" Quaeryt offered a gentle laugh. "I'm afraid I can't remain in Bhorael."

"Well . . . I wouldn't mention that you're on Lord Bhayar's business—except to armsmen or the governor's people. Where you come from doesn't bother the scholars much, but most of the Tilborans don't like the way the armsmen behave. Other than that . . . it's probably like anyplace else. There are places to avoid and places where everyone is friendly and helpful."

After that, Quaeryt steered the talk back to his time with Rhodyn and Darlinka.

A good glass later, he smiled and said, "I fear I have imposed too much, and I should take my leave. Poor Daerlae can barely keep her eyes open."

"Oh, no. I fear we have kept you too late," said Hailae quickly. "You will not be able to find anywhere to stay." She glanced at Jorem. "We do have a guest chamber above the stable. . . . It is modest . . . but it is clean and most private."

"I would not wish to impose. . . ."

"It is not an imposition, not after all the news you have brought us," said Jorem. "And Father would not wish it otherwise. Nor would we."

"That would be most appreciated." Quaeryt paused. "Are you certain?"

"Most certain," said Hailae firmly.

"Let me get a lamp for you, and show you. . . ." Jorem stood.

So did Quaeryt, bowing to Hailae. "My deepest thanks for your hospitality, and for a marvelous dinner." He turned to the sleepy-eyed Daerlae. "And for your company, young lady."

"Am I a lady?" Daerlae looked to her mother.

"You are, and you will be," answered Quaeryt. "If you listen to your parents and mind them." He smiled at Hailae.

She smiled back.

"I heard that," murmured Jorem, returning from the kitchen with a small lamp. "I hope she remembers the last part."

"So do all parents," said Quaeryt with a laugh as he turned to follow the factor down the steps into the factorage and then out to the stable.

24

Quaeryt had intended to slip away early, but Jorem found him in the stable before he had saddled the mare and had insisted on his joining the family for breakfast. Even so, it was well before sixth glass when Quaeryt left the factorage. Daerlae and Jorem stood on the front porch, and Daerlae waved, as the scholar rode northward toward the ferry piers. Quaeryt waved back, a smile on his face at the enthusiasm of the little girl.

Once again, he couldn't help but wonder what lay behind the fracture in the family. It clearly had something to do with Hailae and the fact that she was Pharsi, yet Rhodyn and Darlinka didn't seem to be the kind who would object to their son falling in love with a Pharsi girl, especially one who was attractive and able and who had a family of worth. Not only that, but it was obvious that Hailae and Jorem had endured some hardship and still were deeply in love— without the storminess that Quaeryt had observed from a distance between Bhayar and Aelina.

Absently, he wondered if Vaelora could be as stormy as her brother. Although the tone of her missive had been formal, there had been no mistaking the will behind the words. He shook his head. It would be months before he returned to Solis. Yet . . . why had she written such a formal missive? Why had she written at all? He shrugged. There was little point in speculating, and he certainly wouldn't find out for seasons . . . if he ever did. Yet . . . he had to admit he was intrigued.

The ferry pier was located a half mille or so upstream from where the Albhor River actually entered the harbor and offered several different alternatives, from small boats just for individual passengers all the way up to a donkey-powered paddlewheel craft that could carry two wagons and several horses and their riders. Because the paddlewheel craft was the one that looked the safest and the most ready to depart, Quaeryt paid the five-copper fee, then had to walk the mare into a crude stall and tie her there.

Just as he finished, a one-horse wagon rolled aboard after him, and the teamster paid a silver. When no one else appeared within a quint, not all that surprisingly to Quaeryt, considering that it was early on Samedi, the ferryman groused under his breath and rang a bell. The donkeys began to walk on the slatted platform backed in heavy canvas and wrapped around two rollers, one of which was linked to the rear paddlewheel that churned the gray-brown waters and pushed the unwieldy craft toward the Tilbora ferry piers, close to half a mille away.

Keeping one eye on the mare and the stall, Quaeryt eased over to the ferryman, who was captain, helmsman, and crew, all in one. "Do you know where the Scholars' House is in Tilbora?"

The ferryman looked blank, but did not shift his eyes from the river.

"The place where scholars stay?" prompted Quaeryt.

"Well . . . there's what they call the Ecoliae. It's a hill, sort of northwest from the ferry piers . . ."

The scholar had to strain to understand the man's words; if he happened to be typical, the Tellan Tilborans spoke was almost a different tongue and far more guttural, similar to but not quite the way Chexar had spoken. An instant of sadness came over Quaeryt as he thought about the gruff captain.

". . . and there's an anomen on the next hill to the west . . . and it has a white dome. . . . Might be two milles. Could be three. I don't go that way often. There used to be some teachers there. I suppose there still are . . . unless the Telaryns got rid of them. . . ." The ferryman turned his head and spat.

"There's not a problem with the scholars, is there?"

"No more than anyplace. Not much more, anyways. . . ."

There was a hint of something there, but Quaeryt didn't want to interrupt.

". . . Don't know what all that book learning's good for. They don't cause troubles, anyway. Not like the Telaryn armsmen or the Pharsi types."

"I heard there were troubles years back."

"No more trouble with the Pharsi folk. Good riddance. The armsmen . . . they're still trouble."

Abruptly, the ferryman looked at Quaeryt. "You're a scholar type, aren't you?"

"Yes. I traveled here from Solis to write a history."

"Who'll read it? Other scholars?" The ferryman turned and spat again, his eyes returning to the waters ahead of the ferry. "Leastwise, His Mightiness Lord Bhayar isn't the one writing it. Lord and master of all the east of Lydar, and he's never been here."

"His father was here, and that wasn't exactly what anyone wanted, was it?" asked Quaeryt dryly.

"You got that right, scholar!" After a time, he asked, "What you going to write?"

"One of the reasons I'm here is to talk to people about what happened. What do you think I should write?"

"Write what you want. Who cares?"

"I'd like to write something close to the truth."

"No such thing as truth. Truth is what every man wants it to be for himself. Even the Namer's imagers think their truth is the only one. A course the last one we found around here ended up chained to the sea stones when the tide came in. Couldn't image his way out of all that iron."

Quaeryt kept the wince inside himself. *Does Tilbor view imagers the way Nacliano sees scholars?* "When did that happen?"

"Last week in Juyn, I reckon."

"So, if everyone's got a truth, tell me what you think I should write."

"Someone's got to rule. Someone always has. Most folks don't care so long as they got enough coppers to get by. Too many rulers take too many coppers and don't make things better. That's history. Oh, you got folks with fancy names and fancier clothes, and someone like you writes it all down, what they do, but no one writes about what I do. Don't write what the beggar in the square does. Don't write about the seafarers who sail the storms . . ." The ferryman stopped. "You won't write that, either."

Quaeryt laughed. "You don't care much for scholars, do you?"

"You ever worked, really worked?"

"I ran away and spent six years before the mast. That was work."

"Then you might write about real folk. If you do, them with golds won't read it." The ferryman spat again. "Can't talk no more."

Quaeryt eased away. Even before he reached Tilbora he was getting the feeling that what he had in mind was going to be far, far harder than he'd ever thought . . . and he'd never thought it would be easy. As the donkey ferry neared the piers on the Tilboran side of the river, he couldn't help but note that the northern piers looked more worn and dilapidated than those in Bhorael—and the Bhorael piers had scarcely been pristine.

Once he had led the mare off the ferry and mounted, he set out to find the scholars' place. As was usual in most ports with rivers, there was a road beside the river. This one led northwest from the ferry piers, and Quaeryt rode slowly along it. Unlike the riverside in Nacliano, the ground flanking the river was no more than three or four yards above the water, and many of the structures located between the river road and the water showed watermarks, and stains on the worn wood. Few were constructed of stone above the foundations.

After a mille or so, Quaeryt was sweating in the

midmorning sun, which felt more like summer. Although Tilbora was supposed to be cooler than Nacliano, the heat was more like that in Solis. Before too much longer, he found a wider avenue heading north and in the direction of the hills, the top of one of which appeared to have an anomen situated on its crest. It felt like he had ridden far more than two milles past moderate dwellings and small shops, with but handfuls of people on the streets, early as it was, before he reined up at the bottom of what had to be his destination.

The stone block at the base of the brick-paved lane leading up the gentle slope to the buildings above was inscribed with a single word—ECOLIAE. Quaeryt glanced up. The two-story brick structure that sprawled across the rise was not at all similar in form to the Scholarium in Solis, yet he could feel a certain sameness. All scholarly places exuded a definite feel . . . in some way or another.

He rode up the lane, dismounted, and tied the mare outside the main entrance. A fresh-faced youth in brown, clearly a student, if one likely to be close to finishing his studies, hurried out the door, across the wide covered porch, and down the three, not-quite-crumbing brick steps.

"Good day, sir."

"I'm here from Solis," said Quaeryt, "and would like to stay for a bit. Might I see the scholar princeps?"

"You're fortunate, sir. He is in the front hall at the moment."

"Thank you." Quaeryt walked up the steps and across the mortared bricks of the porch and into the building, whose ancient wooden floor creaked, as if to announce his presence.

The scholar who turned to face Quaeryt had short silver-blond hair and a square-cut beard of the same colors.

"Scholar princeps?" asked Quaeryt.

"I am. What can I do for you?" observed the scholar princeps in Bovarian.

"I'm Quaeryt Rytersyn. I have been traveling, all the way from Solis," replied Quaeryt in the same tongue, "and I had hoped to find room here."

"You know we are not scholars like those in Solis."

"I did not expect that you would be exactly the same. Nor does the moon have sons she acknowledges openly, yet learning exists under moonlight or sunlight, for all that the hunter may be Artiema's guardian."

"Welcome, Quaeryt Rytersyn. I am Zarxes Zorlynsyn. What brings you here?"

"A commission from a patron of scholars in Solis, to update the history of Tilbora." Quaeryt smiled wryly. "I would have been at your doorstep earlier, but . . ." With that opening, he launched into a brief explanation of his travels, omitting his difficulties in Nacliano and how he had handled the reavers, concluding with, ". . . and as a result of holder Rhodyn's kindnesses I have brought missives from him to his sons Syndar and Lankyt."

"Not many scholars arrive with their own mount."

"It was in part a gift from Holder Rhodyn in Ayerne, after the ship I was on was wrecked." In a convoluted way, the mare had been a gift of sorts, because Zachys wouldn't have parted with the mare without Rhodyn's persuasive presence.

"He wanted to assure you completed his tasks. I have met him but once, although he struck me as a man able to know and judge others well. I also thought he might be excellent at persuading them to his ends . . . as necessary."

"About staying here for a week?" prompted Quaeryt.

"For the first night or so, we offer hospitality." Zarxes cleared his throat.

"And after that?" Quaeryt smiled easily.

"A copper a night for the chamber. A copper for every meal. We would appreciate more if possible. The Khanars were always most generous to the scholars. Now . . ."

"Now . . . you must charge for your students and for visiting scholars, as Scholars' Houses do in most of Lydar."

"Unfortunately. Even so, there are months where . . ." Zarxes shrugged.

"I am not wealthy," replied Quaeryt, "but I can certainly forgo any need for hospitality. I am just pleased to be here."

"If you do not mind staying in the west wing . . . there are spacious chambers on the upper level, and the adjoining rooms are currently vacant. The first level can be . . . less than quiet."

"Is that where the student scholars are quartered?"

"You have some knowledge of their habits, I see." Zarxes smiled.

"I was one for many years."

"I thought you might be."

Quaeryt ignored the knowing smile. When he'd been given his names, he'd been too young to know that Ryter was the most common name in Telaryn and that a great proportion of orphans bore the surname "Rytersyn." "My parents died of the Great Plague when I was very young, and in a place where no one knew their names."

The princeps nodded. "You are welcome here. I will have young Gaestnyr fetch Syndar and Lankyt and then ready your chamber. You can wait for them on the porch. These days it is much cooler there."

"Oh . . . and because of the wreck, I will need to make arrangements for another few sets of scholar's garb."

"That should be no problem at all. We have a fine tailor." The princeps strode briskly out the door, and Quaeryt followed, waiting on the shaded porch and standing to catch the light breeze out of the east, while both Zarxes and Gaestnyr vanished in different directions.

Before long, another young man, wearing the uncollared brown shirt and brown trousers of a student, appeared from the east side of the porch, which apparently circled the entire building. He was broad-shouldered and brown-haired and looked much as Rhodyn must have as a young man, Quaeryt thought.

"Scholar . . . the princeps said that you had a missive for me?"

"I have missives for two students," Quaeryt said. "You are?"

"Syndar Rhodynsyn."

Quaeryt lifted both missives from his jacket, looked at the names, and handed one to Syndar. "He wrote this late on Lundi."

"Who did?"

For a moment, Quaeryt didn't answer. Didn't Syndar even know his father's writing? "Your father did. The other missive is for your brother."

"Oh . . ." Syndar nodded. "I'm sorry, scholar. My thoughts were elsewhere. Thank you. I do appreciate your bringing it here."

"You're welcome. I was pleased to do it. Your father and mother were most hospitable and kind."

"They are, indeed." Syndar nodded again. "I do thank you."

Then he turned and left.

Almost as soon as Syndar was out of sight, headed around the east side of the porch, another student, this one far more slender, walked toward the scholar from around the west corner of the porch. His steps were quick, almost eager, and he bowed immediately after stopping short of Quaeryt.

"Scholar Quaeryt, sir? I'm Lankyt Rhodynsyn. The princeps said you might have a missive for me."

"I do indeed." Quaeryt proffered the remaining missive.

As soon as Lankyt saw his name, he smiled. "Thank you so much, sir. Thank you."

"Your father wanted to make sure that you got it, yet . . ." Quaeryt offered a curious expression and let his words die away.

"What is it, sir?"

"Your brother did not seem overjoyed. . . ."

"He has many things on his mind."

"That is what he said, but I'm sure you do as well." Quaeryt paused. "You have another brother. Your mother mentioned him. He's in Bhorael, as I recall." Rhodyn had only said not to mention the letters.

"That's Jorem."

"Your father didn't say much about him. He seemed sad when he mentioned his name."

"Jorem and Father . . . they don't see things the same way."

"I've heard that's often true."

"You must get along well with your parents, sir," said Lankyt with a laugh.

"No. My parents died when I was very small. I was raised by the scholars."

"Oh . . . I'm sorry, sir. I didn't mean . . ."

"That's all right. You were saying . . ."

"It all happened because of the riots . . . and the Telaryn armsmen. Did you hear about the riots?"

"Only that there were riots." At the time, Quaeryt had just returned to Solis and hadn't been that interested in much beside persuading the scholars to take him back. And Jorem had avoided talking about anything like that.

"Old Lord Chayar had told the armsmen to leave the local girls alone. Some of them decided that no one would mind if they took some liberties with the Pharsi girls. Even the Tilborans looked down on them."

Quaeryt let himself wince.

"I see you know about Pharsi women."

"I know that the women are the ones who run the households and that their husbands are usually the ones who do the obeying."

"Some of the soldiers ended up dead, and some were wounded. The governor—the old governor— sent the garrisons out to patrol the streets and then had his engineers destroy the four whole blocks where the armsmen were killed. Some of the dwellings and shops weren't owned by Pharsi families, and the owners protested. The governor ignored them. He said they were all Tilborans, and he didn't care who believed what. People started throwing rocks at the soldiers, and things got worse, and more people and more soldiers got killed, and then the armsmen killed a lot more people . . ." Lankyt shrugged. "I wasn't here then, but that's what the old scholars say happened."

"Those sorts of things can get out of hand, but I

don't understand what that has to do with your brother."

"Oh . . . he rescued a Pharsi girl and her parents. They were visiting their cousins, trying to help them leave Tilbor. The parents were badly hurt in the riots, but Jorem managed to get them all back to Bhorael. They had a produce factorage."

Quaeryt forced himself to wait.

Lankyt finally went on. "He kept seeing Hailae, and they fell in love. After two years, when he was about finished with his studies, he wrote Father saying that he intended to marry Hailae. Father wrote back saying that was fine, and that he looked forward to having his son and new daughter taking over the holding. That was where the trouble started."

"Hailae wanted to stay near her family?" asked Quaeryt.

"She was their only child, and they were ill. Father offered to bring everyone to Ayerne, but Hailae and Jorem said that they wanted to carry on the factorage. He did not wish to ask Hailae to give up all that her parents had sacrificed for, and their injuries were too great for them to run the factorage. Father was hurt, I think. That was when he sent Syndar here to study. I came a year later."

Quaeryt nodded slowly. "Your brother—Syndar—seems rather quiet. Withdrawn, almost."

Lankyt nodded. "He wants to stay and be a scholar. He never liked all that went into running a holding."

"And you?"

"I'm ready to go back to Ayerne any time. Father wants me to stay until Year-Turn. I think he hopes Syndar will change his mind."

Quaeryt wanted to shake his head. So often brothers fought over an inheritance, and in the case of Rhodyn's sons, it seemed as though the father would have preferred either son who didn't want the holding to the one who did. "You really like Ayerne, don't you?"

Lankyt's face brightened once more. "I've always loved it. I've studied about plants and trees, and I think there are things I could do that would make the holding even more prosperous. I've even visited the growers around here, the ones that the scholars say are the most successful . . ."

Quaeryt nodded pleasantly, trying to hide a smile at the young man's enthusiasm, as well as his own sadness, knowing that the expectations of others might well dampen those feelings.

". . . and Caella has already tried some of what I wrote her, and it's working with her orchards."

"Your mother mentioned that."

"They didn't think she could do it, either." Abruptly, Lankyt stopped. "I'm sorry, sir. I didn't mean to . . ."

"You didn't. I think you'll make a fine holder." *If they'll just give you the chance.* "Just remember that no one likes change away from what's familiar. If you can, show them how what you want to change is just another way of accomplishing the familiar. Show them with little things first. It only seems to take longer."

"Sir . . . it only seems . . . ?"

"When you fight to change people's minds, they re-sist. When people resist, it takes longer." Quaeryt laughed. "Now I'm the one who must apologize for acting like a chorister of the Nameless. And I do apologize."

"There is no need to apologize to me, sir . . . and I do thank you for bringing the missive to me. Will you be staying at the Ecoliae?"

"For a few days, a week, perhaps a little longer." After a smile, the scholar added, "I should not keep you longer, and I do need to get my mount out of the sun."

"Oh . . . yes, sir. Thank you again." Lankyt nodded a last time, then hurried off clutching the missive in his hands.

Quaeryt walked down from the porch and untied the mare from the old iron hitching rail, thinking about the differences between the three sons.

As if he had been watching, Gaestnyr reappeared from the west end of the porch. "If you would follow me, sir?"

"I'd be happy to, thank you."

As he led the mare behind young Gaestnyr around to the west end of the main building, presumably to the stable, and then to his quarters, his eyes ranged across the hillside below. Hot as the day was, he saw the signs of how far north Tilbor was. There were far fewer leafy trees, and those that he saw were mainly oaks and maples, while there were evergreens everywhere. Did the kind of trees affect people? Did those who lived around prickly evergreens tend to be more stiff and sharp?

He suspected he would find out before too long.

25

Once he had inspected his chamber, which was larger than the one he had occupied in Solis, as well as cleaner, although it had double shutters, which suggested that the winter would be cold indeed, and left his small amount of gear, Quaeryt reclaimed the mare from the small stable and started on his way down the lane.

To his right, farther west, were larger dwellings, the northern equivalent of villas, with thick walls and windows far smaller than those customary in Solis, or even in Nacliano. None was located on the actual crests of hills, but just slightly down from them, and most had a southern orientation. The lanes leading to them from the roads were angled to climb gently, and the roads themselves were not in the lowest part of the vales.

He could also easily see the Telaryn Palace—what had been the Khanar's Palace until ten years before, when Lord Chayar had taken Tilbora from the west— since it was situated on the highest of the low hills to the north of the city, and its extensive nondescript gray walls and square towers stood out above the golden grasses on the hillsides below. The lower hills flanking the palace were covered with evergreens and held no dwellings or structures that Quaeryt could see, suggesting that they had been reserved for the use of the Khanar—and now probably for the governor.

Quaeryt wasn't about to ride up to the palace—not yet. He wanted to ride through Tilbora and find out what he could before meeting Governor Rescalyn, and he turned the mare eastward onto the narrow but brick-paved road that appeared to lead into the center of Tilbora. For the first half mille or so, the way was bordered by modest dwellings with gardens, but there were no walled gardens or even walled courtyards the way there were in Solis. Even Nacliano had some walled courtyards. Quaeryt saw none. He also saw no grapes or figs, and every courtyard garden in Solis had some variety of one or the other.

He saw wooden rail fences, and occasional stone

and brick walls that were between knee-high and chest-high. The dwellings were smaller and more modest the closer he got to town, but none were built wall-to-wall as they were in other cities he had visited.

After riding another half mille, he came to a brick-paved circle, a crossroads of sorts, in that two roads did cross, but various shops and other structures had been built all the way around the edge of the paved circle, leaving four equal arcs of buildings, each arc set between two roads. More than that, there was ... something about the buildings. None quite looked like those he had passed earlier. All had narrower but longer windows, and every door had an iron grate that closed over it, although all were swung back at the moment. The types of shops seemed normal enough. He could pick out a small woolen shop, a tinsmith's, a fuller, a cooper. One "quarter" held an inn, and the signboard suggested it had been named something different before, because the peeling paint revealed traces of another name, but not enough for Quaeryt to read it.

A woman emptied a bucket of water on the bricks before a shop and then used a worn broom to sweep away dirt and other less benign objects.

Was this a Pharsi area before? Or has it changed as some areas will with time?

He couldn't tell, and he wasn't about to stop and ask. Not at the moment, anyway.

He kept riding, and before that long the narrow road ended at a stone-paved square that served the harbor area. At the east end was a knee-high seawall, also of the same gray stone. The mortar was cracking and missing in places in the wall, and the paving stones were uneven, as if they had not been reset in years. One pier jutted out from the south end of the square, a second from the north end, and a third and smaller pier was set farther to the north.

Quaeryt rode around the edge of the square, past a chandlery and a café of sorts, and all manner of small shops, a number of which bore signboards sporting painted fish. There were fewer women than men on the narrow streets and sidewalks, and most of the women he saw looked older. He kept riding, going up one street and down another, but avoiding the alleys, and eventually ended up back at the harbor square, where he reined up, trying to think over what he'd seen.

The harbor area was far smaller than that of Nacliano, stretching little more than six or seven blocks north and south and three or four to the west from the three piers, none of which approached the length of the smallest in Nacliano, or even the short coastal pier in Solis. In reality, the piers were not even that, but wooden wharves built on what looked to be rough-stripped tree trunks sunk into the harbor floor.

"You'd be looking for something, sir?" The inquiry came from another of the olive-green-clad city patrollers as he walked toward Quaeryt.

"I'm new here, and I was just riding to get my bearings." Quaeryt paused just slightly. "You don't have harbor patrollers here, do you?"

"No, sir. Why would we need them?" The patroller looked up at Quaeryt. His face was lined and ruddy, and his square-cut beard held streaks of gray.

"The last port I was in was Nacliano, and they had harbor patrollers. I've never been here before and didn't know if it might be the same."

The patroller smiled. "We'd not be needing them. Our folk don't take to rowdiness or theft or any of that foolishness. We're here for the times they need a mite of assistance."

"That's good to know."

"You need a good stable . . . you might try Thayl's place. It's two blocks west of the small pier."

Quaeryt smiled at the indirect suggestion that he needed to move on. "If I do, I'll keep that in mind. Thank you." He flicked the reins and guided the mare northward in the general direction of Thayl's, not that he intended to stop there.

When he reached a point opposite the smallest wharf, he did turn the mare in the direction suggested by the patroller. After a single block, he began to grin. Just before Thayl's stable was another building, one with open second-floor windows. Several of the windows were adorned—if that were the proper term—with women wearing the sheerest of cotton shifts or blouses, and some of those blouses were not fastened in the slightest.

The building had no signboard, but then it needed none, and he could see why Thayl might do a fair business stabling mounts for a short period of time. He rode by and took in the scenery. He'd seen better, and he'd seen worse, and in some places, like Nacliano, there wasn't much difference between places like the Sailrigger and a brothel. He'd never patronized either type, not because he didn't appreciate femininity, but because women like Hailae—or especially the not-quite-gangly Vaelora—were more to his taste. At the same time, he couldn't help but wonder exactly how the brothel made its presence known in the depth of winter. Not that he had any intention of being around past Year-Turn to find out.

When he rode back up the lane to the stable behind the main building of the Ecoliae, at close to fourth glass, Quaeryt had a fair understanding of how Tilbora was laid out—a town that had sprawled into a larger town based on the river piers and the harbor with the former Khanar's Palace withdrawn to the northern heights and overlooking the town. Interestingly enough, while there was a good paved road across Tilbora from the palace to the river piers, there was no direct road from the palace to the harbor. That, unfortunately, said far too much about the Khanars and about Chayar and Bhayar.

Also, the men and women he'd seen were taller and leaner than the people of Solis, not that all of them were lean, as evidenced by the view offered by the unnamed brothel, and most of them seemed to have sandy brown hair or blond hair. He'd seen no redheads, and very few people with black hair.

After grooming the mare and seeing to her feed, Quaeryt walked from the stable to the main building, climbing the rear steps to the porch and walking toward the shaded east side. For all the size of the Ecoliae, he saw but a few handfuls of scholars on the wide porch, most of them in two groups in roughly circled chairs.

He didn't feel like intruding, but he also didn't want to turn and walk away. He decided to compromise and walk to the edge of the porch and look down at the small flower bed he had noted earlier. There wasn't much to see, just harvest lilies that were beginning to look scraggly and a line of flowers he didn't recognize, but that appeared similar to sun daisies.

He straightened and turned, debating whether to leave or loiter for a bit longer.

"You must be the visiting scholar. I'm Chardyn . . . Chardyn Traesksyn."

The short scholar who spoke in cultured Tellan, if with a Tilboran accent, and who approached was neither slender nor wiry, but somewhere in the middle and well-muscled. He wore a short straight blond mustache, an affectation Quaeryt had not often seen. In the south, most men èither were clean-shaven or had short beards. From what he'd seen in his ride through Tilbora, most men seemed to have full beards. Then again, Quaeryt hadn't exactly counted.

"The whispered word through the students is that you're on some sort of mysterious quest for some even more mysterious patron."

Quaeryt laughed. "The next thing you know, they'll be saying I'm the bastard son of Lord Bhayar, not that he's old enough to have fathered anyone my age."

Chardyn gestured toward a pair of chairs. "If you wouldn't mind joining me?"

"I'd be pleased."

"Good."

Quaeryt settled himself into one of the chairs and waited until the other had settled himself as well.

"Can you enlighten me as to the truth of the rumors?" Chardyn lifted both eyebrows.

"They're true, except that the quest isn't all that mysterious. Nor is my patron mysterious, except that he prefers to remain unknown because he has discovered that if he ever reveals that he provides scholars with gainful tasks he will be inundated with scholars."

Chardyn laughed, a soft but high-pitched sound. "You have answered what you can about your patron, but what of the quest?"

"There's been very little written about Tilbor and its history in recent times. I'm looking for whoever might have the best understanding of Tilboran history, especially over the last few hundred years."

"That scarcely sounds like the sort of quest most patrons would fund. Most want their names inscribed in tomes more likely to be widely read or upon large and elegantly ugly statues."

"Oh . . . I think he would be most happy with an inscription on a very good recent history. Is there anyone here—you, perhaps—who might be of assistance?"

"Not me. Hardly me. I'm the martial-arts scholar."

"Study or demonstration or both?"

"I've studied a number. I'm relatively proficient in Sansang."

Quaeryt nodded. He'd heard of Sansang, supposedly a discipline that mixed all types of unarmed and nonbladed combat techniques, coming as it had from the ancient High Holder prohibition on the use of bladed weapons by anyone but High Holders, except as armsmen of a High Holder or a ruler, but he'd never met anyone proficient in it. "I'd like to watch your instruction sometime."

"You're welcome any morning at sixth glass on the practice green."

"I'll be there some morning." Quaeryt smiled. "I'm not sure it will be tomorrow, though."

"It won't be. We don't practice on Solayi morning." Chardyn's tone was light.

"Who might be able to help me with the history?"

"Right now, no one speaks much about Tilboran history." Chardyn pursed his lips. "No one else but Sarastyn comes close."

"Could you introduce me?"

The other scholar shook his head. "It's past the third glass of the afternoon. He'll be down soothing his throat, as he puts it. It's best to catch him in the morning. Well . . . not early in the morning, and definitely not early tomorrow morning."

"Doesn't he have tasks . . . ?"

"No. He was the assistant princeps for student studies for twenty years. He must be over seventy now, and as gnarled as winter-heights pine. He claims that his blood is half ale, and I'd believe that. Some men's tongues loosen when they drink. His doesn't. It tightens."

"I met Scholar Zarxes, but I neglected to ask him about the Master Scholar here."

"That's Phaeryn. You can't miss him. Tall, silver-white hair, voice like a deep drum. He's done wonders in keeping everything working since . . ." Chardyn shrugged.

"Since Tilbor became part of Telaryn?"

"That's one way of putting it."

"How would most Tilborans put it?"

Chardyn laughed again, briefly. "Those who are political will say something about the 'unfortunate occurrence.' The merchanters will say something about Lord Chayar wanting to tariff them heavily to pay for his ambitions to rule all Lydar."

"But he died years ago."

"Oh . . . they'll just say that his son is no better."

"What do you say?"

The short scholar smiled. "They're both true. Then there is the fact many will not admit. Eleonyd was not the strongest of Khanars, and the fact that he had no sons and that his daughter refused to marry Bhayar left him in a weakened position. When he died suddenly . . . everyone suspected the hand of Chayar."

"Rhecyrdyl . . . or whatever the Pretender's name was . . . said that was the case, didn't he?"

Another high short laugh followed, a sound that bothered Quaeryt, but he waited.

"Rhecyrd. He was Eleonyd's cousin. He never said anything. In fact, all he did say was that it was too easy to blame Chayar. The Telaryn envoy arrived in Tilbora a few weeks before Eleonyd sickened and died. Then the rumors started, and someone doused the envoy's ship with Antiagon Fire with him still aboard. After that, who could prove anything? It was rather convenient for whoever actually caused Eleonyd's death. More gossip began, this time that Rhecyrd's imager was involved. But he was thirty milles north of Tilbora before and during Eleonyd's illness and death." Chardyn shrugged. "Then Chayar demanded Tilbor submit, and everyone put aside looking into Eleonyd's death . . . for various reasons."

Quaeryt winced.

"For Tilborans, all that was subtle," Chardyn pointed out.

"What happened to the daughter?"

Chardyn shrugged. "She fled to Bovaria with all the jewels she could manage. Some say she married a High Holder there—Iraya or Ryel or something like that. Others say she put Rhecyrd up to everything and then left him to face Chayar. Some think both."

Quaeryt considered what the other had said. He recalled what Bhayar had told him, and nothing that Chardyn had said contradicted that. Supposedly, Chayar had been furious about the treatment of the envoy, but Bhayar had confided to Quaeryt that it had made it easier for his father to justify the war that followed. "What do you think?"

"That was over ten years ago. What does it matter? We all have to do the best we can with things as they are now."

"Zarxes suggested, rather indirectly, that it has been difficult to keep the Ecoliae going in these times."

"Difficult? Yes. Phaeryn has managed well, better than any could have expected. Teaching Bovarian has brought in many children of the wealthier merchants for day studies, and boarding fees for those who live farther away. He has also found other ways to bring in the necessary coins."

"Such as?"

"Offering hospitality to those such as you. Accepting produce and services for teaching the children of merchanters and growers. Using the skills of scholars to rebuild the anomen in return for some support from the chorister. He has been most creative." Chardyn's smile contained a certain hidden amusement.

Quaeryt ignored that amusement, trouble though it suggested, since calling attention to it would only warn the other scholar. "He sounds most able."

"He is indeed." Chardyn rose. "Come, let me introduce you to some of our company."

Quaeryt stood and followed the other, a pleasant smile upon his face.

26

After being introduced to a good half score of older scholars, Quaeryt joined the group for a modest supper at the scholars' dining hall, then listened throughout the meal and for a good glass afterward, before taking his leave. Chardyn bothered him in more ways than one, but since the man had done nothing at all except be friendly, all Quaeryt could do was to be as careful as possible. If his suspicions were correct, it would be a few days before trouble appeared, but he might be too optimistic.

He didn't sleep all that well on Samedi night, not surprisingly, although he did take the precaution of also imaging a clay wedge into place under the heavy door, in addition to sliding the bolt and barring the door. After waking early, he rose, washed and dressed, and went out to the stable to check on the mare. When he returned, he visited the dining hall and ate, waiting to see if Sarastyn appeared.

An older gray-haired and burly scholar appeared just before the servers were about to close the hall. Based on the description Quaeryt had gathered from others the night before, the late arrival was most likely Sarastyn. Quaeryt lingered for a time, then rose from the table where he had been sitting and walked toward the other.

"Scholar Sarastyn, I presume?"

"You are presuming for so early." Sarastyn's voice was harsh, gravel-like.

"Might I join you?"

"It appears you already have." Sarastyn's gesture to the seat opposite him was little more than grudging.

"I'm Quaeryt, and I traveled here from Solis." He smiled politely. "I understand you're the foremost in studying the history of Tilbor."

Sarastyn took a long swallow from his mug before replying. "That might be an overstatement. If it is true, and it doubtless is, it is solely because no one else has bothered to amass any knowledge at all about that collection of anecdotes that some equate with historical scholarship."

"You seem to be suggesting that some scholars merely piece together anecdotes and call it history?"

"Why not?" Sarastyn began to cough.

Quaeryt waited for the other to recover.

The older man took several more sips from the

mug. "Those selfsame individuals piece together mere information and call themselves scholars. How would you define history in scholarly terms?"

Quaeryt thought for a moment. How he replied would doubtless determine whether Sarastyn would prove helpful. "The organization and presentation of past events in a structure that reveals not only what happened, but the patterns behind why it happened."

"Patterns . . . in all the times I've asked that question, you're one of the few who has used the term 'pattern.' Where did you say you were from?"

"Solis."

"Why are you here?"

"To find out more about the recent history of Tilbor, particularly in the years before it was taken over by Telaryn."

Sarastyn nodded slowly. "That would seem simple enough, as would most history, but what seems is not what was." He laughed, a soft sound at odds with his harsh voice. "That is scarcely astonishing when what we think we see and experience is seldom what is. If you ask any three scholars their recollection of an event, you will receive three accounts, and often those accounts are so different as to make one think that there were three different events."

"If one gathers all the recollections . . ." suggested Quaeryt.

"One will have an assembly of nonsense, such as the tomes once racked in that moldy storehouse of a chamber that Zarxes terms a library. One must discern the patterns behind such events."

For a moment, Quaeryt paused, not because he had no response, but because Chardyn had entered the hall and seated himself with two younger scholars.

"You dispute that there are patterns?" asked Sarastyn.

"I've read enough history, sir," said Quaeryt deferentially, "that even I can see that at times the pattern imposed is that of the writer, not of history."

Sarastyn laughed, again softly. "You're young, especially for a scholar. The patterns are there. They're always there, but every generation refuses to see them. Some even ignore them, and replace them with their own patterns, as you suggested. Of those few that do discern the true patterns, most claim that they will escape the patterns of their times. There are few that are intelligent enough both to see the patterns and to understand that men are not all that different, generation to generation, and some of them try to explain to others. Such would-be explainers are either ignored or murdered."

"People see what they want to see," agreed Quaeryt. "Can you tell me which patterns have affected Tilbor over the recent past?"

"All of them."

"I'm sure you're right, but I don't know the history, and no one outside of Tilbor has written it. Chardyn said that you—"

"Ah . . . yes, Chardyn," replied Sarastyn in a lower voice. "He's a pattern, too. He watches all strangers. More than he should, as he is now observing you."

"Why might that be?"

"That . . . you will have to discover for yourself, but it is a pattern that has been consistent for the last few years. He always observes those who do not reside here for long."

"I see." That did confirm some of Quaeryt's suspicions. "He said that you could help with the history. . . ."

"You risk that I may be telling you only my own recollections."

"I'll take that risk."

For the third time, Sarastyn laughed. "It is a lovely day, and the Ice Cleft will not open its doors on a Solayi until the fourth glass of the afternoon. We should repair to the north porch." After a last swallow from the mug, he stood.

Quaeryt rose as well, noting that Chardyn did not turn his head. Quaeryt still felt eyes on his back as he followed the older scholar.

Sarastyn chose a pair of chairs close to the railing, well shaded by the porch roof, but where the building did not block the slight breeze out of the southeast. Quaeryt settled into one of the wooden chairs to listen.

"In what are you interested?"

"Who was Khanar before Eleonyd . . . and was he stronger than his son?"

"It might be best if I started several generations before," suggested Sarastyn, smiling broadly. "Context is often as important as the events themselves. Nidar the Great was the last of the truly strong Khanars—the great-grandfather of Eleonyd. He was the one who rebuilt the harbor here in Tilbora and restructured the old clan levies into the Khanar's Guard and the militia. . . . Not coincidentally, he was the one who thwarted Hengyst's ambitions to conquer Tilbor. . . ."

Quaeryt listened closely as Sarastyn continued, interjecting occasional questions for his own clarification and mentally noting particular references. Over the next glass and more, his interest grew, he had to admit, as Sarastyn's verbal history drew closer to the present.

". . . Tyrena was—I expect she still is—very blond and very strong-willed . . . as good with arms, if not better, than her father. But then, Eleonyd wasn't much good at anything. So long as he listened to his wife . . . he got good advice . . . she died giving birth to Tyrena . . . listened to his daughter, but not enough . . . Rhecyrd . . . raised in the Noiran coast highlands . . . typical norther . . . tall, handsome, and thought everything could be solved with a bow or a blade . . . Eleonyd thought to preserve his lineage by marrying Tyrena to him . . . she wanted to rule in her own right . . . northers objected . . . members of the Khanar's Council from both Midcote and Noira walked out . . ."

Quaeryt nodded as Sarastyn elaborated on what Chardyn had mentioned the night before.

". . . can't say as I blame Tyrena. She didn't have much choice . . ."

"Could she have ruled in her own right?"

Sarastyn offered a rueful smile. "There's never been a Khanara who ruled, but the people of the south preferred her. Rhecyrd started tales that Eleonyd wasn't ill, but that Tyrena was poisoning him . . . most likely that his personal healer was, possibly paid by Rhecyrd . . . Eleonyd started to get better when the healer fell off a balcony and died . . . damage was done by then . . . and Eleonyd never fully recovered . . . got carried off by a nasty form of croup . . . might have been a civil war except the northers are hotheads . . . southers don't like to fight losing battles . . ."

"Except that they did—with Chayar," Quaeryt pointed out.

"No. Most of the southers didn't fight at all. The Guard pulled back to the palace, and Rhecyrd's clans fought. I don't know that either of the Telaryn governors has understood that. Southers, and that's all those south of the Boran Hills, are realists."

"Just don't back them into a corner?" asked Quaeryt.

"Mostly. Except for the Pharsi. They're stiff-necked, but there aren't many left since the riots years ago." Sarastyn coughed several times. "I think I've talked long enough for now. Time for a rest before I take my afternoon medicinals."

"Thank you. Have you written down any of this?"

"Save you, and a few others, who would care?"

"Those who have yet to be born who would also care," suggested Quaeryt.

"You have great faith, Scholar Quaeryt. Few learn from what they observe, and fewer still from the accounts of the mistakes of others."

"I have little enough faith, sir, but I refuse to give up hope."

Sarastyn laughed, openly and without bitterness or malice. "Well said! Well said. So should it be for all scholars." He coughed again. "This has tired me. We should speak later." He rose slowly.

"Are there any books in the library that you or others have written that might be of value?"

"Those I wrote have long since vanished, and the others . . . you can see what you will."

Quaeryt stood and watched as the older man made his way toward the nearest door.

Once he turned to head toward the stables, he saw Chardyn seated at the other end of the porch, seemingly reading a book. He had his doubts that the Sansang scholar had been just engaged in reading.

As Quaeryt stepped off the porch, he glanced to the north and west, but the sky remained clear, without even a trace of haze. While the day felt cooler than it had on Samedi, by late afternoon, it well might be hotter. He shrugged and continued to the stable.

When Quaeryt had finished saddling the mare and led her out into the sunlight, where he mounted, it was close to midday. He didn't see Chardyn on the porch when he rode past the northeast corner, nor any other of the few scholars he might have recalled from the night before. Several students were playing what looked to be a form of turf bowling on the lower lawn in front. He thought one of them might be Lankyt, but the youth didn't look in his direction.

He rode eastward past the anomen, and then farther, past the circular crossroads, which seemed even quieter than the last time he had ridden through it, before he finally came to the broader paved road that led south to the river piers or north to the Telaryn Palace. He turned the mare north.

Less than a hundred yards later, he rode past a produce wagon, filled with baskets of maize, most likely headed toward the river piers. A short distance behind that wagon was another, this one bearing bushels of the red and green apples he'd seen at Jorem's factorage. By the time he was a good half mille, or so he judged, from the lower gate to the causeway serving the palace, he'd ridden past more than a dozen produce wagons, all headed south—and on a Solayi, to boot.

He eased the mare to the shoulder of the road and reined up and studied the Telaryn Palace and its grounds. The long rise ran roughly east to west and had been stripped of all vegetation except grass, and the grass had been grazed regularly enough that it looked to be less than ankle-high in most places. A dry moat some twenty yards across encircled the base of the entire rise, and another road ran parallel to and south of the moat, intersecting the road which Quaeryt had taken at the lower gate that guarded access to the causeway leading up to the palace. Halfway up the slope, the hillside had been carved away to create a wall out of the underlying limestone some three or four yards high. The sole break was where the angled causeway turned straight uphill for a timber bridge that crossed that gap. On the uphill side, the causeway angled back to the east, reaching a stone-framed gate near the eastern end of the gray stone walls.

After taking in the palace, he urged the mare forward and rode slowly toward the gates.

The iron gates were closed, set in gray stone towers that extended back to the moat. A timber bridge crossed the moat, supported in the middle by a single pier rising from the bottom of the dry ditch. A set of towers on the far side of the moat, with cables running to the edge of the bridge on the gatehouse side, suggested that the entire bridge could be lifted.

Two guards, Telaryn armsmen wearing standard green uniforms, were posted in front of the gates, one on each side, each standing under a slanted roof that cast enough shade to keep them from excessive heat. The taller guard, the one on the west side, followed Quaeryt's every motion as he rode past, but did not move or say a word.

Quaeryt continued westward on the road flanking the dry moat, noting with a smile that the stone paving ended about a hundred yards from where the dry moat turned north and away from the road. The wooded hill to the west of the one holding the palace was empty of any dwellings, walls, or fences, but Quaeryt had no doubts that any incursion was likely to result in the appearance of armsmen.

He kept riding, deciding to try to make a large circle back to the Ecoliae.

27

~~~~~~

The circle route that Quaeryt rode on Solayi afternoon had taken him a good three milles north and another mille south to a village so small that it had neither signs nor millestones to give a hint as to its name, and none of the handful of buildings holding shops and crafters had signage, In that, Tilbor clearly resembled the rest of Telaryn, since lettered signs were not exactly common anywhere, although more prevalent in port cities and in Solis. The village almost could have been one anywhere in greater Telaryn, except for the steeply pitched roofs and the narrow windows that hinted at long and cold winters.

After he returned to the Ecoliae and stabled and groomed the mare, Quaeryt washed off the sweat of the day, reminding himself that he needed to purchase more scholars' garments on Lundi.

That evening, with little better to do and hoping to learn more, in one way or another, Quaeryt decided to take in services at the anomen next to the Ecoliae. He had to admit that he was not especially inclined to the worship of anything, particularly a deity as vaguely defined as the Nameless, although from what he had read about the Duodean practices in Caenen, the Nameless seemed far more acceptable, especially with regard to the precepts presented by the choristers.

The midharvest sun was almost touching the hills to the west when Quaeryt walked up the last part of the packed clay and dirt path from the Ecoliae and reached the old yellow-brick archway leading into the anomen. The doors were of antique oak, but recently oiled and in seemingly good repair. The interior was dim, lit only by four wall lanterns of polished brass, two on each side of the meeting hall, a space not quite twenty yards long and about ten wide. The walls were plastered smooth and had been recently whitewashed, but held no decoration or adornment, in keeping with the strict precepts of Rholan.

Quaeryt stood to the south side, halfway back from the sanctuary area, from where he watched as close to thirty students filed into the anomen, led by a scholar whom he did not recognize. Quaeryt picked out both Syndar and Lankyt, although neither appeared to notice him. By the time the chorister stepped to the front of the anomen, in addition to the students, there were close to twenty scholars present, of various ages, but he did not see either Chardyn or Sarastyn. He did see Zarxes and a silver-haired scholar who matched the description Chardyn had provided of Phaeryn.

Despite his short and wavy brown hair, the chorister of the anomen looked old and frail, with the hint of sagging jowls, and high cheekbones that accentuated the gauntness of his face. His wordless invocation warbled and wobbled painfully, so much so that Quaeryt had to conceal a wince.

Thankfully, when the chorister offered the greeting, his voice was stronger. "We gather together in the spirit of the Nameless and to affirm the quest for goodness and mercy in all that we do."

Quaeryt did not sing the opening hymn, something about "the unspoken Namelessness of glory," a song he had never heard.

After that was the confession, which sounded different when spoken in the Tellan of Tilbor. "We name not

You, for Naming presumes, and we presume not upon the creator of all that was, is, and will be. We pray not to You for ourselves, nor ask from You favor or recognition, for such asks You to favor us over others who are also Yours. We confess that we risk in all times the sins of presumptuous pride. We acknowledge that the very names we bear symbolize those sins, for we strive too often to raise our names and ourselves above others, to insist that our small achievements have meaning. Let us never forget that we are less than nothing against Your Nameless magnificence and that we must respect all others, in celebration and deference to You who cannot be named or known, only respected and worshipped."

Quaeryt did chime in with the chorus of "In peace and harmony."

He added a pair of coppers to the offertory basket passed among the worshippers and then watched as the chorister ascended to the pulpit for the homily.

"Good evening."

"Good evening," came the murmured reply.

"Under the Nameless all evenings are good, even those that seem less than marvelous. . . ." The chorister paused and cleared his throat, looking out over the small congregation for a long moment before continuing. "Those of you who are young and strong . . . you say that you are different from those who came before you, because you see them as older. You do not see them as they were when you were young or even unborn, when they were young and strong. But if you are fortunate, you in time will grow old, and those who follow you will in turn claim that they know better because they are young and strong. This insistence that you are right because you are young and strong is but another manifestation of Naming. You place your

appearance above the consideration of what is right
and just. Because men and women are often weak in
spirit, it falls to those who rule to enforce what is right
through strength. Yet because this is so, many claim
that might makes right. That is an argument of the
Namer. All virtues require the support of strength, but
to claim those virtues are only virtues because they
are supported by strength is error indeed. . . ."

Quaeryt couldn't help but think about what the
ancient chorister was saying. How did a ruler convey
virtue beyond the strength with which it was necessarily enforced? How much did people respond to righ-
teousness itself and how much to force? How could
the two best be balanced?

As Quaeryt pondered those questions, he noted
that Zarxes had turned and looked across those scholars attending and had paused in his glances to take in
Quaeryt.

Quaeryt kept a pleasant smile on his face, but ignored the scrutiny, as if it were perfectly normal for the
scholar princeps to ascertain which scholars and students were attending anomen, which, in fact, it doubtless was.

After the benediction, before anyone looked in his
direction, Quaeryt raised a concealment shield and
eased toward the tall silver-haired figure that he
thought was Phaeryn, following him and Zarxes as the
two walked down the rutted path from the anomen
toward the brick lane leading back to the Ecoliae.

Neither scholar spoke until they were well away
from the anomen and seemingly alone. Even then,
Zarxes glanced back through the fading glow of twilight before he spoke.

Close as he was, Quaeryt had difficulty catching all
the words.

"... you see the visiting scholar?"

"... can't say that I did ... haven't met him ... might recall ... only your description ... think he's truly a scholar?"

"He is, most definitely. . . . That might pose a problem . . ."

"Oh?"

"Kellear sent a message the other day ... rumors that Lord Bhayar is sending a scholar assistant to the princeps ... couldn't find out his name. About some things, Straesyr is closemouthed ... worse than Rescalyn, and the governor has little love of us . . ."

"Even after ... ?"

"He's not to be trusted ... used as we can, but not trusted."

"It could be a trap for Kellear. Did you warn him?"

"I'm not about to send messages to him. If he comes to see me, I'll tell him."

"When was the last time he came to see you?"

"Almost a year ago. That's his choice."

Quaeryt tried to fix that name in his memory—Kellear.

Phaeryn did not reply immediately, but finally asked, "You think this visiting scholar—what's his name—might be the one?"

"He gave his name as Quaeryt."

"... can't be his real name . . ."

"... hardly think so. . . . Yet he spent several glasses this afternoon getting Sarastyn to talk about the history he said he was here to write about ... some overheard what he asked, and his questions were detailed ... also delivered letters to two students . . ."

"... must be handled with care . . ."

"... always ... but ... either way ... it would be for the best. He has coin."

"When did he say he would be leaving?"

"A week . . ."

"Have Chardyn or someone get him to give a day where everyone can hear . . ."

"I'd thought something like that . . ."

"Good. What about the plans to deal with Fhae-dyrk?"

". . . he's wily . . . last man we sent drowned . . ."

". . . proving to be a real problem . . . suggest under-paying tariffs to the governor?"

". . . as much as Rescalyn visits them all?"

". . . have to do something. Oh . . . Can you per-suade Cedryk to wait for payment for the lambs?"

"He'll wait another week . . . not that much longer . . ."

Quaeryt let the two slip farther ahead, if slowly, while watching his steps up the paved lane to the Eco-liae. He'd had a feeling about why he'd been given a large, comfortable, and comparatively isolated cham-ber, but it wasn't pleasant to have such a feeling even partly confirmed.

28

While Quaeryt rose before fifth glass on Lundi so that he could observe the students—and Chardyn—at Sansang practice, he raised a concealment shield be-fore he left his chamber and moved as silently as pos-sible down the stairs, which creaked only once or twice under his weight, and out onto the section of the porch overlooking the green. As he watched in the grayish light before sunrise, he could see that Sansang definitely had its roots in nonbladed combat. That suggested that the discipline had grown out of resistance to the Khanars and the High Holders of Tilbor, since he suspected, as was generally the case across all of Lydar, the use of blades longer than the middle finger was most likely forbidden to all except those of high position or their armsmen.

The moves that Chardyn drilled into the students initially involved largely the upper body, but after two quints, the students picked up half-staffs that looked to be slightly less than two yards in length. Chardyn appeared particularly impressive, but Quaeryt had hardly expected anything else.

As the students finished and began to disperse, Quaeryt slipped away to check on the mare. When he entered the stable, he glanced around. Seeing no one, he released the concealment shield. The stable was large enough to hold a dozen mounts in regular stalls, and there were two larger stalls. Each of the larger stalls held a dray horse, but of the dozen other stalls, only six held mounts. By comparison, the stable at the Scholarium Solum held but two drays and two other mounts for occasional use by the senior scholars.

Then, too, he reflected, several mounts might belong to students with wealthy parents. Still . . .

He shrugged. There was no way of telling.

After walking through the stable, studying it, and finding nothing obviously untoward, except a pair of identical saddles with twin scabbards for blades like a sabre, Quaeryt left and walked back to the main building. The dining hall opened at sixth glass, and he made his way through the double doors at a quint past the glass. Before he could seat himself, a rotund older scholar stepped toward him, a man with a slightly angular face and smooth skin that might have belonged to a child, in contrast to the thatch of dull gray hair above the penetrating bright green eyes.

"Scholar Quaeryt?"

"Yes?" Quaeryt smiled politely.

"I'm Nalakyn, the preceptor of students. I had heard that you have come from Solis. I presume you studied at the Scholarium there?"

"I did."

"I was hoping that I could persuade you to talk to the students about Solis and about the government of Lord Bhayar."

"Talking about Solis would be easy, but I know very little more about the government of Lord Bhayar than any other scholar in Solis."

"That is far more than do any of us, and it would be of great value to the students. If you would . . . ?"

Quaeryt offered what he hoped was a helpless smile. "With that understanding, I will offer what I can. Later this morning?"

"Eighth glass would be most appreciated. In the student assembly hall on the west end of the building."

"I will be there."

"I thank you and look forward to hearing what you have to say." Nalakyn nodded and smiled happily before stepping back.

As Quaeryt turned, he wondered, *Did Chardyn or Zarxes put Nalakyn up to that?*

From a table across the hall, Chardyn half-stood and beckoned. Quaeryt raised his hand in acknowledgment and walked toward the end of the table where Chardyn sat, accompanied by a younger scholar.

Chardyn smiled knowingly as he approached. "I might have been mistaken, Scholar Quaeryt, but I don't believe I saw you when we went through our exercises and practice this morning."

Quaeryt offered an embarrassed laugh. "Alas, for all my good intentions, I overslept. Perhaps tomorrow . . ."

"It will be just as early tomorrow." Chardyn nodded in the direction of the dark-haired scholar. "This is Alkiabys. He is training to be my assistant."

"I'm pleased to meet you. Are you also a scholar of Sansang?"

"Yes, sir. I am not half so proficient as Scholar Chardyn."

"It takes time and practice to become good at anything," rejoined Quaeryt as he slipped into the chair across the table from Chardyn.

"You must have expertise in many fields, sir," offered Alkiabys.

"I've been fortunate enough to be able to indulge my love of history."

"Yet few would look at you and see a historian," suggested Chardyn. "You look more like an armsman or an officer."

"I did flee the scholars for a time and served as a ship's apprentice quartermaster. That convinced me that being a scholar was much to be preferred." *Especially for an imager who didn't want to be noticed.* Quaeryt poured a mug of the too-strong tea served at the Ecoliae, then took a small swallow.

"How did that convince you?" asked Chardyn, his voice soft.

"By showing me that knowledge is to be preferred over strength and adventure."

Chardyn nodded. "Still . . . knowledge alone seldom suffices. Not when facing great force."

"Nothing alone suffices," replied Quaeryt, serving

himself several of the flatcakes from a platter put on the table by a student server. He poured a thin berry syrup over the cakes and began to eat, wishing that the syrup happened to be sweeter.

After a time, Quaeryt paused from eating. "By the way, as I told Scholar Princeps Zarxes on Samedi, I need to obtain more garments to replace those lost in my travels. He had said you had a marvelous tailor . . ." Quaeryt let the words hang.

"Naxim is quite good. His shop is on the lower level on the east side. I imagine he will be there soon, if he is not already. Did Nalakyn manage to find you?"

"He did indeed."

"Excellent. I would have hated for you to leave before talking to our students. Whenever they can hear from a scholar who has traveled far and wide it is most beneficial."

"You would seem to be such a scholar yourself," observed Quaeryt.

"My travels have been largely in the library, except, of course, for a brief time when I served the Khanar."

"Might I ask which Khanar?"

"Rhecyrd. That was a most unfortunate time. He had great plans, but . . . there are always those who will turn to treachery when their personal ambitions and whims are thwarted."

"From what Sarastyn has conveyed, that could imply that either Tyrena or Rhecyrd . . . ?" Quaeryt raised his eyebrows.

"Sarastyn has always been a romantic at heart, but romance should not cloud one's view of reality. Tyrena was too young to rule. She refused to see that, and then . . ." Chardyn shrugged.

"You think that she was the one who planned the assassination of Chayar's envoy?"

"Who else? She was the one who drafted the invitation for the envoy to come to Tilbor, on the pretext that she might be available as young Lord Bhayar's consort."

Quaeryt nodded slowly. Chardyn had a plausible point, because Bhayar had been betrothed, but not married, to Aelina at the time, and there was no doubt that Chayar could well have set aside his son's betrothal to unite Tilbor and Telaryn without a war. Except . . . there had been no such letter arriving in Solis. Of that, Quaeryt had been certain, because Bhayar had mentioned that the Khanar had rejected that possibility. Bhayar had never mentioned names to Quaeryt, only the terms "Khanar" and "his daughter." So Chardyn's words were likely an indirect probe. "Was she intelligent and attractive?"

"She doubtless still is, but the man who wed her had best be most cautious."

"You had mentioned that she fled and married a Bovarian High Holder. They are known to keep their wives well in line."

Chardyn laughed. "I would hope so, for his sake, and because she is the type who needs to be on a tight rein."

Quaeryt smiled and continued to eat.

After breakfast, he left Chardyn and found the bursar of the Ecoliae, to whom he tendered enough coppers to pay for the next several days, including more for the feed for the mare, which no one had mentioned, while letting drop that he intended to remain at least through the coming Solayi. Then he took the steps to the lower level and to the tailor shop. Naxim was a tidy man. That Quaeryt could tell the moment he had walked into the small space. He was also not that busy, because, after measuring Quaeryt, he promised to have two sets of scholar browns ready by Meredi afternoon. The price was not inexpensive, but not unreasonable at seven silvers for the pair.

Then Quaeryt hurried up to the main level and to the student assembly hall on the west end of the building, where Nalakyn stood outside the double doors, waiting, along with Zarxes.

The scholar princeps smiled. "I'd thought to increase my knowledge of Solis as well, Scholar Quaeryt."

"I trust I can add at least some small tidbits to your vast array of learning, sir."

"I'm most certain that you can, though they may be small, indeed."

Two more students hurried into the hall, nodding politely as they passed.

"I believe we can begin," said Nalakyn, turning and entering the hall, where he stood beside the doors until the other two scholars entered, then closed the doors.

Zarxes moved to the side of the hall and turned, where he waited. Quaeryt took a position near the front, before thirty students standing in front of benches.

Nalakyn stepped up beside Quaeryt, brushing back his limp gray hair absently. "You may be seated." When all the students were seated, he went on. "I have a special lecture today for you. Scholar Quaeryt is here from the Scholarium Solum in Solis, and he will be telling you about Solis and Lord Bhayar." With a nod to Quaeryt, he stepped aside.

"Young scholars," Quaeryt began, "you have often heard that a little knowledge is most dangerous, and I am about to impart what little knowledge I know about Solis and Lord Bhayar. I hope it is not too dangerous for being so scant. I agreed to do so with the understanding that I studied in Solis at the Scholarium Solum . . . and not anywhere close to the palace of Lord Bhayar . . . although I must say that it is a grand palace that sits on a hill high enough to overlook the harbor without being particularly close to the water or the piers. The Scholarium is much older, and it sits on a smaller hill much closer to the harbor, which has advantages . . . of sorts.

"A few of you, or more, may know that Solis is not the homeland of Lord Bhayar. He and his father, Lord Chayar, were born in Extela, in the mountains of hot mist and fire, and Lord Chayar is the one who spent his life concentrating on truly uniting Telaryn. . . ." From there, Quaeryt gave a brief summary of the various campaigns and battles waged by Chayar's grandsire Bhaeyan to physically control Telaryn, followed by the political reforms of Chayar's father, and then the efforts of Chayar—except those involving the conquest of Tilbor—as well as the shifting of the capital to Solis and the rebuilding of the harbor there, before going on to describe the government under Bhayar. ". . . he has but a handful of ministers, one being charged with the maintaining of rivers, roads, canals, and ports, another with the collection of tariffs, and a third with the operation of the messengers and couriers that serve Lord Bhayar, and a fourth in dealing with envoys and communications with other lands . . ." Quaeryt paused and nodded at Lankyt, whose face bore a puzzled expression. "Yes?"

"You did not mention what minister is in charge of armies and armsmen, sir."

"No . . . I did not. Lord Bhayar himself controls those. His regional governors and his marshals report to him directly. That was the practice of Lord Chayar, and his son has continued it."

"How does he make his will known?" Lankyt persisted.

"He has couriers. I mentioned those before. He also has special companies of armsmen, raised in the mountains, or so it is reported, who are very loyal, and who will remove any official who displeases him. Those who make mistakes are either exiled or sent to unpleasant duties in even more onerous locations. Some even have returned to grace. Those who steal from the Lord or the people are executed." Quaeryt paused. "So it is said. I do not know if that is the case here in Tilbora." He looked to Nalakyn.

"The governor is very strict," admitted the preceptor. "I have not heard about theft going unpunished. He has executed his own soldiers for stealing from the people. Those he has caught, anyway."

That would suggest that few are stealing much, but you'll have to see, thought Quaeryt.

"The Scholarium Solum is both similar to and different from the Ecoliae. . . ." Quaeryt went on to explain in great detail about the scholars in Solis, and then about the port city and capital itself.

He answered more than a score of questions before he finally turned to Nalakyn. "I could talk a great deal longer, but I suspect I've already gone on too long."

"Oh . . . no. It is time to stop, but I'm certain that everyone learned a great deal."

I just hope that Scholar Princeps Zarxes did not.

After leaving the young scholars, Quaeryt searched for Sarastyn, finally locating him almost a glass later on the shaded north porch.

"You have more questions . . . or are you here to enlighten me?" asked the older scholar sardonically.

"I have noticed that I'm not the one learning when I'm talking, sir."

"Don't use 'sir' with me. It makes me feel more decrepit than I already do." Sarastyn gestured to the chair across from him.

"After thinking over what you told me yesterday, I did have a few more questions."

"Well . . . what are they?"

"You mentioned how Nidar the Great had changed from the old clan way of fighting and created the Khanar's Guard, but I was curious about how he could afford having a permanent guard. . . ."

"Oh . . . that was simple enough. He took a copper in tariffs from every gold in timber sales in the three ports—but only for timber leaving Tilbor. Most of that was in Midcote. He did the same thing with the seal and bear pelts taken by the ice hunters north of Noira . . . and he tariffed the white sugar from the south, but not the local molasses . . . not just those, but the same pattern on goods leaving or coming into Tilbor. Of course, there was a great deal more fur trading back then . . ."

Quaeryt listened until Sarastyn stopped and looked at him.

"The Khanar's daughter . . . how exactly did she flee?"

"That was simple enough. She took a boat out to a Bovarian merchanter with her own guards, offered golds if they'd take her to Ephra, and steel if the captain chose to be disinclined."

"And Rhecyrd didn't try to stop her?"

"Why would he? Once she left, no one stood in his way."

"Are there any ironworks in Tilbor now . . ."

"Just the small ones west of here and near Midcote. . . ."

After close to a glass, Quaeryt could tell that Sarastyn was tiring, and he took his leave, walking out to the stable where he saddled the mare and set out on another exploratory ride, this time into the trading and craft sector to the southeast of the Ecoliae. As he had suspected, there were no large manufactories, and only a few handfuls of those that might be considered even of moderate size. While he had heard that much of the timber used to the south of Tilbora came from Tilbor, he could find but one sawmill and two lumbering factorages, confirming in his own mind what Sarastyn had said about Midcote.

When he finally returned to the Ecoliae for supper, he wasn't surprised to find Nalakyn waiting for him beside the dining hall door.

"I appreciated your talk this morning. Very much," said the preceptor of students. "You explained things so very clearly. I cannot believe that you have no experience or personal knowledge of Lord Bhayar."

"Lord Bhayar is such a forceful person that everyone in Solis knows well his wishes and aims," replied Quaeryt with a laugh. "Those who serve him are equally direct and forceful."

"Have you met any of them?"

"I have seen his seneschal, and even the sight of the man made it clear that it was best to avoid him. Fortunately, I had little cause to deal with him." *Or little enough.*

Quaeryt walked through the doors and into the hall. Nalakyn accompanied him. They sat at one end of one of the long tables, and shortly the smallish bursar— Yullyd—joined them.

While the Ecoliae did provide ale or lager with the evening meal, Quaeryt had found the lager bitter and the ale unpalatable, and so had accepted the lager as the lesser evil, although, as he looked at the apple-baked dark fish on the platters set in the middle of the table, he had the feeling that the lager might be the best part of the meal—that and the greasy fried potatoes.

"Master Scholar Phaeryn must be most accomplished to have been able to keep the Ecoliae functioning during the time of the invasion, with all the fighting . . ." offered Quaeryt. "Were you here during that time?"

"Not for the time of the invasion. The Ecoliae was closed then. Master Scholar Phaeryn felt it would not be safe for students or for scholars. We all retreated to his family's timberland in the Boran Hills until the fighting ended."

"He must come from a family of means, then."

"He was the youngest. That was why he became a scholar."

"He said he'd rather be a scholar than a chorister," added Yullyd. "He did serve a year in the Khanar's Guard, too."

"I didn't know that," said Nalakyn.

"Most folks don't."

"Didn't Scholar Chardyn serve as well for a time?"

"He did," said Yullyd. "He left when Lady Tyrena took over command. Not in name, of course, but in fact. That was when Eleonyd got so ill."

Quaeryt could see there were more than a few conflicting stories of that time, but said nothing.

"Master Scholar Phaeryn has done marvels here," said Nalakyn quickly. "The Ecoliae was almost falling down after the war . . ."

Quaeryt listened intently as the preceptor catalogued all of the Master Scholar's virtues and accomplishments. He didn't even have to prod Nalakyn, and that bothered him in more ways than one.

29

After Quaeryt left the dining hall after breakfast on a gloomy and overcast Mardi morning, he was grudgingly grateful for the quantity of flatcakes, which were at least palatable, despite the thinness of the berry syrup. The mutton strips had been almost inedible. He was just three steps into the main corridor when someone called to him.

"Scholar Quaeryt, sir."

He turned to see a student standing against the wall of a side corridor, a position not visible from inside the dining hall. "Yes, Lankyt?"

"I . . . just wanted to thank you . . . for the letter . . . and for the talk, too, but mostly for the letter. I didn't have a chance to talk to you after I read it. I appreciate your bringing it all this way."

"I could scarcely have done less after your father's kindness." Quaeryt moved toward the young man, stopping slightly less than a yard away.

"There's another thing, sir. . . ."

Quaeryt nodded and waited.

"Preceptor Nalakyn . . . he's a good man."

"I got that impression," replied Quaeryt.

"Scholar Chardyn . . . he doesn't care much for anyone who might be in the favor of Lord Bhayar . . . or the governor. I know you said you didn't know much about him, but Da—my father, I mean . . . I think he had a different impression . . . and I wouldn't want . . ."

"I understand, and I thank you. You don't have to say more. Your father is a good man, and I doubt if you could do better than to follow his principles." Quaeryt smiled warmly, trying to disarm the youth. "You could help me with one other matter, if you would."

"Sir?" Lankyt's voice lowered, holding worry.

"Is there a taverna around here with good food?"

The youth grinned, as much in relief as anything, Quaeryt suspected.

"There are only two close. Well, three if you count Sullah's, but no one with any sense goes there. Jardyna has better food, and a singer. The spirits are dear, though. Rufalo's costs less, but the grub is awful. They're both along the road to the west, less than half a mille, almost across from each other. Jardyna is the one with the picture of the garden."

"How do you know all that?"

"I listen a lot, sir. People talk."

Quaeryt laughed. "Keep listening . . . and thank you. I'm not so sure I can take another supper here."

"Some nights I feel like that, sir. I'd better go."

No sooner were the words spoken than Lankyt turned and hurried down the side corridor, leaving Quaeryt alone in the main corridor, if only for a moment.

"Are you still here?" asked Yullyd, coming out of the dining hall. "I thought . . . Did I hear someone else?"

"I just asked a student about tavernas."

"They'd all pick Rufalo's. The lager's cheap there. That's fine, but not if you want to eat. Jardyna's not bad, and if you've got a mount, Terazo on the way into Tilbora is very good. Costly, but good."

Quaeryt paused. "Sarastyn mentioned the Ice Cleft. . . ."

Yullyd laughed. "That was the old name of Rufalo's. It hasn't been called that for years. Rufalo forgets to tariff Sarastyn for half of what he drinks, but then, he probably waters it as well."

"Well . . . I thank you. I'll keep those in mind."

"If you stay here too long, you'll want to keep them more than in mind." Yullyd paused, then asked, "How long will you be here, do you think? Solayi, you'd said."

"I'd thought through Solayi or perhaps Lundi. I need to spend more time with Sarastyn. He can only talk so long before he gets tired. You wouldn't know anyone else who knows history that well?"

"Not here. If the governor will let you into the Khanar's library . . . there's a lot there, I've heard. But I'd tell the governor's people you're from Solis. Things . . . well . . . we avoid the governor, and he avoids dealing with us."

More and more, Quaeryt could see that there were definite tensions between the scholars and the governor, something he'd have to take into account once he reported to the princeps. "I imagine Chardyn would like to look into the Khanar's library."

"I wouldn't know, sir." After another pause, Yullyd added, "You've paid lodging and meals through Jeudi morning. If you want to stay longer, let me know."

"I will."

Before Quaeryt's words had died away, Yullyd was on his way down the corridor to his study. Yullyd's last words had been a reminder to keep paying, as well as an indication of the perilous state of the finances of the Ecoliae.

Quaeryt kept his frown to himself and walked out onto the covered north porch. There he looked in the direction of the Telaryn Palace, where the sky was merely overcast, but a gust of cool wind prompted him to turn to the northwest, where dark clouds had massed and were moving toward Tilbora. Another gust of wind swept the porch, strong enough to shake some of the heavy wooden chairs and to move others fractionally. Then came the patter of rain on the roof, a patter that died away, then repeated itself.

Quaeryt decided against taking a ride, at least for the while. He could always pore over the library, although Sarastyn had been dismissive of the Ecoliae's holdings. Still, there might be something of value there, even if not along the lines of his purported research, and he might find something else that would shed light on better ways for the governor to deal with Tilbor. He reentered the building and walked to the northeast corner.

The library at the Ecoliae was hardly that—just a large chamber some ten yards long and eight wide, filled with wall shelves and two rows of freestanding head-high, back-to-back bookcases. While a thin graying scholar who had been seated at one of the tables near Quaeryt on Solayi night looked up from the table desk near the door, then nodded pleasantly, there were no bars on the windows and no grated doors guarding the library. Quaeryt did note a solid lock on the door and inside shutters on the windows.

Not knowing what was shelved where, and deciding against asking for obvious reasons, since he had no idea who did, or who didn't, inform Zarxes or Chardyn, he began by starting at the top shelf on the outer wall and taking down the first book and opening it to see the title—*The Practice and Profession of Music*. A quick sampling of that set of shelves suggested that all were about music and drama. The books about drama surprised Quaeryt, since only the largest cities had playhouses, and most drama was produced in the smaller theatres of High Holders, as was virtually all orchestral music—except when Lord Bhayar had his band play in the Palace Square on special holidays, such as Year-Turn or Summer-Light.

The next two shelves held various works on philosophy, including one that would have intrigued Quaeryt had he felt he had the time to read it—*Rholan as Philosopher*. The very title might have gotten the author drowned or burned at one time, but when Quaeryt read the name on the title page, he almost laughed. The book had been written by Ryter Rytersyn. He did thumb through the introduction quickly, and one paragraph caught his eye.

> . . . Rholan is revered to this day, and doubtless will be so for generations to come as the voice of the Nameless, as the Unnamer, as the man who destroyed the sacredness of names, yet few, if any, have remarked upon the fact that he used common nouns, names, to do so . . . suggesting either conscious irony or even a great sense of humor . . .

Quaeryt smiled, thinking he might have liked to have met the author, but that was rather unlikely, since, if the date was correct, the man, or possibly the woman, given the pseudonym, had been dead for over a century. Then he moved to the next shelf.

After more than a glass, Quaeryt realized that Sarastyn, if anything, had understated the lack of historical tomes in the library. He found one short shelf of histories, and all seventeen books dealt with other lands—Bovaria, Khel, Tela, Ryntar, Antiago, Ferrum, Jariola—but not Tilbor, or they were rather dated geographies.

His eyes were blurring, almost tearing, when he finally left the library after three odd glasses and made his way outside into the cool air brought by the harvest storm. The heavy rain had begun to turn the brick lane down to the road into a small stream, and the road below into a river. With the rain now coming down in sheets, he wasn't about to take the mare out for a ride . . . and if it kept falling, he'd have to suffer through another evening meal at the Ecoliae.

He did sigh quietly at that thought, then decided to return to the library. Perhaps, amid all the dross and irrelevancies, he might find something of value. Perhaps.

30

The rain was still falling on Meredi morning, if more steadily, rather than in sheeting gusts, but Quaeryt saw no point in trying to ride on roads that were streams if they were paved—which most weren't—and quagmires if they weren't. He didn't see Sarastyn anywhere, and, for lack of anything better to do, he made his way back to the library.

This time he did stop before the quiet scholar apparently in charge of the chamber. "I've seen you here and in the dining hall, but I don't believe we've met. I'm Quaeryt."

"Foraugh. I'm the librarian. I imagine you've guessed that."

The librarian's heavy and thick Tellan accent suggested he might not be from Tilbora, and Quaeryt asked, "I get the feeling you're not from this part of Tilbor. Is that right, or am I just too unfamiliar with the northeast of Lydar?"

"No, sir. You've that right. I'm from the hills south of Midcote. That's the oldest part of Tilbor. That was what my grandpere said, anyway. Usually, he was right. He was a potter, and these days folks will fight over his work."

"How did you come to be a scholar?"

"I spoiled too many pots. My father sent me here. He said that education ruined a man for honest work, but since I was ruined anyway, it couldn't do me any more harm." Foraugh offered a crooked smile.

"How long have you been here?"

"Sixteen years. Five as a student-copyist, and eleven as a scholar."

"The copying paid for your schooling?"

"I doubt that it did, but Master Scholar Phaeryn said it did."

"I noticed there aren't many books on history."

"No. When we returned from the hills after the war, almost all the history references were gone. I've borrowed and copied what I could find . . ."

"Didn't anyone stay here during the war—to look after things?"

"Scholar Chardyn and a few others did. From what he said, I think the partisans may have taken over the Ecoliae for a time."

"The partisans?"

"Oh . . . that was the name they gave themselves. They were the ones who kept fighting after Lord Chayar's soldiers captured and executed Khanar Rhecyrd. The fighting in parts of Tilbora lasted over a year, closer to two."

"It must have seemed the right thing for Scholar

Chardyn to do, then, after his service to Khanar Rhecyrd."

"I would judge so, but he never speaks about that
time. None of us do. Those were the black years."

"I imagine times were very difficult for most people."

"The High Holders didn't fare that badly. They
have their own guards and armsmen, and the governor
didn't want to fight them, not after they attacked High
Holder Jaraul, and lost almost five hundred soldiers to
his two hundred."

"They killed Jaraul?"

"They did, but, later, the governor pardoned him
and granted half the lands back to his widow and surviving son. That was part of the agreement between
the High Holders and Lord Chayar . . . well, the agreement signed on his behalf by the governor. That stopped
the fighting between the High Holders and the governor. After that . . . the partisans had to give up. Mostly,
anyway, except for occasional attacks on careless soldiers."

"The governor caught most of them?"

"Oh, no. They just slipped away, back to whatever
they'd been doing. Well . . . as they could. It didn't
make sense to fight much when they'd been betrayed
by the High Holders."

"For a time, the High Holders gave them support,
until they—the High Holders—reached an agreement
with the governor?"

"I don't know. It seemed that the High Holders used
the partisans as a tool to help force the governor to
come to an agreement. Then they forgot how many
partisans died."

Quaeryt let himself wince. "That seems . . ."

"The way the High Holders always have been, in
any land. Are they any different in Solis?"

"They're . . . less direct, I'd say, but probably no different."

Foraugh offered a sad smile. "You see?"

"None of the students come from their families?"

"They seldom leave their estates, and they have tutors, mainly from Bovaria. The wealthiest of our students would be paupers compared to the poorest children of the High Holders."

That was no surprise to Quaeryt, but the answer he already knew wasn't why he'd asked the question. "Then, the older timbering families, like those of Master Scholar Phaeryn, they're not High Holders?"

"No. They're highlanders and backlanders. They have lands, but not hoards of golds. Not most of them anyway. They also own the timber road to Midcote."

"So most of the timber from Tilbor comes from Midcote?"

"It always has."

Despite talking to Foraugh for another glass, Quaeryt learned little more. Nor did an additional glass in the library turn up anything new of note. When he finally left the library and stepped out onto the porch, the rain had stopped, and the clouds had retreated to a high overcast that appeared to be thinning. He had begun to consider what of those inquiries he had determined to be necessary he might best pursue with Sarastyn when Scholar Princeps Zarxes approached.

"Ah . . . Quaeryt, what do you think of our harvest rains?"

"For the sake of the holders and growers, I hope they had most of their harvesting done—or that what is left is mainly hay . . . or the like."

"You sound like a grower. Do you have relations who are?"

"None that I know of, sir," replied Quaeryt politely. "And you?"

"Not I. Phaeryn and I come from timbering families. I grew up with an ax in my hands, while Phaeryn was raised riding through those lands and marking trees." Zarxes smiled broadly. "I have not seen much of you, except in the dining hall, although I hear you have made many inquiries of Sarastyn. Will you be with us much longer?"

"I anticipate at least until the end of the week, if not longer. I'm learning a great deal from Sarastyn, and even some from Scholar Chardyn."

"Ah, yes. They each know history in a differing fashion. Well . . . I will look forward to reading whatever you write . . . if, of course, you can have a copy made for our poor library."

"That decision, sir, I will have to defer to my patron."

"You never did mention his name, I don't believe."

"I did not. That was his wish."

"His command, perhaps?"

"Hardly. He does not express himself to me in that fashion, for which I am grateful."

Make of that what you will.

"You should be. In that you are most fortunate."

"I suspect it is just that he is perceptive. He is a good patron, and one I would not wish to lose. So I listen, and he sees that."

"Many are not so reasonable, such as Lord Bhayar."

"I have never been in any position to make that judgment," replied Quaeryt with a light laugh. "From what everyone says, I would not wish to be."

"Nor I." Zarxes smiled pleasantly. "It would appear we will have a sunny and pleasant afternoon. Do enjoy it, as you can."

"I have more to learn, but I will." *As I can, while always being aware of what lies behind me.*

Zarxes did not glance back.

Shortly, the sun began to break through the overcast, and then the wind picked up. Directly after the sunshine strengthened, Sarastyn appeared on the south porch, and Quaeryt immediately approached the older man.

"More questions, Scholar Quaeryt?"

"Of course. Once I have thought over what I've learned from you, then I discover I have more questions."

"That is always the way for a scholar." Sarastyn looked out to the south. "The Ice Cleft will be open before all that long. But before that, I will endeavor to provide suitable responses."

"It will be open . . . after all the rain?"

"Especially after all the rain. Here in Tilbor the soil is thin and drains well, too well the growers say, and with this wind, even the muddiest of byways will be passable by tomorrow. The Ice Cleft is on the main road, and I'm careful where I put my feet." Sarastyn raised his thin eyebrows. "Your question, Scholar Quaeryt?"

"Who were the partisans?"

"You might as well ask the name of the wind—or the Nameless," replied Sarastyn gruffly. "Any Tilboran—except a High Holder—could be a partisan at some time or another." The old scholar snorted. "There have been partisans in Tilbor since the first Khanar. Anyone who acts on a grievance against a ruler or a High Holder declares himself a partisan."

"Has anyone written about partisans who changed things—or have any been that successful?"

"Most partisans are more successful in stopping change than making it. To stop change, all you have to do is kill people who can effect change. To make a change in the way a land does things, you have to convince people, and few want to change."

"So the best way to make a change is to convince people you're restoring the old ways that they loved?" Quaeryt's voice was only slightly sardonic.

"If you were a ruler or a governor, Scholar Quaeryt, you might possess the potential to be dangerous. As a scholar, you're merely eccentric, and young for being so. Eccentricity is tolerated in the old, because we are believed unable to accomplish much. In the young, eccentricity is viewed as dangerous or a symptom of mental defect, neither of which is desirable."

"I will attempt to refrain from displaying such," replied Quaeryt. "Are the remaining partisans the ones behind the occasional attacks on the governor's soldiers?"

"By definition, anyone who attacks an occupier of a land is a partisan. I personally suspect that many of those so-called partisans are rather well-dressed, well-armed, and well-fed. They might even be well-mounted. That is only a suspicion, you understand."

"Were I as eccentric and as suspicious as you seem to think," said Quaeryt with a smile, "I would say that a High Holder who professed peaceful intentions while inciting others to violence indirectly might effectively strengthen his position, and that of all High Holders, with the governor."

"You'd not be the first to say so, but if you made that known, and could prove it to the governor, you might well be the first one to remain alive for saying such."

"Even among scholars?"

Sarastyn laughed, softly. "Scholars must live in the world around them, no matter what one studies, and they must accept charity and funds—or take them—where they can. Can it be that one so traveled as yourself has found it otherwise?"

"I wish that I could deny your observation, but . . . alas . . . I cannot."

"Since you cannot, have you other questions . . . of a less present historical nature?"

"When was the Timber Road constructed, and did any High Holders oppose it?"

Sarastyn cocked his head. "Fascinating question . . . fascinating."

The fact that there was no obvious sarcasm in the older scholar's reply bothered Quaeryt far more than sarcasm would have, but he just waited to see what Sarastyn would say.

"When the timbering clans of the Boran Hills began digging the road out of the very rocks of the hillsides, no one noticed. And few others noticed when they bought steads that yielded little—until the road across them appeared. By the time their efforts were too obvious to be concealed, there was little that High Holder Arimyn and High Holder Baelzyt could do, because the timbering clans had also constructed a shorter road from their timber road to the Reserve of the Khanar, a fact which did not escape the eyes of Ciendar—the son of Nidar the Great. Nor was Ciendar exactly displeased when the clans granted him freedom of passage, even for any timber he might wish to sell in Midcote. That strengthened the treasury. . . ." Sarastyn shrugged. "Arimyn and Baelzyt still pay annual tariffs to use the road."

"With all the timber of Tilbor, and all those who fish, why has no Khanar ever developed a fleet?"

"What would have been the point? Outside of timber and fish, neither of which travels well for any great distance, what else do we send on the waves? What would a fleet protect? How would the Khanar have paid for it? Besides, ships require men who can work together day after day and who can take orders." Another laugh followed. "Too few men in Tilbor can do either."

For the next glass Quaeryt asked more questions, not quite at random, but in a variety of areas, because the responses to his more direct questions had been less useful than he would have thought.

Then, after another response, Sasastyn cleared his throat meaningfully. "Again, you have exhausted my voice and my memory, young Quaeryt, and it is time for me to depart and to refresh it." The older man slowly stood.

So did Quaeryt.

The rest of the day was even less productive.

He walked over to the anomen, looking for the ancient chorister, who might have some useful recollections, but the building was empty. He spent almost a glass studying it and found little remarkable there, except for noting that the recent repairs, while not exactly shoddy, looked to be of less than the highest quality of workmanship, almost as if they had been accomplished by students.

They probably were.

Later, he stopped by the tailor shop in the Ecoliae and picked up the garments he had ordered from Naxim. They were of surprisingly good quality, if of wool, which would limit when he could wear them when he returned to Solis, and far better, he had to admit, than those that he had lost in Nacliano.

He wasn't looking forward to another meal in the dining hall, but he also didn't want to walk or ride the still-muddy roads, whether Sarastyn did or not.

31

As Sarastyn had predicted, Jeudi morning dawned bright, clear, and dry, and Quaeryt rode out immediately after breakfast, this time to follow those roads that were brick-paved to the east and north of the Ecoliae. Even with Sarastyn's observations about the soils of Tilbor, he wasn't about to risk the mare on muddy clay or dirt tracks. Others didn't seem so reticent, and by eighth glass, Quaeryt found that there were farm wagons on the road, as well as others, although he did note that many of the wagons had wider wheel rims than those in the south.

In following another brick road that branched off the main road a half mille or so past what he thought of as the circular crossroads, he came to an area of leveled rubble—a space that appeared to encompass four square blocks. Moreover, some of the houses adjoining that area appeared to be deserted, with holes in the walls where windows and doors once had been.

Why had no one rebuilt? Was it considered ill fortune? Had Rescalyn or his predecessor forbidden it? Was it even the area that Lankyt had referred to?

Those were questions he'd have to raise carefully, indirectly, or possibly not at all, if he could get someone to volunteer the information, but he had the feeling that how the Pharsi were treated was something Bhayar would have to consider carefully—given the lord's ambitions. Less than a mille to the northeast from the razed area, after riding past modest but generally well-kept dwellings, he came to a set of brick pillars, one on each side of the road. Beyond the pillars, the narrow road widened into more of an avenue, with larger dwellings, all of them two stories, on each side. All were constructed of a dark reddish brick, but the roofs were not of thatch or tile but of split wooden shingles.

Why wooden shingles when the brick and crafting is so good? He only had to ponder that for a moment before the answer came. *Snow.* Tiles were heavy, and so was slate, and if heavy snow and ice piled on the roofs in the winter, the weight on the roof could be heavy indeed. All the trim was painted, if in dull colors, and all exterior wood was either oiled or painted. Every dwelling had a stable attached by a walled and roofed walkway.

Very cold winters . . .

When Quaeryt returned to the Ecoliae slightly before fourth glass, he felt that he had a basic understanding of what types of people generally lived where in Tilbora, although not necessarily all the reasons why. But he could have spent weeks searching out those factors, and he didn't have weeks.

He managed to get the mare groomed and fed in less than two quints. Then he washed up—his face and hands—at the pump outside the stables and walked to the main building, looking for Chardyn. Despite the fact that he'd asked Yullyd about tavernas, he wanted to see what sort of a reply he would receive from Chardyn.

He didn't get a chance to seek out the Sansang master immediately, because Nalakyn immediately appeared.

"Scholar Quaeryt, I didn't see you around today. I feared you had already left us, and I had some questions I hoped you would address."

"I have a few moments now." Quaeryt gestured toward three vacant chairs, set several yards from a larger grouping of seven scholars, in which the only one he recalled by name and face was Yullyd, although he'd certainly seen the others several times.

"I would appreciate that."

Nalakyn did not move, and, after a moment, Quaeryt headed toward the chairs, where he settled into one and waited for Nalakyn to seat himself before saying, "While I am only a young scholar, as scholars go, and certainly without your length of study, I would be happy to address, as I can, your questions."

"You have traveled, and I have not. When you talked to the students, you outlined the structure of Lord Bhayar's government. The fashion in which you described its organization is unlike any other, and I have not heard or read about that anywhere. Yet you seemed quite conversant with it. I have spent my entire life in Tilbora, and so have others, such as Scholar Chardyn, and none of us could have described the governing of the Khanars as cogently as you did the government of Lord Bhayar. Nor is there any document that does so. Without being a familiar of Lord Bhayar, how did you come by this knowledge?"

Quaeryt smiled easily, even as he wondered if Nalakyn or Zarxes had come up with the question. "Part of that is simply because the Scholarium Solum is but a short walk from the palace of Lord Bhayar, and it is a palace, not an isolated fortress like the palace of the

Khanars. One sees ministers passing by, and those who serve in the palace frequent the same tavernas as do scholars. I've made the acquaintance of some of the palace guards, and I know a scholar who has occasionally played and recited for Lord Bhayar and his ministers. Another fact is that Solis is far warmer than Tilbora, and there are more people, and they talk. Everyone in Solis talks. I have made a practice of listening. Also, the library at the Scholarium is excellent. There are books about the government of Hengyst and even how Rholan the Unnamer affected the way in which Telaryn is governed today. And, upon occasion, scholars are invited to the palace to provide information to ministers. I have not talked with any of Lord Bhayar's ministers myself, but I have certainly heard of them and what they do." Quaeryt shrugged, pleased that he had been able to deliver a perfectly truthful reply that was totally misleading.

"Truly . . . Solis must be a very different place, but if it is so wonderful . . . if I might ask . . . why are you here?"

"I believe I have mentioned that. In all of the wonderful library at the Scholarium there is not a single volume that deals with the recent history of Tilbor. A scholar's future depends in part on his patrons, and in part on his scholarly efforts. In creating such worthwhile contributions, one must provide a patron with a way of . . . shall we say . . . establishing a legacy by means that are not considered acts or tools of the Namer. I suggested that such an updated history might reflect well upon my patron . . . and here I am." He smiled wryly. "Even getting here proved more difficult than I had anticipated, and only Scholar Sarastyn seems to know much about recent history. Riding through Tilbora helps me match what he tells me to the city itself . . . but my task is proving more . . . difficult than I had anticipated." Quaeryt saw Chardyn step out onto the porch, then walk to the railing and look eastward.

"You are, if I might say so, among the younger scholars entrusted with such."

"An older scholar would have more wisdom and knowledge. That is true, but such an older scholar would be far less willing to take such a journey . . . and far less likely to need to do so."

Nalakyn nodded slowly. "I had not thought of that."

"If you will excuse me, I see Scholar Chardyn, and I have been seeking him. I need to make an inquiry of him."

"Of course. Of course . . . and thank you."

Quaeryt rose and smiled pleasantly. "You are most welcome." He walked toward Chardyn.

The Sansang master turned, as if sensing Quaeryt's approach, and waited.

Quaeryt reminded himself to keep Chardyn's almost preternatural awareness in mind, particularly in the future. "Good afternoon."

"The same to you. You have that expression of inquiry, I do believe, Scholar Quaeryt, as befits your name."

"I do, but the inquiry is, alas, most mundane in nature. I think I'd like a change for supper this evening. Are there any good tavernas around?"

"Tavernas?" asked Chardyn. "Are you looking for a good meal, or one of those where it doesn't matter what you eat, so long as you can drink and listen to singers and spend too many coins?"

"A decent meal, and a decent singer or two would be nice," replied Quaeryt.

Chardyn frowned. "Terazo probably has the best food, and the lager's the cheapest at Rufalo's. The food's decent, sometimes better, at Jardyna. All three have singers, and so does Sullah's, but you'd be fortunate to walk away from Sullah's without losing your wallet or more. If you want to ride farther and don't mind spending a silver or two, I've heard that Svaardyn is outstanding."

"That sounds a bit rich for me."

"Of those closer, the food's better at Terazo, and the singing better at Jardyna," offered Chardyn.

"Thank you. I'll have to give each a thought." Quaeryt paused, then went on. "I was talking to Sarastyn the other day, and he mentioned a group who called themselves partisans. He didn't seem to think that highly of them."

Chardyn laughed. "When life is calm, no one likes those who call themselves partisans, but when a ruler becomes tyrannical or a land is ruled by an outsider, the partisans are considered champions by those who feel oppressed."

"And now?"

"Some think they're brigands and thieves, and others think they're champions."

"Who's likely to think they're oppressed?"

"I think every man in Tilbor would have a different opinion," replied Chardyn with a smile.

Quaeryt nodded. "That's likely true anywhere, from what I've seen. Oh . . . by the way, I haven't seen Sarastyn today. Have you?"

"He had a few too many of his 'medicinals' and didn't feel well this morning. Scholar Tharxas has been looking in on him. I'm certain it will pass."

"I do hope so. He has proved most helpful."

"I am certain he has, but . . . he does have . . . certain lapses of memory, certain beliefs that are of the past, rather than the present."

"Such as his belief that the taverna where he takes his 'medicinals' is still the Ice Cleft?"

"Precisely. When names change, more changes than the name."

"That is a very good point." Quaeryt nodded.

"I thought so."

"Thank you . . . and if you will excuse me . . ."

"Of course. . . ."

As he walked westward toward Jardyna, Quaeryt considered several things. He didn't like the fact that Chardyn had known Sarastyn's condition so precisely, but, while Quaeryt couldn't help wondering about Sarastyn, he couldn't very well accuse Chardyn of ill-treating Sarastyn, nor could he keep track of Sarastyn's every move. He also hadn't cared for Nalakyn's inquiries. Both suggested it was time for him to move on . . . and sooner than he had told anyone.

Lankyt's directions proved adequate. It took far less than two quints for Quaeryt to reach the crossroads that held Jardyna on the southeast side and Rufalo's some hundred yards to the north, on the west side, past a local chandlery and wool factorage. The painting of the garden on the signboard was far less artistic than the painting on Jorem and Hailae's factorage, and while the signboard had been touched up, there were still parts where the paint was threatening to peel. The single oversized door, hung with massive iron straps, was of well-oiled oak, and the scents of food did not carry the odor of burned grease.

Quaeryt opened the door and stepped inside. A slender woman dressed in a deep maroon tunic over black trousers turned. While her figure was girlish, the silver and blond hair and the slightly lined face were not.

"Drinks? Or food?"

"Both," replied Quaeryt. "More food than drinks."

"You're from the west, aren't you?"

"From Solis."

"I didn't know Phaeryn was seeking scholars from there."

"He isn't. I had a patron who sent me here."

"He must be indifferent to your wishes, then." The woman's smile was friendly, her tone bantering.

"Not indifferent. Just wanting me to earn his support."

She laughed. "I'm Karelya. You can take any of the small tables that are empty—unless you're expecting more than one person to join you."

"A small table will be fine."

"Pick any one that suits you." She gestured toward her right.

That half of the large room held fifteen or sixteen tables, with a massive ceramic stove in the middle of the end wall. It was covered with plants in pots, most of them flowering. What Quaeryt noted was that the small tables were those set against the oiled pine plank walls, while the larger tables, those seating six or eight and those seating four, were in the middle of the room. Two of the small tables were occupied, one by a white-haired man, and the other by a young couple. Three men wearing the leathers of teamsters sat around a table for four.

"Thank you." Quaeryt smiled, then made his way to the unoccupied table closest to the stove, taking the seat that put his back to the plants on the stove.

He'd no sooner seated himself than Karelya re-appeared.

"Greeter and server?" he asked.

"For the moment, until the evening girls appear. We stay open until ninth glass. That's later than most, but still means we can close down before midnight."

"Unless there's a really good crowd?"

"That sometimes happens on Samedi nights, usually in midfall. In winter, it gets too cold. What will you have?"

"What is there for me to have?"

"The dinners tonight are fowl paprikash with potato dumplings, Skarnan noodles and beef, and mutton cutlets and fried potatoes. Each one is three coppers."

"The fowl, please. What about lagers or ale?"

"Light and heavy lager, gold and brown ale. Two coppers for any of them."

"I'll try the light lager."

"The light lager it is." With a friendly smile, she was gone.

If Jardyna was the less expensive taverna, he didn't want to think about the more expensive places. He glanced to the other side of the taverna, where the tables were all small and crowded together, and where close to fifteen men were already seated and contemplating or drinking from large mugs. Only a surprisingly low murmur oozed into the eating area.

The door opened, and two men entered, attired as if they were factors of some sort, with jackets over linen shirts. They didn't even pause, but made their way to the table for four nearest to Quaeryt, taking as they did.

"Kinnyrd . . . said he'd be here . . ."

". . . believe him? He's always late . . ."

Quaeryt shifted his attention back to Karelya, who appeared with one of the large mugs and set it on the table. He slipped out five coppers.

"Just leave them on the table for now. Selethya will collect them when she brings your meal." With another smile she was gone, moving to the pair of men, who'd been joined by a burlier fellow with an enormous brown beard. "What will you three have? The usual?"

"What else?" rumbled the burly man.

Karelya laughed, although Quaeryt thought the sound was slightly forced. Behind them several more people stepped inside Jardyna, and Quaeryt had the feeling that he'd arrived just a few moments before the customary time for most of those who frequented the place.

Quaeryt sipped the lager slowly as he waited for the meal. If the dark amber brew before him was the "light" lager, he certainly wouldn't be interested in the "heavy" lager or the ale. Then again, maybe the Tilborans needed that heavy a brew in the dark and cold of winter.

Two women, perhaps ten years older than he was, slipped into the table next to him and immediately ordered ale from a serving girl, presumably Selethya, who also wore maroon and who had curly brown hair pulled back from her face and bound at the back of her neck so that the curls flowed down between her shoulder blades.

He tried to listen to the other conversations. That of the women was so low that he could barely hear them.

". . . the sisters . . . worried about backlands partisans . . ."

". . . why? . . . not affect us . . ."

At those words, Quaeryt strained to hear more clearly.

". . . Maera . . . brother said—"

"Not here . . . scholar right behind you."

For several moments, the women said nothing. Then, one spoke again.

"...hear about Waelya?...cannot believe she didn't walk out...family...support her..."

"...pride...we...all have it..."

"...pride be named..."

The three men were far louder, so much so that their conversation drowned that of the women, who were clearly keeping their voices down.

"I told you that the late pears would be soft."

"You're always saying that you told me or someone else, but none of us remember those words."

"You don't want to remember."

"Excuse me!" interrupted Kārelya loudly and cheerfully. "Here you go." She set the three mugs down, one after the other. Then she grinned and added, "The late pears were a trace soft, but I don't think Kinnyrd said anything. Not in here. I would have heard it. So would everyone else."

Even Kinnyrd laughed.

When the three had taken several swallows of whatever was in their mugs, the men's conversation resumed, if in much lower tones.

"...another scholar...haven't seen him before..."

"...trust Phaeryn to find a way..."

"...find a way, yes. Trust, no...backlands timber families can be worse than the High Holders..."

"...could be...also could be related..."

With those words, the three immediately begin talking about whether the snows would come earlier or later.

Quaeryt sipped the lager until the curly-haired Selethya arrived with a platter. "Sir...you had the fowl?"

"I did."

She slipped the platter in front of him.

"Is there a singer tonight?"

"Yes, sir. Daerema will be here in half a glass or so."

"Thank you." He offered her the coppers, plus an extra.

"Thank you, scholar."

The fowl was far better than the fare at the Ecoliae, and the sauce was excellent, especially since the dumplings were a trace firm. Even so, he found he ate everything, doubtless too swiftly. Then he had to sip the lager, slowly, while he waited for the singer. Almost all the tables had come to be filled, and all the conversations blended into a rumble, from which Quaeryt could pick out only phrases, none of which made sense out of context. He found that he had somehow actually finished the lager and ordered another.

The conversation died away when the singer stepped onto the low platform set against the middle of the rear wall, so that those in both halves of the room could hear her. The dark-haired young woman wasn't all that pretty, not with her sharp nose and broad face. She offered no introduction, just lifted the lutelin and began to sing.

> *High upon headland, and clear out to sea,*
> *my true love did sing out his song to me . . .*
> *He sang and he wept and his words sounded true,*
> *that never the night did I think I would rue . . .*

Quaeryt smiled. She might not be a beauty, but her countenance was pleasant, and more important, for a singer, her voice was lovely, and her fingers were deft enough on the five strings of the lutelin that voice and melody blended pleasantly and strengthened the words of the song.

He listened and sipped as she sang, but still kept his eyes moving around the room as he did. After several songs, someone from the taproom side of Jardyna called out, "The wish song!"

"Aye, the wish song!" echoed another voice.

The singer smiled faintly, and raised the lutelin once more.

> *If wishes rained down from the sky,*
> *porkers could talk and whales could fly . . .*
> *if Nidar had lived in these days,*
> *then we'd all be drinking his praise,*
> *oh . . . we'd all be drinking his praise.*
>
> *If Khanar had had a strong son,*
> *or the envoy been roasted well done,*
> *if Nidar had come back to fight,*
> *we'd all be carousing all night,*
> *we'd all be carousing all night.*
> *But wishes don't rain; ice isn't snow,*
> *Boars still snort, and no one will know*
> *the time when the sun and the sea*
> *and the rivers and we run free,*
> *oh . . . the rivers and we run free.*

Cheers followed the song, but as soon as they subsided, the singer immediately began another song, almost as if she wished she hadn't been asked to sing the wish song.

> *My man was a strong man, as strong as life would see,*
> *and he was fair and free and good at loving me . . .*

The murmurs died away, and the room stilled, and Quaeryt glanced around. There were tears in some eyes, and the eyes belonged to both men and women.

. . . but a man and his daughter and a cousin fought,
and now I've a daughter with no father, all for naught . . .

When the singer finished the second song, clearly about the war with Telaryn, she quickly launched into an upbeat tune.

You came home the other night, as tight as you could be,
You woke me up to help you find the finest specialty . . .
But I'm no shop, and not your very private chandlery . . .

Laughter broke out, and Quaeryt laughed with the rest.

After several more songs, he paid Selethya for the second ale, which he'd barely touched, adding two extra coppers, and made his way out of Jardyna.

While he was especially alert on the walk back to the Ecoliae, he couldn't help thinking about the songs that the singer had offered—and that she'd been able to sing the second one without anyone, even from the rowdier taproom side of Jardyna, heckling her . . . and in fact listening respectfully.

That reaction didn't fit with what he'd observed of Chardyn, and that was another aspect of the Ecoliae that disturbed him. But then, there had been the two women talking of the sisters and the partisans . . . and the fact that there had been several tables besides the one adjoining his that had held only women—and that was something he hadn't seen anywhere else in Telaryn, or even in the few Bovarian ports he'd visited years before.

32

As he approached the Ecoliae, Quaeryt felt more and more uneasy. Why? Was it because of the questions by Nalakyn, or Chardyn's remarks? Or the continued interest in when he was likely to depart the Ecoliae? His eyes flicked skyward. Artiema was slightly less than half-full, while the smaller reddish-tinged disk of Erion showed little more than a thin crescent, not that he put much stock in the idea that more violence occurred under the light of a full Erion.

When he reached a spot some fifty yards downhill from the front porch, he imaged a concealment shield. If he happened to be right in his feelings, that would help. If he were wrong, there was no harm done. He slowed his steps so that there was little or no sound from his boots on the bricks of the lane, but it seemed to take forever before he climbed up the steps to the porch. Because there was always a student scholar watching the front door, he walked around the east side of the porch to the east rear side door. It was, naturally, bolted shut, as were all doors except the front one after eighth glass.

That wasn't a problem, or not one that took terribly long, since he imaged away the catch plate, opened the door, and stepped inside, into the dimness of the side hall. Then he imaged the plate back in place and walked slowly and as silently as he could to the narrow staircase at the east end of the building. From there he crept up the steps and then along the long, long hallway toward his chamber on the west end.

He might be overreacting, but he didn't think so.

He stopped in the darkness outside the doorway to his chamber, studying the hallway and then the door. There was no glimmer of light in the thin space between the wooden floor and the bottom edge of the door. Nor did he hear anyone breathing or moving on the other side. All he had to do was lift the latch, because, as was the case with any room in any Scholars' House, there was no lock, only a bar and a bolt that could be slid shut from the inside.

Finally, ever so gently, from beside the door, so that he would not be standing in the doorway, he lifted the latch and then gave the door the slightest push so that it swung inward, creaking slightly. The door came to a halt perhaps three-quarters open.

Quaeryt waited . . . and waited.

The quiet was overwhelming.

Abruptly, as if from nowhere, a dark figure appeared in the doorway, and made two swift passes with a half-staff, one to each side of the door. The second slammed into Quaeryt's left shoulder. He dropped back, managing a side kick to the knee of the other, while he dropped the concealment shield, of little use in the darkness, and concentrated on imaging pitricin into the brain of the other.

A second staff blow hit Quaeryt's arm below the shoulder, and a sharp jab of pain coursed up his arm, before the other convulsed.

Quaeryt managed to jam his forearm across the other man's mouth to keep him from crying out, then half-carried, half-pushed the still-struggling, if less so with every moment, smaller man into the chamber, restraining him for close to a quarter quint before he slumped and stopped breathing.

Only then did Quaeryt lower the body and close the door. From what he could tell, the scuffle had not awakened anyone. That was not totally surprising, since he'd been given the room for just that reason. He'd wondered how many other visitors had "departed early," in one fashion or another, minus coins and goods.

He studied the man on the floor. As he'd suspected, it was Chardyn. Quaeryt was impressed at the other's skills in close to pitch-darkness, although the darkness had effectively reduced the usefulness of his own concealment shield. His shoulder and left arm throbbed. He certainly wouldn't have wanted to face the Sansang master in any sort of combat, or what some, although Chardyn probably hadn't been one of them, would have called a "fair fight."

Quaeryt snorted softly. There was no such thing as a fair fight. Someone, in some way, always had the advantage, and usually the one with the advantage was the one calling it "fair."

Since he doubted anyone but Zarxes and Phaeryn knew what Chardyn had planned, and since none of them could have known exactly when Quaeryt would return to the Ecoliae, he had perhaps a glass, at most, before someone started actively looking for the Sansang master. In that time, Quaeryt needed to dispose of Chardyn's body, or rather get it out of the chamber and down to the stable. Moving unseen wouldn't be the problem. Carrying the body unheard would be. After that, he'd have to conceal the body for the time it took him to return and carry his own clothing and gear back to the stable, because there was no way he'd be able to carry both at once.

The first thing Quaeryt did was to pack all his gear into the canvas bag, except it didn't all fit. So he took the scholar outfits and rolled them up in the thin blanket provided by the Ecoliae and laid the rolled-up garments on the bed beside the bag. Then, with some effort, he hoisted the limp body of Chardyn over his shoulder, raised a concealment shield, and eased his way through the door, latching it behind him.

The trip down the west-end stairs, then out through the west-end rear side door, across the porch, and out to the stable was slow, and painful. Quaeryt was sweating heavily by the time he deposited Chardyn in the empty stall beside the one that held the mare, and Chardyn was far smaller than Quaeryt. Quaeryt took a few moments to catch his breath before he scattered hay and straw over Chardyn, just enough that, if the stable boy did happen to look into the stall, unlikely as that was in the middle of the night, the body wouldn't be immediately visible.

Then he made his way back to his chamber, where he left a silver on the side table before picking up his bag, Chardyn's staff, and the rolled-up garments and making the return trip to the stable.

Once back in the stable, he did light a lamp, if wicked down, in order to saddle the mare. He also had to rummage through the stable to find twine to fasten the rolled-up garments and the canvas bag behind the saddle. Then he had to reclaim Chardyn's body and lift it up and over the front of the saddle before blowing out the lantern and leading the mare out of the stable under a concealment shield.

He mounted and rode down the brick lane to the highway, half-wondering if anyone would hear the sound of hoofs on the bricks and wonder if some sort of spirit or demon horse had left the Ecoliae.

He had just passed the anomen when the bells rang out the first glass after midnight.

Did all that take almost two glasses?

It must have, and that worried him as well. Yet no one had appeared or tried to stop him. For that he could thank the comparative emptiness of the upper level of the west wing. He turned the horse toward the river. He had plenty of time, especially since he wasn't about to try to enter the Telaryn Palace before the seventh glass of the morning.

33

Once he had ridden down the lane from the Ecoliae and was more than a mille away, Quaeryt dropped the concealment shield and continued slowly east and then south until he reached the Albhor River. From there he had to head farther upstream to find an unoccupied wharf from which he could drop Chardyn's body and staff into the dark water. That way, if the body happened to be found, there would be a certain mystery as to how it arrived there, especially with no marks or wounds. If no one ever found it, that would create another mystery as to what had happened to Scholar Chardyn.

Chardyn's disappearance or death should keep Phaeryn and Zarxes from immediately victimizing anyone else . . . and, hopefully, before too long, Quaeryt could find a way to deal with the pair—in a quiet way, because the last thing he wanted was an uproar over a Scholars' House. There were too few of them in

Telaryn as it was, and he didn't want every city regarding scholars the way people seemingly did in Nacliano. And since the scholars and the governor appeared anything but on the most distant of terms, he'd have to bring up the matter slowly . . . and later. *Especially since you'll need scholars to be well-regarded for what else you have in mind.*

After dropping the body, he rode back down the river to the ferry piers, where he turned north on the good road leading to the Telaryn Palace. He was careful to keep the mare well in the middle of the road and away from any shadows. The aching throbbing in his arm and shoulder reminded him that he needed enough time to be able to image a defense.

You might even think about a better way to use imaging as a defense. While that was a wonderful thought, at that moment he didn't have the faintest idea how he might accomplish such a defense. All he'd been able to do was to use imaging to divert, disable, or kill people who were attacking him.

With those thoughts swirling through his head, he kept riding. After another half glass, he stopped and dismounted to water the mare at a public fountain in a small square that was eerily quiet. The square was dark, because Artiema had set, and there were no lamps or lanterns lit, but Quaeryt could see well enough. Then he mounted again and kept riding northward at a leisurely pace. He did worry that his progress through the outskirts of Tilbora was marked by the barking of dogs, but only one actually came anywhere close to the mare before stopping in an alleyway and barking until Quaeryt was well out of sight—or smell.

Even taking his time, before that long Quaeryt was soon on the north side of Tilbora and nearing the Telaryn Palace, and he began to look for a place where he could wait until it was light enough and late enough in the morning to ride up to the gates. He finally found a short hedgerow on the north side of a small field to the southwest of the palace, where he dismounted and tied the mare.

Eventually, dawn came, and then sunrise.

Once there was light, Quaeryt took out the wax-sealed document case, turning it over in his hands under the early light. Then, after looking more closely, he froze. The wax sealing the case had been replaced. It was still sealed, but not as he had sealed it. He'd looked at the case any number of times since leaving Rhodyn and Darlinka, but he hadn't examined it closely.

He swallowed, then took out his belt knife and carefully scraped away the wax, easing open the case. Inside, in addition to the appointment letter and the letter from Vaelora was a small folded paper—and two golds. Quaeryt opened the paper and read the lines, written in Bovarian.

> Please forgive me for this intrusion. While I am trusting, I am not that trusting. Accept these tokens as payment for my lack of trust, and my wishes that may all be well with you.

The signature was that of Rhodyn.

"The old namer-demon," murmured Quaeryt, smiling as he did. He couldn't blame the man for his care. Had the letter from Vaelora helped? Probably only in reinforcing that he was who he'd said he was. There wasn't even a name at the bottom, only her initial.

After a moment, he took both the note from Rhodyn and the letter from Vaelora and slid them into the inside hidden jacket pocket, then slipped the golds into empty slots in his belt. The document case went into the larger inside jacket pocket. He straightened in the saddle and surveyed the lane again. He still had at least a glass to wait before he could approach the gates.

Only a handful of wagons passed the hedgerow lane on the main road while he waited. Finally, he judged that it was late enough that he could make his way to the palace.

As he neared the gates, he rode down through a vale and past a row of cafés and shops he didn't recall from his previous ride through the area, seemingly located amid small plots of lands, and he wondered why they were there. Then his eyes flashed to the Telaryn Palace, and he nodded. *To separate the soldiers from their pay and to provide diversions from boring duties, but away from the main part of Tilbora.*

Before long, Quaeryt reined up short of the two guards before the gates. "Good morning."

"What do you want, scholar?" demanded the shorter and stockier man, wearing the undress green uniform of a Telaryn soldier, set off by black boots and a wide black leather belt, with a matching short sword scabbard on one side and a knife sheath on the other. He was not wearing the uniform jacket, but few soldiers did except in winter—and almost never in Solis.

"I'm supposed to report to Princeps Straesyr. I'm his new scholar assistant."

"And I'm—" began the guard who had spoken first, before the other guard cleared his throat. "What?"

"Seems to me . . . weren't we looking for a scholar . . . ?"

". . . supposed to be here weeks ago . . ."

"The ship I was on got caught in a nor'easter, went on the rocks . . ." Quaeryt said loudly. "That slowed me down."

"He's probably the one. They said he was supposed

to see the princeps first." The taller guard turned back to Quaeryt. "What's your name?"

"Quaeryt Rytersyn, from Solis."

"Sounds like the same name. Better escort him up."

"I'll take him," offered the shorter guard, with a sharp look at the other, before turning and calling, "Gate open!" Then he looked to Quaeryt. "Follow me."

After several moments, the left side of the gate swung back far enough for the guard to walk through, and the scholar followed. The gate closed behind him. A single mount was tethered on the north side of the east tower, and the guard untied it and mounted. Without speaking, he urged the horse onto the planked bridge over the dry moat.

The hoofs of both mounts created a dull echo as they crossed the bridge. The towers on the far side appeared to be exactly as tall as the bridge was wide, and the cables that ran from the top of the towers to iron rings on the south end of the bridge were as thick as the wrists of a large man.

Absently, Quaeryt wondered if anyone had ever tried a winter attack on the palace, since it might have been easier to fill a section of the moat with snow and ice and then let it freeze solid. *But then, how would you shelter and feed a large force in deep winter?*

The angled approach to the palace was a stone-paved road wide enough for two wagons and with a slope gradual enough to be passable in winter.

If shoveled clear, thought Quaeryt, turning to the soldier riding slightly ahead. "Who has the duty of clearing the snow in the winter?"

"Whatever company is assigned," replied the gate guard. "Usually the one with the most troublemakers the week before."

"I suppose that keeps them in line."

"Not always. A fellow can get stir-crazy. It's gray all winter long. A squad in Third Company got so worked up they threw snowballs at the duty guards so that they could get out and shovel. But they're all crazy in Fifth Battalion."

Inwardly, Quaeryt winced, glancing out across the valley below lit in morning sunlight, trying to imagine it dark and gray, covered with ice and snow. He glanced back uphill. On the top of the long rise loomed the gray walls of the palace, walls that looked to extend a good half mille across the front alone. He hadn't realized just how huge the area enclosed by the walls truly was.

When the two neared the top of the approach road and rode toward the gates at the east end of the palace, Quaeryt noted that they were open and swung outward and flush against the flanking towers. Each side was comparatively narrow—less than two yards wide—and extended upward some four yards. When closed, they would fit against the stone on both sides and along the top.

Two more guards stood outside the gates.

"It's the scholar the princeps is expecting."

The guards looked Quaeryt over, but said nothing. The space under the archway between the two towers was effectively a walled tunnel some five yards long. A second set of gates was recessed into the inside walls of the guard towers, and beyond them was a large open courtyard at least seventy yards on a side.

To the right of the capacious entry courtyard were severe stone buildings some three stories in height, looking like troop barracks, and farther to the west were the stables. Behind them were the walls, only a handful of yards higher than the barracks roofs. To

the left and directly beyond the entry courtyard were
gardens, and the scent of flowers was almost over-
powering to Quaeryt.

Gardens? Given the grimness of the stone walls, he
hadn't expected gardens.

A single stone-paved lane, edged by a knee-high
wall, led through the middle of the gardens, and the
escort guard rode toward it. Again, Quaeryt followed.
The terraced gardens were far more than ornamental,
he soon realized, with apple, plum, pear, and sour
cherry trees bordering herb and vegetable gardens,
and an intricate series of stone conduits and miniature
aqueducts between the gardens and trees.

The lane ended abruptly in a circular paved area,
with that part of the arc beside the palace building itself bordered by a covered rotunda. Another pair of
guards stood under the angled roof and before a set
of polished oak doors bound in polished brass.

"The scholar's here to see the princeps."

"You can tie your mount at the end, the iron post,"
said one of the guards.

"Thank you." Quaeryt rode over to the post, where
he dismounted and tethered the mare to the post, then
walked back toward the doors. He had to assume that
his mount and gear would be safe, but, if they weren't,
those would be the least of his worries.

The lower gate guard was already riding back eastward toward the upper palace gates when Quaeryt
reached the two guards.

"Tell the squad leader inside why you're here."

"Thank you." Quaeryt stepped between the two
and opened the door, only to find a second door two
yards on, another sign that the winters were indeed
long and cold.

When he stepped beyond the second door, he stood

in a foyer, a circular space some fifteen yards across, but without the high ceiling he half-expected. The walls were half-paneled with wainscoting up to chest height, above which was white plaster. There were neither paintings nor hangings above the paneling, although vacant niches set into the walls above the paneling and spaced around the foyer once had likely held statues or other decorative items.

Set in the middle of the foyer was a table desk, and seated at the desk was another soldier, this one wearing undress greens, the uniform most officers and aides wore when they met with Bhayar. Quaeryt walked to the desk and stopped.

"Why are you here, scholar?"

"Lord Bhayar sent me. I'm Quaeryt Rytersyn. I was sent to be scholar assistant to Princeps Straesyr."

The squad leader pointed to a bench on the left side of the foyer, but closer to the door than the table desk. "You'll need to wait there while I check with his assistant."

Quaeryt sat, then watched as the squad leader walked past the two guards stationed at the archway leading from the foyer. He was still waiting a quint later, but shortly after that, the functionary finally returned.

"He'll see you shortly. One of his aides will come and take you to his study." The squad leader resumed his position behind the desk.

Another half quint passed before yet another squad leader—this one graying—appeared and said, "Scholar . . . this way."

Quaeryt stood and followed the squad leader past the soldiers guarding the main hallway leading from the foyer. He was beginning to feel as though he had been passing through an endless series of guards. A somewhat worn deep blue carpet runner ran down the center of the polished slate floor, and a series of paintings adorned the walls—in between the doors, all of which were closed. Most of the paintings appeared to be likenesses of past Khanars.

After some thirty yards the corridor opened onto a high ceilinged hall, with a grand marble staircase leading up to the second level and what appeared to be a railed gallery above circling the hall. As he followed the aide up the steps, Quaeryt noted that other corridors branched off the hallway on the lower level . . . and again on the upper level. Quaeryt noted a smaller staircase on the east side of the gallery, whose entry door was open, and he wondered where that led. At the top of the staircase, the squad leader turned right, moving parallel to the stone-pillared railing.

About a third of the way around the circular gallery was another corridor that the squad leader followed. At the end, another forty yards along past other doors, was a set of double doors, one of which was open. Another narrower hallway fronted the doors and extended east and west for about twenty yards in each direction.

Once he was inside the anteroom, Quaeryt again sat and waited for perhaps half a quint before being ushered into the princeps's study—a large room with bookcases on the left-side wall, and an archway on the left, with recessed pocket doors half-open, leading to a room with a long table and chairs. A large and ornately carved desk was set before the waist-high north-facing windows, windows that were closed. The princeps stood behind the desk. Unlike everyone else Quaeryt had seen since he'd ridden up to the lower gates, Straesyr was not wearing a uniform, but a light blue tunic over black trousers. Yet the way he wore them suggested a uniform.

"Good morning. Please be seated." The princeps followed his own words.

Quaeryt sat down in the center chair facing the desk. Straesyr wasn't at all what he had anticipated. He'd pictured the princeps as a slender and bookish figure, but the man who had greeted him was as tall as Quaeryt himself, broad-shouldered, and his voice was warm and pleasant. Only the eyes resembled Quaeryt's preconception, and they looked like pale blue ice, as though Straesyr regarded everything as something to be weighed, measured, or counted.

"You claim to be someone I'm expecting. Can you prove it?"

"I'm most certain that Lord Bhayar has sent you a thorough description of me. I'm Quaeryt Rytersyn, and I have been a scholar to him." Quaeryt eased the document case from his jacket pocket, leaned forward, and extended it.

The princeps took it. "It looks rather worn."

"It's been through a storm and a shipwreck, sir."

"What ship?"

"The *Moon's Son*, out of Tilbora here. She was the first vessel I could get out of Nacliano."

"There weren't any Telaryn ships you could take?"

"Except for the ship that sailed just before I got to Nacliano, not a one that anyone knew of. The port people said that most of the ships that traveled regularly from Nacliano to Tilbora were ported out of Tilbora."

"That's regrettable, if so. It's something I wouldn't know." Straesyr opened the case and extracted the appointment letter, then opened the leather folder on the desk and compared the two. Next, he looked at a second sheet and then at Quaeryt, alternating glances between paper and Quaeryt. Finally, he nodded. "You do seem to be the one Lord Bhayar sent, with an appointment to last until the end of Fevier, if necessary . . ."

He didn't put that date in my letter. The end of Fevier . . . I do hope not. Quaeryt had no intention of staying in Tilbor even into winter, let alone all the way to the end of that frigid season.

". . . I must say that both the governor and I are at a loss why he would send a scholar from Solis to Tilbora. I hope you can enlighten me."

Quaeryt smiled pleasantly. "Lord Bhayar asked me if the people of Tilbor were different because no ruler in the history of Lydar has had so much difficulty in maintaining order so long after a conquest. I made the mistake of saying that I could not offer an opinion because I had not been to Tilbor and because there were no recent histories of Tilbor." Quaeryt offered a helpless shrug. "And so . . . here I am."

After a moment, Straesyr smiled, then shook his head. "You could have said that they were."

"Then he would have asked in what fashion were their differences . . . and every effort on my part would have made my situation worse."

"What exactly are you supposed to do here?" Straesyr returned the battered document case and the appointment letter to the scholar.

"Answer his question, based on what I observe and upon your experiences and those of the governor."

"Why is this important to him, do you think?"

"I don't know. It is possible he just disliked my asking too many questions and wanted to get rid of me or teach me a lesson of some sort. It is possible he is considering an attack on Antiago, or worried about an attack by Bovaria, and wants to see if I can discover some useful information that will make dealing with such easier. It is possible that he has something else in mind."

Straesyr nodded slowly. "It is not particularly useful to second-guess a ruler. Nor is it useful to obstruct others in their duties. Neither the governor nor I would wish to make matters difficult for you to accomplish your report to Lord Bhayar. Likewise, you understand that in seeking the information to answer his inquiry, you should avoid any actions that make our efforts more difficult."

"I understand. That is why, as possible, I would begin by gathering your thoughts and observations on what is different and unique about Tilbor, and then the governor's. After that, I would like to talk with some of the junior officers who must deal with people on a daily basis. Only then would I venture into talking with the people in Tilbor, and that I would do as a visiting scholar."

"That latter task might be both useful and difficult. The scholars here . . . let me just say that they do not seem to be excessively friendly. Anything you might discover that sheds light on that, in one way or another, might make your tasks easier."

Quaeryt was the one to nod. "This is distressing to me. Knowledge that is not used properly is wasted, and there is no one better placed to use knowledge for good than a ruler. As I can, once I have a better understanding of the situation here, I would be more than happy to look into that matter, along with the other aspects of the question, of course."

"Of course. Now . . . there is the matter of quarters. While there is certainly space in the barracks, there are a number of chambers here in the palace proper that would seem more conducive to your efforts, and several also have writing desks. Would those not be preferable?"

"One such would indeed, sir, but I would not wish to be a burden."

"That is not a problem. Not at all. With you in the palace, of course, you will be a member of the junior officers' mess. There is a charge—or deduction from your pay—of a copper a meal, or a silver and a half a week. As with all junior officers away from their postings, there is no charge for quarters. I would have you meet with Governor Rescalyn today, but he has been on an inspection tour to the north. He is not expected to return until Lundi or Mardi. Perhaps tomorrow you and I could meet, and I could brief you on those events and matters that bear upon your task." Straesyr frowned, then smiled. "Seventh glass in the morning would be best."

"Here, sir?"

"Precisely. Now . . . when we finish here, I'll have my messenger conduct you to your quarters. I took the liberty of having your gear sent up already, and the ostler has stabled your mount. Except for today, you are responsible for grooming. In view of your position as one of my assistants, you will have access anywhere in the palace. Once you are briefed by me and have met the governor, you're free to ride where you find it necessary. As with all officers, you are expected to log out and give either a destination or mission and an expected time of return. Is that clear?"

"Yes, sir." *In short, you're confined to the palace until Mardi, and he wants to know where you're going or have been.*

"Ah . . . Scholar Quaeryt," murmured Straesyr, "there is one other small matter."

"Sir?"

The princeps lifted the cover of the folder and took out a sealed missive. "This was sent to you by courier from Solis."

Quaeryt didn't have to counterfeit surprise. *Who would send something to me? Who besides Bhayar even knew where I'd be? Rhodyn? But that wouldn't have come by Telaryn courier.* He took the missive and looked at the seal. He didn't recognize the stylized image of a pen with the hilt of a sabre. A careful look also showed that the seal had been removed, if carefully, and then replaced, but the minute traces of wax on the paper suggested that it had been replaced on the same original paper.

The hand that had written his name was not unfamiliar, but he did not immediately recognize it, and he didn't want to ponder over it with Straesyr looking on. "Thank you, sir. I had not expected correspondence."

"Neither had we expected any for a scholar whose presence we had not anticipated prior to Lord Bhayar's orders." Straesyr rose from behind the desk. "The messenger is waiting."

"Thank you, sir," repeated Quaeryt. "I'll be here at seventh glass tomorrow."

The princeps merely nodded, and Quaeryt inclined his head in reply, then turned and left the study.

The messenger turned out to be a youthful ranker who jumped to attention when Quaeryt stepped back into the anteroom, slipping the missive and the document case inside his jacket.

"You're in the northwest tower, sir. I'll take you down past the officers' mess first, and then to your quarters. That way, you'll know the most direct way to the mess."

"I'd appreciate that."

As he followed the young ranker back to the upper rotunda and down the grand staircase, Quaeryt pondered the implications of what the princeps had said. Bhayar had said he would be quartered in the barracks, but Straesyr had placed him in a chamber in the palace proper. Was that because Rescalyn didn't want him anywhere near the soldiers, or because both the governor and the princeps wanted to keep a close eye on him? Or both? And then, it was clear that Straesyr was more than a little unhappy with the local scholars.

". . . all the chambers for the officers and the mess are in the west wing . . . it's more like a separate building, except it's connected by a covered and walled passageway . . . still cold as a corpse in the winter . . ."

Quaeryt listened attentively as the young man led him along the main corridor and then through the windowless walled passage to the "west wing" and through another two sets of double doors and then past the mess and to the far end of the building and up a narrow staircase to the third level.

". . . think you and the chorister are the only ones up here . . . bathing chambers are all on the main level . . . be quite a cold climb in the winter . . ."

At the top of the stone staircase, they turned right and walked to the first door, which the ranker opened. As promised, Quaeryt's "gear" was in the chamber, the canvas bag and the rolled-up scholars' garments set neatly beside a narrow armoire. There was a wide writing desk, with a sconce above it holding an oil lamp. The bed was single, but wider than a scholar's pallet, and bed linens, two blankets, and a single towel were folded and set on the bottom of the mattress. On one side of the bed was a night table and on the other a narrow three-drawer chest. The door had a sturdy bolt, but no bar and no lock.

". . . captain says that the chambers on this end are for field-grade officers, majors and subcommanders," concluded the ranker.

Once the ranker left, Quaeryt slid the bolt on the door and looked through his gear. It had been searched. That was clear because everything had been more neatly folded than he'd had time to do in his haste in leaving the Ecoliae. Then he hung his spare clothing in the armoire, and put his additional undergarments in the dresser. The chamber had been recently—and hurriedly—cleaned, he suspected, but whoever had done so had been thorough, because there was no dust anywhere.

He walked to the single narrow window and eased it open, enjoying the cool breeze and looking westward, although all he could see were the western walls and the sky above them, which held puffy clouds in the distance.

His room was doubtless one of the coldest in the palace in winter, but possibly one of the more comfortable in harvest and early fall, but it was also the farthest from the palace center where Rescalyn and Straesyr conducted the affairs of the governor on behalf of Lord Bhayar. Definitely, for the moment, at least, they didn't want him too close to anyone.

He sat down at the desk and took out the mysterious missive, studied the script that spelled out his name, then used his belt knife and a touch of imaging to remove the blue wax seal without damaging the imprint. The first words told him the identity of the writer—and had she been anyone but Bhayar's sister, he would have recognized the writing immediately. He just hadn't believed that she would have written him.

Dear Scholar Quaeryt—
I take this liberty in writing you to continue the discussion we
began in Solis, and I hope that this missive finds that you have
arrived in health for your duties on behalf of Lord Bhayar . . .

Lord Bhayar? He shook his head. Without any reference to Bhayar as her brother, anyone who intercepted and read the letter could only assume that the
writer was a woman—from the graceful script—
highly placed in the court in Solis. Only someone who
knew the court would likely understand to whom the
"V" as a signature referred. But the references and the
dispatch by Telaryn courier would make it more likely
that, even if intercepted and read, the missive would
reach him and also, he had to admit, give anyone with
less than charitable intentions toward him some pause
before acting immediately.

Had Vaelora thought that out as well?

Based on both letters he had received so far, he had
to believe that she did—and that meant he was far
more involved in the intrigues surrounding Bhayar
than he'd ever had any intention of being . . . especially
since one of the reasons he'd left Solis was to avoid
such intrigues, knowing that he had no real power in
the court.

. . . also trust that you have had a chance to think over my
previous thoughts, unschooled as they may be, in view of your
own observations . . .

. . . Lord Bhayar has observed on previous occasions that
pursuit of the practical is most necessary for a ruler to be
successful, but, from my own most limited experience, I believe
that what is practical for one man may not be so for another, and
even what is practical for most men may not be so for a woman.
Likewise, what is practical for most women may not be so for most

men. Such questions might seem to some as similar to an attempt to split a hair with a broadsword, yet the very raising of such an inquiry about any law or practice of a ruler can lead the way to greater insight and, one would trust, a more effective ruler.

Many have questioned the value of scholars and others who seek knowledge that has no apparent immediate value. I am no scholar, yet it would seem to me that the ores from which metals are refined have no immediate value, nor does a newborn babe have any immediate value . . .

Quaeryt could not but help smiling as he continued reading and finished the letter. He was also having trouble in not yawning.

He would have to reply to Vaelora, but he wasn't about to try to write a cogent response after a long night with no sleep whatsoever . . . and certainly not when he still had not been able to deduce her motivations for writing. He re-folded the missive, then took both her letters and placed them in the document case.

The bed looked very inviting, and it would only take a few moments to make it up.

34

When Quaeryt woke, it was past noon, and by the time he had walked down to the main level, found the bath chambers, washed and shaved, and climbed back up to his quarters and changed into clean scholars' browns, it was closer to half past first glass. The west wing was apparently deserted, not surprisingly for early afternoon on a working day, and he set out to explore the grounds of the Telaryn Palace, beginning with the area west of where he'd been quartered. Just beyond the west entrance to the building was a stretch of gravel, and beyond that a flat and level area that looked like it might be used for turf bowls.

He walked along the edge of the bowling green to the anomen, located in the shadow of the northwest corner of the walls. It was a comparatively small edifice, dwarfed by the walls, looking from the outside as though it could hold no more than two hundred congregants.

Is it just for the officers? Or does the chorister hold many services? From what Quaeryt knew, there was close to a regiment of Telaryn soldiers and cavalry quartered within the grounds of the palace or nearby.

He studied the anomen closely. The dome had been repainted recently, but the color was more yellow than the traditional gold, and while the main doors had been oiled recently, the oak was still streaked with the white created by too many long winters.

East of the anomen was another stone-paved lane that led back toward the eastern—and only—gates. To the south were more gardens and a narrow orchard, and to the north, what looked more like three-story town houses, set side by side. Quaeryt estimated that they were only six or seven yards wide, but close to ten deep, with their rear wall abutting the defensive walls. He began to count as he walked along the lane. After forty of the narrow houses, there was a small park-like area, where a handful of small children played, watched by a white-haired woman. East of the first forty houses were another forty, and then a large three-story structure with narrow windows that resembled the west wing of the palace, except that the windows were even narrower and closer together.

Housing for the more valued servants? That was Quaeryt's best guess, although he would have guessed that there were tinier rooms beneath the palace itself for others less fortunate.

East of the servants' housing were the structures for the soldiers, more narrow-windowed gray stone buildings, but they were constructed so that the first level held stables, and the two levels above, presumably barracks. After making his way into the stables and asking several ostlers, he found his mare, and she had been groomed and fed, as Straesyr had said, and his saddle carefully cleaned and racked.

When he left the stables, the sound of marching drew Quaeryt back to the entry courtyard. There two companies were drilling, one with pikes, and another carrying sabres. The pike company took up most of the space. He watched for a time, then made his wandering way through the gardens and miniature orchards. During the entire survey of the planted area, which took almost two glasses, and during which he tried to note every different plant and tree, he saw no one except four gardeners.

The more he saw, the more he realized that the "Telaryn Palace" held the equivalent of a small city within the graystone walls.

At just before fifth glass, Quaeryt stepped into the mess in the west wing, to be greeted by a senior squad leader in crisp undress greens. "Scholar Quaeryt?"

"Yes?"

"All officers may sit at any table they please. The exception is at mess nights, when seating is by rank. The princeps has declared that, for purposes of mess night seating, your rank is that of the most junior captain."

"What nights are mess nights?"

"Jeudi nights, unless otherwise announced."

"Thank you." *For quarters, I'm field grade, but to the other officers, I'm a captain?* Quaeryt stepped farther into the mess and quickly studied the tables. There were three long tables, each capable of seating twenty or so. There were but a handful of junior officers already present, and from what he could see of them, all wore the single silver bar of an undercaptain.

"I see you are pondering the anomalousness of being unnamed in a named hierarchy. . . ." The words were delivered from behind Quaeryt with sardonic lightness of tone.

He turned to see a gray-haired man wearing the green uniform of a Telaryn officer, if without rank insignia, but with a black-edged white triangle on each sleeve, recalling the black-edged long white scarf often worn by choristers of the Nameless. Like the other officers, his uniform was clean and pressed, but he did not wear a jacket, presumably because the weather remained too warm. "You must be the governor's chorister."

"More properly, the regimental chorister. Phargos, by name. You are obviously the new scholar."

"Quaeryt."

"A most appropriate appellation and one either greatly more or greatly less vulnerable to the egregiousness of Naming."

"That is one way of describing it," replied Quaeryt with a laugh.

"Would you care to join me?"

"I'd be pleased to."

Phargos led the way to the table farthest from the door and sat in the last chair facing the door at what looked to be the foot of the table, assuming that the

end of the chamber with the crossed banners represented the front.

Quaeryt took the seat across from him. "Phargos . . .
From Montagne?"

"Cintella, actually, but that's only ten milles from
Montagne, farther from the ash and fumes of Mount
Extel." Phargos smiled. "This is where the juniors usually sit, except for the few more senior officers who
occasionally deign to harass me . . . such as the one
now approaching."

Quaeryt half-turned as a deep baritone voice boomed
out. "Phargos . . . I see you're trying to convert another
to nonspecific vagueness."

"If you believe that, then you haven't met too many
scholars. He's likely to have me scrambling to defend
the entire tenet of the Nameless."

"I've never seen you scramble—even when you
were surrounded by those hill brigands." The stocky
major took the seat beside the chorister and across
from Quaeryt.

"The backwoods barons of tall timber? What point
was there in hurrying? The longer I took, the longer
before they attacked, and the more time you had to
reach us."

"I told you they couldn't be converted. They're
worse than the Duodeans . . ." The major broke off and
grinned at Quaeryt. "I'm Skarpa, in charge of Sixth
Battalion, cavalry."

"Quaeryt, recently appointed scholar assistant to
the princeps."

"First a chorister, and then a scholar. Why did you
get posted here?"

Quaeryt shrugged. "The short answer is that I
couldn't give Lord Bhayar an answer he liked."

"What was the question?"

"Whether the people of Tilbor were so much different than other people and whether that was the cause of the continuing problems." Quaeryt offered a wry smile. "I made the mistake of suggesting I couldn't offer a good answer because I'd never been to Tilbor."

Skarpa laughed.

Phargos frowned, then shook his head.

"Why so dour, friend?" asked the major.

"There is no answer to a question such as that."

"Certainly, there is. Every person is similar in some ways to others. Every people is similar to every other in ways, but all peoples are formed by their lands, and that makes them different."

"That is not the answer Lord Bhayar seeks," pointed out the chorister. "Your answer is akin to saying that because all people must have names, all are in some fashion servants of the Namer."

"Arguing again?" interjected another voice.

Quaeryt looked up to see a grizzled captain, apparently far older than the major.

"Why not? It's more entertaining than complaining," replied Skarpa. "Meinyt . . . have you met our new scholar assistant to the princeps?"

"Quaeryt."

"Pleased to meet you. He could use one . . . if he'd listen or read anything besides the regimental ledgers and the Tilboran tariff records."

"Careful . . . the princeps . . ."

"What can he do but complain to the governor? Rescalyn doesn't have anyone else whose company can chase the backlands brigands through the winter snows." Meinyt looked to Quaeryt. "You can even tell the princeps that."

Quaeryt shook his head and laughed. "I'm a scholar,

and I don't think the princeps or the governor is about to listen to my words on military tactics and who's best at what. I've already learned that scholars who say too much about what they don't know are like fish."

Phargos smiled, but said nothing.

"Like fish?" asked Meinyt.

"Did anyone ever catch a fish who kept its eyes open and its mouth shut?"

The two officers laughed, and Meinyt sat down beside Quaeryt.

By then the table was almost full, and as Phargos had said, most of those farther up the table looked to be undercaptains.

"You came all the way from Solis?" asked the captain.

"By sail, with one storm and a shipwreck." Quaeryt offered a wry smile. "I thought it would be easier than riding, and I ended up riding the last part, from the Ayerne north, anyway."

"Sometimes . . . trying to get out of things just gets you in deeper," said Meinyt.

"That's a lesson that's hard to learn." Quaeryt grinned sheepishly.

"Don't tell me we're getting fried squid again," groaned Skarpa, looking at the platter that the server set in the middle of the table. "What's wrong with plain old mutton?"

"It's the season for squid," replied Phargos. "Besides, most of the officers and men like fried squid, and the governor tries to make sure they get the fare they like."

"I know," sighed Skarpa. "But why the Namer do they all like squid?"

Meinyt laughed, and, for the rest of the meal, Quaeryt did his best to listen and say as little as possible.

35

Samedi morning Quaeryt was up early, not because he particularly wanted to be, especially with the soreness and bruises on his upper arm and shoulder, but because the officers' mess was open only from fifth to sixth glass and because he wanted to eat before he met with Straesyr, and he hadn't seen anywhere else around the palace and its grounds to obtain food.

He ended up sitting at the junior officers' table, several spaces from two undercaptains. No one joined him, and he was reluctant to press himself on others. He did listen, but most of what he overheard dealt with duties and routine, except for a brief interchange.

". . . kept talking about the sisters . . ."

". . . so she's got sisters . . ."

". . . no . . . this was something different, like the scholars or the choristers . . ."

"Sisters? Never heard of them . . ."

"Me neither . . . gave me the chills . . . left her right there . . ."

That had been the second time Quaeryt had heard about the sisters, whatever they were, and it sounded like he needed to learn more about them.

After eating a breakfast heavy on oatmeal porridge, which was thicker and more solid than any Quaeryt had sampled almost anywhere else, along with ham strips, dark bread, and even fruit preserves, Quaeryt made certain that he was in the anteroom outside the princeps's study a good half quint before the palace bells rang out seventh glass. Even so, he waited another half quint before the aide at the writing table, upon hearing a bell, said, "You can go in, scholar."

Quaeryt opened the door, entered the study, and closed the door behind himself.

Straesyr did not rise, but gestured to the chairs in front of the table desk. He wore a pale green tunic instead of the blue, with a high collar that reminded Quaeryt of a factor, yet in a way, he wore it almost as if it were a uniform.

"I trust all the arrangements are satisfactory."

"Most satisfactory, sir." Quaeryt settled into the chair on the left. "The food in the mess is quite good."

"The governor insists on good fare for both soldiers and his officers, among other things. He's very particular about that." Straesyr's lips curled momentarily. "Before we begin on dealing with your mission, I'd be curious to know how you became acquainted with Lord Bhayar." The princeps smiled, but his eyes remained icy blue.

"When we were younger, he studied with the same scholars as I did. Lord Chayar sent him to the Scholarium, rather than have him tutored in the palace."

"It's said that Lord Chayar also had him trained in arms, both with the rankers and with junior officers. What do you know of that?"

"Very little, sir. Once, in passing, he made a remark about the sons of High Holders and that they should all spend time being trained like rankers in his father's regiments. That was the only time I recall him saying anything."

"You didn't spend time as a soldier or armsman, then?"

"No, sir."

"So you've been a scholar from birth, essentially."

"No, sir. I was orphaned very young in the Great Plague and raised by the scholars. I left the scholars and spent six years or so before the mast, and then persuaded them to take me back."

"Why did you return to the scholars?"

"Seafaring isn't a way of life that takes to questions. Too much has been learned at the cost of lives, and trying new ways usually doesn't turn out well."

"Isn't that true of most ways of life?"

"It is." Quaeryt smiled wryly. "But a scholar can ask a few more questions and has the time to try to work out better ways. Or to find better reasons why the old ways work as they do, and that sometimes leads to better ways as well."

Surprisingly, to Quaeryt, the princeps nodded. "What better ways are you seeking for Lord Bhayar?"

"He hasn't said." That was certainly true enough. "He wants to know more about why the people of Tilbor are so difficult."

"He could have asked the governor or me."

"Could he, sir?" asked Quaeryt politely, keeping his tone very deferential.

Straesyr stiffened for a moment, then nodded again. "I see your point, scholar. Your presence is the only safe way to raise the question, and that is why Lord Bhayar appointed you as my assistant and not the governor's."

"Lord Bhayar never gave me a reason. He just gave me the appointment."

"His father often did the same. Did you ever meet him?"

"No, sir."

"What about other members of his family?"

"I was briefly introduced to one of his sisters. I have

since received missives from her, inquiring about the prevalence of certain historical practices of rulers."

"You are most careful about your responses," observed the princeps.

"I am a scholar beholden to others, sir. They often have many sources of information, as do you. Untruths would be inadvisable, as well as unwise."

"What do you want to know from me?" asked Straesyr calmly, as if he had discovered what he wished to find out.

"A number of matters . . . but I would begin with the latest. Last night at the mess, I couldn't help but overhear officers talking about the backlanders and the timber barons, as if they remained a considerable problem for you and the governor."

"At one time or another, anyone with arms or power has been a problem," replied Straesyr. "You did, however, hear correctly. Those who are currently fomenting the most trouble are those in the Boran Hills. Even the few . . . disruptions near Tilbora appear to be linked to them. I suspect that they are supported by the landholders there who are not High Holders. I have little trust in the High Holders, either, but whenever possible High Holders attempt to have others shed their blood and spend their golds."

"Why would those landholders in the hills be interested in taking on Lord Bhayar's forces? From what little I know, you and the governor have been fair to all in applying the laws, and that would seem to benefit them more than the High Holders." Those were guesses on Quaeryt's part, but they fit what he had observed so far.

"That is indeed a question. The old Khanars maintained a guard strong enough to defeat any two or three High Holders, but it was not large enough to deal with even a handful of them at once. So the Khanars tended not to upset the High Holders."

"What happened to the Guard?"

"When the Pretender was defeated in battle—just below the palace, in fact—he attempted to retreat behind the walls, but the Guard closed the gates and left the Khanar and his clan followers to face Lord Chayar. The Guard commander claimed that the Pretender wasn't the true Khanar of Tilbor. That made matters easier for Lord Chayar, even though he privately deemed the Guard unworthy. He didn't want to execute all that were left of the two thousand. So he disbanded the Guard and exiled the officers to either Bovaria or Antiago . . . well, also Khel, but that was just before Kharst began his campaign to take over Khel."

"Did any of the Guards take up arms against Lord Chayar later?"

Straesyr shrugged. "I doubt it. Some of them may have, but if they did, it had to be with the backwoods holders."

"None of the High Holders caused trouble?"

"Only one. He refused to pay the overtariff Lord Chayar imposed. Chayar pulled down his holding and killed him. He had me sell off half the lands to pay the tariff and the costs of the attacks, and left the rest to the widow and heirs."

That was a slightly different story than the one Quaeryt had heard from Sarastyn, but he nodded. "After that I take it no one refused to pay tariffs."

"Not so far." The princeps gave a short laugh. "Not in the nine years since."

"How have the merchanters, factors, crafters, and growers done with their tariffs?"

"They pay them. Sometimes a few are late. There

were more who were late until the governor—that was Governor Fhayt, the one before Governor Rescalyn— sent armed squads to collect."

"I'd heard that there have been attacks on soldiers."

"There have been," admitted Straesyr.

"On men alone at night?"

"Oh . . . there have been a few killed by thieves and brigands. That happens everywhere. No. The attacks by their so-called partisans have been on squads on collection duties in the backlands."

"Have you lost any entire squads?"

"Once, last year. Now we send out at least a company. We rotate the companies, except in the winter, when we use those trained in the snow."

"Have you captured any of these partisans?"

"None who know anything. When we have, they've changed their meeting places."

"What sort of weapons do they use?"

"They prefer to pick off soldiers with arrows or quarrels, rather than fight close at hand. That's one reason why the regiment has few archers."

Quaeryt couldn't help frowning. The princeps's statement seemed to make no sense.

"I see I've puzzled you. Tilbor is different. The towns are farther apart. Even the trees in the forests are farther apart. Their archers hide in trees or fire and run. Against these tactics, archers, even mounted archers, are mostly useless. Archers are far more effective against massed bodies of men, especially on foot and in the open. Cavalry or mounted infantry that can move quickly through the woods or on the roads are less of a target and are more effective at chasing the brigands down. The regiment does have one company of archers, but they're seldom used." Straesyr smiled tightly. "I'll talk to the governor when he returns about letting you read the dispatches. I don't see a problem, but that has to be his decision."

"Thank you. Do you or the governor meet often with any of the High Holders?"

"We hold a reception here once every season. I think every single one and his wife have attended at least one a year. Every so often the governor is invited to dinners at the local High Holders' estates, and he makes announced and unannounced visits with a cavalry company to different High Holders on a continuing basis. They do come to meet with the governor when they have problems with a ruling from the governor or Lord Bhayar. I'm the one who meets more often with factors and local merchants. . . ."

Quaeryt listened, asking a question now and again, for almost a glass.

". . . that's about all I can tell you. Do you have any questions that bear on your duties?" Straesyr finally asked.

"Scholars are respected in Solis, if warily, but in Nacliano, they are driven out. How have you seen them regarded here?"

"They have a school and a Scholars' House to the southwest of here. I would say that they are regarded as in somewhat the same fashion as in Solis. Why do you ask?"

"I will need to ride through Tilbora and perhaps farther to gather information. I would rather not be a target."

"You may be anyway, once others discover you are attached to the governor's staff."

Quaeryt laughed softly. "That is possible, but I doubt that most Tilborans would go out of their way to try to find out if one scholar is the one working for the governor as opposed to however many are not."

"You do have a point there, until they come to recognize you."

"Did the Khanar have a library as well, something that might have histories of Tilbor?"

"That's on the first level, and it's open to all officers. There's a guard there, but only to make sure no volumes vanish."

"Are there any records of how the Khanar dealt with the High Holders and . . ."

"There's an entire archive. That's also guarded, but you're welcome to look there. Do you really think . . . ?"

"There's always a possibility. It's probably small, but since you wished me to remain within the palace until after the governor's return, I thought it couldn't do any harm." Quaeryt offered a smile. "And scholars are supposed to dig into old books and records. . . ."

"Ah . . . quite so."

"That's all I can think of for now, sir." Quaeryt waited.

"There is one other matter. You will need a study here in the palace . . . for those times when you are not actively pursuing your tasks or need a place to write where I or the governor can conveniently find you. There is a small vacant chamber three doors to the right as you go out of the anteroom. It is little larger than a small storeroom, but it is suitably appointed and has a window. I expect you to be there at seventh glass from Lundi through Samedi unless you have previously informed me otherwise. I also expect brief written reports weekly, to be on my desk on Lundi morning . . . again, unless you are traveling or otherwise occupied."

"Yes, sir. There may be certain matters not best put in ink. . . ."

"Then just write in the report that you need time to brief me on a matter relating to your duties."

"Yes, sir."

Straesyr smiled wryly. "I had always heard that some seamen were almost as disciplined as soldiers, and I'm pleased to see that you appear able to fit into the regiment. I do hope you will not disappoint the governor and me in that regard."

"Yes, sir."

"That's all I have. Vhorym will show you your study."

"Thank you."

Straesyr nodded a dismissal, and Quaeryt stood, inclining his head before turning and leaving.

The aide who had been seated at the table desk in the anteroom rose. "Sir . . . the princeps asked me to show you your study." He handed the scholar a brass key.

"I'd appreciate that. You're Vhorym?"

"Yes, sir."

"I assume I give my weekly reports to you so that you can put them on the princeps's desk?"

"Yes, sir. I do that for the officers who report to the princeps."

After only a day at the Telaryn Palace, Quaeryt found himself thoroughly reminded just why he'd left the sea and returned to the scholars.

The study to which Vhorym guided Quaeryt was paneled in polished oak. Even the inside shutters were of oiled and polished oak, as was the writing desk, with clean lines and none of the carved ornamentation that distinguished the desk used by the princeps.

Once Vhorym had left, Quaeryt walked to the window and opened the shutters, allowing light to flood into the chamber. Then he sat down before the desk, thinking.

Among other matters, Straesyr's point about Quaeryt's eventually being a target concerned the scholar. He'd always been able to fade into the background with his concealment shields, but, as he'd discovered in dealing with Chardyn, there were times when concealment wasn't enough, and he had the feeling that he would encounter more of those situations in Tilbor, possibly many more. There would also be times when too many people would be watching him for him to appear to vanish. After he'd almost died trying to image gold, he'd become wary of trying to discover new imaging skills, only working to develop those he'd read or seen were possible. There were tales of great feats of imaging, but Quaeryt had more than a few doubts about the veracity of such stories. Yet, for all those doubts, he was plagued by the feeling that he might be too cautious.

Then, too, he'd have to sort out how much of the truth lay in the princeps's version of events, as compared to Chardyn's version, or Sarastyn's, and whether any of them were particularly close to what happened . . . if he even could.

36

In the end, Quaeryt decided he'd begin with the Khanar's library. The young-looking squad leader at the table by the door took a quick glance at Quaeryt, then said, "You know you can't remove any books from the chambers, sir?"

"The princeps made that clear, Squad Leader. I'm likely to be here a while."

"Yes, sir."

Quaeryt nodded, then turned and studied the library. He and the squad leader were the only ones in the library. The door through which he had entered accessed the center chamber of three. At each end of the main chamber was an archway some three yards wide leading into the adjoining room. In the middle of the center chamber, not four yards from him, was a large oval ceramic stove with a freestanding stone chimney. On each end of the stove were open wood bins, half-filled. A series of dark brown leather armchairs were spaced in the middle of the chamber, all facing toward the wall that held the entry door.

Built-in dark wooden bookcases lined every wall and rose from roughly knee level to about two and a half yards above the floor, clearly designed so that most men could reach any volume without resorting to a ladder or a stool. Above the shelves on the wall beyond the stove were windows, each one less than two spans high, but almost a yard wide. Except for two windows, each a third of the way from the walls holding the archways into the other two rooms, the glass was set in frames that did not allow them to be open, and Quaeryt could not see through them. That was because, he realized, there was another pane of glass set perhaps half a handspan behind the first, again except for the two windows that could be opened.

For a moment, he wondered at the arrangement, before realizing it was to allow more light into the library while minimizing draft through the windows by double-glazing all but two.

He began by studying each shelf, taking out a few

books and leafing through them to see if they were shelved in a particular order. Each shelf was comparatively short, roughly two-thirds of a yard long. The first section of shelves all held books, largely slender, dealing with mathematics and measurements. So did the second section The third section dealt with medical matters, as did the fourth, while the fifth held tomes on herbs and their uses.

It took Quaeryt more than two glasses to complete his initial survey of the library, after which he sat down in one of the comfortable dark brown leather armchairs to think and rest his eyes. The history section comprised three sets of shelves, as did volumes on military tactics and statecraft, and there was one section on philosophy, and another on religion. There were almost three sets of shelves holding verse, but only a single set of shelves held plays and works of drama, but two sets of shelves held folders of music. A great many of those books had been read, some very well read.

What does that tell you about the Khanars?

If the books in the library were any indication, they—or some in the palace—were far more knowledgeable than either Bhayar or Chayar, not that such knowledge had availed them in the end.

Quaeryt decided to look more closely through the shelves on history and tactics. The leather bindings of several of the books on the topmost shelf were worn and close to splitting in places. He took down one and opened it to the title page—*Meditations on the Art of Warfare.* The author was a Mhoral Chardynsyn, Commander, Guard of the Khanar. The date was 614 E.K., and that meant nothing to Quaeryt. He leafed through the introduction, smiling as his eyes tracked one phrase.

> . . . any commander must bear in mind that the great-
> est possibility of failure of execution always lies in the
> officers, for well-trained men and mounts seldom be-
> tray their training . . .

He replaced the book and kept looking, immediately passing on *Basics of Foot Strategy* and *Pike and
Blade Tactics*. The next volume was thin and entitled
Course of Instruction in Fortifications. Eventually,
close to a glass later, he came to an older but well-
thumbed volume—*Considerations Behind the Strategy of War*. He almost passed on it, except . . . there
was the slightest gap in pages, and he opened the volume there to find a piece of notepaper and a passage
that had been lightly bracketed with some sort of
markstick. . . .

> . . . while a ruler's force of arms must always be supe-
> rior to those of his holders, use of force should always
> be reserved for when no other alternative will achieve
> the ruler's ends. In such cases, appropriate force should
> be applied before the enemies even know the ruler is
> considering such use. . . . Force of arms can be as lim-
> ited as the assassination of a single enemy commander
> of great skill, or even of a cousin or other relation who
> would plunge a land into chaos, or as great as the con-
> scription of every able-bodied man in the land . . .
> most skillful of rulers can see when to use assassina-
> tion or other tactics to avoid the ruin that follows even
> the most successful of battles . . .

At the last sentence, Quaeryt had to nod. He un-
folded the notepaper, apparently the bottom half of a
larger sheet, on which were written the words "even
ancient writers could see where the greatest dangers

lay . . ." The cursive script looked feminine to Quaeryt, but it had the unnatural precision, he thought, of a young woman still under the direction of a scholar or private tutor. The very words reinforced that impression, because no truly experienced woman would leave such words in a book, even in her own library.

Could the writer have been the Khanar's daughter? Tyrena, was it?

While not new, the paper didn't look that ancient . . . but how many young women had access to the library over the years? On the other hand, how many would dare to leave such an incriminating scrap . . . unless that young woman happened to be untouchable?

He left the paper in the book and replaced it on the shelf.

After another quint of searching he did find a volume that recounted the history of Tilbor from the time of Nidar the Great through the time of Eleonyd's father, who appeared moderately strong, if strangely indifferent. That tome occupied Quaeryt for several glasses, and one phrase particularly caught his attention.

. . . though some thought agreeing to it a weakness, the Charter proved to be the basis of the power of the High Holders and led to the relative decline of those holders who did not agree to its terms . . .

The only problem was that he couldn't find much about the Charter, except that it was an agreement between the Khanar and some of the holders of that time. Quaeryt had the feeling that the Charter was one of those events that everyone at the time knew and therefore wrote little about, only to have the details fade over the years. There was probably a book somewhere, but . . .

He shook his head.

Other books did provide various insights and by the time he needed to leave the library for the day, he thought he had a somewhat better grasp of Tilboran history, at least until the time of Eleonyd.

When Quaeryt finally entered the mess for supper, he could see far fewer officers—roughly half as many as on Vendrei night—but one was Major Skarpa, who motioned for Quaeryt to join him and another major. "This is Quaeryt. He's the scholar assistant to the princeps I told you about. Quaeryt, this is Daendyr. He's in charge of supplies for the regiment."

"I'm pleased to meet you," said Quaeryt as he took the seat across from Skarpa.

"I've never seen a scholar attached to a regiment before."

"He's on the governor's staff," Skarpa said. "They had to give him officer status."

Daendyr nodded.

"What have you been doing today?" Skarpa handed the pitcher of amber lager to Quaeryt, who filled his mug.

"Seeing what was in the Khanar's library. . . ."

"Who reads all that?" asked Daendyr.

"I've read some of them," admitted Skarpa. "A couple of the books on mounted tactics are good."

"Then why didn't they use them?"

"The Khanar's Guard did. They gave us a lot of trouble, even though we outnumbered them." Skarpa shook his head. "Then, all of a sudden, they just withdrew, and left the Khanar and his militia or whatever they were outside the palace moat and walls. We would have taken them sooner or later, but it was a lot easier that way."

"They didn't have any imagers?" asked Quaeryt. "I heard . . ."

"Lord Chayar did something about that. We never heard. It wouldn't matter anyway. Imagers can only do so much, and that doesn't change things in a pitched battle."

"What about the High Holders?" asked Quaeryt.

"What about them? They really didn't fight any more than they had to. The ones here in the south didn't like the Khanar much. They called him the Pretender or some such."

"It sounds like he wasn't very well-liked anywhere."

Daendyr shook his head. "The backwoods and Boran Hills holders liked him, and so did the High Holders around Noira."

"The High Holders in the far north don't count for much. They never have," countered Skarpa.

"Where do the sisters fit in?" asked Quaeryt.

"The sisters?" Daendyr's face screwed up in puzzlement.

"Oh . . . they're a bunch of spinsters who supposedly poison men who beat their wives," explained Skarpa. "Something like that, anyway."

"Where do you get that?" asked Daendyr.

"You hear things."

"Makes me glad I didn't wed a local."

"Have you all been posted here since . . . since the end of the fighting?"

"We have," said Skarpa. "They'll rotate field-grade officers who are married after three years."

"If they ask, and most won't," added Daendyr.

"What about the rankers?"

"They stay for the duration of their term."

"When they're mustered out . . . ?"

"They get their bonus and a ride on a transport wagon back to Solis or the closest large town to where they signed up. If they've done two ten-year terms, they get a stipend for life. It's not much, two silvers a month, but . . ."

"And the marshal sends replacement recruits?"

Daendyr shook his head. "Tilbor's a part of Telaryn. We have to recruit locals now. We have been for more than eight years."

"We haven't had trouble that way at all," added Skarpa. "The governor makes certain the troops get good rations, and the quarters are good. The uniforms are better than what most of them ever wore."

"If it weren't for the backwoods and the northern brigands, it'd be a better life than most of them would ever have."

"It is anyway." Skarpa's tone was wry.

At that moment, a large platter of sliced roast mutton arrived, accompanied by a pitcher of brown gravy and sliced roast potatoes, as well as a large serving dish of spiced stewed apples.

"The mutton's much better than squid," observed Skarpa.

"It's good, but I still like the squid," said Daendyr.

"You're from Thuyl. You would."

Quaeryt smiled and served himself healthy portions of everything before him. It had been a long day since breakfast, and the mess didn't serve a midday meal.

After eating, and mostly listening, as Quaeryt walked back toward his third-floor quarters, thoughts swirled through his mind. He was getting a picture of how matters were going in Tilbor, and it did appear that the troubles facing the governor and the regiment centered on the backwoods holders and the northern High Holders. In that vein, he also found it interesting

that both Phaeryn and Zarxes were from backwoods
holder families. He needed to find out if Straesyr or
the governor knew that, but, since he wanted to avoid
total destruction of the Ecoliae and persecution of
scholars, he definitely couldn't ask directly. He also
wasn't ready to reveal what he'd been doing in the
days before he'd arrived at the Telaryn Palace.

And he did need to write some sort of reply to
Vaelora.

He also couldn't help but wonder about the note
he'd found in *Considerations Behind the Strategy of
War*. If it had been written by Tyrena, given the handwriting, it had likely been written several years before
the war . . . and if it had been that obvious to her . . .

He shook his head.

37

If anything, there were fewer officers at breakfast on
Solayi morning than on Samedi night. Quaeryt ate
alone, then made his way to the chamber in the lowest
level of the palace that held the archives of the khanarate. As the princeps had said, the entry was guarded
by an older ranker.

"Good morning, sir. The assistant to the princeps
said you might be here."

"I'm here. Do you know anything about how the
records are arranged?"

"No, sir." The ranker paused. "Excepting that all
the papers from the last year or so are in the four
wooden boxes on the long table just inside. There." He

pointed. "I'd be guessing that there was no one left to put them in proper order."

"That might have been difficult," agreed Quaeryt. "Thank you."

"My pleasure, sir. Don't see many down here."

Quaeryt stepped into the chamber, a stone-walled and windowless enclosure a good ten yards wide and forty deep. The chamber was so still that he could hear the unevenness of his steps and the scuffing sound of the boot on his bad leg. There were two oil lamps lit, both near the table pointed out by the guard, but the rest of the space faded from gloom into near blackness.

He walked to the box nearest the door and stopped. When he lifted the wooden top off the box, a container a yard long, and half a yard deep and tall, he immediately saw that, if anything, the ranker had understated the lack of organization. Papers of all sizes and types, some in leather folders, but most not, were just crammed in, side by side. Dust billowed out, as if no one had looked in the boxes for some time.

He eased the first box to the rear of the long sturdy table and took out the first span of papers from the right end of the box and then set them on the table in front of the box. He picked up the first sheet, glanced at a cargo manifest of some sort, saw that it dealt with woolens and other types of cloth, and set it aside. The second, third, and fourth sheets comprised a petition from a town council requesting the Khanar improve the bridge over a stream because the horses of the Khanar's Guard had damaged it beyond the ability of the town to repair and it required replacement.

Quaeryt read through three handspans' worth of paper before he came across the first sheet that interested him, a proclamation that declared officers of the "militia of the northern Boran Hills" bore their ranks equivalent to those of the Guard of the Khanar. The document was signed by Rhecyrd, Khanar of Tilbor. He set that aside and kept looking, not that he knew precisely what he sought.

Shortly thereafter, he found a letter addressed to Eleonyd, Khanar and Patriarch of Tilbor, written by one Fhaedyrk, High Holder of Dyrkholm. Most of it was flattery and obfuscation, but one paragraph stood out.

> . . . the wealth of Tilbor lies in two sources, that of its High Holders and that combined which derives from its growers, factors, and crafters. Both create greater wealth from lesser sources, as opposed to the timber holders of the hills, who harvest what they have not grown in greater amounts than the forests will sustain in years to come, and the clans of the north who prey on all who are weaker . . . In all your efforts to improve Tilbor, and in regard to the revisions suggested in tariffs, you and your predecessors have kept these sources in mind, and continuing such may well be in the best interests of the khanarate . . .

He'd heard the name Fhaedyrk, but he couldn't remember where. So he set that letter aside as well and kept reading through the assorted papers. At the end of another glass, he'd found a missive from Chayar's ill-fated envoy announcing his arrival and suggesting that Eleonyd meet with him at his earliest convenience, with the barely veiled suggestion that matters of mutual interest should be considered sooner rather than later, but there was no mention of what those matters might be.

Then, after another few quints, he came across another letter under the crest of the Khanar, this one

signed by Tyrena, as regent for Eleonyd, Khanar of
Tilbor. He almost overlooked it, because it was in the
back of a leather folder behind a flap, and he'd been
about to replace the folder in the box when he realized there was a flap and lifted it. After he finished
reading it, he nodded. Although the bulk of the text
dealt with routine matters before the Khanar's Council, there were several suggestive phrases.

> . . . *as for consideration of tariffs on the timber road, that is a
> matter that will be reviewed at the next session of the Khanar's
> Council* . . .
>   . . . *at this time no funds can be spent on paying for
> enlarging the harbor at Noira* . . . *better funded by the High
> Holders and factors of the north as they are the only ones who
> might benefit* . . .
>   . . . *the matter of the potential marriage of the heiress of
> the Khanar will also be discussed at the next Council meet-
> ing* . . .
>   . . . *discussion of the dispatch from the Autarch of Antiago
> will resume* . . .

While the text had been written by a scrivener, the
signature was different and, from what Quaeryt could
recall, similar to that on the note he'd discovered in the
tactics book, although the signature seemed more ma-
ture. After studying the letter again, Quaeryt checked
back through the other leather folders he had already
looked at, but none contained anything else hidden
behind flaps, and another glass of looking revealed
nothing else dealing with Tyrena.

By midafternoon, his eyes were blurring from all of
the searching through papers and documents, but he
did manage to complete going through the four disorganized boxes of papers, bills of lading, proclama-

tions, even scattered ledger sheets. The one thing that was very clear was that the last days of the khanarate, if the documents were any indication, had been hectic and disorganized. Still, he had perhaps twenty documents that might prove of interest. He slipped them into the folder that had concealed the letter signed by Tyrena, and placed that folder at the end of the third box.

That single letter from Tyrena raised several questions. First . . . if she had acted as regent for her father, why was there only one letter? Or had there been more, and the others removed? That was most likely, given that the single letter he'd found had been tucked behind a flap in a folder containing other papers. But, if there had been others, who had removed them? Rhecyrd? Or one of his assistants, on the Pretender's orders? Would Quaeryt ever know?

He doubted it.

As blurry as his eyes felt by then, roughly at third glass, he left the archives and walked through the gardens and back to his quarters, where he sat down and began to compose a reply to the missive Vaelora had dispatched. He tried to think out each sentence carefully before he wrote it.

Dear Mistress Vaelora—

I arrived in Tilbora on the twenty-seventh of Agostas and received your latest missive then. My journey took longer than I had anticipated because I had to wait for a ship sailing from Nacliano to Tilbora. Unfortunately, the ship encountered a storm and went on the rocks well south of Tilbor. It took a good week for me to recover at the holding of a kindly couple, and then more than another week to ride north to Tilbor. I regret the delay in my replying to your inquiries.

Your last communication raised eloquently the difficulty of

objectively determining what might be the most practical course
of action for a ruler, given that the best possible judgments of
those around the ruler might well differ, even if all had his best
interests in mind. In addition, some might not have those
interests in mind, and often those who are the least inclined to
further a ruler's best interests are also the most eloquent. How
then should he judge whose counsel is of most value? All
circumstances differ, but I would suggest that the ruler offer to
those advising him a plausible course of action in dealing with
the matter at hand, but one which he knows is flawed, and
request their counsel. How they respond may tell him much.

You had also commented upon the value of scholars, and
you might find it of interest to learn that the fashion in
which people perceive scholars varies more widely across
Telaryn than one might suppose. In Nacliano, the Scholars'
House was burned and the scholars dispersed, if not subjected
to worse abuse, because a scholar taught the wife of a City
Patrol chief reading and mathematics because she wished to
aid her husband. Unhappily, what she read and calculated so
horrified the poor woman that she fled, and the Patrol chief
took steps to make sure that scholars troubled Nacliano no
more.

With that much written, Quaeryt set aside his reply
for the moment, since he did not want to dispatch it
immediately, in any case, not until he had met with
the governor.

The mess was more crowded that evening, but
Quaeryt saw that Skarpa was surrounded by other officers. He sat with several undercaptains, mainly listening and offering innocuous pleasantries or simple
factual replies on the few times he was asked questions.

After eating, he made his way to the anomen, largely

because he wanted to see who would be there and hear what Phargos might offer in his homily.

The double doors of the gray stone anomen were of polished but well-weathered oak, and the brass hinges shone. Two lanterns, unlit, given that the sun had not yet set, also gleamed, despite the fact that the anomen lay in the shadow of the massive walls. Inside, which was larger than Quaeryt had originally judged, the wall lanterns were lit and cast a diffuse but warm glow across the officers and rankers gathered there between the oak-paneled walls. Quaeryt had never seen an anomen with paneled walls, not that he'd ever been in more than a handful of anomens, but the walls were without adornment of any sort, as was the fashion. What was strange was that there were far more officers than rankers.

Quaeryt took a position on the east side near the rear and waited. Several undercaptains followed him inside, but no one stood that close to him.

Shortly, Phargos moved to the center of the dais. He did not wear the vestments of a chorister, but his uniform, if with the long scarf that all choristers wore during services. The regimental chorister began with the greeting. "We gather together in the spirit of the Nameless and to affirm the quest for goodness and mercy in all that we do."

Quaeryt's mouth almost dropped open, because Phargos had offered the greeting in perfect Bovarian, not Tellan, and that might well explain the scarcity of rankers among the worshippers.

The opening hymn followed, and it was "Praise Not the Nameless," also sung in Bovarian. Likewise, the confession was also in Bovarian, although Quaeryt could tell some of the more junior officers were stumbling occasionally, but they did seem to have the last words down. "... and deference to You who cannot be named or known, only respected and worshipped."

Quaeryt murmured "In peace and harmony" with the others, and slipped only a copper into the offertory basket. His wallet was getting thin, and he didn't want to try imaging within the stone walls.

Phargos ascended to the pulpit for the homily with the crispness of an officer. "Good evening," he offered in Bovarian.

"Good evening," came the murmured reply.

"Under the Nameless all evenings are good ..."

Although he couldn't help but wonder why the services were being conducted in Bovarian, Quaeryt had no trouble listening. Phargos's voice was resonant and carried, and much of what he said made sense, especially one part.

"... why is the term 'sir' not only respectful, but especially appropriate for an officer of the regiment?" Phargos paused, then went on. "It is appropriate because it conveys respect without using a name, and Naming is not only a sin, but it also undermines the discipline of the regiment. When titles and names are too frequently used, they supersede, with few realizing it, the common purpose of the regiment. Men, even officers, puff themselves up if they hear their titles and name too often. An ancient sage once observed that the surest sign of a land's decline is when the length of the title of its ruler exceeds the length of his name manyfold ... or when both take longer to say than the sentence which follows ..."

A low laugh came from several officers at that. Quaeryt smiled.

After the benediction, Quaeryt lingered, since he saw Meinyt and Skarpa heading in his direction.

"You came to services, scholar," said Skarpa, his tone mock-accusatory.

"I did indeed."

"But are not scholars dubious of the Nameless?"

"We are dubious about everything, but in that regard, we follow the precepts of Rholan, because he was dubious about names. We're dubious about names . . . and a few more things as well."

"Is there anything that you're not dubious about?" asked Skarpa sardonically.

"Only that seasons follow seasons, that rulers will always tariff, and that death comes to all."

"That leaves more doubt in life than most can accept."

"True," replied Quaeryt, "but what men and women will accept and what they believe to be does not make such certain. It only comforts them."

"You sound more cynical than the Namer," observed Meinyt dryly.

"No. The Namer uses names to convey certainty where there is none. False certainty is the hallmark of the Namer."

"You should have been a chorister."

Quaeryt laughed. "I think not." *Not when you're not even certain that there is a Nameless.*

The three walked together back toward the west wing, where Quaeryt took his leave and climbed up to his chamber.

38

On Lundi morning, Quaeryt made certain he was in his assigned study a good half quint before seventh glass, then walked over to the princeps's anteroom.

"Vhorym, is there any special format I should use for my reports?"

"The standard form is like this, sir." The squad leader turned to the wooden box beside his table desk and lifted the hinged cover, removing a thin leather folder and laying it on the desk before extracting a single sheet. "You see? The top line is the addressee, the second is the writer, the third the subject, and the last line of the heading the date." He slipped the sheet back into the folder, and then replaced it in the file box.

"You're very organized."

"The governor . . . and the princeps . . . wouldn't have it any other way, sir."

"Vhorym. One other thing . . . the princeps mentioned that when I do leave the palace grounds, I'm to log out. Where do I do that?"

"In the gatehouse just inside the south side of the main upper gates, sir. There's a log for both missions and individuals."

"Thank you. Later today, if the princeps asks, I'll be down in the archives chamber. I should be there most of the day." With that, Quaeryt returned to his study, where he remained, thinking, until two quints past the bells striking seventh glass. Then he left the

study and made his way down to the lower level of
the palace to continue his perusal of the seemingly in-
numerable boxes of papers in the more than capacious
archives.

While he had hoped to move from box to box,
reading each in place, he ended up carrying a box at a
time to the table under the lamps, because none of the
other wall lamps held oil, and a hand lantern would
have shed so little light that reading the papers would
have been even more difficult.

Thankfully, the documents in the other file boxes
were in fact organized, not only by date, but by subject matter as well. By midmorning, Quaeryt had located and read through a set of files that contained
records of all meetings of the Khanar's Council for the
three years prior to the last year of the khanarate, doc-
umented in a haphazard way by the scattered files in
the first four boxes. He would have liked to have seen
all of them, but what was missing was likely destroyed,
especially anything bearing on the change in rulers.

The Council records were mostly routine. One entire meeting had been devoted to the question of
wastes being dumped into rivers and in particular, the
Albhor River. Another meeting had been on whether
the Khanar should set up a mint in the palace or continue to have coin struck by the gold- and silversmiths
in Tilbora, and yet another had dealt with the penalties
for conviction for logging on the properties of another.
From what he could tell, not a single file was missing
from that period, and all were reported either one
hand or another, only two scripts alternating over the
three years.

Studying all those files took him until the second
glass of the afternoon, when he left for a time to get
some water—from one of the pitchers in the princeps's

anteroom—followed by a walk in the gardens, where he filched a late apple from one of the trees. The apple was crisp, but tart. Then he sat on a stone bench shaded by a well-trimmed juniper and thought about all that he had read so far that day.

There wasn't a single mention in any of the reports about trouble with either timber holders or High Holders in the north. Nor was there any mention about Tyrena, directly or indirectly. The impression he'd received was of a land at peace with itself. That left three likely possibilities. Either Eleonyd was being deceived by everyone on the Council and everyone reporting to him, or he managed the reports to eliminate any mention of unpleasantness, or the land was truly at peace with itself. Since the reports didn't really go anywhere, and no one was ruling over Eleonyd, it was unlikely that the Khanar was having false reports made, or even that someone had substituted reports later, because what would have been the point after the khanarate had fallen?

From what little Quaeryt had seen of Tilbor, except for the backwoods and timber holders, the people didn't seem especially unruly. Stubborn and stiff-necked in a quiet way, but not rebellious . . . and if the regiment had been successfully recruiting for years . . .

He paused—except for the scholars, and that might be because of Phaeryn's and Zarxes's connections to the timber holders. He rose from the bench, stretched, and took a deep breath, then headed back down to the archives.

By two quints past fourth glass, his eyes were again blurring in the dim light of the two lamps in the archives, and it was getting close enough to time for the evening meal. He had to admit that he was surprised not to have found any other mention of Tyrena in any of the papers he'd viewed, but then, in that time period, she'd been old enough that little would have been said, and young enough, if Chardyn and Sarastyn were accurate, that marriage was not yet an issue. Or . . . someone had removed the papers dealing with her.

While that omission bothered him, he doubted that, except for satisfying his own curiosity, it was terribly relevant to his mission for Bhayar. Still . . . until he knew otherwise, he couldn't just dismiss the absence of Tyrena from the records.

He was just heading up the lower staircase when he saw Vhorym coming down.

"Sir? The princeps wanted me to let you know that the governor will see you at ninth glass tomorrow morning."

"Ninth glass. Thank you. Ah . . . where is his study?"

"It's on the other side of the rotunda exactly opposite the princeps's study."

"Thank you."

"My pleasure, sir."

Quaeryt let the squad leader hurry back up the stone steps, then made his way to the wash room near the mess, before returning to join the officers in the mess.

"Scholar . . . come join us!" The call came from a tall captain that Quaeryt didn't even recall seeing before.

Quaeryt smiled and walked toward the table closest to the door, where the captain stood. "I'm Quaeryt, formerly with the Scholarium Sólum in Solis."

"Kalphryn, senior captain, engineers." He gestured to the place across from him.

"Thank you." Quaeryt sat, as did the captain.

"Captain Meinyt said you came out from Solis. What news do you have?"

"Solis is still as hot as ever in summer and harvest,"

Quaeryt said wryly. "Nothing's burned down; no one's at war, or wasn't when I departed; and I should have ridden overland with a courier, even if I'm not quite the worst rider in Lydar, because coming by ship got me wrecked and near-drowned."

Kalphryn smiled; the two captains beside him laughed.

"We heard Rex Kharst had his eyes on Antiago," said Kalphryn.

"He probably does, but the word in the tavernas was that he was still having trouble with Khel."

"Word also is that you're getting dispatches from Solis."

Quaeryt managed to laugh immediately. "Yes . . . I did get a missive from one who would rather be a student of mine, and it asked about how a scholar would determine how to trust those who would give advice."

"He must be wealthy."

"She is . . . and far beyond my reach, especially given her family's proclivity to marry well. I'm doubtless a diversion. As for other news . . . there's a new minister of finance, but I don't recall his name, and there's also a new pleasure house a mere five blocks east of the palace. . . ." Quaeryt went on for a time, trying to recall every bit of news and trivia that he could, occasionally taking a sip of the lager that had appeared in the mug before him, before finally ending, ". . . and on the voyage here, I did discover that the City Patrol chief of Nacliano doesn't like scholars, or bookstores, and that some merchanters are now carrying cannon with shells that hold Antiagon Fire. That's likely to mean that whatever war gets fought next will be largely on land." Quaeryt turned to the engineer captain. "You have more experience in that, far more, than do I. What do you think?"

"Nasty stuff, Antiagon Fire . . . not that much of it, though . . . few imagers can create it . . . still . . . you'd need warships with iron hulls and decks, and they'd be slow and sluggish under sail . . . be costly and take forever to build, too . . ."

Quaeryt nodded and kept listening, even as he took a healthy helping of the sauce-covered cutlets and mashed potatoes on the platter passed down the table.

39

After breakfast on Mardi, Quaeryt went to his small but well-appointed study, where he settled in to think about all the documents he had read over the previous three days and what they had conveyed to him. At half a quint before ninth glass he crossed the second level of the palace to the south side and entered the anteroom to the governor's study.

An undercaptain in pristine greens looked up from the table desk nearest the closed door to the study. "Scholar Quaeryt. Please have a seat. The governor will be ready for you shortly."

Quaeryt sat in one of the wooden captain's chairs set just out from the wall. He'd barely settled himself when the door to the study opened and a trim but muscular man of moderate height stepped out, wearing perfectly tailored undress greens, with the silver starbursts of a marshal on his collars and everything in place from his short blond hair, interspersed with a few silver strands, down to his polished black boots.

The cheerful-looking pale green eyes that flanked a straight strong nose took in Quaeryt, and a smile appeared on the governor's lightly tanned and weathered face.

"So you're the scholar Lord Bhayar sent?"

"Yes, sir. Quaeryt Rytersyn."

"Come in." With another smile, Rescalyn gestured and turned, as if expecting Quaeryt to follow him.

Quaeryt did, and the undercaptain quickly stood and moved to close the study door behind him.

Rescalyn did not seat himself behind the wide but simple table desk that held only a single leather folder. Instead, he stood by the window, not facing toward either it or Quaeryt. "Beautiful day, isn't it? It's hard to believe that in little more than a season, the snow will begin to fall."

Quaeryt knew that the cold struck early in Tilbor . . . but snow in the middle of autumn? "It's a long winter here, I take it."

"Especially compared to Solis . . . if you can call the slight chill there in Ianus and Fevier winter." The governor turned. "Do sit down." He seated himself and waited several moments before speaking again. "The princeps tells me that you're here to find out why the Tilborans are so stiff-necked and ungovernable."

"I don't believe—"

Rescalyn laughed genially and waved off Quaeryt's words. "Spare me the politely worded qualifications and denials. He's the Lord of Telaryn. He wants to know why I continue to need a full regiment, with supporting battalions, and all the golds they require ten years after his father conquered Tilbor. Either that or the High Holders in the rest of Telaryn are complaining about their tariffs, and he needs a better explanation. He's got his hands full with the border problems with Kharst and with the Autarch of Antiago, and the last place he wants to be is another thousand milles farther away. So he sent you. I understand. There's nothing mysterious about it."

Quaeryt couldn't help but be impressed by the governor's words and understanding, not to mention the warmth and understanding in his tone, or the amused smile with which Rescalyn had finished his statement. "He did express concern."

"Of course he did. Any ruler with brains would be concerned, and I'm glad to see that he is. I'll be more than happy to make sure that you see and understand fully the problems we're facing here, and I've already conveyed to the princeps that you're to be given every opportunity to verify anything he or I may tell you—or to find, if you can, anything that contradicts what we may say. I doubt that you'll find anything contrary to what we've reported to Lord Bhayar, but I can definitely understand why he needs to know. The best place to start would be the dispatch files, and when you leave here, I'll have Undercaptain Caermyt take you there."

"I appreciate that."

"I understand you've been studying in the Khanar's library and the archives of the khanarate. What do you think so far?"

"If the archives represent what happened, it appears that Tilbor was relatively well-governed until the last years, and then all internal organization in the palace suffered."

"You're being careful in a scholarly way. When Eleonyd sickened, everything collapsed. That was always the problem with the khanarate. It all rested on the organization and personal strength of the Khanar. If he was strong and disciplined, so was Tilbor. If not . . . well . . . you can see what happened. That's always a problem in governing. If there's not enough structure, and the leadership is weak, the land falls. If there's too much structure, no matter what kind of leadership there is, the land is far weaker than it should be." Another smile followed. "What did you think of the library?"

"I thought it most impressive, frankly."

"So do I. I've read several fascinating books from there . . . when I've had time away from my duties."

"Is there one you'd recommend?"

"The library has so many excellent volumes that I'd be doing it and you a disservice to pick any one out . . . although I will say that there are some outstanding works I've never seen before in among the volumes on history and tactics." A more serious expression appeared. "What arrangements have you made for informing Lord Bhayar of your progress and findings?"

"I had thought that presumptuous until I was here."

"So it would have been." Rescalyn nodded. "I would suggest you send a report with the regimental courier who leaves for Solis every Vendrei morning at seventh glass. I don't want to see your report, only that you make one, and I'll go even farther. You can hand that sealed report to him just before he leaves the palace."

"I'd be happy to—"

"Nonsense. That's your report to your lord. There is one other recommendation I would offer. It's up to you, of course, but I would suggest that you accompany patrols through various areas of Tilbor and see matters for yourself."

"That's very kind of you, sir, and I would like very much to do that. I'd also like to hear what you have to say. Lord Bhayar was most complimentary about your abilities and perception."

"I'm not kind. Just practical." Rescalyn paused. "I will certainly let you know what I think, but I will defer doing so until you have read the dispatches and seen more of Tilbor with regimental patrols. I'd like you to come to some conclusions before I say much."

Quaeryt couldn't argue with that logic, even as he respected the way in which the governor had maneuvered matters. He also had to ask himself why there was something about the governor that bothered him. Rescalyn had been open and polite and direct, and certainly pleasant. He also hadn't mentioned the local scholars, and that suggested, again, that Quaeryt proceed carefully in dealing with that area.

Rescalyn stood. "It's good to meet you, and I'm glad to see that Lord Bhayar shares my concerns about the unsettled nature of the hill country and backwoods here. Caermyt will show you the dispatch room."

"Thank you, sir." Quaeryt inclined his head in respect, then turned and left the study.

The undercaptain was on his feet well before the scholar closed the door to the governor's study. "This way, sir."

As he followed Undercaptain Caermyt down the main staircase, Quaeryt thought about the governor's not-so-veiled order that he needed to accompany Telaryn soldiers into situations that might be dangerous. He couldn't help but wonder why imagers couldn't do more . . . or what they—or he—could do if he were caught in a battle situation. He decided that the lesser danger might be to do a little more in trying to expand his imaging abilities.

At the bottom of the staircase, the undercaptain turned back east along the main-floor center hallway, but only for about ten yards before he produced a key and unlocked the door. Then he handed the key to Quaeryt. "If you would lock the door and return the key to me whenever you're not here, sir, the governor would appreciate it."

"I'll certainly do so, and thank you."

"My pleasure, sir." Caermyt turned and walked quickly back toward the main staircase.

Quaeryt stepped into the room, lit, as was the library, by thin high windows on the outer wall, and closed the door behind him. There were rows and rows of neatly stacked boxes, and a single wide table desk next to the inside wall almost beside the door. A bracket held a pair of lamps, positioned over the desk. Neither was lit, but a striker was set in a holder on the otherwise bare wooden surface.

Almost ten years of dispatches—and where was he supposed to begin?

Quaeryt shook his head and moved toward the last box, the one with the top beside it, rather than covering it. That was as good a place to start as any.

40

Quaeryt spent the rest of Mardi in the dispatch room, with various breaks, until time for the evening meal. While he talked occasionally, he mostly listened through the meal and for a time thereafter, before taking a walk through the gardens and retiring to his quarters.

After a good night's sleep and an early breakfast, he appeared in the study assigned to him on Meredi morning, then retrieved the key from Undercaptain Caermyt and made his way back down to peruse more dispatches. The previous day, he had read the dispatches for most of the past year. While some of the details certainly supported what the governor and the various officers had revealed, he had learned little that was new, only gained more information that shed little light on why matters were as they appeared to be.

After what he had already read, he turned his attention to those from the first months after Lord Chayar had taken the palace—and found there were none. The first dispatches in the files began some four months after the fall of Tilbor, and they were from Governor Fhayt to Lord Chayar. The tone of Fhayt's dispatches was markedly different from that of the later ones sent by Rescalyn. That Quaeryt could see almost from the first. He paused, then read several lines from one sent by Fhayt.

... the northern High Holders complain ceaselessly. They want the port of Noira rebuilt in stone. They want a coastal road from Midcote to Noira...The High Holders of the south are more polite. They ask me to consider how a new paved stone road from the river piers will lead to greater tariff collections. They want more. They say it better...

Quaeryt walked over to one of the first boxes he'd gone through and pulled out a dispatch from Rescalyn, almost at random, reading it in turn.

...tariff collection patrol south of the Boran Hills was attacked, but only one man was wounded. Three brigands were killed, and one captured, but he offered no useful information...now have three farriers trained, which will reduce costs of re-shoeing the cavalry mounts...

He nodded and replaced Rescalyn's dispatch, then went back to reading the ones from Fhayt.

After reading through several months of dispatches, Quaeryt realized something—Fhayt had never mentioned timber holders or backwoods barons or the like. At times, he referred to attacks or incidents near or in the hills, but he never made any attributions as to who or what might be behind them.

By ninth glass, Quaeryt needed a break. He rose, snuffed the twin lamps, and then left the dispatch chamber, locking it behind him. He walked down the long main-level corridor until he reached the library, where he opened the door and stepped inside.

"You're back again, sir."

"There's a lot to learn." Quaeryt smiled. "You're here most of the time, I take it?"

"Yes, sir. Well...me and Khernan, but I'm here in the day, and he's here in the early evening."

"I just wondered if you could help me out. I met with the governor yesterday, and he was commending the library to me, and he mentioned a history volume that he had found especially enlightening . . ." Quaeryt offered a helpless shrug. "I was trying to remember so much. . . . Is there any way . . . ?"

"I couldn't say which book it was, sir."

"Oh . . . I was hoping . . . I hate to have to admit to him that I didn't remember . . ."

"But . . . sir . . . he did insist that I write down any volume he took out of the library. He always returned the books, every one, but I do have a list here . . . that's of the ones he's taken in the last month or so. If you look at it . . . maybe that will jog your memory . . ."

"That would be so helpful. Thank you."

Quaeryt studied the list of six books. One was listed twice. Then he coughed several times, bending over with the list in hand. When he was bent almost double, he concentrated on looking hard at the list and imaging it. Just before he straightened he slipped the second list inside his jacket.

"I'm sorry. I must have caught something in my throat. Thank you. I think it must have been the one called *Historical Elements of Strategy*. I'll see if it's here. Thank you again."

"I'm glad I could help."

"So am I. I would have hated to have had to bother the governor."

"I understand that, sir." The squad leader smiled.

It only took Quaeryt a fraction of a glass to locate *Historical Elements of Strategy* and to repair to one of the comfortable leather chairs. He did not so much skim or read the thin book, but study it, trying to deduce what sections appeared to be more heavily perused.

In the end, he thought three places had been read more often, a guess, based on a short blond hair, a tiny scrap of paper, and what appeared to have been turned-down page corners.

Only a guess, he reminded himself.

> . . . no commander should ever forget that his men are his only resource and that his officers must be an extension of his will and must always set an example and demonstrate through acts that they care for their men. Yet that care must be seen as equal, fair, and above all impartial, and it should also demand that every man do his best in support of his comrades and of the objective to be attained . . . Nor should officers ever arrogate themselves above their men by their mere position. They must be superior in act, ability, and demeanor to those they command . . .

The second passage reflected on power more indirectly.

> . . . the key to ruling is to assure support from those with power, whether that power be control of food supplies, access to rivers, or the ability to turn trade and commerce to one's own ends . . .

One phrase on the third turned-down page struck Quaeryt particularly.

> The best strategy is one carried out in such openness that no enemy, or ally, understands that it is a strategy until the trap is sprung.

Such openness that no one understands?
Quaeryt nodded. Those passages made sense, and

they were practical, commonsense approaches that fit in with what little he'd seen of the governor.

He closed the book, replaced it on the shelf, and returned to the dispatch room.

By close to noon, Quaeryt had struggled through two years of dispatches, most of them dealing with the quiet stubbornness and intransigence of the locals, including the High Holders. Only a few dispatches mentioned attacks on soldiers, and while most took place in or near the hills or timberlands, there were still reports of attacks elsewhere. Then he read a very different dispatch.

> ... grieves me to report the wounding of Governor Fhayt in an unprovoked attack on his way to meet with High Holder Fhaedyrk ... brigands were repulsed by the squad accompanying the governor, although that squad was outnumbered three to one ... governor took three crossbow bolts ... more than twenty brigands killed ...
>
> ... immediately dispatched the Sixth Cavalry Battalion ... followed the surviving brigands for twenty milles ... captured another fifteen ... revealed that the group had been recruited by a former officer of the Khanar's Guard ... only known as "the captain" ... possible ties to timber holders north of the Boran Hills ...
>
> ... as princeps, acting as governor and awaiting your decision, on who should best represent you in Tilbor ...

The dispatch was signed by Straesyr.

For the next two weeks, so was every other dispatch. Then for another two weeks, the dispatches were again signed by Fhayt—including his last, that announced

Rescalyn had arrived as his replacement as regional governor. But all the dispatches signed by either Fhayt or Straesyr seemed to report roughly the same things. While Quaeryt couldn't be absolutely sure, not without counting, and that would have been even more tedious and time-consuming, it appeared to him that the number of attacks on Telaryn troopers was either holding steady or increasing very slightly over the next few years.

At some time close to third glass, there was a knock on the door to the dispatch room. Almost with relief, Quaeryt stood, turned, and opened the door.

Undercaptain Caermyt stood there. "Sir, the governor would like to know if you would like to accompany a patrol tomorrow."

"Yes, I would."

"Then you should be ready to mount up at half past seventh glass. The patrol will be led by Undercaptain Jusaph. He will be expecting you."

"Thank you, and convey my thanks to the governor."

"Yes, sir." Caermyt turned and headed back toward the main staircase.

Quaeryt slowly closed the door and sat back down at the table desk. He hadn't asked where the patrol was going, or what it was doing. He'd assumed it was just a daily patrol . . . but was it?

He looked down at the dispatch he'd been reading and then away, looking blankly at the paneled wall at the end of the chamber.

What exactly do patrols do?

For better or worse, he was about to find out.

He looked back down at the dispatch, finished reading it, and went to the next one.

41

Quaeryt was still thinking over all the dispatches he'd read in two days—close to two-thirds of them, he estimated—when he entered the officers' mess for supper. This time he was earlier and took a place at the far table . . . and found that Phargos and then Skarpa joined him. With the major was a captain who looked to be about Quaeryt's age.

"Taenyd, this is Scholar Quaeryt. He's attached to the princeps's staff."

Taenyd nodded politely. "I heard we had a scholar now. Are you doing a history of the regiment or something?"

"More like a comparative history of Tilbor," replied Quaeryt with a smile, pouring some of the lager. "I'm trying to write an explanation of why some Tilborans are so stiff-necked, especially those in the hills and the forests."

"Most of— If you lived there, you'd be stiff-necked, too. The trees are so tall and thick that it's always gloomy, even in midsummer. In winter, the snow's always drifting down, even when it hasn't snowed for days. It's too cold to bathe, and most of the hill scum stink more than rank sows. . . ."

"Enough . . . enough," protested Skarpa with a laugh. "You tell him too much, and he won't have the scholarly joy of discovering it all on his own."

"Scholarly joy? Isn't that a contradiction in terms?"

countered the captain, immediately flushing and turning to Quaeryt. "I'm sorry, sir."

"For some scholars, you're probably right," admitted Quaeryt cheerfully. "And I'm sure not all Tilborans are stiff-necked. Some seemed very friendly when I rode through Tilbora." He didn't want to say more than that. He took a swallow of the lager—far better than that which he had had at the Ecoliae or Jardyna.

"Most people in Tilbora are. They're practical," said the captain. "That's why they get along with the governor."

"He seems very practical."

"That could be his patronymic," interjected Phargos.

Conversation slowed as the platters appeared, this time a form of ribs stewed in a red sauce, accompanied by seasoned rice with raisins. Quaeryt had to admit that the food in the mess was excellent. After a time, he looked to Skarpa and asked in a low voice, "Is the fare the men get . . . ?"

"Pretty much the same. The setting's not nearly so nice. That's the difference."

Quaeryt nodded and took a swallow of the lager. The ribs were pepper-spiced and every bit as hot as anything he'd had in Solis.

"I saw you at the service on Solayi, scholar," offered Phargos.

"I enjoyed your homily."

The chorister laughed. "That's what those who aren't sure they believe in the Nameless always say."

"I don't believe, and I don't not believe. I just don't know if there is a Nameless." Quaeryt grinned and added, "And if I said I did, wouldn't that be a form of Naming?"

"You scholars . . ." Phargos's voice held humor and exasperation.

"I told you he'd liven things up," added Skarpa.

Quaeryt took more of the ribs, hot as they were, and even more rice. It had been a long day . . . listening as Taenyd talked with the young undercaptain who had seated himself beside him . . .

". . . once you get beyond the lower hills . . . never know when someone's going to let fly with an arrow or a crossbow bolt . . . was that way even for the Khanar's Guard . . ."

". . . don't like anybody very much . . ."

". . . think the hills are theirs . . ."

"Would muskets help at all?" asked Quaeryt, turning to Skarpa.

"Not likely. We've got one company of musketeers. They're not much use except in a set battle. I'd send them to defend Ferravyl in case Kharst attacked there. They're heavy and hard to move. No good in the rain, or in the snow . . . never replace pike and blades, not really. Rather have a halberd company than a musket company, and you know what most officers think of halberds."

Quaeryt didn't, but he let it pass, instead pointing out, "Bows aren't much good in the rain, either."

"No . . . but they're light enough that the archers can get out of the way of a foot or mounted charge. Not that we have any archers right now. Well . . . one company, and that's almost none."

The conversation for the remainder of the meal dealt more with the weather and when the late-harvest rains would come and turn the back roads into quagmires.

Later, when Quaeryt left the mess, he made his way to the gardens to think. A light breeze rustled through the trees and plants, just enough to be pleasant—but he was anything but soothed. As he sat on a bench beside what looked to be a dwarf apple tree—and all the apples in easy reach had been picked, or perhaps harvested and stored for the winter—he couldn't help thinking about the patrol on Jeudi . . . and the matter-of-fact comments by Taenyd. Both reminded him that he'd considered a few times that he needed to expand his imaging abilities.

But how could he forget how he puked his guts out, or the endless days of fever, and the weeks regaining his strength after attempting to image a single gold? How could he not forget that?

Yet . . . if he kept riding on patrols, he'd need more imaging skills . . . and the strength to handle them.

Quaeryt took a deep breath. What exactly could he try to do? He did know that imaging things that were common, like wood or clay or bread, usually didn't have a bad effect on him.

Could he image something like a shield? He frowned. Imaging things out of iron wasn't easy, and iron was heavy. Besides, how could he hold it in place? Something that heavy would just fall to the ground. And trying to image an iron shield—or anything like it—would be useless against arrows or crossbow bolts because he'd have to react, and reacting after he got hit with an arrow wouldn't be terribly useful . . . if he even happened to be in any condition to image anything.

There was water all around, and ice could stop an arrow . . . but ice thick enough to stop an arrow or crossbow bolt would be heavy. Not as heavy as iron, but too heavy to be practical.

He rubbed his forehead. There had to be a way.

Finally, when he could think of no more possibilities, he stood and started back to his quarters. He was tired. He hadn't realized just how tiring reading dispatch after dispatch was. Maybe he could think better in the morning.

He just hoped the patrol wasn't headed where he'd come under attack.

42·

Quaeryt made sure he was in the stables early on Meredi morning, because he was concerned about how long it would take him to saddle the mare. As he checked her before beginning, he could see that she'd been groomed recently . . . although he was supposed to, he recalled belatedly. While he doubted he was anywhere as proficient as the cavalry rankers and officers, he was out in the courtyard in front of the stables and mounted before half past seven. Under a hazy sky that promised another warm day, he glanced around at the column forming up. Two squads, he judged—and that meant that the patrol wasn't going anywhere near the hills.

He was still looking around when an undercaptain close to his own age rode over and reined up. "Scholar Quaeryt?"

"I am. You're Undercaptain Jusaph?"

"Yes, sir. I understand you'll be riding with us this morning."

"If that won't inconvenience you."

"No, sir. This is just a routine patrol along the main road to the river piers, then up the river and then around the inner hill road and back here. I thought you'd ride with me, and I could explain things."

"I'd appreciate that."

From behind them came a series of commands.

"First squad! Form up!"

"Second squad! Form up."

Jusaph rode to the front of the column, then turned in the saddle. "Forward!"

Two outriders led the way through the east gates, down the paved lane and over the moat bridge, and out through the lower gates. Behind them rode the undercaptain and Quaeryt, and the two squads followed.

"Today . . . we'll be taking the main road straight to the river piers," offered Jusaph as his mount crossed the road paralleling the moat. "We'll see teamsters early on, but most of them headed that way will already be near the piers."

"I noticed a group of shops and cafés over that way when I rode in. . . ."

"Yes, sir. That's the vale. That's where the men can go when they're off duty . . . if they want."

"It's frowned on for officers and squad leaders?"

"You might say that. But the men need some place . . . and there was a bad incident years ago. The former governor had to level several blocks more to the south in an older part of the west of Tilbora. Governor Rescalyn made it clear that he never wanted anything like that to happen again. Ever. On Vendrei and Samedi nights we run special patrols through the vale. Anyone who causes trouble gets drummed out of the regiment. Well . . . anyone who causes trouble that's not their fault anywhere gets drummed out."

Quaeryt merely listened as the undercaptain went on.

"One of the reasons for the local patrols is to remind everyone that we're here, and that Tilbor is part of Telaryn. Also, the local patrollers can ask us for help if they need it."

"Has that ever happened to you?"

"When I was a senior squad leader last summer, we chased down a bunch that had looted a silversmith's on the north side of town. We caught every one of them." Jusaph grinned. "We were just lucky to be riding through the square a few moments after it happened. The captain told me later it was the only time he knew we'd done that. But people around there still wave and smile when we ride through." He paused. "The standing orders are that we're to cover the same area each time, but always in a different order and timing."

"That's so no one knows exactly when you'll be somewhere?"

"Yes, sir."

Quaeryt kept listening for a time until Jusaph fell silent, then said, "Might I ask where you're from?"

"Oh . . . I'm from northwest of Tilbora . . . just been promoted from senior squad leader . . . a number of the undercaptains and junior captains are from the south here."

Quaeryt found it amusing that Jusaph referred to Tilbora as "south" when Nacliano and Solis were hundreds of milles farther south, but he only asked, "Isn't Captain Taenyd . . . ?"

"He was one of the first. He's a good officer."

"I have the feeling that the governor doesn't hold much for officers who aren't good, no matter where they come from."

"No, sir. He's made that very clear to all officers."

"Where exactly northwest of Tilbora are you from?" asked Quaeryt conversationally.

"Not too far. Haesylt. It's on the river."

"Your family still lives there?"

"Every last one, except me. They're all river people. They run barges from as far north as Amdermyt, all the way down to the river piers in Tilbora."

"Barges . . . that sounds like a fairly large business."

"Last time I was home, Haermyn showed me the newest one he'd built . . . it was the twenty-first in service . . ."

Quaeryt kept listening.

The column was riding through an area of shops—it might even have been the square where Quaeryt had watered the mare in the middle of the night—when a young man sweeping the steps in front of a cooperage looked up, smiled, and waved to Jusaph.

The undercaptain waved back. "Laernyk. He's a cousin of sorts. That's his wife's father's cooperage, but he's only got daughters, and he treats Laernyk like his own son."

"Is he from Haesylt?"

"His father is my father's cousin, and he moved here before I was born, well back before the fall of the Pretender."

When the patrol reached the river piers, Jusaph had both squads stand down and water the mounts from the public fountain while he rode over to the piers alone and inspected them. He also talked briefly to a ferryman who was awaiting travelers or wagons. After he watered the mare, Quaeryt noted that there were two donkey-powered ferries, although he'd seen only one when he'd crossed the river.

As he waited, he saw a young woman walking along the side of the square that held the fountain. With her was a young boy, scarcely more than a toddler. The two stopped, and the mother pointed at the nearest horse.

"See the horsey? That's a horse. The soldiers ride them. Your uncle Casym is a soldier, and he rides a horse like that."

"Horsey . . . go see."

"Not now . . . dear. You can see Uncle Casym's horse someday."

The mother let her son watch for several moments before she gently urged him along and toward the shops to the north.

Jusaph had taken close to two quints dealing with the three ferrymen at the piers before he returned. Quaeryt walked his mare to the fountain to accompany Jusaph, but stood back while the undercaptain pumped fresh water into the horse trough.

"Is it part of your duties to talk to the ferrymen?"

"We're supposed to be friendly and interested. I just ask them if there's anything we should know about, ask how the river's running . . . try to let them know we're here if they need us."

"It must help that you know the river."

"Only a handful remember when I was a boy bow-poler," replied Jusaph with a laugh. "I hope they don't hold it against me. I wasn't very good."

"How did you end up in the regiment?"

"I always liked horses . . . and I'm the youngest. With five older brothers . . . well . . . it seemed to make sense to do something else, and the governor was offering a two-gold bonus for recruits who made it through training. I did and gave the golds to Diera for her dowry."

"Diera's a sister?"

"Practically raised me. Mother died when I was three. Anyway . . . it's worked out. . . ." He smiled and turned. "Squad leaders! Time to mount up!"

After watering the mare, Quaeryt didn't quite scramble into his saddle, but he certainly wasn't as graceful as the undercaptain.

From the piers, the patrol continued along the river road, the same one that Quaeryt had ridden twice before—although once had been the first time he entered Tilbora, and the second had been in the dark, and he didn't recall a number of structures along the river, but all of them looked more solid than he'd recalled. Was he just getting used to Tilbor, or had he failed to understand at first that everything was built more to withstand the impact of the long winters than for superficial attractiveness?

After riding a good glass, during which several of the rankers—and Jusaph—got waves and smiles, the patrol rode past the road Quaeryt had taken to the Ecoliae and continued along the river road, past even the ramshackle pier where Quaeryt had thrown Chardyn's body into the river. No one came out to tell the undercaptain about a body, but it was likely the river had carried it farther downstream. After another half glass, the undercaptain turned the patrol due north.

"This is the inner hill road," explained the undercaptain. "If we'd ridden another two milles along the river, we would have come to the outer hill road. They both join about a mille west of the palace."

"Do they become the road that runs along the dry moat?"

"That's the one. The next time we patrol, we'll likely go out that way and take the outer hill road. We always have to do the river road."

Again, Quaeryt listened for another quint before asking, "Is there a Scholars' House somewhere around here?"

"Yes, sir." Jusaph pointed eastward. "Do you see

the hillside with the domed building? That's the an-omen for the scholars, and their place—it's called the Ecoliae—is on the next hill toward us. They've got a school there. Most of the students are from trade or holder families. There used to be some from the hill holders, who lived there, but I don't know if there are now."

"I thought the hill holders were the ones who at-tack your patrols. Why . . . ? I'm not sure I under-stand," Quaeryt said.

"They're not the same, sir. Well . . . most aren't. The trouble comes from those who hold timberlands. Most of the hill holders do, but some don't. I think the smaller holders are afraid to displease the larger ones."

"I'd think that would make it difficult. For the gov-ernor, I mean. Scholars usually don't ask about the parents of their students so long as the parents pay for their schooling."

"Our orders are to leave the scholars alone. That's unless they do something against the law, but they never have. Not that anyone's been able to prove."

"I'd thought about visiting them, but I think I'd best refrain until I understand how matters are."

"I'm sure they'd be quite friendly."

"That may be, but since I'm on the governor's staff . . ."

"I see what you mean."

"How old is the scholars' place? Do you know?"

"It's been around for a long time. That's all I know. You're the first scholar I've ever talked to."

Quaeryt understood the question the undercaptain hadn't asked. "I'm afraid I'm not like most scholars. I left the scholars before I finished schooling and went to sea. After six years I came back and pleaded for them to take me back." He hadn't pleaded; he'd bargained, but that wasn't something he wanted to get into with Jusaph. "They took me back."

"I wondered, sir."

For the next half mille, the undercaptain was quiet, and Quaeryt let him have his space. Finally, he did ask, "Will you do a patrol tomorrow or Vendrei?"

"No, sir. The mounts get a rest tomorrow, but the men will spend the day on blade drills. On Vendrei, we'll be at the east maneuver fields practicing full-company exercises."

"They keep you occupied."

"Commander   Myskyl—he's   the   regiment commander—says that there are only two kinds of soldiers: those who are always prepared to fight and those who are dead. Some of the majors think we'll have to fight the Bovarians before long. You've just come from Solis. What do you think?"

"I don't know. I've heard stories that Lord Bhayar's concerned about them, especially after the way Rex Kharst massacred so many of the Khellans."

"That's what Major Skarpa says. You can't trust them. Anyone who does is foolish."

Quaeryt nodded and shifted his weight in the saddle. It was well past the second glass of the afternoon, and most of those four glasses since he'd first mounted up had been in the saddle.

As they neared the Telaryn Palace, Quaeryt couldn't help but think that, for all the concerned tone in the dispatches he had read, he certainly hadn't seen any signs of hostility on the part of the people as the patrol had ridden past. People had looked up, then gone back about their business, some smiling, some frowning, some indifferent, but no one's behavior had seemed to change at the appearance of the patrol.

While he didn't think he'd learn anything new, once

he stabled and groomed the mare, he would finish reading all the rest of the dispatches. With his luck, if he didn't, the one dispatch he missed would be the one that would have told him something he needed to know.

He shifted his weight in the saddle again. With each passing quint, riding got more uncomfortable.

43

After returning from the patrol, Quaeryt stabled and groomed the mare, then made his way up to the second level of the palace, where he stopped to inform Vhorym that he had returned and that he would be heading to the dispatch room.

"You might check your desk before you go to the dispatch room, sir."

"Thank you. I will." Quaeryt managed a smile, then turned and made his way to his study.

There on the desk was an envelope with his name on it, and underneath his name was also written "Scholar Assistant to the Princeps."

Now what?

He opened the letter, took out the single sheet, and read:

THE HONORABLE RESCALYN CALYNSYN,
MARSHAL AND GOVERNOR OF TILBOR,
REQUESTS THE HONOR OF YOUR PRESENCE
AT A RECEPTION IN THE PALACE,
AT THE SIXTH GLASS OF THE EVENING,

SAMEDI, 35 AGOSTAS
IN THE GREEN SALON.

There was no line suggesting a response, but then, since Quaeryt was assigned to the princeps, who reported directly to the governor, the invitation was essentially a command to appear . . . if a very polite one.

He had no formal attire, or even the equivalent of a dress uniform. The new browns were the best he could manage, and he had not worn one of the new sets yet. They'd have to do.

He slipped the invitation—or summons—back inside the envelope and placed the envelope in the single flat drawer in the table desk. Then he left the study and headed over to the governor's anteroom to obtain the key to the dispatch room. He had to wait almost half a quint before Caermyt returned, and he began to wonder if he should image a copy of the key.

No. That's an invitation to trouble, especially if you're found there when Caermyt has the key. He could use an imaging concealment. . . .

He shook his head and waited.

Once he obtained the key, he hurried downstairs, but he'd no more than started to light the lamps in the dispatch room than he realized he had to write a report of his arrival to Bhayar immediately because the weekly dispatch rider left early the next morning . . . and he needed to finish the reply to Vaelora—for more reasons than one.

Rather than return the key, because he intended to finish reading the dispatches after the evening meal, he locked the dispatch room and hurried back to his own quarters, where he retrieved the letter he'd begun to Vaelora, before heading back to his formal study.

Once there, he started in on the report to Bhayar, knowing that it would likely be read long before it reached the Lord of Telaryn. He made it short, and the only inaccuracies were in what he did not report, because he mentioned the travel and the delay in Nacliano, as well as his concerns about the attitude toward scholars, but not his actions there. He also reported the storm and shipwreck, and his illness, possible poisoning, and his recovery, but then noted that after recovering he had traveled to Tilbora and reported to the princeps on the twenty-seventh of Agostas. He concluded by noting the courtesy and the helpfulness of both the princeps and the governor in allowing him full access to all parts of the Telaryn Palace and its records, as well as arranging for him to accompany various patrols.

Finishing the letter to Vaelora took more time. He did add a section about his duties in general and a few words about the one patrol on which he had ridden.

> . . . Although this was the first patrol I accompanied, the governor has assured me that there will be many more so that I can fully experience the difficulties and the successes that he and his regiment have achieved and report most accurately to Lord Bhayar. It does appear that the problems he faces in dealing with Tilbor lie in the areas away from Tilbora, especially in the far north and in the hilly timberlands of the Boran Hills. He has also had much success in recruiting men and junior officers, especially from around Tilbora, where there are warmer feelings toward him and his men. I have not met with any High Holders or merchants but look forward to encountering the latter as time permits. . . .
>
> I offer my deep appreciation for your thoughts and concerns, and especially for your efforts to assure that your correspondence did indeed reach me.

Quaeryt pondered the closing for a time before settling on "In sincerest admiration and appreciation."

By the time he finished, addressed, and sealed both
missives, it was approaching time for supper, and he
slipped both inside the desk drawer, then left the study
to wash up and make his way to the mess.

When Quaeryt stepped into the mess, he saw that
the chamber was already almost completely filled, and
all of the close to a hundred officers were wearing
jackets. He recalled, if belatedly, that Jeudi night was
mess night. He was wearing a jacket, but a scholar's
brown jacket was certainly not as formal as even the
green jackets worn with undress greens.

"Your place is near the bottom of the nearest table,
sir," offered the squad leader by the doorway, "where
the green oblong is. The far table is all for undercaptains."

"Thank you."

Quaeryt walked toward the nearest table, and located the only vacant place—where just to the left
was a green cloth folded into an oblong. He sat down
quickly.

To his left was a black-haired, thin-faced captain.
"Greetings. You must be the scholar. I'm Haestyn."

"Quaeryt. I'm pleased to meet you."

"Dueryl," offered the undercaptain directly across
the table from Quaeryt. "We wondered who was the
new captain. Haestyn's been junior captain for over a
month."

"Scholars don't really have rank," said Quaeryt. "I
think they decided to put me between ranks for just
that reason."

"That sounds like regimental thinking," murmured
someone farther down the table among the undercaptains.

"All rise for the marshal!" boomed out a voice.

Along with the others, Quaeryt rose. He glanced toward the door, where Rescalyn stepped into the mess, also wearing the green undress uniform and jacket.

"As you were!" ordered Rescalyn.

The officers remained standing as Rescalyn walked to the end of the center table where he was greeted by a gray-haired commander, presumably Myskyl, Commander of the Regiment.

Then Rescalyn motioned, and all the officers seated themselves. The governor remained standing. After everyone was seated, he began to speak.

"Gentlemen of the mess . . . I can't ever stand here and look out without feeling a debt of gratitude for the dedication and leadership you all embody." There was a pause and then a grin. "But I'll be the first to apply a boot to your backside if you ever try to rest on it . . . or on your laurels. . . ."

The way in which Rescalyn spoke brought low laughs from the assembled officers.

". . . you may ask why we're working so hard when most of our problems lie in and around the Boran Hills or with a few disgruntled High Holders so far to the north that they're walled off behind ice for all but a few weeks out of the year. The reason is simple. There's a ruler. Rex Kharst." Rescalyn's sardonic delivery brought more chuckles. "He has this habit of massacring people, and he'd like to put all of Lydar under his fat thumb. We have to be ready to deal with him when he tries . . . and after what he did to the good people of Khel, there's no doubt that he'll try, sooner more likely than later. Just keep that in mind.

"Now . . . I'd like to note particularly noteworthy evolutions this past week . . ."

As he listened, Quaeryt couldn't help but note that the governor's delivery was far better than his words and that most officers listened intently.

". . . and like all marshals . . . I've probably used more words to say less . . . and I wish it were the other way around. . . . Enjoy yourselves."

Abruptly, Quaeryt realized something else. Rescalyn had never mentioned Lord Bhayar. In fact, while the governor mentioned Bhayar to Quaeryt, Quaeryt had never heard the governor utter Bhayar's name or title in public, and certainly not before his officers.

"Red or white wine, scholar?" asked Dueryl.

Quaeryt had seen the carafes on the table, but hadn't actually paid them much attention, since he'd been concentrating on Rescalyn. "What's on the platters?"

"Whitefish with a cream sauce or veal cutlets with mushrooms and brown sauce."

"Red, thank you." Quaeryt took the carafe and filled the goblet he'd been provided rather than the mug usually placed before each officer.

"Scholar . . . how soon do you think Kharst will attack?" That came from the captain beside Haestyn.

"I'm more of a historian. Historically, there are more attacks in late spring and summer. Offhand, I don't know of any wars started in late fall or winter. If I had to guess . . ." Quaeryt paused, then went on, "I'd say that if he doesn't attack now in the next week or so, it's unlikely until spring. But, as I said, I'm a historian. What do you think?"

"If he attacked in midfall, we'd have trouble getting from here to the border with Bovaria."

"You'd have to swing south of Montagne," replied Quaeryt, "but that would only add a week or two, and his forces would have trouble in the north, especially if they tried to move on Extela."

"He uses more muskets, and they aren't much good in the rain, and there are a lot of cold rains north of Solis in fall and winter," added someone else.

". . . it rained in Khel, and that didn't stop them . . ."

As the others talked, Quaeryt helped himself to the veal and mushrooms and the seasoned rice, as well as the stewed and sweetened quince slices. Then he began to eat, occasionally adding a comment, but mainly enjoying the fare and the wine.

Later, during a lull in the conversation, Quaeryt looked across at Dueryl. "I've been told we get paid tomorrow, but not the details. . . ."

"Oh . . . they set up a pay table here in the mess for the glass before the evening meal, and if you don't want to take it, they'll just leave it in your pay account until you do."

"That's good to know."

A louder voice rode over the others. "I still say that we'll be at war in less than a year. . . ."

". . . where . . . with Kharst or the Antiagons?"

After leaving the mess, much later, Quaeryt headed back to the main part of the palace. He had to finish reading the remainder of the dispatches.

44

After sitting through mess night, Quaeryt had returned to the dispatch room with the key he'd kept and spent two more glasses reading by lamplight in order to finish reading all the dispatches. None of those he read differed in tone or outlook from all those he'd read before. There were only a few mentions of disturbances in or around Tilbora. As in the dispatches he'd read earlier, almost all the problems mentioned were in or around the Boran Hills, from what he'd been able to tell. He'd gone to sleep Jeudi night more confused than ever.

He was less sore and more rested when he woke on Vendrei morning, but no less confused. He ate quickly, then retrieved both envelopes from his study and hurried out to the dispatch station next to the gatehouse. There the courier waited beside his mount, accompanied by two other hard-faced rankers, already mounted. Quaeryt handed the first envelope to the man.

He looked at it and at Quaeryt, then nodded. "Yes, sir, for Lord Bhayar. The governor told us." The sealed report went into one of the saddlebags. Then he looked at the second, and his eyes widened, doubtless at the addressee—Mistress Vaelora Chayardyr. But he nodded again. "Yes, sir."

"Thank you." Quaeryt handed over a silver—the rate for a private dispatch.

"Thank you, sir."

Quaeryt stepped back, but did not leave until the courier mounted and the other two riders escorted him out through the gates and down the long paved lane to the lower gates. Quaeryt had had his doubts about whether either missive would reach its destination unread, but that was why each had been written in the fashion that it had been.

The bells had just finished ringing out seventh glass when he stepped into the princeps's anteroom. "Vhorym?"

"Yes, sir."

"I'm going to be checking on some matters in the harbor area of Tilbora, in case the princeps inquires."

"Yes, sir. Thank you, sir."

After returning the dispatch-room key to Caermyt, who barely concealed a frown, even after Quaeryt's explanation that he had been reading late, Quaeryt made his way to the stable, groomed and saddled the mare, and then rode to the gatehouse, where he logged out. As he left the upper gates, he looked to the east, since that was the direction from which the wind was blowing and since the sky seemed hazy. He thought there were clouds on the horizon, but he wasn't certain, and the wind was light enough that, if a storm happened to be coming in, he should have several glasses at the least before it hit.

Still . . . he had the feeling that he had less time than he'd counted on to discover exactly what was bothering him. The problem was that there didn't seem to be a problem . . . and yet, he felt that there was.

He didn't press the mare, and it was close to an hour later before he reined up outside Thayl's stable. A burly man with a protruding paunch appeared.

"What's the tariff?"

"Depends on how long."

"No more than a couple of glasses, if that. Are you Thayl?"

"That I am. Couple of glasses is just a copper. Two coppers for all day." The big man grinned.

"I doubt it will be that long, but that's not because of the adjoining establishment. One of the patrollers suggested your stable if I happened to be spending much time around the harbor. He was rather insistent." Quaeryt dismounted and handed the reins to Thayl, along with a copper. "By the way, I'm Quaeryt."

"You with the scholars at the Ecoliae? You don't look familiar."

"No ... I'm a scholar working at the Telaryn Palace for a time."

"Never knew they had scholars there."

"They didn't." Quaeryt smiled. "Take good care of the mare. She's carried me a long ways."

"That I can do, sir." There was a pause. "What do you do there?"

"I was sent to write a history of what's happened in Tilbor since the war ended."

"Not much." Thayl spat into the street. "Could have been better. Could have been a lot worse."

"Do any of the soldiers come here ... next door, I mean?"

"Nope. Governor said that Shariela's place is off-limits. 'Sides, they got their own place out by the palace. Some of the girls went there. Said they made more." The ostler looked directly at Quaeryt again. "You sure you're not with those scholars at the Ecoliae?"

"I'm not. I did deliver a letter to a student there, as a favor to his father."

"What do you think of the place?"

"It seemed to me that it had seen better days."

"Did once. My cousin worked there. They let him go after the war. Said that they couldn't pay him no more. The Khanar used to give the scholars golds. The governor doesn't."

"Do you think he should?"

Thayl spat again. "Nope. Hard on Taxyr, but why should folks who spend all their time in books, begging your pardon, sir, get golds when the rest of us don't?"

"That's true. The Scholars' Houses in other cities don't."

"They don't?"

"No. Scholars who stay more than a night or two have to pay for their food and lodging. Why did the Khanar pay them? Do you know?"

"Always did, from way back in the time of Nidar. Couldn't say why."

"That's the way things are, sometimes." Quaeryt nodded.

"That they are. Don't you be worrying about your mare. She'll be fine."

"I'm sure she's in good hands."

Quaeryt walked from the stable and turned toward the harbor, walking past the unnamed brothel, not gawking at the women who stood just inside the windows, adorning them, after a fashion.

"Do scholars really know how to do it better?" whispered a throaty voice from one of the upper windows.

Quaeryt couldn't help grinning slightly, and he replied, "Knowledge isn't the same as skill or practice, and I defer to you ladies in both."

An amused, if husky, laugh followed.

When he reached the corner, he turned left and crossed the street. The shop on the corner was an apothecary's, and he entered.

The man behind the low counter, with the rows of shelves behind him, looked up. "I'd not be selling to you."

"I'm not looking to buy. I've been sent—"

"You're not from the Ecoliae."

"No. I came from Solis. I'm trying to get information for a history."

The apothecary nodded. "I don't know history."

Quaeryt smiled. "Recent history. What you've lived

through since the time of Eleonyd. That's all history is, except after we're dead, if it's written down, it becomes history. If it isn't, more of the truth is lost."

"Not much to say. Eleonyd was a good Khanar until he got sick. His daughter would have been a good ruler, too. Rhecyrd and the northers and the timber holders didn't like her. The Guard sat on its honor and lost it, and Chayar came in and defeated Rhecyrd and his clan militia. That's what happened. Nothing will change it."

"Why didn't the southers stand up for her?"

"We couldn't. All the men in arms from the south were in the Guard."

"But—"

"I'd rather not talk about it. You're probably not like the others, but let's leave it at that." He turned his back and begin to grind something in a pestle.

Quaeryt eased out of the apothecary's. He could have pressed some, but his reception hadn't been that good to begin with.

When he stepped back outside, the door to the adjoining shop was shuttered and closed. So was the adjoining shop. He didn't think either had been when he entered the apothecary's.

He shook his head and went back across the street. The silversmith's door was shuttered. The next shop was tiny, with but a single narrow window beside the door. While the door was unshuttered, the window was not, but the door opened, and he stepped inside.

"You must have the wrong shop," came a voice from his left.

He turned to see a thin woman adjusting the fabric on a frame shaped like a woman's figure. The woman didn't look to be much older than Quaeryt, although there were streaks of gray in her short-cut hair and lines from the corners of her eyes. "Why? Because you're a dressmaker?"

"I don't see you wearing a dress, and few scholars have either wives or mistresses. Even if you did, you'd not likely have the coins for what I sew." She paused and studied him again. "You are a scholar . . . but you're not from the Ecoliae, are you?"

"Actually, I'm from the Scholarium in Solis. I'm here to study the history of Tilbor."

"You do have the wrong shop."

"I think not. You probably know more of what happened here since just before the war than most."

"The Khanar wasn't strong enough. His daughter was. The north didn't want a Khanara, and neither did the hill people. Those in Tilbora did; the others in the south didn't want a civil war. We all lost. Things turned out better under the governor than they would have under the Pretender. What else is there to say?"

"Well . . ." said Quaeryt with a smile. ". . . there is the question of why it all came to that. What would have been so bad about a Khanara?"

"It wasn't that she was a woman. It was that she was smart, and she saw that Rhecyrd would lead Tilbor into war with Telaryn. She also saw how the timber holders and the northers were evading tariffs. She was keeping her father alive, and she was really the Khanar. But things worked, and no one said anything. Then Rhecyrd brought all his clan militia—and his imager—south, and Eleonyd got sicker and died, and then the imager imaged Antiagon Fire over the envoy from Telaryn. That was because she would have wed Lord Bhayar to save Tilbor, and Rhecyrd knew it."

"And Rhecyrd knew she wouldn't marry him?"

"No woman with any sense would. His wife got sick and died when he needed her out of the way."

"Did you ever meet her?"

"Lady Tyrena? She had me sew several riding out-fits for her . . . she was young then." The seamstress laughed so softly that there was almost no sound. "Weren't we all?"

"What can you tell me about her?"

"What is there to say? She was young, a bit too strong-featured to be beautiful, but attractive in a handsome way. She was very intelligent, more so than her father, I'd say, and Tilbor might not be a part of Telaryn had he listened to her."

"Why do you say that?"

"She was the one who truly commanded the Guard. The old commander—Gustraak—knew she under-stood battles better, and she rode beside him and ad-vised him. Then he died—I still say that he and Eleonyd were both poisoned by Rhecyrd's imager. Commander Traesk refused to listen to her, and she had the imager killed and forced a Bovarian merchanter to take her away with her personal armsmen. Before she left some-one put a knife in Traesk's ribs, and he died, and the Guard retreated to the palace and closed it off. If she'd been in command . . . who knows?"

"Strategy isn't everything," Quaeryt pointed out.

"No. It's not. Soldiers are important, too, and the men of Tilbor make the best soldiers. Why do you think the governor recruits so many of them."

At that moment, a muscular man burst through the rear door and moved quickly toward Quaeryt, a stout club in hand. The scholar barely got up a forearm to deflect the arm with the club.

"Haarl! Stop! He's not one of them!" snapped the woman.

One of whom? The local scholars?

Quaeryt had to block another attempt with the club before the attacker stopped.

"I told you to stop." The woman's voice was acid-tinged.

"They're all the same . . . don't care what Thayl or you say . . ." said the ginger-bearded bear of a man who glared at Quaeryt even as he lowered the club.

Quaeryt wanted to massage his forearm, but he just waited, if warily. "I take it that the local scholars are not exactly in your favor."

"You're not from here. You don't talk like them."

"I told you that, idiot," snapped the woman.

"I wasn't going to wait. Thayl told me one of them was prowling around. Said he was different, as if that mattered . . ."

"You go and tell your brother that he's not one of them. Do you understand?"

Haarl looked at Quaeryt. "Sorry . . . didn't mean to take you for one of them." He turned and walked out. His tone was scarcely apologetic.

Quaeryt looked to the seamstress. "Might I ask what offenses the local scholars have committed?"

"You could. Why would it be to my advantage to tell you?"

"Because I might be able to do something about it."

The woman studied Quaeryt once more. Then she smiled, if faintly. "You might. You'd try, anyway."

He waited.

"The scholars have always been the tool of the timber holders. Eleonyd and the Khanars paid them to run the school, but it was as much tribute as anything. It was cheaper than fighting. In return, the timber holders built their road and allowed the Khanars to use it without tariffing them."

"The governor doesn't pay the scholars for the school. Is that why he is always fighting the timber holders?"

The seamstress shrugged. "I do not know what the governor or the scholars do these days."

"Go ahead. You were going to say more about the scholars."

"It has to do with Commander Traesk. He was one of the few officers from the hills. He joined the Khanar's Guard as a young man. In time, he became an officer, and later, subcommander. All said that he was courageous and a good leader . . . until he betrayed the Khanara. Traesk's son was—he still is, I guess—a scholar. He was also a Guard officer during the fighting. I don't know as he was that good a Guard officer, but he was well-trained in using arms, and he was there to ward his father's back."

"So the scholars supported the Guard?"

She shook her head. "Traesk supported Rhecyrd. Most of the Guard officers supported the Khanara, but they would not break their loyalty to the Guard commander."

"Then who killed Traesk?"

"No man could have killed him."

"Was the Khanara that skilled in weapons?"

"She was the equal of any man."

Quaeryt could see the general outline, but parts of what he thought he saw didn't make sense. "What does this have to do with the scholars?"

"The Khanara had help from . . . some in the south. The . . . scholar has vowed to kill all those who helped her."

Quaeryt looked at the seamstress, taking in the lean muscles he'd thought were merely the sign of lack of privilege. He risked jumping to a conclusion. "He's after all the Sisters?"

Her face tightened.

"I'm not after you . . . or them. I've overheard people talking about the Sisters, but I didn't know what they meant. When you explained, though . . ."

"You are a dangerous man."

"I doubt I'm near as dangerous as you." He paused but briefly. "I do have a question. Do you know the name of Traesk's son? If I ever meet him, I'd like to know it."

"Chardyn . . . Chardyn Traesksyn . . ."

Quaeryt refrained from nodding. That made all too much sense. "And the scholars are still working with the hill timber holders against the governor . . . because they think the people in the south sold out to Lord Chayar?"

"I cannot say. I would judge so." The seamstress offered another smile, faint and knowing. "You are not a scholar . . . or not just a scholar."

"I've been a seaman, but I am a scholar."

"Your eyes say that you are more."

"No more than you," he replied.

She laughed. "You did not give your name."

"Quaeryt Rytersyn."

"Your name says it all."

He frowned.

"The questioner of every man."

"And yours?"

"Syen Yendradyr."

"That says that your mother . . ."

"We do not take our father's names." She nodded. "You know enough for now."

"I might be back."

"Don't come too soon. Talk to others."

"I will." He inclined his head, turned, and departed.

Once he was outside the shop, he shook his head. He'd never thought he'd risked being killed for being a local scholar. Had the patroller who'd recommended Thayl's stable the first time he'd ridden through the harbor done so for reasons other than courtesy?

He massaged his sore forearm with his left hand. The injury, slight as it was, again reminded him that he did need to think more about how to create some sort of shields.

You can't keep putting it off.

He glanced back at the silversmith's, but the door was still shuttered. So he walked past the café and entered the chandlery.

A man within a few years of Quaeryt's age turned, then frowned.

"Greetings," Quaeryt said quickly. "I've recently arrived from Solis."

An expression close to relief crossed the man's face.

"I'm a scholar, and I've been sent to write about the history of Tilbor from the time of the last Khanars until now."

"Were you raised in Solis?"

"I was an orphan left in Solis as a young child when my parents died in the Great Plague. I'd guess I'm as much from Solis as from anywhere."

"Better there than some places."

"I was hoping that you could tell me what you recall . . ." From there Quaeryt went on, asking a question here and there. After two quints, it was clear he wouldn't learn much more, and he left for the next shop.

He visited almost a score of shops, but people were wary, and no one told him as much as Syen had. He never did find a bookstore, nor a cooperage in the harbor area, and it was more than three glasses later when he finally returned to Thayl's and paid the extra copper. Instead of riding back directly, he headed north from the harbor area, through an area of dwellings that were slightly larger than those he'd passed to the northwest of the harbor on his way in, but all had higher-pitched roofs than he'd seen anywhere but in Tilbora, and narrower windows. No one looked askance at him, and several women and older men waved.

By midafternoon, the sky had clouded over, and the wind had shifted from the northwest. A light sprinkling of rain had begun to fall when he finally returned to the palace grounds just after third glass. By the time he'd logged back in, unsaddled and groomed the mare, and washed up, it was close to fourth glass. Even so, he did return to his study, but found no more envelopes and messages.

At half past fourth glass, he made his way down to the mess, where, as Dueryl had explained, there was a pay table. He waited behind several undercaptains until it was his turn.

"Scholar Quaeryt . . . yes . . . here you are, sir." The ranker clerk eased three silvers and five coppers across the pay table.

"I thought meals were a copper each."

"They are, sir, except for mess night, and that's two."

"Oh . . . thank you." Quaeryt certainly didn't mind the charges. The food was better than it would have been in Tilbora, at half the price, and certainly better than at the Ecoliae.

As he stood there, waiting for supper, he couldn't help but wonder about the fare. Yet both the princeps and Major Skarpa had insisted that what the rankers got was about the same as what the officers got. Somehow, if that were true, and he suspected it happened to be so, he doubted that such was the case for rankers elsewhere in Bhayar's service.

45

Samedi morning, Quaeryt lingered over breakfast, talking to another set of undercaptains, not learning anything new, but more of what he'd already picked up, if from a slightly different viewpoint. In a way, that suggested there might not be that much else truly new that he could learn from the junior officers about the regiment itself, at least for the moment, because what he could ask was limited to some extent by what he already knew . . . and what he didn't.

After breakfast, he hurried up to his study, arriving just before seventh glass, where he sat down and tried to think about what he had discovered so far and how he could recommend—if he could—a reduction in troops in Tilbor. If he couldn't, what could he do . . . that wouldn't leave him in a precarious position with Bhayar? The other problem he faced was the scholars. He'd been seeking a way to bolster and improve their position in Telaryn as a first step toward what he really envisioned, but so far all he was discovering was how they were destroying their support among both the landholders and the people.

After a time, he decided to go back down to the library to see if there were any books dealing with scholars. Once there, in less than a glass, he found that there were none, and there hadn't been any references to the scholars in either the governor's dispatches or the records of the Khanar's Council. The lack of mention of the scholars by Rescalyn reinforced Quaeryt's decision to move slowly in dealing with them.

Somewhat discouraged, he decided to make a more thorough survey of everything that lay within the walls of the Telaryn Palace, starting at the west end. That effort took most of the day, from eighth glass until nearly fifth glass. In the process, he did discover that, despite housing more than a full regiment, many of the troop quarters were currently empty, that at least two springs and numerous cisterns supplied and stored water, and that, in effect, the space within the palace walls could house and support more than five thousand people.

With his feet sore from walking on stone pavement and floors for more than seven glasses, something that often happened because of his uneven gait, he returned to his quarters and cleaned up, then made his way to the main part of the palace to find the Green Salon, which he discovered on the third level of the center section of the main palace.

The first person Quaeryt saw—after the senior squad leader in the dress green uniform by the door—when he entered the Green Salon was Princeps Straesyr, wearing a white formal tunic over dark blue trousers. Beyond Straesyr, Quaeryt glimpsed several officers in dress uniforms, including the governor and Commander Myskyl, as well as a woman dressed elegantly in a flowing black gown, and Chorister Phargos.

The princeps stepped toward him. "Master scholar . . . I had forgotten that scholars do not have formal attire. We will have to take care of that. I will request the regimental tailor make you a brown formal jacket of the same cut and cloth as a dress uniform."

Quaeryt didn't have an immediate direct response that would not have been either obsequious or flippant. "I had not anticipated such formality, and I appreciate your thoughtfulness."

"You are likely to be here for a time, and we do want you to be appropriately attired." The princeps gestured toward a sideboard behind him and to his left. "You might try the Noiran white ice wine. It's rather delicate . . . but potent."

"Thank you."

"You're most welcome." With a smile, Straesyr turned and eased back in the direction of those surrounding the governor.

Quaeryt surveyed the salon quickly. The walls of the oval-shaped chamber, a good twenty yards in length and perhaps fifteen in width at its widest point, were cloaked in deep green hangings, flowing down from the gilded crown moldings carved into floral designs. The ceiling rose two levels, at an angle that suggested a mansard exterior, and light—and a gentle breeze—poured in from the open upper-level windows, although the shimmering brass lamps set on protruding brackets at intervals around the salon were also lit. At one end of the salon was placed a clavecin, as if someone might be playing the plucked keyboard instrument later during the reception.

Since no one moved toward him, he stepped toward the sideboard, tended by a ranker in dress greens.

"Sir?"

"The white ice wine, please."

"Very good, sir."

Quaeryt took the goblet, almost tulip-shaped, with

a crest he did not recognize cut into the crystal, and took the smallest sip of the colorless wine. Even that small sip convinced him that the princeps had been right. He'd have to make the wine last a long time.

As several other officers entered the salon, also greeted by the princeps, Quaeryt eased toward those already gathered, not all that far from the end of the clavecin, an instrument whose unadorned but polished wood shimmered.

The gray-haired Commander Myskyl caught sight of Quaeryt and turned, stepping toward him. "Scholar, I don't believe we've met yet."

Quaeryt noted a pattern of faint, but long-healed, scars on the commander's left cheek and jaw. "No, sir. I've only seen you from across the mess."

"What do you think of the regiment so far?"

"I've been very impressed by everything I've seen."

"I understand you've also visited Tilbora and taken a local patrol."

"I have. It appears that your officers and men are held in high regard here."

"Here in the south, that is true."

Behind the commander, Quaeryt heard both Skarpa and Phargos laughing, apparently at something the governor had said. "And elsewhere?"

"We're accepted in the north. We have troubles in the lands bordering and encompassing the Boran Hills."

"I assume you have some sort of post in the north."

"We have posts in Midcote and Noira, just three battalions in Midcote and two in Noira. There aren't that many people in the far north, and most of those are clustered on the lands of the High Holders. The war wiped out most of the northers who would have caused trouble."

"Are the timber holders a problem because they stayed out of the war?"

"They've avoided authority as much as they could from before the time of the Khanars." Myskyl's tone was dryly sardonic. "Have you visited the local scholars?"

"Before the reception I received in Tilbora, until I explained I was a scholar from Solis, I had thought to do so. Now . . . I'm not certain it would be for the best. Not yet, at least. Do you know why those in Tilbora—around the harbor, anyway—feel strongly about scholars?"

"I couldn't say why, except many believe that the scholars are more allied with the timber holders than the rest of the south. I understand they're tolerated because of their school and because they've given no one a reason to attack them . . . and because the governors have declared that any violence will be dealt with severely."

"That's because of the incident involving the Pharsi women?"

Myskyl frowned, if only for a moment. "That was unfortunate. Governor Fhayt did not understand fully how a regiment must be handled following a war."

"Governor Rescalyn understands that clearly, it would seem to me."

The commander nodded. "He understands both war and governing very well."

A bell-like sound echoed across the room, and the conversation died away. Everyone turned toward the governor, who stood, waiting, until the salon was absolutely silent.

"Now that you are all here, I thought we should have some entertainment of . . . shall I say . . . a more refined nature." Rescalyn gestured to the dark-haired woman in black beside him. "Some of you have already heard Mistress Eluisa play, but it is always a joy to listen. She is quite accomplished. She was Bovarian by birth. Her music has made my duties here far more pleasant."

Quaeryt shifted his eyes, but not his head, to observe the princeps. Straesyr merely nodded and offered a polite smile, as did Myskyl.

As the officers formed a semicircle, several yards back from the clavecin, Eluisa settled herself onto the padded bench before the instrument. Quaeryt moved to one side, with the more junior officers, almost beside Major Skarpa. When Eluisa poised her hands above the keys, from where he stood, Quaeryt could not help but notice that her fingers, while slender, were not particularly long.

The music that issued from the clavecin was almost like the flow of a river, dancing, then slowing. Whether that was what the composer had meant, Quaeryt had no idea, only that was the impression he garnered. The second piece was a triumphal march, followed by a gentler melody that seemed half love song, half lullaby. The final presentation was slightly longer, and seemed almost to present a history in music . . . at least to Quaeryt.

All the officers applauded, but after the applause died away, and the more senior officers had presented their compliments, Quaeryt made his way to Eluisa. "What was the last piece that you played?"

"It's an adaptation of a Khellan melody by Covaelyt. He was the court composer to the father of Rex Kharst."

"Why did you flee Variana?" He kept his voice soft, but not too soft, so that the governor would think him merely deferential, rather than secretive.

Her eyebrows lifted.

"You are too beautiful and too talented not to have left except under some sort of . . . duress."

"You compliment as a form of inquiry, master scholar."

"The governor would agree with my compliments, I am most certain."

Her smile was brief. "My sister killed herself. She was extraordinarily beautiful . . ."

"And the Rex used her and spurned her?"

"That was what everyone believed."

"She was too noble for that," suggested Quaeryt.

"How would you know that, master scholar?"

"You are extremely talented, and such ability comes from both training and position. You also have survived in a land strange to you. It is rare, despite the romantic tales, that one daughter in a noble family is weak while another is strong. The daughters of families of high position in Bovaria are always presented in court. I am only speculating, based on what I have heard, but she would not jeopardize your family by any form of outright refusal. Therefore, she did not refuse his advances, and she would likely have been relieved when his attention waned. Except it did not, and his, shall we say, excesses led to her death." Quaeryt was attempting to state the conclusion politely.

For the barest moment, her mouth moved, as if to drop open, before she spoke, her pleasant voice quite level. "Does all Lydar speculate so wildly?"

"My dear Lady Eluisa, the proclivities of any ruler can seldom be kept secret. If those who know them are killed, then the absences are noted, and questions are asked of those who might have carried out the killings, and sooner or later all will know, because a ruler can-

SCHOLAR 343

not kill too many of those who serve him and still remain a ruler. If those who know are not killed, then the proclivities are known sooner."

"Yet women die, and none care. Is it only the death of men that rouses other men to action?"

"That depends, Lady, on the man." Quaeryt bowed his head.

"Or how beloved and highborn the woman is."

"That, too," Quaeryt admitted.

Rescalyn cleared his throat and stepped forward. "You are rather perceptive, scholar, but I would not have your perception recall too many unpleasantnesses for Mistress Eluisa."

"Nor would I." Quaeryt inclined his head to the lady. "My deepest apologies if I have unwittingly injured or offended you."

"You have not," she replied, "so long as matters remain as they are."

"As they shall," promised Quaeryt.

Rescalyn smiled at Eluisa, and she slipped away, moving toward the princeps.

"Master scholar," said Rescalyn cheerfully, "one last word with you before we get on with enjoyment of the evening."

"Yes, sir."

"On Lundi morning, the companies will begin their monthly rotation. Major Skarpa will be taking Sixth Battalion to Boralieu. Since you seem to be on agreeable terms with the major, as well as with one of his captains, Captain Meinyt, I thought that accompanying them and their men to the main hill outpost and riding with them on patrols for a time would provide you a firsthand understanding of the problems we face in the hills."

"I am most certain that it would, and I look forward

to accompanying them and learning what would not otherwise be possible."

"Excellent. Now . . . we have some delightful re- freshments, including slices of a special suckling pig prepared in the Cloisonyt style. Do enjoy yourself." Rescalyn nodded and then walked toward Eluisa and Straesyr.

"He does know how to entertain."

Quaeryt turned to find Phargos at his elbow. "I do believe he does, but that may be the least of his tal- ents."

"Quite so." Phargos smiled.

Quaeryt took another small sip of the ice wine. He would enjoy the refreshments . . . and listen. He'd al- ready talked too much.

46

By midmorning on Solayi, Quaeryt was seated in the shade on a bench under an apple tree, one not exactly a dwarf, but a tree that had been carefully pruned to a size in keeping with the limited space available within the palace grounds, if limited meant an extent more than a half mille from east to west and a third of a mille north to south. His forehead was damp, not so much from the air or the rain that had fallen on the previous day, but because of his efforts in attempting various imaging approaches to creating some sort of shield to protect himself against direct attacks. He'd always relied upon avoiding any direct confrontation, but the events of the last few months had made it clearer and clearer that such an approach was not sufficient for the situation in which he found himself.

You put yourself there.

He had, but . . . over the long run, the alternatives would have been worse.

Over the long run, you'll be dead anyway. Everyone is.

That thought didn't offer much consolation, and, besides, he was where he was, not somewhere else.

He'd tried imaging a net of colorless silk, and ended up with a pile of silk threads. He'd attempted an invisible net like that of a spiderweb, anchoring it between the trees, but it had immediately dragged down the branches, and he'd imaged it away.

What's as light as the air that you could harden?

"Clouds . . . fog . . ." he murmured.

He straightened on the park bench and concentrated on creating a shield of fog—hard misty fog.

The air before him seemed to shiver . . . almost rippling . . . and then tiny ice pellets appeared in mid-air and cascaded down onto the path between the trees, and a wave of chill air washed over him.

For a moment, he felt light-headed, but that passed. He decided to wait for a time to regain his strength and turned his thoughts to another part of his problems—the governor. Everyone seemingly liked the man. He was warm and charming. He spoke well. He certainly took good care of his men, and they all felt he was an outstanding leader. With the strange exception of the timber holders, and possibly a few northers or High Holders in the north, Rescalyn appeared to be extremely effective as a governor, and even the seamstress who had to have been a member of the Sisters had offered testimony to that effectiveness.

Yet . . . Quaeryt had an uneasy feeling about Rescalyn.

The governor definitely knew what was happening in the regiment . . . down to who was friendly with whom—and he'd learned with whom Quaeryt had talked at the mess in less than a matter of days. He'd also opened all the obvious records to Quaeryt without the slightest qualm or hesitation and made it clear that Quaeryt was free to look anywhere.

The scholar/imager shook his head, then straightened.

Time to try something else. But what?

What else was as light as air or lighter?

Smoke?

How could he make smoke into a shield? Especially an invisible one that he could carry all the time?

What about the air itself? Could he just—somehow—harden it?

But how?

What if he visualized the air as tiny shields, hooked together, so that when something struck them, the hooks stiffened?

He concentrated, focusing on the air a yard in front of him. He didn't see anything, but felt as though he were carrying a weight. He stepped forward and extended his hand, palm first. His palm ran into a barrier, one he couldn't see.

He couldn't help but grin. He offered a side kick with his boot, but the barrier remained firm enough that the kick shivered back through his leg. He took out his belt knife and pressed it against the barrier. He didn't thrust it, fearing that the tip of the blade might slip or break. Even with his weight behind the knife, the barrier seemed impenetrable to the blade, and he sheathed it carefully.

At the same time, he felt as though he had been running, and his heart was pounding in his chest. He let go of the feeling of the hooks, and the unseen weight lifted from him. He took one deep breath, and then another, blotting the sweat from his forehead as he did.

When his breathing returned to normal, he tried hardening the air again, this time making the hooks looser. The unseen barrier was far easier to hold, but it bent and the knife cut through it, slowly, as if it were going through soft cheese or even fresh bread.

He was soaked and dripping sweat when he finally settled back onto the bench, breathing heavily. If he hardened the air enough to stop an arrow or a blade, or especially a crossbow bolt, he would be exhausted in less than half a quint. If he didn't, and held what he could with perhaps as much effort as walking, the air slowed things, but didn't stop them. An even "looser" or lighter shield took almost no effort, but barely slowed anything.

Something like the second kind of air shield might keep an arrow from going through you . . . maybe. Or slow a sabre stroke enough for you to dodge.

He just sat there on the bench for a time. He didn't have any other ideas.

But then . . . maybe if he practiced the shields, the way the soldiers drilled, day after day . . . maybe he could build up what the shields could do. In any case, he was exhausted, and there wasn't much else he could do at the moment.

His thoughts drifted back to the reception the night before.

He'd definitely revealed too much in his brief encounter with Mistress Eluisa. *But you've always had a weakness for intelligent and talented women. And you've met so few.*

How was a near-penniless scholar who could come up with a few extra coppers and silvers through imaging ever going to meet someone like that? Watching Eluisa play and talking to her for a few moments . . . or receiving a letter or two from Vaelora . . . those were the few times he'd even come into momentary contact with such women, and such incidents would be few and far between unless his circumstances changed.

. . . or unless you change them.

He smiled ruefully. Accomplishing anything along those lines, when he had little ability in trade or in fighting, was going to take some doing.

Finally he stood. He needed to wash up and rest before dinner . . . and after that he might as well take in services and hear whatever Phargos had to offer with his homily.

47

By midday on Lundi, Quaeryt was riding beside Major Skarpa on the river road, heading northwest from Tilbora, with five companies following them. Fastened behind his saddle was a cylindrical kit bag that had been left in his quarters on Solayi afternoon and that held a spare set of browns and other items that he would need for the time—not ever spelled out, except in general terms along the lines of "as long as it takes to give you a good understanding"—he was supposed to accompany the companies of Sixth Battalion. Those generalities didn't give him the best feelings about what Rescalyn had in mind.

It might have been the first day of Erntyn, the second month of harvest, but the air was hot and heavy, and Quaeryt kept having to blot his forehead and the back of his neck. Part of that was because of the effort he was making to hold very light imaging shields, although he had figured how to link them to his saddle so that he didn't have to keep creating new ones as he rode.

When everything finally appeared settled into a routine, Quaeryt looked to Skarpa and said, "When I talked to the governor for a few moments on Samedi, it was clear that he seems to know anything that goes on in the regiment."

"Good marshals and commanders do. Even as governor, he still holds the rank of marshal. He meets with the regiment commander daily, and he joins the commander's meetings with each battalion major at least once a week. He doesn't ever go around the chain of command. He'll let the commander ask most of the questions, but those meetings aren't a formality. Both he and the commander ask solid questions. Afterward we often get suggestions from the commander, things like differences in training or possible shifts in junior officers. . . ." Skarpa laughed. "I can usually guess which suggestion is from Commander Myskyl and which is from the governor. Either way, they're usually right. Not always. If I can explain why it's not a good idea, the commander doesn't press. He just wants his officers to think things through. So does the marshal."

"What did you think about the reception on Samedi? Does he have them often, or it is something he seldom does?"

"The governor has one every few weeks, and there are always a few majors at each reception. I hadn't been to one in about a year. It was pleasant enough.

Good food, but the receptions are almost like an informal inspection."

Somehow, Quaeryt doubted that his presence and that of Skarpa at the same reception had been any sort of coincidence.

"What did you think, scholar?"

"I thought both the governor and the lady were very impressive. In different ways, of course."

"She's a pretty woman. You talked to her. I saw."

"Just for a few moments, about Variana and Bovaria, and the music she played. The governor is quietly protective."

"He might be. His wife died years ago. They never had any children, and he never found anyone else. That's what Phargos told me. He'd know."

"I haven't seen the governor at services."

"He doesn't attend often. He talks to Phargos, though."

"How did Rescalyn become governor?"

Skarpa laughed. "He was the submarshal under Fhayt, but went back to Solis with Lord Chayar. Then, after Fhayt made that mess with the Pharsi women—do you know about that?"

"I heard that there was trouble between the local women and soldiers. One thing led to another and Fhayt leveled part of Tilbora."

"That's about right. It happened a year or so before Lord Chayar died. Even back then, Straesyr was princeps, but he was in the north, talking to the factors around Noira. Fhayt was always a little hotheaded, and Straesyr usually calmed him down, but . . . he wasn't there. People got hurt, and some more soldiers got killed. The Pharsi mostly moved south, and their tariffs went with them, and Fhayt increased tariffs—"

"Tariffs are higher here? Because of the war? To pay back the cost?"

"That's what Phargos says. In another three years, they go back to the rates for the rest of Telaryn."

Is that why the southers are so calm?

"Chayar was furious, but then some brigands attacked Fhayt while he was on his way to meet with a High Holder, and that made Lord Chayar even more angry. Word was that an attack and an uprising together showed incompetence and stupidity. He sent Rescalyn to replace Fhayt, but he did give Fhayt a stipend. That was if he returned to Solis immediately. If he didn't, he'd be tried for treason and incompetence. It didn't matter. He died of the flux on the trip back." Skarpa's last words were laconically ironic.

"And Straesyr remained as princeps?"

"He's good at it, they say. He was a submarshal in charge of supplies and the like. He can talk to the merchanters and the crafters' guilds. He probably would have been a better governor than Fhayt, but Fhayt was a good battlefield commander."

"Some field commanders aren't so good once they leave the field."

"Some aren't good in the field. Rescalyn's gotten rid of those. There's one good thing about all these little battles with the hill types. We can see which of the undercaptains are good and which aren't, and sometimes pick the good ones when they're still squad leaders."

"I hadn't thought of that, but I'm a scholar, not a soldier," Quaeryt admitted. "How good are the hill fighters?"

"Good? I wouldn't call them good. They're sneaky. Always setting ambushes and traps. You have to keep your eyes open all the time. It took a while to get used to that." Skarpa laughed again. "That's another reason for all the maneuver training when companies come back from the hills. The governor doesn't want the officers and men to forget how they'll need to fight against the Bovarians or the Antiagons."

Quaeryt nodded. "What do you think I'll learn on your patrols?"

"How to keep your eyes open and watch for the smallest signs."

"I meant about Tilbor."

"They're people like people anywhere, except the hill folk are more selfish and meaner. They think everything they see should belong to them. Don't think a thing about putting a shaft through anyone who wanders into their woods, or what they claim as theirs."

"Are they good with bows?"

"I wish they weren't. We usually lose a few men on every rotation, more officers and squad leaders than rankers. They single them out."

"You're still here, after all that?"

Skarpa offered a crooked grin. "I said you need to keep your eyes and ears open for any little thing that's different."

And you're supposed to know what's different when you've never even been here before?

Quaeryt was feeling more uneasy with each mille that he rode from Tilbora.

48

The sun was slanting into his face late on Meredi afternoon as Quaeryt rode beside Captain Meinyt up a dusty road rising gradually to the top of a low rise. For the past day, the battalion had ridden due north from the Albhor River largely through croplands. The wide valley behind them held hundreds of moderately sized fields, each one cultivated by a family, with most of the crop going, Quaeryt suspected, to High Holder Dymaetyn, the local High Holder, according to Meinyt. The rise they traveled was mostly pasture, with scattered brush and trees, but all trees and brush growth had been cleared fifty yards back on each side of the road.

Meinyt's company was the second one in the column, behind more than a hundred mounts, and Quaeryt's kerchief came away from his face tan with sweat and dust.

"You're sweating all the time, scholar. Your mare's the one doing the work, not you," said Meinyt with a laugh.

"I'm a scholar, not a mounted officer. This is work for me," parried Quaeryt as he blotted his forehead and neck once again. He couldn't say for certain, but he thought he was finding it just a touch easier to carry the light shields he imaged for longer and longer—almost a glass at a time. It was still work.

"You should have been here last summer. It was really beastly, almost as hot as Solis, and there was never any wind. In Solis, or Tilbora, at least you can find places where there's a sea breeze. Here, in between the high hills and the lowlands, when it gets hot, it gets really hot."

"I'm glad I wasn't here."

"The winter's worse," continued Meinyt cheerfully. "The clouds are so thick there's never any sun, and when there is it doesn't warm anything up. The snow gets deeper and deeper, and, sometimes, for the last part of Ianus, we can barely get couriers between Boralieu and Tilbora."

From the top of the rise, looking to the left of the road and to the west, Quaeryt could see another valley below, if not nearly so wide as the last, which held a smaller rise about two-thirds of the way across the valley toward the steeper—and largely forested—hills to the west.

"There's Boralieu," announced Meinyt.

Quaeryt blotted his forehead again and studied the "outpost." It scarcely fit his conception of an outpost, looking more like a smaller version of the Telaryn Palace, except the walls were of a reddish brown stone, possibly sandstone, which was far easier to cut and quarry than granite or graystone. Even so, the walls had to be several hundred yards from end to end, and there were certainly a number of stone structures within the walls.

"How many companies are stationed here at any one time?"

"They're really not stationed . . . they're rotated in and out every month, even in winter, except sometimes there's no rotation in the last weeks of Ianus and the first weeks of Fevier. The standing complement is two battalions, sometimes three, and a company of engineers."

Ten companies? Close to twelve hundred men at the least? "How many outposts are there in the hill country?"

"Three others, but the others are smaller, just two companies of mounted foot and the engineers."

"I'd heard about the hill brigands, but I didn't realize that there was so much trouble here."

"It's not that there's so much. It's that they're so scattered. You'd wear down the mounts and men trying to cover all the Boran Hills."

"Are there any other hill areas in Tilbor that have so many problems?"

"There are a few holders in the northern woods, but we've only got a couple of battalions up there, and that seems to be enough. The High Holders there are more helpful in dealing with brigandage and lawlessness."

Quaeryt nodded, but noted Meinyt's views differed somewhat from what he'd heard from both Straesyr and Rescalyn. "And the companies at all the outposts are in addition to the ones at the Telaryn Palace?" He wanted to make sure he understood exactly how many companies there were and where they were.

"Well . . . they're all part of the regiment . . . there are six battalions always at the palace, and that doesn't count those at the outposts. The reason the companies at the outposts are rotated monthly is so all the companies get to deal with the troublemakers and so that no one has to stay more than a month at a time at any outpost."

Quaeryt kept his mental mathematics to himself. "That way everyone is kept ready to deal with the hill types, and it doesn't fall too heavily on one or two battalions."

"Mostly," replied Meinyt dryly. "Some of us end up

doing a bit more. My company is always stationed at the northwest outpost in Ianus."

"That's why you were talking about dealing with brigands in the snow."

"It's usually not too bad."

"Are there any other companies that have winter duties and skills?"

"Chydar's company. That's about it."

Quaeryt was certain he didn't want to be with Meinyt in Ianus, but why were so few companies specified to deal with the worst of the winter conditions? "Do you have special equipment?"

"Most of the men can handle snowshoes or skis."

"Skis?" Quaeryt had never heard of skis.

"They're long wooden slats that you strap to your boots. They keep you on top of the snow—if you don't fall. When you go downhill you can outdistance a wolf or a mount. That's if you're good. Some of the local rankers are very good. It takes practice, but we get a lot of it in Ianus."

"I'm glad I don't have to do that."

"It's not that hard—unless you're chasing brigands."

"They attack in the snow?"

"They attack any time they think you're weak. Besides, what else can they do in the winter except sit in front of a fire and drink?"

Quaeryt let that go. "Who's in charge of Boralieu?"

"That's Commander Zirkyl. He's the post commander." Meinyt looked to the north and the line of clouds over the hills in the distance. "Looks like we'll get to the post and all the mounts stabled before the rain hits."

49

Although he had done very little on Jeudi, Quaeryt was still stiff and sore on Vendrei morning. After eating a hearty breakfast, he walked from the officers' mess—a small room off the end of a larger chamber where the rankers ate—toward the west courtyard and the stables to join Meinyt's company for a patrol. The outpost was obviously far newer than the Telaryn Palace, with competent but not artistic stonework and inside walls of white plaster applied directly to the stone. By looking closely, Quaeryt could see where the cracks in the plaster had been filled and whitewashed over. The walls were clean, as were the stone floors, but there were no decorations or adornments anywhere.

As he walked along the corridor flanking the rankers' dining hall, he couldn't help but overhear a few comments.

"... Waerfyl ... say he's trained a squad of crossbowmen ..."

"... not that much good in the woods ... won't hit many ..."

"... fine ... unless you're the one bolted ..."

Quaeryt agreed with the last observation, but offered no expression as he passed.

"... just have to duck real quick ..."

"... if you're lucky enough to hear anything ..."

How can you hear a crossbow? They wouldn't ever be that close.

Once outside, under a sky that looked partly heat-hazed already, he made his way to the stable. There he saddled the mare and walked her out into the courtyard. At that moment, Meinyt rode over to where Quaeryt was about to mount.

"We'll be riding a good two glasses to the west. It should be an easy ride."

The scholar certainly hoped so. "Good." He climbed into the saddle and rode after the captain to the head of the company.

Quaeryt said little until several quints after the company had left Boralieu, and the company was riding westward along a dirt road uphill through the woods on the far side of the valley that held the outpost. While trees and brush were cut back from the road some ten yards, the woods beyond were dark, although the trees were mostly evergreens and grew far enough apart that a rider—and in some instances, a wagon—could have passed between them.

Since everything seemed to be quiet, Quaeryt spoke. "Major Skarpa didn't tell me whether this is just a routine patrol, or whether you're looking into some sort of problem."

"That's his sense of humor." Meinyt offered a laugh that was more like a bark. "We're logged out as a routine patrol."

Quaeryt could see a glint in the officer's eyes. "Someone's about to make trouble, then, but no one has any proof?"

"More than likely, and it's probably Waerfyl. His lands abut those of High Holder Dymaetyn. Dymaetyn has all the lands to the east and south of Boralieu, and some a little to the southwest. Waerfyl's hold is some eight milles to the southwest of Boralieu, and his holding is almost big enough to make him a High Holder.

Might be bigger, but the other High Holders wouldn't have him as one of them. That's even if he wanted to be, and he doesn't. Dymaetyn says that Waerfyl's men are poaching on his lands. He also claims that Waerfyl's loggers are sneaking into his northern timber stands and logging the best goldenwoods and dragging them out."

"Claims? Doesn't he know?" Quaeryt's words came out more sardonically than he'd intended.

"He knows that there are goldenwood stumps and branches left behind. He knows that Waerfyl's lands are north of his."

"Could they be timber brigands, so to speak?"

"They could. If they are, they're using Waerfyl's lands. It's Waerfyl's responsibility to stop them."

"Why doesn't Dymaetyn? I thought that the High Holders had their own armsmen in numbers large enough to hold off the Khanar's Guard."

"They used to. The governor persuaded them to reduce the numbers. To do that, he had to agree to deal with the backwoods and hill types."

Quaeryt could see the logic in that, because it limited or eliminated the fighting between High Holders, and probably also reduced the temptation for one High Holder to encroach on another. It also lowered the costs of running their holdings, because they didn't have to pay so many armsmen. Did that allow the High Holders to pay higher tariffs and still come out ahead?

Although they had left Boralieu while it was still comfortable, by the time another glass had passed, and the company had taken a fork in the road that led slightly south of due west, Quaeryt was beginning to feel the heat, not to mention the red flies, whose bite was worse than that of a mosquito. He'd lifted his light shields for a time, which extended a yard or so out, and that kept them mostly away from him, but holding them for more than a quint left him tired and sweatier. So he decided to bear the pesky flies and save the shields for when he might really need them.

Another quint passed before one of the scouts rode back and signaled Meinyt. The captain halted the company. "Break for half a quint! Pass it back."

Then he rode forward to talk with the scout.

Quaeryt dismounted, then blotted his face with one kerchief. He was saving the other clean one for later. The trees, even cut back to some ten yards from the road, were high enough in places that the road was a mixture of shade and sun, and the day was getting much warmer. He took a swallow from his water bottle and brushed away one of the red flies with his free hand.

Before long, Meinyt finished conferring with the scout and issued a command. "Squad leaders forward!"

Each squad leader passed the command back, and the five squad leaders converged on the captain at the front of the column. They six were less than ten yards from Quaeryt, but he couldn't hear what Meinyt was saying. The brief conference ended, and the first squad leader returned to his squad just behind Quaeryt, while the others rode back along the shoulder of the road to rejoin their squads.

"... first squad! Listen up! ... brigand tracks ahead ..."

At that moment, Meinyt rode back to Quaeryt. "The scouts found tracks in the side lanes a mille or so ahead, mostly on the south side. That's where the disputes over who owns what lands begin. The old Khanar before the war said that the road was the dividing line. The Pretender said that Waerfyl's lands extended another half mille south. The governor has said that the road marks the boundary."

"Has Waerfyl protested?"

"The hill types protest with bows, blades, and cross-bows." Meinyt turned in the saddle. "From here on, keep your eyes open, and don't hesitate to flatten yourself against your mount."

"I won't." Quaeryt mounted, then brought the mare alongside Meinyt's horse. He raised what he thought of as shields, hoping that they would even work. He needed more practice, and he needed more time holding them to build up his strength.

"Company! Forward!" ordered Meinyt.

Quaeryt rode less than half a mille when he saw a stone pillar on the left side of the road. At one time, it had clearly been higher, possibly with a capstone or something on the top, but someone had battered off the top stones, and they lay in the weeds and grass around the base of the column.

The boundary marker for High Holder Dymaetyn's land? Vandalized by Waerfyl's men?

He didn't ask, because it made little difference. Not at the moment.

"There's the lane," Meinyt said. "The tracks are fresher here, and they've taken a wagon. It's not loaded. Not yet."

What the captain called a lane was more like a path less than four yards wide.

"First squad! Positions!"

Before the command was finished, the troopers in first squad split into two files and turned from the narrow road right into the trees on each side of the lane.

"Second squad!"

The second squad began a quick trot down the lane.

Quaeryt heard a sound like the patter of rain. Mei-nyt flattened himself against his mount's neck. Before Quaeryt could follow that example, something ripped through his thoughts—that was what it felt like—and then slammed into his upper chest near his left shoulder. He looked down to see what looked like a short arrow protruding from his jacket, then hugged the mare's neck, if to one side because he'd done nothing about the quarrel in his shoulder.

"Namer-sows are in the trees—the big oak there and the spreading pine!" someone yelled.

Another pattering sound followed.

Quaeryt kept himself flattened against the mare, who had stopped short. He urged her toward the trees. He certainly didn't want to stay out in the open.

Once he was off the road and so close to a pine he and his mount were partly concealed, Quaeryt straightened, concentrated, and imaged clear spirits into the wound, even as he tested how firm the quarrel was. His eyes watered, and he wanted to scream, except his head was spinning so much that all he could do was to stay in the saddle.

When his head settled somewhat, he forced himself to image the head of the quarrel away. The rest of the quarrel came out, if not easily, without too much effort. Then he puked, barely able to keep the vomit off himself and the mare, and let the remainder of the quarrel fall to the pine needles.

After a time, he straightened and slowly looked around. From what he could tell, he was practically alone, except for a nearby mount that was riderless. He heard yells from the direction of the lane, but those quickly subsided.

He eased the mare toward the riderless mount, and managed to grab the reins, then transferred them to his left hand, hoping the horse didn't try to run. Even holding the reins hurt his shoulder. Then he saw its rider, one of the rankers, barely old enough to be a soldier. He lay on his back on the road. Only the fletched end of the quarrel that had gone through his chest was visible. Even as Quaeryt watched, before he could do anything, the young man tried to open his mouth, then shuddered, and was still.

Quaeryt glanced around, not knowing which way to go, and was about to follow first squad when he heard hoofs. He turned his head, wincing, to see a squad leader he didn't know riding up, followed by a full squad.

"Scholar, sir?"

"They had crossbows. The lead squads went after them." What else could he say?

"Yes, sir. We know." The squad leader rode closer. "You're bleeding, sir. There's a fair amount on you. Best you hold a cloth or something against the wound." He frowned. "What . . . ?"

"Crossbow quarrel. I managed to get it out." Quaeryt fumbled and took out the clean kerchief he hadn't even used, wadded it, then eased it inside the rents in his jacket and brown shirt. The off-white cloth began to turn pink. Quaeryt put more pressure on it.

"That's it. Just stay here. We've cleared out this area, and it won't be long before the captain is back." He turned in the saddle. "Guylart, you and Curyn strap Zaen onto his mount."

Quaeryt relinquished the reins of the other mount to the ranker who rode up. Then he concentrated on trying to stop the bleeding from his shoulder. He seemed to have some success, because the kerchief wasn't getting bloodier, and blood wasn't seeping out from the edges. He almost didn't notice when Meinyt returned.

"How are you doing, scholar?"

"I'm surviving, I think. The bolt wasn't too deep, and I got it out without ripping myself up any more. I've got most of the bleeding stopped."

The captain frowned. "You got it out alone?"

"Yes, sir." Quaeryt blinked. A wave of dizziness passed over him. "What happened?"

"There were five of them in the trees," said Meinyt. "Each one had two crossbows. There were riders, too, but they didn't stay around."

"Did you catch any of them?" Quaeryt continued to hold the cloth against the wound.

"We got three of the bowmen. Two of them are dead. One's in worse shape than you are." Meinyt glanced back down the lane.

"You need to do what you need to do, Captain," Quaeryt said.

"You'll have to go back with the other wounded and half of fifth squad. We need to follow the survivors. Can you ride all the way back to Boralieu?"

"I think so," said Quaeryt, although the throbbing in his shoulder worried him. The wound had felt better before he'd flooded it with clear spirits. So had his head. Yet he knew that the spirits helped. He also knew that sometimes they didn't help enough.

But the shield he'd raised had helped.

"Good. Best of fortune." Meinyt turned his mount.

"The rest of the wounded are back this way, sir," offered the squad leader. "But before you start back, we need to get a field dressing on that wound. Otherwise, you'll bleed out."

Quaeryt winced as he eased the mare around. The ride back was likely to be far longer than the ride out had been. Far longer.

50

Quaeryt had been right. The ride back to Boralieu took slightly more than three glasses, and along the way, another ranker collapsed over his saddle, and the one captive, a broad-faced youth in brown leathers, died.

Since he was one of the least badly wounded, Quaeryt waited another glass in the anteroom to the surgery. One of the aides to the surgeon checked the field dressing on his wound and cleaned the edges while he waited along with a white-faced older ranker with a broken arm.

He had a chance to think while he waited, and the princeps's words—those from his first meeting with Straesyr—came back to him. He'd wondered about archers, and now, unhappily, he understood. The brigands had been out of sight the entire time of the attack. Archers with the company would indeed have been useless. He wanted to shake his head, but feared even that would increase the pain.

After a time, the ranker looked at Quaeryt. "Sir . . . you took a bolt in the chest, didn't you?"

"That's where it hit."

"You worked it out, the squad leader said. Most men die if they do that. The flanges on those bolts are back-barbed tools of the Namer."

"I didn't know that. I didn't know what to do." *That's certainly true.*

"You must be stronger than you look. Sometimes,

it takes two men to get one of those out—but that's after whoever's hit is dead." The young ranker winced as he moved.

"How is the arm?" asked Quaeryt quickly.

"It hurts. Seen enough of these . . . it might be shattered. Hope not. Sometimes you lose the whole arm."

"I hope not, too." *What else can you say?* In hopes of distracting the man, he asked, "Have you been with the regiment long?"

"Too long. Trying to finish a second term and get a stipend."

"How are things now, with the hill holders, compared to when you first came?"

"They're the same nasty bastards. Helped a lot when the governor built the post here. Helped more when he added another squad to each company."

Another squad?

Before Quaeryt could ask more, one of the assistants to the surgeon came and led the ranker away, and Quaeryt sat there alone, but not for long, because the surgeon/healer—a gray-haired captain—appeared. "This way. We need to take a better look at that wound, scholar."

In another small room, the surgeon captain removed the field dressing, carefully, and inspected the wound. "Hmmm . . . fair amount of bruising . . ." He frowned, then touched Quaeryt's collarbone to the left and a touch above the wound. "Does that hurt?"

"It's sore. Everything there is sore."

The surgeon lifted a needle with blackish thread attached. "We'll need to stitch this. Otherwise, every move you make will rip it wider. It's already ripped some. You'll need to keep it in a sling for a few days, too."

The stitches weren't pleasant, but they didn't hurt

nearly so much as either the quarrel hitting him or removing it had.

When he finished, the surgeon shook his head, then smiled. "I wish more turned out like this. You're a fortunate man, scholar, thank the Nameless. Most bolts that hit the collarbone break it. Even a glancing blow will do it. That's just the beginning of the damage. Some slice the big blood vessels, but when that happens, you die right then. The one that hit you didn't do either. It's not shallow, but it's not all that deep, either. It must have been slowed by leaves or small branches. That doesn't mean we don't have to worry, but there's a tincture in there, or spirits, I'd guess. How did you manage that?"

"I had some. How . . . I don't really know. I'd heard it might help."

"Sometimes. At least, the bolt wasn't in the flesh all that long."

"How did you know that?"

A wry expression appeared on the captain's face. "I have seen more than a few wounds like this, scholar."

"I'm sorry. No one even asked me, but you knew."

"Sometimes, I do. It's fairly clean. Clean as possible. Keep it that way. Watch the dressing . . . if there's any greenish pus . . . any smell . . . we'll have to cut and drain . . . If it looks to be healing, don't fool with it. Are your guts upset?"

"They were after I got hit. After that, they've been all right."

"Good. One of my assistants will be bringing you some ale. You're to sit here quietly and drink it slowly. That will help combat the blood loss. From what's on your garments, you lost more than I'd like to see. Don't drink any water for the next few days—just ale or lager. And don't eat very much tonight. Nothing, if

368 L. E. MODESITT, JR.

you can manage it. Oh . . . you can get lager or ale between meals at the mess." With that, the surgeon was gone.

More than a glass later, and after drinking a large mug of bitter ale, with his arm in the sling, Quaeryt walked slowly back toward the main building and the officers' mess. Because he was a little light-headed, he took care with every step. It wouldn't be all that long before the evening meal, and his quarters at Boralieu were almost as small as the room at the Tankard had been.

When he entered the mess, he didn't even have to ask where to find ale or lager. A ranker came up and took in the sling and the caked blood. "Ah . . . lager or ale, sir?"

"Lager, please." Quaeryt took a seat close to the end of the single long table, but it was too high to rest the arm in the sling on. So he pushed back the chair slightly and waited for the lager, which arrived quickly.

He really didn't feel that thirsty, and just sipped it as he could and thought, trying to ignore the combination of sharp stabbing pain and dull throbbing aches in his chest and shoulder. The fact that the surgeon had seen more than a few crossbow-quarrel wounds and that the mess attendant hadn't even asked what he wanted tended to confirm Rescalyn's assessment of the dangers of the hill brigands.

After a time, close to two quints before the bells rang out fifth glass, Skarpa entered the mess, his head moving from side to side until he saw Quaeryt. He immediately hurried over, a puzzled expression on his face. "I'd heard you took a quarrel. I expected you to be laid out in the infirmary. Did I hear wrong?"

"No. I managed to get it out without ripping myself up more. It must have been slowed by leaves or something. It didn't break the bone or cut too deep."

"From all that blood, it wasn't just a scratch, either," Skarpa said.

"No. I'll grant that. The surgeon had to stitch me up. He's still worried about the blood loss and the wound turning bad, but he's done what he can."

"He's had more experience than any one of us would like him to have."

"I certainly learned firsthand just how nasty the hill brigands could be. Getting shot on the first patrol . . ." Quaeryt shook his head.

"It does happen. The governor's always telling the troops that there are no safe patrols in the hill country. Almost every other one has some sort of trouble. One of the rankers who died was on his first patrol out of training."

"I wondered about that. I think he was the one hit when I was. I managed to grab the reins of his mount . . . I mean, after I worked out the quarrel."

Skarpa's eyes widened for just a moment. "You saw him get hit?"

"No. I got hit. Later, I saw him, but he died before I could do anything. Then I got his mount."

"You took a quarrel, worked it out, caught a stray mount, and then rode back here?"

"It wasn't that easy. My . . . guts . . . didn't agree after I got the quarrel out, and I had to hold a cloth over the field dressing most of the way back to keep the bleeding down until it finally stopped."

"You should have been a cavalry officer."

"Me? I was so stupid that I ducked too late. I didn't even realize that pattering sound was quarrels going through leaves." Quaeryt paused. "Why would they shoot through leaves?"

"Because you can't get a totally clean shot in the woods. That's one reason why they use the crossbows. They've got more power, and they don't get stopped as easily."

"I still can't believe I just watched for a moment."

Skarpa laughed. "That's what makes a good officer. Everyone makes mistakes. Those who are smart enough or tough enough to survive become good officers."

Quaeryt had his doubts, but he wasn't about to contradict the major.

What he did know was that, once he felt better, he definitely needed more practice with his shields. He also needed to be too sick to ride back to Tilbora until he was far more healed than anyone thought he was, because he had a very bad feeling about things.

51

For the next five days, all Quaeryt did was eat, rest, and drink lager—and clean off the area around the dressing with small amounts of clear spirits that he imaged when no one else was around. He had bouts of fever, or at least hot sweatiness, but those subsided after several days. He even slept through the time for services on Solayi, not that he'd planned to attend. While he slept a great deal, part of that was because he didn't sleep all that well. He had to stay on his back and prop the arm on his injured side so that it wouldn't move when he drifted off into a state that was more doze than true sleep. By Meredi, especially after the surgeon captain's assessment that morning that the wound was healing nicely, he was feeling improved enough to begin exploring the fortress that was Bora-lieu.

Unlike the Telaryn Palace, Boralieu had been built for the sole purpose of providing an entrenched impregnable base for forces engaged in pursuing and attacking the wayward holders of the hills. The walls were tall enough and thick enough that only massive siege engines could have toppled them, and the post had been built over two springs that supplied water. The windows were double-shuttered and even narrower than those in Tilbora, and most of the open space within the walls was stone-paved to eliminate mud when the heavy winter snows melted. The interior of the post was simple enough that Quaeryt finished walking through it within two glasses, and that was more than soon enough, because he definitely felt tired when he returned to the officers' mess and sank into one of the spare wooden chairs at the table.

During his enforced rest, he'd thought about everything about Tilbor that he could recall, as well as what he might have done, especially in developing better shields. The one thing that he did remember that struck him as both odd and promising was the feeling that something had ripped through his thoughts just before the quarrel had struck him. He had to question if in fact his thoughts were somehow linked to his shields. Yet he wasn't certain how to test that; he didn't want to make himself a target to see, and he wasn't in any condition to do much of great physical effort yet. But the idea held promise.

He couldn't hold the really strong shields for all that long, but could he train his reactions so that such a rip or impact on the lighter shields could instantly

create heavier ones close to him? It was worth looking
into . . . more than worth looking into if he wanted to
survive in Tilbor.

Then there were the larger, if less personal, questions. From what he could figure, there were close to
four thousand officers and men at the Telaryn Palace,
and more than another three thousand in the four
outposts. Together, they represented the largest concentrated force in all Telaryn, and all were controlled
by Rescalyn. Rescalyn had certainly opened every
record to Quaeryt and granted him access everywhere.
So far as Quaeryt could determine, Rescalyn was an
inspiring and effective commander, and one whose acts
benefited Bhayar and all Telaryn, including Tilbor. So
why did Quaeryt feel something was wrong?

For a time, he just sat in the mess and sipped lager,
thinking, not able to put anything in any sort of per-
spective.

Abruptly, he recalled one of the passages in the
book that Rescalyn had read—the one about the best
strategy being the one that was so open that no one
even understood that it was a strategy. He shook his
head ruefully. He'd been looking for what was hidden.
What about what was hidden in plain sight?

"Scholar . . . are you feeling better?" Skarpa paused
at the door to the mess.

As he did, a ranker stepped past the major. Quaeryt
frowned, realizing that in the indirect light where the
two stood, he couldn't tell the difference between their
undress uniforms.

Skarpa stepped inside and walked over to where
Quaeryt sat. "Are you all right?"

"Oh . . . I'm sorry. I was thinking." The scholar gestured to a chair. "Do you have a moment?"

"A few, but not many. Taenyd's company is coming

in from a west valley patrol, and I'll need to debrief
them."

"I was thinking . . . about uniforms. The undress
greens worn by the officers and the rankers are almost
the same except for the collar insignia. . . ."

"Oh . . . that's just good tactics. If the enemy could
easily see who the officers are, they'd concentrate on
them. That's especially important out in the hills. The
brigands always want to get officers."

*So . . . the only one who stood out on that patrol
was one scholar . . .*

"Was that something that the governor came up
with?"

"That was before he was governor. He was stationed in Ferravyl as a commander. You know, watching the Bovarians on the other side of the river.
Sometimes, they'd come downstream and try to pick
off officers from their riverboats with long-range
crossbows. They always targeted officers. He realized
it was because their uniforms were too different. He
persuaded Lord Chayar to make the change. Some of
the older officers didn't approve. They liked their fancy
uniforms. The marshal said they wouldn't like them
near so much if they were leading their men. Then he
suggested that the dress uniforms be as fancy as ever,
because balls and parades were where people paid attention to gilt and glitz. That didn't make him popu-
lar, either. It might have been why Fhayt was appointed
the first governor of Tilbor."

Quaeryt nodded. "Governor Rescalyn's very practical."

"He's a soldier's soldier. The men—and the
officers—would do anything for him. They'd take on
the Namer if the governor told them. They know he'd
be with them. He's not a rear-hilltop marshal."

"I got that impression." Quaeryt paused. "You know. I think when I go on other patrols I should be wearing green also."

"That's probably a good idea," replied Skarpa. "I should have thought of that. We just haven't had a scholar out here before." He frowned. "Weren't you supposed to go back to Tilbora?"

"No one told me anything. I thought I'd just go back when you did." The fact that no one had mentioned his return suggested other possibilities. "In another week or so, I ought to be able to ride."

"Are you sure?"

"I'll see what the surgeon says. I need to see more. One patrol—not even one patrol—won't give me a very good understanding of what you and your men go through."

"I don't know about that," replied Skarpa with a laugh. "You came about as close as anyone to experiencing the worst."

"Then I need to see the best and what's neither."

"Are all scholars so stubborn?"

"No. Only those that have to report back to Lord Bhayar."

Skarpa stood. "I'll see you at supper. I need to find out what Taenyd discovered."

Quaeryt watched the major walk out of the mess. Then he took another swallow of the lager. It wasn't bitter in his mouth, but the conversation with Skarpa had left a bitter residue in his thoughts.

He definitely needed to figure out a way to improve his shields—and soon.

52

On Jeudi morning, before breakfast, Quaeryt went to find the ranker who doubled as the local tailor, where he reclaimed the once-damaged browns—also washed and pressed. He gratefully paid two coppers, well worth it, and thanked the man. Then, after he ate, he headed out to see if he could work out something with his shields. Although he could use his left arm without more than discomfort, he left it in the sling when he wasn't using it, because it still pulled on the wound if he didn't. His first task was to obtain the materials he needed. First, he begged a few sheets of paper from Skarpa's senior squad leader and an old flour sack from the cooks. Then he found pinecones in the tinder bin.

After that, it took him almost a quint to find the head ostler—in the third stable that he entered.

"I was hoping you could help me. I need about five yards of line, and the same of cord."

"Line, sir?" The ostler glanced at Quaeryt's injured arm and at the tattered flour bag that held the paper, pinecones, and thin strips of what might once have been lathing.

Quaeryt concealed a wince. "Line" was the term for sailors. "I'm sorry. That came from my sailing background. Thin rope, stronger than cord, but not the heavy kind used for drays or heavy wagons."

"We might have some in the tack room, sir. Let's go see." The ostler turned.

Quaeryt followed him to the back of the stable and a small room filled with harnesses, spare bridles, traces, and other items he did not recognize hanging everywhere.

"... saw a coil back here the other day ..."

Quaeryt waited.

"Here we are." The ostler glanced back at Quaeryt. "Five yards, you say?"

"If you have it."

"That we do." The ostler began uncoiling rope, quickly measuring out five lengths from fingertip to chest and then adding a few spans. A quick cut with a thin, worn, and sharp belt knife, and the ostler handed the small coil to the scholar. "Cord's over here."

In short order, Quaeryt also had the cord.

"Is there anything else you need, sir?"

"Do you have something broken, iron or bronze, that I could tie to the end of the rope as a weight?"

"Bound to have something like that here somewhere." The ostler bent and rummaged through a barrel. "Thought so!" He straightened. "There you go." He presented Quaeryt with an arc of iron, broken at one end. "Will that do?"

Quaeryt weighed it in his hand. "That's just what I need. Thank you."

"My pleasure, sir."

Quaeryt nodded politely, ignoring the quizzical look from the ostler, then turned and walked out of the stable before heading westward toward the end stable. He stopped suddenly. He realized that the end stable couldn't be empty, because that was where the officers' mounts—and his mare—were stabled. He continued to the stable next to the end one, which was empty, and slipped inside. After closing the doors behind himself, he walked down the center until he found what he sought—a beam close to the ceiling around which he could tie one end of the line, and another ceiling beam less than three yards away, with a pulley suspended from it.

Then it took him time to find a ladder, half-hidden against the rear wall under the opening to a hayloft. With his right hand, he dragged the ladder back to the beams. Then he set to work.

When he finished, he had the broken iron half-hoop or harness trace brace or buckle, whatever it had been, tied to the end of the rope that extended from the first beam, suspended about a yard and a half above the stable floor. The cord ran from the weight to the pulley on the other beam and through it and then down to the floor, where Quaeryt had arranged a framework of slats and the pinecones at an angle so that when the pinecones all rolled off the paper on top of the frame, the change in weight would release the end of the cord.

It took him more than a quint to work out the weight that balanced that of the rope and the iron. The device worked, if jerkily, but that was fine because he didn't want to know when the cord was released.

He flicked one of the pinecones, starting them rolling off the frame, then stepped over to where he'd be in the path of the swinging rope and iron and raised the heavy shields. Several moments later, the iron at the end of the rope banged off the shields.

Quaeryt nodded and reset his contraptions. The second time, he only raised the light shields, concentrating on the feeling when the iron hit the shields— except that it didn't work because even the light shields slowed the iron enough that it nearly stopped before it reached Quaeryt.

The third time, he raised only the lightest of linked-air shields, and the iron slid through them, but Quaeryt could barely sense anything. He took a deep breath and set up the cumbersome makeshift device once more, using slightly heavier shields.

More than a glass later, he was finally able to sense when the iron hit any level of shield.

Although the physical side of the shield training wasn't that hard, he was still sweating, and he sat down on the floor and rested for a quint.

Then he stood and stretched, gingerly.

The next step—he hoped—was to see if he could train his reflexes to create heavier shields without his thinking about it if anything touched the outer shields.

Once more, he reset the framework with the pinecones and the end of the cord.

The first time he tried to link the two sets of shields, nothing happened and the iron thumped into his gut. Nor was the second attempt much better. Nor the third.

Maybe you're looking and anticipating too much.

With that thought in mind, for the fourth attempt, he turned his back . . . and the heavier shield did form, but too far from his body, and then flicked out of existence, and the iron thumped his lower back.

Quaeryt was sweating again . . . more heavily, and he was feeling light-headed.

After two more attempts, he gathered up the pieces of his makeshift apparatus and put them in the corner of one of the unused stalls. Even if someone stumbled over them, they wouldn't know their use.

He smiled. Most likely, they'd think that it was just a pile of junk no one had cleaned up.

Still, while he hadn't figured out how to make things

work enough to protect him, he had proved it was possible.

His steps were slow as he walked toward the mess and another mug of the lager that was beginning to wear on him.

53

By late on Solayi afternoon, just before supper, after four solid days of practice with his ramshackle device, Quaeryt had managed to train his body or his mind or some combination of both to react to any intrusion on light image-created shields, whether he could see it or not. That didn't prove that his improved shields would work in a combat situation or when he was totally surprised, but he was more hopeful than he had been. He also felt that he needed both more work on them and more time to recover from his injury.

With that thought, as he sat in the room serving as the officers' mess, he took another swallow of lager. He looked up to see Skarpa and Meinyt seating themselves across from him.

"Scholar . . . you've been off somewhere a lot lately," offered Meinyt.

"I haven't left Boralieu. I've been thinking, doing some light exercise so my muscles don't stiffen up. And I've been drinking more lager than I ever thought because the surgeon told me to."

"Can't go wrong with that advice," interjected Skarpa.

"I feel like I'll float away at times."

"Does it help?" asked Meinyt.

"It can't be harming him," pointed out Skarpa. "How many men have you seen take a bolt in the chest and shoulder and be up and walking in a week?"

Quaeryt decided against pointing out that the wound hadn't been quite as deep as those suffered by others. It had been deep enough, and it still ached, especially when he forgot to use the sling. "How have things been for you two?"

"We never did find the rest of those poachers," snorted Meinyt. "We may have to go visit Holder Waerfyl personally."

"That's something the commander has to decide," said Skarpa. "He's not here, and that's why I was looking for you. You're a scholar . . . can you talk about the Nameless?"

"I suppose I could talk about Rholan the Unnamer. Why?"

"We don't have a regular chorister for services, and the commander usually serves as chorister, or Captain Fyten of the engineers does, but they've both gone back to see the governor. The commander knows I talk a lot with Phargos. Before he left, he asked if I'd step in or find someone." Skarpa shook his head. "I like Phargos, and I might be able to say things like he does, but no one would believe me if I started talking about the Nameless."

Filling in for a chorister was about the last thing Quaeryt wanted to do. "I could do something for the homily, but I don't know the service."

"Gauswn does. He'll do that. He's a real believer—he might even have considered being a chorister, I heard— but he thinks it's improper for a fresh undercaptain to act as a chorister. No one will think that about you because scholars are supposed to know things like that."

"Am I supposed to give it in Bovarian the way Phargos does, or in Tellan?"

"Out here, even Phargos does it in Tellan. We don't have two services here. But you speak well in either tongue, I think."

"I think you've twisted my very sore arm far enough, Major," answered Quaeryt dryly. "I'll do it." He paused. "You mean tonight? Where are the services?"

"I mean tonight. I wouldn't have asked if you looked like you were dragging. We hold services in the main dining hall—just out there." He pointed through the door to where the troopers were gathered for their meal.

"I should have looked worse," quipped Quaeryt.

"It's too late for that now, scholar," returned Skarpa. "Enjoy your food."

"Because I won't enjoy acting as chorister?" Quaeryt shook his head. "I'm going to have to be more careful around you."

"The captains and undercaptains learn that quickly," said Meinyt.

Skarpa just laughed.

The mess began to fill, and before long, lager, ale, and platters were before those at the table. The sliced mutton, mashed potatoes, and some kind of gourd, all covered with a brown gravy, were decent, but unsurprisingly, not nearly so good as the food at the Telaryn Palace.

Finally, as the officers' mess emptied, Quaeryt stood and adjusted the sling. It had been a long day, and his shoulder was throbbing.

"You sure you'll be all right, scholar?" asked Skarpa.

"I'm a little tired, but I'll be fine. I don't talk with my shoulder." He offered a quick grin.

Less than a quint later, Quaeryt followed Gauswn

into the end of the dining hall, where they faced perhaps a hundred rankers and a handful of officers.
Quaeryt saw Meinyt and Skarpa in the rear to one side.

After a long pause, the undercaptain stepped forward. He wore a plain white scarf over his undress
greens, not nearly so long as those worn by true choristers, but his voice was firm as he began with the
traditional greeting. "We gather together in the spirit
of the Nameless and to affirm the quest for goodness
and mercy in all that we do."

The opening hymn followed, and it was "Praise Not
the Nameless," but sung in Tellan. That wasn't surprising, either, since it was one of the better-known hymns.
Then came the confession, ending with, ". . . and deference to You who cannot be named or known, only
respected and worshipped."

Quaeryt murmured "In peace and harmony" with
the others, but standing where he was, he didn't have
to offer coins for the offertory basket, for which he
was grateful.

Since there was no pulpit, after the offering was
collected he just stepped forward. "Good evening," he
offered in Tellan.

"Good evening," came the murmured reply.

"Under the Nameless all evenings are reckoned as
good . . . but how good . . . well . . . it's not raining,
and for that we can all thank the Nameless."

A low chuckle ran through those assembled.

"A few of you just may have heard about Rholan
the Unnamer." Quaeryt paused, hoping his understate-
ment would at least draw smiles and a few chuckles.

It did, and he went on. "Just before I was posted to
Tilbor, I happened to read about Rholan in an ancient
tome that might not have been opened since it was
written over a century ago. Reading old, old books

often doesn't tell you as much as you hope, but this one, and some of the others, got me to thinking. Rholan is the most famous exponent of the Nameless, yet we know almost nothing about him as a man, as if he tried, in fact, to be as nameless as possible. He was born in Montagne, we think, but do not know for sure, and lived there most of his life. He never traveled more than a two hundred milles from there, and he disappeared after traveling to Cloisonyt in his fifty-third year. Yet his words and acts changed all Lydar.

"You have certainly heard his most famous precepts, such as 'A name does not equal deeds' or 'When the body is a slave to the name, both are servants of the Namer.' You know that every anomen is without adornment within and without because Rholan declared that adornment that serves no function and provides no use is a form of Naming. He made the point that acts always triumph over names, and in a sense his own life proves that. We know little of him, only what he said, only in the questions he raised.

"Yet there is an irony in that, because we tend to revere his name, often ignoring his precepts, and while I am no chorister, I have the feeling that Rholan would rather have been more forgotten than to have his words, and even his questions, ignored in favor of remembering his name. Yet . . . were another such as he to arise, who offered such precepts and questions, would we pay attention to them, or would we require proof of deeds?

"We talk of deeds and acts, but if either a deed or an act is used as a proof of something, is that not also Naming?

"You are all soldiers, and I am a scholar, and it is most unlikely that, even if we wished otherwise, which we should not, our names will outlive us, except in the hearts and thoughts of those closest to us. What will outlive us is our actions, for better or worse, those actions undertaken for the sake of the action itself, and not for fame or glory .. ."

Quaeryt went on to talk about the value of actions, citing a few great military acts along the way, then concluded, ". ... and yet the irony, which we should never forget, is that deeds can only be remembered through words, and words, used too freely, can easily become boasting, and thus a form of Naming. In that, I would observe that, indeed, the hardest part of accomplishing deeds, both great and small, is letting them speak for themselves and resisting the temptation to speak of them."

After the benediction, Quaeryt waited as the worshippers, mainly rankers, filed out of the dining hall.

Then the undercaptain turned to Quaeryt. "You mentioned the coming of another such as Rholan. Do you think that possible?"

"Anything is possible, but I think it unlikely we will ever see another exactly like Rholan. We might see another who raises those questions in another fashion."

"You could be a chorister, Scholar Quaeryt."

"Not week after week, I fear, but thank you anyway."

Skarpa stepped forward, smiling. "I'll have to tell Phargos what you said. After all his homilies I never heard that about Rholan."

Quaeryt laughed softly. "There are some things a scholar should know that not even choristers know."

54

The first part of the week passed relatively uneventfully for Quaeryt. He kept practicing with his contrived system, varying the timing and adding weight to the rope, so that his shields seemed to react instantly to any intrusion. His strength had largely returned, and he had no more incidents of fever, although soreness persisted in his shoulder, and he had trouble sleeping for long periods because he still was limited to sleeping on his back or his right side.

He spent his time, when he wasn't practicing his shields, studying the post, asking questions and listening at meals and in the evening in the officers' mess and trying to learn more about Tilbor and the regiment. While he did find out more, nothing he heard added anything new, but rather filled out with specific details what he already knew.

Finally, at breakfast on Jeudi, he looked across the table at Skarpa. "Major . . . are there any patrols that just stay in the valley?"

"There's one every day. It's tedious. They patrol around the edges of the entire valley looking for tracks or signs that anyone may be scouting the post . . . or causing trouble. It's part training and part precaution."

"I'd like to accompany them today."

Skarpa frowned. "Are you up to that?"

Quaeryt offered a grin. "I can ride. I never was any good with weapons, and I wouldn't be any trouble. And if I get too tired, I can certainly find my way back. There haven't been any brigands in the valley itself in years. That's what Meinyt said."

"That's true." Skarpa frowned, then nodded. "Undercaptain Gauswn has the boundary patrol today. I'll tell him to expect you."

"Thank you. I appreciate it." He didn't point out that he was bored—because he hated to say that—but there was little enough for a scholar to do, with no library and no diversions. Then again, that might have been another reason why the companies spent only a month at a time at Boralieu.

"I don't know as you'll learn all that much."

"I may not, but that's a form of learning, too."

Skarpa shook his head.

After he finished eating, Quaeryt made his way to the end stable. He'd thought about asking around to get a worn green uniform shirt that he could wear over his browns, but hadn't done so. Still, he shouldn't need it, not so long as the patrol stayed in the valley.

He did manage to saddle the mare, if awkwardly. He wouldn't have been able to do so, he realized, if he'd injured his right shoulder. When he led the mare out into the courtyard and mounted, using both hands, but replacing his arm in the sling after settling into the saddle, he saw that clouds were moving in from the north—not thunderclouds, but high thin clouds that might presage nothing or a later rain. The clouds would make the day more pleasant, but not if rain followed.

From the south end of the courtyard, Gauswn turned his horse and rode toward Quaeryt.

The scholar had to admire the ease with which the undercaptain seemed to meld with his mount.

"Greetings, scholar." Gauswn smiled. "Welcome to our very routine patrol."

"That's fine with me. My last patrol had enough excitement."

"Your arm?"

"I can use it if I have to, but I'm supposed to keep it in the sling most of the time for a bit longer."

Gauswn's nod contained a hint of doubt, but he said nothing more as Quaeryt rode beside him toward the head of the column, which looked to consist of two squads, and not a full company.

Once the patrol headed downhill from the sandstone walls of Boralieu, Quaeryt raised his lighter shields, set close to a yard and a half from him. He had already realized that the way his shielding worked, he'd have trouble if he rode too close to anyone. Still . . . if he kept working with them, maybe, just maybe, he could become strong enough to hold the heavier shields all the time. Or he could find a way to make them more selective.

The wind from the north was not stiff, but stronger than a mere breeze, with a hint of chill behind it.

"This won't be much of a patrol," offered Gauswn.

"Major Skarpa said that it was also a training exercise of sorts."

"It is. We put a newer ranker out front with each experienced outrider, and they point out what a scout or an outrider needs to look for. Also, we'll run road drills when we're not near any of the local crofters." Gauswn offered a wry smile. "A quick charge beside a plow horse or a cart horse might spook them, and the commander wouldn't want to hear about that. . . ."

Less than a quint later, as the patrol neared the eastern edge of the valley, Quaeryt saw ahead four large drays. Four draft horses, escorted by a squad of troopers, pulled each as they groaned along the dirt road toward Boralieu.

Gauswn ordered the squads immediately onto the shoulder of the road to wait as the wagons passed.

"Supply wagons," explained Gauswn. "Once a week except in the winter."

"How often then?"

"Whenever they can, but over the next few weeks, they'll bring in extra supplies—the kind that keep—so that the post could last all winter without resupply. The fare isn't what anyone likes, but they're always fed."

"That's the mark of a good commander."

"It is." Gauswn paused, then asked, "Did you ever study to be chorister? You seem to know so much about Rholan and the Nameless."

"Scholars study many things."

"But . . . you knew about Rholan, the way you talked about him. What else do you know?"

Quaeryt hesitated, if but for a moment. If he didn't offer a bit more, he'd seem like a shallow scholar, yet . . . "He's the only follower of the Nameless who is mentioned in any of the hymns or as a subject for homilies in the guidance for choristers."

"Where did you discover that?"

Quaeryt laughed. "I asked several choristers. I have this bad habit of asking questions. So did Rholan, I think." As soon as he uttered the last sentence, he wished he hadn't.

"Rholan asked questions?"

"That's what some of the texts say."

"Such as?"

"Oh . . . some are so familiar everyone's forgotten who first asked them. He was the one who asked, 'What truly is a name?' At least, he was the first to ask that as a serious question. Things like that."

"What else?"

"I'd have to go back to my library in Solis to rediscover the others."

Gauswn looked appraisingly at Quaeryt, but didn't press further.

Skarpa did warn you that he was very devout in his worship of the Nameless.

Once the wagons had passed, the patrol rode no more than another half mille before turning south on a path little more than a dirt track stamped out by patrol after patrol. On the slope to the east were bushes, copses of trees, largely evergreens and birches, and rocky pasture. Quaeryt saw one flock of sheep, tended by a youth or a young girl, farther to the south and higher on the rise.

"This side's easy, but I have the outriders make the new ones name all the tracks they see from the saddle. Too many times, you don't have time to dismount and check, especially not in the woods."

Based on his one experience along those lines, Quaeryt tended to agree.

Close to two glasses later, the patrol reached the southern end of the valley and turned westward. Less than a mille farther, the slopes had become covered with older pines, with but scattered handfuls of birches and only an occasional oak. On the north side of the track were flat fields, most bearing golden wheat corn close to being harvested.

Quaeryt had the feeling that those fertile fields might once have been a shallow lake, generations back.

"It's mostly wheat down here. Farther along, where there's a stream, they grow some maize."

"Do you get any supplies from the locals?"

"Some . . . but they don't grow enough for themselves and all of Boralieu. The governor insists that we pay fair prices for anything we buy and that we make sure to leave enough that they can get through the worst of winters without difficulty."

"He tries very hard to be fair."

"Fairer than the Khanars, some of the old folks say."

As the patrol neared the southwestern corner of the valley, the wind picked up, and Quaeryt could see where the winters could indeed be bitter. Ahead, at the end of a hayfield, one of the last, it appeared to the scholar, a cart was drawn up next to a low stone wall, and a boy was stacking the bundles in the cart while either his father or an older brother was cutting the stalks in the field with a scythe.

As the column approached the cart, a severe gust of wind blasted out of the north, ripping part of the bundle of hay out of the boy's hands and swirling it toward the patrol. Abruptly, Quaeryt's shields triggered, and the hay and dust swirled around him. He dropped the shields quickly, but Gauswn turned with a frown.

"That . . . what was that? The hay and dust, they blew around you . . ."

"They did?" asked Quaeryt. "I didn't notice." *What else can you say?*

"I'm sure they did."

Quaeryt laughed. "Sometimes, the wind does strange things."

Again, the undercaptain looked hard at Quaeryt, who merely offered an amused smile, even as he was thinking, *Why did it have to be Gauswn who saw the effect of the shields?*

"Tell me about what you have the men look for when you patrol along the western edge," said Quaeryt. "Do you get any brigands taking shots at you from the higher slopes?"

The undercaptain looked startled, but, after a moment, replied, "Not since I've been here, but we do see tracks, as if someone is scouting. Not too often, but you can never tell . . ."

Quaeryt remained ready to ask more questions as he listened, but, obviously, he needed to work more, a great deal more, on perfecting the shields if they were to be effective.

55

When he returned from the local patrol, it was a quint or so past second glass, and Quaeryt was so exhausted that he went to his tiny room and took a nap. He woke just before the evening meal sore all over. He limped to dinner, because his bad leg was bothering him more than usual, and managed to sit beside Skarpa in order to avoid Gauswn without really seeming to do so. He listened carefully during and after the meal, while Skarpa, Meinyt, and the other officers talked, but he didn't overhear any references to the wind or hay flying around him.

A long night's sleep left him less tired, but still stiff when he struggled up on Vendrei morning, although he was limping less on the way to the mess. After breakfast, he made his way from the mess to the infirmary. He didn't wait long, because he was the only one there. The surgeon removed the latest dressing and checked the wound.

"You don't need a dressing any longer. Just keep it clean." The captain shook his head. "Most wounds like this don't heal so cleanly or so quickly. If I hadn't seen how deep it was myself, I wouldn't have believed it, scholar."

"When would it be a good idea to go back to riding patrols outside the valley?"

"A good idea? Never. But if that's what you have to do, I'd give it until Lundi. But take two water bottles of lager if you do. You didn't drink any water, did you?"

"No. You told me not to."

"Good. I'd stay away from it for another week, at least mostly. If you do drink water, only drink what you get here in Boralieu. It's clean enough. The hillside streams might look clear, but I've had more than a few rankers who drank from them end up turning their bowels inside out, and you don't need that."

"Do you know why?" Quaeryt couldn't resist asking.

"Might be hill people fouling the water. They're not all that careful. It might be the beavers, or other animals, or who knows what." The surgeon stepped back. "If it gets red or the soreness across your chest gets worse, you need to come back. Otherwise, there's not much else that I can do."

Quaeryt just nodded. *If there's soreness and pain across my chest, there isn't going to be much you or anyone can do.* But there wasn't much point in saying so, and he didn't as he stood and replaced his undershirt and repaired tunic.

After leaving the surgeon, he made his way to the one unused stable, where he set up his apparatus. There he spent almost three glasses experimenting with his apparatus and his shields, trying to figure out how to let small things through the shields . . . but not too small. The tip of an unbarbed crossbow bolt wasn't very large, and he'd seen what that could do.

He wasn't having much success until he thought, *What about the speed of something hitting the outer shields?*

That seemed to make sense, except that he really didn't have much of a way to speed the swinging fall of the iron weight. He could slow it . . . though . . .

After another glass, he felt he was on to something that might work better, but he was feeling tired and not reacting as well as he felt he should.

But you need to improve your shields more or you'll just be a lure for those backwoods crossbowmen.

Improving his shields was taking time, and Bhayar had been rather firm about his returning before the end of winter . . . and Quaeryt himself didn't want to remain for any part of winter. Yet he was convinced that he needed to remain at Boralieu because the hills and the timber holders contained the key to the mystery that was Tilbor, and, if he wanted to survive to discover what that key was, he needed better shields. Even so, he was sweating heavily from exercising, however lightly, in the damp air left from the recent rains, and he needed to cool down and rest.

Some things you can't force.

He hated to admit that, but he hid his makeshift device, then made his way slowly back to his quarters, such as they were, to get the rest he needed and didn't want to spare the time for.

When Quaeryt walked into the mess that night, even before he reached the table, Skarpa intercepted him. "The commander wants to meet you, scholar."

"Me? What did I do . . . or fail to do?"

"Nothing. It's nothing to worry about." The major

guided him toward a black-haired officer in greens with silver starbursts on his collar who stood beside the head of a long table. "Commander Zirkyl, this is Scholar Quaeryt."

"I'm very glad to meet you, scholar." The commander smiled. "All have said that you offered a better homily than most choristers. If you remain here long, we may call upon you again. . . ."

"Thank you, sir, but one homily does not make a chorister out of a scholar."

"I'll take you at your word, scholar . . . with a few doubts. I've heard enough officers speak badly and at length to know that it's unlikely that one who speaks well when asked to do so on short notice will speak badly upon other occasions." Zirkyl smiled. "I might not like what you say all the time, but it's likely you will say it well." He looked to Skarpa. "Have you ever heard him speak poorly?"

"No, sir, but he listens more than he talks."

"I would that some officers followed that practice." Zirkyl laughed and turned back to Quaeryt. "I'm glad to see that you're healing well."

"So am I, sir. Thank you." Quaeryt understood that the commander had said what he wanted, and he inclined his head and stepped back, moving more toward the foot of the table.

Skarpa came with him, then gestured. "We can sit here."

The two sat side by side, directly in front of two pitchers, one of ale and one of lager. Skarpa immediately filled his mug with ale. Quaeryt took lager. In less than half a quint, all the officers were seated, and platters were headed down the table.

Meinyt had taken the seat across from Quaeryt.

"Major Bruelt said the commander especially liked your words about officers and soldiers being remembered for their deeds and not their boasts."

"How did he know what I said?"

"Oh ... Undercaptain Gauswn wrote it down. He's got a good memory."

Quaeryt managed not to wince.

"He's a good undercaptain," Skarpa said. "He works hard, and he's thorough. You rode with him. What do you think?"

"From what I saw, I'd agree, but I'm not a mounted officer."

"With a little training, you'd do better than most," Meinyt said. "Don't know many who could take a quarrel, get it out, catch a loose mount, and then ride back to Boralieu, and be ready to ride again in a few weeks."

"Have any of the companies had any success in dealing with those poachers and hill holders?" asked Quaeryt, trying to change the subject without being totally obvious.

Skarpa, his mouth full of the less than tender mutton, shook his head.

From beside him, Meinyt said, "There haven't been any attacks there since the one on us."

"There have been two near the northwest outpost, though," Skarpa finally said, before taking another swallow of ale.

"What will happen next?"

"The commander is considering paying a visit to Waerfyl—with three companies," said Skarpa quietly. "That's what I hear."

"I think I'd like to accompany you."

"Why do you think I'd be involved?"

"I think both you and Captain Meinyt would be involved. He'd want the best major and company behind him."

Meinyt grinned. "He's got you, Major."

"If . . . if something like that happens, you can go."

"This time I'll wear greens, at least a green shirt," Quaeryt said dryly.

"Good idea."

Is it a good idea? Hardly. You just don't have any better ones. Quaeryt sipped more of the lager he was liking less and less.

56

On Lundi morning, Quaeryt rode out of Boralieu beside Major Skarpa, with three companies from Sixth Battalion behind them, the first one being Meinyt's. Quaeryt had donned, over his browns, a somewhat worn and overlarge green undress uniform shirt he had obtained from the ranker serving as supply clerk, although he had his doubts that such a large force would be attacked. The wind was brisk, under a clear sky.

Commander Zirkyl had decided, regretfully, according to Skarpa, that for the post commander to pay a call on Holder Waerfyl would grant the timber holder far too much importance, both in Waerfyl's own mind and in the eyes of both High Holders and hill holders. Quaeryt couldn't help but wonder if Zirkyl had received a dispatch or other advice along those lines from Rescalyn.

For the first glass, Skarpa's outriders and scouts

followed the same road that Meinyt's company had taken on the patrol where Quaeryt had been wounded. During that part of the ride, Quaeryt kept working with and adjusting his shields, effectively enough that no one noticed. Then, after another few quints, when the scouts reached the point where the road forked, they turned to the right, heading close to due north.

"How far before we reach Waerfyl's holding?" Quaeryt asked the major.

"Another three milles or so to the gate, and about a mille after that."

"Has anyone actually ridden up to his hold?"

"Not often. That's why the outriders will unfurl a friendship banner when we get closer to his holding. He'll be there. Where else would he go?"

Naïve as Skarpa's question sounded superficially, Quaeryt realized that the major had a point. Waerfyl wasn't welcome to visit High Holders, and, from what Quaeryt did know, the hill holders weren't exactly that friendly with each other, just united by a common opposition to any other authority.

Some three quints passed before the scouts—and the column of riders—halted at the gates marking the entry to the estate or hold proper. Unlike the estate gates around Tilbora, or those in Solis, the "gate" to Waerfyl's holding consisted of two pillars constructed of local stones of all sizes a man could lift, mortared together, and standing some four yards apart. Each square pillar was a yard on a side and rose roughly three yards from a flat stone and mortar base. There was no gatehouse or anything resembling such, and no sign of any guards. The road or lane beyond the two gate pillars consisted of gravel unevenly packed into the local clay or mud, but compacted enough by time, hoofs, and wagons that the latest wagon had left barely an indentation on the surface, despite the rain that had fallen on Samedi.

"Horns to the front! With the banner bearers!" ordered Skarpa.

With the hornists riding directly behind the scouts, if separated by several yards, and playing fanfares intermittently, the column rode slowly up the lane that climbed gently through a small area of woods, then crossed a level meadow beside a pond. Both red flies and mosquitoes swarmed toward the riders, and Quaeryt found that his adjustments to his shields did little or nothing to stop the voracious insects. Even fanning them away was of limited usefulness.

The meadow stretched close to half a mille before the ground beyond rose gently to a low ridge, cleared of all trees and brush, on the top of which stood the buildings comprising the hold. That ridge was lower than the one immediately to the north, and only a gentle swale separated the two ridges. What appeared to be a low stone tower stood on the end of the higher ridge closest to the holding buildings.

As Quaeryt rode closer, he could see that the main hold structure looked to be of two stories, although he had the feeling there was a third, lower level dug into the ridge. The walls were of large logs, stripped of their bark and notched or planed to fit together, rising from a foundation composed of stones and mortar that showed a yard above ground. As with all dwellings in Tilbor, the windows, especially on the lower level, were narrow and had thick shutters. The roof was of split slate, rather than tile or thatch—or the wooden shakes he had noticed on larger dwellings in Tilbora.

Why slate here? The snow has to be deeper. Or is the danger from sparks or fire greater? Quaeryt had no way of knowing, but surmised that hill holders had the resources to build structures strong enough to handle snow and minimize dangers from fire.

A handful of men, apparently unarmed and generally wearing leather jackets of various sorts, gathered on the stone-paved expanse that served as an unroofed porch or a terrace and that extended some ten yards on each side of the heavy double doors in the center of the building. The lane split, and one part continued up to where it ran beside the front of the terrace, while the other circled to the right toward the buildings to the east and slightly lower on the ridge.

When the hornists and the banner bearers neared the end of the porch, Skarpa ordered, "Column! Halt!" After several moments, he added, "Welcome fanfare!"

While Quaeryt thought the hornists did their best, the fanfare was ragged and slightly out of tune.

The double doors opened, and a man of medium height stepped out. His bearing declared that he was of import, and he walked to the front of the porch and surveyed the assembled troops. He wore a fine white linen shirt, with a deep red sleeveless vest over it, and brownish black trousers. His brown hair was long, and tied back, but he sported neither mustache nor beard, unlike many of the men Quaeryt had seen around Tilbora or most of those already gathered on the terrace. He looked to be some ten years older than Quaeryt. He just stood on the wide stone platform for a time after the fanfare ended. Then he laughed. "I am honored! Deeply honored that Lord Bhayar's minions would think I am so fearsome that a friendly visit requires so many armed men."

Waerfyl's eyes fixed on Skarpa. "Your approach was rather contradictory, don't you think, Major? A peace banner followed by hundreds of armed cavalrymen?"

"Not at all," replied Skarpa with a brief laugh of his own, riding closer and reining up. "As we have discovered, peaceful behavior here in the hills only seems to happen when one appears with overwhelming force."

"Might I ask, if it is not deemed too impertinent by a mere hill holder in dealing with the force and might of all Telaryn, what might be the purpose of this visit . . . this appearance?"

"You might indeed," replied Skarpa.

Quaeryt could sense that the major was uneasy in speaking, but he had no doubts that Commander Zirkyl had tutored Skarpa carefully in what he wanted said.

After a moment, the major cleared his throat. "I am here to convey the greetings and concerns of the governor. You are the holder over a large expanse of lands, largely timberlands. You are known to have great control over those who serve you. Yet, time after time, groups of men have proceeded from your lands to those of the High Holder whose lands adjoin yours and poached game and removed valuable timber. In addition, some of those men have attacked routine patrols merely riding the roads and, in several cases, killed soldiers. The governor is concerned that you have failed to exercise control over those men. Given the extent of your lands, it is highly unlikely that they could have done what they did without spending a great deal of time on your lands. This suggests a failure to control your own lands, and possibly those who serve you. Your lack of action to exert such control suggests that you either allow or actively support the actions of these men. Neither is acceptable."

Neither Waerfyl nor Skarpa spoke for several moments.

The major continued to look pointedly at the holder.

Finally, Waerfyl offered a cynical smile. "Your words, or should I say the governor's, are most polite. I will say that I am sorry to be unable to respond as well. You accuse me of acts with no proof that these men are in any way connected to me. My lands are large. Not nearly so large as those of High Holder Dymaetyn. They are also hilly and rocky, and there are places that have not seen a man or mount in generations. As you should know, Major, and as the governor certainly knows, it has been strongly suggested by this governor and his predecessor that I avoid raising large numbers of armsmen. I do not have anywhere as many as do the High Holders. Yet they cannot stop such brigands? And I, with far fewer armsmen . . . how can I possibly be held accountable for those who slip through my lands?"

"Holder Waerfyl, I am not here to debate. I am not here to judge. I am here to convey the governor's concerns. You may recall that the fate of those landholders who have ignored those concerns has not been one many would wish to share."

"So . . . you are warning me that if brigands I do not and cannot control continue their actions, the governor will act against me and my family and retainers."

"The governor will do what the governor will do based upon what happens in the future. I am not in his confidences. I cannot say what he will do. I am here to convey his concerns."

"Such a loyal officer." Waerfyl shook his head. "You and your men may take this holding. You may even put it to the torch. If you do, you will never control the hill lands, and any soldier who enters these forests will be at risk, for generations to come. Is that what the governor wants?"

"The governor wishes that the lawbreaking, the attacks, and the thefts stop. Since they come from your lands, it seemed reasonable to convey those concerns to you. I have done so. You have received that conveyance. We will leave the determination of what happens in the future to you." Skarpa inclined his head politely. "Now . . . having conveyed the governor's concerns, we will depart . . . peacefully."

"You may convey to the governor that I can only do what I can do."

"I will do so. Good day, Holder Waerfyl." Skarpa turned his mount. "Column! To the rear!"

Quaeryt followed the major along the side of the lane and down the slope until he was at the rear of the formation, which became the lead as the companies rode back toward the gateposts.

Once the companies were well away from Waerfyl's holding, Quaeryt, again riding beside Skarpa, asked, "Why did he bring up that business about not being able to raise armsmen?"

"There's a decree limiting the numbers of armed men. So far as the hill holders are concerned, it's meaningless. They say that their men are loggers or rangers or whatever, but they're all armed." Skarpa shook his head. "There's no way with all the armed retainers that Waerfyl has that he'd allow outside brigands, but he pleads that he can't patrol because of the decree. If the attacks stop, it's an admission that he's guilty one way or another."

"I can't believe the governor would torch his holding, not with what could happen."

"I can't say whether he will or won't. Lord Chayar didn't have a problem in razing the hold of a High Holder, and the hill holders are getting out of hand. This was a warning to Waerfyl that his raids on Dymaetyn have gotten out of hand and that he shouldn't let his men shoot at soldiers."

"What will happen?"

"Likely what's happened before." Skarpa took a deep breath. "The attacks here will stop . . . for a while. They'll start somewhere else, with some other hill holder against some other High Holder. The hill holders don't really want the governor to turn the regiment against them, and the governor doesn't want to. Not with the threat of the Bovarians in the west. Even the hill holders wouldn't want to change Lord Bhayar for Kharst, not after what Kharst did in Khel. So . . . it's a deadly game, and some of my soldiers get killed or wounded, but the losses are far less than if we had to go in and clean out all of these miserable hill holders." The major shook his head. "I can't say that I like having to use three companies to deliver a warning, but it takes something like that to tell a hill holder you're serious."

"How do the other timber holders get along with each other?"

"They don't. That's another part of the problem. If they don't defend their lands, then another holder will try to log it, or trap on it, so as to save his own lands. . . ."

It's almost as if Rescalyn is using the conflicts between the hill holders and between them and the High Holders as a way of . . . what? Justifying having raised what amounts to a large standing army? Quaeryt didn't like that possibility . . . or any of the other possible answers to his question. Not any of them. Not at all.

He continued riding, keeping a pleasant expression on his face.

57

Quaeryt decided not to press to accompany a company on Mardi or Meredi. While he was improving, and no longer needed to use the sling, the strain of carrying shields tired him more than the riding itself, and he wasn't about to enter the forests without shields, not for long patrols, even if Skarpa had said the patrols would be quiet for a time. He did spend quite a few glasses in the stable working on ways to refine his shields. On Meredi, he accompanied another captain in Sixth Battalion—Duesyn—on a comparatively short patrol through the lower and less wooded hills to the south of the valley that held Boralieu. He still wore the slightly tattered and overlarge undress green shirt over his browns, but the patrol was without event, except that Quaeryt had another chance to work on his shields while in the saddle, but he still couldn't keep insects away without triggering the shields too often.

On Jeudi, he spent more time trying to refine the sensitivity of his shields, wanting to find a way to protect himself from attacks—and from mosquitoes and red flies—without reacting to every other nonthreatening approach. He had little success.

On Jeudi night, Skarpa caught him just before the evening meal. "Tomorrow, Meinyt's taking a patrol to the northeast. High Holder Eshalyn has complained that he's suffering intrusions and attacks from the hill holder next to his lands. Commander Zirkyl thought you might find that useful in your reports to Lord Bhayar."

While Quaeryt hadn't sent any reports to Bhayar, he had written out those reports, but he wanted to hand them to the courier himself. The fewer eyes that saw what he wrote the better.

So . . . on Vendrei morning, Quaeryt pulled on the overlarge green shirt and mounted up, riding out of Boralieu, eastward across the valley, and then north.

"What can you tell me about what you're supposed to be looking for or to stop?" he asked Meinyt, riding to his left, as the patrol neared a thickly wooded slope.

"This time, it's Saentaryn. High Holder Eshalyn isn't worried about poachers, but about raids on one of his mines."

"Mines?" Quaeryt didn't even know there were mines in the area.

"It's a coal mine, and it's not very big, but Eshalyn's family has been mining it to heat their holding and to use in their smithies. They even give the extras to their croppers and tenants. That way they don't have to cut as much timber for firewood. On Mardi, some brigands came in and took two wagons and the coal in them. They killed three miners. The tracks headed north. We're supposed to follow the wagon tracks to see where they go. That's if we can."

"Let me guess," replied Quaeryt. "Until Lord Chayar conquered Tilbor, the mine was on lands claimed by . . . Sentar—"

"Saentaryn," corrected Meinyt. "How did you know that?"

"I didn't. It just seems to be a recurring pattern. Either the hill holders have lost lands under Telaryn, or they're using that as an excuse to grab lands they've always wanted or once had and lost. What do you think?"

"I think they never had them. They just always thought that they should be theirs. Everyone has a glorious past, even if they didn't." Meinyt snorted.

"I wouldn't be surprised if the governor tends to back the High Holders in uncertain claims, just because they keep things more stable."

"There's no question about that. The hill holders aren't trustworthy. They've been fighting each other and the High Holders for generations."

Quaeryt merely nodded, although from what he'd read, the Khanars had tried to cultivate the hill holders to some degree. Why didn't Rescalyn? He certainly could have occasionally been conciliatory toward them. Was it because he believed they couldn't be trusted to keep their word? Or for some other reason?

Once the company entered the woods, Quaeryt stopped talking or asking questions, concentrating instead on the trees on each side of the dirt road. Unlike the roads to the west of Boralieu, the undergrowth and young trees had been cleared back only five yards or so from the packed and rutted dirt. Although that left the road shaded and the troopers out of the sun, the lack of a breeze and the dampness of the air had Quaeryt sweating more than when he had been riding in the open.

Another glass passed before one of the scouts rode back, turning his mount to ride on the side of the captain away from the scholar. "We've got tracks ahead on that road coming from the southeast. They're heavy enough for coal drays."

"That's the side road that's closest to the mine. Any more recent signs of riders?"

"No, sir. Not so far."

"Follow the wagon tracks. We'll be behind you. If you see any recent hoofprints or the wagon ruts turn off the main road, report back."

"Yes, sir."

The side road joined the main road several hundred yards farther north. Quaeryt glanced back as he rode past the junction, noting that the southeast road had a gentler grade than the section of the main road the company had just traveled. Even he could see that the ruts made by the wagons coming from the side road were considerably deeper than the older and half-obliterated ruts made by wagons passing earlier. That suggested to him that the teamsters were indeed familiar with the roads. That and the fact that no one would seize coal unless it didn't have to be carted too far and unless they had a use for it also suggested that High Holder Eshalyn's suspicions were certainly justified.

More than a half glass passed before one of the scouts rode back to report to Meinyt.

"They had problems with one of the wheels up ahead, sir. They were there for a time, possibly a day or so."

"When did they leave?"

"I'd guess sometime early today. It could have been late last night . . ."

"That's not likely. Tell the others to watch closely for anything at all."

"Yes, sir." The scout turned and rode forward.

Meinyt swung his mount to the side. "Squad leaders! Ready arms!"

"Ready arms!" echoed back along the road.

"Forward."

Quaeryt checked his shields, then urged the mare forward to stay beside the captain. After several hundred yards, they reached an area where part of the shoulder was torn up and where a large number of sizable rocks had recently been tossed just beyond the edge of the road.

"They used the rocks to support an axle, it looks like," observed the captain. "Coal's heavy, and those wagons weren't meant to be used here in the hills."

After studying the marks in the road briefly, Meinyt signaled for the company to continue.

Quaeryt kept glancing ahead, but saw nothing but the trees and the road . . . and the low bushes and grass between the two.

The company had covered about another half mille before Meinyt spoke again. "All the tracks on the dirt of the road's shoulder are gone. They've been rubbed out with branches or the like, but the grass is trampled in places."

As the captain turned in the saddle, Quaeryt heard the faintest crackling just ahead and to his right. Then three riders charged directly toward the captain, with three behind them, all carrying blades ready to strike. There might have been more riders farther back, but Quaeryt couldn't tell.

He instantly strengthened and widened his shields, then turned the mare into the charge. He had to grab the pommel of the saddle with his good hand to keep his seat as the two leading attackers and their mounts rebounded from the shields. One mount went down, pinning the rider, and the other two rode into the woods on the west side of the dirt track. The next three turned and rode back down the narrow track whose entry had been disguised with a shield of brush and branches. Quaeryt managed to rein in the mare and circle back to rejoin Meinyt.

The captain didn't look at the scholar. "Column! Halt!"

Two rankers dismounted quickly, and managed to help the fallen horse off the downed rider, who moaned, but did not move. One leg was bent at an angle that suggested it was broken.

"Rough splint that leg and get him back on his mount," commanded the captain. "He might be able to tell us something. Second squad! Hold here, and guard the lane entrance—and the prisoner. Pass it back. We'll check a bit farther along the road."

Less than a mille farther, just over a low rise and halfway around a gentle curve were the beds of two wagons—empty and without wheels, traces, or draft horses.

"Namer-frigged-sows," muttered Meinyt as he reined up, studying the damp shoulder of the road again.

"They brought small carts here and emptied the wagons and stripped them," said one of the scouts. "You can see the tracks heading through the woods there. It's not even a lane."

"Let them go. By now, they've scattered everywhere, and that lane is another ambush waiting to happen."

"How far is it to Saentaryn's holding?" asked Quaeryt.

"A mille, maybe two, up the long hill ahead, and then there's a lane to the east. I haven't been up the lane, but the major says that's where it is. We're not about to go there with only a company and no orders. Let's hope our captive will say more once he's back at Boralieu." Meinyt stood in the saddle. "To the rear . . . ride!"

Quaeryt had to urge the mare to keep up with the

captain as his mount quick-trotted back down the road. The scholar kept looking in all directions, but nothing else jumped out of the woods. Until the company was well away from the stripped wagons and back into the lower hills just north of Boralieu, neither man said much.

Then, abruptly Meinyt turned in the saddle. "What did you do? I haven't seen that brush trick before, and I haven't been in these particular hills for a while; so I didn't remember that little lane."

"I was lucky. I just turned my mount in to them at the last moment. It upset them just enough."

"They were armed. You weren't. How did you manage to avoid that?"

"Like you said . . . I ducked, and let the mare shield me."

"She doesn't even have a cut."

Quaeryt shrugged. "What can I say? I was lucky. After the last time, maybe the Nameless looked on me a bit more favorably today."

"A lot more favorably, I'd say. Fortunate or not, scholar, I appreciate it."

"They targeted you, didn't they?"

"I'd have to think so. They made one pass and rode off. If they'd disorganized the company, they might have stayed around and tried to pick off rankers."

"Is that usual?"

"They don't like pitched fights or anything that lasts. Strike and run. Crossbow quarrels and vanish. They're good at that, but not so good at standing and fighting. So they don't. I have to give them that. They don't do what they're not good at." Meinyt laughed, with a touch of bitterness behind the sound. "That's probably a good rule to follow, but it's not always practical when you've got a mission to carry out."

"That's why you didn't pursue them."

"The major will understand. So will the commander, and the governor will see that the only report that gets to Lord Bhayar is that we were attacked, and captured one brigand and had no casualties. That's not as good as it could be, but better than some patrol reports. That's the way it goes in dealing with the hill holders. Thank the Nameless that the governor understands how they work."

"He understands a great deal," said Quaeryt mildly. "Do you think the princeps does as well?"

"They both do. That's what the major says. The princeps is quieter. Everyone thinks he only knows supplies and figures, but some of the older rankers remember when he was a battalion commander. He wasn't flash, just solid." The captain shrugged. "That's what they say, anyway." He blotted his forehead, brushing away red flies. "Hate patrolling this time of year. Every bug and mosquito known to a soldier is out trying to get the last meals possible before winter hits."

Quaeryt didn't know about the winter, but he definitely agreed about the insects.

58

What Skarpa had predicted after the "visit" to convey the governor's concerns to Waerfyl did in fact come to pass, if after the coal thefts from High Holder Eshalyn. Day after day went by, with Quaeryt accompanying patrol after patrol—and there was no sign of attacks, of poaching, of timber thefts. Nor did any of the High Holders send messages to Boralieu reporting such. What the commander or the major learned from the captive was apparently little, because Skarpa only said that the man had told everything he knew, and that was almost nothing except he'd been ordered to join the raid on the coal mine by a subchief of Saentaryn, and he'd never seen the holder himself.

Quaeryt discovered he had become a much better rider, and his shields worked largely as he had hoped, although he had not been able to make them sensitive enough to keep away predatory insects and still not have them set themselves at the slightest intrusion, but he could live with that. He still wore the undress green shirt on patrols.

He thought he'd be heading back to the Telaryn Palace with Sixth Battalion, but he'd heard no word. By Jeudi the thirty-third of Erntyn, he decided that, even if he didn't get such word, he intended to go—unless someone sent orders forbidding his return. He'd learned all he was likely to learn, for his purposes, in the time he'd spent at Boralieu.

That night at the mess, he sat across the table from Skarpa.

"It's been quiet for a while, and it will be for a few more weeks, maybe even to near the end of Feuillyt or Finitas or into winter," noted the major.

"Did you ever find out more about why Saentaryn ordered the raid?"

"We can't prove he did, and there's been no more trouble. The commander did send the one captive back with a message that suggested there shouldn't be. If there is, we'll probably have to do something." Skarpa shook his head. "There won't be. Not now. Saentaryn doesn't want to risk us torching his hold this close to winter. Besides, he got the coal."

"That doesn't seem . . . right."

"It's not a question of right. It's a question of when you decide you want to lose troopers and what you get for it."

Quaeryt had understood that before he asked the question, but wanted to hear Skarpa's reply. "When will Sixth Battalion get rotated back here?"

"The whole battalion? Not until Avril, most likely. Meinyt's company might have to go to the northwest outpost in Fevier. I haven't heard yet. He might not, since they're here so late in the year. I suggested that to make the company spend three winters in a row on outpost duty wasn't fair to either Meinyt or the men."

"Do you think—"

"The commander's a fair man. He'll make a recommendation to the governor, and unless there's a special reason, the governor will accept it. I'm hopeful Meinyt will be able to enjoy winter in the comparative warmth of Tilbora. Nothing in Tilbor's really that comfortable in winter, but you never really get warm at Boralieu and the outposts. Maybe that's why so many of the hill holders are such Namer-chosen serpents. Nothing ever warms their blood or their hearts."

Quaeryt finished the tough cutlet with the last morsel of tasty sauce, then took a swallow of lager. Tired as he was getting of the lager, the thought of drinking ale was even worse. "What makes a fireplace or a stove far warmer than a fire are the bounds placed on the fire by the containment of the hearth or the stove. Men who recognize no boundaries save those of their own flames of ambition lose the warmth of their hearts without even knowing it."

"You sound like Rholan might."

"Hardly." Quaeryt shook his head.

"I'd have to doubt that, my scholar friend." Skarpa glanced down the long table, grinned, and lowered his voice. "I didn't see you at services on Solayi. Gauswn was disappointed. . . ."

"He seems to think I'm something I'm not. I'm just a scholar who knows a bit about Rholan and the background of those who follow the Nameless."

"You're more than that, even if you're trying to sound like you don't believe in the Nameless."

"I don't disbelieve. I don't know, but I believe in the precepts that Rholan and others set forth."

"For a doubter, you're a powerful chorister."

"That's one of the problems with words. Those who master them think that they've mastered more than the words themselves. Most haven't."

"That sounds even more like Rholan to me, except better."

Quaeryt sighed loudly and dramatically. "I'm not a chorister. I'm not even a scholar of the Nameless."

"You could fool me and most of the officers."

Quaeryt couldn't think what else to say that wouldn't end up with him in the position of protesting so much that he'd end up convincing Skarpa and those around that he was what he wasn't.

"Scholar?" asked a voice from behind Quaeryt's shoulder.

Quaeryt turned, and seeing Commander Zirkyl, immediately stood. "Sir. You surprised me."

"That can be good or bad." Zirkyl's light voice was dry. "By the way, I couldn't help but overhear your comments about the mastery of words convincing people they have greater abilities when they don't. You're right about that. That wasn't what I came over to see you about, though. I'm going to prevail upon

you to speak as chorister at services this coming Solayi. Everyone has said you gave an excellent homily
two weeks ago, and I think they're more than tired of
me. Since you'll be returning to Tilbora with Sixth
Battalion next Meredi, that will be the last chance
many of them will have to avoid hearing me."

While the literal meaning of the commander's words
was correct, since most of those attending would be
leaving when Quaeryt did, the scholar wasn't certain
that was exactly what Zirkyl meant. In any case, all he
could do was nod and say, "If that is your wish, sir, I'll
do my best."

"I'm certain it will be very good. Thank you, scholar."

As the commander walked away, Quaeryt looked
across the mess table at Skarpa. The major was smiling.

"Did you hear that?"

"Every word. I told you the commander was good
at using the resources at his disposal effectively."

"He's very good," agreed Quaeryt. *Too good, in
this case.* He shouldn't have protested so eloquently
or for so long, but then he hadn't seen the commander
slip up behind him.

"Gauswn will be pleased. So will many of the others."

Quaeryt winced.

"Gauswn's a good undercaptain."

"I know he is. He just sees more in me than there is.
Besides, the commander is a good speaker and chorister, I'm certain."

"He is. You're better."

"I think this is a case where familiarity breeds a
desire for difference, and I'm just different." Before
Skarpa could contradict him, Quaeryt asked, "How

early will Sixth Battalion set out on Meredi for the return to Tilbora?"

"I'll let you change the subject this time, scholar, because you still have to give that homily." Skarpa grinned, then added, "By sixth glass."

59

On Samedi morning, Quaeryt rode another uneventful patrol, this one to the southeast, far longer, so that he did not return until just before the evening meal, at which he ended up next to Duesyn, who, he discovered, was actually from Nacliano and had been promoted to captain the past Juyn. The good captain knew nothing about the sad state of affairs concerning scholars in his home city, and said that it must have happened after he had been posted to the regiment from duty near Ruile.

Quaeryt was so tired that he almost slept through breakfast on Solayi and then went back to his quarters and took a nap. By late afternoon, though, he woke feeling famished and made his way to the officers' mess, where he wheedled a lager from the attendants and waited for the evening meal.

He'd barely seated himself when Gauswn stepped into the mess, looked around, spotted him, and then walked over. "Good afternoon, sir."

"Good afternoon."

"You will be speaking tonight, won't you? At services?"

"I will." *As if I had any choice.*

"Thank you. I'm looking forward to hearing what you have to say." After a very polite nod, the under-captain turned and left the mess.

Quaeryt took a long swallow from his mug.

Before long, Skarpa and Meinyt joined him.

"I haven't seen you around today," offered the major as he sat down across from the scholar.

"Yesterday's patrol wore me out. I thought I was almost recovered, but . . ."

"Oh . . . you went with Duesyn on the southern sweep," said Skarpa. "That's long and boring, but we do that one because High Holder Dymaetyn and High Holder Fhaelyn kept asking for it to keep poachers away. They never had any." He shook his head.

"It was a way to show the other High Holders that the governor listens to them," offered Meinyt.

"He listens to all the High Holders. He meets with them all the time. He just doesn't always do what they want," countered the major.

"Has he ever met with the hill holders?" asked Quaeryt.

Skarpa cocked his head. "I can't say as I know. If he does, it isn't often. They said they didn't meet often with the Khanars, either. Most stiff-necked folk in all Tilbor. You were there when I had to deliver the com-mander's message to that young snot Waerfyl, him in his red vest, daring me and the commander to torch his holding."

"I wish you had," murmured Meinyt.

"And then what? We'd have to torch every holding in the hills and abandon them for years or spend hun-dreds of troopers chasing down every man or boy with a bow or crossbow. Armies and regiments aren't meant to fight brigands and outlaws."

Quaeryt wondered about that. With the winters so long and cold, what would happen if most of the holds were destroyed? What would people do in the winter? Rather than raise that point, he just listened.

"What do you do then?" asked Meinyt. "Let them get away with it?"

Skarpa shrugged.

Quaeryt considered the question without commenting as the rest of the officers and the food arrived.

The evening meal consisted of some form of potato dumplings and chunks of meat in a brown gravy so spicy that Quaeryt couldn't begin to determine the origin of the meat, although he guessed it was most likely mutton. The brown bread was hot and moist, though, and that helped.

After eating, as before, Quaeryt followed the officer acting as chorister for the entire service—Commander Zirkyl this time—into the dining hall and stood to one side while the commander led worship from the invocation to confession and through the offertory, before standing aside and letting Quaeryt move forward to deliver the homily.

"Good evening," he offered in Tellan.

"Good evening," came the reply.

"Under the Nameless all evenings are good . . . and even if they weren't, I somehow think that having a less than perfect evening is to be preferred over the alternative of having no evening." Quaeryt didn't expect a laugh, and he didn't get one.

"Some of you may have heard of the term 'nomenclature.' No, it's not a fancy substitute for good old-fashioned swearing. It's the study of names, and the words it comes from mean literally to summon or command a name. For all that, do we really study what names are? We're all familiar with what the names of people and things mean, and even where many of those names come from.

"But what is a name? We say that it is a noun, and a noun describes or is the term or definition of a person, place, or thing. But is that all it is? As people, we need names. They serve a function. They allow us to talk to each other, and to let others know who we are as opposed to other human beings. But let me ask another question." Quaeryt paused.

"Why do we capitalize a name when we write it? That's a simple question, isn't it? In terms of grammar, names are officially 'proper names,' and that is why names are capitalized. But then, would anyone want an improper name?"

A low laugh rippled across the officers and rankers.

"Yet . . . by capitalizing our names and the names of others, we are declaring that we are special, that we have a greater identity or are of greater import to the world than do those objects or creatures who share the same common name, such as trees, or rocks, or pebbles, or ants, or cattle. At times, people name animals, especially those that are loved or that have served faithfully, and those names accord them somehow a higher place than animals that bear no names. Yet no higher power, not even the Nameless, has bestowed our proper names upon us. No . . . we give them to our children, as our parents did to us.

"By what right do we claim a special position in capitalizing our names? Do not all creatures on this earth have a use and a worth, whether or not each has a proper name as opposed to just a creature name? What is our worth and use? Is it measured by a name? Rholan certainly did not believe so. Or is it measured by our usefulness and accomplishments? . . .

"Yet how often do accomplishments become mere

nouns, common names written on the pages of history by struggling scholars far more skilled than I in an effort to capture the essence of those deeds? Do those who read the words understand that essence, or do they only focus on the words and names . . . losing that essence and understanding?

"Rholan understood how easily names, even personal and proper names, could become so much more and so much worse than the sounds we use to identify ourselves as individuals . . . so . . . when we think of a name, especially our own, we should not fall in love with it, but regard it for what it is—a tool like any other tool. Like any tool, it can be most useful, and when misused, it can become dangerous, even deadly. . . ."

Even though the homily was short, Quaeryt knew he'd said enough, perhaps more than enough, and he stepped back to let the commander deliver the benediction.

Only after most of the worshippers had left did Zirkyl turn to Quaeryt. "You amaze me, scholar. To start with a grammar lesson and then tie it into another inspection of Naming . . . I've never heard any chorister do that."

"I haven't either, sir," added Skarpa as he approached.

"You may be wasted as a scholar," continued Zirkyl.

"Alas, sir, that is what I am."

The commander shook his head. "Such a pity."

Quaeryt wasn't about to point out that the prime requisite for a chorister was to believe in the Nameless, and that he was only certain about believing in some of the precepts of the Nameless. Instead, he said, "We cannot be anything we wish; we can only be the best at what we are."

Zirkyl nodded slowly, but then added, "Do not set your sights too low, master scholar."

If you only knew, Commander. If you only knew. "I will keep that very much in mind, sir."

"See that you do." The commander smiled before he turned and left Quaeryt with Skarpa.

"What do you have your sights set on, scholar?" asked Skarpa, his tone half-amused.

"Not to let thoughts of fame and glory impede what I wish to accomplish," replied Quaeryt lightly. "And you?"

"I'd like to be an effective regimental commander."

"You just might be," said Quaeryt, smiling. "Do you want to join me for another lager? I think we can persuade them to serve us."

"Yes . . . but I'll take ale."

The two walked back into the officers' mess.

60

The sun was still above the hills to the west on Jeudi afternoon when Quaeryt rode up the paved road and through the eastern gates into the Telaryn Palace. The brisk winds that had cooled him on the last few glasses of the journey were a definite sign that the hotter weather was beginning to wane, even if it was only the fifth day of autumn. After two days of riding and practicing his shields as often as he could, Quaeryt was pleased that he could hold shields he was certain were strong enough to block a crossbow quarrel—if for less than a quint continuously. He had the feeling he'd need them every bit as much in Tilbora if not more than he had while riding patrols out of Boralieu.

He hadn't sent any reports to Bhayar from Boralieu, but knowing that he'd be returning on a Jeudi, over the previous week he'd written a totally factual report of the events of his month at the outpost, mentioning his injury in passing, but offering nothing about any of his abilities, except an improved capability in the saddle, or any speculations whatsoever. He also had written a summary report of each week's activities for the princeps.

He had barely dismounted in the stable courtyard when a young ranker hurried up.

"Scholar Quaeryt, sir? The princeps would like to see you at your earliest convenience."

Earliest convenience? What exactly does that mean? "Thank you. I'll be there as soon as I take care of my mount."

"Yes, sir. I'll tell him." The ranker hurried off.

After unsaddling and grooming his mount, Quaeryt dumped his gear in his quarters and retrieved his report for Straesyr, then hurried back to the second level of the main section of the palace and into the princeps's anteroom. Vhorym looked up from his table desk, then stood. "The princeps will see you immediately, sir. Just go on in."

Straesyr actually stood as Quaeryt entered his study. "How are you feeling, scholar? How's that chest wound? I heard you'd been wounded on a patrol. The first reports weren't that good."

The princeps's warm voice held concern, and Quaeryt thought that his ice-blue eyes weren't quite as hard and calculating as usual.

Quaeryt felt fine, but he replied, "I'm still sore and bruised, but I'll recover."

"The governor was greatly concerned. He hadn't thought you'd run into such an attack that soon. He'd recommended your going on routine patrols at first."

"It was a routine patrol. Even Captain Meinyt thought so. There were only a few backwoods types. They had crossbows. We lost one ranker, and two others besides me were wounded. Two of the attackers were killed. I didn't do too much, except talk to the officers, after I felt better, for the next few weeks." He extended the sheets of his report. "Here is a consolidated report of the time I spent in Boralieu."

Straesyr smiled and gave a rueful headshake. "It's a pity you're a scholar and not an officer. You're intelligent. You get the job done, and you're obviously durable."

"I'm not terribly good with weapons, sir."

"You think. That's far more important for an officer."

Sometimes you think too much. Quaeryt kept that thought to himself.

"There is one other thing." Straesyr smiled, reached down, picked up a sealed missive off the desk, then handed it to Quaeryt. "This arrived a few days ago by courier. It appears to have been addressed by the same hand as the one awaiting you when you first arrived."

Quaeryt took the missive and looked at the script. "It does look the same."

"Without being too intrusive . . ."

"She is a young lady to whom I was introduced by her aunt just before I left Solis. She posed a number of scholarly issues, and I replied before I departed for Boralieu. While she is charming, I am a scholar, and scholars are not known for their wealth, and I have no family. I will, of course, continue to write, because a woman whose intellect is so sharply honed is rare."

"You phrased that in an interesting fashion, scholar."

Quaeryt laughed softly. "I have found little different in the basic ability of men or women to think. I have found great differences in the proportion of each who are trained to use their thoughts and faculties to the fullest."

"My wife would agree with you, as would my daughter, young as she is," said Straesyr dryly. "I will have to relate your observation to them."

"Are they here in Tilbora?"

"My wife was not about to allow me to remain here unaccompanied. That may be suitable for a widower such as the governor, she said, but not for a handsome and intelligent man. We have quarters in one of the row houses beyond the stables."

"I saw children . . ."

"Doubtless at least one of them was mine." The princeps smiled again. "You have had a long day, and I would not keep you yet longer. You will be in your study in the morning?"

"Yes, sir."

"Good. Until then."

Quaeryt inclined his head and departed.

As he walked back to his quarters to unpack and see what he could do about getting his garments washed, he thought again about the princeps. Behind the open mannerisms, Straesyr concealed a great deal, possibly even more than did Rescalyn. Yet his mention of his wife had been anything but casual, even as easily presented as those words had been.

Not until he was back in his quarters, which had been swept and cleaned in the last day or so, did he study the letter that bore Vaelora's handwriting, although only his name and posting were written on the outside. Interestingly enough, he could detect no sign that the seal had been tampered with, none at all, and he finally broke it and extracted the sheets of paper inside and began to read.

> *Dear Scholar Quaeryt—*
>
> *I am in receipt of your correspondence of 33 Agostas. I do appreciate your thoughtful commentary on the points that I raised previously, and I cannot convey how pleased and relieved I was to learn that you arrived safely in Tilbora, despite the difficulties you encountered in your travels.*
>
> *You had observed certain aspects of my discourse and addressed those with care and consideration. In addition, I would propose, if but tentatively, an additional observation. I believe, and it is, of course, only my belief, that among all people, and particularly among women, those who are often most effective in changing the course of events are those who are many times the least noticed or noticed as having been merely helpful . . .*

Those words struck Quaeryt, and he reread them, then nodded.

> *. . . That being said, there are doubtless many who are effective and well-noticed, and of great accomplishments and meritorious achievement, but, if one can believe the histories and, indeed, the legends, it would appear that of those many a rather large proportion did not live to the ages they might have had they not been so well-noted in their accomplishments. . . .*
>
> *Again, this is but the opinion of a woman, and one who has led a most sheltered life. . . .*

He couldn't help but smile at that line. No one in Bhayar's household led exactly a sheltered life. Protected, but not sheltered. He continued to read through her notes on several books she had read, and her pithy, if carefully couched, observations.

. . . and although fall is approaching, the weather remains
more reminiscent of summer than of fall, or even of harvest. I do
hope my words have not been excessive or terribly less than
scholarly, and I look forward to your reply.

Again, the letter was signed with but her single initial.

As Quaeryt reread the letter, something else nagged
at him, and he retrieved her second letter, and reread it
quickly, then her original letter—and laughed quietly.
While the logic and the validity and structure of the
basic thoughts were still there, the second and third
letters contained far more flowery and self-deprecating
phrases and qualifications, phrases which he believed
not at all, but whose purpose was all too clear. What
remained unclear—and likely would for some time,
perhaps always—was her motivation in writing. Did
she feel so constricted within her palace that such letters were her only escape?

Quaeryt had no way of knowing, and he was not
about to ask, not when he enjoyed receiving those
missives—and replying—and when asking might of-
fend her enough to cause her to cease writing. He immediately sat down to compose a reply, but only
finished slightly more than a page before he realized it
was time to eat—and that he was indeed hungry.

When he reached the mess, he stopped cold, seeing
most of the officers in their jackets and realizing that
it was mess night. He didn't immediately see any of
the officers he had come to know when he entered the
mess, nor did he see Phargos, about which he was
slightly relieved, although he doubted that Gauswn or
the other officers in Sixth Battalion had yet had the
chance or the inclination to discuss his homilies in

Boralieu with the regimental chorister. He shrugged and made his way to his place, where Haestyn and Dueryl greeted him and immediately begin to ply him with questions. Those were cut short by Rescalyn's arrival. The marshal's words were brief, essentially welcoming back the officers of Sixth Battalion.

After Rescalyn's words, Quaeryt bantered with those around him and enjoyed the seasoned roasted fowl with the rice and mushrooms in sauce.

When he returned to his quarters after the evening meal, he struggled through his reply to Vaelora, let it sit on the writing desk while he finished unpacking, and then reread it again.

Mistress Vaelora—

I am in receipt of your letter of 24 Erntyn, although I did not receive it until I returned from a month spent with the cavalry at Boralieu post. I fear I am not cut of the cloth to be a cavalry officer. On the very first patrol I accompanied, I took a crossbow quarrel in the shoulder. As the governor has said to Lord Bhayar in his dispatches, the hill brigands are indeed troublesome types. One even later boasted that action against his holding would incite all the hill holders into revolt. Fortunately, a salutatory visit in force arranged by Commander Zirkyl, who commands the post at Boralieu, convinced the hotheaded holder that his words were most unwise. The injury from the quarrel limited my riding with patrols for several weeks. Fortunately, later patrols were not so eventfully difficult for me . . .

From there, Quaeryt gave a brief summary of his patrols, then addressed her words to him.

While I have not had time to give full consideration to your latest missive, and will not have that time if I am to dispatch

*this tomorrow morning, your words do give rise to some
thoughts, particularly in light of my task to assess the
difficulties of administering a province such as Tilbor. . . .*

*Governor Rescalyn is a good and thoughtful governor, who
has clearly studied the precepts of administration and ruling,
but he is most especially an excellent marshal. The soldiers and
cavalry here are well-trained and extraordinarily devoted to the
marshal. One officer claimed that his men would attack the
Nameless if the governor so ordered. If only Rex Kharst knew
what an effective and disciplined force the marshal has trained.
It must comprise close to two regiments, if not three. How
quickly they would disperse anyone sent against them, but,
having seen, firsthand, the smallest bit of fighting, I would not
wish such on anyone unless it becomes absolutely necessary,
although the forces here could certainly form the spearhead of
any army required to repulse the Bovarians . . . or for any other
purpose necessary. I am most certain that Lord Bhayar
understands far better than I to what uses such a dedicated
force can be applied, for I am but a scholar of history and can
only look back and peruse the dusty tomes dating from even
before the times of the Yaran warlords.*

Given Vaelora's education and personal history,
Quaeryt had every hope that she would understand
the references, and the implications, assuming she ever
received the letter—and that whoever read the correspondence before she did would not. If she did, then he
had no doubts that she would inform Bhayar . . . and
Bhayar was definitely not insensitive to the undercurrents of power.

Finally, he closed the letter.

*Your thoughts and words offer both insight and cheer, and I am
more than glad to receive them, and to reply with what insight
and wit I can offer.*

He used the same closing as before—"In sincerest admiration and appreciation."

Then he blew out the lamp over the writing desk, bolted the door, undressed, and collapsed into bed.

61

Tired as he was, Quaeryt was up early on Vendrei so that he could eat before handing his dispatch to Bhayar and his letter to Vaelora to the courier. He didn't recognize the courier, an older and wiry soldier, but the rider's eyes didn't even widen at the address on the letter. He did accept the silver gracefully and with a quiet "Thank you, sir."

Then Quaeryt went to his study around the corner from Straesyr's anteroom. He sat there for several quints, pondering exactly what he should do next. To keep the local scholars in the good graces of Bhayar, the people of Tilbora, and the High Holders, he needed to separate them from the hill holders, in a way that wasn't terribly obvious or embarrassing to the hill holders while retaining the good features of the Ecoliae. He also needed to verify his various suspicions about the governor, and he needed to determine more precisely the relationship between Straesyr and Rescalyn.

He looked up at the rap on the open door.

Vhorym stood there. "Sir? The princeps would like a word with you."

"Thank you."

Quaeryt rose and walked to the anteroom and into

Straesyr's study. He couldn't help but notice, through the windows behind the princeps, that the sunlight falling on the north walls surrounding the palace definitely seemed weaker. "Yes, sir?"

"Have a seat, Quaeryt."

Quaeryt sat.

"On Mardi, the governor will be riding north to join High Holder Freunyt for a luncheon. Since the High Holder extended the invitation to include others, the governor thought that it might be useful for you to accompany him. I also feel that would be useful. Your reports show you have seen the hill holders. You should visit a High Holder or two as well. The governor and his party will be departing at seventh glass."

"I will be there."

"I also had a pair of coats tailored for you. One is a jacket in the style of an undress uniform, and the other is a dress coat. You need to stop by the regimental tailor's this morning to make sure they fit so that, if they don't, he can make the necessary alterations."

"Thank you, sir."

"You can wear the undress jacket when you accompany the governor and the dress coat to the factors' reception on Samedi. Vhorym has your invitation."

Quaeryt inclined his head. "I must say that I am surprised."

"My duties are to deal with trade, commerce, and the most necessary tariffs that they raise. Certainly, as a scholar assistant to me, you should be visible, especially since several factors have already mentioned your presence in Tilbora. I would like them to meet you so that everyone can see that you are open and about my business."

"Yes, sir." Quaeryt paused, then asked quietly, "Sir?

Might I bring up one other matter for your consideration?"

Straesyr smiled. "If it does not take too long."

"Thank you." The scholar rose and stepped toward the door, this time closing it behind himself before approaching the desk again. He did not sit before he spoke. "I've run across the name of a High Holder Fhaedyrk," offered Quaeryt. "He's mentioned several times in old dispatches and even in the records of the Khanar's Council. What can you tell me about him, sir?"

Straesyr frowned. "I recall the unpleasantness associated with Governor Fhayt. It wasn't Fhaedyrk's fault. That was rather clear, but the governor has not been inclined to test those waters again."

"Would it be untoward if I paid him a visit, perhaps as your intermediary?"

"For what reason?" Straesyr's voice was pleasantly bland.

"I ran across a reference to him in the Khanar's Council reports, and he had enough courage to write the Khanar suggesting that the two strengths of Tilbor were the High Holders and the factors and traders of the south. As I recall, and as you just stated and as your holding a reception for factors emphasizes, your duties include strengthening trade and the tariffs resulting from that trade and commerce."

Quaeryt thought he saw a slight glint in Straesyr's eyes as the princeps nodded slowly and thoughtfully before replying. "And?"

"As your intermediary, who is looking into trade, I could certainly inquire as to his thoughts on the matter."

"I think you have more on your mind than that, scholar."

"Yes, sir. I do. I'd like to see if the High Holder has any ideas about who or what was behind the attack on Governor Fhayt. I am not a great believer in coincidence, and I find it too coincidental that the only attack on a governor was when he was riding to see the sole High Holder who was willing to speak out in favor of the traders and crafters of Tilbor."

"That is an interesting observation, but that happened years ago."

"Yes, sir." Quaeryt said nothing more.

"Well ... it cannot hurt." Straesyr paused. "You know, his holding is almost four glasses to the north, and for that distance, you will need an escort. One squad with a junior officer, an undercaptain, should be appropriate. I will discuss this with the governor, since he will need to approve the escort, and if he approves, I will dispatch a messenger with a request for you to meet with the High Holder in the latter part of next week."

"Thank you, sir."

"If nothing else, it will help convince Fhaedyrk that the governor has thought more of him than merely inviting him to various events and receptions." Straesyr glanced toward the closed study door. "If that is all ... ?"

"Yes, sir." Quaeryt bowed slightly, turned, and left, leaving the study door as it had been before his reentry—half-open. Once he was in the anteroom and neared the table desk, Vhorym stood and handed him an envelope.

"Thank you."

"My pleasure, sir."

"Could you tell me where I might find the regimental tailor?"

"His shop is in the front of the first stables, sir."

Quaeryt did not open the unsealed envelope until he returned to his study. The invitation was to a reception in the Red Room of the palace, honoring the Factors' Association of Tilbora at the third glass of Samedi afternoon, and hosted by the princeps.

After reading the invitation, he immediately left to see the regimental tailor. Once there, he had to wait for half a quint while the tailor took the measurements for new uniforms for a major whose face Quaeryt recognized, but to whom he'd not been introduced. Once the major left, the tailor, a senior ranker, brought out two coats.

"I would guess these are yours, sir."

"Unless there are any other scholars attached to the princeps's staff, I would guess so, too," replied Quaeryt with a soft, warm laugh and a smile.

He tried them both on, beginning with the undress jacket. As he took off the longer dress coat, he looked to the tailor. "They fit perfectly."

"Thank you, sir."

"How did you manage?"

"I had a set of your browns to measure from, sir. I just hoped that they were accurate. It appears that they were."

While Quaeryt had left a set of browns behind in his west wing quarters, he had only glanced at them when he'd returned, because he'd been exhausted the night before and because he'd dressed hurriedly that morning. "Even so, your work is excellent." Quaeryt extended a silver. "I know you're paid fairly by the regiment, but a token of my thanks."

"Sir . . . I can't . . ."

"You're half-right. If . . . if I were an officer, or even

a ranker, you couldn't. I'm not. So.... save it for when you really want an ale or a lager, and it's still days from the paymaster."

"Sir . . ."

"Please don't make me beg to have you take it. I've never owned a coat that fine." That was certainly true enough. "I tell you what. Keep the silver, but only until you find someone who truly needs it. Then . . . give it to them."

The tailor frowned, then shook his head. "I really can't, sir."

"Then I'll have to do that for you. Tell me your name, so that I can tell whoever I give it to that it's from you."

"Oeldyrk, sir."

"You have my word, Oeldyrk, that some poor and deserving individual will benefit, and my gratitude for the jacket and coat." Quaeryt offered a broad smile before he left to take the garments back to his quarters.

After he hung the jacket and coat in his armoire, he headed back to the main section of the palace to pick up the key to the dispatch room. He'd thought about riding into Tilbora, but decided against that because he'd ridden the mare long glasses for the previous two days. Besides, he needed to catch up on the dispatches to see what, if anything, he'd missed.

Caermyt handed over the key, as politely disapproving as ever, and Quaeryt walked quickly down to the dispatch room, where he lit the desk lamps and began to read through the dispatches that had accumulated since his departure from the palace. Part of one was of obvious personal interest.

. . . received word that Quaeryt Rytersyn, the scholar assistant to the princeps, was accompanying a routine patrol when he was seriously wounded by a crossbow quarrel fired by one of the followers of a hill holder, most likely one Waerfyl Aerfylsyn ... indication that the hill holders remain dangerous and that maintaining hill posts and outposts continues to be necessary ...

Quaeryt kept reading. The issues of the poaching and the timber thefts by Waerfyl were mentioned, as were Waerfyl's denial of guilt and his statement that action against him would result in an uprising by all hill holders. There was also Rescalyn's observation that the post commander at Boralieu had conveyed a warning in force to Waerfyl and that transgressions in that area had ceased, but that it was likely others would occur elsewhere. That was confirmed by the next dispatch, which detailed the coal thefts and the attack on Meinyt's patrol.

Less than a glass later, Quaeryt came to the last dispatch, the one sent that morning, which included a single line ...

... Quaeryt Rytersyn, Scholar Assistant to the Princeps, returned to Tilbora largely healed from the wound inflicted by the hill holders ...

Quaeryt nodded, then stopped, and leafed back through the dispatches. He looked again. The only mentions of the hill holders or the actions of the regiment were those relating to the two attacks. The other reports dealt with problems in collecting tariffs from two northern High Holders, and various other difficulties.

There's not really a word that depicts anything positive ... and it's not because Rescalyn is a gloomy sort. He's anything but that.

Quaeryt shook his head. He didn't like what he was discovering—the continuing portrayal of the hill holders as a far greater threat than he suspected that they were. He especially didn't care for the fact that there wasn't anything rock-solid that he could have used as proof of what he was coming to believe. He frowned, then began to look back through the dispatches.

62

On Vendrei night, after he'd returned to his quarters following the evening meal and prepared for bed, he had checked his spare browns, one of the pair tailored at the Ecoliae. Not only were they hanging in the narrow armoire, but they had been cleaned and pressed. That scarcely surprised him. On Samedi morning he donned the same browns he'd worn on Vendrei, deciding to save the clean and pressed ones for the reception, then made his way to the mess. There he ended up sitting with Captain Taenyd and another undercaptain— Haardyn.

"How is your comparative history coming?" asked Taenyd with a smile.

"Matters were slowed somewhat, as you might have heard. A crossbow quarrel, in fact."

"I heard that. I also heard that you're so knowledgeable that you could be a chorister."

"From Undercaptain Gauswn?"

"And from others."

"Alas . . . I'm a scholar of history, not of the Nameless. I'm not sure good scholars always make good choristers."

"Why not?" asked Haardyn.

"Good scholars deal in facts. At least, they should. Choristers present the truth of the Nameless. But there aren't any hard facts that affirmatively prove that there is a Nameless."

"How did the world, the stars, everything come to be, then?" asked Haardyn.

"What if it always was?" Quaeryt smiled ruefully. "Your question presupposes that the Nameless created everything. What if the Namer did? Or there was some other cause? We think we know that the world exists, but what if it doesn't? What if Taenyd and I are merely your imaginings? Or you and Taenyd are mine?"

"You just can't imagine things . . ." Haardyn stopped.

"Exactly," replied Quaeryt. "Imagers can image things into being . . . after a fashion, anyway."

"Then the Nameless could have imaged all of us into being," countered Taenyd, "or the world and whatever was on it that led to us."

"That's possible," agreed Quaeryt. "But so could have the Namer . . . or something else. We don't know. We don't have any proof of any of those causes."

"You don't really believe that we're merely dreams or imaginings," declared Haardyn.

"No, I don't . . . but that's a matter of belief, not facts. How can I tell whether everything around me is real or imagined? I believe it to be real because too many things happen that are unpleasant and that I would not wish to happen . . . but a small part of my mind points out that I often do things which are unwise . . . and that I know are unwise . . . and so, could I not imagine unpleasant or unwise aspects of a world

I might dream?" Quaeryt laughed, then took a swallow of tea from his mug, followed by a mouthful of the egg hash.

The captain and the undercaptain exchanged glances. Finally, Taenyd spoke. "Do you deny the existence of the Nameless?"

"No. I do not *know* whether the Nameless exists. I cannot affirm or deny that which I do not know."

"You still sound like a chorister," said Haardyn with a laugh.

"That's because scholars and choristers both study the world," suggested Taenyd. "They just study it in different ways."

"That's a very good observation." Quaeryt nodded. "And cavalry officers study it in yet another way."

"The good ones do," affirmed Taenyd.

"What do you always look for first?"

"The most likely place from which we might be attacked."

"That's not a bad precept for many situations," replied Quaeryt with a smile.

From there on, the three talked about mounted tactics.

After breakfast, Quaeryt went to his study, then walked to the princeps's anteroom.

Vhorym looked up. "Sir?"

"Could you tell me where the Red Room is, Vhorym?"

The squad leader smiled. "It's on the main level, directly under the Green Salon."

"Thank you. If, by any chance, anyone is looking for me, I'll be in the palace library."

Quaeryt spent the morning and early afternoon in the library, studying the available maps of Tilbor and trying to correlate which High Holders—as listed in a small book he'd discovered earlier—were located where. There was no comparable information on the hill holders, he noted.

As he sat in the library, a thought struck him. He'd seen all the dispatches, and he'd heard Straesyr talk about collecting tariffs, and he'd noted the size of the "regiment." What he hadn't seen any records on was expenses—especially the balancing of expenses against tariffs. The princeps had to be collecting enough tariffs to support the regiment and to send some of those revenues to Bhayar, because Bhayar would have been complaining far more loudly had there been no revenues at all, or scant revenues. Yet how could he raise that issue—or discover the figures—in a way that it did not appear that he was seeking them?

He was still pondering that question, in between other matters, when he had to leave the library to return to his quarters and change into what passed for his finery.

Given the nature of the reception, and the fact that Quaeryt was there as a member of Straesyr's staff, the scholar appeared at the door to the Red Room half a quint before third glass, where he was greeted, unsurprisingly, by Vhorym in a dress green uniform.

"The princeps is over by the sidebar with the wine, sir."

"Thank you." Quaeryt nodded, then walked toward Straesyr, taking in the room and its decor. The chamber was identical to the Green Salon in size and shape, twenty yards in length and perhaps fifteen in width, but the hangings were a deep red and flowed down from the gilded crown moldings carved into floral designs. The ceiling was merely of normal height, and air flowed from a series of brass grates high on the walls. The only light was from the brass lamps set on matching wall brackets at intervals around the room, and, by comparison to the Green Salon, the Red Room was almost gloomy. There was also no clavecin in the chamber.

"Yes," said Straesyr with a nod as Quaeryt approached, "that dress coat makes all the difference, indeed."

"For which I am most grateful," replied Quaeryt. "Is there any point or view you wish me to convey to the factors?"

"Only that you are from Solis, and that you were sent from Solis by Lord Bhayar to gather information for Lord Bhayar. That should be sufficient . . . beyond being pleasant and learning what you can without upsetting people."

"Is there anything special you're interested in discovering?"

"Nothing in particular. One finds out more without an agenda, just by encouraging others to talk about themselves." Straesyr smiled. "You already know that. You might sample the delicacies before others arrive, so that you have more time to listen without your guts interrupting your concentration."

"Yes, sir."

Quaeryt made his way to the side table. From one of the dozen large platters, he picked up a slice of boiled pickled egg set on a petite round of bread and topped with a dollop of a stiff cream topping. The topping was horseradish so hot he never tasted the egg or the bread. The rarish mutton wrapped in thin fried flatbread with a cumin filling was tastier, and he had two of those. He skipped the pickled turtle eggs, but the pâté on dark bread was good enough for two. He finished with one of the small white cakes, then moved to the beverage sideboard.

"Sir?" asked the ranker in dress greens.

"The dry white wine," replied Quaeryt. "Please."

With the goblet in hand, the scholar turned and watched as the first factor entered the Red Room, a thin-faced man with thick and bushy gray hair, and a beard to match, wearing a gray jacket and trousers and a tan shirt. Straesyr greeted him effusively and talked for a moment.

As Straesyr turned from the one factor to greet another entering the Red Room, Quaeryt intercepted the first arrival. "Greetings . . . I'm Quaeryt and an assistant to the princeps."

The factor stiffened for an instant. "Ah . . . Rewhar . . . I'm a brick factor." After another pause, he added, "I had not thought to find a scholar . . . as an assistant to Princeps Straesyr . . ." The factor left the sentence hanging.

"That was not of his choosing. Lord Bhayar sent me from Solis to gather information."

"A scholar to gather information. That makes sense. How are you finding Tilbora?"

"As it is . . . I hope." Quaeryt smiled as winningly as he could.

"What sort of information are you gathering?"

"The condition of the province, its strengths, and its problems, particularly the difficulties posed by the hill holders."

"They are not that much trouble . . . except if one wants to travel the hills. . . ."

"Do they trade much ?"

"They grow or hunt most of what they need, and trade their timber and silver for what else they require."

"Silver? I was not aware . . ."

Rewhar smiled. "They would prefer that few know

of that. Holder Waerfyl and Holder Saentaryn have mines on their lands. So does Zorlyn, but his lands are much farther into the Boran Hills. His mines are also much richer."

"Zorlyn . . . that sounds familiar, but I couldn't say why . . ." Quaeryt had never heard of Zorlyn. At least, he didn't think so.

"Oh . . . he's the one that no one knows beyond his name. One of his youngest sons—and going through three wives, he has many—is a scholar." Rewhar frowned. "He's the princeps of that scholars' place . . ."

"The Ecoliae?" At that moment, the connection struck Quaeryt—Zarxes Zorlynsyn. He didn't want to mention the name Zarxes, because no one at the palace or in Tilbora had ever mentioned Zarxes by name.

"That's it. The fellow's name . . . I can't remember, but it has to start with 'Z.' Zorlyn names all his sons something beginning with 'Z.' I heard that somewhere." Rewhar glanced past Quaeryt toward the serving table.

"Don't let me keep you from enjoying the food. I did find the small mutton rolls and the pâté quite tasty. The sauce on the pickled sliced eggs is rather highly spiced." Quaeryt smiled again and gestured toward the table.

The next two factors to enter and greet the princeps were careful to avoid Quaeryt, and he decided to wait until more had arrived. When a good fifteen or so had appeared, he moved toward a pair standing somewhat away from those clustered around the serving table.

"Honorable factors . . . I'm Quaeryt, the scholar assistant to the princeps. I was sent here from Solis by

Lord Bhayar to offer aid to the princeps and to gather information." He smiled.

"Oh . . ." replied the taller factor. "Jussyt . . . I'm not really a factor so much as a quarryman who became fortunate enough to discover better ways of splitting and dressing stone. They all claim I'm a factor, though. Even Raurem here."

Quaeryt turned to the shorter man.

"Produce, especially apples and the rough grains. But apples . . . they're the most notable fruit of Tilbor. More varieties grown here than anywhere in Lydar. Better, too. It's a pity we can't ship them farther away than the east coast without drying them." Raurem shook his head.

"What's the best eating apple?"

"Ah . . . that depends on when you eat it. Right off the tree or in a day or two, it'd be the black thorn. The best keeper, to eat, that is, is the red mottled, and that'll keep most of the winter in a tight cold cellar, but not one that'll freeze them. You'll just have mush that way . . ."

Quaeryt smiled and kept listening, wondering how much he'd remember about the apples of Tilbor. Then he learned about the gray split slate—the best roofing slate in all Lydar, according to Jussyt. Since neither seemed inclined to discuss scholars, after a time, he slipped away and talked to others, each more than willing to discuss what they did.

Almost a glass later, he eased up to an angular factor, whose left eye had a pronounced tic, but before he could say a word, the other spoke.

"You're the scholar . . . apparently most unlike those in Tilbor . . . from what I hear."

"I couldn't say, not yet. I'm Quaeryt."

"By the way," the factor grinned, "I'm Cohausyt. We have the sawmills north of Tilbora on the river."

"Most seem . . . reluctant to discuss the scholars resident here."

"That is because it is either unwise to do so, or, if one is a High Holder . . . unnecessary."

"Unwise?" Quaeryt did his best to look puzzled.

"Some of those scholars have ties to the hill holders, and they pursue . . . other goals, although it is said that one of those most rumored to be . . . less scholarly . . . recently vanished."

"They actually bear arms and do . . . other unseemly things?"

"We have no need of an assassins' guild here, as they do in Antiago, not with scholars such as those."

Quaeryt winced. "That troubles me. Scholars have a difficult enough time as it is. To have a group behaving so . . ."

"It troubles many in Tilbora as well." Cohausyt leaned forward and lowered his voice. "Can you tell me why the governor ignores such a pox?"

"I did not know that the local scholars were such a pestilence. Because I did not, I never inquired into the matter. I had heard that those here on Lord Bhayar's service were not to deal with the scholars. I had thought that was because Lord Bhayar has always said that his ministers were to leave the scholars alone unless they broke the laws of the land . . ."

"Would that . . ." Cohausyt shook his head. "Enough said."

"I will look into the matter," promised Quaeryt.

"I would that you would . . . but not because any have suggested it."

"I will only say that I overheard some remarks, but could not determine who made them."

For the next two glasses, Quaeryt mixed, mingled, conversed, and mainly listened. While there were more allusions to the local scholars, none of those factors said more, nor did Quaeryt press them. All in all, by the time the last factor left, he felt exhausted. So did Straesyr, he suspected, because the princeps merely said, "We'll talk on Lundi."

That was fine with Quaeryt.

63

On Solayi, Quaeryt took the mare for a ride, telling himself that he needed to try to locate some of the factorages belonging to those whom he had met at the reception. While that was partly true, he also felt he needed to escape the confines of the palace. He did indeed locate Cohausyt's sawmills and saw from a distance stone quarries that might have belonged to Jussyt.

He returned in time to write up his weekly report for Straesyr and then went to the evening meal, and, because he had not been around during the day, he also attended the evening services, presided over by Phargos. Most of the regimental chorister's homily was forgettable, but one phrase did catch Quaeryt's attention and linger in his thoughts.

". . . if there were no higher power, men would do what they would, for then there would be no spirit to face the Nameless and no reckoning to a life ill spent . . ."

Are men and women so weak and so stupid that

they can only do what is right because of the threat of an almighty power? Can they not see that if all behave well, then all benefit more, even the most powerful?

Unfortunately, he feared that Phargos might well be right, and that saddened him.

On Lundi morning, Straesyr was waiting for Quaeryt even before seventh glass and beckoned him into his study.

"Close the door, if you would." The words were pleasant, and the princeps was smiling, not that smiles meant much, Quaeryt had long since discovered.

Quaeryt laid the single sheet that was his weekly report on the desk and took a seat across the desk from the princeps and waited.

Straesyr ignored the paper. "Did you have a pleasant ride yesterday?"

"I did. I spent some time trying to locate factorages, those of factors I met on Samedi."

"What did you find out at the reception?"

"A great deal about the practical side of a number of factorages," replied Quaeryt, "especially stone quarrying, sawmills, and milling, among others. I also overheard some comments about the local scholars . . . and then several factors approached me about them."

Straesyr nodded. "I had hoped some might reveal their concerns. Who might those be?"

"I gave my word not to reveal their names because all were either concerned or actually fearful about their safety if any word of their names were bruited about."

The princeps frowned. "Do you believe them?"

"I fear I do. Perhaps it is time for me to visit the local scholars."

Straesyr fingered his clean-shaven chin. "Do you think that wise?"

"I think it would be unwise not to. As a scholar, I can see what might be amiss. Also, as I reported earlier, many of the shopkeepers I visited in Tilbora were most standoffish until I revealed I had come from Solis and was your assistant."

"If they are dangerous . . ."

"An escort would be helpful," said Quaeryt with a wry smile.

"The governor has already approved your visit to Fhaedyrk. I dispatched a messenger on Samedi. He returned yesterday, and the High Holder will receive you on Meredi afternoon at the second glass. The governor did agree that I could approve any escort of a squad or less for you, with the approval of Commander Myskyl."

"You don't think a squad is sufficient for the scholars?"

"Do you?"

Quaeryt considered for a moment before replying. "I feel that a squad would be either more than sufficient if my doubts are unfounded and most inadequate if they are not."

Straesyr offered a crooked smile in reply. "I fear that we share the same opinion. I will discuss the matter with the governor. It might be best if you remained in the palace until I do. He may wish to speak with you."

"Yes, sir."

"Do you have any questions about the reception?"

"I did wonder how often you hold such."

"Once a season, even in winter. It does remind all of them that they have someone who can listen and who does represent them before the governor and Lord Bhayar. That is useful."

"Are there any particular groups of factors who seldom attend , . . or who never have?"

448 L. E. MODESITT, JR.

"There are a handful whose appearance is less frequent, but they're the ones who are located farther away."

After several more questions, Quaeryt smiled. "I do have another question, sir, but not about the reception."

"What is it?"

"I'm curious about how tariffs are actually collected."

"Why?" Straesyr's voice remained pleasant, almost jovial.

"In most places, factors and others complain about tariffs. Here the only complaints seem to be from the hill holders."

The princeps frowned. "I don't understand the point of your question."

"I'm probably not being as clear as I could be. The captains and majors all talk about how dangerous it is to do anything in small groups in the hills and how so often holders have to be reminded of their . . . obligations . . . by a visit by a company or more. I had the impression that such a show of force was unnecessary elsewhere, but I never asked."

Straesyr smiled. "Your assumption is correct. I send a notice of tariffs due to each crafter, factor, holder, or High Holder at the end of harvest. They can pay here at the palace in the small building across from the east gate guardhouse, or at any post or outpost—or with the town council in towns that have a council, or with the council of the nearest town that has a council. That has seemed to work for all but the most recalcitrant of the hill holders."

"Then you're responsible for consolidating the tariffs and providing the funds to the governor and sending whatever is left to Lord Bhayar?"

Straesyr laughed. "Not exactly. There is a minimum amount of tariff that must be sent to Lord Bhayar. At the end of harvest, I draft and the governor approves or changes a proposed budget for the next year. He sends that to Lord Bhayar, along with the current year's tariffs. We have always been able to exceed the minimum requirements, often by a fifth part or more."

"Thank you. I have no more questions, sir."

"I will see you later, or Vhorym will let you know about the visit to the local scholars."

Quaeryt returned to his study, where he spent some time reflecting upon the meeting with Straesyr. Abruptly, he recalled what the old ranker had told him when Quaeryt had been waiting for the surgeon. He nodded to himself, then rose and walked back to the princeps's study, where he found Vhorym.

"I'll be in the stables for a bit. I want to check on my mare."

"Yes, sir."

It took Quaeryt almost two quints to find the head ostler.

"Sir? What can I do for you?" asked the graying and not-quite-grizzled figure.

"I just wanted a few moments of your time. I'm gathering information for Lord Bhayar, and I thought you've probably been one of those here the longest."

"Yes, sir. I came here with Marshal Fhayt."

"And there's only been one regiment here, with all its horses, since then?"

"Well, sir . . . there were three regiments here right after the fighting stopped, but the second regiment left within two months. The third left in the spring."

"Did the two regiments pretty much fill the stables, then? When both were here?"

"Oh . . . no, sir. We had two empty stables, mayhap

a bit more. We didn't have so many engineers, and the companies were just four squads."

"You don't do much with the other posts or outposts?"

"No, sir."

"But everyone and all the mounts were stabled here for the first few years?"

"Yes, sir. Governor Rescalyn was the one who built the outposts. Good idea. Without them, we were losing too many mounts. Too much time on the road without enough solid fodder, especially in the winter."

"You get all your winter fodder from growers here?"

"Yes, sir. Good fodder and grain. Governor wants the mounts healthy."

"Have you ever seen any of the horses used by the hill holders?"

"Only a few. One came back a week ago. Scrawny underfed thing. Already looking better."

"Are they all like that?"

"I couldn't say, sir. The ones I see are, but maybe those are the ones that let their riders down and get caught."

Quaeryt asked a few more questions before leaving and obtaining the key to the dispatch room. Between what Straesyr had said about budgets and tariffs and what he'd learned from the head ostler, he wanted to check a number of the dispatches.

Almost three glasses later, after having combed through the dispatches, especially the early ones, and those dealing with the budget submissions, he took a deep breath and leaned back in the wooden chair. *In plain sight, indeed. Or rather, the omissions were in plain sight.*

He needed to ask a few more questions of Skarpa

before he could confirm what he thought he'd discovered, but that would have to wait until the evening meal—if Skarpa happened to be there. After returning the dispatch-room key, he made his way back to his study.

He'd been back less than a glass when Vhorym knocked on his half-open door.

"Sir? The princeps asked me to tell you that the governor approved your mission to deal with the scholars. A company from Sixth Battalion will accompany you on Vendrei."

"Thank you, Vhorym."

"My pleasure, sir."

Quaeryt merely nodded, since he truly doubted it was a pleasure at all to the squad leader. He spent the rest of the afternoon calculating and then thinking out what he needed to write in his next letter to Vaelora and his next dispatch to Bhayar, but he committed nothing to paper.

Not yet.

At dinner, Quaeryt sought out Skarpa without seeming to and ended up sitting with Skarpa and Daendyr, the major in charge of supplies. Until they were well into the meal, and both majors had downed a mug of ale, Quaeryt merely listened and bantered.

Finally, as they were finishing the last scraps on their platters, he said, "I'm not an officer type, but the other day I heard a young ranker complaining about the number of patrols. Then an older ranker told him to stop complaining—not in those words—and that he didn't know how much easier it was these days because the companies used to be just four squads."

Skarpa shook his head. "The young ones always think they have it so tough, and the old ones are always reminding them that it was tougher in the old days. But the old ranker had it right. Just four squads, and we were running our mounts into the ground. When Rescalyn took over, he stepped up recruiting and mount procurement and added a squad to every company and another company to every battalion. Made all the difference."

And another battalion as well?

"That, and the outposts," added Daendyr.

"And your supply group," countered Skarpa. "You could supply a whole army."

"Not that much . . ." demurred Daendyr.

"Almost," insisted Skarpa.

After eating and talking a while longer, Quaeryt made his way back to his quarters, still thinking, and more worried than ever. If his calculations were correct, Rescalyn had turned his single "regiment" into a force equivalent to more than three regiments, with his own engineers and his own supply group as well. As Skarpa had inadvertently put it—a whole army— and the way the dispatches on budgets and expenditures were set up and sent to Bhayar, there had never been a mention of the increased number of squads or companies, just the costs of operating and maintaining the "regiment," with various explanations dealing with the cost of the outposts and the like.

All in plain sight.

64

Several quints before tenth glass on Mardi morning, Quaeryt was riding with Rescalyn and Captain Wraelyt from Seventh Battalion, near the head of the captain's company.

"Beautiful day, isn't it?" asked Rescalyn cheerfully. "Not a cloud in the sky, but a cool breeze in our face." He turned to Quaeryt. "How are you finding Tilbor these days, scholar?"

"The present days are to be preferred over my first patrols in Tilbor, sir."

"I can't imagine why," replied Rescalyn with a laugh, "but it's well that you've endured and recovered. Everyone is handed trials. What you do after that is what matters."

"And how you do it," suggested Quaeryt.

"Exactly. Without the regiment and good captains like Wraelyt here, Tilbor would be a far less attractive land. People here appear most pleasant, but that's because they know the alternative would be far worse. They don't mourn the passing of the Khanars, no matter what they say. They were always squabbling and plotting. They couldn't even let the last true Khanar's heir rule—and she'd run the country as well as anyone for years in her father's name."

"Weren't the ones who backed the Pretender mostly the northers, the northern High Holders, and the hill holders?" asked Quaeryt blandly.

"That's what they all claim, but a big part of the

reason why Tilbor fell was that the Khanars never had a strong enough armed force . . . Let me put it another way. They didn't have a large enough strong armed force. The Khanar's Guard was as good a force as any for its size, but it wasn't even the size of an old-style regiment."

Quaeryt concealed a frown. *An old-style regiment?* He was fairly certain that Bhayar had not changed the size of regiments anywhere in Telaryn. He also doubted the Lord of Telaryn was even aware that Rescalyn had done so in Tilbor.

The governor looked to Wraelyt, one of the older captains in the regiment, most likely an officer who had worked his way up through the ranks. "Wouldn't you say that's true, Captain?"

"True enough, sir. If they hadn't decided not to back the Pretender at the end, we'd have lost a lot more good men."

"They couldn't even unite against Telaryn. That tells you how divided they were," asserted Rescalyn cheerfully.

"You do seem to have calmed them down and given them a sense of unity," said Quaeryt. "I notice that many of the junior undercaptains are Tilborans."

"They make good troopers and officers. They'd be a credit to any regiment." Rescalyn gestured ahead. "I see the gates to High Holder Freunyt's estate."

The square gateposts were of dressed graystone, and behind the right post was a gatehouse with a split-slate roof. The twin iron gates were swung open, and two guards in maroon tunics and gray leather vests stood out front, one in front of each open gate.

Beyond the gates, the graystone-paved drive swept to the left around a pond encircled by low grass, upon which swam white geese. To the left of the lane and to the right of the pond were well-tended woods. Quaeryt noted that the paving stones, while mortared securely in place, bore two hollowed pathways, signifying years and years of carriages and wagons traversing the stone. Past the pond, the drive straightened and continued up a gentle slope to a sprawling stone structure close to a hundred and fifty yards long and rising three levels from the low hill. Before the palace-like mansion was a circular drive, in the middle of which was a raised garden, surrounded by a low wall. Quaeryt could smell the mixed perfume-like scents of the flowers.

Rescalyn turned in the saddle. "Captain, we will leave you now."

"Yes, sir."

Obviously, Wraelyt was following a set procedure, because he led the company to the right, down a narrower lane that led to a lower complex of buildings, while the governor and Quaeryt rode around the garden to the left and toward the front entry—with an extended roof wide enough to shade or protect two carriages and their teams end to end. The roof arched over the drive and was supported on the garden side by a series of square stone pillars.

"In the winter," said Rescalyn, "they put wooden panels between the pillars to keep the snow from drifting in front of the entry steps."

Two footmen waited to take the reins of their mounts, and no sooner had Quaeryt dismounted, not unskillfully, but with far less grace than Rescalyn, than a short man stepped out from the gilded double doors, doors that would doubtless have been covered by the folded-back shutter-doors in times of inclement weather.

"Governor . . . the High Holder awaits you in the

terrace salon. If you would come this way ... and you, too, sir," the functionary in maroon added to Quaeryt.

Quaeryt nodded and followed Rescalyn through an entry foyer with a domed ceiling and polished green marble floors to a wide corridor on the left, also with the green marble floor, except that the center held a thick carpet runner of dark green edged in golden yellow. The functionary escorted them past several archways, one of which opened into a darkened but immense dining hall with fireplaces at each end, until they had walked some fifty yards, where he turned down a slightly narrower hallway to an open door. There he stepped aside and gestured for them to enter.

Again, Quaeryt followed the governor, into what had to have been the terrace salon, a chamber almost the size of the Green Salon in the palace, although it was oblong, with wide windows centered on a set of double doors.

"Greetings, greetings, Governor," said the broad-shouldered and muscular figure who turned from the open doors that afforded access to the terrace beyond. High Holder Freunyt wore neither green nor maroon, but black trousers and a sleeveless black vest over a white silk shirt with wide collars. Boots and belt were also black, as was his hair, although there was little enough of that on the top of his head.

"Greetings to you," replied Rescalyn. "It's been too long. Your grounds look spectacular on a day like today."

"They do, don't they? They should, with all the fussing I've had my seneschal do for me. Come ... you've had a dusty ride. Wine ... lager ... what will you have?"

"Some of your estate white, if you still have it."

"And you, scholar?"

"The white, please."

As the High Holder poured the wine from a decanter, Quaeryt studied the room, the walls finished in pale yellow damask with portraits of distinguished looking men and women hung at intervals. The marble floor was largely covered by a thick carpet of green with intertwined cabled designs in gold, with thin lines of black outlining the gold.

"Here you are." Freunyt handed a goblet to Rescalyn and a second to Quaeryt. "Come look at the garden."

Goblet in hand, Quaeryt trailed the two out through the doors onto the terrace, a stone-paved area that extended back a good ten yards and ran ten yards on each side of the doors. At the back of the terrace was a waist-high wall of gray stone, topped with a course of whiter stone. The wall was necessary because, beyond it, the hillside had been cut away and a formal maze garden lay below, with flowers and topiary. There were no fountains, though, Quaeryt noted.

"What do you think?" asked the High Holder, looking to Quaeryt.

"It's beautiful. It's also well laid out." Quaeryt frowned. "The maze design . . ." He wasn't about to blurt it out directly, but looked for a reaction.

"Is it familiar? It might be, to a scholar . . . or a chorister." Freunyt offered an impish smile at odds with his appearance.

"Is that a version of the Path to Namelessness, then?"

"Exactly. With a few alterations to make it a functional maze that children and young people can navigate."

Rescalyn glanced sideways at Quaeryt for a moment,

then turned his attention back to Freunyt. "How have your harvests fared?"

"Well indeed. We've had no drenching rains and the maize and wheat corn are mostly harvested. We'll have a bumper crop of late apples, and even the root crops look good. But the vineyards . . . the best year in ages."

"That will be something, if the year's vintages exceed this." Rescalyn lifted his glass.

"I'm hopeful . . ."

Quaeryt listened, asked a few questions he hoped were innocuous, and listened more until the High Holder glanced back toward the terrace doors and a woman wearing a white lace apron over maroon trousers and tunic.

"I see our fare is waiting." Freunyt turned, and the three men crossed the terrace.

Inside the salon, a moderate-sized circular table had been placed before the center window of the three located on the side of the salon toward the main entrance, and three places had been set, all facing the window. Freunyt took the center place and gestured for Rescalyn to sit to his right. After all three were seated, the server placed a plate in front of each, with a slice of greenish melon garnished with the thinnest strips of a pale meat.

"Honeysweet melon with the tastiest of my cured ham," explained Freunyt.

As he did, a man in maroon refilled the diners' goblets.

The balding Freunyt turned and smiled at Quaeryt. "I never thought to see a scholar here." He lifted his goblet, as if in toast.

"A year ago, sir, I never thought I'd be in Tilbor, but

why did you feel you would not see a scholar here? I know there are scholars in Tilbora, but it is as if most avoid mentioning them."

"I know there are good men among them . . . and their school provides a most needed education for the children of factors and . . . others, but . . . let us say that there is little affection lost between those who lead the scholars and the High Holders of Tilbor." The High Holder smiled at Rescalyn. "That might be a matter which Scholar Quaeryt could look into . . . and see for himself."

"As a matter of fact," replied Rescalyn, "Scholar Quaeryt brought up that matter recently, and I have authorized him to do so over the next week or so."

"Good for you, Governor. It's about time." Freunyt's eyes fixed on Quaeryt. "I would wager that their master scholar, that scoundrel who calls himself Phaeryn, will talk so calmly that you'll think that they're little more than teachers and collectors of books. Don't believe him. Ask him what his so-called Scholar Chardyn did in the fight against the Khanara."

"There was a battle against the Khanara? I thought Tyrena was Eleonyd's daughter and she was acting as regent for her father."

"She was, and rightfully so, until that Pretender Rhecyrd showed up at the head of that mob of hill holders and the norther dissident High Holders. That Scholar Chardyn was up to his elbows in blood, and none of it was his. I wouldn't be surprised if he was the one behind the flaming of Lord Chayar's envoy."

Quaeryt got the strong feeling that what Freunyt had said was new even to Rescalyn, but he replied, "I've asked a few people about that time, and no one ever mentioned anything about a Scholar Chardyn. A

shopkeeper in Tilbora said there was an armsman
named Chardyn who served as a bodyguard for his
father, who was a high officer in the Khanar's Guard."

"Oh . . . that's true enough. It's just not the entire
truth. Chardyn left the scholars for a time to serve
under his father. A very short time. Traesk was the
only hill-bred officer ever to lead the Guard, and it
was a sad day for Tilbor when they picked him. . . ."
The High Holder shook his head. "Enough of such.
We should talk of merrier matters."

*Now that I've been maneuvered to deal with the
situation, I'm certain we will.* But Quaeryt only smiled
and took a sip from his goblet.

65

Even though he had eaten modest portions and limited himself to two glasses of the tasty but powerful
white wine, by the time Quaeryt and the governor
were riding back to the Telaryn Palace, the scholar felt
as though he wouldn't need to eat for days.

It wasn't the quantity, but how rich the food was.
And that richness was something to which he was un-
accustomed.

What Quaeryt didn't understand was why the entire luncheon and meeting had been set up as if to
bring up the matter of the local scholars, especially
when Rescalyn had been avoiding dealing with them
for years.

It's not good, because he's planning something.
Quaeryt also couldn't help but worry about Rhodyn's

sons, especially young Lankyt, and how they might fare if matters went badly. Yet, at the moment, Quaeryt had no idea what Rescalyn had in mind, and that concerned him more than a little. A great deal more than a little, in fact. For that reason, he said little for the first quint after they left Freunyt's estate, and the governor did not press him, as if Rescalyn were doing some thinking of his own.

Then, as they followed the road westward around the base of a hill and the Telaryn Palace came into view, with the sun hanging just above it, Rescalyn asked, "What do you think of High Holder Freunyt, scholar?"

"He's very knowledgeable and cultured . . . especially about wines and history. He also seems to know his lands and his people well."

"That's why he's a successful High Holder. Most of them are educated, and exceptional. They wouldn't stay High Holders if they were not."

"You've met with all of them. Freunyt is the only High Holder with whom I've ever conversed. Would you say he is one of the most astute, or are others more or less astute?"

"I would say he is among the more astute, but there are others just as intelligent, and very few who are incapable of directing their holdings."

"It doesn't appear as though the High Holders have a particularly good opinion of the local scholars, either."

"Either?"

Quaeryt couldn't sense if Rescalyn's gentle single word question happened to be lightly probing or an ironic comment. "At the princeps's reception for factors on Samedi, I overheard a few remarks suggesting the local scholars are not held in great esteem by at least some factors. It was clear I was meant to hear such."

"I had thought so from your request to visit the scholars. It will be interesting to see how they receive you on Vendrei. I would stress to you that you must not allow the scholars to in any way demean the authority you represent. That is one reason why I agreed with the princeps's recommendation that you be escorted by a full company. The officer accompanying you will be ready to have his men use arms . . . if necessary. While I do hope such is not necessary, you should be aware of the possibilities."

"I must say that I was troubled to hear that one of the scholars had been involved in supporting the Pretender. That suggests the hill holders have some influence there."

"That is something you will have to determine. I would find it most useful if you could determine the extent of such influence. So, I suspect, would Lord Bhayar."

"I will do my best, sir, but I am a scholar, not a cavalry officer or an envoy or minister."

"I would scarcely know a true scholar from a false one. You, as a scholar, may well see what others would not."

"That is possible." How could Quaeryt disagree with that observation?

At the same time, another aspect of the luncheon with Freunyt bothered Quaeryt. The governor had asked Quaeryt to accompany him well before Quaeryt had raised the matter of the scholars to the princeps . . . and Quaeryt had scarcely mentioned the scholars at all until the Lundi after the reception. He decided to say nothing more, and since Rescalyn did not inquire further, they rode for a bit longer before the governor spoke again.

"We will be detouring through the vale on the way back to the palace. The vale is an unfortunate necessity, one my predecessor didn't understand. Some of the men, usually the younger ones, do need a place away from the palace grounds in order to feel relaxed or to obtain some measure of female charms ... To keep matters in order, I need to appear there upon occasion ..."

"I'm certain your presence provides a certain reminder ..."

Rescalyn laughed. "It appears to have a salutatory effect. My officers insist it does, and I heed their observations, especially in matters involving their men. I do not always do as they recommend, but I do listen and understand the spirit behind those recommendations. You cannot lead armies if you do not understand those you lead."

"I suspect that is true of anyone leading anybody, sir."

"Indeed, it is." Rescalyn laughed again.

66

On Meredi morning, Quaeryt was up early and the first one into and out of the officers' mess in order to be ready for the long ride to meet with High Holder Fhaedyrk. While Quaeryt had not seen the princeps when he had returned late on Mardi afternoon,

Vhorym had informed Quaeryt that an Undercaptain Skeryl would command the squad escorting him.

Skeryl turned out to be young, at least for an undercaptain, possibly three or four years younger than Quaeryt, slightly round-faced despite a trim and muscular figure, with a cheerful smile and voice. Quaeryt decided to refrain from saying more than general pleasantries until they were well away from the palace walls . . . except that before he could say much, once they were barely beyond the lower gates, Skeryl spoke.

"Did you study to be a chorister before you became a scholar, sir?"

Quaeryt had a good idea from where that question had come, but he only smiled. "I studied history. You can't learn about history without learning about Rholan and how the worship of the Nameless has affected the lands of Lydar."

"And you never were interested in becoming a chorister?"

"I actually left the scholars and spent years before the mast as an apprentice quartermaster. That convinced me I'd rather be a scholar. How did you come to be an undercaptain?"

"I had three older brothers. They were better smiths than I was . . ."

For much of the rest of the ride, Quaeryt asked questions about Skeryl himself, but the kind designed to reveal as much about Tilbor as the undercaptain. He also worked, as he could, on maintaining and improving his shields. After riding, with breaks, some four and a half glasses, they reached the entry to High Holder Fhaedyrk's estate—far less imposing than that of Freunyt, and far more chill in its hilly location. Quaeryt was glad to have worn the undress brown jacket over his regular browns, given the wind gusting downhill.

The gateposts were about the same size as those of Freunyt's entry, but the iron gates were narrower and painted black, and the gatehouse barely large enough to hold the single guard who waved them through, while the paved lane was only wide enough for a single carriage or wagon. No gardens flanked the lane, just meadows with shaggy grasses that had turned the tan brown of fall. The meadows sloped north and upward to the mansion, and behind the dwelling were forests that extended to and over a ridge perhaps a mille uphill of the estate buildings. The main dwelling was of two levels, its walls of a mixture of natural stones, not dressed or cut, with a square tower at the west end, and extended perhaps seventy yards from one end to the other.

As Quaeryt and the squad neared the mansion, he made out a covered entry that extended to the paved lane, but not over it. A long waist-high hedge bordered the lane on the side away from the entry, extending some thirty yards on each side, but there were no gardens in front of the hedge, although the grass had been rough-cut to ankle height.

A wiry blond figure stepped out and halfway down the five wide stone steps, waiting. He wore a brown leather vest, with tooled designs on the leather, pressed brown trousers, and polished brown boots. His shirt was golden yellow and of shining silk.

Quaeryt reined up short of the entry. "Greetings, sir."

"Greetings, master scholar, and welcome to Dyrkholm." The High Holder turned his eyes to Skeryl. "The stables and quarters for resting are the second buildings in the upper side courtyard, Captain. My head ostler is waiting for you. You can water and feed your mounts, as you see fit, and there are refreshments for you and your men."

Skeryl bowed in the saddle. "Our thanks and appreciation, sir."

Fhaedyrk nodded, then turned. "Master scholar . . . again, welcome to Dyrkholm."

Quaeryt hurriedly dismounted, then handed the mare's reins to the ranker who rode forward.

"I will send word to you, Captain, when the scholar is ready to depart."

"Yes, sir."

Quaeryt walked to the steps, stopped at the bottom, and inclined his head. "High Holder."

"Fhaedyrk, if you please. And you are Quaeryt? Fitting name for a scholar. Come."

Quaeryt joined the wiry holder who had appeared shorter than the scholar but turned out to be the same height as they walked through the wide single door of the mansion into a smallish oblong entry foyer, with two staircases, one heading up to the east and one to the west, and then straight back into a modest hallway floored with cut and polished natural stones set in mortar, with a green bordered dark gray carpet runner in the middle.

"I trust you do not mind if my wife joins us for a light meal."

"I'd be delighted." Quaeryt didn't have to counterfeit his pleasure; he had no doubts that Fhaedyrk's wife was most likely to be as intelligent and perceptive as the High Holder, or she would not have been included.

The High Holder stopped at the last door on the right—already open—and gestured. "This is the summer parlor—that's what Laekyna calls it." He extended an arm to the slightly stocky blond woman standing beside the circular table located in a windowed nook and set for three. "Don't you, dear?"

Laekyna smiled, and her entire face came alive. For some reason, although the two looked not at all alike, for that moment, the High Holder's wife reminded Quaeryt of Vaelora. "He does make fun of me, master scholar, but it is the most pleasant room in the summer."

"Any room is pleasant with you in it, dear."

Quaeryt could not miss the obvious affection in word and expression, and it cheered him, even as he warned himself that a man could love his wife and still be a foe not to be trusted.

Fhaedyrk gestured to the table. "We took the liberty of preparing some light fare for you, knowing how far you have ridden." He seated himself in the middle place, and Laekyna was already standing before the place to his right.

Quaeryt took the chair to the High Holder's left and sat down. "You're very kind."

"It was kind of the princeps and governor to send you. Few wish to travel far from Tilbora. I thought we might begin with a cool potato soup."

As Fhaedyrk spoke, a server appeared with a dish and a ladle and began to fill the bowls, set on green porcelain chargers. A second server appeared and placed dark rolls on the small plates beside the chargers.

"The rolls are sweet dark rolls with honeyed raisins. The raisins come from our lower vineyards. I can offer lager, white or red wine, or grape or berry juice."

"What would you recommend?"

"I'm actually going to have lager."

"Fhaedyrk's lager is the best in Tilbor," added Laekyna.

"Then I'll have the lager."

After one swallow, Quaeryt agreed. "It's not just the best lager in Tilbor; it's the best I've had anywhere."

"You see, dearest," said Laekyna. "I told you so."

Just from what was clearly the first course, Quaeryt would not have considered the fare "light" by any means, but suspected the time and terminology had been set for reasons of custom. If asked by other High Holders, Fhaedyrk could say, with perfect honesty, that he had met with Quaeryt in midafternoon and offered light refreshments to the assistant to the princeps, as was only courtesy after such a long ride.

"How was the ride?"

"Pleasant as four-glass rides go. Most of the time, there was a breeze, and that helped."

"Except in the winter," commented Fhaedyrk wryly. "It's usually a gale then."

"Are your winters here as bitter as in the north?"

"They're often more bitter, or so we're told," replied Laekyna. "It has to do with the way the hills channel the winds."

Quaeryt sensed that the meal was for light conversation and held the questions he had in mind. The main course was a meat pie, but the crust was so flaky and the sauce so light that it didn't feel heavy at all.

"You must try the berry custard—it's Laekyna's special recipe."

"My aunt's actually."

"This is your version, and it's better."

Quaeryt needed no urging. When he finished the last tasty spoonful of the custard, he turned to Laekyna. "That was excellent. I've never tasted better."

Laekyna smiled, and blushed slightly. "Thank you."

"I told you," added Fhaedyrk proudly. After the slightest pause, he said, "I had not thought to find the assistant to the princeps to be a scholar."

Quaeryt understood. He also saw that Laekyna was studying him as well.

"I'm from Solis, sir, and I was raised and educated there, but Lord Bhayar sent me here."

"Might I ask why?"

"He expressed concerns about the number of soldiers it takes to keep order. I made the mistake of asking if the people of Tilbor were so different that they needed more order imposed by arms . . . or words to that effect. He said that I asked too many questions and sent me off."

Both listeners smiled.

"What have you discovered?"

"From what I've seen, except for the hill holders, the people and High Holders of Tilbor are a most orderly group that want to get on with their own lives." Quaeryt paused slightly. "Recently, it's come to my attention that some of the scholars may not be what they claim. What is your opinion on that?"

"I would scarcely be in a position to judge that."

"I can understand your reticence to comment, sir, especially given your . . . shall we say . . . strained relations with the scholars at the Ecoliae . . ."

"So far as I know, I have no relations with them." Fhaedyrk's voice turned cool.

Laekyna continued to hold a pleasant expression.

"Exactly." Quaeryt smiled. "Nor would anyone in your position, especially, wish to have any relations with them."

"My position?"

"Governor Fhayt was ambushed and nearly killed coming to visit you. The local scholars have attempted to have you killed at least once, and possibly more often."

470 L. E. MODESITT, JR.

"You have quite an imagination, especially for a scholar."

"Do I?" Quaeryt smiled again. "You also seemed to be one of the few High Holders who actually dared to put into writing in letters to Khanar Eleonyd reasonable observations about the source of Tilbor's prosperity. You're a very far-seeing and practical man. That's one of the many reasons I requested a meeting with you."

"How did you know about my letters, might I ask?"

"I read through the Khanars' archives of the past several years when I first came to Tilbor. It took some time."

"All of them?" asked Laekyna.

"I do not know what was not in the archives. There was an entire chamber. I read all that was there."

Fhaedyrk laughed. "I doubt Khanar Eleonyd read a fraction of what you did."

"Then did Khanara Tyrena?"

"I'm sure that she did," said Laekyna. "Her father, despite all the rumors, relied on her heavily."

Fhaedyrk and his wife exchanged a momentary glance.

"You have traveled a great way, master scholar. Why? Surely not merely to meet me."

"Because you are a far-seeing and practical man, I wanted your thoughts on a matter."

"Oh? Even the governor has not so openly sought my thoughts."

"I'm not the governor. I'm just a scholar assistant to the princeps attempting to find ways to make Tilbor even more peaceful."

"How might I have anything to do with that?"

Quaeryt decided, for the moment, to ignore the direct thrust of the question. "Let us assume, for the moment, that Lord Bhayar would like the scholars in Telaryn to continue to provide schools and teaching. Yet in Tilbor, there are rumors that certain scholars have more of an interest in supporting those who would rather cause unrest. What course of action might preserve the abilities of the scholars to teach while removing their involvement with those who are little more than brigands with lands?"

"You are most kind in your assessment of the hill holders." The sarcasm was delivered gently.

"I am perhaps not impartial. I accompanied a patrol through the hills to seek poachers who were plaguing a High Holder. We attacked no one, not until we were attacked. I took a crossbow quarrel in the shoulder from men who appeared to be minions of a holder Waerfyl. Later, after I recovered, I accompanied another patrol following two wagons full of coal stolen from another High Holder's mine—where a number of miners were killed. In both cases, the men of the hill holder attacked the lands and men of High Holders. That scarcely seems like a protest against Lord Bhayar. Then I recently discovered that certain scholars were involved in actions that might have been construed as undermining the Khanara." Quaeryt looked to Laekyna.

She nodded. "There have been rumors of such. They were more than rumors. So what does this have to do with us?"

"I was curious as to whether you had any idea who was behind the attack on Governor Fhayt and why the only time any governor has been attacked when coming to visit a High Holder happened to occur on a visit to you."

"I doubt there is any proof anywhere as to the identity of the attackers. Yet inquiries have suggested that a certain Sansang master has often been absent from the Ecoliae at the time of certain disruptions."

Laekyna's eyes hardened just a fraction as her husband spoke.

"Because I am a scholar, and because scholars have sometimes behaved unwisely, I find myself in an awkward position. I would like the scholars to be able to study and teach and be accepted, but it appears this would be difficult in Tilbor."

"It would appear so." Fhaedyrk turned to his wife.

"I cannot speak for anyone, master scholar, let alone my husband, but as a poor humble wife, I can see no course of action that would accomplish those ends while the Master Scholar and his princeps remain in charge of the Ecoliae. I will admit that, because my older brother was educated for a year or so at the Ecoliae, I believe Scholar Nalakyn is deeply committed to teaching and little more, and there are others of similar persuasion. Yet for any High Holder to remove either by force . . . many would find that repulsive and high-handed. For a High Holder even to suggest it . . . or mention it . . ." She shrugged.

"There are times when I give my wife liberty to speak her mind," said Fhaedyrk, "but those are her thoughts."

Quaeryt understood the situation all too well. "I understand. You are most considerate in letting her speak her mind. Well . . . you understand my concerns, and I do believe I understand yours. Oh . . . I might also add that the princeps was most impressed with your insight about the source of Tilbor's wealth, and he asked me to convey that appreciation to you."

"That was most kind of him."

"He is much quieter than the governor, but there

are depths under that calm." Quaeryt smiled as he turned to Laekyna. "As is often the case."

"Before you go . . . master scholar . . . you must try a taste of our best brandy."

"I cannot imagine how good that must be, given the excellence of what you called simple fare." Quaeryt shook his head. "I cannot tell you how much I have enjoyed the meal and the afternoon." And he had . . . and hoped they both understood that.

67

Quaeryt was more than glad for the "light fare" provided by Fhaedyrk, because he and Skeryl and the squad didn't return to the palace until after eighth glass on Meredi night. Although he was exhausted from holding shields almost all of the way back, it was close to midnight before he finally got to sleep. After breakfast on Jeudi morning, he made his way to his study, where he wrote his weekly dispatch to Bhayar, and then started in on another letter to Vaelora, spurred in part, he had to admit, by the strange similarity of expression between Laekyna and Bhayar's sister.

Are you sure you're not recalling what you wish to recall?

That was a question for which he had no answer, because, as in so many things, he just did not know. What he did know was that he needed to write her again, for more than one reason.

Mistress Vaelora—

Over the past week I have met with two High Holders, and both were very respectful of the governor. Unfortunately, neither was especially pleased with the views expressed by the local community of scholars, and in particular, both were displeased with rumors about the acts of a very few senior scholars. As a result, tomorrow I will be making an official visit to the Ecoliae, with a company of cavalry at my back. The governor, the princeps, and I all hope that such a force is unnecessary, but it appears as though there may be certain ties between some of the more senior scholars and the hill holders who have created continual difficulties for the governor.

This situation, unhappily, reinforces my belief that scholars serve best when seen as advisors and sources of information. An advisor who is perceived as an instrument of action, either for or against a ruler, whether or not that perception is correct, loses the imprimatur of impartiality, just as an administrator or governor who acts in his own interests, rather than in the interests of the lord of the land, loses the lord's trust. Scholars are more vulnerable, alas, because we lack the power of those who can marshal arms, men, or golds. That is why it is important that any perception of illicit acts be removed as soon as practicable. This must be accomplished in an open manner, while limiting the corrective actions to those who are indeed guilty of such transgressions. I can only hope that I can be of some service to both Lord Bhayar and the honest scholars in this matter.

In your earlier missives, you had discussed the role of those who advise, and the limitations and circumstances that affect how such advice may be received, but I fear the greatest limitation may be that of distance, except, of course, when the advice is lacking in quality and thought, and then distance becomes a blessing . . . but I hope that my distance from you and Lord Bhayar never becomes that particular blessing. . . .

After attempting humorous comments on advice, Quaeryt added a few lines about the weather and Vaelora's kindness in continuing the correspondence, then closed and sealed the letter.

At just before the third glass of the afternoon, Vhorym summoned Quaeryt to the princeps's study. As the scholar entered, Straesyr motioned for him to close the door and sit down. Quaeryt did both . . . and waited to see what the princeps had to say. Not for the first time, Quaeryt had the feeling that Straesyr wore his tunic and trousers—both always crisp—as if they constituted a uniform.

"You are going to see the scholars tomorrow—with a company at your back. This may create certain difficulties, but then, as you have pointed out, the scholars have created a host of other problems. While neither the governor nor I anticipate your having difficulty with the scholars, you are empowered to act with the authority of a battalion major if anything should go awry. If there are significant difficulties, you are not to hesitate to use that authority."

That means you have some expectation of trouble. "Yes, sir."

"There are times when it is best to deliver a message and depart. There are times when it is best to go beyond that. The senior officer present has to decide. Tomorrow, you will be that senior officer. Because you are not normally placed in such a position, I wish to make that clear."

"Yes, sir."

"That's all."

When Quaeryt returned to his study, he was more than a little concerned. He also didn't know whether Straesyr's instructions were designed to make him more vigilant or a subtle way of assuring that he would over-react.

By the time he left his study, he still had not been able to discern what lay behind Straesyr's instructions, but he did remember to stop by his quarters and don his undress jacket to wear to mess night. That took longer than he'd anticipated, and he had to hurry to reach the officers' mess before the governor appeared.

"You had quite a ride the other day, sir," observed Haestyn as Quaeryt approached. "The jacket makes you look like a scholar officer."

"I think that was the princeps's idea," replied Quaeryt with a smile.

"Skeryl was impressed with the fare that High Holder laid out for them."

"High Holder Fhaedyrk was kind and courteous—"

"All rise!"

Since he was still standing, Quaeryt merely stiffened.

"As you were," called out Rescalyn. "Please be seated. I do have a few words."

Chairs shuffled as the officers seated themselves.

"As some of the battalion majors know, the holders in and south of the Boran Hills have been quiet lately. Those of you who have been here a time know that, usually, but not always, such quiet is often followed by some sort of action by not just one holder, but by a number. I would like to say that the hill holders are finally accepting that they are a part of Telaryn. I doubt that I can. If this is like other times, we may need to send reinforcements to Boralieu. I am merely offering you an observation at present. I do hope that it remains such." Rescalyn smiled ironically. "In the meantime, enjoy your fare." He seated himself.

In the momentary silence, Quaeryt poured himself a

lager rather than wine, then took a swallow. It wasn't a fraction as good as what Fhaedyrk had served.

For a time, as the meal progressed he mostly listened.

"It seems like every year we've got a problem with the hill holders," said Dueryl. "I still don't see why."

"It goes way back," replied Haestyn. "Years ago, my uncle said, except I guess it was hundreds of years back, there weren't any High Holders and hill holders. There were only holders. The Khanar offered special privileges to those holders who recognized and supported him, and who limited the number of men-at-arms. He also pledged to defend them against any other holder who attacked them. He called them High Holders. The hill holders and some of the others refused to reduce the size of their forces. They claimed the Khanar couldn't protect them." The captain shrugged. "I don't know if it's true or not, but that's what he said."

"You're a scholar," noted Dueryl, looking to Quaeryt. "Is that true?"

"I don't know. There's nothing in the histories I've read . . ." He paused. What was it that he'd read? He tried to remember for several moments before it came to him. "There is something called the Charter, but I never found anything about what it contained."

"That's what he called it," interjected Haestyn. "Now, I remember."

Quaeryt wanted to hit himself alongside his head. That explained a great deal about the hill holders, but it raised more than a few other questions, such as why the governors hadn't tried to include the hill holders in the similar arrangement later offered to the High Holders. Or had they, and been refused?

He couldn't help wondering if he'd ever understand all undercurrents that swirled through Tilbor.

68

Vendrei morning Quaeryt was up early. He wondered if he'd ever get back into a situation where he could sleep to a decent glass. Early as he was, at least half the regimental officers were already present when he entered the mess. Skarpa rose from where he sat alone at the end of the far table and beckoned to him.

Quaeryt joined the major and poured himself some tea before taking a helping of eggs scrambled with cheese and ham.

"Commander Myskyl ordered me to supply a company to support you today. He said you were going to visit the scholars." Skarpa's tone was even.

Too even, Quaeryt reflected. "I requested an escort. The governor and princeps decided on a company."

"Why does a scholar need such an escort?"

"Because the scholars are tied to the hill holders and backed the Pretender against the Khanara."

Skarpa frowned.

Quaeryt waited.

"I was ordered—ordered, not requested—to send Undercaptain Gauswn and his company, and I don't think that was the regimental commander's idea."

Quaeryt couldn't say he was surprised and didn't. "It's likely it wasn't." He knew full well that the reason Gauswn had been chosen was that he was Tilboran, very junior, least likely to question Quaeryt, and expendable if anything went wrong. For that last reason alone, Quaeryt intended that nothing would go wrong. He also knew that intentions weren't always realized.

"Why not? Do you know?"

"I don't know. I do know the governor brought me to meet with a High Holder last Mardi. The only thing that was discussed was how out of step the scholars were with the High Holders and the people of Tilbor. That was after I went to a reception held by the princeps where I was meant to hear all sorts of comments about the scholars. None of them were favorable."

"This stinks worse than week-old fish in high summer." Skarpa's voice was low.

"What would you suggest?"

"Besides keeping yourself and Gauswn alive? I don't know."

"Rescalyn's remarks last night?"

"They could be a coincidence."

Skarpa didn't sound convinced, and Quaeryt certainly wasn't. "They might be," he offered cautiously.

"You don't believe that."

"Neither do you."

Skarpa laughed, softly, but harshly. Then he shook his head. "Take care of Gauswn. He'll make a good officer in time."

"I'll do what I can."

There wasn't much to be said after that, and Quaeryt and the major ate quietly and then departed on their respective ways.

Quaeryt gave his sealed envelopes to the dispatch rider and parted with another silver, reflecting as he did that he actually had a fair amount of pay coming to him, since he hadn't drawn it the week before . . . something like thirty silvers, after the deductions for the mess. Except that he might not be back in time to draw his pay, not if matters at the Ecoliae were as he feared.

He shook his head as he walked toward the stables.

By a quint past seventh glass, Quaeryt and Gauswn were riding away from the lower gates of the palace toward the Ecoliae. Quaeryt carried the light shields that triggered into heavier shields. He was getting to the point where they felt natural and close to effortless, although the effort of maintaining the heavier shields was akin to that required for a fast walk.

"Can you tell me what this is all about, sir?" asked the undercaptain. "Major Skarpa said that there might be trouble with the scholars, and that I'm under your command."

"I don't know everything," replied Quaeryt. "The problem lies with some of the senior scholars. They seem to have strong ties to the hill holders and have created problems with some High Holders. Neither the factors nor the High Holders trust them, and it shouldn't be that way. We're going there to look into the situation, because the governor thinks that I, as a scholar, should be able to see more."

"What do you think you'll find, sir?"

"Trouble of some sort. I'd be surprised if much force is required, except the force of presence of your company." Quaeryt laughed. "But I've been surprised before, and that's why you and your company are here."

After a moment, Gauswn asked, "What are your orders and instructions?"

"Simply that no one is to leave the Ecoliae until I finish talking with the Master Scholar or, in his absence, the scholar princeps. In carrying out that order, have your men try not to do serious harm to anyone—unless the scholar attempts to do violence to any ranker."

"Yes, sir. Not doing harm unless threatened—that's a standing order. Anything else?"

Quaeryt thought. "Some of the scholars are trained in Sansang. You might caution your men that empty-handed scholars or those with a half-staff can also be dangerous." He hoped Gauswn didn't press him for details on how he knew. He'd rather not evade or lie.

Gauswn turned to the lead ranker riding behind him. "Did you hear that, Fhenoyt?"

"Yes, sir."

"Pass that back to the other squads." Gauswn returned his attention to Quaeryt.

Little more than a glass later, the company reached the base of the hill that held the Ecoliae and started riding up the brick-paved lane, with two scouts before Quaeryt and the undercaptain. Several scholars standing on the front section of the wide covered porch surrounding the main building of the Ecoliae turned and watched as the company of troopers rode from the brick-paved lane and stationed themselves by squads around the main building, positioned to watch the stables as well.

Accompanied by two rankers, Quaeryt rode forward and reined up short of the hitching ring before the front steps, whose bricks still needed repointing. He dismounted and handed the mare's reins to the nearest ranker, then turned toward the steps.

"This is a place of learning. Do not enter if you have aught else on your mind," declared the sharp-faced, dark-haired scholar who stood before the front steps, half-blocking the way.

For a moment, Quaeryt struggled to place the scholar. Then he laughed. "That precept doesn't apply to this House of Scholars, Alkiabys. Not after all that you and Chardyn have done."

"It is still a House of Scholars, and you are no scholar."

"I'm far more a scholar than you or Chardyn. Stand aside. I'm only going to talk to Phaeryn and Zarxes . . . by myself. The troopers are here to see that no one leaves."

Alkiabys stepped back, but Quaeryt strengthened his shields slightly, and made them more sensitive before walking up the steps. As he started to cross the porch, he saw Nalakyn stepping from the center door, his face creased in puzzlement.

"Wait here on the porch, Scholar Nalakyn . . . if you would." Quaeryt softened the last few words before entering the center door.

Both Phaeryn and Zarxes stood in the foyer, waiting for him.

"The prodigal scholar . . ." offered Zarxes sarcastically.

"No . . . just the scholar assistant to the princeps of Tilbor."

"Might I ask exactly why you are here, and under what authority?" asked Phaeryn.

"The authority is that of Lord Bhayar, as approved by Governor Rescalyn. Do you think that anyone could arrive with a company of Telaryn troopers without the governor's approval?"

"There is that," agreed the silver-haired Master Scholar. "Your response, however, begs the question as to why the governor has any interest at all in a group of near-impoverished scholars who have done little but study and teach."

"I do so appreciate your definition of 'little,' Master Scholar Phaeryn." Quaeryt coated his words with irony. "I came to talk to you."

"Then we should repair to my study so that we do not disturb the other scholars," replied Phaeryn.

"Perhaps we should." Quaeryt sensed that was exactly what the other two wanted, but, if matters went as he planned, that would serve his purposes as well.

Zarxes's eyes twitched, as if he had wanted to look to Phaeryn, but had decided against it.

"This way, *Scholar* Quaeryt, if that is truly your name."

"It is, indeed, and always has been." Quaeryt followed the two down the corridor to an open door . . . and inside.

Zarxes shut the door, deftly sliding the bolt, then stepped over beside Phaeryn.

The study was modest in size, if richly paneled in what Quaeryt thought was walnut. A wide desk was set forward of and between two windows flanked by dark green hangings, and three straight-backed chairs faced the desk. The side wall to Quaeryt's right, as he faced the desk, was composed of floor-to-ceiling shelves, although less than a third of the space actually contained books. The wall to his left also held shelves. Two armchairs were set before the shelves on the left.

The silver-haired Phaeryn smiled politely. "You might explain why you need all those troopers if you are here merely to talk."

"Oh . . . they're just here to assure that we do talk. Some people, even scholars, have an aversion to discussing certain matters."

"Might I assume the disappearance of Scholar Chardyn was your doing?" asked Zarxes.

"He disappeared? That would almost be a pity, except for the fact that he was a part of the botched efforts of the Pretender. As for assumptions, you can assume what you wish. All I know is that, if Scholar Chardyn vanished, it was a result of his own acts."

"He disappeared in the middle of the night on the same night you departed . . . and you had nothing to do with it? That's rather unlikely."

"I never said I had nothing to do with it. I intimated that his disappearance was the result of his own decisions. Someone lurked in my room that night. I suspect that Scholar Chardyn discovered that I had been appointed scholar assistant to the princeps of Tilbor. I also suspect he knew what I had discovered." Quaeryt smiled.

"Oh?" asked Phaeryn smoothly, moving toward one of the armchairs, against which rested what appeared to be a walking stick, but was more likely a half-staff. "And what was this dark and mysterious secret you discovered?"

Quaeryt smiled politely as Zarxes took a position before the other armchair, where another half-staff rested. "It was no secret to either of you. Actually, there were several secrets. One was the fact that you'd made several unsuccessful attempts to murder High Holder Fhaedyrk. Another was that you—or, more directly, Chardyn—were behind the bloody attack on Governor Fhayt. That didn't include—"

Both Zarxes and Phaeryn attacked with their Sansang half-staffs. The staffs impacted his shields, and rebounded. Phaeryn's dropped from his hands, while Zarxes dropped his and, drawing a wide-bladed knife from under his brown jacket, turned and slashed Phaeryn's throat, then dropped the knife.

For a moment, that act froze Quaeryt. In that moment, Zarxes turned, took three steps to the shelves, and reached out. The shelves swung aside, revealing a circular staircase.

Quaeryt rushed toward the staircase, but the shelves closed with a dull thud.

He tried pressing or pushing where he'd seen Zarxes put his hand—on a seemingly ornamental protrusion on the bracket holding a lamp—but nothing happened. He glanced back at the still-struggling Phaeryn, whose bloody hands came away from his neck as he pitched forward, dying, if not already dead.

Quaeryt tried to image part of the mechanism away, but nothing happened except that his head felt like it would split where he stood.

Iron-lined . . . or metal anyway . . . behind all that.

Quaeryt sprinted to the study door, fumbled with the bolt, then flung open the door and sprinted down the corridor and out onto the porch. As he started across the porch to issue orders to Gauswn, a figure with a half-staff launched himself at Quaeryt, only to rebound from the scholar's shields. Quaeryt ignored the interruption as he stopped at the edge of the porch. "Gauswn! Send a patrol out to look for a scholar with silver-blond hair and beard! That's Zarxes. He killed the Master Scholar. Have them capture any scholar they see away from the scholarium. Then report back to me inside." Then he whirled and jabbed a finger at the middle-aged and gray-haired scholar who stood waiting. "Nalakyn—find me a sledge and an ax! Bring them to the Master Scholar's study! Now!"

The scholar paled, then swallowed. "Yes, sir."

Quaeryt thought that Zarxes had probably used the hidden staircase to access an escape tunnel, if one happened to be located near the staircase. Quaeryt had few doubts about that, but he needed to make certain, just on the off chance that Zarxes was holed up down below.

He turned in time to see the man who had attacked him—Alkiabys—scurry across the porch and into the building by the eastern front porch door. He took a step in that direction, then stopped. He couldn't afford the time to chase Alkiabys.

"None of you are to leave the porch or the building!" He turned and hurried back inside and down the corridor to Phaeryn's study. Several scholars and students backed away from him as he did. Absently, he realized that neither Lankyt nor Syndar was among them.

He stopped in the study doorway, but the only figure inside was the sprawled and motionless form of the Master Scholar. In a few moments, Nalakyn appeared with a sledge, followed by a young scholar bearing an ax, then by Gauswn.

Quaeryt stepped back. "Nalakyn, Undercaptain, inspect the body. I'd like you to see what happened before anyone else disturbs matters." A few moments wouldn't matter so far as Zarxes happened to be concerned. He was either running—and while the cavalry patrol might catch him, Quaeryt wouldn't—or hidden in the lower levels, in which case he wasn't going anywhere soon.

Gauswn knelt first, away from the blood pooled on the polished but worn wooden floor. "A single cut across the throat. It's deep."

Nalakyn bent over and then straightened. He was pale when he rose, and he swallowed several times. "Why . . . why would Zarxes do that?" He frowned. "Where did he go? None of us saw him."

"I was hoping you could shed some light on why the princeps did that. Think it over. Now . . . there's a hidden staircase behind those shelves. That's how he left. If anyone knows how to open it . . . fine. If not, we need to break through it." He looked to Nalakyn.

"I didn't know there was anything there, sir."

"Which side was swung out, sir?" asked Gauswn, rising to his feet.

Quaeryt concentrated, trying to remember. "The left."

"Then there might be a catch somewhere between the planks that form the edges of the cases there." Gauswn took the ax from the student scholar, hefted it, then stepped toward the seemingly unbroken wall of shelves.

Three deftly aimed strokes of the ax—so precise that Quaeryt had to wonder where the undercaptain had learned to handle it—and one slightly splintered polished support later, the section of shelves leaned forward, but only about a third of a yard, if that.

Gauswn stepped away. "The back is lined with iron, and there's an iron rod affixed to a plate. A long cold chisel would be better. I'll just break the ax, otherwise."

So Quaeryt found himself waiting for another fraction of a quint before another student hurried back with the cold chisel.

Finally, Gauswn snapped the junction between rod and plate and the shelves swung open. "I should go first, sir."

"No. You follow me." Quaeryt stepped around the undercaptain, contracted his shields so that they were close to his body and strengthened them, and then eased down the circular wooden staircase, sturdy enough that it did not even creak once.

At the bottom of the staircase he faced an open space and two doors. Both were closed, but in the dim light that filtered down, he could see bootprints on the dusty stone floor leading to the door on the right. He stepped forward and opened the door—only to find shelves stacked with bottles that looked to hold wine.

He studied the wine closet again, until he saw where the dust had been disturbed. He tried to lift the bottle, but it did not move. He tried to pull it toward him. There was a slight give, but nothing more. He pushed the neck of the bottle, and the entire back of the closet swung away, revealing a long tunnel curving toward the west and angling downhill, a tunnel not quite tall enough for Quaeryt to stand erect.

Quaeryt stepped back into the lower level of the building. "Undercaptain, you might have some men follow the tunnel and see where it leads. But have them be careful."

"Yes, sir."

Quaeryt opened the second door. The shelves there held dusty squat jars. He touched several, but they all also adhered to the wooden shelves on which they rested. He pulled and pushed on almost a score before the back of the closet swung away.

This time, Quaeryt swallowed. Beyond the false closet was a squarish chamber, in which blades were racked on one part of the wall, crossbows on another, seven pikes on another . . . and various other weapons and accouterments, some of which Quaeryt had never seen.

"Mother of the Namer . . ." Gauswn looked to Quaeryt.

"I think we know a little better why not too many people in Tilbora are exactly fond of the dear scholars." Quaeryt shook his head. "This will keep. Go see about getting men to follow the tunnel and see if the patrols had any fortune in finding the good scholar Zarxes. Or the young one who tried to attack me."

"Yes, sir."

The dust suggested that neither the armory nor the tunnel had been used at least in a few weeks, but Quaeryt didn't see any reason to point that out. Quaeryt would have wagered that Alkiabys knew . . . and that raised the question of where Chardyn's assistant had gone. Quaeryt doubted Alkiabys was anywhere near the Ecoliae, and he wouldn't have been surprised if there happened to be another tunnel, and even another armory. In fact, the way matters were going, he would have been shocked if there weren't.

When Quaeryt followed Gauswn up the narrow spiral staircase and emerged back in the Master Scholar's study, he looked at Nalakyn, who had remained, as if frozen. "Nalakyn, I imagine you're the most senior scholar here. I want every scholar to come to the door of the study and see this, but no one is to touch the body. Then I want them all to assemble in the dining hall. The students will have to remain in the building for now, but they don't have to see the body or attend the assembly. Is that clear?"

"Yes, sir."

"After the meeting, we'll discuss arrangements for the pyre. There will be no services and no memorial."

"Sir?"

"I don't think the scholars can afford a memorial to a traitor to Lord Bhayar, and I certainly don't intend to allow it."

"Yes, sir."

"Then you may go." Quaeryt did not take a deep breath until he was momentarily alone. Then he headed for the front porch to see if the company's troopers had been able to find Zarxes. He paused for a moment as he noticed the figure of the ancient chorister walking away from Gauswn, again mounted, but he had to wait only a few moments before the undercaptain rode over.

"Any fortune in finding the princeps?"

Gauswn's reply was simple. "No . . . sir."

"I didn't think they would. What about the other one?"

"They're still looking . . ." Gauswn looked down from his mount at Quaeryt. "What would you have us do now?"

"I'm going to meet with the scholars. After that, I'm going to write a quick report to the governor so that one of your men can ride back and inform him. Then we both wait for orders. In the meantime, no scholar goes anywhere."

"Yes, sir."

Quaeryt walked around the entire porch, but it was empty. After a time, he made his way to the dining hall. As he stepped inside, the murmurs died to absolute silence.

"Please be seated." He waited until everyone was in a chair before he continued. "The reason you are assembled here is very simple. Both your reputations and possibly your lives are in danger. Some scholars have been involved in acts against both High Holders and the former governor of Tilbor. In addition, when I brought this matter up before the Master Scholar and the princeps less than a glass ago, your beloved princeps attacked me with the half-staff of the Sansang and then slashed the throat of Master Scholar Phaeryn. He escaped through the secret tunnel from the study of the Master Scholar. I requested Scholar Nalakyn to have you all view the study so that there would be no mistake about what occurred.

"Hard as it may be for some of you to accept what has happened, the fact is that the roots of the problem lie years in the past. That past is past, and anyone who attempts to use it as a cause or as a reason will suffer. I don't care about the past. Neither does the governor. Nor does the princeps of Tilbor. We all care about the present and what happens from now onward.

"I will be acting as Master Scholar to oversee the transition to a true scholarium, one devoted to scholarship and study, and to education. The school will continue. The practice of Sansang will not. For the moment, Scholar Nalakyn will act as princeps." Quaeryt stopped and waited for several moments. "I trust that is clear. For a time longer, no one will leave the scholarium. Anyone who does leave, when that is allowed, will no longer be considered a scholar, and their name and description will be sent to every scholarium in Telaryn." He turned to Nalakyn. "You may say whatever you think appropriate after I leave. Then join me in the princeps's study."

Quaeryt walked out of the dining hall and to the princeps's study, where he sat down and began to write a summary of exactly what had happened so that Gauswn could send one of the rankers with the report to the governor. When he finished, since Nalakyn had not arrived yet, Quaeryt went to find Gauswn.

The undercaptain was in the rear courtyard and rode over to where Quaeryt stood on the edge of the rear covered porch.

"Here's the report to the governor. Oh . . . could your man go to my quarters at the palace and pick up some gear? I have the feeling I may be here much longer than you or your men."

Gauswn frowned. "Sir . . . is that safe? Staying here?"

"It will be." *One way or another.*

"But with an armory like that . . . ?"

"There's another one somewhere as well, and probably another tunnel, but the scholars responsible are dead or fleeing to the hill holders. Most of those left just want to be scholars, and they never wanted to be anything else. And that's what they will be."

"Yes, sir." Gauswn didn't sound totally convinced.

"If you'd get that report off to the governor . . ."

"Oh . . . yes, sir."

"I need to meet with the preceptor of students. He'll be acting princeps. I'll have to act as Master Scholar for a time."

"You're the only one who could, sir."

Quaeryt couldn't refute that, and didn't try. "I'll be in the princeps's study if you need me." He turned and headed back across the porch, glancing to the northwest, where dark clouds were massing for an autumn-afternoon thunderstorm.

He still had to wait almost half a glass for Nalakyn.

"I'm sorry, sir. It took a while."

"It did. You were in the dining hall a long time. What did they say—besides being outraged?" asked Quaeryt, his tone gently ironic.

"I pointed out that you were a scholar and that you represented Lord Bhayar . . . and that you had the power to remake or destroy the Ecoliae. Some of them didn't like it. I also pointed out that when you left, Chardyn vanished, and that when you returned, Zarxes killed the Master Scholar and fled." Nalakyn shrugged apologetically. "It seems to me that opposing you and

Lord Bhayar isn't a good idea. Most of them understood what I meant. Some of them only understood that you have power."

Quaeryt understood the distinction, and that didn't make him any happier. The next days would be anything but pleasant. At the same time, he had the feeling that, somehow, he'd played into Rescalyn's hands . . . and that bothered him even more.

69

While Quaeryt waited for further orders, he set to dealing with the tasks that needed immediate resolution. The first was finding the other armory and tunnel. That proved much easier than finding the first two had been. He just lined up the scholars and asked, pointing out that no one was going to be happy if he had to take an ax to every wall in the scholarium—that was what he insisted that all the scholars call it from then on—especially if Lord Bhayar's armsmen had to waste time doing it.

Finally, a younger scholar suggested that he try the lower-level laundry room on the east side. There the access to the other tunnel and a larger armory—one without dust—came through two working linen closets. The tunnel ended a quarter mille to the east in the middle of a small garden under a circular stone sculpted with the design of a quill pen. There were bootprints, but no sign of Alkiabys.

Then he had Nalakyn locate a roster of the scholars and students and have a student make a copy for him while he made a top-to-bottom, room-by-room inspection of all the buildings. After that, Nalakyn briefed him on the usual daily and weekly activities of all scholars and students. Gauswn returned and informed him that continuing patrols around the Ecoliae had discovered no sign of either missing scholar.

Late on Vendrei afternoon, just after the pyre that turned Phaeryn into ashes subsided into ashes itself, a ranker courier returned from the Telaryn Palace with a dispatch for Quaeryt—and all of his gear. The dispatch was brief.

> Your handling of the scholars was acceptable. Given the situation, the governor believes you should remain at the Ecoliae for the time and continue your efforts to reorganize the scholars along lines more in keeping with the traditional practices of scholars and in correspondence with the needs of Telaryn as a whole. One squad will remain with you. Report any new developments. You will receive further orders as required.

The brevity and wording of the dispatch—and the arrival of his gear—made two things very clear. Quaeryt would be staying at the scholarium for at least a few more days, and Straesyr was displeased. The latter suggested that Straesyr didn't know or wish to admit what Rescalyn had in mind.

Before receiving the dispatch, he'd worried about taking on authority he didn't have, but he'd justified it to himself by asking how else he could save the scholars from themselves. After the dispatch, he worried about his handling being merely "acceptable." What in the Namer's sake had they expected?

He worried even more about why Zarxes had murdered Phaeryn. Because the Master Scholar would reveal too much? To throw the blame—at least in the minds of the hill holders—on Quaeryt and the governor? Or merely as a self-centered delaying tactic to allow Zarxes himself to escape? Or was there some other reason he hadn't even considered?

Since he had no answers, he'd returned to doing what he could do.

In the end, Quaeryt arranged for second squad to use the former staff rooms above the stable, and he took a second-level room away from any others, barred and wedged it shut, and eventually slept—uneasily. He woke early on Samedi morning, dressed, and immediately checked with the squad leader. Nothing untoward had occurred. Nor had any of the patrols during the night found any sign of either Alkiabys or Zarxes.

After breakfast in the dining hall, where he sat at a table with Squad Leader Rheusyd, he'd made his way back to the Master Scholar's study, which had been cleaned, and began to study the ledgers provided by the bursar that outlined the expenses of the Ecoliae. In less than a quint, he discovered an unexplained entry that appeared every month under "Funds Received." The title was just "scholar stipends," but the sum was the same each month—twenty golds. He went back to the first entry in the ledger he had before him— more than five years earlier—and the entry was the same, with no explanation.

He picked up the ledger and walked to the third door—that to the study of Yullyd, the bursar—opened it, and stepped inside.

"Sir?"

"How long have you been bursar?"

"Four years, sir. I took over when Covean died of consumption."

Quaeryt opened the ledger and pointed to the latest "scholar stipend" entry. "There's no explanation of this, and there's one like it every month from the first page in the ledger. Where did they come from?"

"I don't know where those golds came from, sir. They weren't golds, either. They were new-minted silvers, twenty golds' worth. The Master Scholar never said who sent them and told me not to ask and not to worry. They were always delivered by a barge courier in a canvas bag during the first week of every month. I asked, but the courier didn't know anything except that he was told to meet a barge that came from up-river and take the bag to the Ecoliae."

"Are there any other entries like that in the ledger?"

"No, sir. That's the only one I can't explain."

Quaeryt nodded, if slowly. "Thank you." *Twenty golds' worth of new-minted silvers? Every month?* He closed the ledger and tucked it under his arm, turned, and left the study. He did not return to the Master Scholar's study, but headed toward the princeps's study because the mention of the death of the previous bursar had reminded him of another question.

When he stepped into the princeps's study, Nalakyn was talking with a scholar Quaeryt did not recognize. Both looked up, worried, and the other scholar stood, as if to leave.

"You don't need to go. I just had a quick question for Princeps Nalakyn." Quaeryt turned to Nalakyn. "I haven't seen Sarastyn."

"Oh . . . didn't you know? He died the day after you departed. He had been ill, you know?"

"I knew he was ill, not that he had died. Thank you."

Ill though Sarastyn might have been, reflected Quaeryt as he returned to the Master Scholar's study, he had no doubts that Phaeryn or Zarxes had "helped" that illness along. He couldn't help but wonder what else he might have learned from the old scholar . . . or what Zarxes hadn't wanted him to learn.

He sat down behind the desk and looked at the closed ledger. According to the figures, the Ecoliae was barely getting by . . . and that was with a twenty-gold monthly payment, most likely from one of the hill holders. *But from whom? Why in new-minted silvers?*

The source was likely Zorlyn, because his son had been the scholar princeps, and twenty golds a month wouldn't have hurt a wealthy hill holder, especially if the scholars were furthering Zorlyn's interests. *But what interests exactly? And how?*

At the moment, Quaeryt didn't have an answer to those questions, but he did know that, like it or not, he would have to ask for a similar payment from Stracsyr and Rescalyn in order to keep the scholarium operating—just another task he wasn't exactly antici- pating with anything remotely resembling pleasure.

70

By midday on Solayi, Quaeryt was beginning to won- der what Phaeryn and Zarxes had been doing with their time. He had been through all the files and rec- ords in the studies that had belonged to the Master Scholar and the scholar princeps, and he'd found re- markably little correspondence. All the records of re- ceipts and expenditures had been kept—apparently accurately and in great and clear detail—by Yullyd.

Nalakyn handled the assignment of scholars who taught the students. While Zarxes had been the one to approve expenditures of more than two silvers at a time, there really weren't that many, except for large orders of produce and meat.

What had they done, except plot?

He'd checked the weapons in the second armory, and only a handful were truly sharpened and oiled and in the very best of condition. He'd talked to the ostler, and discovered that the pair of riding horses assigned to the scholars hadn't been used that much, and the pair of dray horses were used almost daily with the wagon for obtaining various supplies. The two geldings used by the Master Scholar and the scholar princeps were ridden almost daily, but where and for what purposes, the ostler didn't know. Finally, after returning to the main building, Quaeryt summoned Nalakyn into the Master Scholar's study.

"Sit down." Quaeryt waited, then asked, "What exactly did the Master Scholar do?"

"He was the Master Scholar, sir."

"I understand that. But you are the one who makes sure everything is done for the school. Yullyd handles receiving and paying out golds and keeping track of them. Chardyn and Alkiabys took care of Sansang training. . . . What did Phaeryn and Zarxes do?"

"They were in charge."

"Did they often ask you about the students or the instruction you were arranging?"

"Master Scholar Phaeryn asked about each student's progress several times each year. He also insisted that they all learn both Tellan and Bovarian reading and writing, and basic arithmetics, the fundamentals of philosophy and rhetoric . . ."

"What about history?"

"He said that was up to me, just so they knew the basics of Tilboran and Lydaran history."

"What else?"

"I had to provide a written assessment of each student's progress each year."

"I understand that. What else do you know that Phaeryn did?"

"He rode a great deal," ventured Nalakyn. "He never said where."

Quaeryt raised his eyebrows.

"Well . . . he did say that he'd had to request that a factor pay for his son's time at the Ecoliae. He said something like that more than once. He often came back from his rides and gave golds or silvers to Yullyd."

Quaeryt nodded. He'd wondered about some of the "board/instruction" entries and their irregularity. "What else?"

"I don't know, sir."

"What about Zarxes?"

"He was gone more often. Sometimes he was gone for days."

"By himself or with others?"

"Sometimes with Chardyn."

"Did all the factors always pay for their children's education?"

"Always." Nalakyn paused. "Sometimes, the Master Scholar had to pay them a visit."

"What else?"

Quaeryt asked more questions. While Nalakyn was more than willing to answer, more often than not he didn't know very much about anything except the school and what the students were taught—that he knew in great detail. Finally, Quaeryt dismissed the precept and returned to studying the ledgers.

Much as he disliked the idea, he knew he needed to

go to services that evening and listen to the ancient chorister, if only to set an example, and that thought kept nagging at him throughout the afternoon. The midfall sun had just touched the hills to the west when Quaeryt stepped through the old yellow-brick archway leading into the anomen. The antique oak doors had not been oiled since his last visit.

Quaeryt moved to the front of the south side and watched as twenty or so students filed into the anomen, led by Nalakyn. It took Quaeryt several moments to find both Syndar and Lankyt. Syndar didn't look in his direction, but Lankyt looked back at Quaeryt for several moments, then offered a nod. From what Quaeryt could tell, almost every scholar was present, and all sneaked surreptitious looks in his direction before the ancient chorister stepped to the front of the anomen. If possible, his wordless invocation warbled and wobbled even more painfully than the last time Quaeryt had heard him. Quaeryt spent as much time watching the worshippers as paying attention to the greeting, murmuring the opening hymn and confession, then adding coppers to the offertory basket.

He wondered exactly what the chorister would say in his homily.

"Under the Nameless all evenings are good, even those that seem less than marvelous. . . ." The chorister cleared his throat, then studied the congregation for a painfully long time before speaking. "We witnessed on Vendrei the results of Naming. Some will say that the Master Scholar died because troopers accompanied a scholar to the scholarium . . ."

Quaeryt was impressed that the ancient chorister used the new term for the Ecoliae.

". . . but the Master Scholar did not die because of

the troopers. The troopers never used their weapons against anyone. The Master Scholar died for another reason. He died because he was a tool of those who have for generations put their names above the needs of all Tilbor. Even the High Holders have considered those needs. You all know I have no love of those who flaunt titles. I have less love for those who sow mistrust and misrepresent what is. Misrepresentation is yet another forming of Naming. It is one of the most pernicious forms of Naming. Those who use misrepresentation take a grain of what is true and then spin a fabric of deceit from that truth. They magnify the importance of a small truth. They make that small truth large enough to conceal their deceit behind it . . ."

Quaeryt listened intently, concealing a smile. The old chorister had seen far more than he had ever revealed, and just as clearly, he had been no true supporter of either Phaeryn or Zarxes.

After the benediction, Quaeryt deliberately avoided the chorister, for to have spoken to him at that moment would have lessened the impact of the homily. Instead, he motioned to Nalakyn. The two walked down the rutted path from the anomen toward the brick lane leading back to the scholarium.

"The chorister knew what Phaeryn and Zarxes were doing." Quaeryt let the words hang.

Nalakyn said nothing for several paces. "I worried about Chardyn more than I did about the Master Scholar. Chardyn had ties to the hill holders, and he was not to be trusted. I thought that Phaeryn kept him so that no one would attack the . . . scholarium . . . or because he feared Chardyn. You know that Chardyn's father was the head of the Khanar's Guard?"

"I learned that."

"Most scholars are not men of action. If you had

watched the Sansang practices, you would have seen
that only a few younger scholars took part. Most of
those who did practice were students. The Master
Scholar allowed Chardyn to require students to learn
some Sansang because they would not be scholars and
because it would benefit them to have some training
in defending themselves without using forbidden
weapons. Most of us were not unhappy when Chardyn vanished." Nalakyn paused.. "You had something
to do with that, did you not?"

"Scholar Chardyn vanished because of his own actions, not because of mine," replied Quaeryt. "There
were others who fell afoul of him, I learned later, and
their golds and silvers found their way back to the
Ecoliae."

"There were rumors . . . but there was never any
proof. I never saw the Master Scholar or Zarxes do
anything untoward."

"Even with the armories and the tunnels?"

"The tunnels were there for escape. The armories
were there for protection. None of us ever took up
weapons—except, it appears, for Chardyn, Phaeryn,
and Zarxes. Perhaps one or two others, but I do not
know who they might be."

As they walked toward the scholarium, Quaeryt
asked questions and listened. He had no doubts that
Nalakyn was kind . . . but the preceptor of students
was also credulous and not the strongest of personali-
ties. Yet who else was respected and could set the right
tone for reforming the scholarium into what Quaeryt
envisioned? Could Yullyd and Nalakyn together manage to keep the school and scholarium operating?

Quaeryt had his doubts . . . but he also didn't see
any other immediate options.

He faced an even larger problem. While his "visit"

to the scholarium and his subsequent inspections and findings had proved, at least to him, that Phaeryn and Zarxes had been linked to the hill holders, why hadn't Rescalyn done something earlier? Surely, the governor had to have known long before Quaeryt had arrived. In fact, Rescalyn couldn't have known that Bhayar was going to send Quaeryt to Tilbora. Bhayar himself hadn't known until Quaeryt had planted the idea.

So why had Rescalyn seized upon the scholars and the Ecoliae so readily? Because it fit in with something he was already planning?

That made an unfortunate kind of sense to Quaeryt—and it also meant that he needed to return and "report" to the governor as soon as possible.

71

On Lundi morning, Quaeryt left the scholarium early enough that he and the two troopers who accompanied him rode through the eastern gates of the Telaryn Palace at half past seventh glass. He had barely reined up in the side courtyard when he saw the form of a ranker being carried on a wooden platform by six men in full uniform. Behind them walked a drummer, playing a slow funereal roll. The ranker had died, presumably in the line of duty, but Quaeryt had received no word about fighting. Besides, anyone who had died in the hills would have been placed on a pyre there, and not at the Telaryn Palace. He glanced to the two rankers beside him.

"Do you know what happened?"

"No, sir." Both shook their heads.

Quaeryt dismounted, then handed the mare's reins to the nearer ranker. "I could be several glasses."

"We'll be near the officers' stable, sir."

"Good."

The scholar turned and, after another look in the direction of the northern part of the courtyard and the funeral party, headed toward the door to the palace.

The duty squad leader looked up from the table desk. "Scholar, sir?"

"What happened? The funeral party?"

"One of the governor's messengers got careless yesterday afternoon. He was running an errand. He slipped and went over one of the railings in the palace . . . fell and hit his head on the stone below."

"Who was it?"

"Kellear . . . he was used mostly as a messenger. Nice young man . . . very pleasant."

Kellear . . . Kellear . . . Quaeryt had heard that name before. He knew he had. "I'm sorry to hear that."

"Accidents happen, sir. We wish they didn't, but they do."

Quaeryt nodded, still puzzling over where he'd heard the name. From the foyer of the palace, he headed down the main corridor and then up the main stairs to the governor's study. At the top, he paused. The railing was more than waist-high . . . and what sort of errand was a ranker running on Solayi, not that the governor couldn't order it? There was also the fact that no one besides the ranker—and the governor— would likely have been in the area above the stairs.

At that moment, he recalled where he'd heard the name before . . . and from whose lips. He stiffened, then took a deep breath, before resuming his steps toward the governor's anteroom, hoping that his deliberate breach of the implied chain of command would yield the results he needed to verify his suspicions.

Undercaptain Caermyt's mouth opened as Quaeryt walked into the anteroom.

"I'm here to report to the governor," announced Quaeryt. "Some matters have come up, of which I feel he should be aware."

"Yes, sir . . . I'll tell him that you're here." The undercaptain rose and walked to the study door, where he knocked. "Scholar Quaeryt is here to report to you."

There was a silence, followed by the words "Have him come in."

Caermyt opened the door and stepped back slightly.

Quaeryt walked to the study, took the door, effectively from Caermyt's hand, closed it, firmly if quietly, behind him, and entered the chamber. He walked to the desk and inclined his head politely. "Sir."

"I must say I am surprised to see you here so soon, scholar." Rescalyn did not rise from behind his table desk.

Behind Rescalyn's smile, Quaeryt sensed there was another emotion. Whether anger, consternation, or concern, he wasn't certain, but he'd definitely gotten a reaction by his presence, and now it was time to see if he could provoke the governor into revealing more.

"I assume you read my report about the hidden armory, sir."

"I did. Surely, you did not ride across Tilbora to question me on what I read?"

"Oh, no, sir. But, after I sent you the first report, I had time to do an even more thorough investigation of the buildings, and I thought you should know immediately of the results."

"A written report, sent through the princeps, would have been more than sufficient."

"There were matters I did not believe should have been put to ink. But first, the buildings. There was a second escape tunnel and also a second hidden armory, concealed in the lower-level armory. Unlike the smaller first armory, whose weapons looked older and which had not been used recently, a number of the weapons in the second armory were in excellent condition and bore signs of recent use and sharpening. Then I undertook an inspection of the ledgers of the Ecoliae. The ledgers were kept by the bursar, but many of the sources of funds were never revealed. What I did determine was that for at least the last five years a monthly sum of golds—twenty to be exact, and in silvers—was delivered by a courier from a barge that came from the Boran Hills and landed at the barge piers in Tilbora. I also ascertained that the Sansang master of the Ecoliae and the Master Scholar and the princeps all have close ties to the hill holders. The Sansang master, who recently vanished, was an officer in the Khanar's Guard, and his father was the last head of the Guard. The princeps and the Master Scholar also served briefly in the Guard, during the time that Lord Chayar took control of Tilbor."

"All that is interesting, but scarcely urgent, scholar."

"Further, I discovered the scholar princeps had placed at least one spy here in the palace, and that the Master Scholar believed that the spy had been discovered and was being watched."

There was only the barest flicker of the eyes from Rescalyn, and Quaeryt continued without pause. "In addition, the scholar princeps—you may recall that he was the one who killed the Master Scholar and fled through the first tunnel—and the Sansang master made many trips into the Boran Hills. Also, the scholar princeps is the son of the hill holder Zorlyn."

Rescalyn smiled with his mouth, but not his eyes. "I admire your diligence, scholar, and I can see why you felt you needed to convey such information personally."

"I thought you would like to have confirmation of what you doubtless already suspected, and perhaps already knew from your own sources. I also wanted to let you know that the scheming and the attacks which resulted from these men were limited to a handful of scholars, two of whom appear to be dead, and two of whom are in flight to the hills." Quaeryt inclined his head politely, wondering if Rescalyn would ask about who happened to be dead.

"Is there any other information you think I should know?"

"I do not know what you know, sir, but I have heard from several factors that the hill holders have their own silver mines, and that they have stockpiled a great deal, perhaps enough to fund a lengthy military action." That was entirely a guess on Quaeryt's part, but a plausible one. He smiled politely. "That is all, sir. It may be that I have thought the information more urgent than you would have judged it, but I am not an officer, although you have accorded me rank as a thoughtful courtesy, and I did not wish to fail you by delaying information you might need."

At that, Rescalyn frowned.

Quaeryt thought the frown was not what the governor felt, but he waited.

Finally, the older man spoke. "I cannot fault you for your diligence, and I can see why you felt I should know." He smiled politely. "You may go."

Quaeryt bowed, turned, and left, before Rescalyn

508   L. E. MODESITT, JR.

could remind him to report to the princeps. The fact
that Rescalyn had not was another small indication
that Quaeryt had upset his thoughts. Once the scholar
was in the corridor outside, he glanced around, and
seeing no one, immediately raised a concealment, then
walked quietly toward the princeps's anteroom. He
did not enter, but turned toward his study and, after
several steps, turned and waited.

Almost half a quint passed before he heard steps.
He immediately moved forward and then trailed the
governor into the princeps's anteroom and then into
the study. Quaeryt barely managed to squeeze into the
study behind Rescalyn, and only because Vhorym was
slow to step forward and close the door behind the
governor.

"Has your scholar assistant reported to you yet?"
Rescalyn's voice was moderate.

Straesyr, clearly startled, rose. "I haven't seen him. I
take it you have."

"Did you tell him to report directly to me?"

"No. He's always been very respectful of the line of
command."

"He left my study just a while ago, and . . ." Rescalyn stopped. "You read his report. What do you think?"

"He seems to have handled matters relatively well,
Rescalyn. No one got killed except for the Master
Scholar, and clever as Quaeryt is, I don't think he could
manage killing a Sansang practitioner with a single
knife slash. It was a single slash, was it not? Also,
Quaeryt doesn't carry that large a blade."

"That was the report from the undercaptain to
Major Skarpa."

"Then you should be pleased that the damage was
so little and that the scholar is reorganizing the Eco-

liae along more traditional lines. You should also be pleased that the two guilty scholars escaped to the hills. That was your intention, wasn't it? That someone escape to warn the hill holders?"

"I'm concerned," said Rescalyn smoothly, "that he may have an agenda of his own."

"That is a surprise to you? Anyone who has survived the palace of Lord Bhayar, and as a seaman, and the situations in which you placed him, has a modicum of intelligence. Any man with intelligence will have his own ideas. The question you might consider is to what degree he is loyal to Lord Bhayar."

"Bhayar thinks him highly loyal. He would not be here otherwise."

"I agree. He also has other contacts in the palace, as I mentioned."

"Yes, you did . . . as I recall."

Straesyr shrugged. "So far, nothing would appear out of the ordinary."

"That may be. I would trust that it will remain so." Rescalyn paused, then added, "Do give my best to your wife."

Straesyr stiffened for a moment, then said coolly, "Thank you. . . ."

Quaeryt could see the impact the mention of Straesyr's wife had, as if the pleasantly spoken words had been a threat, but he concentrated on what followed.

". . . As for matters remaining as they are, as you have intimated, I have no reason for it to be otherwise. Even if Quaeryt has another way of reporting what he has observed, all that you have done is entirely within the purview and discretion of a good governor."

"As I have always been."

"That is true."

Rescalyn nodded brusquely before turning and leaving.

Quaeryt had less trouble exiting the study behind Rescalyn, because the governor did not even try to close the door behind himself.

Quaeryt eased out of the anteroom and down to "his" study, where, after looking in both directions, he dropped the concealment, realizing, belatedly, that holding it had taken almost no effort at all. A result of all his practice with the heavier shields? Most likely.

He unlocked the study door, opened it slightly, and then walked back to the princeps's anteroom, where he heard voices.

". . . shows up, want to see him immediately."

Quaeryt repressed a smile and put on a serious face, stepping into the anteroom.

Straesyr looked up. His expression was not quite grim. "I was trusting you might be here shortly. We need to talk." He turned and walked into his study.

Quaeryt followed and closed the door behind himself.

Straesyr turned. "You're my assistant. Why didn't you report to me first?" While his voice was mild, his eyes were like the coldest blue ice Quaeryt had ever seen.

"I was under the impression, with the governor's orders, that I was under the military chain of command, sir, and had to report to him first. After that, I had to . . . ah . . . and after that I came here, except I saw the governor march into your study. So I waited until he left."

Straesyr opened his mouth . . . then closed it.

Finally, he said, "Scholar Quaeryt, I appreciate cleverness in support, but not in opposition."

"Sir . . . I am in no way opposing you. If my actions appear that way, it is only appearance and not substance."

"Would you mind explaining that?"

"Might I report on what I told the governor, sir?"

"Please do."

Quaeryt repeated, nearly word for word, what he had told Rescalyn, as well as what Rescalyn had said, then added, "I got the impression he thought I was right to tell him, but that he wished I had told you first."

Straesyr nodded. "That's likely to be so." After several moments, he smiled wryly. "The governor is a most capable man. He could achieve great things. Were Telaryn at war, he would doubtless distinguish himself for his forethought, his planning, and even his deep understanding of intrigue and when it is best used and when it is not. I would like to think that in the former areas I have close to equal abilities, but, unlike the governor, I have never been more than adequate in dealing with intrigue, as he has gently reminded me, and as I remind you."

Quaeryt nodded thoughtfully in reply. "I see, sir."

"Knowing from where you come and whom you serve, I believe you do. Need I say more?"

"No, sir." Quaeryt paused. "Will our conversation serve as my weekly report, sir?"

"That, it will. After refreshing yourself, you should return to the Ecoliae . . . the scholarium . . . and continue your work at reforming it. If either the governor or I require your presence, we will summon you."

"Yes, sir."

"And Quaeryt . . . I do appreciate your handling of the situation after you met with the governor. I would not have wished to have had to seek you out."

"No, sir. I never intended that you should."

"I thought as much. Have a pleasant ride back to the scholarium, and do take care."

"Yes, sir."

Quaeryt maintained full shields all the way out of the palace and until he and the two rankers were more than a mille from the lower gates, when he returned to the triggered shields.

For the remainder of the ride back to the scholarium, he reflected on what he had seen and heard that morning. The conversation between the governor and the princeps had been most interesting, for what had been said, what had not been said, and what had been intimated and implied. What Straesyr had said to Quaeryt tended to confirm what Quaeryt believed about Rescalyn's ambitions, especially given Kellear's "accidental" death, the mention of Straesyr's wife, and Straesyr's veiled warning—he'd never told Quaeryt to take care before. Yet Quaeryt had nothing that amounted to hard proof, and he doubted that he ever would. Rescalyn was far too shrewd for that.

72

Mardi passed without incident, as did Meredi. They also passed without any word from either the princeps or the governor. By midday on Jeudi, Quaeryt couldn't help but wonder exactly what was happening at the Telaryn Palace ... or elsewhere in Tilbor. He had the feeling that a storm was looming over the horizon, most likely coming from the Boran Hills, but then ... maybe he'd just misjudged both Rescalyn and the hill holders.

At the knock on the open door of the Master Scholar's study, Quaeryt looked up. He tried not to stare at the ancient chorister who stood there. "Yes ... what can I do for you, chorister?"

"Master Scholar ... a few words with you?"

"I'm not the Master Scholar. I'm just acting as one, trying to reorder matters. You can certainly have a few words and more." Quaeryt paused. "I'm sorry, but I don't know your name."

As he settled into the seat across the desk from Quaeryt, the old man laughed. "That's fitting enough for a servant of the Nameless, don't you think?"

Quaeryt shrugged helplessly and offered an embarrassed smile. "I've heard two of your homilies. I've liked what you had to say in both of them, but no one ever mentioned your name."

"You were there last Solayi. I fear I do not recall the other time. Oh ... I am Cyrethyn."

"That was when I first visited the scholarium, in Agostas. I was only here for a few days. You talked about the arrogance of the young and the strong, equating it in a sense, to Naming."

"You flatter me, Master Scholar, by recalling what I said nearly two months ago. Such flattery is pleasurable, but I do not deserve it. That is why I am here. I am old. I am old in part because I am not brave. I have known for many years that Zarxes and Phaeryn received golds from Zorlyn. I knew that Chardyn had something to do with the death of Lord Chayar's envoy. I knew many things. But I did nothing because I knew nothing would change, and I would die. As I said,

I am not brave. So I am here to do what little I can."
The chorister smiled wryly. "Are you an honest scholar,
Master Quaeryt?"

"I would like to say that I am, but I have been
known to stretch and distort the facts of situations. I
have misrepresented matters upon occasion by not
revealing all that should have been revealed. I have
rationalized that by telling myself that I did so in the
service of seeking greater truths and more information.
I do not know that I have been totally honest in that
regard."

"That you are willing to assess yourself so suggests
you are honest."

"Honest does not mean good," Quaeryt pointed out.

Cyrethyn chuckled. "That might make a good homily."

"It might, at that."

After a brief silence, the chorister spoke again.
"There is one other matter that I believe you should
know."

"What might that be?"

"As in all things, matters are not what they might
seem to be. Your governor—Rescalyn—met with
Phaeryn. That was five years ago. So far as I know, that
was the only time they met."

"That . . . it seems unlikely . . ."

"That may be, but only two people here and alive
know about that meeting. I was one; the other was
Zarxes. I do not sleep well. Many of my age do not. I
was walking well after midnight when I heard a rider.
As I told you, I am not brave. I hid in the bushes near
where the secret tunnel emerges. I was surprised to see
another man walk down the lane. It was Zarxes. They
said little, except that Phaeryn said Rescalyn had offered a workable arrangement. Phaeryn said he had

accepted it. He had no choice, not if he wanted to keep the Ecoliae intact and the golds coming from Zarxes's sire. Zarxes agreed. Neither asked whether the governor could be trusted. Then Phaeryn entered the tunnel, and Zarxes walked the mount back to the stables. No one would have known that the Master Scholar had left the Ecoliae that night."

"Why would they do that?"

"You know why Phaeryn would. The Ecoliae was failing. The only golds outside of fees for the school that he received came from Zorlyn. Yes, I know about the canvas bag sent monthly. As for the governor . . . it had to suit his ends. What those might be, I do not know."

Quaeryt feared he knew exactly what those ends were. "Why did you come here? You don't even know me."

"I know you better than you think, scholar. You are a scholar who offers a better homily than most choristers. You profess not to know whether there is a Nameless, but act in accord with the principles set forth by the best of those who have followed the Nameless. You question more than you declare, and listen more than you speak." Cyrethyn smiled.

"That sounds like you've been talking to a certain undercaptain."

"Why not? I've known him since he was a student here, years ago. He was honest then and seems to have remained so. I saw him ride up, and I begged a few moments of his time."

Quaeryt nodded. That, in a strange way, made sense . . . if anything did.

"I do have one favor to ask, master scholar. I ask that you not disappoint Gauswn. He believes in you."

Quaeryt almost swallowed his tongue. That was the last thing he would have expected.

"For all the goodness you try to conceal, scholar, you are too cynical." The chorister paused. "Then, perhaps, that cynicism is what protects your ideals." He rose, slowly, from the chair. "I hope that what I have told you may assist you in determining your course. Every datum refines a position more accurately. So the experienced quartermasters say."

"Unless it reveals that other sightings are inaccurate." Quaeryt rose.

"You are too careful for that, master scholar." Cyrethyn smiled, and his eyes twinkled. "I just may talk about honest evil on Solayi."

"If I'm still here, I'll be there to listen."

After the old chorister left, Quaeryt sat back down behind the table desk, thinking.

Had Cyrethyn been telling the truth? Quaeryt had no way of verifying that. Yet why would the old chorister lie? Certainly, choristers, for all their professions of sanctity, ranged from the purest in word and deed to those who cloaked pure evil in the raiment of the Nameless. At the same time, every word Cyrethyn had spoken rang with truth ... and, if true, explained more than a few things, and possibly provided an even greater reason why poor Kellear had been killed, because with Phaeryn and Kellear dead, who besides Zarxes would have known about the "agreement" between Rescalyn and Phaeryn? But then, Kellear might not even have known.

Quaeryt shook his head.

73

Vendrei passed without word from the palace, as did Samedi morning. During that time, Quaeryt met several times with Nalakyn about changes in the course of study, adding in more history, and more emphasis on both Bovarian and Tellan. He also spent time with Yullyd formalizing the charges for the services that the scholarium provided, from rooms and meals to visitors to study and board fees for students. He also periodically met with Squad Leader Rheusyd, but the squad watches and patrols had discovered nothing out of the ordinary.

Shortly after midday on Samedi, a student Quaeryt did not know peered into the study. "Master Scholar, there is a Factor Embrayt here to see you."

"Thank you." Quaeryt stood and walked out of the study and out to the front foyer, trying not to limp, because, for some reason, his leg was bothering him more than usual.

The man who stood there was not quite of Quaeryt's stature, square-bearded, and slightly stoop-shouldered. He did not speak.

"Welcome to the scholarium. How might I help you, Factor Embrayt?" Quaeryt smiled politely, holding his shields ready, since he had no idea in these days whether a visitor might be unpleasant or truly inimical.

"Might I have a few words with you?" The factor glanced down the corridor.

"The Master Scholar's study is this way." Quaeryt gestured, then turned.

Embrayt did not speak until he was seated across the table desk from Quaeryt. "I have heard that you are truly a scholar, but not from Tilbor. Your speech would also suggest that."

"But you would like me to confirm that? No ... I am not from Tilbor, at least not in the sense you mean. I do not know where I was born because I'm an orphan. My parents died in Solis while traveling when I was barely more than an infant. I was raised there by the scholars."

Embrayt nodded slowly, and some of the tension seemed to leave his shoulders. "What of ... those who used to be in charge of the ... scholarium?"

"The former scholar princeps slit the throat of the Master Scholar and fled. The Sansang master vanished some weeks before that, and his assistant fled, presumably to the Boran Hills, with the scholar princeps. The governor has requested that I serve for a time as Master Scholar in order to return the scholarium to a place of learning and study, similar to other scholaria throughout Lydar."

"There has been some word of that," admitted the factor.

"I have found that the preceptor of students has always been devoted to the schooling provided by the scholarium. He has also not been involved in those activities that many have found less than scholarly. Likewise, the bursar appears most honest." Quaeryt smiled politely and waited.

"I had not heard ill of the preceptor ... even under the previous Master Scholar."

"Are you considering having one of your children study here?"

Embrayt nodded. "My second son. He is sharp of mind and wit, but . . ."

"His talents do not lie in your factoring?"

"One leg is not as it should be."

"I do understand."

"I noticed. . . ."

Quaeryt nodded. "It has been that way from when I was young, perhaps from birth. How old is your son?"

"He will be twelve in Finitas."

"Would he be amenable to being separated from his family?"

"He would miss us, I am certain. He would not miss those of his age."

Quaeryt also understood that. "Would you like to speak to Scholar Nalakyn about the course of study?"

Embrayt smiled and shook his head. "There is no need. That, I knew before I came. I wished to meet you before we decided. Now I can talk to Emdahl and hope he will agree that his future lies in study." The factor rose.

Quaeryt stood as well. "We will wait on your decision."

"We will see." The factor nodded and turned to leave the study.

Quaeryt moved quickly so that he could escort Embrayt out, and the two walked side by side down the corridor. Quaeryt did open the front door, but he stopped at the top of the steps.

The factor stopped as well, then nodded to Quaeryt. "Good day, master scholar."

"The same to you, and a pleasant ride home."

When Embrayt walked down the steps, Quaeryt turned his study on the waiting coach—painted or stained dark brown with brass trimmings and drawn by a marched pair of chestnuts. The coachman was also dressed in brown. With such a carriage, Embrayt had to be well off, if not more so.

What does he factor? That wasn't the sort of question that he could have asked under the circumstances, but he did wonder as he watched the team and coach leave the scholarium.

"Sir?"

Quaeryt turned to see Lankyt standing at the edge of the porch near the steps.

"Yes, Lankyt?"

"Some of the others say the governor is going to close down the Ecol—I mean, the scholarium. That's because he hates the scholars."

"One never should guess about what is in someone's mind or thoughts. I won't, but I will say that, if the governor wanted to close the scholarium, why would he order me to restructure it so that it is like all the other good scholaria in Telaryn? He could far more easily have instructed me to proceed with closing it down and turning out the scholars and students."

"He still could, sir."

"He could indeed. Is that likely when Lord Bhayar has dispatched a scholar to Tilbor?"

Lankyt frowned, then said quickly, jabbing a finger in the direction of the departing coach, "Is one of his sons going to study here?"

"He is considering it."

"Who is he?"

"His name is Embrayt. He's a factor."

"He's wealthy, then."

"I imagine so, with that coach and team."

"No . . . I've heard his name. He owns a brick factorage and a produce factorage, and some other things, too."

Quaeryt nodded. "What else have you heard?"

"That's all." Another pause followed. "Are you going to stay as Master Scholar?"

"For a time, anyway. Lord Bhayar sent me to be an assistant to the princeps. Even if I go back to the Telaryn Palace, I'd probably still be charged with dealing with the scholarium."

"Lankyt?" called a youthful voice from the east end of the porch.

"I'm coming," replied the student loudly, before turning back to Quaeryt and saying in a much lower voice, "Good day, sir."

Quaeryt couldn't help smiling as the young man hurried off.

74

Solayi arrived, and the day passed with no messages and no word from the palace, from either Straesyr or the governor. The lack of communication tended to confirm that Quaeryt wasn't in the best of graces with either man, but that neither wanted to act against him directly, and until one, especially the governor, or the other could, he was relegated to reforming the scholarium. As part of that effort, he devoted himself, among other matters, to writing out a set of principles for the scholars of the scholarium.

As the time for services approached, he put down the pen, rose from the table desk, and stretched. Then he left the study and walked to the rear porch, since the way to the anomen was shorter from there. He was halfway across the porch when Nalakyn hurried up to join him.

"Are you going to services, master scholar?"

"I am."

"Might I accompany you?"

"Of course." Quaeryt understood that Nalakyn wanted to bring up something.

"Do you know how long you will be . . . posted here as Master Scholar?"

"No. Neither the princeps nor the governor has said."

"You have named me as acting princeps . . ."

Quaeryt understood. "You think that I should formalize who will be in charge in my absence?"

"It would make matters clearer."

Quaeryt smiled faintly. "I can and will write out a plan of succession, but it will be good only with the approval of the governor. It will also only be good for one year after my permanent departure. After that, as in every other scholarium in Telaryn, the Master Scholar must be approved by a majority of the scholars over the age of thirty. I trust that will suffice."

"Ah . . . yes, sir."

"I will also make your position as scholar princeps official, but you will continue as preceptor of students as well."

"Thank you, sir."

"I'm glad you brought it up." And Quaeryt was. What Nalakyn had suggested was something Quaeryt should have done earlier, just to give the scholarium the best chance of survival if anything happened to him. "One other thing—I'm also working on a set of principles for the scholarium. When I've finished the first draft, I'd like your thoughts about any additions or changes you'd like me to consider."

"Yes, sir. I'd be happy to look it over. Perhaps Yullyd . . ."

"I'll have him look at it as well."

Quaeryt didn't have much more to say, and they were almost at the anomen. He just walked in and stood on the left side, about halfway back. Even so, when Cyrethyn appeared, his eyes flicked to Quaeryt, and the chorister gave the faintest of nods.

As usual, Quaeryt did not sing out loudly, but watched the scholars and students. More than a few cast glances in his direction. When the time came for the homily, he waited, wondering if Cyrethyn would deliver what he suggested.

After the opening for the homily, the chorister left no doubt.

"Earlier this week, I visited the Master Scholar. I owe this homily to him. He raised a question that I never heard stated so directly. Can an honest man be evil? Or can he do evil while being honest? My immediate thought was that such was not possible. Yet the more I thought about it, the less convinced I became. What if such a man were honestly convinced that what he did was for the best? Could he not tell the honest truth and still do evil?

"We do not think this is possible because in the life most of us live, we cannot be evil and lie. If you ask the miller if he has given you fair value, he cannot cheat you and give honest reply. Nor can the weaver give you cloth with a thread count that cheats you without lying, if he is asked. But what of those we cannot ask? What of those whose words are true, yet whose actions in accord with those words lead to evil?

"A holder tells his tenants that they must give more of their crop yield to him because his costs have risen. He tells the truth, but is that increased tariff not evil for those tenants? The lord of a land goes to battle, saying the battle is necessary. Even if he tells the truth, does that battle not cause evil for many who are innocent? The words and the names are spoken in truth. Yet evil follows.

"In a similar fashion, that is why Naming can be so evil. We can name a person or a thing honestly, but the name we give it, and the respect we pay that name, conceals its evil. The glory of battle and the tales of heroism conceal the evil of the deaths of young men who believed they were doing right . . . or doing what they had to do, trying to survive. Increasing one's profits honestly, if one is a merchant or a factor, is said to be good. If he does so by increasing his prices, that is an honest act, done openly. Yet if those who must buy his goods are poor and in bad times, that honest act is evil for them, even as it may be necessary for the merchant to keep his shop.

"Likewise, is blind honesty always good? Is it good to tell an elderly widow or a scholar in failing health that death stands waiting . . .

"Claiming that one is honest when one ignores the results of such honesty is indeed a form of Naming. Why? Because the very word 'honesty,' like Naming, places the word above the action and the results of that action . . ."

As he stood there, listening, Quaeryt was troubled by the homily.

75

On Lundi, Quaeryt completed the statement of policies and the document of succession and dispatched a copy to Straesyr with a letter noting that it clearly fell within the princeps's authority since it was a nonmilitary matter. Then, early on Mardi morning, a student rushed into the dining hall and halted at the table where Quaeryt sat with Yullyd and Nalakyn.

"Sir, there are soldiers riding up the lane." The youth's voice cracked with the last words.

Quaeryt stood immediately. "How many?"

"Not all that many. About as many as are here now. Twenty or twenty-five?"

"Then . . . it's not bad news for the scholarium. It might just be a message for me." Quaeryt offered a smile he didn't feel to the other two. "If you'll excuse me . . ."

"You'll let us know?" asked Nalakyn nervously.

"As soon as I can." Quaeryt walked swiftly out of the dining hall and then to the front porch. He arrived just as a squad leader, followed by his men, reined up short of the steps.

"Scholar, sir . . . You're Scholar Quaeryt, are you not?"

"The very same, Squad Leader."

"Yes, sir." The squad leader paused, then said, "The governor requests that you accompany us to join him in the campaign against the hill holders."

"What's happened?" Quaeryt had several thoughts

on the possibilities. With Zarxes's and Alkiabys's disappearance through the secret tunnel, neither the hill holder revolt nor Rescalyn's summons surprised him greatly. He'd half-anticipated that something would happen sooner, but the delay suggested that the hill holders had spent some time organizing and that Rescalyn faced a combined force. Then, that was only his surmise.

"The hill holders have gathered an army. They killed most of one company on a patrol and have besieged Boralieu."

To Quaeryt, that made little sense unless they'd also declared that their quarrel was with the governor or Lord Bhayar and they were urging others to rise against Telaryn. But he doubted that the squad leader would know those details. "What about Rheusyd and second squad? Are they to remain or to join us?"

"They are also to accompany us."

"Are we going back to the palace or are we to meet the governor on the road?"

"He was leaving the Telaryn Palace when we did. We're to rejoin the force on the road."

"I need to tell Rheusyd and his men and gather some gear. I won't be long."

By the time Quaeryt reentered the building, both Yullyd and Nalakyn were standing in the foyer. They both looked at him inquisitively. He gestured toward the Master Scholar's study, and they followed him.

Once inside, with the door shut, he turned. "The hill holders have revolted . . ." He went on to explain, then added, "You're Master Scholar in my absence, Nalakyn. Yullyd, you're the scholar princeps. While nothing is certain, I think it likely that, whatever happens, the scholarium will continue. If the rebels prevail—which is most unlikely—they will wish it. If the governor wins, he certainly won't shut it down."

"What . . . about you . . . sir?" asked Nalakyn.

"I've always served Lord Bhayar and the governor. What happens in the next month or so will determine how I serve them in the future. In the meantime, you two have to carry on." Quaeryt grinned. "And make sure you charge new students the new fees."

"Yes, sir," agreed Yullyd.

"I need to gather my gear and talk to Rheusyd. I'm going to leave some clothing here." *Such as dress and undress jackets and a set of good browns.*

Since Rheusyd wasn't in the dining hall, Quaeryt hurried upstairs, gathered a second set of browns and other items together, including the worn green uniform shirt, and put them in the circular kit bag they had arrived in, then hurried back to the main floor. As he left the building for the stable, Quaeryt saw Lankyt waiting on the rear porch, a worried expression on his face. Recalling what he had told the young man on Samedi, he couldn't help but suspect that Lankyt would be even more worried about the future of the scholarium. Lankyt's fears were justified, despite what Quaeryt had told Nalakyn and Yullyd, because, if anything happened to Quaeryt, while the scholarium would likely remain, who would be left to stand up for the scholars and students against the past not-so-benign neglect of the governor?

"Sir?"

"I've been recalled to duty with the governor's forces. The hill holders have attacked the post at Boralieu."

"They've rebelled?" Lankyt's voice held incredulity.

"They wouldn't call it such," replied Quaeryt dryly.

"I don't think that they've ever believed they owed allegiance to any ruler. They always bargained with the Khanar or ignored him, and the governor has shown that Lord Bhayar won't be bargained with or ignored." *Even if it has been a while coming.*

"They couldn't have done this because the governor sent you here. They couldn't."

"That was just the excuse they were looking for. They've been attacking the patrols out of Boralieu for years." *But they think that Rescalyn double-crossed them over the Ecoliae when his "agreement" with Phaeryn was just designed to set matters up the way Rescalyn wanted it.* It was more than clear to Quaeryt that Rescalyn had promised not to dismantle the Ecoliae so long as the scholars refrained from overt action against the Telaryn Palace—effectively setting up the hill holders as the prime source of opposition, suiting Rescalyn's long-term plans perfectly.

"Will you be back?"

"I don't know."

Lankyt looked down, then raised his eyes. "Best of fortune, sir."

"Thank you." Quaeryt smiled warmly, then hurried toward the stables to find Rheusyd.

Less than a half glass later, Quaeryt rode near the head of the two squads beside Lharym, the leader of the squad sent to fetch Quaeryt. The scholar's gear fit easily behind his saddle.

"They'll be taking the river road for a good twenty milles," offered Lharym.

Quaeryt nodded, forbearing to note that he'd traveled that route twice before. "Do you know if the rebel holders sent any word or declaration to the governor?"

"No, sir. I don't. Captain Theyn didn't, either."

"Has anyone said how many rebels there are under arms?"

"Thousands . . . that's the word."

If there were thousands, a lot of them weren't likely to be all that well trained, unlike Rescalyn's "regiment." But then, Quaeryt reflected, he could be wrong in that assessment.

Almost a glass went by before Quaeryt rode up to the command group, not quite at the front of the long column riding northwest on the river road.

"Scholar! Over here!" Rescalyn's voice boomed over the sounds of men and mounts.

As Quaeryt rode toward the governor, he had to admit that, especially on horseback, Rescalyn was a commanding figure, erect in the saddle and radiating confidence.

"Governor, I'm reporting as you requested."

"You made haste." Rescalyn smiled. "Even with that leg of yours, you'd make a good cavalry officer." He gestured. "Ride with me."

Quaeryt guided the mare alongside the larger black gelding ridden by the governor, noting that the rankers and officers before and behind them moved away, giving Rescalyn space.

"It appears that your efforts to convince the local scholars to abandon their opposition to Lord Bhayar are about to bear fruit—the bitter kind."

"Sir?" Quaeryt was fairly certain he knew what was coming.

"Young Waerfyl, Saentaryn, Demotyl, and Huisfyl have declared their independence from Telaryn. They claim that the imposition of a foreign scholar over the true scholars of Tilbor is an absolute confirmation of the fact that Telaryn intends to destroy all independence of belief and thought in Tilbor. They are the ones who sent the message with a wounded ranker, but they claim other holders have also joined them. Since you precipitated this fracture, I thought you should participate in the aftermath." Rescalyn smiled warmly.

Quaeryt debated for a moment, then spoke. "I'm glad I was able to bring about what you've been seeking, sir."

Rescalyn's momentary frown vanished almost immediately. Then he laughed. "You're far more than a scholar, Master Quaeryt. How did you deduce that?"

"The size of the regiment, the extra companies in each battalion, the rotation so that every company saw action against the hill holders, the building of outposts that also held more troops, the recruiting and training of Tilborans . . . things like that."

"Why do you think I did all that?"

Quaeryt knew full well, but he offered half the answer. "A standard regiment wouldn't suffice against the hill holders. You and the princeps and some of the officers have all indicated, as did the documents I studied, that good as the Khanar's Guard was, it wasn't sufficient to take on the hill holders. Until they're broken, Tilbor won't ever be a secure province."

"You deduced this in less than two months with no experience in Tilbor before?"

"I think I knew after about a month—certainly after getting wounded."

"What did Bhayar really send you for?"

Quaeryt laughed, if ruefully. "To get me out of his hair, sir. He said I asked too many questions, and that I needed to spend time seeing what good governors do. He did say that, if I could find a way to effectively reduce the number of troops in Tilbor to free them for other uses, such a solution would be welcome. From what I can see, the only way to do that is to defeat and destroy the hill holders—or at least all the leaders and their holds."

"We do agree on that."

"Have I misunderstood anything?" asked Quaeryt.

The governor shook his head. "Once we near battle, you will accompany one of Major Skarpa's captains so that you can see matters close at hand and testify as to the results of what good governors do. You do not have to fight, nor to act against the hill rebels, but you must be close enough to see what happens and be able to report to Lord Bhayar."

Close enough to be killed without being ordered to fight. "I had thought that might be the case, sir."

"Tell me. Why does Lord Bhayar's sister write you?"

"That, I cannot honestly say. I met her once, and we talked for less than a half a quint. I never saw her again. Given my position, of course, I cannot afford not to reply with as much length and wit as I can muster."

"I can see that." Rescalyn laughed again. "We have a long ride ahead and time. Tell me. What do you think you have accomplished with the scholars?"

"I've put a true scholar in charge, and a no-nonsense scholar who was also the bursar in place as the scholar princeps. I put forth a set of principles, and I've talked to factors who are now interested in having their children be schooled there. I found that a few of your junior officers were taught there, and, if the scholarium continues, more may be as well. The education will be improved, with more Bovarian being taught and more history. For some reason," Quaeryt said sardonically, "not much history was being taught. Those steps are being taken already. I've also thought about teaching more mathematics and practical science . . ."

"That would be good. Officers need to know that. What else?"

"I abolished the teaching of Sansang. I didn't have a chance to replace that with something less . . . subversive."

"Just teach them half-staff work. It's useful, and the training develops coordination. . . ."

Quaeryt listened, knowing that he had a long, long ride ahead of him, and one on which he would need to watch every word as he tried to convince Rescalyn that he was bright . . . but not too bright.

76

A day and a half later, Quaeryt was still riding with Rescalyn, after a fashion. Although the governor spent more time with Commander Myskyl than with Quaeryt, he returned intermittently to ride with the scholar and even talked to him occasionally, but almost never with any warning, even if his voice was nearly always hearty and cheerful. That heartiness was beginning to irritate Quaeryt. Then that might have been because the governor was never less than always perfectly in command and cheerful, even when no one was looking.

The afternoon wasn't as hot as midsummer, but it was still sultry. Quaeryt's undershirt stuck to his back, and his legs were sore because he'd hardly been riding for the past week, and little enough since he'd returned to Tilbora. The column was headed straight west, possibly less than ten milles from the last line of hills that formed the eastern edge of the valley that held Boralieu.

Abruptly, Rescalyn asked, "Did you actually read all the papers from the Khanar's document room?"

"Yes. Well . . . some of them I just skimmed over after I read the first part."

"Why?"

"Because documents can tell you what it might take years to discover through experience. I was trying to determine if the Khanars had the same sort of difficulties with the hill holders as you have had."

"Did they?"

"It seemed much the same, except there was a kind of bribery on both sides, and less fighting. But then, the hill holders couldn't claim, not in the eyes of most Tilborans, that the Khanar was an outsider."

"Do you really trust what was written?"

"Even when someone isn't writing everything, or they're glossing over things, or misrepresenting them, if you read enough, you can tell things by the way they're written or by what's not there."

"Are you Bhayar's spymaster or one of his top assistant spymasters?"

After a moment, when he was truly surprised, Quaeryt laughed. "No. If he has a spymaster, I have no idea who it is."

"Then why are you here? Why would he send you here?"

"Why not? He likes me, or doesn't dislike me. He's known me since we were students, and he was getting tired of my questions. He's worried about the amount of troops required here, and he doesn't want to leave Solis right now because he's also worried about what

Kharst might do. If I can't tell him, then there's no harm done, and he has several months without me around."

"You almost convince me, scholar." Rescalyn's voice remained cheerful.

"Of what?"

"That you are what you say."

"Everything I've said is true."

"I'm certain it is, but that doesn't mean you've told me everything."

Quaeryt shook his head ruefully. "There's no end to that. To tell you everything about me, or for you to tell me everything about you, would take more time than either of us has."

Abruptly, the sound of a horn echoed from the rear. Quaeryt didn't understand the signal, but Rescalyn did, for he wheeled his mount.

"They're being attacked!" The governor stood in the stirrups. "Column halt! Commander! Take charge here! Scholar! Follow me!"

Quaeryt did indeed follow Rescalyn back along the shoulder of the road, although the distance between them widened with every moment that passed. As the commands passed down the column, companies were turning, and weapons were out and at the ready.

Quaeryt caught up with the governor at the head of the wagons, near the two engineering wagons, and the supply wagons behind them. Rescalyn had reined up and was talking intently to a graying major, who seemed to shrink into his saddle with each word from the governor.

After halting the mare well away from what was clearly some sort of dressing-down, Quaeryt waited and looked to the east. The two last supply wagons were burning fiercely, with black and gray smoke rising into the gauzy sky, seemingly eventually mixing with the high haze. While two companies rode back toward the column from the northeast, Quaeryt saw no sign of any attackers. Suddenly, he realized that he was carrying full shields—and he hadn't even noticed. He almost shook his head, but lowered them to the lighter shields, with the triggers for contact . . . and waited.

After a time, Rescalyn nodded to the major, then turned his gelding and rode back toward Quaeryt. Since the governor didn't stop, Quaeryt turned the mare and swung up alongside Rescalyn, keeping pace with him, but saying nothing.

After several moments, Rescalyn spoke, gesturing back and to the right. "They rode out of a swale back there. They caught the rear guard by surprise." He shook his head. "You'd think that by now . . ."

"They only think that surprises happen in the hills," Quaeryt pointed out.

"You're right." Rescalyn laughed ruefully. "Expecting only what happened before cost a score or more of the rear guard their lives. It could have been worse, if the hill forces had been looking for a fight. I pointed that out to the major."

"They were just trying to destroy supplies?" asked Quaeryt. "With fire arrows?"

"Quarrels filled with flaming pitch . . . or something like that. They're trying to make the point that they can destroy our supplies and attack anywhere."

"The rear guard didn't go that far after them. They were riding back by the time I got to the supply wagons."

"No. There's no point in that. The major did understand that. Before long, we'd be spread over hundreds of milles and be bleeding from scores of cuts."

Quaeryt waited.

"You aren't saying anything, scholar."

"You have a different plan. I was waiting to hear it."

"It's simple enough. Once they return to the woods and hills, they split up. There's no point in trying to track down individuals, but we don't have to. The winters here are long and cold, and without supplies, even the angriest hill holders can't do much. First, we break the siege at Boralieu. By besieging it, they've done us a favor. That concentrates their forces, and we can do more damage to them. Then we move on each hill hold and level it. We take the supplies we can use and destroy the rest. The hill holders have been a plague on Tilbor for too long."

"Won't they just attack the column once you leave Boralieu?"

"That's what scouts are for. It's hard on them, but it cuts overall losses."

While Quaeryt admired the brutal simplicity of the plan, including the fact that it was timed just after most harvests were gathered in, he had to wonder, as he knew he did too often, whether Rescalyn's abilities matched his confidence.

77

By the time the column was riding westward again, more than a glass had passed since the attack. Rescalyn and Myskyl had deployed additional scouts, and the column moved more slowly than it had previously, almost ponderously, as the riders and wagons passed through the fields, pastures, and orchards belonging to High Holder Dymaetyn. Quaeryt saw almost no one, and those few men he did catch sight of vanished almost immediately, very understandably. He saw no women at all, although crofter women often worked fields and orchards. That, too, was more than understandable.

Progress was so slow that when the lower edge of the sun touched the horizon, the vanguard was still a good five milles from the scattered woods at the base of the long and broad ridge-like hills that rose on the eastern side of the valley holding Boralieu, and shadows cloaked the spaces between the trees.

"It's getting late to travel those hills," said Rescalyn cheerfully.

"You think the hill holders are waiting there."

"I'm certain they are. Part of the reason for the attack was to delay us enough that we have to either make camp short of the eastern hills or travel them at dusk or later. Either way offers an opportunity for them to attack again."

"Which way are you choosing, might I ask, sir?"

"What do you think?"

"From what you said earlier, I'd guess—it's only a guess—that you intend to stop and make camp, but have a battalion or two ready at all times."

"Something like that." Rescalyn smiled. "Oh . . . from here on, you're attached to Sixth Battalion. They're three battalions back. You might as well join Major Skarpa now."

"Yes, sir. Do you have any other instructions for me?"

"I'll be interested in your observations after the campaign is over, scholar. I trust you'll be as observant about battles and skirmishes as documents."

"I'll do my best, but documents don't move around the way that soldiers and raiders do."

Rescalyn laughed. "That's just one of the differences." He urged his mount forward to rejoin Commander Myskyl, riding just ahead.

Quaeryt swung the mare wide and out beyond the shoulder. He didn't push her, just let her walk with the low sun on his back, until he saw the ensign with the six on it, carried by a junior ranker.

Skarpa raised an arm in greeting. "I thought we might be seeing you before long, scholar." The major grinned as Quaeryt rode toward him. "The commander said you were being sent to us because the governor wanted you to see all the action."

I'm sure he did . . . and that he hopes I don't return from all that action. Quaeryt was glad he'd thought to bring along the old large uniform shirt. That way, at least he wouldn't stand out too much, but he hadn't wanted to wear it yet . . . and not around the governor. "I think he feels scholars need to get out of books and documents and see what really happens."

"For all that you're a scholar, and maybe even a chorister of sorts, Master Quaeryt, I don't see you as one buried in books."

"I like the books, but the governor has indicated that books and documents aren't enough for what I must report to Lord Bhayar. As for being a chorister, I'm not friendly enough with the Nameless for that."

"You don't sound fond of the governor or the Nameless."

"I have no doubt that Governor Rescalyn is an excellent commander, and a most effective governor. He can't help but resent that a young scholar has been sent from Solis and ordered to serve on his staff. It's my fortune to have both Lord Bhayar and Governor

Rescalyn wanting me somewhere else. Under those circumstances, I'd rather be where I am—with Sixth Battalion." Quaeryt didn't want to say more about the Nameless, not unless he was pressed.

"We're glad to have you."

The next glass passed quickly enough, and before that long, the regiment was setting up camp on a low knoll a good half mille from the nearest tendril of woods on the lower section of the hills. There were no cookfires once the force stopped. The evening meal, such as it was, consisted of hard yellow cheese and harder biscuits. There was also mutton jerky, but Quaeryt had lost his taste for dried mutton that was hard enough to break teeth years before.

As the twilight deepened, and a warm light breeze carried the scent of dry grasses out of the south, Skarpa turned to the scholar. "We'll be the early guard on the trail from the south. Fifth Battalion will hold the trail on the north side of camp. The hill types won't come from there or from the south trail. The commander and the governor both know it. Oh ... they might send a patrol or a company that way to mislead us, but they'll never attack us where we're waiting, not at night. The governor will make sure the hill forces know where we're posted."

"They'll come out of the trees when we're least likely to be ready?"

"They know the usual watch schedules, and they'll attack during the time guards and standby forces are being changed." Skarpa smiled coldly.

"Somehow ... I think you'll be ready."

"We'll see. They may decide not to attack. I'm wagering they will."

"Why?"

"Just a feeling I have." The major paused, then

asked, "Do you want to join Meinyt or one of the other captains or undercaptains?"

Quaeryt understood his only choice was which company he would join. "Meinyt . . . if he's willing."

"He'd hoped you would. He says you bring good luck."

Quaeryt winced.

"Oh . . . I brought something for you. It's a little old, but it was the best I could do. I figured since you spent time before the mast, it would work better for you than a sabre." Skarpa grinned as he extended a half-staff. "Might be harder on horseback, but I couldn't stand the thought of you going into battle without some sort of weapon." The major laughed. "I know you're just supposed to observe, but it's hard just to observe when you're in the middle of a fight."

Quaeryt had already figured that out. He took the staff. Old as it might have been, it was polished and iron-tipped on both ends, with two iron bands around the wood equidistant from the ends and from each other. It was finely balanced, possibly the best half-staff he'd ever held. "This is a good staff. Where did you get it?"

"I sent one of the rankers to the armory when I got word from Commander Myskyl that you'd be accompanying Sixth Battalion."

"Thank you."

"There's one other thing." Skarpa tossed something like a ball to Quaeryt.

The scholar caught the ball, only to discover that it consisted of wound leather thongs.

"Those are used to hold an ensign. They should hold that staff. Fasten them to the saddle."

Quaeryt nodded.

Skarpa nodded. "Best you find Meinyt."

Quaeryt walked from where he left the mare tethered with the other mounts of the Sixth Battalion officers and made his way toward Meinyt, still carrying the half-staff. He waited until the captain finished talking to a squad leader, then stepped forward.

"You've decided to join us, I see," offered the older captain. "Don't know as that staff will help much."

"It's the only weapon I know how to use, and I don't have much experience—except at getting wounded. I need to be around someone who does."

"You're better than some."

Quaeryt didn't know what to say to that. So he said nothing.

"We've got about a glass before we take the guard on the south trail. We'll have duty for two glasses. Figure they'll attack sometime after the first glass of duty. It will be full dark then. That's when we'd usually change companies."

"Is that duty mounted?"

Meinyt shook his head. "Scouts and outriders will be mounted. They can see better from the saddle. They're also better targets, but there's not much moonlight tonight, just a bit from bloody Erion. All the squads will be afoot by their mounts, ready to ride."

Quaeryt nodded. "What did you think of that attack on the wagons?"

"That was about what I'd have expected. The last two wagons usually have stuff we can do without if we need to."

"They don't know that?"

"They've never had to fight far from home."

While Quaeryt hadn't thought about that, it certainly made sense. He stepped back as another squad leader approached. The last thing he wanted to do was interfere with Meinyt. Besides, he had to figure out how to attach the lance or ensign holder to the saddle.

Just as Meinyt had predicted, some two glasses later, as Quaeryt waited beside the captain, a warning echoed across the still-warmish evening.

"Attackers on the way!"

"Company mount! Form up! Double interval!"

Quaeryt wasn't the very last one in the saddle, but he was far from the first. He even managed to get his staff in the leathers.

"Company! Forward! Fast walk!"

Quaeryt raised full shields and kept the mare close to the captain.

The faintest of rustling sounds seeped through the darkness, and a flight of arrows—but no quarrels from what Quaeryt could see—sleeted down into the company. Most missed. None struck his shields, but he heard one moan from a ranker somewhere to his left.

"Stand fast!" ordered Meinyt.

Even before his command was finished, Quaeryt heard hoofs galloping southward, diminishing into the night. From the sound, he doubted that the attackers had numbered more than a squad or two.

He glanced around, his eyes moving to the west, noting that Meinyt was already watching, although the captain kept looking back to the south.

Then, little more than a half mille away, from the slight bulge in the trees, black figures emerged, riding dark mounts through grasses close to waist-high, so that they looked very low to the ground—or grass. In the faint reddish light of Erion—less than a quarter full—they were more like moving shadows.

"Shouldn't we do something?" asked Quaeryt in a low voice.

"Watch."

As the wave of dark riders neared the camp perimeter, abruptly shadow after shadow halted, then fell, and the screams of injured and dying horses began to fill the night, followed by yells and the sounds of weapons and men using them. Quaeryt couldn't see what was happening, other than mounts and men going down.

In a fraction of a quint, only a comparative handful of the shadows turned and sprinted back toward the cover of the trees. The rest soon vanished into the grass.

"The governor figured they'd do that," murmured Meinyt. "He had Fourth Battalion there with pikes, hidden in the grass. The pikes were all blackened. The hill riders never saw them, not until their mounts started getting spitted. Seventh Battalion is set up the same way on the northwest side of camp."

"He planned that all along."

"Knowing him, most likely."

"Will they attack again . . . tonight?"

"Who knows what the hill types will do? I wouldn't think so, but you never know. In the meantime, you might try to get some sleep. Rest, anyway. Tomorrow will be worse when we have to cross the ridge."

Quaeryt felt he'd be fortunate even to doze.

78

Surprisingly, Quaeryt did sleep for several glasses on Meredi night, despite worries about another attack . . . and having only a thin blanket between him and the ground. If an attack happened, he didn't hear it. No one said anything about one when he rose in the pale gray light before sunrise, stiff and sore, enough so that he was limping more than usual when he went to check on the mare before eating more biscuits and cheese.

"You did sleep, I see," offered Meinyt.

"Enough that I'm sore all over." Quaeryt took another bite of the hard biscuit, followed by a modest swallow from his water bottle, because otherwise he wouldn't be able to eat the biscuit.

"Better sore than tired."

"What happens next?"

"We either go north or south or follow the road until we get attacked."

Quaeryt knew that much already. He ate another biscuit.

"North would take us through a swamp," Meinyt finally said. "South would take another day. Then, when we got back to the main road again, we'd still have to worry about being attacked from both sides. I'd get your gear rolled up. Whatever the governor has in mind, it won't be long. I'm about to find out." With a wry smile, he hurried off.

Quaeryt barely had taken out the overlarge green uniform shirt and then finished fastening his gear behind his saddle, and readjusting the leathers to hold the staff, when Meinyt returned from wherever he'd been.

"The rebels hold the heights on the last ridge on the east side of the valley. We're to circle to the south, just far enough to get out of sight, and then ride back up through the trees. It's a gradual rise. The trees aren't that close together."

"We? All of Sixth Battalion?"

"And Fourth. The rest of the regiment will follow the road. The governor's keeping it simple. We're to keep them from retreating south."

"And they'll end up backed up against the swamp if they go north?"

Meinyt nodded.

"They can still go west." Quaeryt pulled the uniform shirt on over his browns, glad that the morning was comparatively cool.

"They could . . . and there's· enough ground between the eastern hills and Boralieu that they might escape . . . but that would also give Commander Zirkyl a chance to strike them on one side while we press the other. Or something like that. The governor's the one who makes those decisions, not me. We need to mount up." Meinyt paused. "Good idea with the shirt."

"I'd prefer not to stand out too much."

The captain just nodded and headed for his mount.

Quaeryt mounted and then followed Meinyt as the company formed up by squads. Then they rode south and slightly west. Quaeryt let the mare trail the captain slightly, so as not to interfere with the officer's line of sight.

After about two milles, Meinyt raised his arm, and ordered, "Five-man front!"

When the company came to a halt some fifty yards

short of where the trees began, intermittently spaced, Quaeryt glanced to his right toward the next company, noting that it was the one commanded by Gauswn, although the undercaptain did not glance in Quaeryt's direction, not that Quaeryt noticed.

"We're not to give quarter in battle, but we're also to leave the fallen alone." Meinyt snorted. "The major made that clear."

Quaeryt understood. Stopping to deal with the fallen simply weakened the attack, and Rescalyn wanted to destroy the hill holders as a force for generations to come—if not forever.

"Fourth Battalion will be to our right, just beyond Gauswn's company. We'll move when the governor orders the horn signal to break camp. That might confuse the hill folks, since they do know our signals."

Almost another quint passed before the notes of the horn—off-key—drifted southward.

"Sixth Battalion! Weapons ready! Forward! Standard walk!"

As the first light of sunrise spread from the east, Quaeryt again took station on Meinyt, who rode about a half length back of the leftmost ranker in the front line. There were no sounds of birds or insects, only those of underbrush occasionally crackling and crunching under hoofs. Quaeryt kept his eyes moving, but he saw nothing but tree trunks and low-hanging branches. The trees thickened as he rode northwest with the others. Since most of the trees were evergreens that had left a carpet of needles on the ground between the trunks, there was comparatively little undergrowth, and he could see between ten and twenty yards ahead most of the time. Every so often there was a massive oak or maple that looked to have been there far longer than the pines and spruces.

What bothered him, even carrying his shields, was that anyone waiting or watching could also see the riders of the two battalions.

After a quint, or perhaps slightly longer, another horn signal, far closer, sounded.

Within moments, there were yells and then the sound of a wounded horse. Meinyt and the company kept moving.

Then . . . there was that pattering sound, like rain, followed by a grunt, and one of the riders ahead and to the right of Quaeryt doubled over in the saddle.

"Deliberate speed!" ordered Meinyt. "Deliberate speed!"

Quaeryt wanted to follow the captain, but couldn't because of a fallen tree trunk he hadn't seen quickly enough, and he edged the mare to the right, around another massive trunk. He glanced forward, and slightly up, as another volley of shafts swept past him. Ahead was a young, scared-looking man, wearing what looked to be a leather shirt and britches and straddling a wide oak branch some three yards above the forest floor. He held a crossbow, aimed directly at Quaeryt.

The quarrel's impact on the scholar's shields threw Quaeryt back in the saddle. He struggled forward to regain his balance. The youth leapt from the oak toward Quaeryt—a pair of glittering knives in his hands—then slammed against the scholar's shields, dropped to the ground, and staggered back. Before Quaeryt could even think of stopping the mare, the weight of the horse and the shields threw the rebel into the thick trunk of a pine. There might have been a *crack*, but Quaeryt didn't hear it. What he saw was the young man's neck snap forward, hanging loosely, before his dead body slid down the trunk.

"Keep moving!" ordered Meinyt, not necessarily to Quaeryt. "You slow down and you're a potted pigeon."

Quaeryt remembered, belatedly, that he did have a half-staff and struggled to get it clear of the leather straps as another leather-clad rider plunged through the trees in his direction. When he raised the staff, the rider veered toward Meinyt, apparently not seeing the captain, whose sabre slammed into the hill rider's neck.

Quaeryt tried to keep up with the others, but he was more abreast of the second line than just behind Meinyt, and he urged the mare forward.

The strain of holding the shields as far out from him as he had been was getting to Quaeryt. He contracted them until they were more like a skin. That would also allow him to use the half-staff. As he did, he wondered why he hadn't thought of the closer shields earlier. *Because the kind of imaging you knew how to do needed distance? How many other things haven't you thought of because—*

"That one!"

Quaeryt glimpsed two riders ahead, one looking over his shoulder, and the other lifting what looked to be a short lance.

If that lance hits you, shields or not . . .

At the last moment, he flattened himself against the mare's neck, but grasped the staff firmly with both hands and braced it against the front edge of the saddle pommel, letting it stick out.

The lance missed him—and his shields—but the staff struck something, and the other rider lurched backward in his saddle. Quaeryt's hands felt bruised and mangled, and without the reinforcement of the shields, he would have lost the staff as well. He barely managed to hang on, and he had no idea what had happened to the man he thought he'd struck.

He straightened in the saddle and had managed to bring the staff forward when he had the feeling that, suddenly, the woods seemed to fill with thunder and the sound of hoofs. With those sounds he saw what looked to be scores of riders, seemingly one or two or even three riding abreast filling all the spaces between the trees, charging down the gentle slope. All seemed headed directly at him, and several had short, but pointed, lances.

Quaeryt reined the mare up just short of two pines, with enough space for a rider on either side of him, then projected his shields forward and around the pines, so that they were anchored to the trees.

Let's hope this works. . . .

He raised his half-staff, as if in futile defense, and two of the charging hill riders charged directly at him.

The impact of the two mounts and riders on the shields still lifted Quaeryt up from his saddle, then dropped him hard on the leather. Both horses lay in a heap. One screamed, horribly. Neither rider moved, and neither looked as if he ever would again.

Quaeryt's head was a splitting mass of pain, and he tried to shrink the shields back to cover his body alone. That hurt so much that it felt as though knives were jabbing into his skull through his eyes and ears, and he had to release the shields. That reduced the pain somewhat, but he could still barely see, although he could sense the other riders passing him.

He eased the mare back enough to get around the pine to his right, and then urged her forward. With no shields, he'd have to be even more careful—except, from what he'd experienced already, being too cautious was more deadly than being too rash.

Ahead of him, he saw yet another hill rider angling from behind a copse of low evergreens, almost galloping toward a gap between the ranker forward of Quaeryt and to his right and the rankers of the company farther to the west. Then he realized the ranker didn't see the attacker, and he urged the mare forward, yelling as he did, "Ahead! Right!"

The ranker paid no attention.

Quaeryt jabbed his heels into the mare's flank, and she bolted forward. This time, Quaeryt held the half-staff forward at an angle, again braced against the front edge of the pommel.

The hill rider didn't seem to see Quaeryt until the last moment, just before the half-staff took him at the edge of his chest and then caught his arm, twisting him in the saddle. After that, Quaeryt had to hang on because the mare definitely hadn't appreciated the boot heels in her flanks—or maybe that had told her she was free to run.

For the next half quint or so, Quaeryt was more worried about staying in the saddle and dodging trees than defending or attacking the enemy. Yet . . . when he slowed the mare, and took stock, he was within a few yards of the western outrider of Gauswn's company . . . at least, that was what he thought he saw through eyes still tearing and stabbing with muted pain. Fortunately, there didn't seem to be any more hill riders around.

He turned the mare more to the west, angling behind the staggered remnants of the first lines of Meinyt's company and riding until he could make out the figure of the older captain, barely, given his blurred vision, who had reined up at the edge of a wide clearing bordering the south edge of the road to Boralieu. On the road were other Telaryn riders, roughly ranked. Quaeryt could see a battalion ensign, but couldn't read it the way his eyes were twitching. He glanced to the west, looking for the sun.

Somehow : . . it was approaching noon. He reined up, not knowing what else he was supposed to do.

"Are you all right, scholar?" asked Meinyt.

The pain in Quaeryt's eyes was so great that even squinting he couldn't make out the captain's expression.

"You've got blood on your sleeve," added Meinyt.

Quaeryt looked down at his left arm. There was indeed a large smear of blood, but there was no cut in the cloth. He gingerly felt the forearm . . . sore already and probably bruised, but it didn't feel like there was any wet blood or stickiness beneath.

"Someone else's blood, I think. I'm bruised all over."

The captain turned his head, but said nothing.

"I wedged the staff under the pommel of the saddle and stuck it out sideways . . . well, up a little. It worked, but it strained every muscle in my arms and shoulders. Then I blocked lances and a sabre somehow, but I've got bruises everywhere. . . ."

"I saw it, Captain, sir," called a ranker. "He wedged himself sort of between two trees and stopped two mounts and their riders. Both went down so hard . . . never get up."

"Why . . . ?" Meinyt never finished the question.

"They had very sharp lances, and they were aimed at me. You said we weren't supposed to let them pass. I did what I could."

Meinyt looked back to the ranker.

"He stopped 'em, sir. Stopped dead. Didn't see how . . . had to worry about some others."

Meinyt nodded to the ranker, then, abruptly, laughed. "Trees and staffs . . . never heard of such."

Quaeryt just hoped that none of the other rankers had seen any more. And, as sore as he'd been that morning, he had no doubts that he'd feel worse the next morning.

79

By less than a glass áfter midday, Major Skarpa had all the companies of Sixth Battalion in position on the west side of the hillside clearing overlooking the valley that held Boralieu. Quaeryt's vision had largely returned, although his head still throbbed, and even the idea of raising shields was painful. He'd also rolled up the green shirt, which he thought of as his patrol and combat shirt, and wore just his browns.

As he stood just beyond the shoulder of the road, looking westward, he could see that the valley was very different from what he recalled. Most of the ground for a good half mille east of Boralieu, perhaps even a full mille, was dotted with ponds, lakes, and flooded fields. Although it was hard to tell, the flooding appeared to encircle the entire knoll on which the post had been built. A timber palisade had also been erected on a smaller knoll to the east of the walls, overlooking the raised road leading across the flooded land. For several moments, he stood there, considering the change, before Meinyt walked up beside him.

"What are you looking at, scholar?"

"The ground . . . the fields just east of Boralieu. Look closely."

"What the Namer . . ." muttered Meinyt. "Never seen that before."

"They must have diverted a stream or something," said Quaeryt.

"Why would they . . . ? Oh . . . the road's the only easy way to the post."

"Or from it, and that would restrict the ability of the companies at Boralieu to attack that temporary fort unless they wanted to take a lot of casualties."

Meinyt gave a sound that was half grunt, half assent before he turned to face Quaeryt full on. "According to the men, scholar, you did a lot of damage with your little staff today. One man even claims you saved his life by unhorsing someone he didn't see."

"I yelled, but he didn't hear me. I had to do something."

Meinyt snorted. "Too many dead heroes felt that way."

"The man who was attacking him didn't see me."

"That's more the way it should be. Officers shouldn't try to be heroes. They should be officers. Otherwise, who's left to lead the men?"

That was another thing Quaeryt hadn't considered. But then, he wasn't an officer, not really, and he certainly wasn't in the chain of command. Still . . . were he in Meinyt's position, where would he draw the line?

"Good. You're thinking," said the captain.

Quaeryt didn't retort that he always tried to think. He merely nodded.

The sound of a horn blared from somewhere nearby.

"Officers' meeting . . ." Meinyt turned and headed in the direction of the horn.

Quaeryt decided to trail along, although he planned to be as inconspicuous as possible, browns or not, at the back of the officers gathering. The air was dusty, not surprisingly, with all the horses around, and there was already a faint odor of decay.

The number of officers wasn't quite so great as Quaeryt had expected, although there were certainly more than fifty, and he positioned himself behind two taller men and waited. Shortly, there was another horn call—this one calling the officers to attention. Quaeryt stiffened with the rest of the officers, then waited as Rescalyn vaulted up onto the back of the supply wagon, likely moved into the middle of the temporary encampment for just that purpose.

The governor stood there for a moment, before commanding, "At ease, officers."

Those around Quaeryt relaxed, but only slightly.

"So far . . . things are going more our way than theirs. If you've looked down at the valley, you'll notice that it looks a great deal wetter than any of you recall. That's because the hill renegades breached some of the irrigation dams and diverted the streams. They didn't think too far ahead . . . or they miscalculated your abilities. It could be both, but I'm proud of the way you all handled your men and the way they responded this morning. All Telaryn should be proud, not that most will ever know. The enemy casualties were considerable, and ours were comparatively light.

"Because of the flooding in the valley, we're going to shift our plan of attack . . . slightly. The main body of hill renegades has retreated to the west, out of the valley, but they've left a garrison behind those palisade walls. We're not going to storm their little fort. Instead, the engineers have a way to deal with that. They'll only need the support of Eighth Battalion, but I'm asking Seventh to stand by just in case.

"The rest of you can use the remainder of the day to re-form and recover. We won't be entering Bora-lieu . . . for obvious reasons . . ."

It took Quaeryt a moment to realize that, if the regiment entered the post, the rebels could easily return, and the governor's forces would be the ones hemmed in and hampered by all the flooded ground.

". . . If all goes as planned, we'll be moving out at dawn. I'll be giving specific orders to individual battalion commanders." Rescalyn smiled. "That's all. Dismissed to duties."

Quaeryt slipped away, moving back toward the general area that held Sixth Battalion. He was still looking for Meinyt when he saw Skarpa approaching.

"Major."

"Scholar, Meinyt told me that you managed to hold your own this morning . . . a bit more than that, even."

"By the end, I was in the second or third line. I still don't ride as well as most of them."

"I'll have to tell Phargos that you fight too well to be a good chorister."

"I was just fortunate. One encounter doesn't prove anything."

At that, Skarpa nodded. "Just remember that, and you'll make it through." After a moment, he added, "I need to meet with the commander and the governor in a few moments. I'll see you and the other officers after I meet with them."

"Best of fortune with that."

The major barked a short laugh, then turned.

Standing there and watching Skarpa depart, Quaeryt felt a sharp pin-like jab in his upper arm, but discovered that it was only a dried pine needle that had worked its way through his sleeve. He found several others, and almost wondered why he hadn't noticed them before.

A good glass later, Skarpa had not returned, but a squad leader walked toward Quaeryt, who had found a shady spot under an oak, then stopped. "The governor would like to see you. If you'd come with me, sir."

"Of course." Quaeryt stood and followed the squad leader toward the middle of the temporary camp. Within a few moments, he saw their destination—and awning, or perhaps the top of a tent without walls, under which were three camp chairs and a folding table. Two of the chairs were vacant. Rescalyn sat in the third, apparently studying a map. The area around the tent was clear to a distance of some ten or fifteen yards on every side, with rankers posted at intervals to maintain the separation.

The squad leader did not cross that invisible perimeter, but motioned for Quaeryt to approach.

The scholar did, halting in the shade just under the canvas. "Sir, you requested my presence."

"Have a seat, scholar." Rescalyn pointed to the middle chair.

Quaeryt took it and waited.

"You've seen the flooding to the west, I take it?"

"Yes, sir."

"The last skirmish was hardly over, and a messenger from High Holder Dymaetyn arrived. He blames me—oh, it was far more politely worded than that—for the destruction of valuable lands. How do you think Lord Bhayar would expect me to reply?"

"Sir, I have no instructions to give you. Lord Bhayar asked me to observe you as an example of a good governor."

Rescalyn laughed. "You are persistently consistent, scholar. Then, in your own capacity as a scholar, how would you suggest that I respond?"

"I would express concern for the damage, but note that the problems created by the hill holders long predate your tenure as governor and stretch back well into the reigns of the Khanars. You might also observe that, had the Khanars and the High Holders of the past been more willing to deal firmly with the hill holders, such recent events as the flooding might never have come about. Then you could note that, since harvest is over and it appears that his lands have indeed been harvested, additional moisture should only be beneficial for most of them, provided, of course, that the dams, streams, and levees are returned to their previous courses prior to the onset of winter. That will require some effort, but certainly not so much as that which you are making on behalf of both Lord Bhayar and Telaryn to permanently resolve a problem that should have been dealt with generations back."

"Just on behalf of Telaryn, I'd think," mused Rescalyn, before saying, "Go on."

"If you wish to be conciliatory, you might offer the expertise of some of your engineers in helping develop the work plans for his efforts at restoration."

"He won't like that." Rescalyn's voice was heartily bland.

"He won't like anything except having you and your men repair everything and then pay him compensation. If you do that—"

"Then every last one of them will want the same. I can see that. In fact, what you suggested follows closely what I already wrote. I do like the offer of a few engineers to assist him in planning. That way, he can't say we did nothing at all . . . and all of them complain that we don't do enough. There's nothing new about that." Rescalyn fingered his chin.

Quaeryt waited.

"How are you finding Sixth Battalion?"

"I'm working to observe and help and not interfere."

Rescalyn rose. "Good. That's all."

Quaeryt stood immediately. "Yes, sir." He nodded politely, then turned and left.

Was all that just to see how I looked after a battle . . . or skirmish? Most likely, but it was more than that. Quaeryt kept walking, heading back to the Sixth Battalion area.

The more Quaeryt met with Rescalyn, the less he trusted the man—or his motives. And the one comment Rescalyn had made about "on behalf of Telaryn" reminded Quaeryt, again, that he'd never heard the governor speak of Bhayar . . . and that went along with the slight dig in his speech about no one in Telaryn knowing what the officers and men had done.

80

By early Jeudi afternoon, Quaeryt understood all too well what Rescalyn had in mind for the timber fort. The engineers set up portable bombards, just out of bow range, and used them to hurl crocks of burning bitumen at the palisade walls as well as within. In less than two glasses everything was aflame. A good many of the defenders escaped by running into and through the waters and swamps they had created. Almost as many ran into Seventh Battalion and did not survive.

Even those who reached the immediate safety of the watercourses and swamps might not live all that long, Quaeryt knew, since stagnant waters held their own dangers, from whitemouth snakes to the bloody flux. When full night fell, the site of the palisade still glowed in the darkness, and the smell of burning wood and other less pleasant odors filled the valley and even drifted as far eastward as the regimental camp. Quaeryt wondered if the hill holders understood what Rescalyn intended for them.

He doubted it, and, in a way, that bothered him as well, because they were plaques in the governor's game and had no idea how they were being played. Yet, at the moment, it was too early for Quaeryt to act, especially since he still needed to survive the coming battles, or skirmishes, as Rescalyn called them. Besides, from what he'd experienced, he had little love for the hill holders, who seemed to think that they could do whatever they wanted with comparatively few repercussions.

For whatever reason, possibly simply sheer exhaustion, Quaeryt did sleep better on Jeudi night, and, true to his words, Rescalyn had the regiment on the road well before sunrise on Vendrei.

Once they reached the valley floor, they stayed on the main road for close to three milles before heading southward on a dirt lane that, in turn, led to another lane, that rejoined the road leading westward from Boralieu—the one that Quaeryt had ridden many times during his time at the post. While no one had actually said so, Quaeryt gained the impression that the regiment was headed directly toward Waerfyl's hold.

Sixth Battalion formed the rear guard, following the supply wagons, which followed the engineering wagons. Rescalyn had given that position to the battalion, according to Skarpa, because Sixth Battalion had taken among the heaviest impacts of the fighting in the hills. Quaeryt had refrained from pointing out that the very first attack on the regiment had been on the rear guard.

Since he was concerned about his ability to carry heavy shields for any length of time, Quaeryt held the lightest of shields with trip points set to register any intrusion and strengthen his shields. Even so, he still worried, because every impact against the shields weakened him, and he'd seen enough to know that he needed shields to survive. He just wasn't that good a warrior.

"I've been riding this road for years," said Meinyt in a low voice. "Still looks different every time. It's not just the light, either."

"Trees grow and change," suggested Quaeryt.

"More than that."

Quaeryt had no answer. He just nodded.

Another glass or so passed, when the faintest patter alerted Quaeryt to the incoming volley, and he immediately flattened himself against the mare's neck.

"From the right!" snapped Meinyt. "First and second squads!"

That didn't include Quaeryt, but he didn't see any point in staying on the road, not by himself. Because continuing alone would have made him an even more obvious target, he followed Meinyt across the yards of cleared ground flanking the road and toward the trees, keeping himself low on the mare, while trying to extract the half-staff from its leathers. He almost had it free when he entered the trees. In the predawn gloom, he thought he saw riders ahead, but he wasn't certain.

He definitely heard another volley of arrows and quarrels, but none touched him or his shields. Just as he congratulated himself on that, a figure appeared ahead and to his left and hurled something at him—a large throwing ax. While his shields did stop the weapon, he could still feel the muted impact.

The astonishment of the hill raider froze him for a moment, long enough for Quaeryt to bring up the staff and catch the man at the juncture of arm and shoulder and fling him from the branch to the ground. Quaeryt kept moving, following Meinyt and keeping low until he heard the sound of the recall horn, when he eased in beside the captain, and the two trotted back to the road, without speaking.

As they cleared the trees, Meinyt turned. "You didn't have to come with the squads."

"It seemed like a better idea than staying on the road alone."

"You might be right on that."

Quaeryt didn't think the captain sounded totally convinced.

Another glass passed before there was another horn signal, this one from the front of the column. All in all, after that, two more quick attacks occurred before late midafternoon, when a ranker rode back to inform the captains and undercaptains to ride forward to meet with Major Skarpa.

That meeting didn't take long, because in little more than a quint Meinyt came riding back to rejoin his company. "We'll be setting up camp in a meadow about two miles ahead."

"Won't they try a night attack?" asked Quaeryt.

"They might, but the meadow's large enough that they'll have to leave the trees even to get within bow-shot range."

So we'll lose sentries. . . .

"It is war, scholar," replied the older captain, as if he'd read Quaeryt's thoughts. "They know the governor's serious now. It's not just skirmishes."

But then, Quaeryt was so tired that he might have actually spoken the words. He did remind himself that he needed to keep his feelings hidden, in the fashion in which he'd had no difficulty in Solis or in the Telaryn Palace. *Is there something about the possibility of death in battle that makes men less guarded . . . or is it just because you're still not really used to this?*

He suspected it was the latter, since few of the officers revealed anything on their faces.

The encampment on Vendrei night was unlike the others, with patrols encircling the large meadow that held the camp site, and a sense of worry among more than a few of the officers. From what Quaeryt could remember, the regiment had halted only slightly beyond a point two-thirds of the way from Boralieu to Waerfyl's hold, seemingly not all that far from where Quaeryt had been wounded on that first "routine" patrol.

Supper was cold, again, biscuits, cheese, and mutton jerky. This time, Quaeryt forced himself to chew some of the jerky. It wasn't quite as bad as he recalled, but that might have been because he was hungry . . . and so exhausted that he was asleep not all that long after full darkness.

Quaeryt was so tired that he wasn't certain whether he heard first the horn call to arms or the shouts of "Repel attackers!" It took him a moment to pull on his boots and raise his shields, and he had to grope around for his staff.

By the time he was on his feet and fully alert, the attackers had retreated to the woods surrounding the camp site. He glanced skyward, catching sight of the crescent Artiema and the slightly less than half-full Erion It had to be his imagination, but the smaller moon seemed redder, bloodier, than usual.

Imagination, he told himself firmly.

"Pack up and mount up!" ordered Meinyt from somewhere to Quaeryt's left.

"Now, sir?" asked a figure in the gloom.

"Now! The governor said that it's not that long until dawn so that we might as well head out. None of you'd sleep anyway."

Quaeryt had to agree with that. He wouldn't. *Not now.*

He returned to where he'd abandoned his blanket and gear, arranged them, and then rolled everything up and put it in his kit bag. He stood carefully and looked around. Most of the others in the company were already heading toward their mounts.

As Quaeryt trailed the rankers toward where the mounts were tethered, his boot slipped. He looked down. Under the boot on his bad leg was a crossbow quarrel. He reached down and retrieved it, bringing it close enough to his face that he could see it better. In the dim light, it appeared similar to the one that had wounded him. He quickly slipped it under the cords with which he'd tied his kit bag to the rear of his saddle. He'd study it later.

81

The sun was well up, although it was barely mid-morning, when the hill holders attacked again, this time out of the trees on both sides of the road and into the middle of the column. The column slowed, but kept moving, and before long, Quaeryt saw leather-clad bodies lying alongside the road, more than two score, left where they had fallen, and untouched, except that their weapons had been removed. Since he hadn't seen anyone loading weapons into the wagons ahead, he suspected that they'd just been strapped to spare or captured mounts. He also thought there were more than a few bodies in the trees flanking the road. Again, he was carrying light shields, because it was going to be a long day.

Just before noon, the column halted near a stream, where company by company, the horses were watered, and the men had a chance to stretch their legs.

"How soon before another attack, do you think?" Quaeryt asked Meinyt.

"Sometime in the next few glasses. Surprised that they weren't laying for us here." The captain paused. "Except they would have had to make good time through the woods. The road is faster. If they split their forces . . ."

"It would be even harder to regroup."

Meinyt nodded.

A glass later, there was another halt, but no signal of any sort of attack, but Quaeryt could see several engineers and one wagon pull onto the shoulder and head forward.

A bridge out? He didn't recall any bridges on the road ahead.

More than two quints passed before the column began to move again, and Quaeryt rode almost a mille before he came to a section of the road where it appeared that the rebels had dug a trench across the road, almost a yard wide. There were also bodies beside the road there, one of them a Telaryn mount.

After yet another glass, ahead Quaeryt could see the column turning to the right and moving uphill, doubtless through the two pillars that served as "gates" to Waerfyl's hold proper. Before long, the wagons before Sixth Battalion had lumbered through the natural stone posts, but they only continued for another fifty yards before coming to a halt.

Once more, Meinyt left for a quick meeting with Skarpa and then returned to give orders to the squad leaders.

"We'll be forming up once we leave the trees. That's another three or four hundred yards up. Five-man front. We need to take enough ground to get the engineers within a few hundred yards of the hold, and we'll have to hold that ground . . ."

When the horn signaled again, the column rode slowly up the lane that climbed gently through a small area of woods, then crossed a level meadow beside a pond. The red flies and mosquitoes seemed less numerous than on Quaeryt's last visit, but that might have been because they had far more men and mounts on which to feast and were just spread out over more victims, but for whatever reason, he was glad that only a few pestered him, few enough that he could fan most of them away.

Once past the pond, the regiment re-formed on the meadow, with perhaps a third of a mille between the front ranks and the beginning of the gentle upslope to the top of the low ridge on which were located the holding buildings. Archers crowded the top of the modest stone tower at the end of the higher adjoining ridge, and shafts arched toward the regiment under the high gray clouds, but all fell short. All the shutters on the narrow windows of the hold buildings were fastened shut, and not a person was to be seen.

Quaeryt glanced back. While he could not see what was happening, he had no doubts that the engineers were assembling their bombards. He looked forward, but outside of the archers he saw none of Waerfyl's retainers. Nor did he while the engineers continued to work.

Less than half a glass later, after several ranging stones, the first crock flew over the regiment and hit the stone terrace, short of the heavy log walls, but the chunks of flaming bitumen skidded across the stone, some coming to rest against the logs. More crocks flew. One never burned. Several burned out without igniting the walls, but the engineers kept up the bombardment. Before long, a corner of the large hold building showed signs of beginning to catch fire.

At that point, hundreds of men in leathers, perhaps as many as five hundred, less than a third of them mounted, poured out from behind the hold and over the ridge and down toward the regimental formation.

"Hold until they're on the flat!" ordered Meinyt.

Quaeryt could hear other captains giving the same order.

A horn signal followed, and the regiment charged as one. Quaeryt let the captain take the lead, keeping himself in the second line. This time he had the staff ready long before the horsemen of the battalion crashed into the hill forces.

Almost immediately, the lines mixed, and there were footmen in leathers, horsemen in uniform, and those in leathers, all thrown together. Unlike the skirmishes in the trees, Quaeryt found, here there was only a little room to move, but he saw a footman with an ax, and he thrust with the staff, catching the man in the chest—and a Telaryn mounted ranker slashed down with a sabre.

Even as he thrust away a leather-clad rider, he had to wonder why he'd joined the charge, but he had little time for wonderment as another rider pressed between two rankers toward him. He used the staff to knock aside the oversized blade carried by the hill attacker, then managed to swing the staff over the mare to catch another rider on the back of the head before he slashed a ranker on his unprotected side.

For the next quint or so, he used the staff and his shields as much to beat back the men on foot who were trying as much to cripple or kill the mare and other mounts as they were interested in attacking the horses' riders, although a few more times, he thrust at hill riders . . . and might even have injured one or two.

Before long, on the top of the ridge, the holding house was burning so fiercely that Quaeryt could feel the heat on his face, as he struggled just to keep men from the mare. Then, in a space of what seemed moments, the opposition faded away, and seemingly abruptly, the soldiers of the regiment were left alone. The main hold building was burning fiercely, but only the closest outbuilding was also afire.

Quaeryt found that he was panting and that his arms burned. He lowered the staff. Blood was smeared across the end, some of it already dried. He didn't recall hitting anyone in a way that would have drawn blood. He looked to Meinyt, but the captain had eased his mount over to a ranker.

"You're the squad leader now, Noyan. You know what to do."

"Yes, sir."

"Give me a report as soon as you can."

Quaeryt eased the mare back and tried to inspect her from the saddle. He saw no injuries, and she wasn't limping. He did not look eastward at the bodies strewn across the matted grass at the base of the ridge, or those lying across the slope, not for more than a few moments.

"See you're still with us, scholar," called Meinyt as he turned his mount.

"So far."

"Sixth Battalion officers!" Skarpa's voice rang over the hubbub.

Meinyt rode toward the major, and Quaeryt followed to where Skarpa had gathered the battalion officers, staying back and listening.

"I'll need reports in the next quint. We'll camp here and head out early tomorrow. Odds are that there will be more attacks. They'll be more vicious . . ."

Quaeryt could understand that. What he didn't understand was why the hill holders had thought that the governor would ignore them forever. Or had that been because the Khanars had let them do as they pleased, at least among themselves, so long as they paid token allegiance to the Khanar?

In a way, Rescalyn acted as the Khanars had until he had the force to do otherwise.

Yet Rescalyn had been able to do it with less tariff revenue, effectively, than had the Khanars. Because the princeps was more efficient at getting and using tariff golds? For all the answers Quaeryt thought he had, there were still many questions for which he had none.

"... Commander announced that sow's ass Waerfyl was one of those killed. He was with the first attackers. His people didn't even seem to miss him. Likely some of the other holders will be better commanders. Each holding attack is going to be harder than the last, but there won't be any peace in Tilbor until we've gotten rid of the worst of these arrogant leeches."

Quaeryt's lips quirked. Clearly, Skarpa hadn't forgotten his last meeting with the late holder Waerfyl.

82

As Quaeryt rode past where the natural stone gateposts had been, well before sunrise on Samedi morning, all he saw was a pile of rubble and stone. Behind them, he knew, they had left the smoldering ruins of Waerfyl's hold, with every building burned and leveled, and all stores either taken or destroyed, but with several wagons commandeered and filled with food, grain, and other fodder. When he saw the gateposts destroyed as well, he shivered. Rescalyn was making it very plain what the cost was for attacking Telaryn.

But how much of that is to make the point not to cross him personally?

The road that the regiment took angled to the northeast and was one that Quaeryt had never seen before. Sixth Battalion now rode as the first full battalion back from the vanguard and directly behind Rescalyn and the command group, with Meinyt's company leading

the battalion. For that reason, Quaeryt rode with both
Skarpa and Meinyt, since Skarpa usually rode at the
head of his battalion. Quaeryt also had refrained from
wearing the overlarge green shirt, since he could occasionally see the governor, and that meant Rescalyn
could see him.

A good glass after riding out, and just as the sun
was beginning to rise, Quaeryt said, "I haven't been
on this road before. Where are we headed?"

"This is the direct back road to Saentaryn's," replied Meinyt. "In a few glasses, we'll join the road
where we dealt with the coal wagons."

"And where from there? After Saentaryn?"

Meinyt shrugged. "No one's told me, but the next
closest hill hold belongs to Demotyl. . . ."

"Are all the holders who signed that message neigh-
bors of Waerfyl?"

"What message?" demanded Skarpa.

"Oh . . . I thought you knew. Waerfyl and some
other hill holders sent a missive saying they'd had
enough of Telaryn interference. It was signed by Waerfyl, Demotyl, Huisfyl, and Saentaryn."

"Demotyl and Saentaryn adjoin Waerfyl's lands.
Huisfyl's are farther into the hills, and then you get to
one of the biggest holdings. That's Zorlyn's." Skarpa
frowned. "How did you know about the message?"

"The governor told me before he sent me to Sixth
Battalion," admitted Quaeryt.

"That's good to know. The governor hasn't told
me, or any of the battalion commanders. Not in our
meetings, anyway."

"We're likely to reach Saentaryn's hold by right after midday, aren't we?" asked Quaeryt.

"That's likely."

"Will we attack this afternoon?"

"That's up to the governor. I would. Men and mounts will be a bit tired, but Saentaryn won't expect it that soon." Skarpa shrugged. "Then I'd give the regiment a day to recover before moving on. More if the men need it."

"Demotyl's holding is more than twenty milles north," added Meinyt. "No way anyone could get there and then get back to attack in less than a day and a half, maybe more. Any other hill holding's more than twice that far."

Slightly past midmorning, the horn signal for an attack was sounded from the rear, but the column never even slowed, and several quints later, word reached Skarpa that only a small group of attackers had appeared, and that they'd been driven off with minimal casualties.

"Most of the survivors from Waerfyl's hold likely retreated deeper into the hills," observed the major. "Saentaryn's likely on his own."

"Wasn't Waerfyl?" asked Quaeryt.

"He was, but he's always had more lands and men," said Meinyt. "That was one reason, I'd guess, Saentaryn raided the coal mine. They couldn't cut enough timber for the winter."

"Or they hadn't, and realized it too late," added Skarpa dryly.

Less than a glass later, a volley of arrows arched from the trees toward the command group, but two squads from the vanguard charged out even as the shafts were falling, and no more were fired. But the squads didn't find anyone, either.

"Less than a mille to the gates," said Meinyt.

"They won't let us much past there," predicted Skarpa.

The major was right.

Before the regiment was even out of the trees beyond the gates, attackers swarmed toward the column from all sides, again, both those mounted and those on foot. The initial numbers seemed so great to Quaeryt that he couldn't help wondering who'd thought that Saentaryn had fewer fighters.

Two riders surged through a gap between squads and charged Quaeryt. He braced the staff against the saddle pommel, so that it extended on each side, then ducked, urged the mare forward, and angled the staff until the forward tip slammed into the gut of the man on the right. The momentum of the impact twisted the staff so that the left side crashed into the back of the shoulder of the other attacker, whose blade had glanced off Quaeryt's shields at an angle.

He'd barely straightened in the saddle when a slender figure on foot appeared from nowhere with a sharp and bloody blade, bringing it up as if to gut the mare.

Quaeryt struck down with all the force he could muster, the iron-tipped end of the staff cracking into the temple of the attacker. Even with the din and shouts around him, he could hear and feel the crunch of breaking bone. As he pulled the staff back, trying to recover his balance, an edge ripped of the attacker's leather cap-like helm, and a cascade of dark hair revealed that the attacker he'd killed was a young woman.

He had little time to think about that, not when another rider charged him, swinging one of the overlarge blades that the hill riders seemed to prefer. He tried to slide the blade with the staff, but its weight and the momentum of the rider almost ripped the staff out of his hands, and the blade came down on his shielded shoulder—and shattered.

That scarcely helped Quaeryt, because the impact rattled him inside the shields like a dried pea in a cup, so that he could barely stay on the mare and hang on to the staff. Another ranker to his left took on the disarmed rebel, and Quaeryt tried to keep moving and gather himself together.

After that, he jabbed, thrust, swung, and tried to avoid getting hit too many times, but by the time the field, such as it was, cleared, his head was throbbing, and he was having trouble seeing, although he did catch sight of men in leathers riding out, trying to shield others on foot from pursuing squads. But, following Rescalyn's orders, the troopers did not follow far into the woods, only enough to assure that those they had pursued were truly fleeing.

Quaeryt was exhausted, bruised in more places than he wanted to count, and grateful to be alive—and that was using imaging shields. Without them, he'd have been long since dead. He was definitely no warrior, and his respect for the rankers and officers continued to increase.

This time, Rescalyn had not ordered the engineers to bombard the dwellings, not that he'd had the time or the ground to allow that before the initial attacks. Once the area around the building was secured, two squads from Seventh Battalion went through the structures, one at a time. They emerged without wounds, and without captives.

Quaeryt waited, still mounted, with Meinyt's company, surveying the edge of the trees and the open ground beyond, well short of the holding buildings, where much of the fighting had taken place. His eyes dropped to his sleeves, and he realized that he'd never put on the green shirt, and that the browns barely showed the blood splatters. He looked up again, forcing his eyes to look at individual bodies. During the attack, he'd felt as though there were thousands, yet there were probably less than two hundred bodies, and many, he suspected, were youths and women, some of whom had fought with little more than knives. He swallowed, trying to keep the bile down.

Yet . . . what else can any ruler do with holders who continually flount authority?

Finally, Skarpa relayed the order to dismount and deal with what needed to be done immediately . . . tending to the wounded, checking mounts, cleaning weapons.

After meeting briefly with the governor and the other battalion commanders, Skarpa returned and summoned his officers. Quaeryt joined them and listened.

"We'll be able to use the buildings and some of the supplies. That'll be good, especially if there's rain tonight. Some provisions are gone. Not that many, but the best. There's plenty of fodder and grain for the horses. They didn't have time or the wagons to move much. We'll be able to give the men decent cooked meals. It'll take time, but we have that. We won't be moving out until Lundi. But it'll be early Lundi. Now . . . see to your men."

Quaeryt had to admit that Rescalyn had been correct in his decision as to when to attack. But then, Quaeryt had considerable regard for the governor's tactical and strategic abilities, just as he had significant suspicions about Rescalyn's ambitions.

83

Quaeryt was so tired that, when he woke up in the small shed with most of Meinyt's company on Solayi, he had no idea at first where he was or how he'd gotten there. When he tried to move, he was reminded instantly. He just lay there on a pile of pine branches that was better than bare ground, but not much, thinking.

Solayi . . . the day of rest. . . . Rest from what? Killing?

He wanted to laugh at the irony of it all, but he was almost afraid that, if he did, he wouldn't be able to stop. So he rolled over and struggled to his feet.

"That leg bothering you, again, sir?" asked a ranker.

"It does more in the morning. I'll be all right in a bit." He didn't bother rolling up his gear, not when they'd be there one more night. He walked out of the shed into a grayish morning. While it was still early, the gray was because of the featureless clouds that had rolled in, not because it was before dawn. He made his way toward one of the cookfires, where he saw Skarpa talking with another major.

By the time he reached the cookfires, the two had walked away, deep in conversation, and Quaeryt didn't follow them. After a breakfast of egg and mutton hash inside a rolled flatcake, accompanied by some very bad ale—likely the dregs from Saentaryn's stores—that he had to pour into his own water bottle, Quaeryt still had a headache and was still sore and stiff. He went to check the mare, but she looked and acted better than he felt.

He'd no sooner returned to the area that held Sixth Battalion than a ranker hurried toward him. Quaeryt had the feeling he knew who was seeking him.

"The governor would like to see you, scholar."

"Where is he?"

"He's inside, in the main hall of the hold."

Quaeryt nodded and walked toward the hold building, not dawdling, but not rushing, not with the way his leg felt. When he got there, two guards blocked the open double doors. "Not yet, sir."

After more than a quint, one of the guards called, "Sir, the governor will see you now."

Quaeryt stepped through the open double doors into a large foyer, although the ceiling was not raised above normal height or open to the upper level. The floor was wooden, and oiled, but showed the marks of years of wear, and the grain suggested it was oak. The walls were oak-paneled, and lighter oblongs suggested that paintings had hung there and been removed, either by Saentaryn's retainers earlier or at Rescalyn's direction later. Quaeryt wasn't about to ask which.

"Sir . . . the governor's that way." A squad leader pointed to the square archway to the left. "He's expecting you."

The large hall—obviously a dining hall—had been roughly cleared, with the long tables and benches pushed against the walls. A shorter table stood before the natural stone hearth and chimney, but well out from the stonework. Rescalyn sat behind the table.

He motioned to Quaeryt.

Quaeryt approached and bowed slightly. "Sir."

"Scholar, I understand you give a passable homily . . . and that Undercaptain Gauswn knows the service fairly well."

"I'm no chorister, sir, but I can speak to some of the teachings of Rholan and the Nameless. From what I've observed, Undercaptain Gauswn is quite familiar with the order of the service."

"Good. I will leave the arrangements for this evening's service to the two of you. I do trust that the subject of the homily will be appropriate."

"Yes, sir."

"That is all, scholar."

Quaeryt inclined his head, turned, and departed.

Once he was outside the hold, he moved to the south end and kept walking until he could step into a space between two junipers. There he raised a concealment shield and slowly and carefully made his way back to the hold entrance, where, after a time, he slipped past the ranker guards and into the foyer, and then into the hall.

It was empty, but the papers left on the table suggested that Rescalyn would return.

Quaeryt waited almost two quints, standing beside the massive stone hearth and chimney, before the governor returned, accompanied by Commander Myskyl.

For a time, the talk centered on logistics, including three wagons the engineers had found in the wagon shed and were inspecting to see how usable they might be. Eventually, the two began to discuss subjects of greater interest to Quaeryt.

". . . should be able to get to the staging point on that flat ridge a good glass before sunset if we leave at dawn tomorrow."

"If it doesn't rain, that shouldn't be a problem, sir."

"The clouds are still high. If we do get rain, it won't be more than a light drizzle for the next few days. After that, it won't matter as much."

"A few prayers to the Nameless wouldn't hurt," replied Myskyl ironically.

"Speaking of the Nameless, what you do think of the scholar?"

"I've asked around, as you requested. Quietly." Myskyl paused. "He's careful. He's also courageous. The officers and the men respect him."

"How does he handle that staff?"

"Like a seaman, mostly."

Rescalyn shook his head. "He's never what he says he isn't . . . but that doesn't mean he's not more than he is."

"You know he's Lord Bhayar's man."

"It's too bad, really. We'll just have to see, though. We'll put Sixth Battalion in the center when we face Demotyl's retainers . . . and later at Zorlyn's . . . if it comes to that."

"Will it?"

"I'll offer terms to Zorlyn to appear magnanimous, because he didn't sign their declaration, but he won't accept. Besides, it will take Zorlyn's fall to convince those in the south. Do we have any word from the north?"

"I'm certain Commander Pulaskyr can flatten Vurlaent's hold. After that, the others will likely capitulate."

"I trust that will be so. That will give us the winter to rebuild. Without the threat of the hill holders, we'll pick up more rankers. We might pick up a few deserters as well."

"More than a few, I'd wager. Enough to add another full battalion."

"It would be helpful if they were archers. We'll need another two companies by then."

Quaeryt stood in the space beside the massive hearth for more than a glass, but the rest of the conversation with Commander Myskyl and those with other officers all dealt with the conduct of the campaign. Finally, behind his concealment shield, he slipped away and out of the hold house that held little of value that could have been moved. He found a shaded space behind a large juniper at the south end of the dwelling, where he released the concealment, then headed back to find the officers of Sixth Battalion.

Again . . . what he'd heard wasn't totally conclusive, but it was more than suggestive, especially the words about archers, because archers were supposedly only good in pitched battles. For what pitched battles was Rescalyn planning?

It took him almost half a glass to find Gauswn, whose company was located in an outlying sheep shed that no longer held sheep—only pungent odors that made it clear that the ovine presence had been most recent.

"Sir?" asked the undercaptain on seeing Quaeryt approach.

"The governor has requested that you and I conduct services this evening, much the way we did at Boralieu."

"Yes, sir."

"By the way, Cyrethyn speaks most highly of you. I'm not certain he doesn't think you should be a chorister."

"No, sir. I couldn't think up things the way either of you do."

"That just comes with practice and experience in life."

"I think it takes more than that, sir."

Quaeryt wasn't about to argue on that point and said, "You know the openings, the invocation . . . the confession . . ."

"Yes, sir."

"I think we should skip the offertory."

Gauswn nodded.

In less than a quint, the two had completed the arrangements and organization for the evening services. After that, Quaeryt found a quiet spot in the rear and very rustic herb and vegetable gardens to think about a homily that was true to the precepts of the Nameless and also "appropriate," as Rescalyn had put it. He didn't like being put in the position of delivering homilies under the auspices of a deity of whose existence he was most uncertain, and especially doing so in the middle of what was turning into a very bloody campaign. Yet . . . refusing to do so helped no one, including the rankers who were the ones shedding most of the blood. It also wouldn't help him or Lord Bhayar or his goals for scholars and eventually imagers— goals he thought were worthwhile.

But doesn't everyone with a mission believe their goals are worthwhile? Doesn't Rescalyn?

He knew the answers to those questions, and they didn't offer much comfort.

All too soon the rest of the afternoon and supper passed, and Quaeryt and Gauswn stood on the flat space north of the hold house, facing several hundred men and officers. Gauswn handled the invocation and confession, and skipped the offertory, then turned to Quaeryt.

"Under the Nameless . . . all evenings are good," Quaeryt began. "But we all know that some are better than others." He'd hoped the dryness of the way he delivered those words would get at least a few smiles . . . and he saw some. "We've all been through some long days lately, and there might be a few questions about how it all came to this. Well . . . I can't claim any insight into what the Nameless might think, but I have seen, now and again, as have most of you, what happens when people, even rulers, think that they don't have to abide by the laws and rules of a land . . . when they think they're above those rules. In an important way, acting as though you're above the laws is no different from Naming. It's just another way of claiming that you're better than anyone else. . . ."

Quaeryt paused and gestured toward the hold house. "Holder Saentaryn didn't want to pay his tariffs like other holders. He stole coal from other holders and killed hardworking miners . . . and what was his reward for his Naming? Who will remember his name or his evil . . . or even any good he may have done? I can't say whether it's exactly the will of the Nameless, but those who attempt to exalt their names through evil and greed and reaching beyond their true abilities . . . well . . . all too often, it doesn't go well for them.

"Now . . . it's easy to look at someone in power, especially one who has fallen from power or someone evil, and say they deserve what happens, but we can fall into that trap in our day-to-day life, to justify weighted bones in gaming with a comrade who's not quite so sharp . . . or just tired, or to bet more than he can cover . . . or even . . . you all know the little tricks that those who don't care enough about their comrades can come up with. But there's a problem with this sort of little Naming, just as there is with big Naming. In fights and battles, we all need each other. If any of you have been shorting your comrades, one way or another, can you be certain they'll make every effort to protect your back? Even if they're honorable, and almost everyone is, will that worry hamper you when things get tight? . . ." Quaeryt went on to strengthen those points, trying to stress how the values of the Nameless strengthened the regiment and benefited each and every man and officer.

After the benediction, Rescalyn appeared and walked toward Quaeryt. "Most appropriate, scholar. Thank you."

"You're welcome, sir."

As the rest of the men and officers slipped away, Gauswn turned to Quaeryt. "I still say you'd make an excellent chorister, sir."

"Thank you . . . but I think both the Nameless and I would be happier if I weren't, Undercaptain. I have too many doubts to be a good chorister, much as I believe in the values for which the Nameless stands."

"We all have doubts, sir. What matters is what we do, given those doubts."

Quaeryt couldn't have agreed more, but he worried a great deal about whether his own actions met those standards . . . and whether they would in the days and weeks ahead.

84

The regiment left the smoking ruins of Saentaryn's holding slightly before sunrise on Lundi. Everything that could not be used or transported immediately had been put to the torch or otherwise destroyed shortly after dawn. While there were no attacks on the column during the morning, scouts did report seeing mounted figures in the trees by late in the afternoon.

"Why no attacks now?" Quaeryt had asked.

"Those who are Saentaryn's see no point. Not now. Those who serve others are saving every man to defend the hold," replied Skarpa.

And every woman and youth. Quaeryt kept that thought to himself.

For whatever reason, either that expressed by Skarpa, or for some other, there were no attacks on the regiment during the ride. The column drew up and camped on a flat less than two milles from the approach to Demotyl's holding, presumably the same flat that Myskyl and Rescalyn had discussed the day before. That night, there were no attacks, either, although scouts verified that there was activity at the holding, and a gathering of forces there.

Well before true dawn, the regiment moved through a misty fog that was almost a drizzle toward the heights to the east of Demotyl's holding. Unlike at Waerfyl's hold, all the buildings were of stone, with split-slate roofs, and there was a low wall on the south edge of the flat ridge on which the structures were set, a wall overlooking terraced fields that had been harvested days or weeks earlier.

As the Sixth Battalion drew up in the trees in the center of the wedge, a good half mille from the main hold house, and positioned so that the battalion didn't have to deal with the southern wall, Quaeryt glanced upward at the thickening clouds, barely visible through the drizzling mist. He shook his head.

"You're asking why now, scholar?" Meinyt offered a crooked grin. "Because the rain will really come down later, and everything will be slop for days. The governor wants to take the place before it does and hole up there while things dry out."

"... and we'll get the holes, and he'll dry out," came a murmur from the ranks behind.

Meinyt glanced back sharply, if but for a moment. There were no more comments, low-voiced or otherwise.

The attack began with two squads from another battalion—Quaeryt didn't know which—riding to one of the outlying barns and breaking down the doors and loosing the horses that had been herded inside. But no one emerged from any of the buildings.

"They're going to play turtle," predicted Meinyt. "It'll cost them dear."

No matter what they do, it will cost them dearly. Quaeryt did not voice the thought.

For a time, the only sounds were those of horses, the air so chill that their breath was sometimes a hot fog that drifted upward from their nostrils before dissipating. Then a team pulled in an engineers' wagon, and the engineers unloaded various lengths of wood and other items. Before long, they had positioned a bombard less than a hundred yards from the north end of the main hold building. Shortly, the weapon began to hurl moderate-sized boulders, no more than two or three stones in weight, at the shuttered upper window. Not all hit the shutters, and those that didn't merely bounced off the thick stone walls, but after a half glass or so, the shutters were gone and the narrow window gaped open. Then came the crocks of flaming bitumen.

To the east just below Sixth Battalion, another bombard attacked the center lower window. As the bitumen crocks began to fly at that open window, two things happened. Cold rain began to pelt down, and every door in the holding opened—side doors, barn doors, cellar doors—and armed figures swarmed toward the bombards. The engineers retreated in full run, and the horn sounded the charge.

Once more, Quaeryt followed Meinyt, his staff out and ready, as Sixth Battalion crossed the open ground from the trees and swept toward the defenders.

The holders had a definite strategy, because they came at the cavalry in pairs, one man with a long spear or something resembling a pike, and the other with a shorter blade or ax, with each pair targeting a given horseman.

"Beware the pikes! 'Ware the pikes!" came an order, but at least one or two leading riders ended up with their mounts brought down, and several horses screamed.

Quaeryt saw an opening and guided the mare between a pair of holders concentrating on another rider, then turned her, and slammed the staff into the pikeman's head. He realized that, for a moment, he had an advantage in being partly behind the pikes. He kept moving sideways and trying to strike or otherwise upset each man with the long spear or pike, and he managed to upset or incapacitate five or so before he saw three pikemen ahead bracing their weapons against him.

He couldn't stop the mare fast enough, and he momentarily extended his shields, hoping he could hold them. For an instant, he felt as though he'd been impaled in two places, but the pain passed, if leaving him light-headed in doing so, and he eased the mare around, trying to rejoin the company.

Another youth lunged at the mare, and Quaeryt

knocked him aside. The mare struck him in passing, and he went down under another horse. Quaeryt kept moving, knowing that standing still was an invitation for the mare to be gutted and him to be trapped under her or dragged off and having his throat cut. He tried to keep the staff in play as well, so that anyone near him couldn't determine where he might strike. He couldn't get too close to the main building; it was now engulfed in flames.

Already, men and mounts were slipping in the mud, and the battle had deteriorated into what amounted to hand-to-hand fighting, where the mounted soldiers had an advantage because four hoofs had better footing than two boots in the slop that seemed to be everywhere. But as soon as battalions had wiped out one group of defenders, more appeared from somewhere.

Quaeryt couldn't help but wonder if some of the defenders had come from those who had fled Waerfyl's hold, but it didn't matter where they came from, only that they were cut down or rendered out of combat.

How long the fighting lasted, Quaeryt had no idea, because the icy rain and clouds blocked the sun and turned everything into mud covering mud, but . . . after a long time, Quaeryt discovered the only figures around him were other Telaryn riders. After another interval, the horn sounded, out of tune, signaling a recall to re-form by squad and company.

Again . . . while there were more than a few bodies, there weren't so many as Quaeryt felt there had been all around him. Did a battle—a skirmish—do that to judgment—make it seem like there were more enemies than there were?

As he pondered thát, Quaeryt kept looking for Sixth Battalion, finding the companies in one of the livestock wintering barns. While it wasn't all that warm, Quaeryt was more than glad to be out of the cold rain and mud and in a dry covered space. His fingers were so numb that it took an effort to let go of the staff and dismount.

"We're just fortunate that we're not in Eighth Battalion," said Meinyt, looking back out through the wide doors of the barn into the mixture of rain and snow that fell even more heavily. "They were held in reserve. They got ordered to round up all the horses they loosed earlier. They'll take casualties from the holders in the woods, and they'll freeze their asses to their saddles before the afternoon's over."

". . . might end up with the bloody flux," muttered someone from farther back in the shed.

"Not likely," said the captain sharply. "Not if you take care of yourselves."

"Yes, sir."

Meinyt walked his mount past each of the remaining rankers. Although Quaeryt couldn't tell for certain, he had the feeling that the captain had lost more than a squad in the fight to take the hold, although "taking" it wasn't exactly what had happened because, despite the snow and rain, the main building had turned into a conflagration that was still burning, if not nearly so fiercely as earlier.

Skarpa returned from wherever he'd been in the large wintering barn and stopped by Quaeryt, who was doing his best to remove the cold and near-frozen mud from the mare.

"Good thing you did out there, scholar," said the major.

"I saw a chance. They weren't expecting a rider with something as long as a staff."

"You saved close to a squad doing that. They almost took you down. Don't see how you managed to knock aside three pikes with that staff, but I'm glad you did."

Quaeryt snorted. "I doubt I could do it again. I didn't know what I was doing, except that I knew if I could make a gap in the pikes . . ."

"There's some officers couldn't figure that out so quick . . . not in a mess like this."

"You're kind, Major. We just do what we can."

"Maybe . . . but I appreciate it. Some of the rankers won't even know, but I do." Skarpa nodded. "Have to report to the commander."

Quaeryt returned to the task of removing cold mud from the mare and from himself and his gear. He glanced outside and shuddered.

And this is early fall. It's still fairly hot in Solis right now.

He didn't even have a winter jacket.

85

The cold rain abated for a time late on Lundi afternoon, only to be followed by a chilling north wind, which created thin ice on top of the mud, and then by a driving snow that was already ankle-deep by the time Quaeryt collapsed into his blanket that night, where, despite the comparative warmth provided by the combination of horses and men, he shivered through the night, even wearing his browns, his brown jacket, and another shirt. When he finally rose on Mardi, the snow was more than boot-deep, and it continued to fall intermittently throughout the long gray day.

The cooks did manage a hot meal on Mardi night, another hash-like offering, with mutton that had been dried before it was cooked, with potato strips, but it was warm, and for that Quaeryt was thankful. As he sat after eating, perched on a support beam in the barn beside Skarpa, he asked, "Why doesn't the regiment have its archers here?" He'd heard what Straesyr had said, but he wanted to hear what the major said.

"We have a company or so. What would we use them for? They're useful in pitched battles, but a man with a blade is more effective here in the hills for what we do. You've seen the attacks. An archer wouldn't even know where to aim most of the time, and they're not good at close-in fighting. I think I saw our company. They're here. Commander's likely saving them for where they'll do the most good."

Quaeryt considered. Given the hit and run tactics of the hill holders; he could see that. The hill rebels had only massed at Waerfyl's and only for a few moments. Archers really wouldn't have helped much so far. "How long will we be here, do you think?"

"The sky's clearing now. Tomorrow will be warmer, enough to melt the snow, and we'll be back on the road by Jeudi, Vendrei at the latest," predicted the major.

"With the snow this deep?" Quaeryt had a hard time believing that. Was Skarpa jesting . . . or was the weather that changeable?

Skarpa looked at Quaeryt and laughed. "You'll see."

Quaeryt did indeed.

Meredi dawned clear, and by late afternoon the air was warm, and the snow was mostly gone, with that which remained having turned largely to slush ... and mud, gloopy gray mud. The battalions spent the day cleaning gear and preparing to resume the campaign. That didn't happen until Vendrei morning, because Rescalyn decided another day would provide more rest ... and drier and more secure roads.

Again ... before sunrise, the regiment leveled everything, putting all that could not be removed to the torch, and moved out, the wounded in commandeered wagons heading back to Boralieu, along with the valuables salvaged from the holding. The main body took the road that led in its winding way northwest toward Huisfyl's holding.

The roads were mostly dry, but the horses threw up enough mud that Quaeryt's trousers were spattered below the knees. Again, there were no attacks from the roadside, but that wasn't unexpected, because while the snow had melted in the areas reached by the sun, such as the roads and lanes, much still remained in the depths of the woods.

The sky remained clear throughout Vendrei, but the warmth of Meredi and Jeudi slipped away, and a light but chill breeze blew consistently out of the north.

By late afternoon, Quaeryt was feeling chilled, and he turned in the saddle toward Meinyt, riding to his right. "What happened to the warm day we had yesterday?"

"That's the way fall is in Tilbor," replied Meinyt. "Rain, snow, warm, cold, frost, warm ... it changes every day. Each time it warms up, it's not as warm as the last time. By the end of Finitas, it just doesn't ever warm up again. Not until mid-Maris. Then everything melts at once, and you get two-three weeks of mud."

Quaeryt was glad he didn't have to be around for winter and the mud that followed. The shiver he felt at that thought wasn't just from the chill breeze that gusted around him.

86

Vendrei evening the regiment stopped at and took over one of the few hamlets in the Boran Hills, consisting of less than a score of dwellings, including what passed for a chandlery or store, a blacksmith's shop, and an inn that had but five rooms to let, and a public room. Even using stables, barns, and sheds, and the porches of the inn, less than a third of the regiment was under roof that night, but at least the wind abated . . . or was less fierce in the sheltered location of the hamlet.

Since there had been no resistance, when the regiment pulled out on Samedi morning, the hamlet was much as it had been. Rescalyn had been most firm about not harming property or inhabitants of those who welcomed or did not resist Telaryn forces.

At close to eighth glass that morning, as the regiment neared Huisfyl's hold . . . arrows arched down on the lead elements of the column from the top of a low bluff a hundred yards away. Since the arrows showed no sign of ceasing, Rescalyn sent two companies from Fourth Battalion through the woods, which still held some traces of snow, but they returned empty-handed, and with five men wounded, one of whom had taken a shaft in the chest and was unlikely to survive.

By ninth glass, the regiment drew up in the trees to the south of Huisfyl's hold, more of a compound than a hold, since it was unlike any of the others Quaeryt had seen. A rough stone wall, no more than chest-high, formed an irregular oval around a series of buildings set almost at random on the rough but gently sloped ground that ran from a low point above a creek in the west to a higher level in the northwest. Paths, rather than lanes, ran from building to building. Some fifty yards above the northwest section of the wall, the forest resumed, like a bastion of massive pines and spruces. The largest dwelling within the wall, less than a quarter the size of the smallest of the holds of the three that had fallen so far, was located as the highest structure on the hill, but the structures below seemed to alternate between outbuildings, sheds, barns, and smaller dwellings, and all were constructed of large logs in the same general fashion as Waerfyl's hold had been. The roofs were not of split slate, either, but of some form of shake or shingle that had weathered to a grayish shade similar to that of pale slate.

This time, the engineers began to set up the bombards a hundred yards back from the south side of the wall, approximately halfway up the slope, in the roughly cleared land holding low bushes and autumn-browned high·grasses. The first target was the large dwelling at the top of the compound.

Barely had the first stone—used for ranging, rather than wasting a crock of bitumen—thudded into the ground below the dwelling than a bell clanged and a good hundred hill fighters in furs and leathers appeared from structures all over the compound and raced toward the bombards. Rescalyn waited until they cleared the wall before ordering the charge by Fourth Battalion.

Once the riders left the trees, half the hill fighters halted and immediately lifted bows, loosing shafts directly at the horsemen. While several riders went down, almost no horses did, and the hill fighters broke and retreated behind the wall.

Quaeryt, seated on the mare beside Meinyt, waited to see what the governor would order next. Rescalyn recalled Fourth Battalion, and as they rode back across the uneven ground, the engineers resumed calibrating the two bombards.

When the first crock of bitumen sprayed flame across the main hold house, the compound bell rang again, and even more figures in furs and leathers appeared and advanced toward the engineers, but the engineers managed to get two more shots away before withdrawing and leaving the field to the cavalry.

This time Fourth and Fifth Battalion charged the defenders. The locals did not retreat, but attempted to stand their ground. Almost a third were cut down in the initial charge, but another wave of defenders appeared and rushed over the walls. Many of the reinforcements carried pikes, long spears, or even just sharpened poles.

"Sixth Battalion. Stand ready!" ordered Skarpa.

"Standing ready!" came the reply from the company officers.

When the signal to attack came, Skarpa stood in the stirrups for an instant. "To the right! On me!"

As Quaeryt followed Meinyt in the company's advance, he saw exactly what Skarpa had in mind: Sixth Battalion would angle uphill, almost to the stone wall, then turn and charge downhill, in an effort to catch the defenders on their flank. If they tried to set their pikes and spears against Sixth Battalion, then Fourth and Fifth Battalion would have a clearer path of attack.

If the defenders held to a position to halt Fourth and Fifth Battalion, Sixth Battalion could cut them down from the side.

Quaeryt managed to stay close to Meinyt until the company was almost upon the defenders, some of whom swung their spears and makeshift pikes to face uphill. Not enough did, and most of the company's riders avoided being spitted or brought down by the long pointed weapons.

Quaeryt found a pointed pole aimed at him, with the defender firmly anchoring the butt in the hillside. He jerked the reins to the left at almost the last moment, then immediately brought the mare back to the right so that her weight levered the defender off his feet before she knocked down another who hadn't seen Quaeryt coming.

The scholar managed to beat down a third man with the staff, before again swinging behind Meinyt. In moments, the longer pikes were dropped amid the low bushes and high grasses rapidly being trampled flat. Then the defenders came up with long knives and did their best to slash at the legs of the company's mounts.

Horses began to fall, but not so swiftly as did the defenders, and as the numbers of the defenders who fell increased, the Telaryn riders could move more freely to avoid the slashes of those who remained. Quaeryt was appalled to see, even while he continued to use his staff, that the defenders never retreated. They stood and fought until they fell.

The regiment advanced, almost ponderously, to the wall, while the engineers returned and resumed the bombardment of the largest dwelling. Other engineers moved forward to create gaps in the wall, through which the regiment advanced. Sixth Battalion moved uphill inside the wall, from point to point, building to building, often with long pauses in the action before the movement to the next structure. Above them all, the main dwelling flamed and then steadily burned down into a glowing mass of smoking embers.

Quaeryt's arms were sore, his back and legs stiff when Meinyt brought the company back together on the narrow flat below the ashes and coals that were all that remained of the holder's main dwelling. He glanced downhill, his eyes studying the slope and spaces between buildings. In the late-afternoon sun, everywhere he looked were scattered bodies, most of them in leathers and fur. Many were women and youths, almost as many, it appeared, as the full-bearded men, all of whom seemed to bear multiple wounds.

Quaeryt tried to count the company. When he finished, he was so surprised that he counted once more. While he doubtless was less than completely accurate, his enumeration revealed that Meinyt had lost only five men in a melee in which Quaeryt had been more than certain at least a squad's worth of troopers had perished. He counted a third time, but the numbers remained unchanged.

87

Solayi dawned bright, clear, and chill, with gusty winds that were warm only by comparison to those of the night before. Quaeryt had spent the night in the hayloft of a barn, but he'd been surprised to see that,

even so late as it was in the year, the first day of Finitas, the last month of the year, with just that month
left before full winter descended on Tilbor, the loft
was but half-filled with hay and wild grasses. Still,
sleeping there had been far softer and warmer than
where he had spent the previous nights. He almost felt
guilty—almost—that he hadn't had to do the night
patrols assigned to Meinyt's company or to join in the
parties that carried bodies to the several pyres that had
been built. That alone convinced Quaeryt that Rescalyn intended to have the regiment stay for at least several days, because in the past, the bodies had simply
been disposed of in the buildings that were burned.

At close to the second glass of the afternoon, a
ranker arrived to summon Quaeryt to meet with the
governor. As he accompanied the ranker, Quaeryt suspected that he'd once more be asked to deliver a homily. He only wondered if, this time, Rescalyn would
suggest a subject.

Rescalyn was waiting in the main room of the
quarters attached to what might be called a coach or
equipment house, seated at one end of a battered dining table, with two oil lamps on each side of the maps
he studied. He gestured for Quaeryt to approach, but
did not rise.

"Sir?" Quaeryt wasn't about to ask why he'd been
summoned.

"Tell me, scholar . . . why do you fight?" Rescalyn's
voice remained cheerfully hearty, as it seemed to be
most of time, at least from what Quaeryt had heard
every time he'd been around the governor.

"You assigned me to Sixth Battalion, sir. What else
would you have me do when they're fighting?"

"You were only required to observe."

"It has appeared to me that an observer in a battle or skirmish faces all of the risks with none of the advantages of a combatant."

"Do you not believe that to be true in life, as well, scholar?"

Quaeryt smiled carefully. "I suppose that would depend on whether one's circumstances place them in a situation resembling a battle."

"So it would. But is not most of life arranged in that fashion, if more concealed and obscured by custom, golds, and fashion?"

"Certainly, some philosophers have claimed that to be so."

"What do you think?"

"I do not believe it is always so, but it is more so than most would care to admit."

"That is a careful and scholarly reply, as befits a scholar." Rescalyn smiled. "Neither life nor war are always either careful or scholarly . . . as I hope you have observed in your time with the regiment."

"I have indeed, sir. Might I ask what you plan next?"

"You may ask. I'll answer in general terms. We have crushed the four hill holders who declared rebellion. I have sent a courier under a parley flag to hill holder Zorlyn, with a message. That message offers a cease-fire to him and all remaining hill holders provided they swear immediate allegiance to Telaryn and its lord . . . and offer additional tariffs of two parts in ten. I wrote him that Telaryn is making the offer because he did not join the declared rebels. If he does not so swear, then he will suffer the fate of the deceased rebel holders . . . as will any holder who does not do so."

"Do you expect him to do so?"

"What do you think, scholar?"

"I have my doubts, sir."

"So do I, but, by making the offer, I appear reasonable."

"You also show the High Holders that, if tariffs need to rise, you will back such increases with force."

"That, too," replied Rescalyn with a smile. "Oh . . . I expect another homily tonight . . . and would you convey to Undercaptain Gauswn that his services will also be required? You can use the large wintering barn."

Quaeryt had expected that "request." He only had been surprised that Rescalyn hadn't begun with it. "Yes, sir."

"That's all, scholar."

Quaeryt nodded and departed.

When he returned to the barn, Gauswn was waiting for him.

"Sir . . . are we—"

"Yes, the governor has requested that we conduct services tonight in the large wintering barn. It appears we'll be here for several days. If you'll excuse me for a few moments, I need to report to Major Skarpa."

"He's at the north end, sir."

"Thank you." Quaeryt walked to the far end of the barn.

Skarpa turned from the senior squad leader with whom he had been talking. "Scholar."

"Major . . . I just returned from talking with the governor. He asked that Gauswn and I perform the services tonight—in the large wintering barn. He also said that he'd sent a message to Holder Zorlyn, suggesting the holders acknowledge the primacy of Telaryn and its lord. He is awaiting a reply."

"I hadn't heard that, but he has called for an all-officers' meeting in a glass. We'll be here for several days, then. At least two more. Thank you."

"I thought you should know, if you didn't already."

"I appreciate it."

Quaeryt headed back to find Gauswn and discuss the service. He also needed to find another "appropriate" topic for his homily.

A glass later, he was sitting on a post in the corner of the barn, below the hayloft, thinking . . . and murmuring ideas to himself.

"Youth and strength as Naming . . . no . . . Cyrethyn mentioned that. Who is better remembered—Caldor, Hengyst, or Rholan? No . . . that suggests that rulers aren't to be trusted as much as followers of the Nameless . . . Rholan . . . the creation of a legend . . ."

He paused. *What about the idea that creating a legend is a form of cultural Naming . . . that legends effectively destroy truth . . . and why is it that most great men so wish to be a legend in their own time?*

Quaeryt smiled. He could do something with that idea . . . something that he could directly tie in to the acts and behaviors of the hill holders . . . while suggesting that form of Naming existed in great and powerful men of accomplishment everywhere . . . and that sometimes, only the intervention of the Nameless prevented even greater disasters. He wouldn't mention that powerful men often claimed that the Nameless had made their excesses, which they regarded as triumphs, possible.

88

Quaeryt's homily was well-received on Solayi night, and Rescalyn had seemed pleased, even with the words about the intervention of the Nameless to prevent complete disasters. Lundi morning was warmer. The wind had died down, and Quaeryt managed to wash the worst of the mud and blood off the one set of his trousers and tunics and hang them up in the barn, hoping that they would dry before the regiment moved on—whether against Zorlyn or back to Boralieu.

He did spend some time, when he retreated to a quiet corner of the loft, studying the quarrel he had retrieved days earlier, and practicing some different types of imaging, beginning with imaging shafts of straw into barn beams, so that they protruded. Even if someone had been watching, it would have been highly unlikely that they would have seen a straw seemingly appear stuck to the ancient wood, not in the middle of a hayloft.

After that, he checked the mare, thought, talked about matters with Meinyt, and fretted.

Just before supper on Lundi evening, Skarpa appeared in the barn holding Sixth Battalion. "The governor's called an officers' meeting." His eyes went to Quaeryt. "That includes you, scholar."

Quaeryt inclined his head.

"I don't think it's good," added the major.

"I wouldn't expect so. The hill holders have regarded themselves as beyond anyone's law but their own for far too many years."

"Why did he even send a message, then?"

"So that, after we've destroyed Zorlyn and a few more holders totally, he can make an offer again for those few remaining."

"They could just abandon their holds and wait him out," pointed out Skarpa.

"Do you really think so? You've told me how hard the winters are. Second, no one's ever succeeded in carrying this kind of war to them before. They don't really believe it can be done. They've been too isolated, and they've never dealt with someone who has the skill, determination, and the number of trained troops that the governor has. Even so, he's just starting the destruction. He's counting on the winter to largely finish it."

Skarpa nodded slowly. "I need to tell the other officers. We're to meet immediately."

"I'll come with you, then."

The two walked toward Gauswn, some twenty yards away, standing back from the east doorway.

Quaeryt said nothing more as Skarpa gathered his officers, and they all walked to the meeting—in the same chamber where Rescalyn had received Quaeryt the day before. Once all the officers had appeared, the governor entered the room. He wasted little time on greetings of formalities.

"As I reported to all of you yesterday," he began, his voice shorn of the heartiness it so often possessed, "I sent a courier with escorts to Holder Zorlyn. My message offered an amnesty for those hill holders who had not taken up arms against Telaryn, provided they swore allegiance to Telaryn and its lord and provided that they paid tariffs equal to the rates of other High

602 L. E. MODESITT, JR.

Holders, with an addition of two parts in ten for the
next several years." Rescalyn paused, then went on.
"We received a reply less than a glass ago. The courier
and his escorts were returned . . . and released three
milles from here. When they reached our camp, two
escorts were dead, strapped to their mounts; two were
alive but wounded; and the courier was alive—but
with a letter pinned to his chest with a knife. . . ."

Quaeryt felt like wincing. *The idiots . . . the absolute, boar-headed insufferable egotistical sow-
slutted . . . They're playing the plaques exactly as he
had planned they would.* And yet, there was no real
proof, only his suspicions. Was he justified in planning
what he did with only what he knew and sensed? And
yet, waiting too long would create another problem.

"I will read you the letter," said Rescalyn, coldly.
He cleared his throat.

> "To the one called governor—
>
> "The message you sent is an insult to Tilbor. It is also an
> insult to any self-respecting Tilboran, let alone to a holder
> whose lands have remained self-governing in his family for
> generation upon generation. Not even the most absolute of the
> Khanars ever insisted upon such outrageous tariffing. Nor did
> they bring in foreign scholars to change the way those who
> received their education at the Ecoliae were taught. Nor did
> they elevate mere crafters and merchants to the levels of those
> who have stewarded their lands wisely for all these many
> generations. After such acts, then for you to attempt to destroy
> all those who stand up for their time-honored rights and
> traditions is an even greater outrage, and one for which you
> and every man in your regiment will perish.
>
> "There can be but one reply to such ignorant arrogance and
> such self-serving egotism . . . and that is the reply you receive.

I spare those whom I have returned solely so that you may know
that I indeed am the one who sends this message . . ."

Rescalyn paused. "The courier and the two surviving ranker escorts told me that Zorlyn himself personally read them these words in the great hall of his
hold, before two of them were cut down, and the others were maimed."

Rescalyn let the silence speak for him. Only after it
became oppressive did he speak again. "I have offered
amnesty and mercy twice. It has been spurned in the
cruelest way. We will begin destroying this hold at
dawn tomorrow. We will ride out by sunrise." He
paused but momentarily before saying, "That is all.
Pass the word to your men." This time, he stood silently as the officers, and Quaeryt, filed out.

As he walked back to the barn, Quaeryt couldn't
help but admire Rescalyn's planning and understanding of the hill holders.

89

Mardi morning was clear, but the skies to the northwest showed a haze that promised a change in the
weather. The wind also blew from the northwest, hard
enough to fan the fires set in all the structures in Demotyl's holding into infernos within less than a quint
after they had been set. By midmorning, the regimental column and its wagons, almost twice as many as
had left Boralieu as a result of those recovered from

the various holdings, had covered more than seven milles, and a third of the sky was covered with low, thick, gray clouds. The wind had turned intermittently biting.

The first attack on the vanguard started at ninth glass, when several hundred riders galloped across the matted brown grasses of an upland meadow to within two hundred yards of the road and the lead companies. There they reined up and began to loose volleys of arrows at the Telaryn forces.

Rescalyn called on Fifth Battalion to attack by circling from the right. The hill riders waited until the first company was within fifty yards before loosing three volleys directly at the cavalry. Fifth Battalion ran down those too slow to escape and cut them down on the spot, perhaps fifty, according to the messenger who rode up and passed the work to Skarpa. Fifth Battalion suffered almost that many casualties, and more than twenty men were killed or wounded in the vanguard.

Rescalyn sent out more outriders and scouts.

All during the time between noon and the first glass of the afternoon, arrows and quarrels arched intermittently from the woods or from hills or bluffs down on the column, occasionally striking riders before one of the squads detailed to chase the archers away neared the attackers and they faded into the trees. The column scarcely slowed at all.

Shortly after that, a ranker rode back and summoned Quaeryt to ride forward to see the governor. When Quaeryt approached, Rescalyn motioned for him to ride next to him, but the governor did not speak immediately.

After they had ridden more than a hundred yards, Rescalyn asked, "Scholar . . . what did you think, honestly, of Zorlyn's reply?"

"Foolish . . . and predictable."

"Zorlyn is anything but a fool."

"I am certain that is so, sir, but intelligent and perceptive men still make foolish statements and attempt unwise acts when they fail to realize they are captive to perceptions or beliefs that are in error. Zorlyn has never faced a determined foe whose desire is to obliterate what he stands for. Neither have any of his forebears. The Khanars always compromised, and the hill holders believe that all rulers will do so, rather than fight and lose more men than is seen to be worth their while. Zorlyn, like all hill holders, assumes that your interest and that of Lord Bhayar is merely to collect tariffs. He also assumes that you will not pay the price for your actions. Were his assumptions correct, then his defiance would be justified. But those assumptions are incorrect."

"How does a man tell when he is captive to erroneous perceptions or beliefs?"

"Some men never do. Others discover the errors of their ways when they fail or are about to die from those errors. Seldom do they discover such errors except through some form of trial or pain. Even then, some do not."

"You could unsettle any man, master scholar," replied Rescalyn with a hearty laugh.

"I doubt it. Those who might be unsettled usually refuse to see."

"You are a cynical man, even for a scholar."

"When people disagree with what stands there for all to see, they often call those who observe events with accuracy cynical. One such might call you cynical for observing and acting on the fact that the hill holders will not capitulate to reason until you have effectively destroyed the majority of those with power."

Rescalyn laughed again, if with a slightly bitter edge.

Before the governor could speak, Quaeryt pressed on. "I have to ask . . . once you've destroyed Zorlyn and his holding and men, how many more will you have to obliterate before the remaining hill holders surrender? All of them?"

Rescalyn frowned. "One or two more, at the most. We have already destroyed three of the four most powerful holdings in the Boran Hills. Zorlyn's is the most powerful. On Samedi I received word that Commander Pulaskyr has done the same for the two strongest hill holders in the north. The remaining five hill holders in the south can likely muster together fewer men—and women and youths—than Zorlyn can alone. The remaining four in the north pose little problem. They'd just as soon be minor High Holders, but feared the others. We may have to destroy one more here in the south to prove that we will go after even the weaker hill holders. We could destroy them all, if need be. . . ."

"But you still must best Zorlyn."

"That we must . . . but I have a few surprises for him—and you, perhaps—as well."

"You have formidable talents, sir. You may well surprise me, but I will not underestimate you."

"You always have an interesting way of putting things, master scholar."

"I try to be accurate, sir. Or, as some might say, cynical."

"So . . . cynicism is merely accuracy when no one wishes to accept that accuracy?" Rescalyn shook his head.

"Sir!" A scout rode toward the governor.

"You may return to Sixth Battalion, scholar."

As Quaeryt eased his mount onto the shoulder and back toward Sixth Battalion, he reflected. There was no doubt that Rescalyn was brilliant and a good commander, and he inspired his men. Yet, beneath the genial facade, he was ruthless, far more so than Bhayar, and he certainly had continually deceived Bhayar, scarcely a laudable trait. Quaeryt smiled ruefully. There was also the simple fact that Bhayar, for all his impatience, had befriended Quaeryt and that he listened ... and might well help Quaeryt achieve his goals of better positions in Telaryn for scholars and imagers. Rescalyn's continual efforts to place Quaeryt in harm's way suggested all too strongly that Quaeryt would never be able to trust the governor.

Once Quaeryt eased the mare back alongside Skarpa at the head of Sixth Battalion, the major looked at the scholar, but did not speak.

"The governor wanted to know what I thought of Zorlyn's reply. . . ." Quaeryt went on to recount most of the rest of the conversation.

He had no more than finished summarizing what had been said when the ranker riding in front of them, the last rider in Fifth Battalion, stiffened, flailed, grabbing at his neck, and then slumped in the saddle, a crossbow quarrel through his throat.

Quaeryt felt the impact on his shields and glanced ahead and to the left. "They're up behind those bushes!"

"First squad!" snapped Meinyt from behind Quaeryt and Skarpa.

"Where, sir?"

Quaeryt looked around. The archer had vanished, but he'd marked where at least one man had been. "This way!" he called, urging the mare onto the shoulder of the road and then at an angle uphill.

"Follow the scholar!"

Quaeryt guided the mare through the low bushes that stretched for a good thirty yards back from the road, keeping his head down and close to the mare's neck. As he neared the top of the slope, the mare's hoofs slipped once in the slushy snow that remained in patches between the bushes, but Quaeryt kept riding toward where he'd seen the archer, then was surprised when three other figures, wearing white cloth over their leathers, rose out of the bushes and let fly their shafts.

They missed.

More archers rose, and Quaeryt kept riding. Another shaft struck his shields, but it must have been at an angle because he barely sensed the impact. He could feel the squad had almost caught up with him.

The archers turned and began to run.

One stumbled, and another tripped. The squad leader swept past Quaeryt, then leaned forward and slashed down across the back of one man's neck.

More arrows flew from the trees, and Quaeryt turned his mount directly toward the archers, but had covered no more than a few yards before the volleys stopped. He could hear the sounds of crackling underbrush and then of horses. He reined up, as did the rankers around him.

"First squad . . . return to the company!" called the squad leader, who then added, "Sir . . . we're not to follow into the trees once they stop shooting."

Quaeryt turned the mare, seeing two figures who had fallen amid the bushes and the remnants of slushy snow. Red stained their white overgarments.

One of the rankers bent down in the saddle, so easily that Quaeryt was amazed, and grabbed the crossbow from where it lay caught in the bushes beside one of the hill archers, while another retrieved a bow and quiver.

By the time the mare carried Quaeryt down the slope and forward to Sixth Company—which, with the rest of the column, had kept moving—Quaeryt wondered, exactly, why he'd done what he had.

Behind him, the squad leader reported to Meinyt, "We got two stragglers, sir, before the rest got to the woods and rode off."

Skarpa looked at Quaeryt. "Don't tell me you wouldn't make an officer."

"I said I wouldn't make a good one," Quaeryt said dryly. "A good officer would have described where to go in a few words. I couldn't find the words quickly enough. So the only thing I could do was lead."

"That's what officers do. They act when things go wrong. Anyone with any sense can handle matters when they go right."

Quaeryt wasn't about to argue, especially since, suddenly, large wet snowflakes were pelting the riders and mounts.

"Good thing they're large," observed Meinyt from behind Quaeryt and Skarpa. "The large flakes mean the storm won't last long. The small really cold ones mean a storm can last for days."

The heavy snow continued for almost a glass, until everything was covered, before it subsided into occasional flurries. For Quaeryt, that glass seemed all too long.

90

More scattered attacks occurred on Mardi afternoon
and evening, as did more snow flurries, but the regiment again took over a hamlet that evening, one supposedly situated less than two milles from the gates of
Zorlyn's holding. There were no attacks on Mardi
night, but that might have been because Rescalyn had
posted sentries and supporting patrols all the way
around the hamlet, which was named, unsurprisingly
to Quaeryt, Zaemla. It also might have been because
cold and snow flurries continued through the night.

Early on Meredi morning, with Rescalyn having
assigned Sixth Battalion as the vanguard, the regiment
moved out under high clouds, down from which
drifted occasional small flakes of snow. Even wearing
his browns and another shirt, Quaeryt was chilled after riding less than a quint.

His first glimpse of Zorlyn's holding affirmed his
suspicions, because he saw it from a good mille away,
situated on a low hill or ridge, facing to the south. The
stone-walled and slate-roofed structure was close to
as large as the central palace building of the Telaryn
Palace, but without its wings and all the other structures held within the walls that had sheltered the
Khanars. Although there were some ornamental trees
near the hold, and there looked to be, from the tops of
trees protruding, a walled garden adjoining the hold
on the southwest side, effectively there was no way to
approach the hold without being exposed. Halfway

up the hill and close to a half mille downhill from the lowest of the outbuildings was a stone wall of close to two yards in height that encircled the entire hill. Quaeryt could see but a single gate, which served the road on which the regiment approached, but there might have been another on the north side. Not only were the iron-grilled double gates closed, but large stones had been stacked in front of them to the height of the wall on each side.

Rows of archers stood on the sloping ground about fifty yards back of the wall and gate. But Quaeryt did not see any other men-at-arms, not that he doubted that there were a good thousand or more somewhere nearby.

The regiment halted some three hundred yards from the gate and wall. Horn signals followed until the horse battalions were in formation side by side. What Quaeryt didn't understand, though, was why they remained in files of two, rather than with the five-man front used for attack. For another half quint, the regiment waited.

Then two strange-looking wagons appeared. The long wagon beds were filled with bags of some sort, and at the rear of each wagon was a wooden shield that rose a good two yards. Behind the shield were six horses, with far wider spacing than in a normal hitch, and a single teamster rode astride one of the rear horses. The wagons moved forward along the road no faster than a man could walk, creaking and groaning. As they approached the wall, the archers let fly, but the arrows either missed or stuck in the timber shield or the bags in the wagon bed. One wagon turned gradually and slightly to the right and one to the left until they were lined up to reach the wall on each side of the blocked gates.

More arrows flew, but the wagons continued to

move forward slowly until they reached the wall. Then they stopped. For a time, it appeared to Quaeryt that nothing happened, even as arrows sleeted down, but were blocked by the wooden shields that were beginning to resemble hedgehogs. He realized that there were two teamsters and that they were doing something with the hitches and turning the big dray horses. Then the horses began to pull again—except that the wagons did not move, but began to tilt until the front end lifted and kept rising until it was as high as the wall. At the same time, the wagon bed stretched.

Quaeryt's mouth opened. Indeed, Rescalyn had some surprises prepared. Then another set of planks emerged, winched from somewhere, that began to extend over the wall. The scholar watched as both wagons became ramps.

"Fifth Battalion! Forward! By twos!"

The companies of Fifth Battalion galloped to the wall, then slowed, as each rider guided his mount up the ramp and then down the other side.

The archers targeted the riders, and several were hit. One mount and rider went down on the ramp, then slid to the bottom, but Fifth Battalion kept coming.

"Sixth Battalion! Forward! By twos!"

As he rode forward, Quaeryt could see a flood of men hurrying downhill from one of the structures near the top of the knoll, but they had close to a half mille to cover. At the same time, more than a few riders and mounts from Fifth Battalion had fallen, but the others were riding toward the archers, and the closer they got, the less time the bowmen had to nock and release the next volley.

He glanced to his right, where he saw two engineers' wagons being driven toward the gate, with a ranker holding a wide shield in front of the teamster.

There had to be more engineers in the wagons, and Quaeryt could only hope that they were going to try to sap the gates or create more ways for the regiment to get through or over the walls.

Except that will be too late for you.

Quaeryt forced his concentration back to the road and Meinyt in front of him, trying to ignore the fact that arrows had to be falling around him. Then, before he expected it, the wagon ramp was ahead of him.

"One mount at a time! Pass it back!" ordered Meinyt.

Quaeryt could feel the ramp shake and shiver as the mare climbed up it, and at the top an arrow—more likely a quarrel from the force—smashed into his shields so hard that he rocked back in the saddle, barely keeping his seat as the mare carried him down. He managed to yell back, "One mount at a time! Pass it back!" before he was down and off the ramp, heading toward the archers who were retreating in stages, while still loosing shafts.

He was scarcely ten yards from the ramp when he heard an ominous crack, and then a yell, and an agonized scream from a mount. He forced himself to concentrate on the hillside ahead, a slope gentle enough that it rose perhaps one yard in every ten—steep for a wagon, but not that steep for a man or mount.

"On your squad leaders!" ordered Meinyt.

Half-staff out and now in hand, Quaeryt just followed the older captain uphill and toward the left side of the archers still loosing shafts. The slight vibration of his shields suggested that another arrow had grazed them.

The armsmen who had been hurrying down the slope halted fifty yards or so above the archers, some of whom were already beginning to fall to the blows from the leading riders in the remnants of Fifth Battalion, others of whom were retreating uphill. The newly arrived defenders immediately formed a solid line some four or five men deep that stretched across a front some two hundred yards wide. They all carried small round shields—larger than bucklers and seemingly strapped to the forearm—with blades longer than sabres but shorter than hand-and-a-half blades, a combination Quaeryt had never seen, but then there were many aspects of arms about which he knew nothing.

At the sound of a tattoo on a bass drum, the remaining archers fled, running up the gentle slope to try to escape the several hundred riders remaining from Fifth Battalion, who in turn immediately did their best to pursue and cut down the fleeing bowmen.

"Sixth Battalion! At the defenders!" ordered Skarpa, from somewhere to Quaeryt's right.

Quaeryt understood. Once the defenders let the archers slip through their ranks, the bowmen could move uphill, turn, and again target the attacking Telaryn forces. He took a quick glance over his shoulder back downslope. As he had feared, one of the ramps had collapsed, and all other riders were using the remaining ramp while the engineers worked frantically to clear the stones and open the gate.

He urged the mare forward, but found most of Meinyt's squad moving uphill faster than he was. So he angled the mare to the left more, in order to stay out of the way of better riders, and readied the staff. The defenders worked in pairs—one attacking the rider, and the other trying to disable his mount. Seeing that, as he rode toward the defenders, whose breath was creating a fog of sorts along the hillside, he extended his shields, feeling the effort. Yet what else could he do? He certainly wasn't agile enough to lean forward in the saddle and strike anyone trying to slash the mare's legs.

Before he realized that he'd closed on the defenders, two jumped toward him, one high and one low. He let the shields take the impact, then contracted them enough that he could hammer the one aiming at the mare, then brought the staff up in an ungainly thrust, so awkward that the defender didn't see it coming as his blade came down on Quaeryt's shielded arm. Even as the defender collapsed, Quaeryt almost dropped his staff, because the sword had slammed into his shields so forcefully that his entire body shook for a moment.

Another shock shivered him, as yet another defender attacked while he tried to clear his head.

Not supposed to be like this. . . .

He tried to turn the mare, but found himself in a press of bodies, those of mounts and men, with blades being used more like crowbars than cutting weapons, and his shields being hammered more often than not while he tried to use the staff. Before that long the hammering on his shields ceased, as more and more defenders dropped or, wounded, did their best to scramble or crawl out of the way. More than a few fell victim to hoofs as the companies of Sixth Battalion pressed up the slope.

Another wave of defenders advanced downhill, taking a position some fifty yards behind the lowest line of armsmen, the last of whom were slowly being separated and cut down or wounded. Abruptly, at the sound of a tattoo on a bass drum, the remaining defenders on the lower part of the hill all turned and turned and ran uphill, but at an angle, toward one end of the new defense formation or the other.

Fifth and Sixth Battalion, as well as Fourth, and then Eighth, continued uphill toward the secondary line of defense. Quaeryt thought there were almost as many new defenders as there had been in the last line.

How many armsmen does Zorlyn have?

Quaeryt had the feeling that they'd already faced more than two thousand . . . and that meant that Zorlyn had more troops than the old Khanars had mustered. No wonder the Khanars and High Holders hadn't wanted to press the hill holders that much.

Regardless of what he wanted, the press of riders was carrying him toward the next formation of defenders, and to try to fight his way clear would make him far too obvious. Yet he was breathing heavily, and his head was throbbing. He compromised by riding with the others, but not pressing to get to the front.

Once more, the defenders attempted to cut mounts down, and the attacking Telaryn troopers tried to cut down the men attacking them, rather than the mounts, before lower-down defenders could get to the mounts. Most of the time, the riders were the more successful . . . but not always, as a mount went down in front of Quaeryt.

The mare stumbled, but caught her balance and danced to the left, where Quaeryt used the staff to good effect on a defender trying to slash at her forelegs, and then on his partner. He ended up using the staff to block blows from hitting his shields, because every time a blade struck the shields it hurt, and he felt as though his ability to hold shields was draining away, quint by quint, if not moment by moment.

He kept warding off blows, but saw that they were coming less frequently, and that Sixth Battalion and the other battalions had turned the tide and were beginning once more to thin the defenders to the point where they would have to either break or be slaughtered where they stood.

A massive bass drumroll echoed down the hillside.

Quaeryt couldn't help but look up. Yet another set of fighters, all in black, rode into sight at the top of the hill—under a banner with a black "Z" encircled in gold. Quaeryt swallowed. There had to be almost the equivalent of more than another battalion in that group, over five hundred riders. He glanced downhill. Surrounded by Seventh Battalion, Rescalyn and his command group had ridden through where the main gates had been—Quaeryt hadn't even known that the engineers had gotten them open or removed them—and uphill toward the battle.

Clearly the governor felt he needed to commit every man to meet the latest wave of defenders, but Quaeryt couldn't help but worry. *What if Zorlyn has even more defenders concealed somewhere else?*

As Zorlyn's elite force—if that was what they were—swept downhill, Quaeryt noted that all wore helms, breastplates, and greaves, and that their sabres were curved somewhat. *Heavy cavalry.* Where that phrase came from he didn't know. He also saw that there was one man, in the center, whose breastplate bore a "Z." Zorlyn himself? Or his eldest son?

Quaeryt would have wagered that that it was Zorlyn himself, but who would know until the battle was decided one way or another?

At the sounds of the bass drum, the center of the defenders parted, and the heavy cavalry knifed toward the center of the Telaryn forces.

At that moment, flights of arrows arched into the heavy cavalry.

Quaeryt glanced around, and finally located the company of Telaryn archers to the side of the slope, where they had apparently been for a time. The arrows cut into the heavy cavalry, cutting down scores and slowing the charge until the rebel riders were within yards of the Telaryn forces.

Even so, the rebel riders pushed back the Telaryn forces for some thirty yards before slowing to little more than a walk, and then less than that, as Seventh Battalion reached the edges of the center.

For the next half quint, blades battled blades, and Quaeryt just tried to protect the mare and to keep from getting struck directly by either footmen or the handfuls of heavy cavalry that had moved out of the center of the heaviest fighting.

Then, again, from the top of the hill came the sound of hoofs. Quaeryt glanced up, fearing to see more riders in black. Instead, he beheld the ensign of Telaryn and at least three more battalions of riders as they charged down on the rear of Zorlyn's forces.

Commander Zirkyl's forces . . . held in reserve and coming in from the north when Zorlyn had committed everything.

Seventh Battalion—and Rescalyn—continued to fight uphill toward the center of Zorlyn's forces—and the "Z" banner, and Zorlyn himself.

Quaeryt forced himself to concentrate on where he was—just in time to see two riders with breastplates bearing down on Meinyt, who was defending himself against three men on foot.

Quaeryt urged the mare forward at an angle to the hill rider closest to Meinyt, bracing the staff against the pommel and turning it at the last moment. The one attacker swayed back in his saddle, and Quaeryt jabbed at the second one, not hitting him squarely, but hard enough that he was past Meinyt before he regained full control of his blade.

Quaeryt turned the mare, catching sight of the center of the hillside field, where the forces around Zorlyn surged inward, and horseman by horseman, the defenders fell. Yet the black-clad riders fought as though they faced the Namer and his demons.

And they probably believe that.

Did Quaeryt dare? Did he dare not?

Quaeryt urged the mare downhill slightly and then tried to make his way eastward toward the remaining thick of the battle.

Ahead and uphill of him, the "Z" banner waved and dipped, then rose again, as if it had been handed to another ensign carrier. The knot of black-clad riders around it was getting smaller, perhaps as few as fifty.

Another black-clad rider charged Quaeryt. The scholar barely got his staff up to block the vicious slash . . . but the rider handled the sabre so well that the staff seemed to bend in Quaeryt's hands and he barely could hold it in hands that felt numb as his attacker rode past. For a moment, Quaeryt was in a space where he was almost alone.

Where was Rescalyn? Quaeryt found that he could barely see . . . that he was squinting to make out where the governor was. He concentrated and squinted harder. He finally made out the Seventh Battalion banner, and well back of it, the muscular figure of the governor, well protected by his personal guard.

Quaeryt tried to shift his attention to the "Z" banner, where only a handful of black-clad riders surrounded Zorlyn, if indeed he was the rider with the marked breastplate.

Was the outcome certain? Did he dare wait any longer?

His mouth was so dry that he couldn't even swallow, and pain jabbed through his eyes like needles *Where is Rescalyn?* He struggled to find the governor, but his eyes wouldn't focus.

You have to find him. Otherwise . . .

His eyes fixed on the Seventh Battalion banner, then slowly moved to the well-guarded governor.

Quaeryt focused all his energy into what he had to do.

As he imaged the quarrel toward its target, his shields vanished, and he felt as though the mightiest sabre he'd ever tried to block had shattered them, and turned his concentration into jelly. He swayed in the saddle, just trying to hold his seat.

Then another black-clad rider plunged out of the contracting mass around Zorlyn and aimed himself directly at Quaeryt, his sabre flashing toward the scholar.

Quaeryt threw up the staff, feeling that he was too late . . . too slow . . .

The sabre caught the staff, ripped it backward . . . and Quaeryt with it . . . and he felt himself being hurled backward off the mare.

He heard someone yelling, but though he knew the words, they were unintelligible.

Then . . . he felt nothing.

91

The next thing Quaeryt remembered was lying somewhere while someone did something to his arm. That
created so much pain that sounds and sights blurred
into a haze. When that blurred haze finally began to
fade, he was surrounded by darkness, lying on blankets with a heavy weight on his chest. That weight, he
realized, was his left arm, encased in something. Slowly,
he managed to sit up, but every movement caused
pain somewhere, especially when he moved his arm.

"The scholar's awake. Tell the major," said someone.

Quaeryt couldn't tell who spoke because it was
dark and because his vision remained somewhat
blurred.

After a time, a figure approached. "You're finally
back with us." Skarpa sat on a stool that he'd dragged
from somewhere.

"I've been here. I just didn't know I was. Where are
we? What happened?" Quaeryt's voice was hoarse
and cracked now and again. He hoped he hadn't been
yelling or screaming.

"We've got a barn. Maybe it was a sheep shed. Better than some barracks the men have had at times.
Zorlyn—his place is better than some High Holders'
estates. Maybe better than any of them."

"It looked that way. How bad . . . did we lose too
many?"

"More than a battalion's worth. There'll be more

that won't make it. Sixth Battalion . . . we took it pretty heavy. Well over a hundred—a hundred eight at last count, with five who'll be fortunate to pull through, and another thirty with wounds that should. Like you."

Quaeryt looked down at the heavy wooden splint bound in strips of cloth.

"The surgeon said you were easy. He said it was a clean break, and that might heal before all the bruises you've got."

His arm might have suffered a clean break, but it felt as though the Namer was jabbing red-hot pokers into his arm. *You don't believe in the Namer. . . .* Maybe not, but that was the way it felt.

"The last thing I remember, I was trying to block the attack of one of the black riders. I didn't do it very well. Zorlyn was still fighting, but there weren't many of his personal guards left. What happened after that?"

Skarpa snorted. "It was mostly over by then, even if we didn't know it. Both Gauswn and Meinyt saw you go down. There was some sort of flash around you, Gauswn said. He was seeing things. No one else did, but that happens. He fought through some of those black-clad guards to get you." Skarpa snorted. "That was when Zorlyn and his guards almost broke free. Might have, too, except Gauswn's company got in the way. It wasn't what the governor planned—I think he wanted to capture the bastard—but they broke through the guards. Gauswn actually killed Zorlyn. He said he had to . . . or they would have trampled you."

Quaeryt wasn't about to say anything. That wasn't quite what he'd anticipated.

"Everything was a mess, then, but Myskyl and Zirkyl took over and settled things down."

"They took over?" asked Quaeryt, trying to sound confused.

"You didn't know? Oh . . . how would you? One of their last archers put a shaft right through Rescalyn's chest. A quarrel, really. I didn't see any crossbowmen, but it was the same kind of quarrel they've been using all along. That's what the commander said."

"You might recall that I'm familiar with those quarrels," Quaeryt said.

"One of them got you in the chest. You were more fortunate than the governor. He died right there. Didn't even get to see that everything worked out the way he planned it."

"He planned well. I couldn't believe those wagons that turned into ramps."

"There were two on the north side, too."

A ranker appeared with a large mug. "Here's the ale for the scholar, sir."

"You need to drink this and rest," said Skarpa. "We won't be doing much else for a while, anyway. It's snowing again, already almost boot-deep. Good thing the larders here are full. Zorlyn didn't think he'd ever lose."

"The hill holders never did before." *Not until now.*

"First time for everything." Skarpa rose.

Quaeryt took the mug in his good hand and began to sip. He appreciated Skarpa's sending for the ale. He wasn't sure he could have walked any distance at all, let alone gotten to his feet. He didn't even care that it was ale and not lager.

92

The snow lasted for only another day and tapered off near late afternoon on Jeudi. The sun returned on Vendrei, warmer than in days, and began to melt away everything that had accumulated. Vendrei afternoon, Quaeryt received a summons to meet with Myskyl, who was acting marshal for the regiment—or what remained of it.

The scholar limped up the hill, slowly following his escort, because his bad leg was worse, and his "good" leg was bruised in places all the way down from hip to just above the ankle. There were bruises across his chest and thighs as well, already turning yellow-purple, and others in places he couldn't see but certainly could feel.

When he reached what could only be called a manor house or mansion, even a small palace, he was escorted into the study by a junior squad leader, a study every bit as large as the one the governor had used at the Telaryn Palace, and at least as lavishly appointed, with dark paneled walls, and deep green hangings.

Myskyl turned from where he had been looking out the bay window overlooking the walled garden and walked back to the ornately carved goldenwood desk. "Please be seated, scholar." He sat behind the desk and waited for Quaeryt to ease himself into the cushioned wooden armchair before speaking. "I'm not an envoy or a courtier, scholar. I'm a soldier. I don't pretend to be anything else. I speak what I think. You present a puzzle. You're as brave and as resourceful as any junior officer I have, more so than most. Your courage is unquestioned. You've saved countless other officers and men. Yet . . . the governor was troubled by you. So am I. I'm also disturbed by the fact that he was killed by a crossbow quarrel at the end of the battle when no one saw any archers. No one has yet found a crossbow anywhere on the field. I'm even more troubled because that quarrel went straight through the plate the governor wore under his shirt and jacket. That can happen. It did happen. But it has to happen at close range."

I imaged the quarrel through plate? No wonder I lost shields . . . a wonder I'm alive. "I don't know what to say, sir. You seem to think I might know something about his death. Major Skarpa can tell you that I did not even know that the governor had died when I finally could think and talk again."

"Strange things happen around you, scholar. Tell me why you are here. I know you told the governor. But tell me."

"It's no secret I was sent by Lord Bhayar. It's no secret that Lord Bhayar is concerned about the costs and the numbers of soldiers required to keep order in Tilbor. It's no secret that Lord Bhayar believed that Governor Rescalyn was an outstanding commander and a good governor. The way he planned and conducted the campaign against the hill holders proves that point. I reported all that. Well . . . I did, except for the last part of the campaign, but that's exactly what I will report."

"The governor said something to the effect that you were always everything you said you were, but that you were more than that. What else are you?" Myskyl's voice was cool.

"I am what I am, sir. Many men are more than what they say they are. Governor Rescalyn was more than he said he was. You know that. I am truly sorry he was killed. He was a great commander, and that is how he will be remembered. It is also how he should be remembered." Quaeryt smiled faintly. "Don't you think so?"

Myskyl was silent, but his eyes never left Quaeryt. Finally, he cleared his throat. "How did you manage it?"

"I managed nothing, sir. If you will ask every single person who saw me on the field, you will find that I was struck down before the last part of the fighting ended." Quaeryt looked down at the heavy splint.

Myskyl shook his head. "I have asked everyone. They all say what you have told me. Yet the governor is dead. He was killed by a hill holder quarrel that should not have been able to penetrate his plate. It did. I do not believe in coincidences."

"Nor do I, sir. Yet it happened. Sometimes, things happen that we cannot explain. One can deny that they should have, but they did. One can claim it was the work of the Namer or the Nameless, but nothing changes."

"No . . . they do not." Myskyl moistened his lips. "What will you do now?"

"Why are you asking, scholar?"

"I still have to report to Lord Bhayar."

"So you do." A short bitter laugh followed before the commander continued. "As the governor planned, I've sent messages to the remaining hill holders. I sent a company with each messenger as well."

"Will they agree to terms?"

"Rescalyn didn't think they would. I think they might. We'll see."

"What are you going to do with Zorlyn's holding, sir?"

"That's up to the princeps. He's the acting governor. He may not even know yet, unless the couriers have reached him, but it's his decision. After we finish with the other hill holders, I've recommended that we move two or three battalions here and make it a permanent base. We'd have control, and all the crop tithes would support the base here. We'd have to reduce the numbers at Boralieu. The lands of the other holdings will become Lord Bhayar's."

"That sounds like a good plan, sir."

"It was the governor's."

"He was a good commander and a good governor." *Just one who was far too ambitious.*

"He was." Myskyl stood. "You'll be going back to Boralieu with the rest of the wounded when the roads firm up. From there, when the fighting's over, one way or another, you'll go back to Tilbora."

"Yes, sir." Quaeryt struggled to his feet.

"I'd hope there won't be any more strange occurrences."

"So do I, sir." Quaeryt inclined his head, then turned. He could feel the commander's eyes on his back as he walked out of the study.

He hadn't liked what he'd done. But he'd seen enough to know just where Rescalyn's unbridled ambition would lead, both for Bhayar and for himself.

. . . and yet . . . would Rescalyn have made a better ruler of Telaryn than Bhayar?

Quite possibly, if he merely succeeded Bhayar, reflected Quaeryt, as he limped back toward Sixth Battalion, but what he would have had to do to consolidate his rule would have negated his abilities. And . . . Bhayar was a good ruler, for all his faults. The cost of a civil war to everyone, and the deaths and the unrest, would have far outweighed the benefits of a ruler who *might* have been a better ruler. Then, too, there was the problem that Rescalyn had no heirs, and succession was yet another problem, while Bhayar already had two sons.

The risks for Telaryn—and you—were too great.

He kept walking.

93

A sunny Samedi followed Vendrei, and an even warmer Solayi followed Samedi—and Myskyl, thankfully, did not request that Quaeryt offer a homily at the evening services. Quaeryt avoided attending, afraid that he would hear either a eulogy of some sort to Rescalyn or thanks for the great victory over Zorlyn. While it had been a significant victory, and the one that, for all intents and purposes, broke the power of the hill holders, even if Myskyl might have to ravage another holding, going to those services would have reminded Quaeryt of all the costs that were never mentioned . . . and his own part in how matters turned out. So he remained with those of Sixth Battalion who did not attend.

On Mardi morning, a column of the riding wounded, those, like Quaeryt, who were on the way to recovery, left Zorlyn's holding and made their way back to Boralieu. Quaeryt rode an almost-broken-down gelding, since no one seemed to know where the mare was—or if she had even survived the battle. She'd carried him through so much . . . and to have her vanish . . . He tried not to think about that . . . as well as other matters—at least not until he felt better.

They arrived at Boralieu well after sunset on Meredi, but before total darkness. Quaeryt had not heard whether the remaining hill holders had agreed to terms when they left, and no one of the small contingent that remained at Boralieu had any word on what had occurred when they arrived.

Over the next two days, Quaeryt forced himself to write up a report for Bhayar, one that summarized exactly what had happened during that part of the campaign in which he had participated, but which said nothing at all about his personal efforts. Between the physical effort of writing it one-handed, which took more care than he had anticipated, and the mental effort of seeking exactly the right words and phrases, the report took far longer than he had thought it would.

Because the mess was more suited to writing, because he felt the walls of his small quarters were pressing in on him, because the bunk was uncomfortable for sitting and the chairs in the mess were far more comfortable than the single rickety one in his quarters, he spent most of his time in the officers' mess. Late on Vendrei afternoon, Quaeryt was again sitting at the long table there when he heard riders outside in the courtyard. He debated getting up to see who they were, and if they had news, but decided he'd find out before long. Besides, walking any distance was still painful, especially as the day wore on.

He saw several captains and undercaptains he did not know coming and going, and that suggested that a fair-sized contingent had returned. In turn, that indicated a high likelihood that the remaining hill holders had capitulated . . . but that was only an indication.

Almost a glass later, a ranker peered into the mess from the door. "Scholar Quaeryt, sir?"

"Yes?"

"Commander Zirkyl would like to see you, sir. He's in his study."

"I'll be right there." Quaeryt rose carefully, then followed the ranker down the adjoining corridor to the open study door.

"Come in, scholar."

Quaeryt did close the door behind him, then settled into one of the chairs in front of Zirkyl's table desk. "I did not know you were among those who returned, sir."

"I brought back those who had accompanied me from here to deal with the hill holders at Zorlyn's holding. We arrived back here less than a glass ago. On Jeudi, Commander Myskyl received word from the last of the hill holders, accepting the terms he offered. Once that happened, he dispatched us." Zirkyl looked directly at Quaeryt. "You've been sending reports to Lord Bhayar, I understand?"

"Yes, sir."

"Commander Myskyl's couriers will be leaving here tomorrow morning, one for Tilbora to inform the acting governor, and one to Solis to report on the result of the campaign against the hill holders. Commander Myskyl asked me to tell you that you are welcome to have the courier carry your report to Solis as well. If you wish to do so, you should have it ready by seventh glass."

"It is largely written, sir, except I did not know that the remaining holders had accepted terms."

"I doubt that they were overjoyed . . . but defying the commander now would have been turning bare backs to the Namer."

"Where should I bring the report? To the courtyard by the gates?"

"By the guardhouse. I'll let the courier know that you will have a dispatch for him."

"Thank you, sir."

"Don't thank me. According to the commander, Lord Bhayar's the one who should be thanking you." Zirkyl offered a sad smile. "That is all I wanted to tell you. I do have a few other matters . . ."

"Yes, sir." Quaeryt stood, as gracefully as he could, then turned and limped from the commander's study and headed back toward the mess.

While he would have liked to send a letter to Vaelora, he decided that asking a special courier to carry it would not be a good idea, besides which, he frankly wasn't certain what he would—or should— write, given the way matters stood in Tilbor. Or if he could find the right words in the time he had.

94

What with one thing and another, almost a week passed before Quaeryt joined Sixth Battalion on its return to Tilbora the following Jeudi. Once more, he rode with Skarpa, still awkwardly because the splinted arm, even in a sling, tended to unbalance him, although he had been reunited with the mare.

"How did you find her?" he had asked when one of Skarpa's rankers had led her out to him before they left Boralieu.

"I didn't," Skarpa had replied. "Gauswn did. While

we were waiting for the hill holders to decide, he had his men search for her. It took a couple of days to find her. Seventh Battalion had her. He said it wasn't right that she wasn't with you."

"I do appreciate it." He'd reminded himself to thank the undercaptain with more than words, for both saving his life and finding the mare, although he had ridden across the courtyard to Gauswn and offered those words of gratitude almost immediately.

Gauswn had insisted that he'd only done what was right and went on to say, "You'll change things, sir. You will. Like Rholan."

That comparison had appalled Quaeryt, but he couldn't say that, not when he likely owed the undercaptain his life . . . and the mare. All he'd been able to do was reiterate his thanks and gratitude. But Gauswn's words and worshipful attitude had preyed on him throughout the journey.

Finally, on Vendrei afternoon, as Sixth Battalion turned off the river road and headed directly along the back road toward the Telaryn Palace, Quaeryt again turned to Skarpa.

"I've been thinking about Gauswn. I worry that he thinks I'm something that I'm not. I'm just a scholar trying to do the best I can."

Skarpa laughed. "I'll grant that you're a scholar. I'll not grant that you're just a scholar. No officer and man in Sixth Battalion would say you're *just* a scholar. You're as good a chorister as many, and you're a better officer than many who wear the bars. There's a lot more I don't know. I do know that Commander Myskyl wouldn't cross you."

"He wouldn't cross me? I'm a near-penniless scholar." Quaeryt laughed.

"You were sent by Lord Bhayar. You get letters from his family . . ."

Quaeryt managed not to wince. Did the entire regiment know that?

". . . and you've survived battles and wounds. I recall you also got through storms and a shipwreck. Myskyl knows that. He wouldn't cross you for all the new-minted silvers he found in Zorlyn's strong room."

"Didn't he have a silver mine?" asked Quaeryt, deciding to change the subject as quickly as he could, especially since he'd wondered about the Ecoliae's receipt of new-minted silvers. "Someone said . . ."

"He does. Or he did."

"And he was minting his own silvers?"

Skarpa looked quizzically at Quaeryt. "One of the majors said they found coin dies. Why does it matter? Silver's silver."

"It would help explain how Zorlyn could afford to pay so many armsmen, for one thing." *And for another, it would explain why Rescalyn needed to take Zorlyn's lands and holding.*

Skarpa nodded. "It would. Some of us wondered about that, even with all his lands."

Quaeryt's thinking about Zorlyn brought to mind Zarxes. "Do you know if they found two scholars among the captives there?"

"The two that ran off from the scholarium? Can't say that I do."

Quaeryt wondered if he'd ever find out, or if Alkiabys and Zarxes had been part of the heavy cavalry that had been largely killed at the end of the battle. He shook his head.

There are always things left unresolved, no matter how much you want to know how they turn out. That's life.

After a long silence, Skarpa finally spoke again. "Tell me. What will you do now?"

"I don't know. I'm only supposed to be the scholar assistant to the princeps until close to the end of winter. I'm supposed to return to Solis before the first day of spring."

"No offense . . . but should you be traveling before that arm has healed more? And all those bruises?"

"Some of the bruises have healed."

"Not all, I'd wager."

"Not all of them," Quaeryt admitted. Not wanting to dwell on the possibility of spending a long cold winter in Tilbora, he asked, "What will Myskyl do with the regiment now? Has he said?"

"That's up to the princeps—I'd guess he's the acting governor for now. He'll need to step up recruiting. That won't be a problem now. Some of the senior squad leaders will be trained to be undercaptains, maybe even a few squad leaders."

"And you?"

"I'll keep being a major. What else do I know? It's a better life than many." Skarpa laughed. "I've got some golds put by, enough to live quiet-like if I go out on an injury stipend or make it to full-stipend age. We'll all get battle pay. You, too, I'd guess."

Quaeryt hadn't even thought about pay or golds— but he hadn't drawn his pay in something like two months. At half a gold a week—even with the deductions for the mess—that would total more than four golds.

He smiled, if faintly. The golds had never meant that much to him, but that was probably because he'd never wed or had family to think about. And, the way his life was going, he never would.

95

Quaeryt needed to report to Princeps Straesyr. So, on Samedi morning, just after seventh glass, he made his way from "his" study to the anteroom to the princeps's study.

"He thought you might be here early," replied Vhorym, in a manner more pleasant than Quaeryt recalled. "You can go on in, sir."

"Thank you." Although his arm was still splinted and in a sling, it felt somewhat better, but every movement still hurt as Quaeryt limped into the princeps's study and closed the door behind himself.

You'd think you'd feel better than this after two weeks. . . .

The first thing Quaeryt noted was that Straesyr no longer wore a tunic. Instead, he wore a marshal's uniform. The second thing that the scholar noted was that the acting governor appeared far more comfortable in the uniform.

Straesyr did not rise, but gestured to the chairs before the desk. "You're still recovering, I see."

"It's likely to be a while, sir." Quaeryt eased himself into the nearest chair.

"I've received several reports from Commander Myskyl, and the few remaining hill holders have agreed to terms and have even tendered part of their tariffs as evidence of good faith."

As evidence of fear, I suspect. "I had not heard

about their payments, sir. I did know that they had
agreed to terms."

"They did indeed. Myskyl sent along their letters of
agreement. Every one of them practically groveled.
Not surprising."

"Do you know how the High Holders feel?"

"The ones I've heard from are pleased, naturally."
Straesyr's lips curled into a sardonic smile. "I've had
three inquiries about purchasing the lands of the rebel
holders. I wrote back that, if they wished, they could
inquire of Lord Bhayar, since the lands were now his.
I've heard nothing further." He paused. "I also received an interesting report from the commander
about you. You were most effective in battle. What
was also unusual, apparently, was the difficulty the
rebels had in actually striking you, and the fact that
you managed to evade most blows you did not seem
to see coming . . ."

*Did Myskyl interrogate every ranker in Sixth Bat-
talion?*

". . . Several officers seem to think that you're under
the protection of the Nameless, for all that you protest
that you don't know if the Nameless exists. Yet you are
a most effective chorister in delivering homilies. Everyone the commander talked to insists that you asked for
no special treatment." Straesyr paused, then asked,
"What are you? Why are you here? Most important,
what really happened to the governor?"

"I'm sure you already know that, sir. He was hit in
the chest with a crossbow quarrel. The quarrel was
the kind the hill holders used, but no one could find
who did it."

"That's another question. Who could put a quarrel
through solid plate armor? Your name suggests it
all—there are just too many questions around you."

"That may be, sir, but there are the same questions around everyone. There were as many questions around the governor, but no one even thought of asking them."

"Rescalyn was a good commander and strategist. Do you even understand, scholar . . ."

"I understand quite well, sir. He understood that the hill holders could fight forever against company-sized or even battalion-sized attacks. He built the regiment to the size necessary to destroy the major hill holds, if not more, and expanded the engineers. While he was doing that, he was giving the hill holders the illusion that they were holding their own, but he was consolidating support for himself and Telaryn everywhere outside of the hills, and using the hill holders as an example of brigandry. Then he attacked and destroyed the major holds one after the other. He removed the key holds . . . and then sent—well, Commander Myskyl did, but it was the governor's plan—terms to those few surviving, demanding tribute and submission—or their destruction—and their agreement to follow the rules governing all the High Holders. After he took Zorlyn's hold and destroyed most of his supporters, the others, all of them much weaker, capitulated."

"Will they remain so?"

"You know the answer to that, sir. You may have to marshal the regiment once more against some recalcitrants to prove the point. But . . . if you make that point to all the officers . . . you may not. Word will get out." Quaeryt paused, then added, "Rescalyn's strategy wouldn't have worked in a warmer clime, because the fighters could live off the land after the regiment left, but the winters are so harsh and long here that without stockpiles and supplies, that's not feasible—and that's why Waerfyl, Saentaryn, Zorlyn, and the others fought rather than scattering into the hills. . . ."

"You saw this . . . when?"

"Some of it within weeks of arriving . . . some of it not until the campaign was well along."

"It's a tragedy that one of the last hill brigands was able to kill Rescalyn . . . if that's what happened. Do you know how to use a crossbow?"

"I've never even picked one up, sir. As all the rankers and officers will tell you, I can barely defend myself with a half-staff. I've been wounded and injured twice and feel fortunate to have survived." Quaeryt wasn't about to raise the point that he'd been forced to learn to defend himself because Rescalyn had detailed him to assignments with Sixth Battalion that had continually exposed him to danger.

A flash of puzzlement crossed Straesyr's face.

Quaeryt continued. "Rescalyn's life ended with the reputation as a great strategist, an excellent commander, and a good governor. That's how he will be remembered, and everyone will regard his death as a tragedy. That's how it should be, rather than with Telaryn being torn apart."

"You don't really think—"

"Governor," Quaeryt said firmly, "and you are governor in fact, at least until Bhayar decides otherwise, you know as well as I do what would have happened with the near-fanatical loyalty of the regiment to Rescalyn. He was a hero. It's best left there."

"Lord Bhayar is fortunate to have scholars such as you, Master Quaeryt." Straesyr's voice was surprisingly mild, almost at odds with the words he spoke.

"No, sir. Lord Bhayar is wise enough to use the talents of those who serve him loyally." Quaeryt had a certain doubt that Bhayar always did so, but he had no doubts whatsoever that what Rescalyn had intended, after rebuilding the "regiment," would have created far more death and devastation than anyone could have envisioned.

"How much of this is Lord Bhayar and how much is because of you? You never trusted Rescalyn from the first, did you?"

"Let us just say that I worried about his ambitions being greater than were in the interests of Lord Bhayar."

"How did you know?"

"From his acts, his behavior, and even from the books he read. He wanted to be another Hengyst."

"You may well be right, but where is the proof?"

"Rescalyn was far too brilliant to leave a written plan, or even footprints. But if one looks at the way he reorganized the regiment without ever letting on to Lord Bhayar actually how many men he had or how every dispatch emphasized in one way or another, never overplayed, the dangers of the hill holders . . ."

"That kind of proof is thin indeed."

"And the way in which he used your wife's safety against you." Rather than reveal how he knew that, Quaeryt went on, "I suspected that in the way you mentioned family. Then, there was the warning you gave me, telling me to take care at a time when I wasn't going into battle. More than anything, it was that the sum total of all the little things pointed to one end. He never mentioned in any dispatch the way he'd reorganized the regiment on the company and battalion level. Why did he leave the scholars alone when he knew their ties and links? His excessive efforts to build personal loyalty among the officers and men . . . his failure to ever mention Lord Bhayar to them . . . all those things . . ."

Straesyr shook his head. "You're a dangerous man,

scholar, to deduce so much, so accurately, from such small indicators."

"What about you?" Quaeryt asked bluntly.

"Me? I've been ambitious, the Nameless knows, but I'd be more than pleased to end my days as governor here, not that such is likely now . . . and my family would be as well. That would never have suited Rescalyn."

"You don't know what Lord Bhayar will do. For what it's worth, my words about you will be favorable."

Straesyr's smile was both rueful and wintry.

Quaeryt waited.

"That leaves the matter of what to do with you."

"My term as your assistant lasts until the end of Finitas." Not that Quaeryt wanted to stay in Tilbor even that long.

"That's not exactly true," replied Straesyr. "The letter from Lord Bhayar said that you were to be rèleased in time to reach Solis before the end of winter. According to the surgeon—I did ask about your condition—you shouldn't be riding as much as you did. You'll be here longer than you had hoped. I don't have to release you by the end of Finitas."

Quaeryt didn't answer immediately. Winter in Tilbor? What would Bhayar say? He'd suggested that Quaeryt might as well stay in Tilbor if he didn't return by the end of winter. But how could Quaeryt even meet that deadline if he didn't leave before winter truly set in?

Before Quaeryt could speak, Straesyr went on. "I'm going to have to handle both positions. At the very least, scholar, I'll need assistance, and I expect such, especially in matters dealing with the scholarium."

After a moment, Quaeryt replied, "I can help

there . . . and with anything else you feel comfortable with me doing."

"Comfortable?" Straesyr raised his eyebrows. "You're more than competent, but I can't say I'm comfortable. As I said a moment ago, you're a dangerous man." He paused. "The biggest immediate problem will be all the prisoners Commander Myskyl is marching back. What would you do with them?"

"Apprentice out the youths. Relocate the adults as you can. Foster the orphaned children under five. The scholarium could help there, although they'd need some golds for clothing and food. You might have to offer some silvers for apprentices to begin with."

"The scholarium would need golds anyway. You had that in mind all along."

"I did . . . if I thought the new Master Scholar could make matters work."

"It appears as though he is . . . or rather, his scholar princeps is."

"I thought it might work out that way."

"A number of matters have worked out the way you thought. A man would be wise to consider your views. Did Rescalyn ever ask you yours?"

"Only when he thought I might agree with him."

"Did you ever raise questions about his acts or views? To him directly?"

"I hinted that the size of the regiment was large enough for other endeavors after dealing with the hill holders. He avoided dealing with that, and assigned me to Sixth Battalion for the attack on Zorlyn's holding. Sixth Battalion was always in the fore and was one of the two lead battalions."

"That is representative of his methods." Straesyr nodded. "Scholar . . . there is one other thing."

"Sir?"

Straesyr's countenance broke into a smile as he extended an envelope. "This arrived with the last courier."

As Quaeryt took the envelope, his eyes dropped to the script—Vaelora's hand. "Thank you, sir." For reasons he wasn't certain he wanted to investigate at that moment, the existence of the missive seemed to lift a burden off his shoulders.

Is that because she writes because she wants to?

He looked to Straesyr. "Is there anything else, sir?"

"Not for the moment. We should talk on Lundi morning. You look like you could use some rest. I won't need any written reports from you. You can just tell me anything you haven't already then."

"Thank you, sir." Quaeryt stood slowly, nodded, and retreated to his study.

Once there, he opened the letter.

My Dearest Scholar Quaeryt—

"My Dearest"? Rhetorical excess? Or does she have dreams . . . more like delusions . . . or are the delusions yours? Quaeryt frowned, then swallowed. *If she really feels that way . . .* Bhayar would be anything but pleased. *Anything but pleased.* He took a deep breath before he continued reading.

Your latest missive was most entertaining as well as informative, so much so that I had to share it with members of my family. Unhappily, some were not so amused as was I, but even the sternest acknowledged your perception and wit . . .

Good . . . but will that be enough now that your brother has since discovered that he no longer has a "good governor" and undoubtedly superior com-

mander? And that you address me as "Dearest"—or
was that a way to assure I got the letter? He hoped so,
or he might be marooned in Tilbor forever.

> . . . and the wisdom behind such fascinating observations,
> although I must, as a mere young woman of no great worldly
> experience, defer to those with far greater apperception of the
> world as it is and not as I would have it.
>
> I must also confess that I miss hearing your wit and
> perceptive comments in person, although in truth, I needs
> must also acknowledge that such occasions were far fewer in
> number than I, and I hope you, would otherwise have wished.
> For, as you know from your observations of the palace and the
> court, how could matters have been otherwise? Yet, in these
> times and perhaps in all times, a wise woman, or a young
> woman who is intelligent enough to seek the counsel of
> women far wiser and more powerful, must learn to seek where
> she can the company of minds who are not unsympathetic to
> her deepest feelings and convictions, be that company in
> correspondence, in conversation, or more happily otherwise.
> Wherever that dialogue may occur, it is to be valued and
> cherished, for even one so sheltered as I have been knows that
> it is rare indeed in any company, and so do I cherish those
> words you dispatch to me.
>
> It may be that the news of other happenings has not reached
> you, in view of your duties and responsibilities, but it appears
> as if the Autarch of Antiago is tending to forget his most
> felicitous past relationships with Telaryn and is responding to a
> courtship of sorts from the Rex of Bovaria. . . .

Quaeryt read quickly through the next few para-
graphs, which recounted various bits of news from
Solis, all of which suggested that Rex Kharst was bent
on annexing Antiago in one fashion or another in the
years ahead . . . if not sooner.

. . . all of these events have given much pause, it is said, to Lord Bhayar, and those who know him well are given to suggesting that he has devoted much thought to readying Telaryn to weather the tempests that appear on the horizon. What preparations he will make and in what fashion has not been made known to any, only that he is about to undertake such, and that much may well change in the months and years to come. What this bodes for us, and for this most felicitous correspondence, I do not know, only that your words and the thoughts of receiving them have enlightened and warmed me, and that I would most earnestly hope that I will be able to count on continuing to receive such.

Quaeryt swallowed at the closing—"Your devoted Vaelora."

Was her life that constricted in the palace that his comparatively few letters afforded such pleasure? Were her words rhetorical excess, based on the wistful fancies of a young woman who felt totally imprisoned by who she was?

He shook his head. Whatever the reason for the plea, he could not fail to reply to her, perhaps because he had seen—in the persons of Rescalyn's exiled Bovarian mistress, of Hailae, and even of Tyrena, if only through the vista of a vanishing past—the way in which events could stifle the spirit of brilliant and accomplished women. He could not free Vaelora, but he could, he hoped, offer words that would stimulate and perhaps comfort, although, given the fierceness of her spirit, he could not ever be condescending or pitying.

And yet . . . even the act of replying to such a missive, even if carefully, oh so carefully accomplished, increased the risk of Bhayar's displeasure . . . and for that matter the displeasure of anyone of power who wanted to form an alliance or gain greater power or access to Bhayar. Such displeasure could easily turn into attacks that might be difficult for even an accomplished imager to stop or divert.

For all that . . . you will reply . . .

He eased, awkwardly, a sheet of paper from the desk drawer.

96

Quaeryt barely made the mess on Solayi morning and had no more than seated himself when a figure walked swiftly toward him—Phargos.

"I was hoping to catch you," said the chorister, settling into the seat across from Quaeryt. "I'm not going to ask you to deliver a homily." A wide smile followed. "From what I've heard, mine would be most unfavorably compared to yours."

"I'm certain that wouldn't be true," replied Quaeryt. "The homilies of yours that I've heard have always been enlightening."

"I'm afraid it would be. Undercaptain Gauswn is convinced you're the second coming of Rholan. So are a few others."

"I'm nothing of the sort. You, of all people, know that." Quaeryt poured tea into his mug, carefully, still feeling awkward in only having one hand to use.

"I do. I'm just not sure exactly what you are. You're almost all things to all people. You're a good officer to Skarpa and those who saw you in combat. You're a good chorister to those who have heard your homilies. You're obviously a good scholar to those who value scholarship." Phargos shook his head. "I don't think anyone, even you yourself, knows truly what you are." The smile returned. "That's not why I wanted to talk to you. Did you know that Gauswn wants to leave the regiment when his time is up and become a chorister?"

"I didn't know. I can't say I'm surprised, though. When would that be?"

"His commitment ends on the thirty-fifth of Erntyn next year. Cyrethyn would like for him to study with both of us and succeed him as the chorister for the scholarium. We've gotten some good junior officers from there, and it would help to have a chorister who's friendly to Telaryn and the regiment. Those are my thoughts on the matter. What are yours?"

Quaeryt grinned. "You don't want my thoughts. You want to know if I'd approve of him. Yes, I would. He's good at heart, and intelligent. He'd represent change, even though it wouldn't be that great a change, and the scholarium could use that." Quaeryt paused. "You don't even need my approval. What's the problem?"

"Cyrethyn is frail. He's very frail. I worry he may not live another year."

"Do you want me to talk to Straesyr to see if he'd release Gauswn early on the condition he starts immediately at the scholarium?"

"Cyrethyn is far more frail than he lets on."

"I'll do what I can."

"Thank you." Phargos rose. "Unlike with some, with you, those words mean what they say."

Quaeryt served himself one of the thick cooling cheese omelets and scarcely warm bread, then took a sip of his tea. As he ate, he couldn't help but think about Phargos's comment, especially as it applied to Vaelora. Was he something he wasn't to her? He'd certainly never tried to deceive her—perhaps to mislead anyone who intercepted and read his words, but not her. For those reasons, composing a response to her latest missive had been difficult, and he had yet to finish that reply, but he did have a few days before another courier would leave for Solis.

What did he feel about her?

He shook his head. Did what he felt really matter? At best, all he'd ever be would be a correspondent who provided a window of sorts to a world her brother would never let her enter. And that, he could and would do.

Except . . . you'd like to do more for her.

He pushed that thought away. Anything more was beyond his power—even as a hidden imager.

The remainder of the day he divided his time between working on his reply to Vaelora, considering how to improve the scholarium, what he would say to Straesyr on Lundi in regard to Gauswn, and even resting. He was least successful at resting, with his thoughts swirling in so many different directions that he finally rose from his bunk feeling more exhausted than when he had stretched out on it.

After the evening meal, he did make his way to the palace anomen and take in services, as much as to hear what Phargos had to say as anything, in hopes that the chorister's words might offer some wisdom to settle his thoughts.

Phargos began his homily with the standard opening, the one that Quaeryt had always heard. ". . . under the Nameless all evenings are good. . . . Almost all of you have just returned from a campaign against the hill holders. I have already heard tales of endless attacks and total destruction, and pondered what had led to such. The easy answer is Naming and the

Namer . . . but easy answers are not always good answers.

"Recently, I talked to a man. Some of you know him. Some don't. I asked for his help in a matter some would call small and some would not. He said that he would do what he could. From this man, those words meant what they said. At the same time, I realized that so often we equate words with Naming. That is not so. Words followed by honest action are not Naming. Empty words or duplicitous words are the same as Naming. Promising help and not helping is a form of Naming. Saying good things in public about someone and undermining them in private are Naming, and so often empty words or deceptive words build on each other and lead to devastation and destruction . . ."

Quaeryt had to agree with those sentiments, although the indirect reference to him—he thought it was to him, but perhaps it was not—bothered him. Still . . . what Phargos said about words was right— even if Quaeryt still had no idea of whether there even happened to be a Nameless.

97

Lundi morning, Quaeryt woke to gusty winds that filled his quarters with chill drafts and rattled the shutters. Outside under gray skies, fine light snowflakes danced on the gusty winds. As he shivered his way into his browns, he knew that it was bound to be far colder with far more snow falling in the Boran Hills, and that meant a much slower and more laborious return for those battalions not remaining at Zorlyn's hold or at Boralieu.

After breakfast, he made his way to meet with Straesyr. He had to wait almost a quint in the anteroom before the princeps arrived.

"You're always prompt, scholar. Come on in."

Quaeryt entered after the princeps and closed the door, then took a seat in front of the desk.

"Why don't you tell me your view of the campaign? I'd like your views on what worked well, what didn't work so well, and why."

"Yes, sir." Quaeryt shifted his weight in the armchair, enough so that he could rest the splint on the short wooden arm, then cleared his throat. "Governor Rescalyn planned the campaign exceedingly well. He also understood from the beginning the need not to become unduly distracted by the continual attacks from small forces of hill rebels . . ." He went on to talk for almost a glass about what he had seen and the need for the kind of campaign Rescalyn had planned and executed. ". . . all the destruction was necessary because nothing less would have ended the power of the hill holders to disrupt and restrict formal governing from either Tilbora or Solis."

"I've already heard from several High Holders that they think the additional tariffs on the remaining hill holders are too low. They complain that they've paid for more than their fair share. What would you tell them, master scholar?"

"That the price paid by the dead hill holders was far greater than what they have paid, that the higher tariff levels on the remaining hill holders will continue for several years, and that harvesting a ram's wool for years is more productive than slaughtering or starving it."

"That won't make them happy."

"Nothing will make them happy. If they're happy, you're not tariffing enough, because that means they feel like they're paying less than what they should."

"You sound like Rescalyn."

"I never disagreed with his governing."

"As we discussed, you will, of course, continue to supervise the scholarium."

"Of course."

"And I will have you study the ledgers so that you can begin to watch the tariffs and expenses . . ." Straesyr went on to outline other duties and details he had in mind for Quaeryt. When he finished that enumeration, he looked to the scholar. "Are there other matters we need to discuss?"

"There is one that Chorister Phargos brought to my attention."

"Oh?"

"Undercaptain Gauswn—from Sixth Battalion— had at one time studied to be a chorister of the Nameless. Gauswn would like to leave the regiment when his time is up to become a chorister. That isn't a problem, I would believe, but the problem lies in the fact that the current chorister at the scholarium is quite frail, and his years are numbered, perhaps even limited to months. Phargos feels, and I agree, that Gauswn would make an excellent replacement for Cyrethyn, but it would be beneficial for all, I believe, if Gauswn could be released earlier to study with Cyrethyn before the old chorister is no longer able to impart his knowledge."

"Gauswn . . . he's the one who kept you from being trampled, isn't he?"

"He is. He's also the one who's often conducted services at Boralieu when Commander Zirkyl was unavailable. Chorister Phargos made the point that some good young officers have come from the scholarium, and that having Gauswn be chorister there would be beneficial to Telaryn. If Cyrethyn dies before Gauswn's service ends . . ." Quaeryt shrugged.

Straesyr frowned. "I'd like to talk to Myskyl when he returns. That should be within the week. What do you think?"

"I think it's a good idea. It will also aid in continuing to change the outlook at the scholarium. You'd likely lose Gauswn anyway, and this way, Major Skarpa has more time to groom his replacement."

"That makes sense. We can work it out." The princeps nodded slowly. "I'll still have to talk to the commander. You're not to say a word to anyone, even Phargos."

"I understand, sir. I will tell him that I asked you, and you and Commander Myskyl will decide."

"Is there anything else?"

"Not at the moment, sir."

"Then you should get on with those matters." But Straesyr did smile warmly as Quaeryt slowly rose from the chair.

Quaeryt didn't return to his own small study until almost ninth glass, where he began on the various tasks the princeps had assigned him.

Given his physical condition, the remainder of the week passed, steadily, if not swiftly. On Jeudi, Quaeryt spent a good glass with Straesyr and several more with the chief accounts clerk and a stack of ledgers, learning enough about the tariff and expense accounts so that he could assist Straesyr at least until Bhayar sent word as to what he intended to do about who would be governor, if not Straesyr, and who would be princeps if the princeps became governor.

On Vendrei, Quaeryt dispatched his reply to Vaelora,

one on which he had labored long and carefully. Commander Myskyl returned, in another light snowstorm that tapered off around sunset, with those battalions—and the engineers—who would not be immediately posted to the Boralieu or to Zorlyn's hold, now being called Rescalyt. With Myskyl came several hundred prisoners . . . or refugees.

Quaeryt was not included in the discussions between the governor and the commander, which was probably a good idea, he decided upon reflection.

On Samedi morning, the princeps informed Quaeryt that many of his recommendations had been taken and that the scholarium would need to foster some twenty-one orphans. He also gave his decision regarding Undercaptain Gauswn, and on that afternoon Quaeryt rode, with the escort of a squad from Sixth Battalion, to the scholarium, where he spent the rest of the day with Nalakyn and Yullyd over those matters and a quint with Cyrethyn informing him about the acting governor's decision to release Gauswn from his obligation at the end of Finitas. While there, he recovered the gear and clothing he had left—and everything was as he had left it.

Quaeryt actually rested on Solayi. He did not attend services.

On Lundi morning, a courier delivered a letter to the Telaryn Palace, a letter that made its way up to the princeps's anteroom, from where Vhorym delivered it to Quaeryt in his small study.

There were two names on the outside of the envelope. One indicated it was from Jorem Rhodynsyn, and the other was given as "Scholar Quaeryt, Telaryn Palace."

Why was Jorem writing him? Another Pharsi problem? Had something happened to Rhodyn? He opened the envelope, extracted the single sheet, and began to read.

Dear Scholar Quaeryt:

I have heard from many that you are a person of position in Tilbor. I would not impose on you for any favor for myself. I know of no one else to whom I can turn. Hailae has a young cousin named Chartyn. He is barely a youth, but he has been discovered as an imager. As such, and as a Pharsi, his very life will be endangered. Young Chartyn is most industrious and intelligent. He would make a good scholar, but we cannot afford the fees to pay for such an education. . . .

Quaeryt set the letter aside and took a deep breath. Finally, he picked it up and finished the last lines. He supposed he could include Chartyn as a sort of fosterling and ask Nalakyn to look after the boy. Perhaps even Lankyt would help.

Outside, the wind howled, reminding him that winter was little more than a week away.

He shivered.

98

Quaeryt returned to the Telaryn Palace at just past second glass on Meredi afternoon. He'd spent more than a glass at the scholarium persuading Nalakyn and Yullyd that young Chartyn needed discipline and support, and that to accept young Chartyn would be to everyone's advantage, not to mention that the scholarium owed the governor/princeps for agreeing to a forty gold a month payment for fostering and other services. Their acquiescence had been better than grudging and less than heartily enthusiastic, and the returning ride had been in a cold and biting wind.

He had barely gotten the worst of the chill out of his bones and his arm, which only pained him intermittently, if especially when he was tired, and was seated back in his study, looking at a ledger that held the tariff collections for the factors in southern Tilbor, when he heard horns and the sound of horses. He didn't get up because he couldn't see much of the courtyard and because he was tired and the riders were most likely the battalion that Straesyr had ordered transferred from Midcote to Tilbora.

More than a glass later, he'd finished checking the autumn receipts when Vhorym knocked on his door. "You're needed in the governor's study, sir."

"Do you know why?"

"No, sir. I wasn't told."

Quaeryt rose, but he couldn't help but notice an odd expression, one he couldn't identify, on the squad leader's face. "Are you all right, Vhorym?"

"Yes, sir. You'd best hurry . . . as you can."

Quaeryt still limped, as he always had, but the pain of his other injuries had almost vanished, unless he bumped into something with a few parts of his body where the bruises had been especially deep.

Vhorym did not accompany Quaeryt to the governor's anteroom, where Undercaptain Caermyt stood by the door to the study. Otherwise the anteroom was empty.

"You're to go right in, sir." Caermyt opened the door.

Quaeryt saw Straesyr standing behind the governor's desk. Another man, brown-haired and in traveling grays, stood beside him, but continued to look away from the door. Straesyr motioned Quaeryt forward, his face pleasant, but unsmiling.

As the study door closed, the man in grays turned, and his dark blue eyes fixed on Quaeryt. The scholar managed not to gape. He inclined his head. "Lord Bhayar."

"Scholar." Bhayar did not smile, but looked to Straesyr. "You may go, Governor. We will finish our talk later."

"Yes, sir." Straesyr nodded, turned, and walked toward the study door. He avoided looking at Quaeryt.

Only when the door closed did Bhayar look directly at Quaeryt. The scholar immediately noted the circles under Bhayar's eyes and the fact that the wiry lord appeared thinner, if possible, than the last time Quaeryt had seen him.

Quaeryt waited.

"It appears as though you have been busy," said Bhayar in formal Bovarian, his voice calm, not quite flat. "If not exactly in the manner which you had suggested upon your departure from Solis. You know, scholar, this has been an arduous trip. We rode from Solis, pressing all the way. We did accomplish some good along the way. We wiped out the last of the ship reavers, and we enjoyed the hospitality of a holder—Rhodyn, I think his name was—who thought quite highly of you. Still . . . I do believe you exceeded the charge with which I sent you. Especially by requiring, in effect through a missive to my sister, that I come to Tilbor or risk losing my rule."

For a moment, Quaeryt hesitated, before replying in Bovarian, "I did what I thought best and in your interests, sir."

"As I recall," replied Bhayar, "you said you would

recommend how to reduce the number of soldiers required in Tilbor. You didn't say that you would take matters into your own hands and make it happen— regardless of the consequences. You didn't happen to mention that you intended to have a governor vanish—and in a fashion that no one can possibly trace to you—or that you'd make a princeps whose greatest value was to keep tariffs honestly flowing to Solis into his successor, or that . . ." Bhayar did not finish what he might have said, instead pausing, then asking, "What exactly did you have in mind?"

"To stop Rescalyn from turning a fanatically loyal regiment that he'd built into the size of three regiments with your tariffs and all the silvers from Zorlyn's mine into a weapon for overthrowing you and visiting chaos, death, and destruction on Telaryn at exactly the time you face challenges in the west."

Bhayar nodded. "I made a few inquiries of my own, and it appears that you have always been more than you represented, even while you were in Solis. Here in Tilbor, you did happen to be correct. You also resolved the problem, somehow, by setting up the would-be usurper as a hero who died in serving me. You also appear to have reorganized the local scholars and gained the respect of the officers and men of the regiment, as well as that of the new governor. What, might I ask in the shadow of the Nameless, makes you any different from Rescalyn?"

"I did what I did to enhance your rule, not to undermine it."

"Yet . . . you have proven to be one of those men who can use the smallest levers of power to great effectiveness. Such men are as dangerous as they are useful. What can I do with you to maintain that usefulness without endangering myself?"

Quaeryt thought, but couldn't come up with a quick answer. Still . . . he had to try. "You could—"

Bhayar held up his hand. "Spare me. There are some matters where I still have better ways of dealing with the problem at hand. I have looked into all aspects of your acts and your life, and I have found a solution."

Quaeryt had a very uneasy feeling, although the almost mischievous smile on Bhayar's face was at odds with Bhayar's usual means of dealing with those who displeased him. Still . . . if he had to, he could image a distraction and raise concealment.

Bhayar pointed at Quaeryt. "Stay where you are." He walked past Quaeryt and stood by the study door, then half-turned. "You may not like it at first, but I assure you that you both will come to enjoy it . . . or you should."

Both? What exactly does he have in mind?

Bhayar opened the study door. He gestured.

The woman who stepped through the door had light brown wavy hair, brown eyes, and light honey-clear skin. She still wore riding trousers and a winter jacket, if now open. She smiled.

Vaelora? What . . . Quaeryt could only look at her, somehow older, perhaps partly because of the circles under her eyes as well, and . . . knowing . . .

Bhayar shut the study door behind her. "You do look appropriately stunned," he said dryly to Quaeryt. "I believe you two have met. I even believe you have exchanged some considerable correspondence. Considerable, at least, given her position and yours, scholar."

Before either Vaelora or Quaeryt could speak, Bhayar held up his hand again. "I have given this some thought. My sister has insisted that she will not marry some High Holder for reasons of state. Nor will she marry someone she does not respect. Yet there are few indeed she respects, and none presently of position. Moreover, I will be badgered and pestered by every High Holder and would-be power-seeker so long as she remains unwed. Likewise, scholar, you are powerful in ways I do not claim to understand. So I have decided on several things. First, scholar, I am appointing you princeps of Tilbor." He looked to his sister, whose smile had faded to an expression between surprise and exasperation. "That is partly so that my sister cannot claim that she gained a marriage that did not have a purpose of state. It is also so that you can continue to build ties between Tilbor and the rest of Telaryn. Of necessity, she will reinforce your loyalty. Of necessity, you will have to maintain her respect because I will not have my sister *ever* disrespected. This marriage and your appointment will also reinforce in the minds of the High Holders and others of power in Tilbor that I do in fact have a personal interest in the welfare and future of the people of Tilbor. It will also tell the officers and soldiers of the regiment that deeds of selflessness are sometimes rewarded. And . . . because I have been too long already from Solis, the wedding will take place here in the palace on Solayi." The Lord of Telaryn grinned, one of the few times Quaeryt had ever seen that expression. "That way, I can return to Solis in peace, and you two can spend *all* of the very long winter here keeping each other warm."

Quaeryt remained speechless.

"We will find a way to tailor a jacket over that splint, dearest," said Vaelora warmly.

TOR

Award-winning authors
Compelling stories

Please join us at the website
below for more information
about this author and other great
Tor selections, and to sign up for
our monthly newsletter!